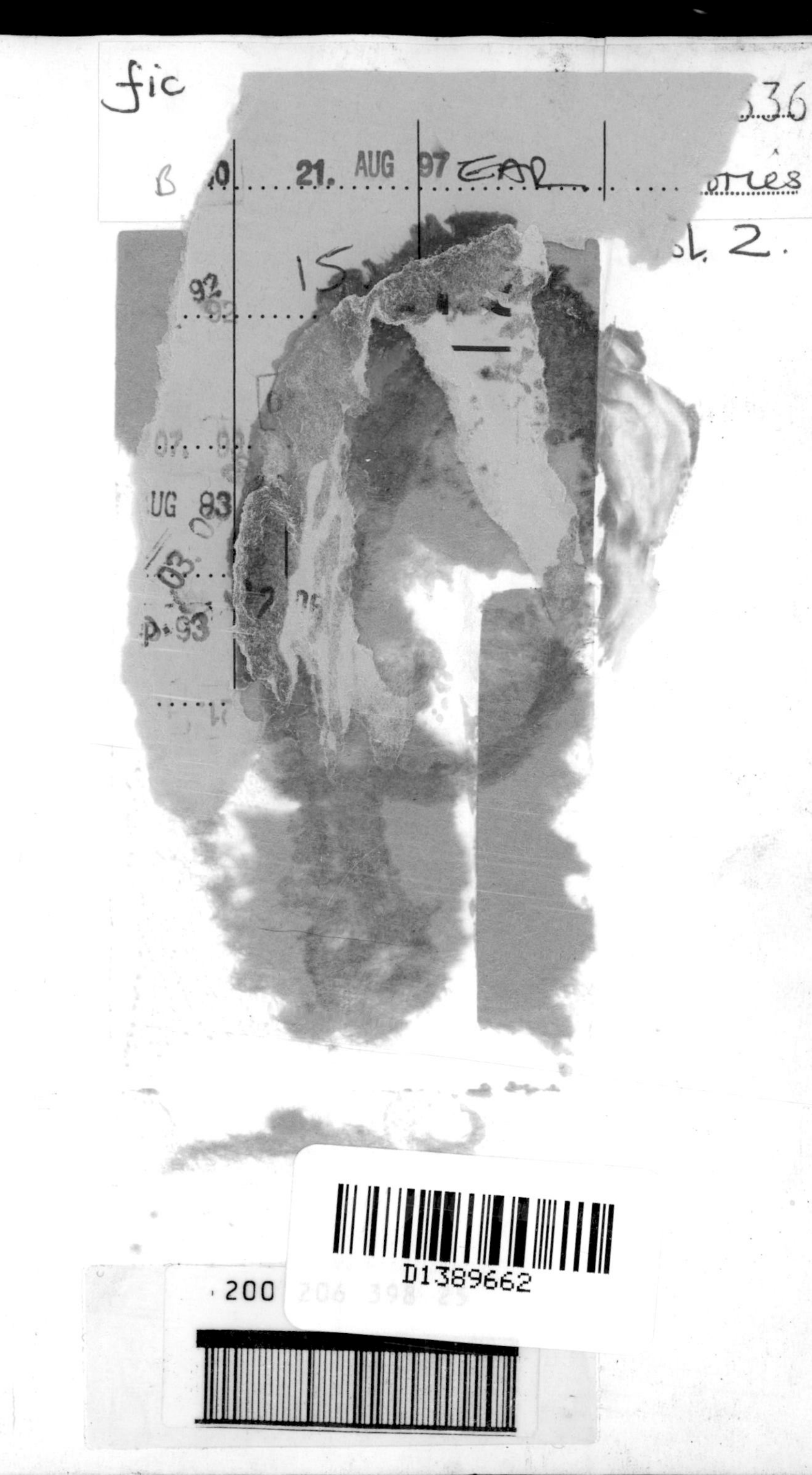
fic
21. AUG 97
D1389662
200

The Complete Short Stories
Volume two

Guy de Maupassant

CASSELL · LONDON

CASSELL & COMPANY LTD
35 Red Lion Square, London, WC1
Melbourne, Sydney, Toronto
Johannesburg, Auckland

First 3-volume edition 1970

S.B.N. 304 93483 6

Reproduced and Printed by
Redwood Press Limited
Trowbridge & London

F. 969

CONTENTS

CONTENTS

CONTENTS

29

29
32
27
88

MISS HARRIET

THERE WERE SEVEN OF US IN THE DRAG, FOUR WOMEN AND three men, one of whom was on the box-seat beside the coachman. We were following, at a walking pace, the winding coast road up the hill.

Having set out from Étretat at daybreak to visit the ruins of Tancarville, we were still half asleep, benumbed by the fresh air of the morning. The women, especially, who were little accustomed to early rising, let their eyelids fall every moment, nodding their heads or yawning, quite insensible to the glory of the dawn.

It was autumn. On both sides of the road the bare fields stretched out, yellowed by the stubble of oats and wheat which covered the soil like a badly-shaved beard. The misty earth looked as if it were steaming. Larks were singing in the air, while other birds piped in the bushes.

At length the sun rose in front of us, a bright red on the edge of the horizon; and as it ascended, growing clearer from minute to minute, the country seemed to awake, to smile, to stretch itself, to slip off its night-gown of white mist, like a young girl leaving her bed. The Comte d'Etraille, who was seated on the box, cried:

"Look! look! a hare!" and he stretched out his arm to the left, pointing to a patch of clover. The animal scurried along, almost concealed by the field, only its large ears visible. Then it swerved across a deep furrow, stopped, started off again at top speed, changed its course, stopped anew, uneasy, spying out every danger, and undecided as to the route it should take. Suddenly it began to run, with great bounds of its hind legs, disappearing finally in a large patch of beetroot.

All the men had wakened up to watch the animal's movements.

René Lemanoir then exclaimed :

" We are not at all gallant this morning," and looking at his neighbour, the little Baroness de Sérennes, who was struggling with drowsiness, he said to her in a subdued voice : " You are thinking of your husband, Baroness. Reassure yourself ; he will not return before Saturday, so you still have four days."

She replied, with a sleepy smile :

" How silly you are." Then, shaking off her torpor, she added : " Now, let somebody say something that will make us all laugh. You, Monsieur Chenal, who have the reputation of having more successes than the Duc de Richelieu, tell us a love-story in which you have been involved, anything you like."

Léon Chenal, an old painter, who had once been very handsome, very strong, very proud of his physique and very popular, took his long white beard in his hand and smiled ; then, after a few moments' reflection, he became suddenly grave.

" Ladies, it will not be an amusing tale ; for I am going to relate to you the most lamentable love-affair of my life, and I sincerely hope that none of my friends may ever inspire a similar passion."

I

" At that time I was twenty-five years old, and I was daubing along the coast of Normandy. I mean by ' daubing ' wandering about, with a knapsack on one's back, from inn to inn, under the pretext of making studies and sketches from nature. I know nothing more enjoyable than that happy-go-lucky wandering life, in which you are perfectly free, without shackles of any kind, without a care, without a single preoccupation, without even a thought of to-morrow. You go in any direction you please, without any guide save your fancy, without any counsellor save what pleases your eyes. You pull up, because a running brook seduces you, or because you are attracted, in front of an inn, by the smell of fried potatoes. Sometimes it is the perfume of clematis which decides you in your choice, or the glance of the servant at an inn. Do not despise these rustic affections. These girls have souls as well as bodies, firm cheeks and fresh lips; their vigorous kisses are strong and fragrant, like wild fruits. Love is always worth while, come whence it may. A heart that beats when you make your appearance, an eye that weeps when you go away, these are things so rare, so sweet, so precious, that they must never be despised.

"I have had rendezvous in ditches full of primroses, behind the stable in which the cattle slept, and among the straw in garrets still warm from the heat of the day. I have memories of coarse grey linen on supple, strong bodies, and of hearty, fresh, free kisses, more delicate, in their sincere brutality, than the subtle joys accorded by charming and distinguished women.

"But what one chiefly loves in these pilgrimages of adventure is the country, the woods, the sunrises, the twilights, the light of the moon. For the painter these are honeymoon trips with Nature. You are alone with her in a long, quiet rendezvous. You go to bed in the fields amid marguerites and wild poppies, and, with eyes wide open, under the bright sunlight, you regard far away some little village, with pointed clock-tower which sounds the hour of noon.

"You sit down by the side of a spring which gushes out from the foot of an oak, amid a covering of tall, fragile weeds, glistening with life. You go down on your knees, bend forward, and drink the cold and pellucid water, wetting your moustache and nose; you drink it with a physical pleasure, as though you were kissing the spring, lip to lip. Sometimes, when you find a deep hole along the course of these tiny brooks, you plunge into it, quite naked, and on your skin, from head to foot, like an icy and delicious caress, you feel the swift and gentle quivering of the current.

" You are gay on the hills, melancholy on the shores of the lagoons, exalted when the sun is drowned in an ocean of blood-red clouds and wakes red reflections in the rivers. And at night, under the moon, as she passes across the roof of heaven, you think of things, singular things, which would never have occurred to your mind under the brilliant light of day.

" So, in wandering through this same country where we are this year, I came one day to the little village of Bénouville, on the rocky coast between Yport and Étretat. I came from Fécamp, following the cliff, the tall cliff, perpendicular as a wall, with its bastions of chalk falling sheer down into the sea. I had walked since morning on the close-clipped grass, as smooth and yielding as a carpet, which grows along the edge of the cliff, fanned by the salt breezes of the ocean. Singing lustily, I walked with long strides, looking sometimes at the slow, curving flight of a gull, with its sweep of white wings sailing over the blue heavens, sometimes at the green sea, or at the brown sails of a fishing bark. In short, I had passed a happy day, a day of liberty and freedom from care.

" I was told there was a little farmhouse where travellers were put up, a kind of inn kept by a peasant, which stood in a Normandy courtyard, surrounded by a double row of beeches.

" Leaving the cliff, I reached the hamlet, which was shut in by great trees, and I presented myself at the house of Mother Lecacheur.

" She was an old country woman, wrinkled and austere, who always seemed to receive customers reluctantly, with a kind of contempt.

" It was the month of May : the flowering apple-trees covered the court with a roof of perfumed flowers, with a whirling shower of pink blossoms which rained unceasingly upon the people and upon the grass.

" I said :

" ' Well, Madame Lecacheur, have you a room for me ? '

" Astonished to find that I knew her name, she answered :

" 'That depends; everything is let; but all the same, there will be no harm in looking.'

" In five minutes we had come to an agreement, and I deposited my bag upon the earthen floor of a rustic room, furnished with a bed, two chairs, a table, and a wash-stand. The room opened into the large, smoky kitchen, where the lodgers took their meals with the people of the farm and with the woman herself, who was a widow.

" I washed my hands, after which I went out. The old woman was making a chicken fricassee for dinner in a large fire-place, in which hung the stew-pot, black with smoke.

" 'You have visitors, then, at the present time?' I said to her.

" She answered in an offended tone of voice:

" 'I have a lady, an English lady, of a certain age. She is occupying the other room.'

" For an extra five sous a day, I obtained the privilege of dining out in the court when the weather was fine.

" My place was accordingly set in front of the door, and I began to champ the lean limbs of the Normandy chicken, to drink the clear cider, and to munch the hunk of white bread, which, though four days old, was excellent.

" Suddenly the wooden gate which opened on to the highway was opened, and a strange person walked toward the house. She was very thin, very tall, enveloped in a Scotch shawl with red checks. You would have believed that she had no arms, if you had not seen a long hand appear just above the hips, holding a white tourist's umbrella. The face of a mummy, surrounded with sausage-rolls of plaited grey hair, which shook at every step she took, made me think, I know not why, of a pickled herring adorned with curling-papers. Lowering her eyes, she passed quickly in front of me, and entered the house.

" This singular apparition amused me. She undoubtedly was my neighbour, the 'English lady of a certain age' of whom our hostess had spoken.

"I did not see her again that day. The next day, when I had begun to paint at the end of the beautiful valley which you know, which extends as far as Étretat, lifting my eyes suddenly, I perceived something singularly attired standing on the crest of the declivity; it looked like a pole decked out with flags. It was she. On seeing me, she disappeared.

"I returned to the house at midday for lunch, and took my seat at the common table, so as to make the acquaintance of this eccentric old creature. But she did not respond to my polite advances, was insensible even to my little attentions. I perseveringly poured water out for her, I passed her the dishes with an air. A slight, almost imperceptible movement of the head, and an English word, murmured so low that I did not understand it, were her only acknowledgments.

"I ceased taking any notice of her, although she had disturbed my thoughts. At the end of three days, I knew as much about her as Madame Lecacheur did herself.

"She was called Miss Harriet. Seeking a secluded village in which to pass the summer, she had stopped at Bénouville, some six weeks before, and did not seem disposed to leave it. She never spoke at table, ate rapidly, reading all the while a small book of Protestant propaganda. She gave a copy of this book to everybody. The *curé* himself had received no less than four copies, at the hands of an urchin to whom she had paid two sous' commission. She said sometimes to our hostess, abruptly, without the slightest preliminary leading up to this declaration:

"'I love the Saviour above all; I worship Him in all creation; I adore Him in all nature; I carry Him always in my heart.'

"And she would immediately present the old woman with one of her brochures destined to convert the universe.

"In the village she was not liked. In fact, the schoolmaster had declared that she was an atheist, and a kind of stigma attached to her. The *curé*, who had been consulted by Madame Lecacheur, responded:

" 'She is a heretic, but God does not wish the death of the sinner, and I believe her to be a person of pure morals.'

"These words, 'atheist,' 'heretic,' words which no one could precisely define, threw doubts into some minds. It was asserted further, that this Englishwoman was rich, and that she had passed her life in travelling through every country in the world, because her family had thrown her off. Why had her family thrown her off? Because of her impiety, of course.

"She was, in reality, one of those people of exalted principles, one of those obstinate puritans of whom England produces so many, one of those good and insupportable old women who haunt the *tables d'hôte* of every hotel in Europe, who spoil Italy, poison Switzerland, render the charming cities of the Mediterranean uninhabitable, carry everywhere their fantastic manias, their petrified vestal morals, their indescribable toilettes, and a certain odour of india-rubber, which makes one believe that at night they slip themselves into a case of that material. When I met one of these people in a hotel, I used to flee like the birds when they see a scarecrow in a field.

"This woman, however, appeared so singular that she did not displease me.

"Madame Lecacheur, hostile by instinct to everything that was not peasant, felt in her narrow soul a kind of hatred for the ecstatic extravagances of the old maid. She had found a phrase by which to describe her, a phrase assuredly contemptuous, which had sprung to her lips I know not how, invented probably by some confused and mysterious travail of soul. She said: 'That woman is a demoniac.' This phrase, applied to that austere and sentimental creature, seemed to me irresistibly comic. I, myself, never called her now anything else but 'the demoniac,' feeling a singular pleasure in pronouncing this word aloud on seeing her.

"I would ask Mother Lecacheur: 'Well, what is our demoniac doing to-day?' To which the peasant would respond with a scandalised air:

" 'What do you think, sir? She picked up a toad with a crushed paw, carried it to her room, put it in her wash-stand, and dressed its wound as if it were a human. If that is not profanation, I should like to know what is!'

" On another occasion, when walking along the shore, she had bought a large fish which had just been caught, simply to throw it back into the sea again. The sailor, from whom she had bought it, though paid handsomely, was greatly provoked at this act—more exasperated, indeed, than if she had put her hand into his pocket and taken his money. For a whole month he could not speak of the circumstance without getting into a fury and denouncing it as an outrage. Oh yes! She was indeed a demoniac, this Miss Harriet, and Mother Lecacheur must have had an inspiration of genius in thus christening her.

" The stable-boy, who was called Sapeur, because he had served in Africa in his youth, entertained other opinions. He said, with a knowing air: 'She is an old hag who has had her day.' If the poor woman had but known.

" Céleste, the little servant, did not like waiting on her, but I was never able to understand why. Probably her only reason was that she was a stranger, of another race, of a different tongue, and of another religion. She was a demoniac, in brief!

" She passed her time wandering about the country, adoring and searching for God in nature. I found her one evening on her knees in a cluster of bushes. Having discovered something red through the leaves, I brushed aside the branches, and Miss Harriet at once rose to her feet, confused at having been found thus, looking at me with eyes as frightened as those of an owl surprised in open day.

" Sometimes, when I was working among the rocks, I would suddenly see her on the edge of the cliff, standing like a semaphore signal. She gazed passionately at the vast sea, glittering in the sunlight, and the boundless sky empurpled with fire. Sometimes I would distinguish her at the bottom of a valley, walking quickly, with her elastic English step; and I would go towards her, mysteriously attracted, simply to see her visionary expression, her dried-up, ineffable features, full of an inward and profound happiness.

"Often I would encounter her in the corner of a field sitting on the grass, under the shadow of an apple-tree, with her little Bible lying open on her knee, while she looked meditatively into the distance.

"I could no longer tear myself away from that quiet country neighbourhood, bound to it as I was by a thousand links of love for its soft and sweeping landscapes. I was happy at this farm, which was out of the world, far removed from everything, but in close proximity to the soil, the good, healthy, beautiful green soil, which we ourselves shall fertilise with our bodies some day. And, I must confess, there was perhaps a certain amount of curiosity which kept me at Mother Lecacheur's. I wished to become acquainted a little with this strange Miss Harriet, and to learn what passes in the solitary souls of those wandering old English dames."

II

"We became acquainted in a rather singular manner. I had just finished a study which I thought good, and so it was. It was sold for ten thousand francs, fifteen years later. It was as simple as twice two make four, and had nothing to do with academic rules. The whole of the right side of my canvas represented a rock, an enormous jagged rock, covered with sea-wrack, brown, yellow, and red, across which the sun poured like a stream of oil. The light fell upon the stone, and gilded it as if with fire, but the sun itself was behind me and could not be seen. That was all. A foreground dazzling with light, blazing, superb.

"On the left was the sea, not the blue sea, the slate-coloured sea, but a sea of jade, greenish, milky, and hard under the deep sky.

"I was so pleased with my work that I danced as I carried it back to the inn. I wished that the whole world could have seen it at one and the same moment. I can remember that I showed it to a cow which was browsing by the wayside, exclaiming, at the same time: 'Look at that, my old beauty; you will not often see its like again.'

"When I had reached the front of the house, I immediately called out to Mother Lecacheur, bawling with all my might:

"'Look at this! You won't see anything like it in a hurry.'

"The woman came and looked at my work with stupid eyes, which distinguished nothing, and did not even recognise whether the picture represented an ox or a house.

"Miss Harriet was coming into the house, and she passed behind me just at the moment when, holding out my canvas at arm's length, I was exhibiting it to the old innkeeper. The 'demoniac' could not help but see it, for I took care to exhibit the thing in such a way that it could not escape her notice. She stopped abruptly and stood motionless, stupefied. It was her rock which was depicted, the one which she usually climbed to dream away her time undisturbed.

"She uttered a British 'Oh,' which was at once so accentuated and so flattering, that I turned round to her, smiling, and said:

"'This is my latest study, Mademoiselle.'

"She murmured ecstatically, comically, and tenderly:

"'Oh! Monsieur, you understand nature in a most thrilling way!'

"I coloured up, indeed I did, and was more excited by that compliment than if it had come from a queen. I was seduced, conquered, vanquished. I could have embraced her—upon my honour.

"I took my seat at the table beside her, as I had always

done. For the first time, she spoke, following out her thought aloud:

"'Oh! I love nature so much.'

"I offered her bread, water, wine. She now accepted these with a slight, dry smile. I then began to converse with her about the scenery.

"After the meal, we rose from the table together and walked leisurely across the court; then, attracted by the fiery glow which the setting sun cast over the surface of the sea, I opened the outside gate which faced in the direction of the cliff, and we walked on side by side, happy as two persons are who have just learned to understand and penetrate each other's motives and feelings.

"It was a misty, relaxing evening, one of those enjoyable evenings which impart happiness to mind and body alike. All is joy, all is charm. The luscious and balmy air, loaded with the perfume of grass, with the tang of seaweed, with the odour of the wild flowers, caresses the nostrils with its wild perfume, the palate with its salty savour, the soul with a penetrating sweetness. We were walking as on the brink of the abyss which overlooked the vast sea, which rolled its little waves a hundred yards below our feet.

"We drank, with open mouth and expanded chest, that fresh breeze from the ocean which glides slowly over the skin, salted by long contact with the waves.

"Wrapped in her plaid shawl, with a look of inspiration as she faced the breeze, the Englishwoman gazed fixedly at the great sun ball as it descended toward the horizon. Far off in the distance a three-master in full sail was outlined on the blood-red sky and a steamship, somewhat nearer, passed along, leaving behind it a trail of smoke on the horizon. The red sun-globe sank slowly lower and lower and presently touched the water just behind the motionless vessel, which, in its dazzling effulgence, looked as though framed in a flame of fire. We saw it plunge, grow smaller and disappear, swallowed up by the ocean.

" Miss Harriet gazed in rapture at the last gleams of the dying day. She seemed longing passionately to embrace the sky, the sea, the whole landscape.

" She murmured : ' Ah ! I love—I love——' I saw a tear in her eye. She went on : ' I wish I were a little bird, so that I could mount up into the firmament.'

" She remained standing as I had often before seen her, perched on the cliff, her face as red as her shawl. I should have liked to have sketched her in my album. It would have been a caricature of ecstasy.

" I turned away so as not to laugh.

" I then spoke to her of painting as I would have done to a fellow-artist, using the technical terms common among the devotees of the profession. She listened attentively, eagerly seeking to divine the meaning of the terms, so as to understand my thoughts. From time to time she would exclaim : ' Oh ! I understand, I understand. It is very interesting.'

" We returned home.

" The next day, on seeing me, she approached me, cordially holding out her hand ; and we at once became firm friends.

" She was a good creature who had a kind of soul on springs, which became enthusiastic at a bound. She lacked equilibrium, like all women who are spinsters at the age of fifty. She seemed to be preserved in vinegary innocence, but her heart still retained something of youth and of girlish effervescence. She loved both nature and animals with a fervent ardour, a love like old wine, mellow through age, a sensual love that she had never bestowed on men.

" One thing is certain : a bitch feeding her pups, a mare roaming in a meadow with a foal at its side, a bird's nest full of young ones, squeaking, with their open mouths and enormous heads, and no feathers, made her quiver with the most violent emotion.

" Poor solitary beings ! Sad wanderers from *table d'hôte* to *table d'hôte*, poor beings, ridiculous and lamentable, I love you ever since I became acquainted with Miss Harriet !

" I soon discovered that she had something she would like to tell me, but dared not, and I was amused at her timidity. When I started out in the morning with my box on my back, she would accompany me to the end of the village, silent, but evidently struggling inwardly to find words with which to begin a conversation. Then she would leave me abruptly, and walk away quickly with her jaunty step.

" One day, however, she plucked up courage :

" ' I would like to see how you paint pictures ? Will you show me ? I have been very curious.'

" And she coloured up as though she had given utterance to words of extreme audacity.

" I conducted her to the bottom of the Petit-Val, where I had commenced a large picture.

" She remained standing near me, following all my gestures with concentrated attention. Then, suddenly, fearing, perhaps, that she was disturbing me, she said to me : ' Thank you,' and walked away.

" But in a short time she became more familiar, and accompanied me every day, with visible pleasure. She carried her folding-stool under her arm, would not consent to my carrying it, and she sat by my side. She would remain there for hours immovable and mute, following with her eye the point of my brush in its every movement. When I would obtain, by a large splotch of colour spread on with a knife, a striking and unexpected effect, she would, in spite of herself, give vent to a half-suppressed ' Oh ! ' of astonishment, of joy, of admiration. She had the most tender respect for my canvases, an almost religious respect for that human reproduction of a part of Nature's divine work. My studies appeared to her as a species of holy pictures, and sometimes she spoke to me of God, with the idea of converting me.

" Oh ! He was a queer creature, this God of hers. He was

a sort of village philosopher without any great resources, and without great power; for she always pictured him to herself as being in despair over injustices committed under his eyes, as if he were helpless to prevent them.

"She was, however, on excellent terms with him, affecting even to be the confidante of his secrets and of his whims. She said: 'God wills,' or 'God does not will,' just like a sergeant announcing to a recruit: 'The colonel has commanded.'

"At the bottom of her heart she deplored my ignorance of the intentions of the Eternal, which she strove to impart to me.

"Every day I found in my pockets, in my hat when I lifted it from the ground, in my box of colours, in my polished shoes, standing in the mornings in front of my door, those little pious brochures, which she, no doubt, received directly from Paradise.

"I treated her as one would an old friend, with unaffected cordiality. But I soon perceived that she had changed somewhat in her manner, though, for a while, I paid little attention to it.

"When I was painting, whether in my valley or in some country lane, I would see her suddenly appear with her rapid, springy walk. She would then sit down abruptly, out of breath, as though she had been running or were overcome by some profound emotion. Her face would be red, that English red which is denied to the people of all other countries; then, without any reason, she would turn ashy pale and seem about to faint away. Gradually, however, her natural colour would return and she would begin to speak.

"Then, without warning, she would break off in the middle of a sentence, spring up from her seat and walk away so rapidly and so strangely that I was at my wits' ends to discover whether I had done or said anything to displease or wound her.

"I finally came to the conclusion that those were her normal manners, somewhat modified no doubt in my honour during the first days of our acquaintance.

"When she returned to the farm, after walking for hours on the windy coast, her long curls often hung straight down, as if their springs had been broken. This had hitherto seldom given her any concern, and she would come to dinner without embarrassment, all dishevelled by her sister, the breeze.

"But now she would go up to her room in order to adjust what I called her lamp-glasses. When I would say to her, with familiar gallantry, which, however, always offended her: 'You are as beautiful as a star to-day, Miss Harriet,' a little blood would immediately mount into her cheeks, the blood of a young maiden, the blood of sweet fifteen.

"Then she became very shy, and ceased coming to watch me paint. I thought:

"'This is only a fit of temper. It will pass.'

"But it did not pass away. When I spoke to her now, she would answer me, either with an air of affected indifference, or in a sullen anger; and she became by turns rude, impatient, and nervous. I never saw her except at meals, and we spoke but little. I concluded, at length, that I must have offended her in something: and, accordingly, I said to her one evening:

"'Miss Harriet, why have you changed towards me? What have I done to displease you? You are causing me much pain!'

"She responded in an angry tone, which was very funny: 'I have not changed towards you. It is not true, not true,' and she ran upstairs and shut herself up in her room.

"At times she would look upon me with strange eyes. Since that time I have often said to myself that those condemned to death must look thus when informed that their last day has come. In her eye there lurked a species of madness, an insanity at once mystical and violent—something more, a fever, an exasperated desire, impatient and impotent, for the unrealised and unrealisable!

"It seemed to me that there was also going on within her a combat, in which her heart struggled against an unknown force that she wished to overcome—perhaps, even, something else. But what could I know? What could I know?"

III

"It was indeed a singular revelation.

"For some time I had been working as soon as it got light on a picture the subject of which was as follows:

"A deep ravine, enclosed, surmounted by two thickets of rushes and trees, extended into the distance and was lost, submerged in that milky vapour, in that cloud-like cotton-down that sometimes floats over valleys at daybreak. And at the extreme end of that heavy, transparent fog one saw, or rather guessed, two human figures, a youth and a maiden, their arms interlaced, embracing, she with her head raised towards him, he bending over her, their lips joined.

"A first ray of the sun, glistening through the branches, pierced that fog of the dawn, illuminated it with a rosy reflection just behind the rustic lovers, framing their vague shadows in a silvery background. It was good; really good.

"I was working on the declivity which led to the valley of Étretat. On this particular morning I had, by chance, the sort of floating vapour which I needed.

"Suddenly something rose up in front of me like a phantom; it was Miss Harriet. On seeing me she was about to flee. But I called after her, saying: 'Come here, come here, Mademoiselle. I have a nice little picture for you.'

"She came forward, though with seeming reluctance I handed her my sketch. She said nothing, but stood for a long time motionless, looking at it. Suddenly she burst into tears. She wept spasmodically, like men who have been struggling hard against shedding tears, but who can do so no longer, and abandon themselves to grief, resisting still. I got up, trembling, moved myself by the sight of a sorrow I did not understand, and I took her by the hand with a gesture of brusque affection, a real French impulse, in which action outruns thought.

" She let her hands rest in mine for a few seconds, and I felt them quiver, as if her whole nervous system were on the rack. Then she withdrew her hands abruptly, or, rather, tore them out of mine.

" I recognised that shiver as soon as I had felt it; I knew it perfectly. Ah! the love-thrill of a woman, whether she is fifteen or fifty years of age, whether she is of the people or in society, goes so straight to my heart that I never have any difficulty in understanding it!

" Her whole frail being trembled, vibrated, swooned. I knew it. She walked away before I had time to say a word, leaving me as surprised as if I had witnessed a miracle, and as troubled as if I had committed a crime.

" I did not go in to breakfast. I took a walk on the edge of the cliff, feeling that I could just as soon weep as laugh, looking on the adventure as both comic and deplorable, and my position as ridiculous, believing her unhappy enough to go mad.

" I asked myself what I ought to do. I decided that my only course was to leave the place, and at once made up my mind to do so.

" Somewhat sad and perplexed, I wandered about until dinner-time, and entered the farmhouse just when the soup had been served.

" I sat down at the table as usual. Miss Harriet was there, eating away solemnly, without speaking to anyone, without even lifting her eyes. Her manner and expression were the same as usual.

" I waited patiently till the meal had been finished, then, turning toward the landlady, I said: ' Well, Madame Lecacheur, it will not be long now before I shall have to take my leave of you.'

" The good woman, surprised and troubled, replied in her

drawling voice : ' My dear sir, what's this ? You are going to leave us after I have become so accustomed to you ?'

" I glanced at Miss Harriet out of the corner of my eye. Her countenance did not change in the least. But Céleste, the little servant, looked up at me. She was a fat girl of about eighteen, rosy, fresh, as strong as a horse, and possessing the rare attribute of cleanliness. I had kissed her at odd times in out-of-the-way corners, after the manner of travellers—nothing more.

" The dinner being at length over, I went to smoke my pipe under the apple-trees, walking up and down from one end of the enclosure to the other. All the reflections which I had made during the day, the strange discovery of the morning, that passionate and grotesque attachment for me, the recollections which that revelation had suddenly called up, recollections at once charming and perplexing, perhaps also that look which the servant had cast on me at the announcement of my departure—all these things, mixed up and combined, put me now in a reckless humour, gave me a tickling sensation of kisses on the lips, and in my veins a something which urged me on to commit some folly.

" Night was coming on, casting its dark shadows under the trees, when I descried Céleste, who had gone to fasten up the poultry-yard at the other end of the enclosure. I darted towards her, running so noiselessly that she heard nothing, and as she got up from closing the small trap-door by which the chickens got in and out, I clasped her in my arms and rained on her coarse, fat face a shower of kisses. She struggled, laughing all the same, as she was accustomed to do in such circumstances. Why did I suddenly loose my grip of her ? Why did I at once experience a shock ? What was it that I heard behind me ?

" It was Miss Harriet, who had come upon us, who had seen us and who stood in front of us motionless as a spectre. Then she disappeared in the darkness.

" I was ashamed, embarrassed, more sorry at having been

thus surprised by her than if she had caught me committing some criminal act.

"I slept badly that night. I was completely unnerved and haunted by sad thoughts. I seemed to hear loud weeping, but in this I was no doubt deceived. Moreover, I thought several times that I heard someone walking up and down in the house and opening the hall-door.

"Towards morning I was overcome by fatigue and fell asleep. I got up late and did not go downstairs until the late breakfast, being still in a bewildered state, not knowing what kind of expression to put on.

"No one had seen Miss Harriet. We waited for her at table, but she did not appear. At length, Mother Lecacheur went to her room. The Englishwoman had gone out. She must have set out at break of day, as she often did to see the sun rise.

"Nobody seemed surprised at this and we began to eat in silence.

"The weather was hot, very hot, one of those still, sultry days when not a leaf stirs. The table had been placed out of doors, under an apple-tree; and we drank so much that Sapeur had to go constantly to the cellar to replenish the cider-jug. Céleste brought the dishes from the kitchen, a ragout of mutton with potatoes, a cold rabbit, and a salad. Afterwards she placed before us a dish of cherries, the first of the season.

"As I wanted to wash and freshen these, I begged the servant to go and bring a pitcher of cold water.

"In about five minutes she returned, declaring that the well was dry. She had lowered the pitcher to the full extent of the cord, and had touched the bottom, but on drawing the pitcher up again, it was empty. Mother Lecacheur, anxious to examine the thing for herself, went and looked down the hole. She returned announcing that there must be something in the well, something altogether unusual. Doubtless a neighbour had thrown some bundles of straw down, out of spite.

"I wanted to look down the well, too, thinking I could

better make out what it was. I leaned over the brink. I perceived, indistinctly, a white object. What could it be? I then conceived the idea of lowering a lantern at the end of a cord. The yellow flame danced on the stone walls, and gradually sank deeper. All four of us were leaning over the opening, Sapeur and Céleste having now joined us. The lantern rested on a black and white, indistinct mass, singular, incomprehensible. Sapeur exclaimed:

" 'It is a horse. I see the hoofs. It must have escaped from the meadow during the night, and fallen in.'

" But suddenly a cold shiver attacked my spine, I first recognised a foot, then a leg which protruded; the whole body and the other leg were submerged.

" I groaned and trembled so violently that the light of the lamp danced hither and thither over the object.

" 'It is a woman, who—who—is down there! It is Miss Harriet.'

" Sapeur alone did not flinch. He had witnessed worse things in Africa.

" Mother Lecacheur and Céleste began to scream piercingly, and ran away.

" But the corpse had to be recovered. I attached the boy securely by the loins, then I lowered him slowly, by means of the pulley, and watched him disappear in the darkness. In his hands he had a lantern, and another rope. Soon his voice, seeming to come from the centre of the earth, cried:

" 'Stop.'

" I then saw him fish something out of the water. It was the other leg. He bound the two feet together and shouted anew:

" 'Haul up.'

" I commenced to wind him up, but I felt as if my arms were broken, my muscles relaxed, and I was in terror lest I should let the boy fall to the bottom. When his head appeared over the brink, I asked:

" 'Well,' as if I expected he had a message from the woman lying at the bottom.

" We both got on to the stone slab at the edge of the well, and, face to face, leaning over the aperture, hoisted the body.

" Mother Lecacheur and Céleste watched us from a distance, hidden behind the wall of the house. When they saw the black slippers and white stockings of the corpse emerge from the hole, they disappeared.

" Sapeur seized the ankles, and we pulled up that poor, chaste woman in the most immodest posture. The head was in a shocking state, bruised and black; and the long, grey hair, hanging down, out of curl for ever, was muddy and dripping with water.

" 'Good Lord, how thin she is!' exclaimed Sapeur, in a contemptuous tone.

" We carried her into the room, and as the women did not put in an appearance, I, with the assistance of the lad, dressed the corpse for burial.

" I washed her sad, disfigured face. By the touch of my hand an eye was slightly opened; it fixed me with that pale stare, with that cold, that terrible look which corpses have, a look which seems to come from the beyond. I plaited up, as well as I could, her dishevelled hair, and I arranged on her forehead a novel and singular coiffure. Then I took off her dripping wet garments, baring, not without a feeling of shame, as though I had been guilty of some profanation, her shoulders and her chest, and her long arms, slim as the twigs of branches.

" Then I went to fetch some flowers, poppies, corn-flowers, marguerites, and fresh, sweet-smelling grass, with which to strew her funeral couch.

" Being the only person near her, it was necessary for me to fulfil the usual formalities. In a letter found in her pocket written at the last moment, she asked that her body be buried in the village in which she had passed the last days of her life.

A frightful thought then oppressed my heart. Was it not on my account that she wished to be laid at rest in this place?

"Towards evening, all the female gossips of the locality came to view the remains of the deceased; but I would not allow a single person to enter; I wanted to be alone; and I watched by the corpse the whole night.

"By the light of the candles, I looked at the body of this miserable woman, wholly unknown, who had died so lamentably and so far away from home. Had she left no friends, no relatives behind her? What had her infancy been? What had been her life? Whence had she come, all alone, a wanderer, like a dog driven from home? What secrets of suffering and of despair were sealed up in that uncouth body, like a shameful defect, concealed all her life beneath that ridiculous exterior, which had driven away from her all affection and all love?

"What unhappy beings there are! I felt that upon that human creature weighed the eternal injustice of implacable nature! Life was over with her, without her ever having experienced, perhaps, that which sustains the most miserable of us all—the hope of being once loved! Otherwise, why should she thus have concealed herself, have fled from others? Why did she love everything so tenderly and so passionately, everything living that was not a man?

"I understood, also, why she believed in a God, and hoped for compensation from him for the miseries she had endured. She had now begun to decompose, and to become, in turn, a plant. She would blossom in the sun, and be eaten up by the cattle, carried away in seed by the birds, and as flesh by the beasts, again to become human flesh. But that which is called the soul had been extinguished at the bottom of the dark well. She suffered no longer. She had changed her life for that of others yet to be born.

"Hours passed away in this silent and sinister communion with the dead. A pale light announced the dawn of a new day, and a bright ray glistened on the bed, casting a line of fire on the bed-clothes and on her hands. This was the hour she had so much loved, when the waking birds began to sing in the trees.

"I opened the window wide, I drew back the curtains, so that the whole heavens might look in upon us. Then bending toward the glassy corpse, I took in my hands the mutilated head, and slowly, without terror or disgust, imprinted a long, long kiss upon those lips which had never before received the salute of love."

Léon Chenal was silent. The women wept. We heard the Comte d'Etraille on the box-seat blow his nose several times in succession. Only the coachman nodded. The horses, no longer feeling the sting of the whip, had slackened their pace and were dragging us slowly along. And the brake hardly moved at all, having become suddenly heavy, as if laden with sorrow.

THE LOCK

THE FOUR GLASSES IN FRONT OF THE DINERS WERE STILL nearly half full, which is a sign, as a general rule, that the guests are quite so. They were beginning to speak without waiting for an answer; no one took any notice of anything except what was going on inside him; voices grew louder, gestures more animated, eyes brighter.

It was a bachelors' dinner of confirmed old celibates. They had instituted this regular banquet twenty years before, christening it "The Bachelors'," and at the time there were fourteen of them, all fully determined never to marry. Now there were only four of them left; three were dead and the other seven were married.

These four stuck firmly to it, and, as far as lay in their power, they scrupulously observed the rules which had been laid down at the beginning of their curious association. They had sworn hand in hand, to turn aside every woman they could from the right path, and their friends' wives for choice, and more especially those of their most intimate friends. For this reason, as soon as any of them left the society, in order to set up in domestic life for himself, he took care to quarrel definitely with all his former companions.

Besides this, they were pledged at every dinner to relate most minutely their last adventures, which had given rise to this familiar phrase among them: "To lie like a Bachelor."

They professed, moreover, the most profound contempt for woman, whom they talked of as a "beast of pleasure." Every moment they quoted Schopenhauer, who was their god, and his well-known essay "On Women"; called for the reintroduction of harems and towers, and had the ancient maxim:

" *Mulier, perpetuus infans*," woven into their table-linen, and below it, the line of Alfred de Vigny: " *La femme, enfant malade et douze fois impure*." So that by dint of despising women they lived only for them, while all their efforts and all their desires were directed toward them. Those of them who had married called them old fops, made fun of them, and—feared them.

The confidences of this Bachelors' dinner were due to begin exactly when the champagne was served.

On the day in question, these old fellows, for they were old by this time, and the older they grew the more extraordinary strokes of luck in the way of love-affairs they had to relate, were quite talkative. For the last month, according to their own accounts, each of them had seduced at least one woman a day. And what women! the youngest, the noblest, the richest, and the most beautiful!

After they had finished their stories, one of them, he who had spoken first and had therefore been obliged to listen to all the others, rose and said:

" Now that we have finished drawing the long bow, I should like to tell you, not my last, but my first adventure—I mean the first adventure of my life, my first fall for it is a moral fall after all, in the arms of a woman. Oh! I am not going to tell you my first—what shall I call it?—my first appearance; certainly not. The leap over the first ditch (I am speaking figuratively) has nothing interesting about it. It is generally rather a muddy one, and one picks oneself up rather abashed, with one charming illusion the less, with a vague feeling of disappointment and sadness. That realisation of love the first time one experiences it is rather repugnant; we had dreamed of it as being so different, so delicate, so refined. It leaves a physical and moral sense of disgust behind it, just as when one has happened to put one's hand on a toad. You may rub your hand as hard as you like, but the sensation remains.

" Yes! one very soon gets quite used to it; there is no

doubt about that. For my part, however, I am very sorry it was not in my power to give the Creator the benefit of my advice when He was arranging these little matters. I wonder what *I* should have done? I am not quite sure, but I think, with the English savant, John Stuart Mill, I should have managed differently; I should have found some more convenient and more poetical combination, yes—more poetical.

"I really think that the Creator showed Himself to be too naturalistic—too—what shall I say? His invention lacks poetry.

"However, what I am going to tell you is about my first woman of the world, the first woman in society I ever made love to. I beg your pardon, I ought to say the first woman of the world that ever triumphed over me. For at first it is *we* who allow ourselves to be taken, while, later on—it is the . . . same thing!

"She was a friend of my mother, a charming woman in every way. When such women are chaste, it is generally from sheer stupidity, and when they are in love they are furiously so. And then—we are accused of corrupting them! Yes, yes, of course! With them it is always the rabbit that begins and never the sportsman. I know all about it; they don't seem to lure us, but they do it all the same, and do what they like with is, without its being noticed, and then they actually accuse us of having ruined them, dishonoured them, degraded them, and all the rest of it.

"The woman in question certainly had a great desire to be 'degraded' by me. She may have been about thirty-five, while I was scarcely two-and-twenty. I no more thought of seducing her than I did of turning Trappist. Well, one day when I was calling on her, and while I was looking at her dress with considerable astonishment, for she had on a morning wrapper which was open as wide as a church door when the bells are ringing for mass, she took my hand and squeezed it—squeezed it, you know, as they will do at such moments—and said, with a deep sigh, one of those sighs, you know, which come right from the bottom of the chest: 'Oh! don't look at me like that, child!' I got as red as a tomato, and felt more nervous than usual, naturally. I was very much inclined to bolt, but she held my hand tightly, and putting it on her well-developed bust, she said: 'Just feel how my heart beats!' Of course it was beating, and I began to understand what was the matter, but I did not know what to do. I have changed considerably since then.

"As I remained standing there, with one hand on the soft covering of her heart, while I held my hat in the other, and continued to look at her with a confused, silly smile—a timid, frightened smile—she suddenly drew back, and said in an irritated voice:

"'Young man, what are you doing? You are indecent and badly brought up.'

"You may be sure I took my hand away quickly, stopped smiling, and stammering out some excuse, got up and took my leave as if I had lost my head.

"But I was caught, and dreamed of her. I thought her charming, adorable; I fancied that I loved her, that I had always loved her, and I determined to see her again. I decided to be enterprising, to be more than that even.

"When I saw her again she gave me a shy smile. Oh, how that little smile upset me! And she shook hands with a long, significant pressure.

"From that day it seems that I made love to her; at least, she declared afterward that I had ruined her, captured her, dishonoured her, with rare Machiavellism, with consummate cleverness, with the calculations of a mathematician, and the cunning of an Apache Indian.

"But one thing troubled me strangely: where was my triumph to be accomplished? I lived with my family, and on this point my family was most particular. I was not bold enough to venture into a hotel in broad daylight with a woman on my arm, and I did not know whom to ask for advice.

" Now, my fair friend had often said in joke that every young man ought to have a room for himself somewhere or other from home. We lived in Paris, and this was a sort of inspiration. I took a room, and she came. She came one day in November; I should have liked to put off her visit because I had no fire, and I had no fire because the chimney smoked. The very evening before, I had spoken to my landlord, a retired shopkeeper, about it, and he had promised that he would come himself with the chimney-expert in a day or two to see what could be done.

" As soon as she came in, I said:

" 'There is no fire because my chimney smokes.'

" She did not even appear to hear me, but stammered: 'That does not matter, I have plenty of fire'; and when I looked surprised, she stopped short in confusion, and went on: 'I don't know what I am saying; I am mad. I have lost my head. Oh! what am I doing? Why did I come? How unhappy I am! What a disgrace, what a disgrace!' And she threw herself sobbing into my arms.

" I thought that she really felt remorse, and swore that I would respect her. Then, however, she sank down at my knees, sighing: 'But don't you see that I love you, that you have overcome me, that it seems as though you had thrown a charm over me?'

" Then I thought it was about time to show myself a man. But she trembled, got up, ran, and hid behind a wardrobe, crying out: 'Oh! don't look at me; no! no! If only you did not see me, if we were only in the dark! I am ashamed in the light. Cannot you imagine it? What a nightmare! Oh! this light, this light!'

" I rushed to the window; I closed the outside shutters, drew the curtains, and hung a coat over a ray of light that peeped in, and then, stretching out my hands so as not to fall over the chairs, with my heart beating, I groped for her, and found her.

"Then the two of us set out again, feeling our way with our hands united, toward the other corner where the alcove was. I don't suppose we went straight, for first of all I knocked against the mantelpiece and then against a chest of drawers, before finding what we wanted. Then I forgot everything in a frantic ecstasy. It was an hour of folly, madness, superhuman joy, followed by a delicious lassitude, in which we slept in each other's arms.

"I was half dreaming; but in my dream I fancied that someone was calling me and crying for help; than I received a violent blow, and opened my eyes.

"'Oh—h!' The setting sun, magnificent and red, shone full into the room through the door, which was wide open. It seemed to look at us from the verge of the horizon, illuminating us both, especially my companion, who was screaming, struggling, and twisting, and trying with hands and feet to get hold of a corner of a sheet, a curtain or anything else, while in the middle of the room stood my landlord in a morning-coat with the concierge by his side, and a chimney-sweep, as black as the devil, all three staring at us with stupid eyes.

"I sprang up in a rage, ready to jump at his throat, and shouted:

"'What the douce are you doing in my room?'

"The chimney-sweep laughed so that he let his brush fall on to the floor. The concierge seemed to have gone mad, and the landlord stammered:

"'But, Monsieur, it was—it was—about the chimney—the chimney, the chimney which——'

"'Go to the devil!' I roared. So he took off his hat, which he had kept on in his confusion, and said, in a confused but very civil manner:

"'I beg your pardon, Monsieur; if I had known I should

not have disturbed you; I should not have come. The concierge told me you had gone out. Pray excuse me.' And they all went out.

"Ever since that time I never draw the curtains, but I am always very careful to lock the door."

SUICIDES

HARDLY A DAY GOES BY WITHOUT OUR READING IN SOME newspaper the following paragraph

"On Wednesday night the people living in No. 40 Rue de —— were awakened by two shots in succession. They seemed to come from the apartment occupied by M. X——. The door was broken in and the man was found bathed in his blood, still holding in one hand the revolver with which he had taken his life.

"M. X—— was fifty-seven years of age, enjoying a comfortable income, and had everything necessary to make him happy. No cause can be found for his action."

What terrible grief, what unknown suffering, hidden despair, secret wounds drive these presumably happy persons to suicide? We search, we imagine tragedies of love, we suspect financial troubles, and, as we never find anything definite, we apply to these deaths the word "mystery."

A letter found on the desk of one of these "suicides for motive unknown," and written during his last night, beside his loaded revolver, has come into our hands. We think it rather interesting. It reveals none of those great catastrophes which we always expect to find behind these acts of despair; but it shows us the slow succession of the little vexations of life, the disintegration of a lonely existence, whose dreams have disappeared; it gives the reason for these tragic ends, which only nervous and high-strung people can understand.

Here it is:

"It is midnight. When I have finished this letter I shall kill myself. Why? I shall attempt to give the reasons, not for those who may read these lines, but for myself, to kindle my waning courage, to impress upon myself the fatal necessity of this act which could only be deferred.

" I was brought up by simple-minded parents who were unquestioning believers. And I believed as they did.

" My dream lasted a long time. The last veil has just been torn from my eyes.

" During the last few years a strange change has been taking place within me. All the events of Life, which formerly had to me the glow of a beautiful sunset, are now fading away. The true meaning of things has appeared to me in its brutal reality ; and the true reason for love has bred in me disgust even for romantic love. ' We are the eternal toys of foolish and charming illusions, which are always being renewed.'

" On growing older, I had become partly reconciled to the awful mystery of life, to the uselessness of effort ; when the emptiness of everything appeared to me in a new light, this evening, after dinner.

" Formerly, I was happy ! Everything pleased me : the passing women, the appearance of the streets, the place where I lived ; and I even took an interest in the cut of my clothes. But the repetition of the same sights has had the result of filling my heart with weariness and disgust, just as one would feel were one to go every night to the same theatre.

" For the last thirty years I have been rising at the same hour ; and, at the same restaurant, for thirty years, I have been eating at the same hours the same dishes brought me by different waiters.

" I have tried travel. The loneliness which one feels in strange places terrified me. I felt so alone, so small on the earth that I quickly started on my homeward journey.

" But here the unchanging expression of my furniture, which has stood for thirty years in the same place, the worn armchairs that I had known when quite new, the smell of my apartment (for, with time, each dwelling takes on a particular odour) each night, these and other things disgust me and make me sick of living thus.

"Everything repeats itself endlessly. The way in which I put my key in the lock, the place where I always find my matches, the first object which meets my eye when I enter the room, make me feel like jumping out of the window and putting an end to those monotonous events from which we can never escape.

"Each day, when I shave, I feel an inordinate desire to cut my throat; and my face, which I see in the little mirror, always the same, with soap on my cheeks, has several times made me cry from sadness.

"Now I even hate to be with people whom I used to meet with pleasure; I know them so well, I can tell just what they are going to say and what I am going to answer. Each brain is like a circus, where the same horse keeps circling around eternally. In spite of our efforts, our detours, the wall is near, round and round for ever, no unexpected way, no door to the unknown. We must circle round always, around the same ideas, the same joys, the same pleasures, the same habits, the same beliefs, the same sensations of disgust.

"The fog was terrible this evening. It enfolded the boulevard, where the street lights were dimmed and looked like smoking candles. A heavier weight than usual oppressed me. Perhaps my digestion was bad.

"For good digestion is everything in life. It gives inspiration to the artist, amorous desires to young people, clear ideas to thinkers, the joy of life to everybody, and it also allows one to eat heartily (which is really the greatest pleasure). A sick stomach induces scepticism, unbelief, nightmares, and a desire for death. I have often noticed this fact. Perhaps I should not be killing myself, if my digestion had been good this evening.

"When I sat down in the arm-chair where I have been sitting every day for thirty years, I glanced around me, and just then I was seized by such a terrible distress that I thought I must go mad.

" I tried to think of what I could do to run away from myself. Every occupation struck me as being worse even than inaction. Then I bethought myself of putting my papers in order.

" For a long time I have been thinking of clearing out my drawers ; for, for the last thirty years, I have been throwing my letters and bills pell-mell into the same desk, and this confusion has often caused me considerable trouble. But I feel such moral and physical laziness at the sole idea of putting anything in order that I have never had the courage to begin this tedious business.

" I therefore opened my desk, intending to choose among my old papers and destroy the majority of them.

" At first I was bewildered by this array of documents, yellowed by age, then I chose one.

" Oh ! if you cherish life, never disturb the burial-place of old letters !

" And if, perchance, you should, take the contents by the handful, close your eyes that you may not read a word, so that you may not recognise some forgotten handwriting which may plunge you suddenly into a sea of memories ; carry these papers to the fire ; and when they are in ashes, crush them to an invisible powder, or otherwise you are lost—just as I was lost an hour ago.

" The first letters which I read did not interest me greatly. They were recent, and came from living men whom I still meet quite often, and whose presence does not move me to any great extent. But all at once one envelope made me start. My name was traced on it in a large, bold, handwriting ; and suddenly tears came to my eyes. That letter was from my dearest friend, the companion of my youth, the confidant of my hopes ; and he appeared before me so clearly, with his pleasant smile and his hand outstretched, that a cold shiver ran down my back. Yes, yes, the dead come back, for I saw him! Our memory is a more perfect world than the universe: it gives back life to those who no longer exist.

"With trembling hand and dimmed eyes I re-read everything that he told me, and in my poor sobbing heart I felt a wound so painful that I began to groan as a man whose bones are slowly being crushed.

"Then I travelled over my whole life, just as one travels along a river. I recognised people so long forgotten that I no longer knew their names. Their faces alone lived in me. In my mother's letters I saw again the old servants, the shape of our house and the little insignificant odds and ends which cling to our minds.

"Yes, I suddenly saw again all my mother's old gowns, the different styles which she adopted and the several ways in which she dressed her hair. She haunted me especially in a silk dress, trimmed with old lace; and I remembered something she said one day when she was wearing this dress. She said: 'Robert, my child, if you do not stand up straight you will be round-shouldered all your life.'

"Then, opening another drawer, I found myself face to face with memories of tender passions: a dancing-pump, a torn handkerchief, even a garter, locks of hair and dried flowers. Then the sweet romances of my life, whose living heroines are now white haired, plunged me into the deep melancholy of things. Oh, the young brows where blond locks curl, the caress of the hands, the glance which speaks, the hearts which beat, that smile which promises the lips, those lips which promise the embrace! And the first kiss—that endless kiss which makes you close your eyes, which drowns all thought in the immeasurable joy of approaching possession!

"Taking these old pledges of former love in both my hands, I covered them with furious caresses, and in my soul, torn by these memories, I saw them each again at the hour of surrender;

and I suffered a torture more cruel than all the tortures invented in all the fables about hell.

" One last letter remained. It was written by me and dictated fifty years ago by my writing master.

" Here it is :

" ' My Dear Little Mamma,—

" ' I am seven years old to-day. It is the age of understanding. I take advantage of it to thank you for having brought me into this world.

" ' Your little son, who loves you,

" ' Robert.'

" It is all over. I had gone back to the beginning, and suddenly I turned my glance on what remained to me of life. I saw hideous and lonely old age, and approaching infirmities, and everything over and gone. And nobody near me !

" My revolver is here, on the table. I am loading it. . . . Never re-read your old letters ! "

And that is how many men come to kill themselves ; and we search in vain to discover some great sorrow in their lives.

THE KISS

My little darling: so you are crying from morning until night and from night until morning, because your husband leaves you; you do not know what to do and so you ask your old aunt for advice; you must consider her quite an expert. I don't know as much as you think I do, and yet I am not entirely ignorant of the art of loving, or, rather, of making one's self loved, in which you are a little lacking. I can admit that at my age.

You say that you are all attention, love, kisses and caresses for him. Perhaps that is the very trouble; I think you kiss him too much.

My dear, we have in our hands the most terrible power in the world: love.

Man is gifted with physical strength, and his weapon is force. Woman is gifted with charm, and she rules with caresses. It is our weapon, formidable and invincible, but we should know how to use it.

We are the mistresses of the visible world. To tell the history of Love from the beginning of the world would be to tell the history of man himself. Everything springs from it, the arts, great events, customs, wars, the overthrow of empires.

In the Bible you find Delilah, Judith; in fables, Omphale, Helen; in history the Sabines, Cleopatra, and many others.

Therefore we reign supreme, all-powerful. But, like kings, we must make use of delicate diplomacy.

Love, my dear, is made up of imperceptible sensations. We know that it is as strong as death, but also as frail as glass. The slightest shock breaks it, our power crumbles, and we are never able to build it up again.

We have the power of making ourselves adored, but we lack one tiny thing, understanding of the various shades of caresses, the subtle feeling for what is excessive in the manifestations of our tender feelings. When we are embraced we lose the sentiment of delicacy, while the man over whom we rule remains master of himself, capable of judging the foolishness of certain words. Take care, my dear; that is the defect in our armour. It is our Achilles' heel.

Do you know whence comes our real power? From the kiss, the kiss alone! When we know how to offer and give up our lips we can become queens.

The kiss is only a preface, indeed, but a charming preface. More charming than the realisation itself. A preface which can always be read over again, whereas one cannot always read over the book.

Yes, the meeting of lips is the most perfect, the most divine sensation given to human beings, the supreme limit of happiness. It is in the kiss alone that one sometimes seems to feel this union of souls after which we strive, the intermingling of swooning hearts, as it were.

Do you remember the verses of Sully-Prudhomme:

> "All our caresses are but vain endeavour
> The eternal, fruitless yearning of our love;
> For bodies meet, but souls are blended never."

One caress alone gives this deep sensation of two beings welded into one—it is the kiss. No violent delirium of complete possession equals this trembling approach of the lips, this first moist and fresh contact, and then the long, lingering, motionless rapture.

Therefore, my dear, the kiss is our strongest weapon, but we must take care not to dull it. Do not forget that its value is only relative, purely conventional. It continually changes according to circumstances, the state of expectancy and the ecstasy of the mind. I will give an example of what I mean.

Another poet, François Coppée, has written a line which we all remember, a line which we find delightful, which moves our very hearts.

After describing the expectancy of a lover waiting in a room one winter's evening, his anxiety, his nervous impatience, his terrible fear of not seeing her, he describes the arrival of the beloved, who at last enters hurriedly, out of breath, bringing with her a breath of winter, and he exclaims :

"Ah, first, delicious kisses through the veil!"

Is that not a line of exquisite sentiment, a delicate and charming observation, a perfect truth? All those who have hastened to a clandestine meeting, whom passion has thrown into the arms of a man, well do they know these first, delicious kisses through the veil; and they tremble at the memory of them. And yet their sole charm lies in the circumstances, from being late, from the anxious expectancy, from the purely—or, rather, impurely, if you prefer—sensual point of view, they are detestable.

Think! Outside it is cold. The young woman has walked quickly; the veil is moist from her cold breath. Little drops of water shine in the lace. The lover seizes her and presses his burning lips to her liquid breath. The moist veil, which discolours and carries the dreadful odour of chemical dye, penetrates into the young man's mouth, moistens his moustache. He does not taste the lips of his beloved, he tastes the dye of this lace moistened with cold breath. And yet, like the poet, we would all exclaim:

"Ah, first, delicious kisses through the veil!"

Therefore, the value of this caress being entirely a matter of convention, we must be careful not to abuse it.

Well, my dear, I have several times noticed that you are very clumsy. You are not, indeed, alone in that fault; the majority of women lose their authority by abusing the kiss with untimely kisses. When they feel that their husband or their lover is a little tired, at those times when the heart as well as the body needs rest, instead of understanding what is going on within him they persist in giving inopportune caresses, tire him by the obstinacy of begging lips and give caresses lavished with neither rhyme nor reason.

Trust my experience. First, never kiss your husband in public, in the train, at the restaurant. It is bad taste; do not give in to your desires. He would feel ridiculous and would never forgive you.

Beware of useless kisses lavished in intimacy. I am sure that you abuse them. For instance, I remember one day that you did something quite shocking. Probably you do not remember it.

All three of us were together in the drawing-room, and, as you did not stand on ceremony before me, your husband was holding you on his knees and kissing you at great length on the neck, the lips and throat. Suddenly you exclaimed: "Oh! the fire!" You had been paying no attention to it, and it was almost out. A few lingering embers were glowing on the hearth. Then he rose, ran to the wood-box, from which he was, with great efforts, dragging two enormous logs, when you came to him with begging lips, murmuring:

"Kiss me!" He turned his head with difficulty and tried to hold up the logs at the same time. Then you gently and slowly placed your mouth on that of the poor fellow, who remained with his neck out of joint, his sides twisted, his arms almost dropping off, trembling with fatigue and tired from his desperate effort. And you kept drawing out this torturing kiss, without seeing or understanding. Then when you freed him, you began to grumble: "How badly you kiss!" No wonder!

Oh, beware! We all have this foolish habit, this stupid and inconsiderate impulse to choose the most inconvenient moments. When he is carrying a glass of water, when he is putting on his shoes, when he is tying his cravat—in short, when he finds himself in any uncomfortable position—then is the time which we choose for a caress which makes him stop for a whole minute in the middle of what he is doing, with the sole desire of getting rid of us!

Do not think that this criticism is insignificant. Love, my dear, is a delicate thing. The least little thing offends it: everything depends on the tact of our caresses. An ill-placed kiss may do any amount of harm.

Try following my advice.

Your old aunt,

COLLETTE.

DENIS

MONSIEUR MARAMBOT OPENED THE LETTER WHICH HIS SERVANT Denis gave him, and smiled.

For twenty years Denis had been a servant in this house. He was a short, stout, jovial man, who was known throughout the country-side as a model servant. He asked:

"Is Monsieur pleased? Has Monsieur received good news?"

M. Marambot was not rich. He was an old village chemist, a bachelor, who lived on an income acquired with difficulty by selling drugs to the farmers. He answered:

"Yes, my boy. Old Malois is afraid of the lawsuit with which I am threatening him. I shall get my money to-morrow. Five thousand francs will not hurt the account of an old bachelor."

M. Marambot rubbed his hands with satisfaction. He was a man of quiet temperament, more sad than gay, incapable of any prolonged effort, careless in business.

He could undoubtedly have amassed a greater income had he taken advantage of the deaths of colleagues established in more important centres, by taking their places and carrying on their business. But the trouble of moving and the thought of all the preparations had always stopped him. After thinking the matter over for a few days, he would just say:

"Bah! I'll wait until the next time. I'll not lose anything by the delay. I may even find something better."

Denis, on the contrary, was always urging his master to new enterprises. Of an energetic temperament, he would continually repeat:

"Oh! If I had only had the capital to start out with, I could have made a fortune! One thousand francs would do me."

M. Marambot would smile without answering and would go out in his little garden, where, his hands behind his back, he would walk about dreaming.

All day long, Denis sang the joyful refrains of the folk-songs of the district. He even showed an unusual activity, for he cleaned all the windows of the house, energetically rubbing the glass, and singing at the top of his voice.

M. Marambot, surprised at his zeal, said to him several times, smiling:

"My boy, if you work like that there will be nothing left for you to do to-morrow."

The following day, at about nine o'clock in the morning, the postman gave Denis four letters for his master, one of them very heavy. M. Marambot immediately shut himself up in his room until late in the afternoon. He then handed his servant four letters for the mail. One of them was addressed to M. Malois; it was undoubtedly a receipt for the money.

Denis asked his master no questions; he appeared to be as sad and gloomy that day as he had seemed joyful the day before.

Night came. M. Marambot went to bed as usual and slept.

He was awakened by a strange noise. He sat up in his bed and listened. Suddenly the door opened and Denis appeared, holding in one hand a candle and in the other a carving-knife, his eyes staring, his face contracted as though moved by some deep emotion; he was as pale as a ghost.

In his astonishment M. Marambot thought that he was sleep-walking, and he was going to get out of bed and assist him when the servant blew out the light and rushed at the bed. His master stretched out his hands to ward off the shock, which knocked him over on his back; he was trying to seize the hands of his servant, whom he now thought to be crazy, in order to avoid the blows which the latter was aiming at him.

He was struck by the knife; once in the shoulder, once on

the forehead and the third time in the chest. He fought wildly, waving his arms around in the darkness, kicking and crying:

"Denis! Denis! Are you mad? Listen, Denis!"

But the latter, gasping for breath, kept up his furious attack, always striking, always repulsed, sometimes with a kick, sometimes with a punch, and rushing forward again furiously.

M. Marambot was wounded twice more, once in the leg and once in the stomach. But, suddenly, a thought flashed across his mind, and he began to shriek:

"Stop, stop, Denis, I have not yet received my money!"

The man immediately ceased, and his master could hear his laboured breathing in the darkness.

M. Marambot then went on:

"I have received nothing. M. Malois takes back what he said, the lawsuit will take place; that is why you carried the letters to the mail. Just read those on my desk."

With a final effort, he reached for his matches and lit the candle.

He was covered with blood. His sheets, his curtains, and even the walls, were spattered with red. Denis, standing in the middle of the room, was also bloody from head to foot.

When he saw the blood M. Marambot thought himself dead, and fell unconscious.

At break of day he revived. It was some time, however, before he regained his senses, and was able to understand or remember. But, suddenly, the memory of the attack and of his wounds returned to him, and he was filled with such terror that he closed his eyes in order not to see anything. After a few minutes he grew calmer and began to think. He had not died immediately, therefore he might still recover. He felt weak, very weak; but he had no real pain, although he noticed an uncomfortable smarting sensation in several parts of his body. He also felt icy cold, and all wet, and as though wrapped up in bandages. He thought that this dampness came from the blood which he had lost; and he shivered at the dreadful thought of this red liquid which had come from his veins and covered his bed. The idea of seeing this terrible spectacle again so upset him that he kept his eyes closed with all his strength, as though they might open in spite of himself.

What had become of Denis? He had probably escaped.

But what could he, Marambot, do now? Get up? Call for help? But if he should make the slightest motions, his wounds would undoubtedly open up again and he would die from loss of blood.

Suddenly he heard the door of his room open. His heart almost stopped. It was certainly Denis who was coming to finish him up. He held his breath in order to make the murderer think that he had been successful.

He felt his sheet being lifted up, and then someone feeling his stomach. A sharp pain near his hip made him start. He was being very gently washed with cold water. Therefore, someone must have discovered the misdeed and he was being cared for. A wild joy seized him; but prudently, he did not wish to show that he was conscious. He opened one eye, just one, with the greatest precaution.

He recognised Denis standing beside him, Denis himself! Mercy! He hastily closed his eye again.

Denis. What could he be doing? What did he want? What awful scheme could he now be carrying out?

What was he doing? Washing him, of course, in order to hide the traces of his crime! And he would now bury him in the garden, under ten feet of earth, so that no one could discover him! Or perhaps in the wine-cellar under the bottles of old wine! And M. Marambot began to tremble like a leaf. He kept saying to himself: "I am lost, lost!" He closed his eyes in order not to see the knife as it descended for the final stroke. It did not come. Denis was now lifting him up and bandaging him. Then he began carefully to dress the wound on his leg, as his master had taught him to do when he was a pharmacist.

There was no longer any doubt. His servant after wishing to kill him was trying to save him.

Then M. Marambot, in a dying voice, gave him the practical piece of advice :

" Wash the wounds in a diluted solution of carbolic acid ! "

Denis answered :

" That is what I am doing, Monsieur."

M. Marambot opened both his eyes. There was no sign of blood either on the bed, on the walls, or on the murderer. The wounded man was stretched out on clean white sheets.

The two men looked at each other.

Finally, M. Marambot said calmly :

" You have been guilty of a great crime."

Denis answered :

" I am trying to make up for it, Monsieur. If you will not betray me, I will serve you as faithfully as in the past."

This was no time to anger his servant. M. Marambot murmured as he closed his eyes :

" I swear not to betray you."

Denis saved his master. He spent days and nights without sleep, never leaving the sick-room, preparing drugs, broths, potions, feeling his pulse, anxiously counting the beats, attending him with the skill of a trained nurse and the devotion of a son.

He continually asked :

" Well, Monsieur, how do you feel ? "

M. Marambot would answer in a weak voice :

" A little better, my boy, thank you."

And when the sick man would wake up at night, he would often see his servant seated in an arm-chair weeping silently.

Never had the old chemist been so cared for, so fondled, so spoiled. At first he had said to himself :

" As soon as I am well I shall get rid of this rascal."

He was now convalescent, and from day to day he would

put off dismissing his murderer. He thought that no one would ever show him such care and attention, for he held this man through fear; and he warned him that he had left a document with a lawyer denouncing him to the law if any new accident should occur.

This precaution seemed to guarantee him against any future attack; and he then asked himself if it would not be wiser to keep this man near him, in order to watch him closely.

Just as formerly, when he would hesitate about taking some larger place of business, he could not make up his mind to any decision.

"There is plenty of time," he would say to himself.

Denis continued to show himself an admirable servant. M. Marambot was well. He kept him.

One morning, just as he was finishing breakfast, he suddenly heard a great noise in the kitchen. He hastened in there. Denis was struggling with two gendarmes. An officer was taking notes on his pad.

As soon as he saw his master, the servant began to sob, exclaiming:

"You betrayed me, Monsieur, that's not right, after what you had promised me. You have broken your word of honour, Monsieur Marambot; that's not right, that's not right!"

M. Marambot, bewildered and distressed at being suspected, lifted his hand.

"I swear to you before God, my boy, that I did not betray you. I haven't the slightest idea how the police could have found out about your attack on me."

The officer started:

"You say that he attacked you, M. Marambot?"

The bewildered chemist answered:

"Yes—but I did not betray him—I haven't said a word—I swear it—he has served me excellently from that time on——"

The officer pronounced severely:

"I will take down your testimony. The law will take

notice of this new action, of which it was ignorant, Monsieur Marambot. I was commissioned to arrest your servant for the theft of two ducks surreptitiously taken by him from M. Duhamel, of which act there are witnesses. I shall make a note of your information."

Then, turning toward his men, he ordered:

"Come on, let us start!"

The two gendarmes dragged Denis out.

The lawyer used the plea of insanity, contrasting the two misdeeds in order to strengthen his argument. He had clearly proved that the theft of the two ducks came from the same mental condition as the eight knife-wounds in the body of Marambot. He had cunningly analysed all the phases of this transitory condition of mental aberration, which could, doubtless, be cured by a few months' treatment in a reputable sanatorium. He had spoken in enthusiastic terms of the continued devotion of this faithful servant, of the care with which he had surrounded his master, wounded by him in a moment of alienation.

Touched by this memory, M. Marambot felt the tears rising to his eyes.

The lawyer noticed it, opened his arms with a broad gesture, spreading out the long black sleeves of his robe like the wings of a bat, and exclaimed:

"Look, look, gentlemen of the jury, look at those tears. What more can I say for my client? What speech, what argument, what reasoning would be worth these tears of his master? They speak louder than I do, louder than the law; they cry: 'Mercy, for the fleeting aberration!' They implore, they pardon, they bless!"

He was silent and sat down.

Then the judge, turning to Marambot, whose testimony had been excellent for his servant, asked him:

"But, Monsieur, even admitting that you consider this man insane, that does not explain why you should have kept him. He was none the less dangerous."

Marambot, wiping his eyes, answered :

" Well, your honour, what can you expect ? Nowadays it's so hard to find good servants—I could never have found a better one."

Denis was acquitted and put in a sanatorium at his master's expense.

THE DONKEY

THERE WAS NOT A BREATH OF AIR STIRRING ; A HEAVY MIST was lying over the river. It was like a layer of dull white cotton placed on the water. The banks themselves were indistinct, hidden behind strange shapes of fog that looked like mountains. But day was breaking and the hill was becoming visible. At its foot, in the dawning light of day, the plaster houses began to appear like white spots. Cocks were crowing in the barnyards.

On the other side of the river, hidden behind the fog just opposite Frette, a slight noise from time to time broke the dead silence of the quiet morning. At times it was an indistinct plashing, like the cautious advance of a boat, then again a sharp noise like the rattle of an oar and then the sound of something dropping in the water. Then silence.

Sometimes whispered words, coming perhaps from a distance, perhaps from quite near, pierced through these opaque mists. They passed by like wild birds which have slept in the rushes and fly away at the first light of day, fly forever and forever ; and one glimpses them a moment, piercing the mist in full flight, uttering their soft, timid cry, which wakes their brethren all along the banks.

Suddenly, near the bank, opposite the village, a barely perceptible shadow appeared on the water. Then it grew, became more distinct and, coming out of the foggy curtain which hung over the river, a flat-boat, manned by two men, pushed up on the grass.

The man who was rowing rose and took a pailful of fish from the bottom of the boat, then he threw the dripping net over his shoulder. His companion, who had not moved, exclaimed: "Get your gun, Mailloche, and see if we can't land some rabbits in the dunes."

The other one answered: "All right. I'll be with you in a minute." Then he disappeared to hide their catch.

The man who had stayed in the boat slowly filled his pipe and lighted it. His name was Labouise, but he was called Chicot, and was in partnership with Maillochon, commonly called Mailloche, practising the doubtful and undefined profession of scavengers.

They were sailors of a low class, but only sailed really when things were short. The rest of the time they were scavengers. Rowing about on the river day and night, watching for any prey, dead or alive, water-poachers, night-hunters, skimmers of drains; sometimes hunting deer in the forest of Saint-Germain, sometimes looking for drowned people and searching their clothes, picking up floating rags, empty bottles, empty bottles which sway drunkenly in the current, neck upwards, bits of wood carried down-stream; thus did Labouise and Maillochon live easily.

At times they would set out on foot about noon and stroll along at random. They would dine in some inn on the shore and leave again side by side. They would remain away for a couple of days; then one morning they would be seen rowing about in the tub which they called their boat.

At Joinville or at Nogent some boatman would be looking for his boat, which had disappeared one night, probably stolen, while twenty or thirty miles from there, on the Oise, some shopkeeper would be rubbing his hands, congratulating himself on the bargain he had made when he bought a boat the day before for fifty francs, which two men offered him as they were passing.

Maillochon reappeared with his gun wrapped up in rags. He was a man of forty or fifty, tall and thin, with the restless eye of a man worried by legitimate troubles, or of a hunted animal. His open shirt showed his hairy chest, but he seemed never to have had any more hair on his face than a short brush of a moustache and a few stiff hairs under his lower lip. He was bald around the temples. When he took off the dirty cap that he wore like a helmet, his scalp seemed to be covered with a fluffy down, like the body of a plucked chicken ready for the spit.

Chicot, on the contrary, was red, fat, short and hairy. He looked like a raw beefsteak hidden in a fireman's cap. He continually kept his left eye closed, as if he were aiming at something or at somebody, and when people jokingly cried to him: "Open your eye, Labouise!" he would answer quietly "Never fear, sister, I open it when there's cause to."

He had a habit of calling every one sister, even his fellow-scavenger.

He took up the oars again, and once more the boat disappeared in the heavy mist, which was now turning milky-white in the pink-tinted sky.

"What kind of lead did you take, Maillochon?" Labouise asked.

"Very small, number nine; that's the best for rabbits."

They were approaching the other shore so slowly, so quietly that no noise betrayed them. This bank belongs to the forest of Saint-Germain, and is the boundary-line for rabbit hunting. It is covered with burrows hidden under the roots of trees, and the creatures frisk about at daybreak, running in and out of the holes.

Maillochon was kneeling in the bow, watching, his gun hidden on the floor. Suddenly he seized it, aimed, and the report echoed long throughout the quiet country.

Labouise, in a few strokes, touched the beach, and his companion, jumping to the ground, picked up a little grey rabbit, still quivering.

Then the boat once more disappeared into the fog to get to the other side, and keep away from the gamekeepers.

The two men seemed to be riding easily on the water. The

weapon had disappeared under the board which served as a hiding-place and the rabbit was stuffed into Chicot's loose shirt.

After about a quarter of an hour Labouise asked : " Well, sister, shall we get one more ? "

" All right, come on," answered Maillochon.

The boat started swiftly down the current. The mist, which was hiding both shores, was beginning to rise. The trees could be barely perceived, as through a veil, and the little clouds of fog were floating up from the water. When they drew near the island, the end of which is opposite Herblay, the two men slackened their pace and began to watch. Soon a second rabbit was killed.

Then they went down until they were half-way to Conflans. Here they stopped, tied their boat to a tree and went to sleep in the bottom of it.

From time to time Labouise would sit up and look over the horizon with his open eye. The last of the morning mist had disappeared and the large summer sun was climbing up the blue sky.

On the other side of the river the vineyard-covered hill stretched out in a semicircle. One house stood out alone at the summit. Everything was silent.

Something was moving slowly along the tow-path, advancing with difficulty. It was a woman dragging a donkey. The stubborn, stiff-jointed beast stretched out a leg now and then, yielding to its companion's efforts when further resistance was impossible, and it proceeded thus, with outstretched neck and ears lying flat, so slowly that one could not prophesy when it would ever be out of sight.

The woman, bent double, was pulling, turning round occasionally to strike the donkey with a stick.

When he saw her, Labouise exclaimed : " Hey, Mailloche ! "

Mailloche answered : " What's the matter ? "

" Want to have some fun ? "

" Of course ! "

" Then hurry, sister ; we're going to have a laugh."

Chicot took the oars. When he had crossed the river he stopped opposite the woman and called : " Hey, sister ! "

The woman stopped dragging her donkey and looked.

Labouise continued : " What are you doing—going to the locomotive show ? "

The woman made no reply. Chicot continued : " Your Neddy must have won a prize at the races. Where are you taking him at that speed ? "

At last the woman answered : " I'm going to Macquart, at Champioux, to have him killed. He's worthless."

Labouise answered : " You're right. How much do you think Macquart will give you for him ? "

The woman wiped her forehead on the back of her hand and hesitated, saying : " How do I know ? Perhaps three francs, perhaps four."

Chicot exclaimed : " I'll give you five francs and your errand's done ! How's that ? "

The woman considered the matter for a second and then exclaimed : " Done ! "

The two men landed. Labouise grasped the animal by the bridle. Maillochon asked in surprise : " What do you expect to do with that carcass ? "

Chicot this time opened his other eye in order to express his gaiety. His whole red face was grinning with joy. He chuckled : " Don't worry, sister, I've got my idea."

He gave five francs to the woman, who then sat down by the road to see what was going to happen. Then Labouise, in great humour, got the gun and held it out to Maillochon, saying : " Each in turn ; we're going after big game, sister. Don't get so near or you'll kill it right off ! You must make the pleasure last a little."

He placed his companion about forty paces from the victim. The ass, feeling itself free, was trying to crop the tall grass on the bank, but it was so exhausted that it swayed on its legs as if it were about to fall.

Maillochon aimed slowly and said: " A little pepper for the ears; watch, Chicot!" And he fired.

The tiny shot struck the donkey's long ears and he began to shake them in order to get rid of the stinging sensation. The two men were doubled up with laughter and stamped their feet with joy. The woman, indignant, rushed forward; she did not want her donkey to be tortured, and she offered to return the five francs. Labouise threatened her with a thrashing and pretended to roll up his sleeves. He had paid, hadn't he? Well, then, he would take a shot at her skirts, just to show that it didn't hurt. She went away, threatening to call the police. They could hear her protesting indignantly and cursing as she went her way.

Maillochon held out the gun to his comrade, saying: " It's your turn, Chicot."

Labouise aimed and fired. The donkey received the charge in his thighs, but the shot was so small and came from such a distance that he thought he was being stung by flies, for he began to thrash himself with his tail on the legs and back.

Labouise sat down to laugh more comfortably, while Maillochon reloaded the weapon, so happy that he seemed to sneeze into the barrel. He stepped forward a few paces, and, aiming at the same place that his friend had shot at, he fired again. This time the beast started, tried to kick and turned its head. At last a little blood was running. It had been wounded and felt a sharp pain, for it tried to run away with a slow, limping, jerky gallop.

Both men darted after the beast, Maillochon with a long stride, Labouise with the short breathless trot of a little man. But the donkey, tired out, had stopped, and, with a bewildered look, was watching his two murderers approach. Suddenly he stretched his neck and began to bray.

Labouise, out of breath, had taken the gun. This time he

walked right up close, as he did not wish to begin the chase over again.

When the poor beast had finished its mournful cry, like a last call for help, the man called : " Hey, Mailloche ! Come here, sister ; I'm going to give him some medicine." And while the other man was forcing the animal's mouth open, Chicot stuck the barrel of his gun down its throat, as if he were trying to make it drink a potion. Then he said : " Look out, sister, here she goes ! "

He pressed the trigger. The donkey stumbled back a few steps, fell down tried to get up again and finally lay on its side and closed its eyes. The whole body was trembling, its legs were kicking as if it were trying to run. A stream of blood was oozing through its teeth. Soon it stopped moving. It was dead.

The two men stopped laughing. It was over too quickly ; they had not had their money's worth. Maillochon asked : " Well, what are we going to do now ? "

Labouise answered : " Don't worry, sister. Get the thing on the boat ; we're going to have some fun when night comes."

They went and got the boat. The animal's body was placed on the bottom, covered with fresh grass, and the two men stretched out on it and went to sleep.

Toward noon Labouise drew a bottle of wine, some bread and butter and raw onions from a hiding-place in their muddy, worm-eaten boat, and they began to eat.

When the meal was over they once more stretched out on the dead donkey and slept. At nightfall Labouise awoke and shook his comrade, who was snoring like a buzz-saw. " Come on, sister," he ordered.

Maillochon began to row. As they had plenty of time, they went up the Seine slowly. They coasted along the reaches covered with water-lilies, perfumed by hawthorn which dipped its white tufts over the stream ; and the heavy, mud-coloured boat slid over the great, flat leaves of the water-lilies and bent down their flowers, pale, round, split like a dancer's belt, which rose behind their passing.

When they reached the wall of the Éperon, which separates the forest of Saint-Germain from the park of Maisons-Laffitte, Labouise stopped his companion and explained his idea to him. Maillochon was moved by a prolonged, silent laugh.

They threw into the water the grass which had covered the body, took the animal by the feet and hid it behind some bushes. Then they got into their boat again and went to Maisons-Laffitte.

The night was perfectly black when they reached old Jules' wine shop and inn. As soon as the dealer saw them he came up, shook hands with them and sat down at their table. They began to talk of one thing and another. By eleven o'clock the last customer had left and old Jules winked at Labouise and asked : " Well, have you got any ? "

Labouise made a motion with his head and answered : " Perhaps, perhaps not ! "

The dealer insisted : " Perhaps you've got nothing but greys ? "

Chicot dug his hand into his flannel shirt, drew out the ears of a rabbit and declared : " Three francs a pair ! "

Then began a long discussion about the price. They agreed on two francs sixty-five and the two rabbits were handed over. As the two men were getting up to go, old man Jules, who had been watching them, exclaimed : " You have something else, but you won't say what."

Labouise answered : " Possibly, but it is not for you ; you're too stingy."

The man, growing eager, kept asking : " What is it ? Something big ? Perhaps we might make a deal."

Labouise, who seemed perplexed, pretended to consult Maillochon with a glance. Then he answered in a slow voice : " This is how it is. We were in the bushes at Éperon when something passed right near us, to the left, at the end of the wall. Mailloche takes a shot and it drops. We skipped on account of the game people. I can't tell you what it is, because I don't know. But it's big enough. But what is it? If I told you I'd be lying, and you know, sister, between us everything's above-board."

The man asked, shaking with excitement: "Think it's a deer?"

Labouise answered: "Might be and then again it might not! Deer?—might be a little big for that! More like a doe. Mind you, I don't say it's a doe, because I don't know, but it might be."

Still the dealer insisted: "Perhaps it's a buck?"

Labouise stretched out his hand, exclaiming: "No, it's not that! It's not a buck. I should have seen the horns. No, it's not a buck!"

"Why didn't you bring it with you?" asked the man.

"Because, sister, from now on I sell on the spot. Plenty of people will buy. All you have to do is to take a walk over there, find the thing and take it. No risk for me."

The innkeeper, growing suspicious, exclaimed: "Supposing it's gone by now!"

Labouise once more raised his hand and said: "It's there, I swear!—first bush to the left. What it is, I don't know. But it's not a buck, I'm positive. It's for you to find out what it is. Twenty francs, cash down!"

Still the man hesitated: "Couldn't you bring it?"

Maillochon then became spokesman:

"Then there is no bargain. If it is a buck, it will be fifty francs, if it is a doe, seventy; that's our price."

The dealer decided: "Done for twenty francs!"

And they shook hands over the deal.

Then he took out four big five-franc pieces from the cash drawer, and the two friends pocketed the money. Labouise arose, emptied his glass and left. As he was disappearing in the shadows he turned round to explain: "It isn't a buck.

I don't know what it is!—but it's there. I'll give you back your money if you find nothing!"

And he disappeared in the darkness. Maillochon, who was following him, kept punching him in the back to express his delight.

AN IDYLL

THE TRAIN HAD JUST LEFT GENOA, IN THE DIRECTION OF Marseilles, and was following the rocky and sinuous coast, gliding like an iron serpent between the sea and the mountains, creeping over the yellow sand edged with silver waves and entering suddenly into the black-mouthed tunnels like a beast into its lair.

In the last carriage, a stout woman and a young man sat opposite each other. They did not speak, but occasionally they would glance at each other. She was about twenty-five years old. Seated by the window, she silently gazed at the passing landscape. She was from Piedmont, a peasant, with large black eyes, a full bust and fat cheeks. She had deposited several parcels under the wooden seat and she held a basket on her knees.

The man might have been twenty years old. He was thin and sunburned, with the dark complexion that denotes work in the open. Tied up in a handkerchief was his whole fortune; a pair of heavy boots, a pair of trousers, a shirt and a coat. Hidden under the seat were a shovel and a pickaxe tied together with a rope.

He was going to France to seek work.

The sun, rising in the sky, spread a fiery light over the coast; it was toward the end of May and delightful odours floated in the air and penetrated through the open windows of the railway carriage. The blooming orange and lemon-trees exhaled a heavy, sweet perfume that mingled with the breath of the roses which grew in profusion everywhere along the line, in the gardens of the wealthy, in front of cottage doors, and even wild.

Roses are at home along this coast! They fill the whole region with their dainty and powerful fragrance and make the atmosphere taste like a delicacy, something better than wine, and as intoxicating.

The train was going at slow speed as if loath to leave behind this wonderful garden. It stopped every few minutes at small stations, at clusters of white houses, then went on again leisurely, emitting long whistles. Nobody got in. One would have thought that all the world had gone to sleep, unable to stir, on that sultry spring morning. The plump peasant woman from time to time closed her eyes, but opened them suddenly as her basket began to slide from her lap. She would catch it, replace it, look out of the window a little while and then doze off again. Tiny beads of perspiration covered her brow and she breathed with difficulty, as if suffering from a painful oppression.

The young man had let his head fall on his breast and was sleeping the sound sleep of the labouring man.

All of a sudden, just as the train left a small station, the peasant woman woke up and opening her basket, drew forth a piece of bread, some hard-boiled eggs, and a flask of wine and some fine, red plums. She began to eat.

The man had also wakened and he watched the woman, watched every morsel that travelled from her knees to her lips. He sat with his arms folded, his eyes set and his lips tightly compressed.

The woman ate like a glutton, with relish. Every little while she would take a swallow of wine to wash down the eggs and then she would stop for breath.

Everything vanished, the bread, the eggs, the plums and the wine. As soon as she finished her meal, the man closed his eyes. Then, feeling ill at ease, she loosened her blouse and the man suddenly looked at her again.

She did not seem to mind and continued to unbutton her dress.

The pressure of her flesh causing the opening to gape, she revealed a portion of white linen chemise and a portion of her skin.

As soon as she felt more comfortable, she turned to her fellow-traveller and remarked in Italian: "It's too hot to breathe."

He answered, in the same tongue and with the same accent: "Fine weather for travelling."

She asked: "Are you from Piedmont?"

"From Asti."

"And I'm from Casale."

They were neighbours. They began to talk.

They exchanged the commonplace remarks that working people repeat over and over and which are sufficient for their slow-working and narrow minds. They spoke of their homes. They had mutual acquaintances.

They quoted names and became more and more friendly as they discovered more and more people they knew. Short, rapid words, with sonorous endings and the Italian cadence, gushed from their lips.

After that, they talked about themselves. She was married and had three children whom she had left with her sister, for she had found a situation as nurse, a good situation with a French lady at Marseilles.

He was going to look for work.

He had been told that he would be able to find it in France, for they were building a great deal, he had heard.

They then fell silent.

The heat was becoming terrible; it beat down like fire on the roof of the railway carriage. A cloud of dust flew behind the train and entered through the window, and the fragrance of the roses and orange-blossoms had become stronger, heavier and more penetrating.

The two travellers went to sleep again.

They awakened almost at the same time. The sun was

nearing the edge of the horizon and shed its glorious light on the blue sea. The atmosphere was lighter and cooler.

The nurse was gasping. Her dress was open and her cheeks looked flabby and moist, and in an oppressed voice, she breathed :

" I have not nursed since yesterday ; I feel as if I were going to faint."

The man did not reply ; he hardly knew what to say.

She continued : " When a woman has as much milk as I, she must nurse three times a day or she'll feel uncomfortable. It feels like a weight on my heart, a weight that prevents my breathing and just exhausts me. It's terrible to have so much milk."

He replied : " Yes, its bad. It must hurt you."

She really seemed ill and almost ready to faint. She murmured : " I only have to press and the milk flows out like a fountain. It is really interesting to see. You wouldn't believe it. In Casale, all the neighbours came to see it."

He replied : " Ah ! really."

" Yes, really. I would show you, only it wouldn't help me. You can't make enough come out that way."

And she paused.

The train stopped at a station. Leaning on a fence was a woman holding a crying infant in her arms. She was thin and in rags.

The nurse watched her. Then she said in a compassionate tone : " There's a woman I could help. And the baby could help me, too. I'm not rich ; I'm leaving my home, my people and my baby to take a place, but still, I'd give five francs to have that child and be able to nurse it for ten minutes. It would quiet him, and me too, I can tell you. I think I would feel as if I were being born again."

She paused again. Then she passed her hot hand several times across her wet brow and moaned : " Oh ! I can't stand it any longer. I believe I shall die." And with an unconscious motion, she opened her dress altogether.

Her right breast appeared all swollen and stiff, with its brown teat, and the poor woman gasped: "Ah! gracious Heaven! What shall I do?"

The train had left the station and was running on, while the flowers breathed out their penetrating fragrance on the warm evening air.

Sometimes they saw a fishing-boat, which seemed asleep on the blue sea with its motionless white sail, which was reflected in the water as though another boat were there, head down.

The young man, embarrassed, stammered: "But—madam—I—might perhaps be—be able to help you."

In an exhausted whisper, she replied: "Yes, if you will be so kind, you'll do me a great favour. I can't stand it any longer, really I can't."

He got on his knees before her; and she leaned over to him with a motherly gesture as if he were a child. In the movement she made to draw near to the man, a drop of milk appeared on her breast. He absorbed it quickly, and, taking this heavy breast in his mouth like a fruit, he began to drink regularly and greedily.

He had passed his arms around the woman's waist and pressed her close to him in order not to lose a drop of the nourishment. And he drank with slow gulps, like a baby.

All of a sudden she said: "That's enough, now the other side!" Docilely, he took the other.

She had placed both hands on his back and now was breathing happily, freely, enjoying the perfume of the flowers carried on the breeze that entered the open windows.

"What a lovely smell," she said.

He made no reply and drank on at the living fountain of her breast, closing his eyes as though to savour it better

But she gently pushed him from her.

" That's enough. I feel much better now. It has put life into me again."

He rose and wiped his mouth with the back of his hand.

While she replaced her breasts inside her dress, she said :

" You did me a great favour. I thank you very much ! "

And he replied in a grateful tone :

" It is I who thank you, for I hadn't eaten a thing for two days ! "

THE STRING

ALONG ALL THE ROADS AROUND GODERVILLE THE PEASANTS and their wives were coming toward the little town, for it was market-day. The men walked with slow steps, their whole bodies bent forward at each movement of their long twisted legs, deformed by their hard work, by the weight on the plough which, at the same time, raises the left shoulder and distorts the figure, by the reaping of the wheat which forces the knees apart to get a firm stand, by all the slow and painful labours of the country. Their blouses, blue, starched, shining as if varnished, ornamented with a little design in white at the neck and wrists, puffed about their bony bodies, seemed like balloons ready to carry them off. From each of them a head, two arms, and two feet protruded.

Some led a cow or a calf at the end of a rope, and their wives, walking behind the animal, whipped its haunches with a leafy branch to hasten its progress. They carried on their arms large wicker-baskets, out of which a chicken here, a duck there, thrust out its head. And they walked with a quicker, livelier step than their husbands. Their spare, straight figures were wrapped in a scanty little shawl, pinned over their flat bosoms, and their heads were enveloped in a piece of white linen tightly pressed on the hair and surmounted by a cap.

Then a wagon passed, its nag's jerky trot shaking up and down two men seated side by side and a woman in the bottom of the vehicle, the latter holding on to the sides to lessen the hard jolts.

In the square of Goderville there was a crowd, a throng of human beings and animals mixed together. The horns of the cattle, the rough-napped top-hats of the rich peasants, and the head-gear of the peasant women rose above the surface of the crowd. And the clamorous, shrill, screaming voices made a continuous and savage din which sometimes was dominated by the robust lungs of some countryman's laugh, of the long lowing of a cow tied to the wall of a house.

It all smacked of the stable, the dairy and the dung-heap, of hay and sweat, giving forth that sharp, unpleasant odour, human and animal, peculiar to the people of the fields.

Maître Hauchecorne, of Bréauté, had just arrived at Goderville, and was directing his steps toward the square, when he perceived upon the ground a little piece of string. Maître Hauchecorne, economical like a true Norman, thought that everything useful ought to be picked up, and he stooped painfully, for he suffered from rheumatism. He took the bit of thin cord from the ground and was beginning to roll it carefully when he noticed Maître Malandain, the harness-maker, on the threshold of his door, looking at him. They had once had a quarrel together on the subject of a halter, and they had remained on bad terms, being both good haters. Maître Hauchecorne was seized with a sort of shame to be seen thus by his enemy, picking a bit of string out of the dirt. He concealed his find quickly under his blouse, then in his trousers pocket; then he pretended to be still looking on the ground for something which he did not find, and he went towards the market, his head thrust forward, bent double by his pains.

He was soon lost in the noisy and slowly-moving crowd, which was busy with interminable bargainings. The peasants looked at cows, went away, came back, perplexed, always in fear of being cheated, not daring to decide, watching the vendor's eye, ever trying to find the trick in the man and the flaw in the beast.

The women, having placed their great baskets at their feet, had taken out the poultry, which lay upon the ground, tied together by the feet, with terrified eyes and scarlet crests.

They heard offers, stated their prices with a dry air and

impassive face, or perhaps, suddenly deciding on some proposed reduction, shouted to the customer who was slowly going away: "All right, Maître Anthime, I'll give it to you for that."

Then little by little the square was deserted, the Angelus rang for noon, and those who lived too far away went to the different inns.

At Jourdain's the great room was full of people eating, as the big yard was full of vehicles of all kinds, carts, gigs, wagons, nondescript carts, yellow with dirt, mended and patched, raising their shafts to the sky like two arms, or perhaps with their shafts on the ground and their backs in the air.

Right against the diners seated at the table, the immense fire-place, filled with bright flames, cast a lively heat on the backs of the row on the right. Three spits were turning on which were chickens, pigeons, and legs of mutton; and an appetising odour of roast meat and gravy dripping over the nicely browned skin rose from the hearth, lightened hearts and made mouths water.

All the aristocracy of the plough ate there, at Maître Jourdain's, tavern keeper and horse dealer, a clever fellow who had money.

The dishes were passed and emptied, as were the jugs of yellow cider. Every one told his affairs, his purchases, and sales. They discussed the crops. The weather was favourable for the greens but rather damp for the wheat.

Suddenly the drum began to beat in the yard, before the house. Everybody rose, except a few indifferent persons, and ran to the door, or to the windows, their mouths still full, their napkins in their hands.

After the public crier had stopped beating his drum, he called out in a jerky voice, speaking his phrases irregularly:

"It is hereby made known to the inhabitants of Goderville, and in general to all persons present at the market, that there was lost this morning, on the road to Benzeville, between nine and ten o'clock, a black leather pocket-book containing five hundred francs and some business papers. The finder is requested to return same to the Mayor's office or to Maître Fortuné Houlbrèque of Manneville. There will be twenty francs reward."

Then the man went away. The heavy roll of the drum and the crier's voice were again heard at a distance.

Then they began to talk of this event discussing the chances that Maître Houlbrèque had of finding or not finding his pocket-book.

And the meal concluded. They were finishing their coffee when the chief of the gendarmes appeared upon the threshold.

He inquired :

" Is Maître Hauchecorne, of Bréauté, here ? "

Maître Hauchecorne, seated at the other end of the table, replied :

" Here I am."

And the officer resumed :

" Maître Hauchecorne, will you have the goodness to accompany me to the Mayor's office ? The Mayor would like to talk to you."

The peasant, surprised and disturbed, swallowed at a draught his tiny glass of brandy, rose, even more bent than in the morning, for the first steps after each rest were specially difficult, and set out, repeating : " Here I am, here I am."

The Mayor was awaiting him, seated in an arm-chair. He was the local lawyer, a stout, serious man, fond of pompous phrases.

" Maître Hauchecorne," said he, " you were seen this morning picking up, on the road to Benzeville, the pocket-book lost by Maître Houlbrèque, of Manneville."

The countryman looked at the Mayor in astonishment, already terrified by this suspicion resting on him without his knowing why.

" Me ? Me ? I picked up the pocket-book ? "

" Yes, you, yourself."

" On my word of honour, I never heard of it."

" But you were seen."

" I was seen, me? Who says he saw me?"

" Monsieur Malandain, the harness-maker."

The old man remembered, understood, and flushed with anger.

" Ah, he saw me, the clodhopper, he saw me pick up this string, here, Mayor." And rummaging in his pocket he drew out the little piece of string.

But the Mayor, incredulous, shook his head.

" You will not make me believe, Maître Hauchecorne, that Monsieur Malandain, who is a man we can believe, mistook this cord for a pocket-book."

The peasant, furious, lifted his hand, spat at one side to attest his honour, repeating :

" It is nevertheless God's own truth, the sacred truth. I repeat it on my soul and my salvation."

The Mayor resumed :

" After picking up the object, you stood like a stilt, looking a long while in the mud to see if any piece of money had fallen out."

The old fellow choked with indignation and fear.

" How anyone can tell—how anyone can tell—such lies to take away an honest man's reputation! How can anyone——"

There was no use in his protesting, nobody believed him. He was confronted with Monsieur Malandain, who repeated and maintained his affirmation. They abused each other for an hour. At his own request, Maître Hauchecorne was searched. Nothing was found on him.

Finally the Mayor, very much perplexed, discharged him with the warning that he would consult the Public Prosecutor and ask for further orders.

The news had spread. As he left the Mayor's office, the old man was surrounded and questioned with a serious or bantering curiosity, in which there was no indignation. He began to tell the story of the string. No one believed him They laughed at him.

He went along, stopping his friends, beginning endlessly his statement and his protestations, showing his pockets turned inside out, to prove that he had nothing.

They said:

"Ah, you old devil!"

And he grew angry, becoming exasperated, hot and distressed at not being believed, not knowing what to do and always repeating himself.

Night came. He had to leave. He started on his way with three neighbours to whom he pointed out the place where he had picked up the bit of string; and all along the road he spoke of his adventure.

In the evening he took a turn in the village of Bréauté, in order to tell it to everybody. He only met with incredulity.

It made him ill all night.

The next day about one o'clock in the afternoon, Marius Paumelle, a hired man in the employ of Maître Breton, husbandman at Ymauville, returned the pocket-book and its contents to Maître Houlbrèque of Manneville.

This man claimed to have found the object in the road; but not knowing how to read, he had carried it to the house and given it to his employer.

The news spread through the neighbourhood. Maître Hauchecorne was informed of it. He immediately went the circuit and began to recount his story completed by the happy climax. He triumphed.

"What grieved me so much was not the thing itself, as the lying. There is nothing so shameful as to be placed under a cloud on account of a lie."

He talked of his adventure all day long, he told it on the highway to people who were passing by, in the inn to people who were drinking there, and to persons coming out of church the following Sunday. He stopped strangers to tell them about it. He was calm now, and yet something disturbed him without his knowing exactly what it was. People had the air of joking while they listened. They did not seem convinced. He seemed to feel that remarks were being made behind his back.

On Tuesday of the next week he went to the market at Goderville, urged solely by the necessity he felt of discussing the case.

Malandain, standing at his door, began to laugh on seeing him pass. Why?

He approached a farmer from Criquetot, who did not let him finish, and giving him a thump in the stomach said to his face:

" You clever rogue."

Then he turned his back on him.

Maître Hauchecorne was confused, why was he called a clever rogue?

When he was seated at the table, in Jourdain's tavern he commenced to explain " the affair."

A horse-dealer from Monvilliers called to him:

" Come, come, old sharper, that's an old trick; I know all about your piece of string!"

Hauchecorne stammered:

" But the pocket-book was found."

But the other man replied:

" Shut up, papa, there is one that finds, and there is one that brings back. No one is any the wiser, so you get out of it."

The peasant stood choking. He understood. They accused him of having had the pocket-book returned by a confederate, by an accomplice.

He tried to protest. All the table began to laugh.

He could not finish his dinner and went away, in the midst of jeers.

He went home ashamed and indignant, choking with anger and confusion, the more dejected that he was capable with his

Norman cunning of doing what they had accused him of, and even of boasting of it as of a good trick. His innocence seemed to him, in a confused way, impossible to prove, as his sharpness was known. And he was stricken to the heart by the injustice of the suspicion.

Then he began to recount the adventure again, enlarging his story every day, adding each time new reasons, more energetic protestations, more solemn oaths which he imagined and prepared in his hours of solitude, his whole mind given up to the story of the string. He was believed so much the less as his defence was more complicated and his arguing more subtle.

" Those are lying excuses," they said behind his back.

He felt it, consumed his heart over it, and wore himself out with useless efforts. He was visibly wasting away.

The wags now made him tell about the string to amuse them, as they make a soldier who has been on a campaign tell about his battles. His mind, seriously affected, began to weaken.

Towards the end of December he took to his bed.

He died in the first days of January, and in the delirium of his death struggles he kept claiming his innocence, reiterating.

" A piece of string, a piece of string—look—here it is."

WAITER, A BOCK

WHY DID I GO INTO THAT TAVERN ON THAT PARTICULAR evening? I do not know. It was cold; a fine rain, a flying mist, veiled the gas-lamps with a transparent fog, made the sidewalks reflect the light that streamed from the shop-windows, lighting up the soft slush and the muddy feet of the passers-by.

I was going nowhere in particular; was simply having a short walk after dinner. I had passed the Crédit Lyonnais, the Rue Vivienne, and several other streets. I suddenly perceived a large tavern which was more than half full. I walked inside, with no object in view. I was not the least thirsty.

I glanced round to find a place that was not too crowded, and went and sat down by the side of a man who seemed to me to be old, and who was smoking a cheap clay-pipe, which was as black as coal. From six to eight saucers piled up on the table in front of him indicated the number of bocks he had already absorbed. I did not look at him closely. At a glance I recognised a bock-drinker, one of those frequenters of beer-houses who come in the morning when the place opens, and do not leave till evening when it is about to close. He was dirty, bald on top of his head, with a fringe of iron-grey hair falling on the collar of his frock-coat. His clothes, which were much too large for him, appeared to have been made for him at a time when he was corpulent. One guessed that these trousers never held up, that he could not take ten steps without having to stop to put them straight and adjust them. Did he wear a waistcoat? The mere thought of his boots and of that which they covered filled me with horror. The frayed cuffs were perfectly black at the edges, as were his nails.

As soon as I had seated myself beside him, this individual said to me in a quiet tone of voice:

" How goes it?"

I turned sharply round and scanned his features, whereupon he continued:

" I see you do not recognise me."

" No, I do not."

" Des Barrets."

I was stupefied. It was the Comte Jean des Barrets, my old school-friend.

I seized him by the hand, and was so dumbfounded that I could find nothing to say. At length I managed to stammer out:

" And you, how goes it with you?"

He responded placidly:

" I get along as best I can."

" What are you doing now?" I asked.

" You see what I am doing," he answered quite resignedly.

I felt my face getting red. I insisted:

" But every day?"

" Every day it is the same thing," was his reply, accompanied with a thick puff of tobacco smoke.

He then tapped with a sou on the top of the marble table, to attract the attention of the waiter, and called out:

" Waiter, two bocks."

A voice in the distance repeated:

" Two bocks for the fourth table."

Another voice, more distant still, shouted out shrilly:

" Here!"

Immediately a man with a white apron appeared, carrying two bocks at a run, and spilling some of the yellow liquid on the sandy floor in his haste.

Des Barrets emptied his glass at a single draught and replaced it on the table, while he sucked in the foam that had been left on his moustache. Then he asked:

"What news?"

I really had nothing new to tell him. I stammered:

"Nothing, old man. I am a business man."

In his monotonous tone he said:

"Indeed, does it amuse you?"

"No, but what can I do? One must do something!"

"Why should one?"

"To have an occupation."

"What's the use of an occupation? I never do anything, as you see, nothing at all. When one has not a sou I can understand why one should work. But when one has enough to live on, what's the use? What is the good of working? Do you work for yourself, or for others? If you work for yourself, if you do it for your own amusement, that's all right; if you work for others, you are a fool."

Then, laying his pipe on the marble table, he called out anew:

"Waiter, a bock." And continued: "Talking makes me thirsty. I am not accustomed to it. Yes, yes, I do nothing. I let things slide, and I am growing old. In dying I shall have nothing to regret. My only remembrance will be this tavern. No wife, no children, no cares, no sorrows, nothing. That is best."

He then emptied the glass which had been brought him, passed his tongue over his lips, and resumed his pipe.

I looked at him in astonishment, and said:

"But you have not always been like that?"

"Pardon me; ever since I left college."

"That is not a life, my dear fellow; it is simply horrible. Come, you must have something to do, you must love something, you must have friends."

"No. I get up at noon, I come here, I have my lunch, I drink bocks, I remain until the evening, I have my dinner, I drink bocks. Then about half-past one in the morning, I go home to bed, because the place closes up; that annoys me more than anything. In the last ten years I have passed fully six years on this bench, in my corner; and the other four in my bed, nowhere else. I sometimes chat with the regular customers."

"But when you came to Paris what did you do at first?"

"I studied law . . . at the Café de Médicis."

"What next?"

"Next I crossed the water and came here."

"Why did you take that trouble?"

"Well, one cannot remain all one's life in the Latin Quarter. The students make too much noise. Now I shall not move again. Waiter, a bock."

I began to think that he was making fun of me, and I continued:

"Come now, be frank. You have been the victim of some great sorrow; some disappointment in love, no doubt! It is easy to see that you are a man who has had some trouble. What age are you?"

"I am thirty-three, but I look at least forty-five."

I looked him straight in the face. His wrinkled, ill-shaven face gave one the impression that he was an old man. On the top of his head a few long hairs waved over a skin of doubtful cleanliness. He had enormous eyelashes, a heavy moustache, and a thick beard. Suddenly I had a kind of vision, I know not why, of a basin filled with dirty water in which all that hair had been washed. I said to him:

"You certainly look older than your age. You surely must have experienced some great sorrow."

He replied:

"I tell you that I have not. I am old because I never go out into the air. Nothing makes a man deteriorate more than café life."

I still could not believe him.

"You must surely also have been married? One could not get as bald-headed as you are without having loved greatly."

He shook his head, shaking dandruff down on his coat as he did so.

" No, I have always been virtuous."

And, raising his eyes toward the chandelier which heated our heads, he said :

" If I am bald, it is the fault of the gas. It destroys the hair. Waiter, a bock. Are you not thirsty ? "

" No, thank you. But you really interest me. Since when have you been so morbid ? Your life is not normal, it is not natural. There is something beneath it all."

" Yes, and it dates from my infancy. I received a great shock when I was very young, and that turned my life into darkness which will last to the end."

" What was it ? "

" You wish to know about it ? Well, then, listen. You recall, of course, the house in which I was brought up, for you came there five or six times in the holidays. You remember that large grey building, in the middle of a great park, and the long avenues of oaks which opened to the four points of the compass. You remember my father and mother, both of them so ceremonious, solemn, and severe.

" I worshipped my mother ; I was afraid of my father ; but I respected them both, accustomed as I was to see every one bow before them. They were *Monsieur le Comte* and *Madame la Comtesse* to all the country round, and our neighbours, the Tannemares, the Ravelets, the Brennevilles, showed them the utmost consideration.

" I was then thirteen years old. I was happy, pleased with everything, as one is at that age, full of the joy of life.

" Well, toward the end of September, a few days before returning to school, as I was playing about in the shrubbery of the park, among the branches and leaves, as I was crossing a path, I saw my father and mother walking along.

" I recall it as though it were yesterday. It was a very windy day. The whole line of trees swayed beneath the gusts of wind, groaning, and seeming to utter cries—those dull, deep cries that forests give out during a tempest.

" The falling leaves, turning yellow, flew away like birds, circling and falling, and then running along the path like swift animals.

" Evening came on. It was dark in the thickets. The motion of the wind and of the branches excited me, made me tear about as if I were crazy, and howl in imitation of the wolves.

" As soon as I perceived my parents, I crept furtively toward them, under the branches, in order to surprise them, as though I had been a veritable prowler. But I stopped in fear a few paces from them. My father, who was in a terrible passion, cried:

" ' Your mother is a fool; moreover, it is not a question of your mother. It is you. I tell you that I need this money, and I want you to sign this.'

" My mother replied in a firm voice:

" ' I will not sign it. It is Jean's fortune. I shall guard it for him and I will not allow you to squander it with vile women as you did your own inheritance.'

" Then my father, trembling with rage, wheeled round and, seizing his wife by the throat, began to strike her with all his force full in the face with his disengaged hand.

" My mother's hat fell off, her hair became loosened and fell over her shoulders; she tried to parry the blows, but she could not do so. And my father, like a madman, kept on striking her. My mother rolled over on the ground, covering her face with her hands. Then he turned her over on her back to strike her again, pulling away her hands which were covering her face.

" As for me, my friend, it seemed as though the world was coming to an end, that the eternal laws had changed. I experienced the overwhelming dread that one has in the presence of things supernatural, of irreparable disasters. My childish mind was bewildered, distracted. I began to cry with all my might, without knowing why; a prey to a fearful dread, sorrow, and astonishment. My father heard me, turned round, and, on seeing me, started toward me. I believe that he wanted to kill me, and I fled like a hunted animal, running straight ahead into the thicket.

"I ran perhaps for an hour, perhaps for two. I know not. Darkness set in. I sank on the grass, exhausted, and lay there dismayed, frantic with fear, and devoured by a sorrow capable of breaking for ever the heart of a poor child. I was cold, hungry, perhaps. At length day broke. I was afraid to get up, to walk, to return home, to run farther, fearing to encounter my father, whom I wished never to see again.

"I should probably have died of misery and of hunger at the foot of a tree if the gamekeeper had not discovered me and led me home by force.

"I found my parents looking as usual. My mother alone spoke to me:

"'How you frightened me, you naughty boy. I lay awake the whole night.'

"I did not answer, but began to weep. My father did not utter a single word.

"A week later I returned to school.

"Well, my friend, it was all over with me. I had witnessed the other side of things, the bad side. I have not been able to perceive the good side since that day. What took place in my mind, what strange phenomenon warped my ideas, I do not know. But I no longer had a taste for anything, a wish for anything, a love for anybody, a desire for anything whatever, any ambition, or any hope. And I always see my poor mother on the ground, in the park, my father beating her. My mother died some years later; my father is still alive. I have not seen him since. Waiter, a bock."

A waiter brought him his bock, which he swallowed at a gulp. But, in taking up his pipe again, trembling as he was, he broke it. "Confound it!" he said, with a gesture of annoyance. "That is a real sorrow. It will take me a month to colour another!"

And he called out across the vast hall, now reeking with smoke and full of men drinking, his everlasting: "Waiter, a bock—and a new pipe."

REGRET

Monsieur Saval, who was called in Mantes "Father Saval," had just got out of bed. It was raining. It was a dull autumn day; the leaves were falling. They fell slowly in the rain, like a heavier and slower rain. M. Saval was not in good spirits. He walked from the fire-place to the window, and from the window to the fire-place. Life has its sombre days. It would no longer have any but sombre days for him, for he had reached the age of sixty-two. He was alone, an old bachelor, with nobody to look after him. How sad it is to die alone, all alone, without anyone who is devoted to you!

He pondered over his life, so barren, so empty. He recalled former days, the days of his childhood, his home, the house of his parents; his school-days, his escapades, the time he studied law in Paris, his father's illness, his death. He then returned to live with his mother. They lived together very quietly, and desired nothing more. At last the mother died. How sad life is! He had lived alone since then, and now, in his turn, he, too, would soon be dead. He would disappear, and that would be the end. There would be no more of Paul Saval upon the earth. What a frightful thing! Other people would love, would laugh. Yes, people would go on amusing themselves, and he would no longer exist! Was it not strange that people could laugh, amuse themselves, be joyful under that eternal certainty of death? If this death were only probable, one could then have hope; but no, it is inevitable, as inevitable as night following day.

But if only his life had been full! If he had only done something; if he had had adventures, great pleasures, success, satisfaction of some kind or another. But no, nothing. He had done nothing, nothing but get up, eat at the same hours, and go to bed again. And he had gone on like that to the age of sixty-two years. He had not even married, as other men do. Why not? Yes, why was it that he had not married? He might have done so, for he possessed considerable means. Had he lacked an opportunity? Perhaps! But one can create opportunities. He was indifferent; that was all. Indifference had been his greatest drawback, his defect, his vice. How many men wreck their lives through indifference! It is so difficult for some natures to get out of bed, to move about, to take long walks, to speak, to study any question.

He had not even been loved. No woman had slept in his arms, in a complete abandon of love. He knew nothing of the delicious anguish of expectation, the divine vibration of a hand in yours, of the ecstasy of triumphant passion.

What superhuman happiness must overflow your heart, when lips encounter lips for the first time, when the grasp of four arms makes one being of two, a being unutterably happy, two beings mad for one another.

M. Saval was sitting before the fire, his feet on the fender, in his dressing-gown. Assuredly his life had been a failure, a complete failure. Yet he had loved. He had loved secretly, sadly, and indifferently, in a manner characteristic of him in everything. Yes, he had loved his old friend, Madame Sandres, the wife of his old school-friend Sandres. Ah! if he had known her as a young girl! But he had met her too late; she was already married. Unquestionably, he would have asked her hand! How he had loved her, nevertheless, without respite, since the first day he set eyes on her!

He recalled his emotion every time he saw her, his grief on leaving her, the many nights that he could not sleep for thinking of her.

In the morning he always woke up rather less in love than on the night before. Why was that?

How pretty she used to be, so dainty, with fair curly hair, and always laughing. Sandres was not the man she should have chosen. She was now fifty-eight. She seemed happy. Ah! if she had only loved him in days gone by ; yes, if she had only loved him! And why should she not have loved him, Saval, seeing that he loved her, Madame Sandres, so much?

If only she could have guessed. Had she not guessed anything, seen anything, comprehended anything? What would she have thought? If he had spoken, what would she have answered?

And Saval asked himself a thousand other things. He reviewed his whole life, seeking to recall a multitude of details.

He recalled all the long evenings spent playing cards at Sandres' house, when his wife was young, and so charming.

He recalled things that she had said to him, the intonations of her voice, the little significant smiles that meant so much.

He recalled their walks, the three of them together, along the banks of the Seine, their luncheon on the grass on Sundays, for Sandres was employed at the sub-prefecture. And all at once a clear remembrance came to him of an afternoon spent with her in a little wood on the banks of the river.

They had set out in the morning, carrying their provisions in baskets. It was a bright spring morning, one of those days which intoxicate one. Everything smells fresh, everything seems happy. The voices of the birds sound more joyous, and they fly more swiftly. They had luncheon on the grass, under the willow-trees, quite close to the water, which glittered in the sun's rays. The air was balmy, charged with the odours of fresh vegetation ; they drank it in with delight. How pleasant everything was on that day!

After lunch, Sandres went to sleep on his back. "The best nap he had in his life," said he, when he woke up.

Madame Sandres had taken Saval's arm, and the two went off along the river bank.

She leaned on his arm. She laughed and said to him: "I am intoxicated, my friend, I am quite intoxicated." He looked at her, his heart going pit-a-pat. He felt himself grow pale, fearful that he might have looked too boldly at her, and that the trembling of his hand had revealed his passion.

She had made a wreath of wild flowers and water-lilies, and she asked him: "Do I look pretty like that?"

As he did not answer—for he could find nothing to say, he would have liked to go down on his knees—she burst out laughing, a sort of annoyed, displeased laugh, as she said: "Great goose, what's the matter? You might at least say something."

He felt like crying, but could not even yet find a word to say.

All these things came back to him now, as vividly as on the day when they took place. Why had she said this to him?—"Great goose, what's the matter? You might at least say something!"

And he recalled how tenderly she had leaned on his arm. And in passing under a shady tree he had felt her ear brush his cheek, and he had moved his head abruptly, lest she should suppose he was too familiar.

When he had said to her: "Is it not time to return?" she had given him a queer look. Yes, she had certainly looked at him very strangely. He had not thought of it at the time, but now the whole thing appeared to him quite plain.

"Just as you like, my friend. If you are tired let us go back."

And he had answered: "I am not tired; but Sandres may be awake now."

And she had said: "If you are afraid of my husband's being awake, that is another thing. Let us return."

On their way back she remained silent, and leaned no longer on his arm. Why?

At that time it had never occurred to him to ask himself "why." Now he seemed to notice something that he had not then understood.

Could it be . . . ?

M. Saval felt himself blush, and he got up at a bound, as if he were thirty years younger and had heard Madame Sandres say, " I love you."

Was it possible ? The idea which had just entered his mind tortured him. Was it possible that he had not seen, had not guessed ?

Oh ! if that were true, if he had let this opportunity of happiness pass without taking advantage of it !

He said to himself : " I must know. I cannot remain in this state of doubt. I must know ! " He thought : " I am sixty-two years old, she is fifty-eight ; I may ask her that now without giving offence."

He started out.

The Sandres' house was situated on the other side of the street, almost directly opposite his own. He went across and knocked at the door, and a little servant opened it.

" You here at this hour, M. Saval ! Has some accident happened to you ? "

" No, my girl," he replied ; " but go and tell your mistress that I want to speak to her at once."

" The fact is, Madame is preserving pears for the winter, and she is in the preserving-room. She is not dressed, you understand."

" Yes, but go and tell her that I wish to see her on a very important matter."

The little servant went away, and Saval began to walk with long, nervous strides, up and down the drawing-room. Yet he did not feel in the least embarrassed. Oh ! he was merely going to ask her something, as he would have asked her about some cooking recipe. He was sixty-two years old !

The door opened ; she appeared. She was now a large woman, fat and round, with full cheeks and a sonorous laugh. She walked with her arms away from her sides and her sleeves tucked up, her bare arms all covered with fruit juice. She asked anxiously :

"What is the matter with you, my friend? You are not ill, are you?"

"No, my dear friend; but I wish to ask you one thing, which to me is of the first importance, something which is torturing my heart, and I want you to promise that you will answer me frankly."

She laughed, "I am always frank. Say on."

"Well, then. I have loved you from the first day I ever saw you. Can you have any doubt of this?"

She responded, laughing, with something of her former tone of voice.

"Great goose! what is it? I knew it from the very first day!"

Saval began to tremble. He stammered out: "You knew it? Then. . ."

He stopped.

She asked:

"Then? . . . What?"

He answered:

"Then—what did you think? What—what—what would you have answered?"

She broke into a peal of laughter. Some of the juice ran off the tips of her fingers on to the carpet.

"I? Why, you never asked me. It was not for me to declare myself!"

He then advanced a step toward her.

"Tell me—tell me. . . . You remember the day when Sandres went to sleep on the grass after lunch . . . when we had walked together as far as the bend of the river, below. . . ."

He waited, expectantly. She had ceased to laugh, and looked at him, straight in the eyes.

"Yes, certainly, I remember it."

He answered, trembling all over:

"Well—that day—if I had been—if I had been—venturesome—what would you have done?"

She began to laugh as only a happy woman can laugh, who has nothing to regret, and responded frankly, in a clear voice tinged with irony :

" I would have yielded, my friend."

She then turned on her heels and went back to her jam-making.

Saval rushed into the street, cast down, as though he had met with some disaster. He walked with giant strides through the rain, straight on, until he reached the river bank, without thinking where he was going. He then turned to the right and followed the river. He walked a long time, as if urged on by some instinct. His clothes were running with water, his hat was out of shape, as soft as a rag, and dripping like a roof. He walked on straight in front of him. At last, he came to the place where they had lunched on that day so long ago, the recollection of which tortured his heart. He sat down under the leafless trees, and wept.

MY UNCLE JULES

A POOR OLD MAN WITH WHITE HAIR BEGGED US FOR ALMS. My companion, Joseph Davranche, gave him five francs. Noticing my surprised look, he said :

" That poor unfortunate reminds me of a story which I shall tell you, the memory of which continually haunts me. Here it is :

" My family, which comes from Havre, was not rich. We just managed to make both ends meet. My father worked hard, came home late from the office, and earned very little. I had two sisters.

" My mother suffered a good deal from our reduced circumstances, and she often had harsh words for her husband, veiled and sly reproaches. The poor man then made a gesture which used to distress me. He would pass his open hand over his forehead, as if to wipe away perspiration which did not exist, and he would answer nothing. I felt his helpless suffering. We economised on everything and never would accept an invitation to dinner, so as not to have to return the courtesy. All our provisions were bought at reduced prices, whatever was left over in the shops. My sisters made their own gowns, and long discussions would arise on the price of a piece of braid worth fifteen centimes a yard. Our meals usually consisted of soup and beef prepared with every kind of sauce. They say it is wholesome and nourishing, but I should have preferred a change.

" I used to go through terrible scenes on account of lost buttons and torn trousers.

" Every Sunday, dressed in our best, we would take our walk along the pier. My father, in a frock-coat, tall hat and kid gloves, would offer his arm to my mother, decked out and beribboned like a ship at a fête. My sisters, who were always ready first, would await the signal for leaving; but at the last minute someone always found a spot on my father's frock-coat, and it had to be wiped away quickly with a rag moistened with benzine.

"My father, in his shirt-sleeves, his silk hat on his head, would await the completion of the operation, while my mother hurried about, putting on her spectacles, and taking off her gloves in order not to spoil them.

"Then we set out ceremoniously. My sisters marched on ahead, arm-in-arm. They were of marriageable age and had to be shown off. I walked on the left of my mother and my father on her right. I remember the pompous air of my poor parents in these Sunday walks, their stern expression, their stiff walk. They moved slowly, with a serious expression, their bodies straight, their legs stiff, as if something of extreme importance depended upon their appearance.

"Every Sunday, when he saw the great steamers returning from unknown and distant countries, my father would invariably utter the same words:

"'What a surprise it would be if Jules were on that one! Eh?'

"My Uncle Jules, my father's brother, was the only hope of the family, after being its only fear. I had heard about him since childhood, and it seemed to me that I should recognise him immediately, knowing as much about him as I did. I knew every detail of his life up to the day of his departure for America, although this period of his life was spoken of only in hushed tones.

"It seems that he had led a bad life, that is to say, he had squandered a little money, which action, in a poor family, is one of the greatest crimes. Among rich people a man who amuses himself only 'sows his wild oats.' He is what is smilingly called a sportsman. But among needy families a boy who forces his parents to break into capital becomes a good-for-nothing, a rascal, a scamp. And this distinction is just, although the action be the same, for consequences alone determine the seriousness of the act.

"Well, Uncle Jules had visibly diminished the inheritance on which my father had counted, after he had swallowed his own to the last penny. Then, according to the custom of the times, he had been shipped off to America on a freighter going from Havre to New York.

"Once there, my uncle began to sell something or other, and he soon wrote that he was making a little money and that he hoped to be able shortly to indemnify my father for the harm he had done him. This letter caused a profound emotion in the family. Jules, who up to that time had not been worth his salt, suddenly became a good man, a kind-hearted fellow, true and honest like all the Davranches.

"One of the captains told us that he had rented a large shop and was doing an important business.

"Two years later a second letter came, saying: 'My dear Philippe, I am writing to tell you not to worry about my health, which is excellent. Business is good. I leave to-morrow for a long trip to South America. I may be away for several years without sending you any news. If I shouldn't write, don't worry. When my fortune is made I shall return to Havre. I hope that it will not be too long, and that we shall all live happily together. . . .'

"This letter became the gospel of the family. It was read on the slightest provocation, and it was shown to everybody.

"For ten years nothing was heard from Uncle Jules; but as time went on my father's hope grew, and my mother, also, often said:

"'When that good Jules is here, our position will be different. There is one who knew how to get along!'

"And every Sunday, while watching the big steamers

approaching from the horizon, pouring out a stream of smoke, my father would repeat his eternal question :

" 'What a surprise it would be if Jules were on that one! Eh?'

" We almost expected to see him waving his handkerchief and crying :

" 'Hey! Philippe!'

" Thousands of schemes had been planned on the strength of this expected return; we were even to buy a little house with my uncle's money—a little place in the country near Ingouville. In fact, I wouldn't swear that my father had not already begun negotiations.

" The elder of my sisters was then twenty-eight, the other twenty-six. They were not yet married, and that was a great grief to every one.

" At last a suitor presented himself for the younger one. He was a clerk, not rich, but honourable. I have always been morally certain that Uncle Jules' letter, which was shown him one evening, had swept away the young man's hesitation and definitely decided him.

" He was eagerly accepted, and it was decided that after the wedding the whole family should take a trip to Jersey.

" Jersey is the ideal trip for poor people. It is not far; one crosses a strip of sea in a steamer and lands on foreign soil, as this little island belongs to England. Thus, a Frenchman, in a two-hours' sail, can observe a neighbouring people at home and study their customs.

" This trip to Jersey completely absorbed our ideas, was our sole anticipation, the constant thought of our minds.

" At last we left. I see it as plainly as if it had happened yesterday. The boat was getting up steam against the quay at Granville; my father, bewildered, was superintending the loading of our three pieces of baggage; my mother, nervous, had taken the arm of my unmarried sister, who seemed lost since the departure of the other one, like the last chicken of a brood ; behind us came the bride and bridegroom, who kept lagging behind, which often made me turn round.

" The whistle sounded. We got on board, and the vessel, leaving the pier, forged ahead through a green, marbled sea. We watched the coast disappear in the distance, happy and proud, like all who do not travel much.

" My father was swelling out his chest in the breeze, beneath his frock-coat, which had that morning been very carefully cleaned ; and he spread around him that odour of benzine which always made me recognise Sunday. Suddenly he noticed two elegantly-dressed ladies to whom two gentlemen were offering oysters. An old, ragged sailor was opening them with his knife and passing them to the gentlemen, who would then offer them to the ladies. They ate them in a dainty manner, holding the shell on a fine handkerchief and advancing their mouths a little in order not to spot their dresses. Then they would drink the liquid with a rapid little motion and throw the shell overboard.

" My father was probably pleased with this delicate manner of eating oysters on a moving ship. He considered it good form, refined, and, going up to my mother and sisters, he asked :

" 'Would you like me to offer you some oysters ?'

" My mother hesitated on account of the expense, but my two sisters immediately accepted. My mother said in a provoked manner :

" 'I am afraid that they will make me sick. Offer the children some, but not too much, it will upset them.' Then, turning toward me, she added :

" 'As for Joseph, he doesn't need any. Boys shouldn't be spoiled.'

" So I remained beside my mother, chafing at this unjust discrimination. I watched my father as he pompously conducted my two sisters and his son-in-law toward the ragged old sailor.

" The two ladies had just left, and my father showed my sisters how to eat them without spilling the liquor. He even tried to give them an example, and seized an oyster. He attempted to imitate the ladies, and immediately spilled all the liquid over his coat. I heard my mother mutter :

" ' He would do far better to keep quiet.'

" But, suddenly, my father appeared to be worried ; he retreated a few steps, stared at his family gathered around the old shell-opener, and quickly came toward us. He seemed very pale, with a peculiar look. In a low voice he said to my mother :

" ' It's extraordinary how like Jules that man opening the oysters looks.'

" Astonished, my mother asked :

" ' What Jules ? '

" My father continued :

" ' Why, my brother. If I did not know that he was well off in America, I should think it was he.'

" Bewildered, my mother stammered :

" ' You are mad ! As long as you know that it is not he, why do you say such foolish things ? '

" But my father insisted :

" ' Go on over and see, Clarisse ! I would rather have you see with your own eyes.'

" She arose and walked to her daughters. I, too, was watching the man. He was old, dirty, wrinkled, and did not lift his eyes from his work.

" My mother returned. I noticed that she was trembling. She exclaimed quickly :

" ' I believe that it is he. Why don't you ask the captain ? But be very careful that we don't have this rogue on our hands again ! '

" My father walked away, but I followed him. I felt strangely moved.

" The captain, a tall, thin man, with blond whiskers, was

walking along the bridge with an important air as if he were commanding the Indian mail steamer.

" My father addressed him ceremoniously, and questioned him about his profession, adding many compliments :

" ' What might be the importance of Jersey ? What did it produce ? What was the population ? The customs ? The nature of the soil ? ' etc., etc.

" ' You have there an old shell-opener who seems quite interesting. Do you know anything about him ? '

" The captain, whom this conversation began to weary, answered dryly :

" ' He is some old French tramp whom I found last year in America, and I brought him back. It seems that he has some relatives in Havre, but that he doesn't wish to return to them because he owes them money. His name is Jules—Jules Darmanche or Darvanche or something like that. It seems that he was once rich over there, but you can see what's left of him now.'

" My father turned ashy pale and muttered, his throat contracted, his eyes haggard :

" ' Ah ! ah ! very well, very well. I'm not in the least surprised. Thank you very much, Captain.'

" He went away, and the astonished sailor watched him disappear. He returned to my mother so upset that she said to him :

" ' Sit down ; someone will notice that something is the matter.'

" He sank down on a bench and stammered :

" ' It's he ! It's he ! '

" Then he asked :

" ' What are we going to do ? '

" She answered quickly :

" ' We must get the children out of the way. Since Joseph knows everything, he can go and get them. We must take good care that our son-in-law doesn't find out.'

" My father seemed absolutely bewildered. He murmured :

" ' What a catastrophe ! '

" Suddenly growing furious, my mother exclaimed :

" ' I always thought that that thief never would do anything, and that he would drop down on us again ! As if one could expect anything from a Davranche ! '

" My father passed his hand over his forehead, as he always did when his wife reproached him. She added :

" ' Give Joseph some money so that he can pay for the oysters. It would be the last straw if we were recognised by that beggar. That would be pleasant indeed ! Let's go down to the other end of the boat, and take care that that man doesn't come near us ! '

" They gave me five francs and walked away.

" Astonished, my sisters were awaiting their father. I said that mamma had felt a sudden attack of sea-sickness, and I asked the shell-opener :

" ' How much do we owe you, Monsieur ? '

" I wanted to say, ' uncle ' ! He answered :

" ' Two francs fifty.'

" I held out my five francs and he returned the change. I looked at his hand ; it was a poor, wrinkled, sailor's hand, and I looked at his face, an unhappy old face. I said to myself :

" ' That is my uncle, the brother of my father, my uncle ! '

" I gave him a tip of half a franc. He thanked me :

" ' God bless you, my young sir ! '

" He spoke like a poor man receiving alms. I felt that he must have begged over there ! My sisters looked at me, surprised at my generosity. When I returned the two francs to my father, my mother asked me in surprise :

" ' Was there three francs' worth ? That is impossible.'

" I answered in a firm voice :

" ' I gave ten sous as a tip.'

" My mother started, and, staring at me, she exclaimed :

" ' You must be crazy ! Give ten sous to that man, to that vagabond——'

" She stopped at a look from my father, who was pointing at his son-in-law. Then everybody was silent.

" Before us, on the distant horizon, a purple shadow seemed to rise out of the sea. It was Jersey.

" As we approached the breakwater a violent desire seized me once more to see my Uncle Jules, to be near him, to say to him something consoling, something tender. But as no one was eating any more oysters, he had disappeared, having probably gone below to the dirty hold which was the poor wretch's home."

ON THE JOURNEY

I

THE RAILWAY CARRIAGE WAS FULL AS WE LEFT CANNES. We were chatting, for everybody was acquainted. As we passed Tarascon someone remarked : " Here's the place where they assassinate people."

And we began to talk of the mysterious and untraceable murderer, who for the last two years had taken, from time to time, the life of a traveller. Every one made his guess, every one gave his opinion ; the women shudderingly gazed at the dark night through the carriage windows, fearing suddenly to see a man's head at the door. We all began telling frightful stories of terrible encounters, meetings with madmen in an express train, of hours passed opposite a suspicious individual.

Each man knew an anecdote to his credit, each one had intimidated, overpowered, and throttled some evil-doer in most surprising circumstances, with an admirable presence of mind and audacity.

A physician, who spent every winter in the south, desired, in his turn, to tell an adventure :

" I," said he, " never have had the luck to test my courage in an affair of this kind ; but I knew a woman, now dead, one of my patients, to whom the most singular thing in the world happened, and also the most mysterious and pathetic.

" She was a Russian, the Comtesse Marie Baranow, a very great lady, of exquisite beauty. You know how beautiful Russian women are, or at least how beautiful they seem to us, with their fine noses, their delicate mouths, their eyes of an indescribable colour, a blue-grey, and their cold, rather hard grace! They have something about them, mischievous and seductive, haughty and sweet, tender and severe, altogether charming to a Frenchman. At the bottom, it is, perhaps, the difference of race and of type which makes me see so much in them.

"Her physician had seen for many years that she was threatened with a disease of the lungs, and had tried to persuade her to come to the south of France; but she obstinately refused to leave St. Petersburg. Finally, last autumn, deeming her lost, the doctor warned her husband, who directed his wife to start at once for Mentone.

"She took the train, alone in her carriage, her servants occupying another compartment. She sat by the door, a little sad, seeing the fields and villages pass, feeling very lonely, very desolate in life, without children, almost without relatives, with a husband whose love was dead and who cast her thus to the end of the world without coming with her, as one sends a sick footman to hospital.

"At each station her servant Ivan came to see if his mistress wanted anything. He was an old servant, blindly devoted, ready to execute any order she might give him.

"Night fell, and the train rolled along at full speed. She could not sleep, being wearied and nervous.

"Suddenly the thought struck her to count the money which her husband had given her at the last minute, in French gold. She opened her little bag and emptied the shining flood of metal on her lap

"But all at once a breath of cold air struck her face. Surprised, she raised her head. The door had just opened. The Comtesse Marie, in terror, hastily threw a shawl over the money spread upon her lap, and waited. Some seconds passed, then a man in evening dress appeared, bareheaded, wounded in the hand, and panting. He closed the door, sat down, looked at his neighbour with gleaming eyes, and then wrapped a handkerchief around his wrist, which was bleeding.

"The young woman felt herself fainting with fear. This man, surely, had seen her counting her money and had come to rob and kill her.

"He kept gazing at her, breathless, his features, convulsed, doubtless ready to spring upon her.

"He suddenly said:

"'Madame, don't be afraid!'

"She made no response, being incapable of opening her mouth, hearing her heart-beats, and a buzzing in her ears.

"He continued:

"'I am not a criminal, Madame.'

"She continued to be silent, but by a sudden movement which she made, her knees meeting, the gold coins began to run to the floor as water runs from a spout.

"The man surprised, looked at this stream of metal, and he suddenly stooped to pick it up.

"Terrified, she rose, casting her whole fortune on the floor, and ran to the door to leap out on to the track.

"But he understood what she was going to do, and springing forward, seized her in his arms, seated her by force, and held her by the wrists.

"'Listen to me, Madame,' said he, 'I am not a criminal; the proof of it is that I am going to gather up this gold and return it to you. But I am a lost man, a dead man, if you do not assist me to pass the frontier. I cannot tell you more. In an hour we shall be at the last Russian station; in an hour and twenty minutes we shall cross the boundary of the Empire. If you do not help me I am lost. And yet I have neither killed anyone, nor robbed, nor done anything contrary to honour. This I swear to you. I cannot tell you more.'

"And kneeling down he picked up the gold, even hunting under the seats for the last coins, which had rolled to a distance. Then, when the little leather bag was full again he gave it to his neighbour without saying a word, and returned to seat himself in the other corner of the compartment. Neither of them moved. She kept motionless and silent, still faint from terror, but gradually growing quieter. As for him, he made no gesture, no motion, but remained sitting erect, his eyes staring in front of him, very pale, as if he were dead. From time to time she threw a quick look at him, and as quickly turned her glance away. He appeared to be about thirty years of age, and was very handsome, with the air of a gentleman.

" The train ran through the darkness, giving at intervals its shrill signals, now slowing up in its progress, and again starting off at full speed. But suddenly its progress slackened, and after several sharp whistles it came to a full stop.

" Ivan appeared at the door for his orders.

" The Comtesse Marie, her voice trembling, gave one last look at her companion; then she said to her servant, in a quick tone:

" ' Ivan, you will return to the Comte; I do not need you any longer.'

" The man, bewildered, opened his enormous eyes. He stammered:

" ' But, *barine*——'

" She replied:

" ' No, you will not come with me; I have changed my mind. I wish you to stay in Russia. Here is some money for your return home. Give me your cap and cloak.'

" The old servant, frightened, took off his cap and cloak, obeying without question, accustomed to the sudden whims and caprices of his masters. And he went away, with tears in his eyes.

" The train started again, rushing toward the frontier.

" Then the Comtesse Marie said to her neighbour:

" ' These things are for you, Monsieur—you are Ivan, my servant. I make only one condition to what I am doing: that is, that you shall not speak a word to me, neither to thank me, nor for anything whatsoever.'

" The unknown bowed without uttering a syllable.

" Soon the train stopped again, and officers in uniform visited the train.

" The Comtesse handed them her papers and, pointing to the man seated at the end of the compartment, said :

" ' That is my servant Ivan, whose passport is here.'

" The train started again.

" During the night they sat opposite each other, both silent.

" When morning came, as they stopped at a German station, the unknown man got out ; then, standing at the door, he said :

" ' Pardon me, Madame, for breaking my promise, but as I have deprived you of a servant, it is proper that I should replace him. Have you need of anything ? '

" She replied coldly :

" ' Go and find my maid.'

" He went to summon her. Then he disappeared.

" When she alighted at some station for luncheon she saw him at a distance looking at her. They reached Mentone."

II

The doctor was silent for a second, and then resumed :

" One day, while I was receiving patients in my office, a tall young man entered. He said to me :

" ' Doctor, I have come to ask you news of the Comtesse Marie Baranow. I am a friend of her husband, although she does not know me.'

" I answered :

" ' She is lost. She will never return to Russia.'

" And suddenly this man began to sob, then he rose and went out, staggering like a drunken man.

" I told the Comtesse that evening that a stranger had come to make inquiries about her health. She seemed moved, and told me the story which I have just related to you. She added:

"'That man, whom I do not know at all, follows me now like my shadow. I meet him every time I go out. He looks at me in a strange way, but he has never spoken to me!'

"She pondered a moment, then added:

"'Come, I'll wager that he is under the window now.'

"She left her reclining-chair, went to the window and drew back the curtain, and actually showed me the man who had come to see me, seated on a bench at the edge of the side wall with his eyes raised toward the house. He perceived us, rose, and went away without once turning around.

"Then I understood a sad and surprising thing, the silent love of these two beings, who were not acquainted with each other.

"He loved her with the devotion of a rescued animal, grateful and devoted to the death. He came every day to ask me, 'How is she?' understanding that I had guessed his feelings. And he wept frightfully when he saw her pass, weaker and paler every day.

"She said to me:

"'I have never spoken but once to that singular man, and yet it seems as if I had known him for twenty years.'

"And when they met she returned his bow with a serious and charming smile. I felt that—although she was given up, and knew herself lost—she was happy to be loved thus, with this respect and constancy, with this exaggerated poetry, with this devotion, ready for anything.

"Nevertheless, faithful to her superexcited obstinacy, she absolutely refused to learn his name, to speak to him. She said:

"'No, no, that would spoil this strange friendship. We must remain strangers to each other.'

"As for him, he was certainly a kind of Don Quixote, for he did nothing to bring himself closer to her. He intended to keep to the end the absurd promise never to speak to her which he had made in the railway carriage.

"Often, during her long hours of weakness, she rose from her reclining-chair and partly opened the curtain to see whether he were there, beneath the window. When she had seen him, always motionless upon his bench, she went back and lay down with a smile upon her lips.

"She died one day about ten o'clock. As I was leaving the hotel he came up to me with a distracted face; he had already heard the news.

"'I should like to see her, for one second, in your presence,' said he.

"I took him by the arm and went back into the house.

"When he was beside the couch of the dead woman he seized her hand and kissed it long and tenderly and then fled away like a madman."

The doctor again was silent, then continued:

"This is certainly the strangest railway adventure that I know. It must also be said that men sometimes do the maddest things."

A woman murmured, half aloud:

"Those two people were not so crazy as you think. They were—they were——"

But she could not continue, she was crying so. As we changed the conversation to calm her, we never knew what she had wished to say.

MOTHER SAVAGE

I

I HAD NOT RETURNED TO VIRELOGNE FOR FIFTEEN YEARS. I went back there to hunt in the autumn, staying with my friend Serval, who had at last rebuilt his château, which had been destroyed by the Prussians.

I was infinitely fond of that country. There are delicious corners in this world which have a sensual charm for the eyes. One loves them with a physical love. We folk whom nature attracts, keep certain tender recollections for certain springs, certain woods, certain ponds, certain hills, which have touched us like happy events. Sometimes even memory returns toward a forest nook, or a bit of a river bank, or a blossoming orchard, seen only once, on some happy day, which has remained in our heart like those pictures of women seen in the street, on a spring morning, with a white, transparent costume, which leave in our soul and flesh an unappeased, unforgetable desire, the sensation of having just missed happiness.

At Virelogne, I loved the whole country, which was dotted with little woods and traversed by brooks which ran through the soil like veins bringing blood to the earth.

We fished in them for crayfish, trout, and eels! Divine happiness! We could bathe in some places and often found woodcock in the tall grass which grew on the banks of those little narrow streams.

I went, light as a goat, watching my two dogs forage in front of me. Serval, a hundred yards away, on my right, was beating up a field of lucerne. I went around the thickets which formed the boundaries of the Sandres Forest, and I perceived a ruined hut.

Suddenly I recollected that I had seen it for the last time in 1869, neat, vine-clad, with chickens before the door. What is sadder than a dead house with its skeleton standing, dilapidated and sinister?

I recalled also that a woman had given me a glass of wine there, on a day when I was very tired, and that Serval had then told me the story of the inhabitants. The father, an old poacher, had been killed by the gendarmes. The son, whom I had seen before, was a tall, weather-beaten fellow, who was likewise considered a ferocious killer of game. People called them the Savage family.

Was it a name or a nickname? I hailed Serval. He came with his long stride, as if he were walking on stilts.

I asked him: "What has become of those people?" And he told me this adventure.

II

"When war was declared, the younger Savage, who was then about thirty-three years old, enlisted, leaving his mother alone in the house. People did not pity the old woman very much, because they knew that she had money.

"So she stayed all alone in this isolated house, so far from the village, on the edge of the woods. She was not afraid, however, being of the same race as her men, a strong, tall, thin, old woman, who seldom laughed, and with whom no one joked. The women of the fields do not laugh much, anyway. That is the men's business! They have a sad and narrow soul, leading a life which is gloomy and without bright spots.

"The peasant learns a little of the noisy gaiety of the pot-house, but his wife remains serious, with a constantly severe expression of countenance. The muscles of her face never learn the motions of laughter.

"Mother Savage continued her usual existence in her hut,

which was soon covered with snow. She came to the village once a week to get bread and a little meat: then she returned to her cottage. As people spoke of wolves, she carried a gun on her shoulder, her son's gun, rusty, with the stock worn by the rubbing of the hand. She was a curious sight, this tall Savage woman, a little bent, walking with slow strides through the snow, the barrel of the weapon extending beyond the black head-dress, which imprisoned the white hair that no one had ever seen.

"One day the Prussians arrived. They were distributed among the inhabitants according to the means and resources of each. The old woman, who was known to be rich, had four soldiers billeted upon her.

"They were four big young men with fair flesh, fair beards, and blue eyes, who had remained stout in spite of the fatigues they had endured, and good fellows even if they were in a conquered territory. Alone with this old woman, they showed themselves full of consideration for her, sparing her fatigue and expense as far as they could do so. All four might have been seen making their toilette at the well in the morning, in their shirt-sleeves, splashing their pink and white flesh, the flesh of the men of the north, in the water, on cold snowy days, while Mother Savage came and went preparing their soup. Then they might have been observed cleaning the kitchen, polishing the floor, chopping wood, peeling potatoes, washing the clothes, doing all the household duties, like four good sons around their mother.

"But she thought continually of her own son, the old mother, of her tall, thin boy with his crooked nose, brown eyes, and stiff moustache which made a cushion of black hair on his upper lip. She asked each of the soldiers installed at her hearth:

"'Do you know where the French regiment has gone, the Twenty-third Infantry? My boy is in it.'

"They answered: 'No, don't know, know nothing.'

" And understanding her grief and worry they, who had mothers at home, rendered her a thousand little services.

" She liked them very well, her four enemies : for peasants have no patriotic hatreds : that is confined to the upper classes. The humble, those who pay the most because they are poor, and because every new burden rests upon them, those who are killed in masses, who form the true cannon-fodder because they are the " masses," those who, in a word, suffer most cruelly the atrocious miseries of the poor, because they are the weakest and the most unresisting, understand little of those bellicose ardours, the excitable points of honour and those pretended political combinations which exhaust two nations in six months, the victorious as well as the vanquished.

" They said in the country, speaking of Mother Savage's Germans : ' There are four who have found a snug berth.'

" Now, one morning, as the old woman was alone in the house, she perceived afar off on the plain a man coming toward her home. Soon she recognised him : it was the postman on his round. He handed her a folded paper, and she drew from their case her spectacles which she used for sewing, and read :

" ' Madame Savage, this is to give you sad news. Your son Victor was killed by a cannon-ball yesterday, which pretty well cut him in two. I was very near, as we were side by side in the company and he had asked me to tell you the same day if anything happened to him.

" ' I took his watch from his pocket to bring it to you when the war is finished.

" ' I remain your friend,

" ' Césaire Rivot.

" ' Soldier of the 2d Class, in the 23d Infantry.'

" The letter was dated three weeks back.

" She did not weep. She stood motionless, so astounded that she did not yet suffer.

" She thought : ' Victor is killed ! '

" Then little by little the tears came to her eyes and grief overwhelmed her heart. Ideas came to her one by one, frightful, torturing ideas. She would never kiss him again, her big boy, never again. The gendarmes had killed the father, the Prussians had killed the son. He had been cut in two by a cannon-ball. And it seemed to her that she saw the thing, the horrible thing : the head falling, the eyes open, while he gnawed the end of his big moustache, as he did in moments of anger.

" What had they done with his body afterwards ? If they had only sent her boy back to her, as they had her husband, with a bullet in his forehead.

" But she heard a sound of voices. It was the Prussians, who were returning from the village. She quickly hid the letter in her pocket, and received them tranquilly, with her ordinary expression on her face, having had time to wipe her eyes.

" They were all four laughing, in high spirits, for they were bringing back a fine rabbit, stolen no doubt, and they made a sign to the old woman that they were going to have something good to eat.

" She applied herself at once to the duties of preparing the breakfast ; but when it came to killing the rabbit, her heart failed her. And yet it was not the first. One of the soldiers killed it with a blow behind the ears.

" Once the animal was dead, she took the red body out of the skin ; but the sight of the blood which she touched, which covered her hands, of the warm blood which she felt getting cold and coagulating, made her tremble from head to foot ; and she kept seeing her tall boy cut in two and all bleeding, like this still palpitating animal.

" She sat at the table with her Prussians, but she could not eat, not even a mouthful. They devoured the rabbit without troubling about her. She looked at them aside without speaking, nursing an idea, with her countenance so impassive that they perceived nothing.

" Suddenly she said : ' I don't even know your names, and it is a month since we have been together.' They understood, not without difficulty, what she wished and gave her their names. That was not enough, she made them write them for her on a piece of paper, with the address of their families, and resting her spectacles on her large nose she scanned this unknown handwriting, then she folded the sheet and put it in her pocket, with the letter which told of the death of her son.

" When the meal was finished, she said to the men :

" ' I am going to work for you.'

" And she began to carry straw to the garret in which they slept.

" They were astonished at this act. She explained to them that they would be less cold ; and they assisted her. They piled the bundles of straw up to the roof, and thus they made for themselves a sort of big room with four walls of forage, warm and sweet-smelling, where they would sleep wonderfully.

" At dinner one of them was disturbed to see that Mother Savage did not eat anything. She asserted that she had cramps. Then she lighted a good fire to warm herself, and the four Germans climbed to their lodging by the ladder which they used every evening.

" As soon as the trap-door was closed, the old woman took away the ladder, then she noiselessly opened the outside door and returned to get more bundles of straw, with which she filled the kitchen. She went out barefooted in the snow, so softly that the men heard nothing. From time to time she listened to the deep and uneven snores of the four sleeping soldiers. When she thought her preparations were sufficient, she threw into the fire one of the bundles of straw, and when it had ignited she piled it on the others, and then went out again and looked.

" A brilliant light illuminated in a few seconds all the interior of the cottage; then it became a frightful brazier, a gigantic, glowing furnace, whose gleams shone through the narrow window and cast a dazzling light upon the snow.

"Then a great cry came from the top of the house; there was a clamour of human shrieks, of heart-rending appeals of anguish and terror. Then the trap-door having sunk down into the interior, a whirlwind of fire leaped through the attic, pierced the thatched roof, and ascended to the sky like the flame of a great torch; and the whole cottage was burning.

"Nothing more was heard inside but the crackling of the flames, the crumbling of the walls, and the crashing of the beams. The roof suddenly fell in, and the glowing remnant of the house shot up into the air, amid a cloud of smoke, a great fountain of sparks.

"The white field, lighted up by the fire, glistened like a cloth of silver tinted with red.

"A bell in the distance began to ring. Old Savage stood erect before her ruined home, armed with a gun, her son's, for fear one of the men should escape.

"When she saw that her work was finished, she threw the weapon in the fire. A report rang out.

"The people arrived, peasants and Prussians.

"They found the woman sitting on the trunk of a tree, tranquil and satisfied.

"A German officer who could speak French like a Frenchman, asked her:

"'Where are the soldiers?'

"She stretched her thin arm toward the red mass of flames, which were now dying down, and answered in a strong voice:

"'They are in there!'

"All pressed around her. The Prussian asked:

"'How did the fire start?'

"She replied:

"'I set the house on fire.'

"They did not believe her, thinking that the sudden disaster had made her mad. Then, as everybody gathered around and listened, she related the whole thing from beginning to end, the arrival of the letter to the last cry of the men, burned with the house. She did not forget a single detail of what she had felt nor what she had done.

"When she had finished she drew two papers from her pocket, and, to distinguish them in the last gleams of the fire, she again put on her spectacles. Then she said, showing one of them: 'This is the death of Victor.' Showing the other, she added, nodding her head toward the red ruins: 'And this is the list of their names, so that someone may write the news home about them.'

"She quietly handed the white sheet to the officer, who took her by the shoulders, and she resumed:

"'You will write how it happened, and you will tell their relatives that it was I who did it, Victoire Simon, the Savage; don't forget.'

"The officer shouted some orders in German to the soldiers; they seized her, and threw her against the wall of the house, which was still hot. Then a squad of twelve men drew up in a rank opposite her, at a distance of twenty yards. She did not stir. She had understood. She waited.

"An order resounded, which was followed by a long report of muskets. One late shot went off all alone, after the others.

"The old woman did not fall. She sank down as if someone had mowed off her legs.

"The Prussian officer approached. She was cut almost in two, and in her shrivelled hand she held her letter, bathed in blood."

My friend Serval added:

"It was by way of reprisal that the Germans destroyed the château of the district, which belonged to me."

I thought of the mothers of the poor gentle young fellows burned there; and of the atrocious heroism of that other mother, shot against the wall.

And I picked up a little pebble, still blackened by the fire.

THE ORIENT

AUTUMN IS HERE! WHEN I FEEL THE FIRST TOUCH OF winter I always think of my friend who lives down yonder on the Asiatic frontier.

The last time I entered his house I knew that I should not see him again. It was towards the end of September, three years ago. I found him stretched out on his divan, dreaming under the influence of opium. Holding out his hand to me without moving, he said:

"Stay here. Talk and I will answer you, but I shall not move, for you know that when once the drug has been swallowed you must stay on your back."

I sat down and began to tell him a thousand things about Paris and the boulevards.

But he interrupted me.

"What you are saying does not interest me in the least, for I am thinking only of countries under other skies. Oh, how poor Gautier must have suffered, always haunted by the longing for the Orient! You don't know what that means, how that country takes hold of you, how it captivates you, penetrates you to your inmost being and will not let you go. It enters into you through the eye, through the skin, all its invisible seductions, and it holds you by an invisible thread, which tugs at you without respite, in whatever spot on earth chance may have flung you. I take the drug in order to muse on that land in the delicious torpor of opium."

He stopped and closed his eyes.

"What makes it so pleasant to you to take this poison?" I asked. "What physical joy does it give, that people take it until it kills them?"

" It is not a physical joy," he replied ; " it is better than that, it is more. I am often sad ; I detest life, which wounds me every day on all sides, with all its angles, its hardships. Opium consoles for everything, makes one resigned to everything. Do you know that state of mind that one might call gnawing irritation ? That is my normal, usual state. And there are two things that can cure me of it : opium or the Orient. As soon as I have taken opium I lie down and wait, perhaps one hour and sometimes two. Then, when it begins to take effect, I feel first a slight trembling in the hands and feet, not a cramp, but a vibrant numbness ; then little by little I have the strange and delicious sensation of feeling my limbs disappear. It seems to me as if they were taken off, and this feeling grows upon me until it fills me completely. I have no longer a body ; I retain merely a kind of pleasant memory of it. Only my head is there, and it works. I dream. I think with an infinite, material joy, with unequalled lucidity, with a surprising penetration. I reason, I deduce, I understand everything. I discover ideas that never before have come to me ; I descend to new depths and mount to marvellous heights ; I float in an ocean of thought, and I taste the incomparable happiness, the ideal enjoyment of the chaste and serene intoxication of pure intelligence."

Again he stopped and closed his eyes. I said : " Your longing for the Orient is due only to this constant intoxication. You are living in a state of hallucination. How can one long for that barbarous country, where the mind is dead, where the sterile imagination does not go beyond the narrow limits of life and makes no effort to take flight, to expand and conquer ? "

" What does practical thought matter ? " he replied. " What I love is dreaming. That only is good, and that only is sweet. Implacable reality would lead me to suicide, if dreaming did not permit me to wait.

" You say that the Orient is the land of barbarians. Stop,

wretched man! It is the country of the sages, the hot country where one lets life flow by, where angles are rounded.

"We are the barbarians, we men of the West who call ourselves civilised; we are hateful barbarians who live a painful life, like brutes.

"Look at our cities built of stone and our furniture made of hard and knotty wood. We mount, panting, a high, narrow stairway, to go into stuffy apartments into which the cold wind comes whistling, only to escape again at once through a chimney which creates deadly draughts that are strong enough to turn a windmill. Our chairs are hard, our walls cold and covered with ugly paper; everywhere we are wounded by angles—angles on our tables, on our mantels, on our doors, and on our beds. We live standing up or sitting in our chairs, but we never lie down except to sleep, which is ridiculous, for in sleeping you are not conscious of the happiness there is in being stretched out flat.

"And then to think of our intellectual life! It is filled with incessant struggle and strife. Worry hovers over us and preoccupations pester us; we no longer have time to seek and pursue the two or three good things within our reach.

"It is war to the finish. And our character, even more than our furniture, is full of angles—angles everywhere.

"We are hardly out of bed when we hasten to our work, in rain or snow. We fight against rivals, competition, hostility. Every man is an enemy whom we must fear and overcome and with whom we must resort to ruse. Even love has with us its aspects of victory and defeat: that also is a struggle."

He reflected for some moments and then continued:

"I know the house that I am going to buy. It is square, with a flat roof and wooden trimmings, in the Oriental fashion. From the terrace you can see the sea, where white sails like pointed wings are passing, and Greek or Turkish vessels. There are hardly any openings on the outside walls. A large garden, where the air is heavy under the shadow of palms, is in the centre of this abode. A jet of water rises from under the trees and falls in spray into a large marble basin, the bottom of which is covered with golden sand. I shall bathe there at any hour of the day, between two pipes, two dreams, two kisses.

" I will not have any servant, any hideous maid with greasy apron, who kicks up the dirty bottom of her skirt with her worn shoes. Oh, that kick of the heel which shows the yellow ankle ! It fills my heart with disgust, and yet I cannot avoid it. They all do it, the beasts.

" I shall no longer hear the tramping of shoes on the floor, the loud slamming of doors, the crash of breaking dishes.

" I will have beautiful black slaves, draped in white veils, who run barefoot over heavy carpets.

" My walls shall be soft and rounded, like a woman's breasts ; and my divans, ranged in a circle around each apartment, shall be heaped with cushions of all shapes, so that I may lie down in all possible postures.

" Then, when I am tired of this delicious repose, tired of enjoying immobility and my eternal dream, tired of the calm pleasure of well-being, I shall have a swift black or white horse brought to my door.

" And I shall ride away on it, drinking in the air which stings and intoxicates, the air that whistles when one is galloping furiously.

" And I shall fly like an arrow over this coloured earth, which intoxicates the eye with the effect of the flavour of wine.

" In the calm of the evening I shall ride madly toward the wide horizon, which is tinged rose-colour by the setting sun. Everything is rosy down there in the twilight, the scorched mountains, the sand, the clothing of the Arabs, the white coat of the horses.

" Pink flamingos rise out of the marshes under the pink sky, and I shall shout deliriously, bathed in the illimitable rosiness of the world.

" I shall no longer see men dressed in black, sitting on uncomfortable chairs and drinking absinthe while they talk of business, or walking along the pavements in the midst of the deafening noise of cabs in the street.

" I shall know nothing of the state of the Bourse, the fluctuations of stocks and shares, all the useless stupidities in which we waste our short, miserable and treacherous existence. Why all this trouble, all this suffering, all these struggles? I shall rest, sheltered from the wind, in my bright, sumptuous home.

" And I shall have four or five wives in luxurious apartments —five wives who have come from the five continents of the world and who will bring to me a taste of feminine beauty as it flowers in all races."

Again he stopped, and then he said softly:

" Leave me."

I went, and I never saw him again.

Two months later he sent me these three words only: " I am happy."

His letter smelled of incense and other sweet perfumes.

A MILLION

It was a modest clerk's household. The husband, who was employed in a Government office, was conventional and painstaking, and he always was very careful in the discharge of his duties. His name was Léopold Bonnin. He was a mediocre young man who held the right opinions about everything. He had been brought up a Christian, but he was inclined to be less religious since the country had begun to move in the direction of the separation of Church and State. He would say in loud tones at the office : " I am a believer, a true believer, but I believe in God, not in the clergy." His greatest claim was that he was an honest man. He would strike his chest as he said so. And he was an honest man, in the most humdrum sense of the word. He arrived punctually at his office and left as punctually. He never idled and was always very straight in " money matters." He had married the daughter of one of his poor colleagues, whose sister, however, was worth a million, having been married for love. She had had no children, which was a deep disappointment for her, and, consequently, she had no one to whom she could leave her money except her niece. This legacy was the constant preoccupation of the family. It haunted the house, and even the office. It was known that " the Bonnins would come in for a million."

The young couple were also childless, a fact which did not distress them in the least, as they were perfectly satisfied with their humdrum, narrow life. Their home was well kept, clean and thrifty ; they were both very placid and moderate in all things, and they firmly believed that a child would upset their lives, and interfere with their habits.

They would not have endeavoured to remain without heirs; but, since Heaven had not blessed them in that particular respect, they thought it was no doubt for the best.

The wealthy aunt, however, was not to be consoled, and was profuse with practical advice. Years ago, she had vainly tried a number of methods recommended by clairvoyants and her women friends, and since she had reached the age where all thought of offspring had to be abandoned, she had heard of many more, which she supposed to be unfailing, and which she persisted in revealing to her niece. Every now and then she would inquire: "Well, have you tried what I told you about the other day?"

Finally she died. The young people experienced a delighted relief which they sought to conceal from themselves as well as from the outside world. Often one's conscience is garbed in black while the soul sings with joy.

They were notified that a will had been deposited with a lawyer, and they went to the latter's office immediately after leaving the church.

The aunt, faithful to her lifelong idea, had bequeathed her fortune to their first-born child, with the provision that the income was to be used by the parents until their decease. Should the young couple have no offspring within three years, the money was to go to the poor and needy.

They were completely overwhelmed. The husband collapsed and stayed away from the office for a week. When he recovered, he resolved with sudden energy to become a parent.

He persisted in his endeavours for six months, until he was but the shadow of his former self. He remembered all the hints his aunt had given and put them into practice conscientiously, but without results. His desperate determination lent him a factitious strength, which, however, proved almost fatal.

He became hopelessly anæmic. His physician threatened him with tuberculosis, and terrified him to such an extent that he forthwith resumed his peaceful habits, even more peaceful than before, and began a restorative treatment.

Broad rumours had begun to float around the office. All the clerks had heard about the disappointing will, and they made much fun over what they termed the " million franc deal."

Some ventured to give Bonnin facetious advice; while others dared to offer themselves for the accomplishment of the distressing clause. One tall fellow, especially, who had the reputation of being quite a roué and whose many affairs were notorious throughout the office, teased him constantly with veiled allusions, broad hints and the boast that he, Morel, could make him, Bonnin, inherit in about twenty minutes.

However, one day, Léopold Bonnin became suddenly infuriated, and jumping out of his chair, his quill behind his ear, he shouted: " Sir, you are a cur; if I did not respect myself, I would spit in your face."

Seconds were dispatched to the antagonists, and for days the whole department was in an uproar. They were to be found everywhere, in and out of the offices, meeting in the halls to discuss some important point and to exchange their views of the affair. Finally a document was drawn up by the four delegates and accepted by the interested parties, who gravely shook hands and mumbled a few words of apology in the presence of the departmental chief.

During the month that followed, the two men bowed ceremoniously and with affected courtesy, as became adversaries who had met on the field of honour. But one day, they happened to collide against each other in the hall, outside of the office, whereupon Monsieur Bonnin inquired with dignity: " I trust I did not hurt you?" And Monsieur Morel replied: " Not in the least."

After that encounter, they saw fit to speak a few words whenever they met. And little by little they became more friendly, appreciated one another and grew to be inseparable.

But Léopold was unhappy. His wife kept taunting him with allusions, torturing him with thinly-veiled sarcasm.

And the days were flitting by. One year had already elapsed since the aunt's demise. The inheritance seemed lost to them.

When sitting down to dinner Madame Bonnin would remark: "We have not very much to eat; it would be different if we were well off."

Or, when Léopold was ready to start for the office, his wife would hand him his walking-stick and observe: "If we had an income of fifty thousand francs, you would not have to kill yourself working, you poor quill-driver."

When Madame Bonnin went out on a rainy day, she would invariably murmur: "If we had a carriage, I should not be compelled to ruin my clothes on a day like this."

In fact, at all times, she seemed to blame her husband, rendering him alone responsible for the state of affairs and the loss of the fortune.

Finally, growing desperate, he took her to a well-known physician, who, after a lengthy consultation, expressed no opinion and declared he could discover nothing unusual; that similar cases were of frequent occurrence; that it was the same with bodies as with minds; that, after having seen so many couples separated through incompatibility of temper, it was not surprising to find some who were childless because of physical incompatibility. The consultation cost forty francs.

A year went by, and war was declared between the pair, incessant, bitter war, almost ferocious hatred. And Madame Bonnin never stopped saying over and over again: "Isn't it dreadful to lose a fortune because one happens to have married a fool!" or "To think that if I had married another man, to-day I would have an income of forty thousand francs!" or again: "Some people are always in the way. They spoil everything."

In the evening, after dinner, the tension became wellnigh insufferable. One night, fearing a terrible scene, and not knowing how to ward it off, Léopold brought his friend,

Frédéric Morel, with whom he had almost had a duel, home with him. Soon Morel became the friend of the house, the counsellor of husband and wife.

The expiration of the delay stipulated in the will was drawing near; only six months more and the fortune would go to the poor and needy. And little by little Léopold's attitude toward his wife changed. He, too, became aggressive, taunting, would make obscure insinuations, mentioning in a mysterious way wives of clerks who had built up their husbands' careers.

Every little while he would bring up some story of promotion that had fallen to the luck of some obscure clerk. "Little Ravinot, who was only a temporary clerk, five years ago, has been made assistant chief clerk." Then Madame Bonnin would reply: "You're certainly not the man to accomplish anything like that."

Léopold would shrug his shoulders.

"As if he did more than anyone else! He has a bright wife, that is all. She captivated the head of the department and now gets everything she wants. In this life we have to look out that we are not fooled by circumstances."

What did he really mean? What did she infer? What occurred? Each of them had a calendar on which the days which separated them from the fatal term were marked; and every week they were overcome by a sort of madness, a desperate rage, a wild exasperation, so that they felt capable of committing a crime if necessary.

And then one morning Madame Bonnin, with shining eyes and a radiant face, laid her hands on her husband's shoulders, looked at him intently, joyfully, and whispered: "I believe that I am pregnant." He experienced such a shock that he almost collapsed; and suddenly clasping his wife in his arms, he drew her down on his knee, kissed her like a beloved child, and, overwhelmed by emotion, sobbed aloud.

Two months later, doubt was no longer possible. He went with her to a physician and had the latter make out a certificate which he handed to the executor of the will The lawyer stated that, inasmuch as the child existed, whether born or unborn, he could do nothing but bow to circumstances, and would postpone the execution of the will until the birth of the heir.

A boy was born, whom they christened Dieudonné, in remembrance of the practice in royal households.

They were very rich.

One evening, when M. Bonnin came home—his friend Frédéric Morel was to dine with them—his wife remarked casually : " I have just requested our friend Frédéric never to enter this house again. He insulted me." Léopold looked at her for a second with a light of gratitude in his eyes, and then he opened his arms ; she flew to him and they kissed each other tenderly, like the good, united, upright little couple that they were.

And it is worth while to hear Madame Bonnin talk about women who have transgressed for love, and those whom a great passion has led to adultery.

TOINE

I

OLD TOINE WAS KNOWN FOR TWENTY MILES AROUND, FAT Toine, Toine-ma-Fine, Antoine Mâcheblé, *alias* Brûlot, the innkeeper at Tournevent.

He had made famous this hamlet, buried in the depths of the valley which ran down to the sea, a poor peasant hamlet, composed of a dozen Norman houses surrounded by ditches and trees. The houses were huddled together in this ravine, covered with grass and furze, behind the curve of the hill which had given the village the name of Tournevant. As birds conceal themselves in the furrows during a storm, they seemed to have sought a shelter in this hollow, a shelter against the fierce salt winds of the sea, which gnawed and burned like fire, and withered and destroyed like the frosts of winter.

The whole hamlet seemed to be the property of Antoine Mâcheblé, *alias* Brûlot, who was, besides, often called Toine, and Toine-ma-Fine, because of a phrase which he constantly used. " My *fine* is the best in France," he would say. His *fine* was his cognac, of course. For twenty years he had soaked the country-side in his cognac, for, whenever his customers said : " Well, what is it going to be, my boy ? " he invariably replied : " Try a brandy, old son. It warms the guts and clears the head ; there is nothing better for your health." He called everybody " old son," although he had never had a son of his own.

Ah, yes, every one knew old Toine, the biggest man in the district, or even in the country. His little house seemed too ridiculously small to contain him, and when one saw him standing in his doorway, where he spent the greater part of every day, one wondered how he could enter his home. But he did enter, each time a customer presented himself, for Toine-ma-Fine was invited, as by right prescriptive, to levy a glass on all who drank in his house.

His café bore on its sign the legend "The Rendezvous of Friends," and old Toine was truly the friend of all the country round. People came from Fécamp and Montivilliers to see him and laugh at his stories—for this great, good-natured man could bring a smile to the most solemn face. He had a way of joking without giving offence, of winking his eye to express what he dared not utter, and of slapping his thigh in his bursts of mirth, which made one laugh in spite of oneself. And then it was a curiosity just to see him drink. He drank all that was offered him by everybody, with a joy in his wicked eye, a joy which came from a double pleasure: first, the pleasure of regaling himself, and then the pleasure of heaping up money at the expense of his friends.

The local wits would ask:

"Tell us now, Toine. Why don't you drink up the sea?"

And he would reply:

"There are two objections. First, it is salty, and second, it would have to be bottled, since my paunch prevents me from stooping down to that cup."

The quarrels of Toine and his wife were Homeric! It was such a good show that one would have paid to see it. They had squabbled every day through the whole thirty years of their married life. Only Toine was good-natured over it, while his wife was furious. She was a tall peasant woman who walked with long, stilt-like strides, her thin, flat body surmounted by the head of an ugly screech-owl. She spent her whole time in rearing poultry in the little yard behind the inn, and was renowned for the success with which she fattened her fowls.

When any of the great ladies of Fécamp gave a feast to the people of quality, it was necessary to the success of the repast that it should be garnished with the celebrated fowls from mother Toine's poultry-yard.

But she was born with a vile temper and had continued to be dissatisfied with everything. Angry with everybody, she was particularly so with her husband. She jeered at his gaiety, his popularity, his good health, and his fatness; she treated him with the utmost contempt because he got his money without working for it, and because, as she said, he ate and drank as much as ten ordinary men. Not a day passed without her declaring, in exasperated tones: "Wouldn't a hog like that be better in the sty with the pigs! He's that fat, it makes me sick in the stomach." "Wait a little, wait a little," she would shriek in his face, "we shall soon see what is going to happen! This great wind-bag will burst like a sack of grain!"

Toine laughed, tapping his enormous belly, and replied: "Ah, old skin-and-bones, let is see you try to make your chickens as fat as this."

And rolling up his sleeve he showed his brawny arm. "There's a wing for you!" he would cry. And the customers would strike their fists on the table and fairly writhe with joy, and stamp their feet and spit upon the floor in a delirium of delight.

The old woman grew more furious than ever, and shouted at the top of her lungs: "Just wait a bit, we shall see what will happen. You will burst like a sack of grain."

And she rushed out, maddened with rage at the laughter of the crowd of drinkers.

Toine, in fact, was a wonder to see, so fat and red and short of breath had he grown. He was one of those enormous creatures with whom Death seems to play, with tricks, and jokes, and treacherous buffooneries, making irresistibly comic the slow work of destruction. Instead of behaving as he did towards others, showing the white hairs, shrunken limbs, wrinkles, and general feebleness which makes one say with a shiver: "Heavens, how he has changed!" Death took pleasure in fattening Toine ; in making a droll monster of him, in reddening his face and giving him the appearance of superhuman health ; and the deformities which he inflicted on others became in Toine's case laughable and diverting instead of sinister and pitiable.

" Wait a little, wait a little," muttered mother Toine, as she scattered the grain about her poultry-yard, " you will see what will happen ! "

II

One day, indeed, Toine had a seizure, and fell down with a paralytic stroke. They carried the giant to the little chamber partitioned off at the rear of the café in order that he might hear what was going on on the other side of the wall, and converse with his friends, for his brain remained clear while his enormous body was prone and helpless. They hoped for a time that his mighty limbs would recover some of their energy, but this hope disappeared very soon, and Toine was forced to pass his days and nights in his bed, which was made up but once a week, with the help of four friends who lifted him by his four limbs while his mattress was turned. He continued to be cheerful, but with a different kind of good humour ; more timid, more humble, and with the pathetic fear of a little child in the presence of his wife, who scolded and raged all the day long. " There he lies, the booser, the good-for-nothing, the idler ! " she cried. Toine replied nothing, only winking his eye behind the old woman's back, and turned over in the bed, the only movement he was able to make. He called this change " making a move to the north, or a move to the south." His only entertainment now was to listen to the conversation in the café and to join in the talk across the wall, and when he recognised the voice of a friend he would cry : " Hello, old son ; is that you, Célestin ? "

And Célestin Maloisel would reply: "It is me, father Toine. How are the legs to-day, my boy?"

"I can't run yet, Célestin," Toine would answer, "but I am not growing thin, either. The shell is good." Presently he invited his intimates into his bedroom for company, because it pained him to see them drinking without him. He would say: "Boys, what knocks me is not to be able to have a glass. I don't care a hoot about anything else, but it's terrible not to drink."

Then the screech-owl's head of mother Toine would appear at the window, and she would cry: "Look, look at him! this great hulking idler, who must be fed and washed and scoured like a pig!"

And when she disappeared a red-plumaged rooster sometimes perched on the window-sill, and, looking about with his round and curious eye, gave forth a shrill crow. And sometimes two or three hens flew in and scratched and pecked about the floor, attracted by the crumbs which fell from father Toine's plate.

The friends of Toine-ma-Fine very soon deserted the café for his room, and every afternoon they gossiped around the bed of the big man. Bedridden as he was, this rascal Toine still amused them; he would have made the devil himself laugh, the jolly fellow! There were three friends who came every day: Célestin Maloisel, a tall, spare man with a body twisted like the trunk of an apple-tree; Prosper Horslaville, a little dried-up old man with a nose like a ferret, malicious and sly as a fox; and Césaire Paumelle, who never uttered a word, but enjoyed himself all the same. They brought in a board from the yard which they placed across the bed and on it they played dominoes from two o'clock in the afternoon until six. But mother Toine soon interfered: she could not endure that her husband should amuse himself by playing dominoes in his bed, and, each time she saw the game begin, she bounded into the room in a rage, overturned the board, seized the dominoes, and carried them into the café, declaring that it was enough to feed this great lump of fat, without seeing him amuse himself at the expense of hard-working people. Célestin Maloisel bent his head before the storm, but Prosper Horslaville tried to further excite the old woman, whose rages amused him. Seeing her one day more exasperated then usual, he said : " Hello, mother Toine ! Do you know what I would do if I were in your place ? "

She waited for an explanation, fixing her owl-like eyes upon him. . He continued :

" Your husband, who never leaves his bed, is as hot as an oven. I should set him to hatching out eggs."

She remained stupefied, thinking he was jesting, watching the thin, sly face of the peasant, who continued :

" I would put five eggs under each arm the same day that I set the yellow hen ; they would all hatch out at the same time ; and when they were out of their shells, I would put your husband's chicks under the hen for her to bring up. That would bring you some poultry, mother Toine."

The old woman was amazed. " Is it possible ? " she asked.

Prosper continued : " Why not ? If one can hatch out eggs in a warm box, one can hatch them out in a warm bed."

She was greatly impressed with this reasoning, and went out completely quieted down and thoughtful.

Eight days later she came into Toine's chamber with her apron full of eggs, and said : " I have just put the yellow hen to set with ten eggs under her ; here are ten for you ! Be careful not to break them ! "

Toine was astonished. " What do you mean ? " he cried.

" I mean that you shall hatch them, good-for-nothing."

Toine laughed at first, then as she insisted he grew angry, he resisted and obstinately refused to allow her to put the eggs under his great arms, that his warmth might hatch them. But the baffled old woman grew furious and declared : " You shall have not a bite to eat so long as you refuse to take them—there, we'll see what will happen ! "

Toine was uneasy, but he said nothing. When he heard the clock strike twelve he called to his wife : " Hey, mother, is the soup ready ? " The old woman shouted from the kitchen : " There is no dinner for you to-day, you lazy thing ! "

He thought at first she was joking, and waited. Then he begged and prayed and swore by fits ; turned himself " to the north " and " to the south," grew desperate under the pangs of hunger and the smell of the viands, and pounded on the wall with his great fists, until at last, worn out and almost famished, he allowed his wife to introduce the eggs into his bed and place them under his arms. After that he had his soup.

When his friends arrived, they believed Toine to be very ill ; he seemed constrained and uneasy.

Then they began to play dominoes as formerly, but Toine appeared to take no pleasure in the game, and put forth his hand so gingerly and with such evident precaution that they suspected at once something was wrong.

" Is your arm tied ? " demanded Horslaville.

Toine feebly responded : " I have a feeling of heaviness in my shoulder."

Suddenly someone entered the café, and the players paused to listen. It was the mayor and his assistant, who called for two glasses of cognac and then began to talk of the affairs of the country. As they spoke in low tones, Toine Brûlot tried to press his ear against the wall ; and forgetting his eggs, he gave a sudden lunge " to the north," which resulted in his lying down on an omelet. At the oath he uttered, mother Toine came running in, and divining the disaster she uncovered him with a jerk. She stood a moment too enraged and breathless to speak, at the sight of the yellow poultice pasted on the flank of her husband. Then, trembling with fury, she flung herself on the paralytic and began to pound him with great force on the body, as though she were pounding her dirty linen on the banks of the river. She showered her blows upon him with the force and rapidity of a drummer beating his drum.

The friends of Toine were choking with laughter, coughing, sneezing, uttering exclamations, while the frightened man parried the attacks of his wife with due precaution in order not to break the five eggs he still had on the other side.

III

Toine was conquered. He had to turn broody. He had to renounce the innocent pleasure of dominoes, to give up any effort to move, for his wife deprived him of all nourishment every time he broke an egg. He lay on his back, with his eyes fixed on the ceiling, his arms extended like wings, warming against his immense body the incipient chicks in their white shells. He spoke only in low tones as if he feared a noise as much as a movement, and he asked often about the yellow hen in the poultry-yard, who was engaged in the same task as himself.

" Did the yellow one eat last night ? " he would say to his wife.

The old woman went from the hen to her husband, and from her husband to the hen, possessed and preoccupied with the little broods which were maturing in the bed and in the nest. The country people, who soon learned the story, came in, curious and serious, to get the news of Toine. They entered on tiptoe as one enters a sick-chamber, and inquired with concern :

" How goes it, Toine ? "

" That's all right," he answered ; " but it is so long, I get very hot. I feel cold shivers galloping all over my skin."

One morning his wife came in very much disturbed, and exclaimed : " The yellow hen has hatched seven chicks ; there were three bad eggs ! "

Toine felt his heart beat. How many would he have ?

" Will it be soon ? " he asked, with the anguish of a woman who is about to become a mother.

The old woman, who was tortured by the fear of failure, answered angrily :

" It is to be hoped so ! "

They waited.

The friends, seeing that Toine's time was approaching, soon became uneasy themselves. They gossiped about it in the house, and kept all the neighbours informed of the progress of affairs. Towards three o'clock Toine grew drowsy. He slept now half the time. He was suddenly awakened by an unusual ticking under his arm. He put his hand carefully to the place and seized a little beast covered with yellow down, which struggled between his fingers. His emotion was so great that he cried out and let go the chick, which ran across his breast. The café was full of people. The customers rushed into the room and circled round the bed, as if they were at a circus, while mother Toine, who had arrived at the first sound, carefully caught the fledgeling as it nestled in her husband's beard. No one uttered a word. It was a warm April day ; one could hear through the open window the clucking of the yellow hen calling to her new-born. Toine, who perspired with emotion and agony, murmured : " I feel another one now under my left arm."

His wife plunged her great, gaunt hand under the bed-clothes and drew forth a second chick with all the precautions of a midwife.

The neighbours wished to see it and passed it from hand to hand, regarding it with awe as though it were a phenomenon. For the space of twenty minutes no more were hatched, then four chicks came out of their shells at the same time. This caused great excitement among the watchers.

Toine smiled, happy at his success, and began to feel proud of this singular paternity. Such a sight had never been seen before. This was a droll man, truly ! " That makes six," cried Toine. " By heavens, what a christening there will be ! " and a great laugh rang out from the public. Other people now crowded into the café and filled the doorway, with outstretched necks and curious eyes.

"How many has he?" they inquired.

"There are six."

Mother Toine ran with the new fledgelings to the hen, who, clucking distractedly, puffed up her feathers and spread wide her wings to shelter her increasing flock of little ones.

"Here comes another one!" cried Toine. He was mistaken—there were three of them. This was a triumph! The last one broke its shell at seven o'clock in the evening. All Toine's eggs were good! He was delivered, and, delirious with joy, he seized and kissed the frail little creature on the back. He could have smothered it with caresses. He wished to keep this little one in his bed until the next day, moved by the tenderness of a mother for this being to whom he had given life; but the old woman carried it away, as she had done the others, without listening to the supplications of her husband.

The spectators went home delighted, talking of the event by the way, and Horslaville, who was the last to leave, said: "You will invite me to the first fricassee, won't you, Toine?"

At the idea of a fricassee, Toine's face brightened and he answered:

"Certainly I will invite you, my son."

FRIEND PATIENCE

" Do you know what has become of Leremy ? "

" He is captain in the Sixth Dragoons."

" And Pinson ? "

" He's a subprefect,"

" And Racollet ? "

" Dead."

We tried to remember other names which would remind us of youthful faces under the caps of young officers. Later in life we had met some of these old comrades, bearded, bald, married, fathers of several children, and the realisation of these changes had given us an unpleasant shudder, reminding us how short life is, how everything passes away, how everything changes. My friend asked me :

" And Patience, fat Patience ? "

I almost howled :

" Oh ! as for him, just listen to this. Four or five years ago I was in Limoges, on a tour of inspection, and I was waiting for dinner-time. I was seated before the big café in the Place du Théâtre, bored to tears. The tradespeople were coming by twos, threes or fours, to take their absinthe or *vermouth*, talking all the time of their own or other people's business, laughing loudly, or lowering their voices in order to impart some important or delicate piece of news.

" I was saying to myself : ' What am I going to do after dinner ? ' And I thought of the long evening in this provincial town, of the slow, uninteresting walk through unknown streets, of the overwhelming sadness inspired in the solitary traveller by the people who pass, strangers in all things, the cut of their provincial coats, their hats, their trousers, their customs, their accent, their houses, shops, and carriages of singular shape. And then the ordinary sounds to which one is not accustomed, the harassing sadness which makes you hasten your step gradually, until you feel as if you were lost in a dangerous country, which oppresses you and you wish yourself back at the hotel, the hideous hotel, where your room preserves a thousand suspicious odours, where the bed makes you hesitate, and the basin has a hair stuck in the dirt at the bottom.

"I thought about all this as I watched them light the gas, feeling my isolated distress increase as the shadows fell. What was I going to do after dinner? I was alone, entirely alone, and lamentably lonesome.

"A big man came in, seated himself at a neighbouring table, and commanded in a formidable voice:

"'Waiter, my bitters.'

"The 'my' in the phrase sounded like the report of a cannon. I understood immediately that everything in existence was his, belonged to him and not to any other, that he had his character, and, by Jove! his appetite, his trousers, *his* no matter what, after his own fashion, absolutely, and more completely than anybody else in the world. He looked about him with a satisfied air. They brought him his bitters and he called:

"'My paper.'

"I asked myself: 'Which is his paper, I wonder?' The name of that would certainly reveal to me his opinions, his theories, his hobbies, and his nature.

"The waiter brought the *Temps*. I was surprised. Why the *Temps*, a grave, dull, doctrinaire, heavy paper? I thought:

"'So he is a wise man, of serious ways, regular habits, in short, a good citizen.'

"He placed his gold eyeglasses on his nose, turned around and, before commencing to read, cast another glance all around the room. He noticed me and immediately began to look at me in a persistent, uneasy fashion. I was on the point of asking him the reason for his attention, when he cried out from where he sat :

" 'By Jove, if it is not Gontran Lardois !'

" I answered : 'Yes, sir, you are not mistaken.'

" Then he got up brusquely and came towards me with outstretched hands.

" 'Ah ! my old friend, how are you ?' asked he.

" My greeting was constrained, as I did not recognise him at all. Finally I stammered :

" 'Why—very well—and you ?'

" He began to laugh : 'I bet you do not know me.'

" 'No, not quite—— It seems to me—however——'

" He tapped me on the shoulder :

" 'There, there ! Don't try to fool me. I am Patience, Robert Patience, your chum, your comrade.'

" I recognised him. Yes, Robert Patience, my school-friend. It was he. I pressed the hand he extended to me and said :

" 'Everything going well with you ?'

" 'With me ? Like a charm.'

" His laugh rang with triumph. He inquired :

" 'What has brought you here ?'

" I explained to him that I was an inspector of finances, making the rounds.

" He replied, observing my order : 'Then you are successful ?'

" I replied : 'Yes, fairly ; and you ?'

" 'Oh ! I ? Very, very !'

" 'What are you doing now ?'

" 'I am in business.'

" 'Then you are making money ?'

" 'Lots of it. I am rich. But, come to lunch with me to-morrow at noon, No. 17 Rue du Coq-qui-chante ; then you will see my place.'

" He appeared to hesitate a second, then continued :

" 'You are still the good pal you used to be ?'

" 'Yes—I hope so.'

" 'Not married?'

" 'No.'

" 'So much the better. And you are still fond of a little beer and skittles?'

"I commenced to find him deplorably commonplace. I answered, nevertheless: 'Yes.'

" 'And pretty girls?'

" 'Yes, certainly.'

"He began to laugh, with a good, hearty laugh:

" 'So much the better, so much the better,' said he. 'You recall our first night at Bordeaux, when we had supper at Roupie's? Ha! what a night!'

"I did remember that spree; and the memory of it amused me. Other facts were brought to mind, and still others. One of us would say:

" 'Do you remember the time we shut up the usher in old Latoque's cellar?'

"And he would laugh, striking his fist upon the table, repeating:

" 'Yes—yes—yes—and you remember the face of the professor of geography, M. Marin, when we sent off a cracker on the map of the world just as he was orating on the principal volcanoes of the earth?'

"Then suddenly, I asked him:

" 'And you, are you married?'

"He cried: 'For ten years, my dear fellow, and I have four children, most astonishing kids; but you will see them and their mother.'

"We were talking loudly; the neighbours were looking around at us in astonishment. Suddenly my friend looked at his watch, a chronometer as large as a turnip, and cried out:

" 'Heavens! what a nuisance, but I shall have to leave you; I am not free this evening.'

" He rose, took both my hands and shook them as if he wished to break off my arms, and said:

" ' To-morrow at noon, you remember?'

" ' All right.'

" I passed the morning working at the General-Treasurer's. He wished to keep me for luncheon, but I told him that I had an appointment with a friend. As he was going out, he accompanied me. I asked him:

" ' Do you know where the Rue du Coq-qui-chante is?'

" ' Yes,' he replied, ' it is five minutes from here. I've nothing to do, I will take you there.'

" And we set out. Soon, I noticed the street we were looking for. It was wide, pretty enough, on the extreme outskirts of the town. I looked at the houses and found No. 17. It was a kind of mansion with a garden at the back. The front, ornamented with frescoes in the Italian fashion, appeared to me in bad taste. There were goddesses hanging to urns, and others whose secret beauties were hidden by a cloud. Two stone Cupids held up the number.

" I said to the Treasurer: ' Here is where I am going.'

" And I extended my hand to say good-bye. He made a brusque and singular gesture, but said nothing, and shook the hand I had held out to him. I rang. A maid appeared. I said:

" ' M. Patience, if you please. Is he at home?'

" She replied: ' Yes, sir—— Do you wish to speak with him?'

" ' Yes.'

" The vestibule was ornamented with paintings from the brush of some local artist. Paul and Virginia were embracing under palms drowned in a rosy light. A hideous Oriental lantern hung from the ceiling. There were many doors, masked by showy hangings. But that which struck me particularly was the odour—a permeating, perfumed odour, recalling rice powder and the mouldiness of cellars—an indefinable odour in a heavy atmosphere, as overwhelming and as stifling as the furnaces in which human bodies are burned. Following the maid, I went up a marble staircase which was covered by a carpet of some Oriental kind, and was led into a sumptuous drawing-room.

" Left alone, I looked about me.

" The room was richly furnished, but with the pretension of an ill-bred parvenu. The engravings of the last century were pretty enough, representing women with high, powdered hair and half naked, surprised by gallant gentlemen in interesting postures. Another lady, lying on a huge disordered bed, was teasing with her foot a little dog buried in the sheets. Another resisted her lover complacently, as his hand strayed under her petticoat. One sketch showed four feet whose bodies could be divined, although concealed behind a curtain. The vast room, surrounded by soft divans, was entirely impregnated with this enervating odour, which had already taken hold of me. There was something suspicious about these walls, these stuffs, this exaggerated luxury, in short, the whole place.

" I approached the window to look into the garden, of which I could see but the trees. It was large, shady, superb. A broad path circled the lawn, where a fountain was playing in the air, flowed under some bushes, and reappeared some distance off. And suddenly three women appeared, down at the end of the garden, between two hedges of shrubs. They were walking slowly, arm-in-arm, clad in long, white tea-gowns covered with lace. Two were blondes and the other was dark-haired. Almost immediately they disappeared again behind the trees. I stood there entranced, delighted with this brief and charming apparition, which brought to my mind a whole world of poetry. They had scarcely allowed themselves to be seen, in just the proper light, in that frame of foliage, in the midst of that mysterious, delightful park. It seemed to me that I had suddenly seen before me the great ladies of the last century, who were depicted in the engravings on the wall. And I began to think of these happy, joyous, witty and amorous times when manners were so graceful and lips so approachable.

"A deep voice made me jump. Patience had come in, beaming, and held out his hands to me.

"He looked into my eyes with the sly look which one takes when divulging secrets of love, and, with a Napoleonic gesture, he showed me his sumptuous parlour, his park, the three women, who had reappeared in the background. Then, in a triumphant voice, in which the note of pride was discernible, he said:

"'And to think that I began with nothing—my wife and my sister-in-law!'"

THE DOWRY

No one was surprised at the marriage of Maître Simon Lebrument and Mlle Jeanne Cordier. Maître Lebrument had just bought the practice of Maître Papillon, the notary; he needed money, of course, with which to pay for it; and Mlle Jeanne Cordier had three hundred thousand francs clear, in notes and bearer bonds.

Maître Lebrument was a handsome fellow, who had style, the style of a notary, a provincial style, but, after all, a style of sorts, and style was a rare thing at Boutigny-le-Rebours.

Mlle Cordier had grace and freshness; the grace was a little awkward, and the freshness a little artificial; but she was, nevertheless, a pretty girl, desirable and entertaining.

The wedding ceremonies turned Boutigny topsy-turvy. The married couple were much admired, and they returned to the conjugal domicile to conceal their happiness, having resolved simply to take a little trip to Paris, after they had spent a few days together.

These few days together were charming, for Maître Lebrument knew how to manage his early relations with his wife with a delicacy, a directness, and a sense of fitness that was remarkable. He took for his motto: "Everything comes to him who waits." He knew how to be patient and energetic at the same time. His success was rapid and complete.

After four days Madame Lebrument adored her husband. She could not bear to be a moment away from him. He must be near her all day long, that she might caress his hands, his beard, his nose, etc. She would sit upon his knees and, taking him by the ears, would say: "Open your mouth and shut your eyes." He opened his mouth with confidence, shut his eyes half-way, and then would receive a very long, sweet kiss that gave him great shivers down his back. And in his turn, he never had enough caresses, enough lips, enough hands, enough of anything with which to enjoy his wife from morning until evening, and from evening until morning.

As soon as the first week had passed away he said to his young companion:

"If it suits you, we might leave for Paris next Tuesday. We shall be like lovers who are not married; go about to the theatres, the restaurants, the open-air concerts, and everywhere, everywhere."

She jumped for joy. "Oh! yes, yes," she replied, "let us go as soon as possible."

"And, as we must not forget anything, you might ask your father to have your dowry ready; I will take it with me, and at the same time pay Maître Papillon."

She answered: "I will speak to him about it to-morrow morning."

Then he seized her in his arms and renewed those little tendernesses she had learned to love so much in eight days.

The following Tuesday, the father-in-law and the mother-in-law accompanied to the station their daughter and son-in-law who were leaving for the capital. The father-in-law remarked:

"I tell you it is imprudent to carry so much money in your pocket-book." And the young notary smiled.

"Do not be disturbed, father-in-law," he answered, "I am accustomed to these things. You know that in my profession it often happens that I have nearly a million about me. By carrying it with me, we escape a lot of formalities and delays, to say the least. Do not worry yourself."

Then the porter cried out: "Paris train. All ready!" and they hurried into a compartment where they found themselves with two old ladies.

Lebrument murmured in his wife's ear: "How annoying! Now I cannot smoke."

She answered in a low tone: "I am sorry too, but not on account of your cigar."

The engine puffed and started. The journey lasted an hour, during which they could not say anything of importance, because the two old ladies did not go to sleep.

When they were in the Saint-Lazare station, in Paris, Maître Lebrument said to his wife:

"If you like, my dear, we will first go and breakfast on the boulevard, then return at our leisure to find our trunk and give it to the porter of some hotel."

She consented immediately: "Oh! yes," said she, "let us breakfast in some restaurant. Is it far from here?"

"Yes, rather far, but we will take an omnibus."

She was astonished: "Why not a cab?" she asked.

He began smilingly to scold her: "Is that the way you economise? A cab for five minutes' ride, at six sous per minute! You do not deprive yourself of anything!"

"That is true," said she, a little confused.

A large omnibus was passing, with three horses at a trot. Lebrument hailed it: "Conductor! eh, conductor!"

The heavy vehicle stopped. The young notary pushed his wife inside, saying hurriedly, in a low voice:

"You get inside while I go up on top and smoke at least a cigarette before breakfast."

She had not time for any answer. The conductor, who had seized her by the arm to aid her in mounting the steps, pushed her into the bus, where she landed, half frightened, upon a seat, and in a sort of stupor watched the feet of her husband through the windows at the back, as he climbed to the top.

She remained motionless between a large gentleman who smelled of a pipe and an old woman who smelled of a dog. All the other travellers, in two mute lines—a grocer's boy, a workman, a sergeant of infantry, a gentleman with gold-rimmed spectacles and a silk hat with an enormous brim, like a gutter, and two ladies with an important, mincing air, which seemed to say: 'We are here, although we should be in a better place.' Then there were two nuns, a little girl with long hair, and an undertaker's mute. The assemblage looked like a collection of caricatures in a freak museum, a series of expressions of the human countenance, like a row of grotesque puppets which one knocks down at a fair.

The jolts of the carriage made them toss their heads a little, and as they shook, the flesh of their cheeks trembled; and the disturbance of the rolling wheels gave them an idiotic or sleepy look.

The young woman remained inert: "Why did he not come with me?" she asked herself. A vague sadness oppressed her. He might, indeed, have deprived himself of that cigarette!

The nuns gave the signal to stop. They alighted, one after the other, leaving an odour of old and faded skirts.

Soon after they were gone, the bus stopped again. A cook got in, red and out of breath. She sat down and placed her basket of provisions upon her knees. A strong odour of dish-water pervaded the omnibus.

"It is further than I thought," said the young woman to herself.

The undertaker got out and was replaced by a coachman who smelled of a stable. The long-haired girl was succeeded by an errand-boy who exhaled the odours of his deliveries.

The notary's wife perceived all these things, ill at ease and so disheartened that she was ready to weep without knowing why.

Some others got out, still others came in. The omnibus went on through the interminable streets, stopped at the stations, and began its route again.

"How far it is!" said Jeanne. "Especially when one has nothing to amuse oneself, and cannot sleep!" She had not been so much fatigued for many days.

Little by little all the travellers got out. She remained alone, all alone. The conductor shouted:

"Vaugirard!"

As she blushed, he again repeated: "Vaugirard!"

She looked at him, not understanding that this must be addressed to her as all her neighbours had gone. For the third time the man said: "Vaugirard!"

Then she asked: "Where are we?"

He answered in a gruff voice: "We are at Vaugirard, of course; I've told you twenty times already."

"Is it far from the boulevard?" she asked.

"What boulevard?"

"The Boulevard des Italiens."

"We passed that a long time ago."

"Ah! Will you be kind enough to tell my husband?"

"Your husband? Where is he?"

"On the outside."

"On the outside! It has been a long time since there was anybody there."

She made a terrified gesture. Then she said:

"How can it be? It is not possible. He got up there when I entered the omnibus. Look again; he must be there."

The conductor became rude: "Come, my girl, that's enough talk. If there is one man lost, there are ten to be found. Be off, now! You will find another in the street."

The tears sprang to her eyes. She insisted: "But, sir, you are mistaken, I assure you that you are mistaken. He had a large pocket-book in his hand."

The employee began to laugh: "A large pocket-book? I remember. Yes, he got out at the Madeleine. That's right! He's left you behind! Ha! ha!"

The carriage was standing still. She got down and looked up, in spite of herself, to the roof, with an instinctive movement of the eye. It was totally deserted.

Then she began to weep aloud, without thinking that anyone was looking at or listening to her. Finally she said :

" What is going to become of me ? "

The inspector came up and inquired : " What's the matter ? "

The conductor answered in a jocose fashion :

" This lady's husband has left her on the way."

The other replied : " All right. It doesn't matter. Attend to your own business." And he turned on his heels.

Then she began to walk ahead, too much frightened, too much excited to think even where she was going. Where was she going ? What should she do ? How could such an error have occurred ? Such an act of carelessness, of disregard, of unheard-of distraction !

She had two francs in her pocket. To whom could she apply ? Suddenly she remembered her cousin Barral, who was a clerk in the Ministry of Marine.

She had just enough to hire a cab ; she would go to him. And she met him just as he was starting for his office. Like Lebrument, he carried a large pocket-book under his arm.

She leaned out of the carriage and called : " Henry ! "

He stopped, much surprised.

" Jeanne," said he, " here ?—and alone ? Where do you come from ? What are you doing ? "

She stammered, with her eyes full of tears : " My husband is lost somewhere——"

" Lost ? where ? "

" On the omnibus."

" On the omnibus ! Oh ! "

And she related to him the whole story, weeping much over the adventure.

He listened reflectively, and then asked :

" This morning ? And was his head perfectly clear ? "

" Oh, yes ! And he had my dowry."

" Your dowry ? The whole of it ? "

" Yes, the whole of it—in order to pay for his practice."

"Well, my dear cousin, your husband, whoever he is, is probably well on his way towards the Belgian frontier by this time."

She did not yet comprehend. She stammered: "My husband—you say——"

"I say that he has run off with your—your capital—and that's all about it."

She remained standing there, choking with grief, murmuring: "Then he is—he is—is a wretch!"

Then, overcome with emotion, she fell on her cousin's shoulder, sobbing violently.

As people were stopping to look at them, he guided her gently into the doorway of his house, and with his arm around her waist, he helped her up the stairs. When his astonished servant opened the door he said:

"Sophie, run to the restaurant and bring breakfast for two. I shall not go to the office to-day."

FEMININE MEN

HOW OFTEN WE HEAR PEOPLE SAY, "THAT MAN IS CHARMING, but he is a woman, a regular girl." They are alluding to the feminine men, the bane of our country.

For all we men in France are feminine, that is, fickle, fanciful, innocently treacherous, without consistency in our convictions or our will, violent and weak, as women are.

But the most irritating of the species is assuredly the Parisian and the boulevardier, in whom the appearance of intelligence is more marked, and who combines in himself all the attractions and all the faults of charming lights o' love, accentuated by his masculine temperament.

Our Chamber of Deputies is full of feminine men. They form the greater number of the amiable opportunists whom one might call "the charmers." It is they who govern by soft words and deceitful promises, who know how to shake hands in such a manner as to win hearts, how to say "My dear friend" in a certain tactful way to the people they know the least, to change their minds without even realising that they do so, to be carried away by each new idea, to be sincere in their weathercock convictions, to let themselves be deceived as they deceive others, to forget the next morning what they affirmed the day before.

The newspapers are full of feminine men. That is probably where one finds them most, but it is also where they are most needed. Certain papers, like the *Journal des Débats* and the *Gazette de France*, are exceptions.

Admitted, every good journalist must be something of a prostitute—that is, at the command of the public, supple enough to follow unconsciously the shades of public opinion, wavering and varying, sceptical and credulous, spiteful and devout, a braggart and a true man, enthusiastic and ironical, and always convinced while believing in nothing.

Foreigners, our anti-types, as Mme Abel called them, the stubborn English and the heavy Germans, regard us with a certain amazement mingled with contempt, and will continue to regard us so till the end of time. They consider us frivolous. It is not that, we are feminine. And that is why people love us in spite of our faults, why they come back to us despite the evil they speak of us; these are lovers' quarrels! . . .

The feminine man, as you meet him in this world, is so charming that he captivates you after five minutes' chat. His smile seems made for you; you cannot believe that his voice does not assume specially tender intonations on your account. When he leaves you it seems as if you had known him for twenty years. You are quite ready to lend him money if he asks for it. He has enchanted you, like a woman.

If he does not act quite straight with you, you cannot bear any malice, he is so nice when you meet him next. If he asks your pardon you long to ask his. Does he tell lies? You cannot believe it. Does he put you off indefinitely with promises that he does not keep? You lay as much store by his promises as though he had moved heaven and earth to render you a service.

When he admires anything he goes into such raptures that he convinces you. He once adored Victor Hugo, whom he now treats as a back number. He would have fought a duel for Zola, but now he has abandoned him for Barbey d'Aurevilly. And when he admires, he permits no qualifications, he would slap your face for a word. But when he becomes scornful, his contempt is unbounded and allows of no protest.

In short, he understands nothing.

Listen to two girls talking.

"Then you are angry with Julia?" "I should say so. I slapped her face." "What had she done?" "She told

Pauline that I was broke thirteen months out of twelve, and Pauline told Gontran—you understand." "You were living together in the Rue Clanzel?" "We lived together, four years ago, in the Rue Bréda; we quarrelled about a pair of stockings that she said I had worn—it wasn't true—silk stockings that she had bought at Mother Martin's. Then I slapped her face and she left me at once. I met her six months ago and she asked me to come and live with her, as she has rented a flat that is twice as big as she needs."

You go on your way and miss the end of the story. But on the following Sunday, when you are going to Saint-Germain two young women get into the same railway carriage. You recognise one of them at once, it is Julia's enemy. The other is—Julia!

And there are endearments, caresses, plans. "Tell me, Julia—listen, Julia," etc.

The man of the species has friendships of this kind. For three months he cannot bear to leave his old Jack, his dear Jack. There is no one but Jack in the world. He is the monopoly of intelligence, sense, talent. He alone is somebody in Paris. You meet them everywhere together, they dine together, walk about in company, and every evening see each other home, walking back and forth without being able to part.

Three months later, if Jack is mentioned:

"There is a cad, a bounder, a scoundrel for you. I know him well, you may be sure. And he is not even honest, and ill-bred," etc., etc.

Three months later, and they are living together.

But one morning you hear that they have fought a duel, then embraced each other, amid tears, on the duelling ground.

For the rest, they are the dearest friends in the world, furious with each other half the year, abusing and loving each other by turns, squeezing each other's hands till they almost crush the bones, and ready to run each other through the body for a misunderstanding.

For the relations of these feminine men are uncertain. Their temper is governed by fits and starts, their enthusiasms unexpected, their affection subject to sudden revulsions, their excitement is liable to eclipse. One day they love you, the next day they will hardly look at you, for they have, in fact, a girl's nature, a girl's charm, a girl's temperament, and all their sentiments are like the affections of girls.

They treat their friends as kept women treat their pet dogs.

Their friends are like the little doggie which they hug, feed with sugar, and allow to sleep on the pillow, but may quite well throw out of a window in a moment of impatience; which they swing round, holding it by the tail, squeeze in their arms till they almost strangle it, and plunge, without any reason, in a pail of cold water.

Then, what a strange thing it is when a feminine man falls in love with a real harlot! He beats her, she scratches him, they execrate each other, cannot bear the sight of each other and yet cannot part, linked together by no one knows what mysterious bonds of the heart. She deceives him, he knows it, sobs and forgives her. He sleeps in the bed which another man is paying for, and firmly believes his conduct is irreproachable. He despises and adores her without seeing that she would be justified in despising him. They are both atrociously unhappy and yet cannot separate. They cast invectives, reproaches and abominable accusations at each other from morning till night, and when they have reached the climax and are vibrating with rage and hatred, they fall into each other's arms and kiss each other ardently, their strumpets' souls and bodies united.

The feminine man is brave and a coward at the same time. He has, to an exceptional degree, the exalted sentiment of honour, but is lacking in the sense of simple honesty, and, circumstances favouring him, he would defalcate and commit infamies which do not trouble his conscience, for he obeys without questioning the oscillations of his ideas, which are always impulsive.

To him it seems permissible and almost right to cheat a shopkeeper. He considers it honourable not to pay his debts, unless they are gambling debts—and therefore somewhat shady. He dupes people whenever the laws of society admit of his doing so. When he is short of money he uses every resort to borrow money, not being in the least scrupulous as to tricking the lenders, but he would, with sincere indignation, run his sword through anyone who would even suspect him of lacking in delicacy.

THE MOUSTACHE

CHÂTEAU DE SOLLES,
MONDAY, JULY 30, 1883.

MY DEAR LUCY,—

I have no news. We live in the drawing-room, looking out at the rain. We cannot go out in this frightful weather, so we have theatricals. My dear, how stupid these drawing-room plays are nowadays! Everything is forced, coarse, heavy. The jokes are like cannon-balls, smashing everything in their passage. No wit, nothing natural, no good humour, no elegance. These literary men really know nothing of society. They are perfectly ignorant of how people think and talk in our set. I do not mind if they despise our customs, our conventions, and our manners, but I do not forgive them for not knowing them. When they want to be humorous they make puns that would entertain a sergeants' mess; when they try to be jolly, they give us jokes that they must have picked up on the outer boulevards, in those beer-houses artists are supposed to frequent, where one has heard the same students' jokes for fifty years.

So we have taken to theatricals. As we are only two women, my husband takes the part of a soubrette, and, in order to do that, he has shaved off his moustache. You cannot imagine, my dear Lucy, how it changes him! I no longer recognise him—by day or at night. If he did not let it grow again I think I should no longer love him; he looks so horrid like this.

In fact, a man without a moustache is no longer a man. I do not care much for a beard; it almost always makes a man look untidy. But a moustache, oh, a moustache is indispensable to a manly face. No, you would never believe how pleasant these little hair bristles on the upper lip are to look at and . . . in other ways. I have thought over the matter a great deal, but hardly dare to write my thoughts. I would like to whisper them to you. Words look so different on paper and the subject is so difficult, so delicate, so dangerous that it requires infinite skill to tackle it.

Well, when my husband appeared, shaven, I understood at once that I never could fall in love with a strolling actor nor a preacher, even if it were Father Didon, the most charming of all! Later when I was alone with him (my husband) it was worse still. Oh, my dear Lucy, never let yourself be kissed by a man without a moustache; their kisses have no flavour, none whatever! They no longer have the charm, the mellowness and the snap—yes, the snap—of a real kiss. The moustache is the spice.

Imagine placing to your lips a piece of dry—or moist—parchment. That is the kiss of the man without a moustache. It is not worth while.

Whence comes this charm of the moustache, will you tell me? Do I know myself? It tickles your face, you feel it approaching your mouth and it sends a little shiver through you down to the tips of your toes.

And on your neck! Have you ever felt a moustache on your neck? It intoxicates you, makes you feel creepy, goes to the tips of your fingers. You wriggle, shake your shoulders, toss back your head. You wish to get away and at the same time to remain there; it is delightful, but irritating. But how good it is!

And then . . . really I am afraid to say it! A husband who loves you, absolutely, I mean, knows a lot of little corners to be kissed, places one never could think of alone. These kisses, without a moustache, also lose much of their flavour. In fact they become indecent. Can you explain this? I think I know why. A lip without a moustache is like a body without clothing; and one must wear clothes, very few, if you like, but still some clothing. The Creator (I dare not use any other word in speaking of such things) took care to cover all the parts of our body that were made for love. A shaven lip makes me think of trees that have been felled around a fountain where one hoped to quench one's thirst and rest.

I recall a sentence (uttered by a politician) which has been running in my mind for three months. My husband, who keeps up with the newspapers, read me one evening a very singular speech by our Minister of Agriculture, who was called M. Méline. He may have been superseded by this time. I do not know.

I was paying no attention, but the name Méline struck me. It recalled, I do not exactly know why, the "Scènes de la vie de bohème." I thought it was about some grisette. That shows how scraps of the speech entered my mind. This M. Méline was making this statement to the people of Amiens, I believe, and I have ever since been trying to understand what he meant: "There is no patriotism without agriculture!" Well, I have just discovered his meaning, and I affirm in my turn that there is no love without a moustache. When you say it that way it sounds comical, does it not?

There is no love without a moustache!

"There is no patriotism without agriculture," said M. Méline, and he was right, that minister; I now understand why.

From a very different point of view the moustache is essential. It gives character to the face. It makes a man look gentle, tender, violent, a monster, a rake, enterprising! The hairy man, who does not shave off his whiskers, never has a refined look, for his features are concealed, and the shape of the jaw and the chin betrays a great deal to those who understand.

The man with a moustache retains his own peculiar expression and his refinement at the same time.

And how many different varieties of moustaches there are!

Sometimes they are twisted, curled, coquettish. Those seem to be chiefly devoted to women.

Sometimes they are pointed, sharp as needles, and threatening. That kind prefers wine, horses and war.

Sometimes they are enormous, overhanging, frightful. These big ones generally conceal a fine disposition, a kindliness that borders on weakness and a gentleness that savours of timidity.

But what I adore above all in the moustache is that it is French, altogether French. It came from our ancestors, the Gauls, and has remained the insignia of our national character.

It is boastful, gallant and brave. It sips wine gracefully and knows how to laugh with refinement, while the broad-bearded jaws are clumsy in everything they do.

I recall something that made me cry my heart out, and also —I see it now—made me love a moustache on a man's face.

It was during the war, when I was living with my father. I was a young girl then. One day there was a skirmish near the château. I had heard the firing of the cannon and of the artillery all the morning, and that evening a German colonel came and quartered himself in our house. He left the following day. My father was informed that there were a number of dead in the fields. He had them brought to our place so that they might be buried together. They were laid all along the great avenue of pines as fast as they brought them in, on both sides of the avenue, and as they began to smell, their bodies were covered with earth until the deep trench could be dug. Thus one saw only their heads, which seemed to protrude from the earth and were almost as yellow, with their closed eyes.

I wanted to see them. But when I saw those two rows of frightful faces, I thought I should faint. However, I began to look at them, one by one, trying to guess what kind of men these had been.

The uniforms were concealed beneath the earth, and yet

immediately, yes, immediately, my dear, I recognised the Frenchmen by their moustaches!

Some of them had shaved on the very day of the battle, as though they wished to be elegant up to the last; others seemed to have a week's growth, but all wore the French moustache, very plain, the proud moustache that seems to say: "Do not take me for my bearded friend, dear; I am a brother."

And I cried, oh, I cried a great deal more than I should if I had not recognised them, the poor dead fellows.

It was wrong of me to tell you this. Now I am sad and cannot chatter any longer. Well, good-bye, dear Lucy. I send you a hearty kiss. Long live the moustache!

JEANNE.

BED NO. 29

WHEN CAPTAIN ÉPIVENT PASSED IN THE STREET ALL THE ladies turned to look at him. He was the perfect type of a handsome hussar officer. He was always on parade, always strutted a little and seemed preoccupied and proud of his leg, his figure, and his moustache. He had superb ones, it is true, a superb moustache, figure and leg. The first-mentioned was blond, very heavy, falling martially from his lip in a beautiful sweep the colour of ripe wheat, carefully turned at the ends, and falling over both sides of his mouth in two powerful sprigs. His waist was thin as if he wore a corset, while a vigorous masculine chest, bulged and arched, spread itself above his waist. His leg was admirable, a gymnastic leg, the leg of a dancer, whose muscular flesh outlined each movement under the clinging cloth of his red trousers.

He walked with muscles taut, with feet and arms apart, and with the slightly swinging gait of the horseman, who knows how to make the most of his limbs and his carriage, and who seems a conqueror in a uniform, but looks commonplace in a mufti.

Like many other officers, Captain Épivent did not look well in civilian clothes. He had no elegance as soon as he was clothed in the grey or black of the shop assistant. But in his proper setting he was a triumph. He had, besides, a handsome face, the nose thin and curved, blue eyes, and a good forehead. He was bald, and he never could understand why his hair had fallen out. He consoled himself with the thought that a slight baldness on top is not unbecoming with a heavy moustache.

He scorned everybody in general, with a difference in the degrees of his scorn.

In the first place, for him the middle class did not exist. He looked at them as he would look at animals, without according them more of his attention than he would give to sparrows or chickens. Officers, alone, counted in his world; but he did not esteem all officers equally. He only respected handsome men; the real, the only attribute of the military man being a fair presence. A soldier was a gay fellow, a devil, created for love and war, a man of brawn and muscle, with hair on his chest, nothing more. He classed the generals of the French Army by their figures, their bearings, and the stern looks of their faces. Bourbaki appeared to him the greatest warrior of modern times.

He was greatly amused at the officers of the line who are short and fat, and puff while marching. And he had a special scorn for the poor recruits from the École Polytechnique, those thin, little men with spectacles, awkward and unskilful, who looked as appropriate in a uniform as a bull in a china shop, as he often asserted. He was indignant that they should be tolerated in the army, those lanky abortions, who marched like crabs, did not drink, ate little, and seemed to love equations better than pretty girls.

Captain Épivent himself had constant successes and triumphs with the fair sex.

Every time he took supper in company with a woman, he thought himself certain of finishing the night with her upon the same mattress, and, if unsurmountable obstacles prevented victory that evening, he was sure, at least, that the affair would be "continued in our next." His comrades did not like him to meet their mistresses, and the shopkeepers who had pretty wives at the counter knew him, feared him, and hated him desperately. When he passed, the shopkeepers' wives, in spite of themselves, exchanged glances with him through the glass of the front windows; those looks that avail more than tender words, which contain an appeal and a response, a desire and an avowal. And the husbands, impelled by a sort of instinct, suddenly turned, casting a furious look at the proud, erect silhouette of the officer. And, when the Captain had passed, smiling and content with his impression, the shopkeepers, nervously shifting about the objects spread out before them, would declare :

" What a big fool ! When shall we stop feeding all these good-for-nothings who go clattering their ironmongery through the streets ? For my part, I would rather be a butcher than a soldier. Then if there's blood on my table, it is the blood of beasts, at least. And he is useful, is the butcher ; and the knife he carries has not killed men. I do not understand how these murderers are tolerated, walking on the public streets, carrying with them their instruments of death. It is necessary to have them, I suppose, but at least, let them conceal themselves, and not dress up in masquerade, with their red breeches and blue coats. The executioner doesn't dress himself up, does he ? "

The woman, without answering, would shrug her shoulders, while the husband, divining the gesture without seeing it, would cry :

" One must be a fool to watch those fellows parading up and down."

Nevertheless, Captain Épivent's reputation for conquests was well established in the whole French Army.

Now, in 1868, his regiment, the One Hundred and Second Hussars, came into garrison at Rouen.

He soon became known in the town. He came every evening, towards five o'clock, to Boïeldieu Mall, to take his absinthe and coffee at the Comedy ; and, before entering the establishment, he would always take a turn upon the promenade, to show his leg, his figure, and his moustaches.

The shopkeepers of Rouen who also promenaded there with their hands behind their backs, preoccupied with business affairs, speaking of the ups and downs of the market, would sometimes throw him a glance and murmur:

"Egad! that's a handsome fellow!"

But when they knew him, they remarked:

"Look! Captain Épivent! A fine chap, say what you will!"

The women on meeting him had a very queer little movement of the head, a kind of shiver of modesty, as if they felt weak or unclothed in his presence. They would lower their heads a little, with a smile upon their lips, wanting to be found charming and have a look from him. When he walked with a comrade the comrade never failed to murmur with jealous envy, each time that he saw the same by-play:

"This rascal Épivent has all the luck!"

Among the kept ladies of the town it was a struggle, a race, to see who would carry him off. They all came at five o'clock, the officers' hour, to Boïeldieu Mall, and sauntered in pairs up and down the length of the walk, while the lieutenants, captains, and majors, two by two, trailed their swords along the ground before entering the café.

One evening the beautiful Irma, the mistress, it was said, of M. Templier-Papon, the rich manufacturer, stopped her carriage in front of the Comedy and, getting out, made a pretence of buying some paper or some visiting-cards at M. Paulard's, the engraver's, in order to pass before the officers' tables and cast a look at Captain Épivent, which seemed to say: "When you will," so clearly that Colonel Prune, who was drinking the green liquor with his lieutenant-colonel, could not help muttering:

"Confound that fellow! He is lucky, that scamp!"

The Colonel's remark was repeated, and Captain Épivent, moved by this approbation of his superior, passed the next day and many times after that under the windows of the beauty, in full uniform.

She saw him, showed herself, and smiled.

That same evening he was her lover.

They attracted attention, made an exhibition of their attachment, and mutually compromised themselves, both of them proud of their adventure.

Nothing was talked of in town except the amours of the beautiful Irma and the officer. M. Templier-Papon alone was ignorant of their relation.

Captain Épivent beamed with glory; every instant he would say:

"Irma happened to say to me—Irma told me to-night—or, yesterday at dinner Irma said——"

For a whole year they walked about and displayed this love in Rouen like a flag taken from the enemy. He felt his stature increased by this conquest, he was envied, surer of his future, surer of the decoration so much desired, for the eyes of all were upon him, and it is sufficient to be well in the public eye in order not to be forgotten.

But war was declared, and the Captain's regiment was one of the first to be sent to the front. Their farewells were lamentable, lasting the whole night long.

Sword, red breeches, cap, and jacket were all overturned from the back of a chair upon the floor; robes, skirts, silk stockings, also fallen down, were spread around and mingled with the uniform abandoned on the carpet; the room upside down as if there had been a battle; Irma, wild, her hair unbound, threw her despairing arms around the officer's neck, straining him to her; then, leaving him, rolled upon the floor, overturning the furniture, catching the fringes of the arm-chairs, biting their feet, while the Captain, much moved, but not skilful at consolation, repeated:

"Irma, my little Irma, do not cry so, it is necessary."

He occasionally wiped a tear from the corner of his eye with the tip of his finger. They parted at daybreak. She followed her lover in her carriage as far as the first stopping-place. Then she kissed him before the whole regiment at the moment of separation. People even found this very pretty, worthy, and very romantic; and the comrades pressed the Captain's hand and said to him:

"You lucky dog. She had a heart, that child."

It really seemed somehow a patriotic gesture.

The regiment was sorely proved during the campaign. The Captain conducted himself heroically and finally received the cross of honour. Then, the war ended, he returned to Rouen and the garrison.

Immediately upon his return he asked news of Irma, but no one was able to give him anything definite. Some said she had been enjoying herself with the Prussian staff-officers. Others, that she had gone to her parents, who were farmers in the suburbs of Yvetot.

He even sent his orderly to the mayor's office to consult the registry of deaths. The name of his mistress was not to be found.

He cherished a great sorrow, and was at no pains to conceal it. He even took the enemy to task for his unhappiness, attributing to the Prussians, who had occupied Rouen, the disappearance of the young girl, declaring:

"In the next war they shall pay well for it, the beggars!"

Then, one morning as he entered the mess at lunch-time, an old porter, in a blouse and oilcloth cap, gave him a letter, which he opened and read:

"My Darling,—I am in hospital, very ill, very ill. Will you not come and see me? It would give me so much pleasure!

"Irma."

The Captain grew pale and, moved with pity, declared:

"It's too bad! The poor girl! I will go there as soon as I have had lunch."

And during the whole time at the table, he told the officers that Irma was in hospital, and that he, by God, was going to get her out. It must be the fault of those unspeakable Prussians. She had doubtless found herself alone without a sou, broken down with misery, for they must certainly have stolen her furniture.

" Ah ! the dirty swine ! "

Everybody listened with great excitement. Scarcely had he slipped his napkin in his wooden ring, when he rose and, taking his sword from the peg, and thrusting out his chest to make his waist thin, hooked his belt and set out with hurried step to the city hospital.

But entrance to the hospital building, where he expected to enter immediately, was sharply refused him, and he was obliged to find his Colonel and explain his case to him in order to get a word from him to the director.

This man, after having kept the handsome Captain waiting some time in his anteroom, gave him an authorised pass and a cold and disapproving greeting.

Inside the door he felt himself constrained in this asylum of misery and suffering and death. A boy in the service showed him the way. He walked upon tiptoe, that he might make no noise, through the long corridors, where floated a musty odour of illness and medicines. An intermittent murmur of voices alone disturbed the silence of the hospital. Here and there, through an open door, the Captain perceived a dormitory, with its rows of beds whose clothes were raised by the forms of bodies. Some convalescents were seated in chairs at the foot of their beds, sewing, and clothed in the uniform grey cloth dress with white cap.

His guide suddenly stopped before one of these corridors filled with patients. He read on the door, in large letters: " Syphilis." The Captain started ; then he felt that he was blushing. An attendant was preparing some medicine at a little wooden table at the door.

"I will show you," said she, "it is bed 29."

And she walked ahead of the officer. She indicated a bed: "There it is."

There was nothing to be seen but a bundle of bed-clothes. Even the head was concealed under the coverlet. Everywhere faces rose out of the beds, pale faces, astonished at the sight of a uniform, the faces of women, young women and old women, but all seemingly plain and common in the humble regulation garb.

The Captain, very much disturbed, carrying his sword in one hand and his cap in the other, murmured:

"Irma."

There was a sudden motion in the bed and the face of his mistress appeared, but so changed, so tired, so thin, that he would scarcely have known it.

She gasped, overcome by emotion, and then said:

"Albert!—Albert! It is you! Oh! I am so glad—so glad." And the tears ran down her cheeks.

The attendant brought a chair. "Won't you sit down, sir?" she said.

He sat down and looked at the pale, wretched countenance, so little like that of the beautiful, fresh girl he had left. Finally he said:

"What is the matter with you?"

She replied, weeping: "You know well enough, it is written on the door." And she hid her eyes under the edge of the bed-clothes.

Dismayed and ashamed, he continued: "How did you catch it, my poor girl?"

She answered: "It was those beasts of Prussians. They took me almost by force and then poisoned me."

He found nothing to add. He looked at her and kept turning his cap around on his knees.

The other patients gazed at him, and he believed that he detected an odour of putrefaction, of contaminated flesh, in this corridor full of girls tainted with this ignoble, terrible malady.

She murmured : " I do not believe that I shall recover. The doctor says it is very serious."

Then she noticed the cross upon the officer's breast and cried :

" Oh ! you have been decorated ; now I am happy. How contented I am ! If I could only embrace you ! "

A shiver of fear and disgust ran through the Captain at the thought of this kiss. He had a desire to make his escape, to be in the clear air and never see this woman again. He remained, however, not knowing how to say good-bye, and finally stammered :

" You took no care of yourself, then."

A flame flashed in Irma's eyes : " No, the desire to avenge myself came to me when I should have broken away from it. And I poisoned them too, all, all that I could. As long as there were any of them in Rouen, I had no thought for myself."

He declared, in a constrained tone in which there was a little note of gaiety : " So far, you have done some good."

Getting animated, and her cheek-bones getting red, she answered :

" Oh ! yes, there will more than one of them die from my fault. I tell you I had my revenge."

Again he said : "So much the better." Then rising, he added : " Well, I must leave you now, because I have only time to meet my appointment with the Colonel——"

She showed much emotion, crying out : " Already ! You leave me already ! And you have scarcely arrived ! "

But he wished to go at any cost, and said :

" But you see that I came immediately ; and it is absolutely necessary for me to be at the Colonel's at four o'clock."

She asked : " Is it still Colonel Prune ? "

" Still Colonel Prune. He was twice wounded."

She continued: "And your comrades? Have some of them been killed?"

"Yes. Saint-Timon, Savagnat, Poli, Saprival, Robert, de Courson, Pasafil, Santal, Caravan, and Poivrin are dead. Sahel had an arm carried off and Courvoisin a leg crushed. Paquet lost his right eye."

She listened, much interested. Then suddenly she stammered: "Will you kiss me, say, before you leave me? Madame Langlois is not there."

And, in spite of the disgust which came to his lips, he placed them against the wan forehead, while she, throwing her arms around him, scattered random kisses over his blue jacket.

Then she said: "You will come again? Say that you will come again—— Promise me that you will."

"Yes, I promise."

"When, now. Can you come on Thursday?"

"Yes, Thursday——"

"Thursday at two o'clock?"

"Yes, Thursday at two o'clock."

"You promise?"

"I promise."

"Adieu, my dear."

"Adieu."

And he went away, confused by the staring glances of the dormitory, bending his tall form to make himself seem smaller. And when he was in the street he took a long breath.

That evening his comrades asked him: "Well, how is Irma?"

He answered in a constrained voice: "She has a trouble with the lungs; she is very ill."

But a little lieutenant, scenting something from his manner, went to headquarters, and, the next day, when the Captain went into mess, he was welcomed by a volley of laughter and jokes. They had got vengeance at last.

It was learned further that Irma had led a very gay life with the Prussian General Staff, that she had gone through the country on horseback with the colonel of the Blue Hussars, and many others, and that, in Rouen, she was no longer called anything but the " Prussians' woman."

For eight days the Captain was the victim of his regiment. He received by post and by messenger, notes from those who can reveal the past and the future, circulars of specialists, and medicines the nature of which was inscribed on the package.

And the Colonel, catching the drift of it, said in a severe tone :

" Well, the Captain had a pretty acquaintance. I send him my compliments."

After some twelve days he was called by another letter from Irma. He tore it up in a rage, and made no reply to it.

A week later she wrote him again that she was very ill and wished to see him to say farewell.

He did not answer.

After some days more he received a note from a chaplain of the hospital.

> " The girl Irma Pavolin is on her death-bed and begs you to come."

He dared not refuse to follow the chaplain, but he entered the hospital with a heart swelling with wicked anger, with wounded vanity, and humiliation.

He found her scarcely changed at all and thought that she had deceived him. " What do you want with me ? " he asked.

" I wish to say farewell. It appears that I am near the end."

He did not believe it.

" Listen," said he, " you have made me the laughing-stock of the regiment, and I do not wish it to continue."

She asked : " What have I done ? "

He was irritated at not knowing how to answer. But he said :

"Don't imagine I am coming back here to be joked by everybody on your account."

She looked at him with languid eyes, where shone a pale light of anger, and answered :

"What have I done to you? Have I not been nice to you, perhaps! Have I even asked for something? But for you, I would have remained with M. Templier-Papon, and would not have found myself here to-day. No, you see, if anyone has reproaches to make it is not you."

He answered in a clear tone : "I have not made reproaches, but I cannot continue to come to see you, because your conduct with the Prussians has been the shame of the town."

She fell back suddenly in the bed, as she replied :

"My conduct with the Prussians? But when I tell you that they took me, and when I tell you that if I took no thought of myself, it was because I wished to poison them! If I had wished to cure myself, it would not have been so difficult, I can tell you! But I wished to kill them, and I have killed them, come now! I have killed them!"

He remained standing : "In any case," said he, "it was a shame."

She seemed to choke, and then replied :

"Why is it a shame for me to cause them to die and try to exterminate them, tell me? You did not talk that way when you used to come to my house in the Rue Jeanne d'Arc. Ah! it is a shame! You have not done so much, with your cross of honour! I deserve more merit than you, do you understand, more than you, for I have killed more Prussians than you!"

He stood dazed before her, trembling with indignation. He stammered : "Be still—you must—be still—because those things—I cannot allow—anyone to touch upon——"

But she was not listening : "What harm have you done the Prussians? Would it ever have happened if you had kept them from coming to Rouen? Tell me! It is you who should stop and listen. And I have done more harm than you, I, yes, more harm to them than you, and I am going to die for it, while you are singing songs and making yourself fine to inveigle women——"

Upon each bed a head was raised and all eyes looked at this man in uniform, who stammered again :

" You must be still—more quiet—you know——"

But she would not be quiet. She cried out :

" Ah ! yes, you are a pretty poser ! I know you well. I know you. And I tell you that I have done them more harm than you—I—and that I have killed more than all your regiment together—come now, you coward."

He went away, in fact he fled, stretching his long legs as he passed between the two rows of beds where the syphilitic patients were becoming excited. And he heard the gasping, hissing voice of Irma pursuing him :

" More than you—yes—I have killed more than you——"

He tumbled down the staircase four steps at a time, ran off and shut himself up in his room.

The next day he heard that she was dead.

THE PATRON

HE WOULD NEVER HAVE DARED TO HOPE THAT SUCH GOOD fortune would be his! The son of a provincial Sheriff, Jean Marin had come to Paris, like so many others, to study law in the Latin Quarter. In the various cafés which he had successively patronised, he had made friends with a number of talkative students, who chattered about politics as they drank their beer. He developed great admiration for them and became their follower, even paying for their drinks when he happened to have any money.

Afterwards, he practised law and handled some suits, which he lost, when, one morning, he read in the papers that a friend of his student days had become a deputy. Again he became his faithful servant, the friend who discharges all the troublesome errands, whom one sends for when he is wanted, and with whom one stands on no ceremony.

But it so happened, by the chance of politics, that the deputy became a minister, and six months afterwards, Jean Marin was appointed State Councillor.

At first, he was so puffed up with pride that he almost lost his head. He would take walks just to show himself off, as if the people he met in the street could guess his position just by looking at him. He always managed to say to the various tradespeople he dealt with, as well as to the news-dealers and even the cabmen:

"I, who am a State Councillor. . . ."

He naturally experienced, as the direct result of his profession and his newly-acquired dignity, an imperative desire to patronise. He would offer his influence to every one he met, at all times, and with inexhaustible generosity.

When he ran up against a man he knew on the boulevard, he would rush up to him in a delighted manner, shake hands, inquire after his health and then, without waiting for any inquiry, would blurt out:

"You know I am State Councillor, and I am absolutely at your service. If there is anything I can do for you, I hope you will call on me unhesitatingly. In my position, a man can do a lot for his friends."

Then he would go into some café with this friend and ask for some writing-paper and a pen and ink—"just one sheet, waiter, I want to write a letter of introduction."

He wrote quantities of these letters, sometimes twenty, thirty, and fifty a day. He wrote them at the Café Américain, at Bignon's, at Tortoni's, at the Maison-Dorée, at the Café Riche, at the Helder, at the Café Anglais, at the Napolitain, everywhere. He addressed them to every official in the Republic, from magistrates to ministers. And he was happy, thoroughly happy.

One morning, as he was leaving his rooms to go to the State Council it began to rain. He was inclined to take a cab, but did not, finally deciding that he would walk.

The shower became very heavy, soaking the pavements, and inundating the streets. M. Marin was compelled to seek shelter in a doorway. An old priest had already taken refuge there, an old, white-haired priest. Before he had been appointed State Councillor, M. Marin did not care much for the clergy. But now, ever since a Cardinal had consulted him regarding some delicate matter, he treated the clergy with consideration. The downpour was so heavy that the two men were forced to take refuge in the concierge's box, to avoid getting splashed. M. Marin, who was constantly impelled to brag about himself, declared:

"A very bad day, Monsieur l'Abbé."

The old priest bowed:

"Ah! yes, Monsieur, and it is all the more disagreeable when one is in Paris for a few days only."

"Ah! so you live in the provinces?"

"Yes, Monsieur, I am only passing through Paris."

"Indeed, it is most annoying to have rain when one is spending a day or so in the capital. We officials, who live here all the year round, do not mind it."

The abbé made no reply and looked into the street, where the rain was beginning to stop a little. And suddenly clutching his gown in both hands, he resolved to brave the elements.

M. Marin, seeing him depart, shouted

"You will get drenched, Monsieur l'Abbé. Wait a few minutes more, the rain will stop."

The old man wavered and then said:

"Well, I'm in a great hurry. I have a very urgent engagement."

M. Marin appeared very much concerned.

"But you will certainly be wet through. May I ask where you are going?"

The priest seemed to hesitate a moment, but then he said:

"I am going in the direction of the Palais-Royal."

"Well then, if you will allow me, Monsieur l'Abbé, I will offer you the shelter of my umbrella. I am going to the State Council. I am a State Councillor."

The old priest raised his eyes, looked at the speaker and exclaimed:

"I am greatly obliged to you, Monsieur, and accept your offer with pleasure."

Then M. Marin took him by the arm, and they set out. He led him along, watching over him and giving advice:

"Be careful of this gutter, Monsieur l'Abbé. Look out for the carriage-wheels, they throw mud all over one. Mind the umbrellas! Nothing is more of a danger to the eyes than the sharp ends of an umbrella! The women, especially, are so careless; they never mind anything and thrust their sunshades and their umbrellas right under people's noses. And they never go out of anyone's way, either. They seem to think that they own the whole city. I think myself that their education has been sadly neglected."

And M. Marin chuckled gleefully.

The priest made no reply. He picked his way carefully along the streets, slightly bent, choosing with discrimination the dry spots on the pavement so as not to bespatter his shoes and gown.

M. Marin went on:

" I suppose you are in Paris for a little rest?"

The old man retorted:

" No, I have come on business."

" Oh! anything important? Might I inquire what it is? If I can be of service to you, I would only be too glad."

The abbé looked embarrassed. He mumbled:

" Oh! it's a little personal matter. A little difficulty with—with my bishop. It could hardly interest you. It is something about the adjustment—the adjustment of some ecclesiastical matter."

M. Marin became eager.

" Why, these matters are always referred to the State Council. In this case I wish you would make use of me."

" Yes, it is to the State Council I am going. You are most kind. I have an appointment with M. Lerepère and M. Savon, and maybe I will interview M. Petitpas also."

M. Marin came to a stop.

" Why, they are my friends, Monsieur l'Abbé, my dearest friends, fine fellows, all of them. I shall warmly recommend you to them. Rely on me."

The priest thanked him and protested his undying gratitude. M. Marin was delighted.

" Oh! you can thank your stars, Monsieur l'Abbé, that you met me. You will see how smoothly everything will go now."

They finally reached the State Council. M. Marin conducted the priest to his office, installed him before the open fire and then sat down at his desk and wrote:

"My dear colleague, allow me to recommend most heartily to you a very worthy priest, M. l'Abbé. . . .'
He paused and inquired:
"Your name, please?"
"Abbé Ceinture."
M. Marin wrote:
"M. l'Abbé Ceinture, who needs your intercession in a little matter which he will lay before you.
"I am glad of this opportunity which allows me, my dear colleague. . . ."

And he concluded with the customary compliments.
After he had written the three letters, he handed them to his protégé, who departed amid renewed protestations of gratitude.

M. Marin attended to his official duties, went home, spent a quiet day and slept peacefully that night. The next morning he woke up happy, dressed and sat down to read the papers. The first one he opened was a radical organ. He read:

"Our Clergy and our Officials.
"There seems to be no end to the misdeeds of the clergy. A certain priest named Ceinture, convicted of having conspired against the existing government, accused of infamous acts, that we will not even mention, suspected besides of being a former Jesuit transformed into an ordinary priest, revoked by his bishop for reasons which are said to be unprintable, and summoned to Paris to explain his conduct, has found a warm partisan in the State Councillor, Marin, who did not hesitate to give this cassocked rascal the most enthusiastic letters of recommendation to all his Republican colleagues.
"We wish to call the minister's attention to the unqualifiable attitude of this State Councillor. . . ."

M. Marin sprang to his feet, slammed down the paper and rushed off to see his colleague Petitpas, who exclaimed :

" Well you must have gone crazy to recommend that old conspirator to me."

Thoroughly bewildered, M. Marin retorted :

" No . . . no . . . you see, I was deceived myself. He looked like such a good man . . . he tricked me . . . he tricked me most shamefully. I beg of you to condemn him severely, most severely. I shall go myself to the Attorney-General and the Archbishop of Paris, yes, to the Archbishop. . . ."

And he sat down abruptly at M. Petitpas' desk and wrote :

" My Lord,—I have the honour to inform Your Grace that I have been made a victim of the intrigues and lies of a certain Abbé Ceinture, who shamefully took advantage of my good faith.

" Misled by the protestations of this priest, I was induced. . . ."

Then, after he had signed his name to the letter and sealed it, he turned to his colleague and remarked :

" Look here, my dear friend, I hope this will be a lesson to you never to recommend anyone."

OLD MONGILET

IN THE OFFICE OLD MONGILET WAS LOOKED ON AS A "character." He was an old employee, a good-natured creature, who had never been outside Paris but once in his life.

It was the end of July, and we all went every Sunday to roll in the grass, or bathe in the river in the country near by. Asnières, Argenteuil, Chatou, Bougival, Maisons, Poissy, had their habitués and their ardent admirers. We argued about the merits and advantages of all these places, celebrated and delightful to all employees in Paris.

Old Mongilet would say:

"You are like a lot of sheep! A nice place, this country you talk of!"

And we would ask:

"Well, how about you, Mongilet? Don't you ever go on an excursion?"

"Yes, indeed. I go in an omnibus. When I have had a good luncheon, without any hurry, at the wine shop below, I look up my route with a plan of Paris and the time table of the lines and connections. And then I climb up on top of the bus, open my umbrella and off we go. Oh, I see lots of things, more than you, I bet! I change my surroundings. It is as though I were taking a journey across the world, the people are so different in one street and another. I know my Paris better than anyone. And then, there is nothing more amusing than the entresols. You would not believe what one sees in there at a glance. One can guess a domestic scene simply by seeing the face of a man shouting; one is amused on passing by a barber's shop to see the barber leave his customer all covered with lather to look out in the street. One exchanges heartfelt glances with the milliners just for fun, as one has no time to alight. Ah, how many things one sees!

"It is the drama, real, true, natural drama that one sees as the horses trot by. Heavens! I would not give my excursions in the omnibus for all your stupid excursions in the woods."

"Come and try it, Mongilet, come to the country once just to see."

"I was there once," he replied, "twenty years ago, and you will never catch me there again."

"Tell us about it, Mongilet."

"If you wish to hear it. This is how it was: You knew Boivin, the old clerk, whom we called Boileau?"

"Yes, perfectly."

"He was my office chum. The rascal had a house at Colombes and always invited me to spend Sunday with him. He would say:

"'Come alone, Maculotte (he called me Maculotte for fun). You will see what a nice walk we shall take.'

"I let myself be trapped like an animal, and set out one morning by the eight o'clock train. I arrived at a kind of town, a country town where there is nothing to see, and I at length found my way to an old wooden door with an iron bell, at the end of an alley between two walls.

"I rang, and waited a long time, and at last the door was opened. What was it that opened it? I could not tell at the first glance. A woman or an ape? The creature was old, ugly, covered with old clothes that looked dirty and wicked. It had chickens' feathers in its hair and looked as though it would devour me.

"'What do you want?' she said.

"'M. Boivin.'

"'What do you want of him, of M. Boivin?'

"I felt ill at ease on being questioned by this fury. I stammered: 'Why—he expects me.'

"'Ah, it is you who are coming to lunch?'

" 'Yes,' I stammered, trembling.

" Then, turning toward the house, she cried in an angry tone:

" 'Boivin, here is your man!'

" It was my friend's wife. Little Boivin appeared immediately on the threshold of a sort of barrack of plaster covered with zinc, that looked like a foot-warmer. He wore white duck trousers covered with stains and a dirty Panama-hat.

" After shaking my hands warmly, he took me into what he called his garden. It was at the end of another alleyway enclosed by high walls and was a little square the size of a pocket-handkerchief, surrounded by houses that were so high that the sun could reach it only two or three hours in the day. Pansies, pinks, wallflowers and a few rose bushes were languishing in this airless well which was as hot as an oven from the refraction of heat from the roofs.

" 'I have no trees,' said Boivin, 'but the neighbours' walls take their place. I have as much shade as in a wood.'

" Then he took hold of a button of my coat and said in a low tone:

" 'You can do me a service. You saw the wife. She is not agreeable, eh? To-day, as I had invited you, she gave me clean clothes; but if I spot them all is lost. I counted on you to water my plants.'

" I agreed. I took off my coat, rolled up my sleeves, and began to work the handle of a kind of pump that wheezed, puffed and rattled like a consumptive as it emitted a thread of water like a Wallace drinking-fountain. It took me ten minutes to fill the watering-pot, and I was in a bath of perspiration. Boivin directed me:

" 'Here—this plant—a little more; enough—now this one.'

" The watering-pot leaked and my feet got more water than the flowers. The bottoms of my trousers were soaking and covered with mud. And twenty times running I kept it up, soaking my eet afresh each time, and perspiring anew as I worked the handle of the pump. And when I was tired out and wanted to stop, Boivin, in a tone of entreaty, said as he put his hand on my arm :

" 'Just one more watering-potful—just one, and that will be all.'

" To thank me he gave me a rose, a big rose, but hardly had it touched my buttonhole than it fell to pieces, leaving of my decoration only a hard little green knot. I was surprised, but said nothing.

" Mme Boivin's voice was heard in the distance : 'Are you ever coming ? I tell you lunch is ready ! '

" We went towards the foot-warmer. If the garden was in the shade, the house, on the other hand, was in the blazing sun, and the sweating-room of a Turkish bath is not so hot as my friend's dining-room was.

" Three plates, at the side of which were some half-washed forks, were placed in a table of yellow wood. In the middle stood an earthenware dish containing warmed-up boiled beef and potatoes. We began to eat.

" A large water-bottle full of water lightly coloured with wine attracted my attention. Boivin, embarrassed, said to his wife :

" 'See here, my dear, just on a special occasion, are you not going to give us a little undiluted wine ? '

" She looked at him furiously.

" 'So that you may both get tipsy, is that it, and stay here gabbing all day ? A fine special occasion ! '

" He said no more. After the stew she brought in another dish of potatoes cooked with bacon. When this dish was finished, still in silence, she announced :

" 'That is all ! Now get out ! '

" Boivin looked at her in astonishment.

" 'But the pigeon—the pigeon you plucked this morning ? '

" She put her hands on her hips :

" 'Perhaps you have not had enough ? Because you bring

people here is no reason why we should devour all that there is in the house. What is there for me to eat this evening?'

"We rose. Boivin whispered:

"'Wait for me a second, and we will skip.'

"He went into the kitchen where his wife had gone, and I overheard him say:

"'Give me twenty sous, my dear.'

"'What do you want with twenty sous?'

"'Why, one does not know what may happen. It is always better to have some money.'

"She yelled so that I should hear:

"'No, I will not give it to you! As the man has had luncheon here, the least he can do is to pay your expenses for the day.'

"Boivin came back to fetch me. As I wished to be polite I bowed to the mistress of the house, stammering:

"'Madame—many thanks—kind welcome.'

"'That's all right,' she replied. 'But do not bring him back drunk, for you will have to answer to me, you know!'

"We set out. We had to cross a perfectly bare plain under the burning sun. I attempted to gather a flower along the road and gave a cry of pain. It had hurt my hand frightfully. They call these plants nettles. And, everywhere, there was a smell of manure, enough to turn your stomach.

"Boivin said, 'Have a little patience and we will reach the river bank.'

"We reached the river. Here there was an odour of mud and dirty water, and the sun blazed down on the water so that it burned my eyes. I begged Boivin to go under cover somewhere. He took me into a kind of shanty filled with men, a river boatmen's tavern.

"He said:

"'This does not look very grand, but it is very comfortable.'

"I was hungry. I ordered an omelet. But lo and behold,

at the second glass of wine, that cursed Boivin lost his head, and I understand why his wife gave him water in his wine.

"He got up, declaimed, wanted to show his strength, interfered in a quarrel between two drunken men who were fighting, and, but for the landlord, who came to the rescue, we should both have been killed.

"I dragged him away, holding him up until we reached the first bush, where I deposited him. I lay down beside him and apparently I fell asleep. We must certainly have slept a long time, for it was dark when I awoke. Boivin was snoring at my side. I shook him; he rose, but he was still drunk, though a little less so.

"We set out through the darkness across the plain. Boivin said he knew the way. He made me turn to the left, then to the right, then to the left. We could see neither sky nor earth, and found ourselves lost in the midst of a kind of forest of wooden stakes, that came as high as our noses. It was a vineyard and these were the supports. There was not a single light on the horizon. We wandered about in this vineyard for about an hour or two, hesitating, reaching out our arms without coming to the end, for we kept retracing our steps.

"At length Boivon fell against a stake that tore his cheek and he remained in a sitting posture on the ground, uttering with all his might long and resounding hallos, while I screamed 'Help! Help!' as loud as I could, lighting wax-matches to show the way to our rescuers, and also to keep up my courage.

"At last a belated peasant heard us and put us on our right road. I took Boivin to his home, but as I was leaving him on the threshold of his garden, the door opened suddenly and his wife appeared, a candle in her hand. She frightened me horribly.

"As soon as she saw her husband, whom she must have been waiting for since dark, she screamed, as she darted toward me:

"'Ah, scoundrel, I knew you would bring him back drunk!'

"My, how I made my escape, running all the way to the station, and as I thought the fury was pursuing me I shut myself in an inner room, as the train was not due for half an hour.

"That is why I never married, and why I never go out of Paris."

THE CLOSET

After dinner we were talking about women, for what else is there to talk about, among men? One of us said:

"By the way, I had a curious adventure of that kind." And this is what he told us:

"One evening last winter, I was suddenly taken with one of those depressing, overwhelming fits of lassitude, which seize upon one, body and soul, from time to time. I was at home and alone, and I knew well that if I remained there I should have a frightful attack of despondency, of the kind that must lead to suicide when they return often.

"I put on my overcoat and went out, without knowing at all what I was going to do. Having descended to the boulevard, I began to walk along past the cafés, which were nearly empty, for it was raining. One of those fine rains was falling that dampen the spirits as much as the clothes; not one of those good showers that strike one in a cascade and drive pedestrians into doorways out of breath, but a rain so fine that you do not feel the drops, a humid rain that unceasingly deposits upon you imperceptible droplets and covers your clothing with a cold, penetrating moisture.

"What should I do? I went up and down, seeking some place to spend a couple of hours, and discovering, for the first time, that there was not a place of amusement in all Paris in the evening. Finally, I decided to enter the Folies-Bergères, that amusing woman-market.

"There were very few people in the huge auditorium. In the long, semicircular promenade there were only people of no importance, whose vulgarity was apparent in their walk, their clothing, the cut of their hair and beard, their hats, and their complexion. There was hardly one man who looked clean, perfectly clean, and whose clothes looked as though they fitted him. As for the girls, they are always the same, those dreadful girls you know, plain, weary, drooping, walking with that hunter's step and that air of imbecile disdain which they assume, I know not why.

" I reflected that indeed not one of these cow-like creatures, greasy rather than fat, bloated in one place, skinny in another, with paunches like a cardinal and scraggy knock-knees like a stork, was worth a pound—that hard-earned pound they get, after asking for five.

" But suddenly I perceived a little one that looked nice; not very young, but fresh, droll, and provoking. I stopped her and, stupidly, without thinking, set my price for the night. I did not wish to return home alone, all alone; I preferred rather the company and embraces of this creature.

" And so I followed her. She lived in a tall, tall house in the Rue des Martyrs. The gas was already extinguished on the staircase. I mounted slowly, constantly lighting wax-matches, striking the steps with my feet, stumbling and ill at ease, following a petticoat, the rustle of which I heard before me.

" She stopped at the fourth story, and having shut the outside door, she asked .

" 'And you wish to remain until to-morrow?'

" 'Yes. You know that was the agreement.'

" All right, dearie, I only wanted to know. Wait for me here a minute. I'll be back in a moment.

" And she left me in the darkness. I heard her close two doors, then it seemed to me she was speaking with somebody. I was surprised and disturbed. The idea of blackmail occurred to me. But I have fists and solid muscles. 'We shall see,' thought I.

" I listened with all attention, both of ear and mind. Someone was moving, walking about, but with great precaution.

Then another door was opened, and it seemed to me that I still heard talking, but in a very low voice.

" She returned, bringing a lighted candle. 'You can come in now,' she said.

" She spoke familiarly, as a sign of possession. I entered, and after having crossed a dining-room, where it was evident nobody ever dined, I entered a room like all these girls' rooms, a furnished room, with red curtains, and eider-down silk quilt with suspicious-looking spots.

" She went on : 'Make yourself at home, dearie.'

" I inspected the apartment with a mistrustful eye. There seemed nothing disquieting, however. She undressed herself so quickly that she was in bed before I had my overcoat off. Then she began to laugh :

" 'Well, what is the matter with you ? Are you changed into a pillar of salt ? Come ! Make haste !'

" I imitated her and joined her. Five minutes later I had a foolish desire to dress again and go out. But the overwhelming lassitude which had seized me at my house returned to me, depriving me of all strength to move, and I remained, in spite of the disgust which I felt for this public bed. The sensual charm which I fancied I saw down there, under the lights of the theatre, had disappeared in my arms, and I had with me, flesh to flesh, only a vulgar girl, like all the rest, whose indifferent and complaisant kiss had an after-taste of garlic.

" I began to talk to her :

" 'Have you been here long ?' said I.

" 'Six months the fifteenth of January.'

" 'Where were you before that ?'

" 'I was in the Rue Clauzel. But the concierge made so much trouble that I left.'

" And she began to relate an interminable story of the concierge, who had made some scandal about her.

" Suddenly I heard something moving near us. At first

there was a sigh, then a slight but distinct noise, as if someone had stirred in a chair.

"I sat up quickly in bed and asked: 'What was that noise?'

"She answered with tranquil assurance: 'Don't disturb yourself, my dear, it is my neighbour. The partition is so thin that we hear everything as if they were here. What rotten holes these are. They are made of pasteboard.'

"My indolence was so strong that I got down under the clothes again. We continued our talk. Incited by the curiosity which drives all men to question these creatures upon their first adventure, to wish to raise the veil from their first fault in order to find in them some far-off trace of innocence, that we may find something to love, perhaps, in the rapid recital evoked by their candour and the shame of long ago, I asked her about her first lover.

"I knew that she would lie. What did it matter? Among all the lies I might discover, perhaps, some sincere or touching incident.

"'Come,' said I, 'tell me who he was.'

"'He was a boater, dearie.'

"'Ah! Tell me about it. Where were you?'

"'I was at Argenteuil.'

"'What were you doing there?'

"'I was maid in a restaurant.'

"'What restaurant?'

"'At the Marin d'Eau Douce. Do you know it?'

"'Well, yes; Bonanfan's.'

"'Yes, that's the one.'

"'And how did he pay his court, this boater?'

"'While I was making his bed. He violated me.'

"But suddenly I recalled the theory of a doctor of my acquaintance, an observant, philosophic doctor who, in his practice in a great hospital, had daily examples of these girl-mothers and prostitutes, and knew all the shame and misery of women, the poor women who become the hideous prey of the wandering male with money in his pocket.

" 'Invariably,' he told me, 'a girl is debauched by a man of her own class and station in life. I have made volumes of observations upon it. It is customary to accuse the rich of culling the flower of innocence from the children of the people. That is not true. The rich pay for the culled bouquet. They cull also, but at the second flowering; they never cut the first.'

" Then turning toward my companion, I began to laugh:

" 'Come now, I know all your story by heart. The boater was not the first, as you well know.'

" 'Yes he was, dearie, I swear it!'

" 'You are lying.'

" 'Oh! no, I promise you I am not.'

" 'You are lying. Come, tell me the truth.'

" She seemed to hesitate, astonished. I continued:

" 'I am a sorcerer, my good child, a hypnotist. If you do not tell me the truth, I shall put you to sleep, and then I can find out.'

" She was afraid, being stupid like her kind. She murmured:

" 'How did you ever guess it?'

" I replied: 'Come, speak.'

" 'Oh! the first time, it was almost nothing. There was a country holiday and a chef was called in for the occasion, M. Alexander. As soon as he came he had it all his own way in the house. He ordered everybody about, even the master and the mistress, as if he had been a king. He was a tall, handsome man who had hardly enough room to stand in front of the stove. He was always shouting: "Here, some butter—some eggs—some Madeira!" And you had to run to him with everything at once, or he would get angry and say things to you that would make you blush all over your body.

" 'When the day's work was done he installed himself in front of the door and began to smoke. And, as I passed in front of him with a pile of plates, he said to me: "Here, child, won't you come down to the edge of the river and show me the country?" I went, like a fool; and scarcely had we arrived at the bank when he violated me so quickly that I did not even know that it was done. And then he went away by the nine o'clock train, and I never saw him again after that.'

"I asked: 'Is that all?'

"She stammered: 'Oh! I believe Florentin is his?'

"'Who is Florentin?'

"'He is my little boy.'

"'Ah! very well. And you made the boater believe that he was the father, did you not?'

"'Yes.'

"'Had this boater money?'

"'Yes, he left me an income of three hundred francs for Florentin's support.'

"I began to be amused, and continued:

"'Very well, my girl, very well. You are all less stupid than one would believe. And how old is Florentin now?'

"She answered: 'Twelve years old. He will take his first communion in the spring.'

"'That is good; and since that you have conscientiously followed your profession?'

"She sighed resignedly: 'One does what one can.'

"A loud noise in another part of the room made me leap out of bed with a bound; it was the noise of someone falling, then rising and groping with his hands upon the wall. I had seized the candle and was looking about, frightened and furious. She got up also and tried to hold me back, saying:

"'It is nothing, dearie, I assure you it is nothing.'

"But I had discovered on which side of the wall this strange noise was. I went straight toward a concealed door at the head of the bed and opened it suddenly—and perceived there a poor little boy, trembling and staring at me with frightened eyes, a pale, thin little boy beside a large chair filled with straw, from which he had fallen.

" When he saw me, he began to cry and, opening his arms to his mother :

" ' It was not my fault, mamma, it was not my fault. I was asleep and I fell. You mustn't scold me, for it was not my fault.'

" I turned toward the woman and said :

" ' What does he mean ? '

" She seemed sad and embarrassed. But finally she said in a broken voice :

" ' What can you expect ? I do not earn enough to put the child to school ! I must take care of him somehow, and I cannot afford to hire another room. He sleeps with me when I have no one. When someone comes for an hour or two, he can stay in the closet very well and keep quiet ; he knows how. But when one remains all night, as you have, his muscles are fatigued from sleeping on the chair—and it is not the child's fault. I would like to see you—you—sleep all night on a chair—you would sing another song——'

" She was angry, wrought up, and was shouting.

" The child was still crying. A poor, weakly, timid child, a true child of the closet, of the cold, dark closet, a child who came from time to time to get a little warmth in the bed when, for a moment, it was empty.

" I, too, had an inclination to weep.

" I returned home to my own bed."

BOMBARD

Life often seemed very hard to Simon Bombard! He was born with an incredible capacity for doing nothing and with an immoderate desire to follow this vocation. All effort, whether moral or physical, every movement accomplished for a purpose, appeared to him beyond his strength. As soon as he heard anyone speak of anything serious he became confused, his mind being incapable of tension or even attention.

The son of a linen-draper in Caen, he took things easily, as they said in the family, until he was twenty-five years of age. But as his parents were always nearer bankruptcy than fortune, he suffered greatly for want of money.

He was a big, tall, fine-looking fellow, with red whiskers, cut Norman fashion, florid of face and blue of eye, stupid and good-humoured, with an incipient paunch, and dressed with the swagger elegance of a provincial on a holiday. He laughed and gesticulated on every occasion, displaying a noisy good nature with the assurance of a commercial traveller. He believed that life was made solely for love and laughter, and as soon as it became necessary to curb his noisy enjoyment, he fell into a kind of chronic somnolence, being incapable of sadness.

His need of money harassed him until he formed the habit of repeating a phrase which became celebrated in his circle of acquaintance: "For ten thousand francs a year, I would become an executioner."

Now, he went each year to Trouville for a fortnight. He called this "spending the season." He would install himself at the house of his cousins, who gave him the use of a room, and from the day of his arrival to that of his departure he would promenade along the board walk which extends along the great stretch of seashore.

He walked with an air of confidence, his hands in his pockets or crossed behind his back, always clothed in ample garments, with light waistcoats and showy cravats, his hat somewhat over his ear and a cheap cigar in one corner of his mouth.

He went along, brushing up against the elegantly-dressed women and staring contemptuously at the men like a fellow ready for a fight, and seeking—seeking—really seeking.

He was seeking a wife, counting upon his face and his physique. He said to himself: "Why the devil, in all the crowd that comes here, should I not be able to find what I want?" And he hunted with the scent of a foxhound, with the keen instinct of a Norman, sure that he would recognise the woman who would make him rich, the moment he perceived her.

One Monday morning he murmured: "Hello! hello! hello!" The weather was superb, one of those yellow and blue days of the month of July, in which it rains heat, so to say. The vast beach covered with figures, dresses, colours, looked like a garden of women; and the fishing-boats with their brown sails, almost immovable upon the blue water which reflected them upside down, seemed asleep under the hot ten o'clock sun. There they remained, opposite the wooden pier, some near, some further off, some still further, as if overcome by summer day idleness, too indifferent to seek the open sea, or even to return to port. And in the distance one could vaguely perceive in the mist the coast of Havre, showing two white points on its summit, the lighthouses of Sainte-Adresse.

He said to himself: "Hello, hello, hello!" For he had passed her now for the third time and felt her look resting on him: the look of a mature, experienced, bold woman, inviting response. He had noticed her before, because she seemed also in quest of someone. She was an Englishwoman, rather tall, a little thin, one of these bold Englishwomen whom circumstances and much journeying had made a kind of man. Not bad, on the whole, walking along slowly with short steps, soberly and simply clothed, but wearing a queer sort of hat as Englishwomen always do. She had rather pretty eyes, high cheek-bones, a little red; her teeth were too long and always visible.

When he came to the pier, he retraced his steps to see if she would meet him again. He met her and threw her an ardent glance, a glance which seemed to say: "Here I am!"

But how should he speak to her? He returned a fifth time, and when he was again face to face with her she dropped her parasol. He rushed forward, picked it up and presented it to her, saying:

"Permit me, Madame——"

She responded: "Oh, you are very kind!"

And then they looked at each other. They had nothing more to say. But she blushed. Then becoming courageous, he said:

"We are having beautiful weather here."

And she answered: "Oh, delicious!"

And then they again faced each other, embarrassed, neither thinking of going away. It was she who finally had the audacity to ask: "Are you going to be here long?"

He answered, laughing: "Oh! yes, about as long as I care to." Then suddenly he proposed: "Would you like to go down to the pier? It is pretty there on a day like this."

She simply said: "I should be much pleased."

And they walked along side by side, she with her stiff, rigid movements, he with the rolling swagger of a gander showing off in a farmyard.

Three months later the leading merchants of Caen received one morning a square white card which said:

"M. and Mme Prosper Bombard have the honour to

announce the marriage of their son, M. Simon Bombard, to Mme Kate Robertson."

and on the other side:

"Mme Kate Robertson has the honour of announcing her marriage to M. Simon Bombard."

They settled in Paris. The bride's fortune amounted to fifteen thousand francs a year free of incumbrances. Simon wished to have four hundred francs a month for his personal expenses. He had to prove that his tenderness merited this amount; he did prove it easily and obtained what he asked for.

At first everything went well. Young Mme Bombard was indeed no longer young, and her freshness had undergone some wear; but she had a way of exacting things which made it impossible for anyone to refuse her. She would say, with her grave, imperious English accent: "Oh! Simon, now we must go to bed," which made Simon start toward the bed like a dog that had been ordered "to his kennel." And she knew how to have her way by day and night, in a manner there was no resisting.

She did not get angry; she made no scenes; she never raised her voice; she never had the appearance of being irritated or hurt, or even disturbed. She knew how to talk, that was all; and she spoke to the point, and in a tone that admitted no contradiction.

More than once Simon was on the point of rebelling; but against the brief and imperious desires of this singular woman he found himself unable to stand out. Nevertheless, when the conjugal kisses began to be meagre and monotonous, and he had in his pocket what would bring to him something better, he stood himself all he wanted, but with a thousand precautions.

Mme Bombard perceived all this, without his knowing how; and one evening she announced to him that she had rented a house at Mantes where they would live in the future.

Then existence became harder. He tried various kinds of pastimes, which did not at all compensate for the feminine conquests for which he longed.

He fished, learned how to tell the places which the gudgeon liked, which the roach and carp preferred, the favourite spots of the bream and the kinds of bait that the different fish will take.

But in watching his floater as it trembled on the surface of the water, other visions haunted his mind. Then he became the friend of the chief clerk at the Sub-prefecture, and the captain of the police; and they played whist in the evening at the Café du Commerce, but his sorrowful eye would disrobe the queen of clubs or of diamonds, while the problem of the absent legs on these two-headed figures would confuse the images awakened in his mind.

Then he conceived a plan, a typical specimen of Norman cunning. He made his wife take a maid who suited him; not a beautiful girl, a coquette, or dressy, but a gawky woman, rough and strong-backed, who would not arouse suspicions and whom he had carefully coached in his plans.

She was recommended to them by the collector of tolls, his accomplice and obliging friend, who guaranteed her in every way. And Madame Bombard accepted with confidence the treasure they brought to her.

Simon was happy, happy with precaution, with fear, and with unbelievable difficulties. He could never escape the watchful eye of his wife, except for a few short moments from time to time, and then without security. He sought some plan, some stratagem, and he ended by finding one that succeeded perfectly.

Madame Bombard, who had nothing to do, retired early, while Bombard, who played whist at the Café du Commerce, returned each evening at half-past nine, exactly. He got Victorine to wait for him in the passageway of his house, under the hall steps, in the darkness.

He only had five minutes at the most, for he was always

in fear of a surprise ; but five minutes from time to time sufficed for his ardour, and he slipped a louis into the servant's hand, for he was generous in his pleasures, and she would quickly remount to her garret.

And he laughed, he triumphed all alone, and repeated aloud, like King Midas's barber fishing for whitebait in the reeds on the river bank : " Fooled, old girl ! "

And the happiness of having fooled Madame Bombard made up to him in great part for the imperfection and incompleteness of his salaried conquest.

One evening he found Victorine waiting for him as usual, but she appeared to him more lively, more animated than usual, and he remained perhaps ten minutes at the rendezvous in the corridor.

When he entered the conjugal chamber, Madame Bombard was not there. He felt a cold chill run down his back and sank into a chair, tortured with fear.

She appeared with a candlestick in her hand. He asked trembling :

" You have been out ? "

She answered quietly : " I went to the kitchen for a glass of water."

He forced himself to calm his suspicions of what she might have heard ; but she seemed tranquil, happy, confident, and he was reassured.

When they entered the dining-room for breakfast the next morning, Victorine put the cutlets on the table. As she turned to go out, Madame Bombard handed her a louis which she held up delicately between her two fingers, and said to her, with her calm, serious accent :

" Here, my girl, here are twenty francs which I deprived you of last night. I return them to you."

And the flabbergasted girl took the gold piece, gazing at it stupidly, while the terrorised Bombard looked at his wife with wide-open eyes.

ROOM NO. ELEVEN

"WHAT! YOU DO NOT KNOW WHY PRESIDENT AMANDON was transferred?"

"No, not at all."

"As far as that is concerned, he never knew either. But it is the strangest of stories."

"Tell me."

"You must remember Madame Amandon, that pretty brunette, thin, and so distinguished and pretty that she was called Madame Marguerite in all Perthuis-le-Long?"

"Yes, perfectly."

"Very well, then. You recall also how much she was respected and considered, and the most popular person in the town; she knew how to receive, how to organise a fête or a charity fair, how to find money for the poor, and how to please the young people in a thousand ways.

"She was very elegant and very coquettish, nevertheless, but in a Platonic fashion, and with a charming provincial elegance, for she was a provincial, this pretty little woman, an exquisite provincial.

"The poets and writers, who are all Parisian, sing to us of the Parisian woman and of her charm, because they know only her; but I declare here that the woman from the provinces is a hundred times better, when she is of superior quality.

"The provincial has an attraction all her own, more discreet than that of the Parisienne, more humble, promising nothing and giving much, while the Parisienne, for the most part, promises much but gives nothing when she is undressed.

"The Parisian woman is the elegant and brazen triumph of artificiality; the provincial is the modesty of truth.

" Yet a wide-awake provincial, with her air of homely alertness, her deceitful, schoolgirl candour, her smile which means nothing, and her good little passions, narrow but tenacious, is capable of a thousand times more deceit, artifice, and feminine invention than all the Parisiennes together, for gratifying her own tastes or vices, and that without awakening suspicion, or scandal or gossip in the little town which watches her with all its eyes from all its windows.

" Madame Amandon was a type of this rare but charming race. Never had anyone suspected her, never had anyone thought that her life was not as limpid as her look, a sly look, transparent and warm, but seemingly so honest—you should have seen it !

" Then she had admirable tact, a marvellous ingenuity and power of invention, and unbelievable simplicity.

" She picked all her lovers from the army and kept them three years, the time of their sojourn in the garrison. In short, she gratified, not her heart but her senses.

" When some new regiment arrived at Perthuis-le-Long, she informed herself about all the officers between thirty and forty years of age—for, before thirty one is not discreet, and after forty, one is often weak.

" Oh ! she knew the list of officers as well as the Colonel did. She knew everything, everything, the habits, manners, instruction, education, physical qualities, the power of resistance to fatigue, the character, whether patient or violent, the fortune, and the tendency to closeness or prodigality of each of them. Then she made her choice. She gave preference to men of calm exterior, like herself, but they must be handsome. She also wished them to have had no previous entanglements, any passion which might have left traces, or have made a scandal. Because the man whose loves are mentioned is never very discreet.

" After having decided upon the one she would love for the three years of his regulation sojourn, it remained for her to throw him the gage.

" How many women would find themselves embarrassed, would have taken ordinary means, following the way of others, let themselves be courted, marking off all the stages of conquest and resistance, allowing their fingers to be kissed one day, their wrist the next, their cheek the following, then the lips, then the rest. She had a method more prompt, more discreet, and more sure. She gave a ball.

" The chosen officer invited the mistress of the house to dance. Then, in waltzing, led on by the rapid movement, bewildered by the intoxication of the dance, she would press against him as if surrendering herself, and hold his hand with a nervous, continued pressure.

" If he did not understand, he was only a fool, and she passed on to the next, classed as number two on the list of her desires.

" If he understood, the thing was done, without fuss, without compromising gallantries, without numerous visits.

" What could be simpler or more practical?

" How well women might follow a similar procedure, in order to let us know that they like us! How many difficulties, hesitations, misunderstandings that would obviate! How often we pass by, without knowing it, a possible happiness—without suspecting it, because we are unable to penetrate the mystery of thought, the secret abandon of the will, the mute appeal of the flesh, the unknown soul of a woman whose mouth preserves silence, whose eye is impenetrable and clear.

" When the man understood, he asked for a rendezvous. But she always made him wait a month or six weeks in order to watch and be sure that he had no dangerous faults.

" During this time he was racking his brain to think of some place where they could meet without peril, and imagining combinations difficult and unsafe.

" Then, at some official luncheon, she would say to him in a whisper:

" ' Go on Tuesday evening, at nine o'clock, to the Hôtel du

Cheval d'Or, near the ramparts, on the Vouziers road, and ask for Mademoiselle Clarisse. I shall be waiting for you. And be sure to be in mufti.'

"For eight years she had in fact rented this furnished room by the year, in this obscure inn. It was an idea of her first lover, which she found practical, and after the man departed, she kept the nest.

"Oh! it was a mediocre nest; four walls covered with grey paper adorned with blue flowers, a deal bedstead under muslin curtains, an arm-chair bought at her order by the inn-keeper's wife, two chairs, a bedside rug, and some necessary articles for the toilette—what more was needed?

"Upon the walls were three large photographs. Three colonels on horseback; the colonels of her lovers! Why not? It would not do to preserve the true likeness, the exact likeness, but she could perhaps keep some souvenirs by proxy.

"And had she never been recognised by anyone in all these visits to the Cheval d'Or, you ask?

"Never, by anyone!

"The means she employed were admirable and simple. She had thought out and organised some charity reunions and religious meetings, some of which she attended, others she did not. Her husband, knowing her good works, which cost him a lot of money, lived without suspicions. Then, when a rendezvous had been agreed upon, she would say at dinner, before the servants:

"'I am going this evening to the Association for making flannel bandages for the paralysed old men.'

"And she went out about eight o'clock, went straight to the Association, came out again immediately, passed through divers streets, and, finding herself alone in some little street, in some sombre corner without a light, she would take off her hat, replace it by a maid's cap which she carried under her cape, fold a kerchief after the same fashion and tie it over her shoulders, carrying her hat and the garment she had worn in a napkin; she would go trotting boldly along like a good little maid that had been sent upon some errand; and sometimes she would even run, as if she were in a great hurry.

" Who could have recognised in this trim, lively servant the wife of President Amandon?

" She would arrive at the Cheval d'Or, go up to her room, to which she had the key, and the big proprietor, Maître Trouveau, seeing her pass his desk, would murmur:

" 'There is Mademoiselle Clarisse coming to meet some lover.'

" He had indeed guessed something, the rogue, but did not try to learn more, and he would certainly have been much surprised to find that his client was Madame Amandon, or Madame Marguerite, as she was called in Perthuis-le-Long. And this is how the horrible discovery took place:

" Never had Mademoiselle Clarisse come to her meeting-place two evenings in succession, never! being too nice and too prudent for that. And Maître Trouveau knew this well, since not once in eight years had he seen her come the next day after a visit. Often, therefore, in days of need, he had disposed of her room for a night.

" Now, last summer, Monsieur Amandon absented himself from home for a week. It was in July. Madame was ardently in love, and as there was no fear of being surprised, she asked her lover, the handsome Major Varangelles, one Tuesday evening on leaving him, if he wished her to return the next day.

" He replied: 'How can you ask!'

" And it was agreed that they should return at the usual hour on Wednesday. She said to him in a low tone:

" 'If you arrive first, my dear, you can wait for me in bed.'

" Then they embraced and separated. The next day, as Maître Trouveau sat reading the *Tablettes de Perthuis*, the Republican organ of the town, he cried out to his wife, who was plucking a fowl in the courtyard:

"'Here! the cholera has broken out in the country. There was a man died yesterday of it in Vauvigny.' But he thought no more about it, his inn being full of people, and business very good.

"Towards noon a traveller presented himself on foot, a kind of tourist, who ordered a good lunch, after having drunk two absinthes. And, as he was very warm, he absorbed a bottle of wine and two bottles of water at least. Then he took his coffee, and his little glass of liqueur, or rather three little glasses, and feeling rather drowsy he asked for a room where he might sleep for an hour or two. There was no longer a vacant room, and the proprietor, after consulting his wife, gave him Mademoiselle Clarisse's.

"The man went in there and, about five o'clock, as he had not been seen coming out, the landlord went to wake him. What was his astonishment to find him dead!

"The innkeeper went down to find his wife: 'Listen,' he whispered to her, 'the tourist I put in No. 11, I believe is dead.'

"She raised her arms, crying: 'It's not possible! Lord God! It is the cholera!'

"Maître Trouveau shook his head:

"'I should rather believe that it was a cerebral congestion, seeing that he is as black as the dregs of wine.'

"But the mistress was frightened and kept repeating:

"'We must not mention it. We must not talk of it. People will say it is cholera. Go and make the report and say nothing. They will take him away in the night, and no one will know about it. "What the eye doesn't see the heart doesn't grieve over."'

"The man murmured: 'Mademoiselle Clarisse was here yesterday, the room will be free this evening.'

"And he found the doctor who made out the certificate, 'From congestion after a copious repast.' Then he made an agreement with the commissioner of police to remove the dead body towards midnight, so that there might be no suspicion about the hotel.

"It was scarcely nine o'clock when Madame Amandon went secretly up the staircase of the Cheval d'Or, without being seen by anyone. She reached her room, opened the door, and entered. A candle was burning upon the chimney-piece. She turned toward the bed. The major, she thought, was already there and had closed the curtains.

"She said to him: 'One minute, darling, and I am coming.'

"And she undressed with a feverish haste, throwing her boots upon the floor and her corset upon the arm-chair. Then, her black dress, and skirts having fallen in a circle around her, she stood in her red silk chemise like a flower that has just blossomed.

"As the major said not a word, she asked:

"'Are you asleep, dear?'

"He did not answer, and she began to laugh, murmuring:

"'Wait! He is asleep. It is too funny!'

"She kept on her black silk openwork stockings and, running to the bed, slipped in quickly, seizing him full in her arms and kissing him on the lips, in order to wake him suddenly. It was the cold dead body of the traveller.

"For one second she remained immovable, too frightened to comprehend anything. But the cold of this inert flesh penetrated her own, giving her an atrocious fright before her mind had time to reflect.

"She made a bound out of the bed, trembling from head to foot; then running to the chimney-piece, she seized the candle, returned, and looked! And she perceived a frightful face that she had never before seen, black, swollen, with eyes closed, and a horrible grimace of the jaw.

"She uttered a cry, one of those piercing interminable cries which women utter in their fright, and, letting fall the candle, she opened the door and fled, unclothed, down the passage, still screaming in frightful fashion. A commercial traveller in his socks, who occupied room No. 4, came out immediately and received her in his arms.

" He asked, much startled : ' What is the matter, my pretty dear ? '

" She stammered out, terrified : ' Someone has been killed—in—my room ! '

" Other guests appeared. The landlord himself ran out.

" And suddenly the tall figure of the major appeared at the end of the corridor. When she saw him, she threw herself toward him, crying :

" ' Save me, save me, Gontran—someone has been killed in our room.'

" Explanations were difficult. Maître Trouveau, however, told the truth and demanded that they release Mademoiselle Clarisse, for whom he vouched with his own head. But the commercial traveller in socks, having examined the dead body, declared that a crime had been committed, and he convinced the other guests that Mademoiselle Clarisse and her lover should not be allowed to depart.

" They were obliged to await the arrival of the police commissioner, who gave them their liberty, but was not discreet.

" The following month, President Amandon received promotion with a new place of residence."

A WOMAN'S HAIR

THE WALLS OF THE CELL WERE BARE AND WHITE-WASHED. A narrow, barred window, so high that it could not easily be reached, lighted this bright, sinister little room; the madman, seated on a straw chair, looked at us with a fixed eye, vague and troubled. He was very thin, with wrinkled cheeks and almost white hair that had evidently grown white in a few months. His clothes seemed too large for his dried-up limbs, his shrunken chest, and hollow body. One felt that this man had been ravaged by his thoughts, by a thought, as fruit is by a worm. His madness, his idea, was there in his head, obstinate, harassing, devouring. It was eating his body, little by little. It, the Invisible, the Impalpable, the Unseizable, the Immaterial Idea gnawed his flesh, drank his blood, and extinguished his life.

What a mystery, this man killed by a Thought! He is an object of fear and pity, this madman! What strange dream, frightful and deadly, can dwell in his forehead, to fold such profound and ever-changing wrinkles in it?

The doctor said to me: "He has terrible paroxysms of rage, and is one of the strangest lunatics I have ever seen. His madness is of an erotic, macabre kind. He is a sort of necrophile. He has written a journal which shows as plainly as daylight the malady of his mind. His madness is visible, so to speak. If you are interested, you may run through this document."

I followed the doctor into his office and he gave me the journal of this miserable man.

"Read it," said he, "and give me your opinion about it."

Here is what the little book contained:

"Up to the age of thirty-two years I lived quietly, without love. Life appeared to me very simple, very good, and very easy. I was rich. I had a taste for so many things that I had never felt a passion for anything. It was good to live! I awoke happy each day, to do things which it pleased me to do, and I went to bed satisfied, with a calm hope for the next day and a future without care.

"I had had some mistresses without ever having my heart torn by desire or my soul bruised by love after the possession. It is good to live thus. It is better to love, but it is terrible. Still, those who love like everybody else should find happiness, less than mine, perhaps, for love has come to me in an unbelievable manner.

"Being rich, I collected old furniture and antiques. Often I thought of the unknown hands which had touched these things, of the eyes that had admired them, and the hearts that had loved them—for one does love such things! I often remained for hours and hours looking at a little watch of the last century. It was so dainty, so pretty with its enamel and gold embossing. And it still went, as on the day when some woman had bought it, delighted in the possession of so fine a jewel. It had not ceased to palpitate, to live its mechanical life, but had ever continued its regular tick-tack, although a century had passed. Who then had first carried it upon her breast, in the warmth of the dress—the heart of the watch beating against the heart of the woman? What hand had held it at the ends of its warm fingers, then wiped the enamelled shepherds, tarnished a little by the moisture of the skin? What eyes had looked upon this flowered dial awaiting the hour, the dear hour, the divine hour?

"How I should have liked to see her, to know her, the woman who had chosen this rare and exquisite object. But she is dead! I am possessed by a desire for women of former times; from afar I love all those who loved long ago. The story of past tenderness fills my heart with regrets. Oh!

the beauty, the smiles, the caresses of youth, the hopes! Should not these things be eternal!

"How I have wept, during whole nights, over the women of old, so beautiful, so tender, so sweet, whose arms opened to love, and who now are dead! The kiss is immortal! It goes from lip to lip, from century to century, from age to age! Men take it and give it and die.

"The past attracts me, the present frightens me, because the future is death. I regret all that which is gone, I weep for those who have lived; I wish to stop the hour, to arrest time. But it goes, it goes on, it passes away, and it takes me, from second to second, a little of me for the annihilation of to-morrow. And I shall never live again.

"Farewell, women of yesterday, I love you.

"But I am not to be pitied. I have found her whom I awaited, and I have tasted through her inconceivable pleasures.

"I was roaming around Paris one sunny morning, with joyous foot and happy soul, looking in the shops with the vague interest of a stroller. All at once I saw in an antique shop an Italian piece of furniture of the seventeenth century. It was very beautiful, very rare. I decided it must be by a Venetian artist, named Vitelli, who belonged to that epoch. Then I passed on.

"Why did the remembrance of this piece of furniture follow me with so much force that I retraced my steps? I stopped again before the shop to look at it, and felt that it tempted me.

"What a singular thing is temptation! You look at an object, and, little by little, it seduces you, troubles you, takes possession of you like the face of a woman. Its charm enters into you, a strange charm which comes from its form, its colour, and its physiognomy. Already you love it, wish for it, desire it. A need of possession seizes you, a pleasant need at first, because timid, but increasing, becoming violent and irresistible. And the dealers seem to suspect, from the look of the eye, this secret, increasing desire. I bought that piece of furniture and had it carried to my house immediately. I placed it in my room.

" Oh! I pity those who do not know this honeymoon of the collector with the object which he had just acquired. He caresses it with his eye and hand as if it were flesh; he returns every moment to it, thinks of it continually, wherever he goes and whatever he may be doing. The thought of it follows him into the street, into the world, everywhere. And when he re-enters his house, before even removing his gloves or his hat, he goes to look at it with the tenderness of a lover.

" Truly, for eight days I adored that piece of furniture. I kept opening its doors and drawers; I handled it with delight and experienced all the intimate joys of possession.

" One evening, in feeling the thickness of a panel, I perceived that there might be a hiding-place there. My heart began to beat and I passed the night in searching out the secret, without being able to discover it.

" I came upon it the next day by forcing a piece of metal into a crevice in the panelling. A shelf slipped, and I saw, exposed upon a lining of black velvet, a marvellous head of woman's hair!

" Yes, a head of hair, an enormous twist of blond hair, almost red, which had been cut off near the skin and tied together with a golden cord.

" I stood there stupefied, trembling and disturbed! An almost insensible perfume, so old that it seemed like the soul of an odour, arose from this mysterious drawer, this surprising shrine.

" I took it gently, almost religiously, and lifted it from its resting-place. Immediately it unwound, spreading out its golden billows upon the floor, where it fell, thick and light, supple and brilliant, like the fiery tail of a comet.

" A strange emotion seized me. To whom had this belonged? When? Under what circumstances? Why had this hair been shut up in this piece of furniture? What adventrue, what drama was hidden beneath this souvenir? Who had cut it off? Some lover, on a day of parting? Some husband, on a day of vengeance? Or, perhaps, the woman herself, whose hair it was, on a day of despair? Was it at the hour of entering the cloister that she had thrown there this fortune of love, as a token left to the world of the living? Was it the hour of closing the tomb upon the young and beautiful dead, that he who adored her took this diadem off her head, the only thing he could preserve of her, the only living part of her body that would not perish, the only thing that he could still love and caress and kiss, in the transport of his grief?

"Was it not strange that this hair should remain there thus, when there was no longer any vestige of the body with which it was born?

"It curled about my fingers and touched my skin with a singular caress, the caress of death. I felt myself affected, as if I were going to weep.

"I kept it a long time in my hands, then it seemed to me that it had some effect upon me, as if something of the soul still remained in it. And I laid it upon the velvet again, the velvet blemished by time, then pushed in the drawer, shut the doors of the closet, and betook myself to the street to dream.

"I walked straight ahead, full of sadness, and full of trouble, of the kind of trouble that remains in the heart after the kiss of love. It seemed to me I had lived in former times, and that I had known this woman.

"And Villon's lines rose to my lips, like a sob:

'Tell me now in what hidden way is
Lady Flora the lovely Roman?
Where's Hippatchia, and where is Thais,
Neither of them the fairer woman?
Where is Echo, beheld of no man,
Only heard on river and mere,—
She whose beauty was more than human? . . .
But where are the snows of yester-year?

. . . .

'White Queen Blanche, like a queen of lilies,
With a voice like any mermaiden,—
Bertha Broadfoot, Beatrice, Alice,
And Ermengarde the lady of Maine,—
And that good Joan whom Englishmen
At Rouen doomed and burned her there,—
Mother of God, where are they then? . . .
But where are the snows of yester-year?'[1]

"When I returned to my house I felt an irresistible desire to see my strange treasure again. I took it up and felt it, and in touching it a prolonged thrill ran through my body.

"For some days, however, I remained in my normal state, although the thought of this hair never left me. Whenever I came in, it was my first desire to look at it and handle it. I would turn the key of the desk with the same trembling that one has in opening the door of one's mistress, for I felt in my hands and in my heart a confused, singular, continual, sensual desire to bury my fingers in this charming rivulet of dead hair.

"Then, when I had finished caressing it, when I had returned it to its resting-place, I always felt that it was there, as if it were something alive, concealed, imprisoned; I felt it and I still desired it; again I felt the imperious need of touching it, of feeling it, of enervating myself to the point of weakness by contact with this cold, smooth, irritating, exciting, delicious hair.

"I lived thus for a month or two, I no longer know how long, with this thing possessing me, haunting me. I was happy and tortured, as in the expectation of love, as one is after the avowal which precedes the embrace.

"I would shut myself up alone with it in order to feel it upon my skin, to bury my lips in it, to kiss it, and bite it. I would roll it around my face, drink it in, drown my eyes in its golden waves, to see the high lights through it.

[1] Translation by D. G. Rossetti.

"I loved it! Yes, I loved it. I could no longer live away from it, nor be contented an hour without seeing it. I expected —I expected—what? I know not—her!

"One night I was suddenly awakened with a feeling that I was not alone in my room. I was alone, however. But I could not go to sleep again; and, as I was tossing in the fever of insomnia, I rose and went to look at the twist of hair. It appeared to me sweeter than usual, and more animated.

"Could the dead return? The kisses with which I warmed it made me faint with happiness, and I carried it to my bed and lay down with it, pressing it to my lips, as a man presses his mistress before he takes her.

"The dead returned! She came! Yes, I saw her, touched her, possessed her as she was when alive in former times, tall, fair, plump, with cool breasts, and with hips in the form of a lyre. And I followed with my caresses that divine, undulating line from the throat to the feet, in all the curves of the flesh.

"Yes, I possessed her, every day and every night. The Dead returned, the beautiful Dead, the Adorable, the Mysterious, the Unknown, she returned every night.

"My happiness was so great that I could not conceal it. I found in her a superhuman delight, the profound, inexplicable joy of possessing the Impalpable, the Invisible, the Dead! No lover ever tasted joys more ardent or more terrible.

"I knew not how to conceal my happiness. I loved her so much that I could not bear to leave her. I carried her with me always, everywhere. I walked with her through the city, as if she were my wife, took her to the theatre and to restaurants as one would a mistress. But they saw her—and guessed—they took me, and threw me into prison, like a malefactor. They took her away—oh! misery!——"

The manuscript stopped there. And suddenly, as I raised my wondering eyes to the doctor, a frightful cry, a howl of fury and exasperated desire filled the asylum.

" Listen," said the doctor, " that obscene maniac has to be doused with water five times a day. Sergeant Bertrand is not the only man who fell in love with the dead."

I stammered, moved with astonishment, horror, and pity: " But that hair—did it really exist? "

The doctor got up, opened a closet full of vials and instruments, and threw me, across his desk, a long, thick rope of blond hair, which flew towards me like a golden bird.

I trembled as I felt upon my hands its caressing, light touch. And I stood there, my heart beating with disgust and desire, the disgust we have in coming in contact with objects connected with crimes, and the desire which comes with the temptation to test some infamous and mysterious thing.

Shrugging his shoulders, the doctor added: " The mind of man is capable of anything."

YVETTE

I

As they left the Café Riche, Jean de Servigny said to Léon Saval :

" We'll walk, if you don't mind walking. It's too fine to take a cab."

" It will suit me perfectly," answered his friend.

" It's barely eleven," continued Jean. " We shall be there long before midnight, so let us go slowly."

A restless crowd swarmed on the boulevard, the crowd which on summer nights is always to be seen there, contented and merry, walking, drinking, and talking, streaming past like a river. Here and there a café flung a brilliant splash of light on to the group which sat outside, drinking at round little tables loaded with bottles and glasses, and obstructing the hurrying crowd of passers-by. And in the road the cabs, with their red, blue, and green eyes, passed swiftly across the harsh glare of the lighted front, and for an instant revealed the silhouette of the thin, trotting horse, the profile of the driver on the box, and the dark, square body of the vehicle. The Urbaine cabs gleamed as the light caught their yellow panels.

The two friends walked slowly along, smoking their cigars. They were in evening dress, their overcoats on their arms, flowers in their buttonholes, and their hats a little on one side, with the careless tilt affected by men who have dined well and find the breeze warm.

Ever since their school-days the two had been close friends, profoundly and loyally devoted to each other.

Jean de Servigny, small, slim, slightly bald, and frail, very elegant, with a curled moustache, bright eyes, and thin lips, was one of those night-birds who seem to have been born and bred on the boulevards; inexhaustible, though he wore a perpetual air of fatigue, vigorous despite his pallor—one of those slender Parisians to whom gymnastics, fencing, the cold plunge, and the Turkish bath have given an artificial nervous strength. He was as well known for his conviviality as for his wit, his wealth, and his love-affairs, and for that geniality, popularity, and fashionable gallantry which are the hall-mark of a certain type of man.

In other ways, too, he was a true Parisian, quick-witted, sceptical, changeable, impulsive, energetic yet irresolute, capable of anything and of nothing, an egoist on principle and a philanthropist on impulse. He kept his expenditure within his income, and amused himself without ruining his health. Cold and passionate by turns, he was continually letting himself go and pulling himself up, a prey to conflicting impulses, and yielding to all of them, following his instinct like any hardened pleasure-seeker whose weathercock logic bids him follow every wind and profit from any train of events, without taking the trouble to set a single one of them in motion.

His companion, Léon Saval, rich also, was one of those superb giants who compel women to turn round and stare after them in the street. He had the air of a statue come to life, of a racial type: he was like one of those models which are sent to exhibitions. Too handsome, too tall, too broad, too strong, all his faults were those of excess. He had broken innumerable hearts.

As they reached the Vaudeville, he inquired:

"Have you let this lady know that you're bringing me?"

Servigny laughed.

"Let the Marquise Obardi know! Do you let a bus-driver know in advance that you're going to get on to his bus at the corner of the boulevard?"

"Well, then, exactly who is she?" asked Saval, slightly perplexed.

"A parvenue," replied his friend, "a colossal fraud, a charming jade, sprung from Lord knows where, who appeared one day, Lord knows how, in the world of adventurers, in which she is well able to make herself prominent. Anyhow, what does it matter? They say her real name, her maiden-name—for she has remained a maiden in every sense but the true one—is Octavie Bardin, whence Obardi, retaining the first letter of the Christian name and dropping the last letter of the surname. She's an attractive woman, too, and with your physique you're certain to become her lover. You can't introduce Hercules to Messalina without something coming of it. I ought to add, by the way, that though admission to the place is as free as to a shop, you are not obliged to buy what is on sale. Love and cards are the stock-in-trade, but no one will force you to purchase either. The way out is as accessible as the way in.

"It is three years now since she took a house in the Quartier de l'Étoile, a rather shady district, and opened it to all the scum of the Continent, which comes to Paris to display its most diverse, dangerous, and vicious accomplishments.

"I went to the house. How? I don't remember. I went, as we all go, because there's gambling, because the women are approachable and the men scoundrels. I like this crowd of decorated buccaneers, all foreign, all noble, all titled, all, except the spies, unknown to their ambassadors. They all talk of their honour on the slightest provocation, trot out their ancestors on no provocation at all, and present you with their life-histories on any provocation. They are braggarts, liars, thieves, as dangerous as their cards, as false as their names, brave because they must be, like footpads who cannot rob their victims without risking their necks. In a word, the aristocracy of the galleys.

"I adore them. They're interesting to study, interesting

to meet, amusing to listen to, often witty, never commonplace like the dregs of French officialdom. Their wives too are always pretty, with a little flavour of foreign rascality, and the mystery of their past lives, half of which were probably spent in a penitentiary. Most often they have glorious eyes and wonderful hair, the real professional physique, a grace which intoxicates, a seductive charm that drives men mad, a vicious but wholly irresistible fascination! They're the real old highway robbers, female birds of prey. And I adore them too.

"The Marquise Obardi is a perfect type of these elegant jades. A little over-ripe, but still beautiful, seductive, and feline, she's vicious to the marrow. There's plenty of fun in her house—gambling, dancing, supper . . . all the distractions of the world, the flesh, and the devil, in fact."

"Have you been, or are you, her lover?" asked Léon Saval.

Servigny answered:

"I haven't been, am not, and never shall be. It's the daughter I go there for."

"Oh, there's a daughter, then, is there?"

"There is indeed! She's a marvel. At present she's the principal attraction. A tall, glorious creature, just the right age, eighteen, as fair as her mother is dark, always merry, always ready for fun, always laughing at the top of her voice, and dancing like a thing possessed. Who's to have her? Who has had her? No one knows. There are ten of us waiting and hoping.

"A girl like that in the hands of a woman like the Marquise is a fortune. And they don't show their hands, the rogues. No one can make it out. Perhaps they're waiting for a catch, a better one than I am. Well, I can assure you that if the chance comes my way I'll take it.

"This girl, Yvette, absolutely nonplusses me. She's a mystery. If she isn't the most finished monster of perverse ingenuity that I've ever seen, she's certainly the most extraordinary scrap of innocent girlhood to be found anywhere. She lives there among that disgraceful crew with easy and triumphant serenity, exquisitely wicked or exquisitely simple.

" She's an extraordinary girl to be the daughter of an adventuress, sprung up in that hotbed, like a beautiful plant nourished on manure, or she may be the daughter of some man of high rank, a great artist or a great nobleman, a prince or a king who found himself one night in her mother's bed. No one can understand just what she is, or what she thinks about. But you will see her."

Saval shouted with laughter.

" You're in love with her," he said.

" No, I am one of the competitors, which is not the same thing. By the way, I'll introduce you to my most serious rivals. But I have a real chance. I have a good start, and she regards me with favour."

" You're in love," repeated Saval.

" No, I'm not. She disturbs me, allures me and makes me uneasy, at once attracts me and frightens me. I distrust her as I would a trap, yet I long for her with the longing of a thirsty man for a cool drink. I feel her charm, and draw near it as nervously as if I were in the same room with a man suspected of being a clever thief. In her presence I feel an almost absurd inclination to believe in the possibility of her innocence, and a very reasonable distrust of her equally possible cunning. I feel that I am in contact with an abnormal being, a creature outside the laws of nature, delicious or detestable, I don't know."

For the third time Saval declared :

" You're in love, I tell you. You speak of her with the fervour of a poet and the lyricism of a troubadour. Come now, have it out with yourself, search your heart and admit it."

" Well, it may be so, after all. At least she's always in my mind. Yes, perhaps I am in love. I think of her too much. I think of her when I'm falling asleep and when I wake up ;

that's fairly serious. Her image haunts me, pursues me, is with me the whole time, in front of me, round me, in me. Is it love, this physical obsession? Her face is so sharply graven in my mind that I see it the moment I shut my eyes. I don't deny that my pulses race whenever I see her. I love her, then, but in an odd fashion. I long for her passionately, yet the idea of making her my wife would seem to me a monstrous, absurd folly. I am also a little afraid of her, like a bird swooped upon by a hawk. And I'm jealous of her too, jealous of all that is hidden from me in her incomprehensible heart. I'm always asking myself: 'Is she a delightful little guttersnipe or a thoroughly bad lot?' She says things that would make a trooper blush, but so do parrots. Sometimes she's so brazenly indecent that I'm inclined to believe in her absolute purity, and sometimes her artlessness is so much too good to be true that I wonder if she ever was chaste. She provokes me and excites me like a harlot, and guards herself at the same time as though she were a virgin. She appears to love me, and laughs at me; in public she almost proclaims herself my mistress, and when we're alone together she treats me as though I were her brother or her footman.

"Sometimes I imagine that she has as many lovers as her mother. Sometimes I think that she knows nothing about life, absolutely nothing.

"And she has a passion for reading novels. At present, while waiting for a more amusing position, I am her bookseller. She calls me her librarian.

"Every week the Librairie Nouvelle sends her, from me, everything that has appeared; I believe she reads through the whole lot.

"It must make a strange hotchpotch in her head.

"This literary taste may account for some of her queer ways. When you see life through a maze of fifteen thousand novels, you must get a queer impression of things and see them from an odd angle.

"As for me, I wait. It is certainly true that I have never felt towards any woman as I feel towards her.

"It's equally certain that I shall never marry her.

"If she has had lovers, I shall make one more. If she has not, I shall be the first to take my seat in the train.

"It's all very simple. She can't possibly marry, ever. Who would marry the daughter of the Marquise Obardi, Octavie Bardin? Clearly, no one, for any number of reasons.

"Where could she find a husband? In society? Never; the mother's house is a public resort, and the daughter attracts the clients. One can't marry into a family like that. In the middle classes, then? Even less. Besides, the Marquise has a good head on her shoulders; she'd never give Yvette to anyone but a man of rank, and she'll never find him.

"In the lower classes, perhaps? Still less possible. There's no way out of it, then. The girl belongs neither to society nor to the middle class, nor to the lower classes, nor would marriage jockey her into any one of them. She belongs, by her parentage, her birth, her upbringing, heredity, manners, habits, to the world of gilded prostitution.

"She can't escape unless she becomes a nun, which is very unlikely, seeing that her manners and tastes are already what they are. So she has only one possible profession—love. That's where she'll go, if she has not already gone. She can't escape her destiny. From being a young girl, she'll become just a—'woman.' And I should very much like to be the man who brings about the transformation.

"I am waiting. There are any number of lovers. You'll come across a Frenchman, Monsieur de Belvigne, a Russian who calls himself Prince Kravalow, and an Italian, Chevalier Valréali. These have all definitely entered themselves for the race, and are already training. There are also a number of camp-followers of less account.

"The Marquise is on the look-out. But I fancy she has her

eye on me. She knows I'm very rich and she knows less about the others.

"Her house is the most extraordinary place of the kind that I have ever seen. You meet some very decent fellows there; we're going ourselves and we shall not be the only ones. As for the women, she has come across, or rather picked out, the choicest fruit on the professional stall. Lord knows where she found them. And she was magnificently inspired to make a point of taking those who had children of their own, daughters for choice. The result is that a greenhorn might think the house was full of honest women!"

They had reached the Avenue of the Champs Élysées. A faint breeze whispered among the leaves, and was now and again wafted against their faces, like the soft breath of a giant fan swinging somewhere in the sky. Mute shadows drifted under the trees, others were visible as dark blots on the benches. And all these shadows spoke in very low tones, as though confiding important or shameful secrets.

"You cannot imagine," went on Servigny, "what a collection of fancy titles you come across in this rabbit-warren. By the way, I hope you know I'm going to introduce you as Count Saval. Saval by itself would not be at all popular, I assure you."

"No, damn it, certainly not!" cried his friend. "I'm hanged if anyone is going to think me fool enough to scrape up a comic-opera title even for 'one night only,' and for that crowd. With your leave, we'll cut that out."

Servigny laughed.

"You old idiot! Why, I've been christened the Duc de Servigny. I don't know how or why it was done. I have just always been the Duc de Servigny; I never made trouble about it. It's no discomfort. Why, without it I should be utterly looked down on!"

But Saval was not to be persuaded.

"You're a nobleman, you can carry it off. As for me, I

shall remain, for better or worse, the only commoner in the place. That will be my mark of distinctive superiority."

But Servigny was obstinate.

"I tell you it can't be done, absolutely cannot be done. It would be positively indecent. You would be like a rag-and-bone man at an assemblage of emperors. Leave it to me; I'll introduce you as the Viceroy of Upper Mississippi, and no one will be surprised. If you're going to go in for titles, you might as well do it with an air."

"No; once more, I tell you I won't have it."

"Very well, then. I was a fool really to try persuading you, for I defy you to get in without someone decorating you with a title; it's like those shops a lady can't pass without being given a bunch of violets at the door-step."

They turned to the right down the Rue de Berri, climbed to the first floor of a fine modern mansion, and left their coats and sticks in the hands of four flunkeys in knee-breeches. The air was heavy with the warm festive odour of flowers, scent, and women; and a ceaseless murmur of voices, loud and confused, came from the crowded rooms beyond.

A sort of master of ceremonies, a tall, upright, solemn, pot-bellied man, with a face framed in white whiskers, approached the new-comers and, making a short, stiff bow, asked:

"What name, please?"

"Monsieur Saval," replied Servigny.

Whereupon the man flung open the door and in a loud voice announced to the crowd of guests:

"Monsieur le Duc de Servigny. Monsieur le Baron Saval."

The first room was full of women. The eye was filled at once by a vast vision of bare bosoms lifting from billows of white lace.

The lady of the house stood talking to three friends; she turned and came forward with stately steps, grace in her bearing and a smile upon her lips.

Her low, narrow forehead was entirely hidden by masses

of black, gleaming hair, thick and fleecy, encroaching even on her temples. She was tall, a little too massive, a little too fat, a little over-ripe, but very handsome, with a warm, heady, and powerful beauty. Her crown of hair, with the large black eyes beneath it, provoked entrancing dreams and made her subtly desirable. Her nose was rather thin, her mouth large and infinitely alluring, made for speech and conquest.

But her liveliest charm lay in her voice. It sprang from her mouth like water from a spring, so easily, so lightly, so well pitched, so clear, that listening to it was sheer physical joy. It thrilled the ear to hear the smooth words pour forth with the sparkling grace of a brook bubbling from the ground, and fascinated the eye to watch the lovely, too-red lips part to give them passage.

She held out her hand to Servigny, who kissed it, and, dropping the fan that hung from a thin chain of wrought gold, she gave her other hand to Saval, saying:

"You are welcome, Baron. My house is always open to any friend of the Duc's."

Then she fixed her brilliant eyes on the giant to whom she was being introduced. On her upper lip was a faint smudge of black down, the merest shadow of a moustache, more plainly visible when she spoke. Her scent was delicious, strong and intoxicating, some American or Indian perfume.

But other guests were arriving, marquises, counts, or princes. She turned to Servigny and said, with the graciousness of a mother:

"You will find my daughter in the other room. Enjoy yourselves, gentlemen. The house is yours."

She left them in order to greet the new arrivals, giving Saval that fugitive smiling glance with which women let men know that they have found favour.

Servigny took his friend's arm.

"I'll be your pilot," he said. "Here, where we are at present, are the women; this is the Temple of the Flesh, fresh or otherwise. Bargains as good as new, or better; very superior articles at greatly reduced rates. On the left is the gambling. That is the Temple of Money. You know all about that.

"At the far end, dancing; that is the Temple of Innocence. There are displayed the offspring, if we may believe it, of the ladies in here. Even lawful unions would be smiled on! There is the future, the hope . . . of our nights. And there, too, are the strangest exhibits in this museum of diseased morals, the young girls whose souls are double-jointed, like the limbs of little clowns who had acrobats for parents. Let us go and see them."

He bowed to right and left, a debonair figure, scattering pretty speeches and running his rapid, expert glance over every pair of bare shoulders whose possessor he recognised.

At the far end of the second room an orchestra was playing a waltz; they stopped at the door and watched. Some fifteen couples were dancing, the men gravely, their partners with fixed smiles on their lips. Like their mothers, they showed a great deal of bare skin; since the bodices of some were supported only by a narrow ribbon round the upper part of the arm, there were occasional glimpses of a dark shadow under the armpits.

Suddenly a tall girl started up and crossed the room, pushing the dancers aside, her absurdly long train gathered in her left hand. She ran with the short quick steps affected by women in a crowd, and cried out:

"Ah, there's Muscade. How are you, Muscade!"

Her face was glowing with life, and radiant with happiness. She had the white, golden-gleaming skin which goes with auburn hair. Her forehead was loaded with the sheaf of flaming, gleaming tresses that burdened her still slender neck.

She seemed made for motion as her mother was for speech, so natural, gracious, and simple were her movements. A sense of spiritual delight and physical contentment sprang from the mere sight of her as she walked, moved, bent her head or raised her arm.

"Ah, Muscade," she repeated. "How are you, Muscade?"

Servigny shook her hand vigorously, as though she were a man, and said:

"This is my friend, Baron Saval, Mam'selle Yvette."

She greeted the new-comer, then stared at him.

"How do you do? Are you always as tall as this?"

"Oh, no, Mam'selle," answered Servigny, in the mocking tone he used to conceal his uneasiness in her presence. "He has put on his largest size to-day to please your mother, who likes quantity."

"Oh, very well, then," replied the girl in a serio-comic voice. "But when you come for my sake, please be a little smaller; I like the happy medium. Muscade here is about my size," and she offered him her little hand.

"Are you going to dance, Muscade?" she asked. "Let's dance this waltz."

Servigny made no answer, but with a sudden swift movement put his arm round her waist, and away they went like a whirlwind.

They danced faster than any, turning and twirling with wild abandon, so tightly clasped that they looked like one. Their bodies held upright and their legs almost motionless, it was as though they were spun round by an invisible machine hidden under their feet. They seemed unwearying. One by one the other couples dropped out till they were left alone, waltzing on and on. They looked as though they no longer knew where they were or what they were doing, as though they were far away from the ballroom, in ecstasy. The band played steadily on, their eyes fixed on this bewitched pair; every one was watching, and there was a burst of applause when at last they stopped.

She was rather flushed; her eyes were no longer frank, but strangely troubled, burning yet timid, unnaturally blue, with pupils unnaturally black.

Servigny was drunk with giddiness, and leaned against a door to recover his balance.

" You have a poor head, Muscade," she said. " You don't stand it as well as I do."

He smiled his nervous smile and looked at her with hungry eyes, a savage lust in his eyes and the curve of his lips.

She continued to stand in front of the young man, her throat heaving as she regained her breath.

" Sometimes," she continued, " you look just like a cat about to make a spring. Give me your arm, and let us go and find your friend."

Without speaking he offered her his arm, and they crossed the large room.

Saval was alone no longer ; the Marquise Obardi had joined him, and was talking of trivial things, bewitching him with her maddening voice. Gazing intently at him, she seemed to utter words very different from those on her lips, words that came from the secret places of her heart. At the sight of Servigny she smiled and, turning to him, said :

" Have you heard, my dear Duc, that I've just taken a villa at Bougival for a couple of months ? Of course you'll come and see me ; you'll bring your friend, won't you ? I'm going down there on Monday, so will you both come and dine there next Saturday, and stay over the week-end ? "

Servigny turned sharply to Yvette. She was smiling a serene, tranquil smile, and with an air of bland assurance said :

" Of course Muscade will come to dinner on Saturday ; there's no need to ask him. We shall have all kinds of fun in the country."

He fancied that he saw a vague promise in her smile, and an unwonted decision in her voice.

The Marquise thereupon raised her great black eyes to Saval's face, and said :

" And you also, Baron ? "

There was nothing equivocal about her smile.

He bowed.

" I shall be only too pleased."

" We'll scandalise the neighbourhood—won't we, Muscade ?—and drive my admirers wild with rage," murmured Yvette, glancing, with a malice that was either candid or assured, towards the group of men who watched them from the other side of the room.

" To your heart's content, Mam'selle," replied Servigny; by way of emphasising the intimate nature of his friendship with her, he never called her " Mademoiselle."

" Why does Mademoiselle Yvette always call my friend Servigny ' Muscade ' ? " asked Saval.

The girl assumed an air of innocence.

" He's like the little pea that the conjurers call ' Muscade.' You think you have your finger on it, but you never have."

" Quaint children, aren't they ? " the Marquise said carelessly, obviously thinking of far other things, and not for an instant lowering her eyes from Saval's face.

" I'm not quaint, I'm frank," said Yvette angrily. " I like Muscade, and he's always leaving me ; it's so annoying."

Servigny made her a low bow

" I'll never leave you again, Mam'selle, day or night."

She made a gesture of alarm.

" Oh, no, that would never do ! In the day-time, by all means, but at night you'd be in the way."

" Why ? " he asked imprudently.

With calm audacity she replied :

" Because I don't expect you look so nice with your clothes off."

" What a dreadful thing to say ! " exclaimed the Marquise, without appearing in the least excited. " You can't possibly be so innocent as all that."

" I entirely agree with you," added Servigny in a jesting tone.

Yvette looked rather hurt, and said haughtily :

" You have just been guilty of blatant vulgarity ; you

have permitted yourself far too much of that sort of thing lately."

She turned her back on him, and shouted :

" Chevalier, come and defend me ; I have just been insulted."

A thin, dark man came slowly towards them.

" Which is the culprit ? " he asked, forcing a smile.

She nodded towards Servigny.

" That's the man ; but all the same I like him better than all of you put together ; he's not so boring."

The Chevalier Valréali bowed.

" We do what we can. Perhaps we are not so brilliant, but we are at least as devoted."

A tall, stout man with grey whiskers and a deep voice was just leaving.

" Your servant, Mademoiselle Yvette," he said as he passed.

" Ah, it's Monsieur de Belvigne," she exclaimed, and turning to Saval, she introduced him.

" Another candidate for my favour, tall, fat, rich, and stupid. That's how I like them. He's a real field-marshal—one of those who hold the door open at restaurants. But you're taller than he is. Now what am I going to christen you ? I know ! I shall call you Rhodes Junior, after the colossus who must have been your father. But you two must have really interesting things to discuss, far above our heads, so good night to you."

She ran across to the orchestra, and asked them to play a quadrille.

Madame Obardi's attention seemed to be wandering.

" You're always teasing her," she said softly. " You're spoiling the child's disposition and teaching her a number of bad habits."

" Then you haven't finished her education ? " he replied.

She seemed not to understand, and continued to smile benevolently.

But observing the approach of a solemn gentleman whose breast was covered with orders, she ran up to him :

" Ah, Prince, how delightful ! "

Servigny took Saval's arm once more and led him away, saying :

" There's my last serious rival, Prince Kravalow. Isn't she a glorious creature ? "

" They're both glorious," replied Saval. " The mother's quite good enough for me."

Servigny bowed.

" She's yours for the asking, old chap."

The dancers elbowed them as they took their places for the quadrille, couple by couple, in two lines facing one another.

" Now let's go and watch the Greeks for a bit," said Servigny.

They entered the gambling-room.

Round each table a circle of men stood watching. There was very little conversation ; sometimes a little chink of gold, thrown down on the cloth or hastily mixed up, mingled its faint metallic murmur with the murmur of the players, as though the voice of gold were making itself heard amid the human voices.

The men were decorated with various orders and strange ribbons ; and their diverse features all wore the same severe expression. They were more easily distinguished by their beards.

The stiff American with his horseshoe beard, the haughty Englishman with a hairy fan spread over his chest, the Spaniard with a black fleece reaching right up to his eyes, the Roman with the immense moustache bequeathed to Italy by Victor Emmanuel, the Austrian with his whiskers and clean-shaven chin, a Russian general whose lip was armed with two spears of twisted hair, Frenchmen with gay moustaches—they displayed the imaginative genius of every barber in the world.

" Aren't you going to play ? " asked Servigny.

" No ; what about you ? "

" I never play here. Would you like to go now ? We'll

came back one day when it's quieter. There are too many people here to-day; there's nothing to be done."

"Yes, let us go."

They disappeared through a doorway which led into the hall.

As soon as they were out in the street, Servigny asked:

"Well, what do you think of it all?"

"It's certainly interesting. But I like the women better than the men."

"Good Lord, yes! Those women are the best hunting in the country. Don't you agree with me that love exhales from them like the perfumes from a barber's shop? These are positively the only houses where one can really get one's money's worth. And what expert lovers they are! What artists! Have you ever eaten cakes made by a baker? They look so good, and they have no flavour at all. Well, the love of an ordinary woman always reminds me of baker's pastry, whereas the love you get from women like the Marquise Obardi—that really is love! Oh, they can make cakes all right, can these confectioners. You have to pay them twopence halfpenny for what you would get anywhere else for a penny, that's the only thing."

"Who is the man running the place at present?" asked Saval.

Servigny shrugged his shoulders to express utter ignorance.

"I have no idea," he said. "The last I knew certainly was an English peer, but he left three months ago. At the moment she must be living on the community, on the gambling and the gamblers, very likely, for she has her whims. But it's an understood thing, isn't it, that we are dining with her at Bougival on Saturday? There's more freedom in the country, and I shall end by finding out what notions Yvette has in her head!"

"I ask for nothing better," replied Saval. "I'm not doing anything that day."

As they returned down the Champs Élysées, under the

embattled stars, they passed a couple lying on a bench, and Servigny murmured :

"How ridiculous, yet how utterly indispensable, is this business of love ! A commonplace, and an ecstasy, always the same and always different ! And the clown who is paying that girl a franc is only seeking the very thing I buy for ten thousand from some Obardi who is perhaps no younger or more fascinating than that drab ! What folly ! "

He was silent for some minutes, then said :

"All the same, it wouldn't be a poor thing to be Yvette's first lover. For that I'd give . . . I'd give. . . ."

He did not make up his mind what he would give. And Saval bade him good night at the corner of the Rue Royale.

II

The table had been laid on the veranda that overlooked the river. Villa Printemps, the house that the Marquise Obardi had taken, stood half-way up the hillside, just where the Seine made a turn, running round in front of the garden wall and down towards Marly. Opposite the house the island of Croissy formed a background of tall trees, a mass of leafage. A long reach of the broad river was clearly visible as far as the floating café, La Grenouillère, half hidden in the branches.

Night was coming down, calm and still, after a flaming riverside sunset ; one of those tranquil evenings that bring with them a vague sense of happiness. Not a breath of air stirred the branches, no gust of wind disturbed the smooth, translucent surface of the Seine. The air was warm, but not too hot ; it was good to be alive. The grateful coolness of the river banks rose to the quiet sky.

The sun was disappearing behind the trees, wheeling towards other lands. The serene calm of the sleeping earth soothed the visitors' senses; under the vast quiet dome of the sky they felt the effortless surge of universal life.

The scene enchanted them when they came out of the drawing-room and sat down at the dinner-table. A tender gaiety filled their hearts; they all felt it very good to be dining out there in the country with that broad river and glorious sunset for scenery, and breathing that limpid, heady air.

The Marquise had taken Saval's arm, Yvette Servigny's.

These four made up the little party.

The two women were not in the least like their Parisian selves. Yvette was the more altered of the two; she spoke very little, and seemed tired and grave.

Saval hardly recognised her, and asked:

"What's the matter with you, Mademoiselle? I find you very changed since last week. You have become quite a reasonable being."

"It's the effect of the country," she answered. "I am not the same here; I feel quite strange. And besides, I never am the same two days together. To-day I behave like a lunatic, to-morrow I'll be like a funeral oration; I change like the weather, I don't know why. I'm capable of absolutely anything—at the right time. There are days when I could kill people; not animals—I could never kill animals—but people, certainly; and then there are days when I cry for just nothing. A hundred different ideas rush through my head. It depends, too, on my feeling when I get up in the morning. Every morning when I wake up I know just what I shall be like all day. Perhaps our dreams decide that sort of thing. Partly it depends on the book I have just been reading."

She was dressed in white flannel; the soft, delicate folds of material covered her from head to foot. The bodice was loose, with big pleats, and suggested, without too rigidly defining, the firm sweeping contour of her already well-formed bosom. Her slender neck rose from fold upon fold of frothy lace, drooping languidly, its warm gleaming flesh even whiter than her dress and weighed down with its heavy burden of golden hair.

For a long minute Servigny gazed at her, then said:

"You are adorable to-night, Mam'selle—I wish I could always see you like that."

"Don't propose to me, Muscade," she said, with a touch of her wonted archness. "On a day like this I should take you at your word, and that might cost you dear."

The Marquise looked happy, very happy. She was dressed severely in black; the fine folds of the gown set off the superb, massive lines of her figure. There was a touch of red in the bodice, a spray of red carnations fell from her waist and was caught up at her side, a red rose was fastened in her dark hair. There was a flame in her to-night, in her whole being, in the simple dress with the blood-red blossoms, in the glance that lingered on her neighbour, in her slow voice, in her rare movements.

Saval, too, was grave and preoccupied. From time to time, with a gesture familiar to him, he stroked his brown Vandyke beard, and seemed sunk in thought.

For some moments no one spoke.

"There is sometimes a saving grace in silence," said Servigny at last, as the trout was being handed. "One often feels nearer one's fellow-creatures when silent than when speaking; isn't that so, Marquise?"

She turned slightly towards him and replied:

"Yes, it's true. It is so sweet to think together of the same delightful thing."

She turned her burning gaze on Saval; for some moments they remained looking into one another's eyes. There was a slight, an almost imperceptible movement under the table.

"Mam'selle Yvette," continued Servigny, "you'll make me think you're in love if you continue to behave so beautifully. Now with whom can you be in love? Let's think it out together. I leave the vulgar herd of sighing swains on one side and go straight for the principals. How about Prince Kravalow?"

At this name Yvette was roused.

"My poor dear Muscade, what *are* you thinking about? The Prince looks like a Russian in the waxworks, who has won a medal at a hairdressers' competition."

"Very well. The Prince is out of it. Perhaps you have chosen the Vicomte Pierre de Belvigne?"

This time she broke into a fit of laughter and asked:

"Can you see me hanging round Raisiné's neck"—she called him Raisiné, Malvoisie, or Argenteuil, according to the day of the week, for she nicknamed every one—"and whispering in his ear: 'My dear little Pierre,' or 'My divine Pedro, my adored Pietri, my darling Pierrot, give your dear fat poodle-head to your darling little wifie because she wants to kiss it'?"

"Away with Number Two, then," said Servigny. "We are left with the Chevalier Valréali, whom the Marquise seems to favour."

Yvette was as much amused as before.

"What, Old Lachrymose? Why, he's a professional mourner at the Madeleine; he follows all the high-class funerals. Whenever he looks at me I feel as though I were already dead."

"That's three. Then you've fallen hopelessly in love with Baron Saval, here present."

"With Rhodes Junior? No, he's too strong. It would feel like being in love with the Arc de Triomphe de l'Étoile."

"Well, then, Mam'selle, it is plain that you're in love with me, for I'm the only one of your worshippers that we haven't already dealt with. I had kept myself to the end, out of modesty and prudence. It only remains for me to thank you."

"You, Muscade!" she replied with charming gaiety. "Oh, no, I like you very much . . . but I don't love you. . . . Wait, I don't want to discourage you. I don't love you yet. . . . You have a chance . . . perhaps. . . . Persevere, Muscade, be devoted, ardent, obedient, take plenty of trouble and all possible precautions, obey my lightest whims, be prepared to do anything I may choose . . . and we'll see . . . later."

"But, Mam'selle, I'd rather do all this for you after than before, if you don't mind."

"After what . . . Muscade?" she asked him with the ingenuous air of a soubrette.

"Why, deuce take it, after you've shown me that you love me."

"Well, behave as though I did, and believe it if you want to."

"But, I must say. . . ."

"Be quiet, Muscade. That's enough about it for this time."

He made her a military salute and held his tongue.

The sun had gone down behind the island, but the sky still glowed like a brazier, and the quiet water of the river was as though changed to blood. The sunset spilled a burning light over houses, people, everything; the scarlet rose in the Marquise's hair was like a drop of crimson fallen upon her head from the clouds.

Yvette was looking into the distance; her mother laid her hand on Saval's, as though by accident. But the young girl turned, and the Marquise quickly snatched away her hand and fumbled at the folds of her bodice.

Servigny, who was watching them, said:

"If you like, Mam'selle, we'll go for a walk on the island after dinner."

She was delighted with the idea.

"Oh, yes; that will be lovely; we'll go by ourselves, won't we, Muscade?"

"Yes, all by ourselves, Mam'selle."

Once more they were silent.

The calm of the wide landscape, the restful slumber of eventide weighed on their hearts, their bodies, their voices. There are rare, quiet hours wherein speech is almost impossible. The servants moved noiselessly about. The flaming sky burnt low; slowly night folded the earth in shadow.

"Do you propose to stay here long?" asked Saval.

"Yes," replied the Marquise, dwelling upon each word, "for just as long as I'm happy here."

As it was now too dark to see, lamps were brought. They flung across the table a strange, pale light in the hollow darkness. A rain of little flies began falling upon the cloth. They were tiny midges, burnt as they flew over the glass chimneys of the lamps; their wings and legs singed, they powdered the table-linen, the plates, and the glasses with a grey, creeping dust. The diners swallowed them in their wine, ate them in the sauces, watched them crawling over the bread. Their faces and hands were perpetually tickled by a flying swarm of innumerable tiny insects.

The wine had constantly to be thrown away, the plates covered; they took infinite precautions to protect the food they were eating. Yvette was amused at the game; Servigny carefully sheltered whatever she was raising to her lips, guarded the wine-glass and held his napkin spread out over her head like a roof. But it was too much for the fastidious nerves of the Marquise, and the meal was hastily brought to an end.

"Now let's go to the island," said Yvette, who had not forgotten Servigny's suggestion.

"Don't stay long, will you?" advised her mother languidly. "We'll come with you as far as the ferry."

They went off along the tow-path, still two and two, the young girl in front with her friend. They could hear the Marquise and Saval behind them talking very fast in very low voices. All round them was black, a thick, inky blackness. But the sky, swarming with seeds of fire, seemed to spill them out on the river, for the dark water was richly patined with stars.

By this time the frogs were croaking; all along the banks their rolling, monotonous notes creaked out.

The soft voices of innumerable nightingales rose in the still air.

Yvette remarked abruptly:

"Hallo! They are no longer following us. Where are they?"

And she called: "Mother!"

There was no answer. "They can't be far away," continued the young girl. "I heard them a moment ago."

"They must have gone back," murmured Servigny. "Perhaps your mother was cold." He led her on.

A light shone in front of them; it was the inn of Martinet, a fisherman who also ran a tavern. At their call a man came out of the house, and they boarded a large boat moored in the grasses on the bank. The ferryman took up his oars, and the heavy boat advanced, waking the stars slumbering on the water and rousing them to a frenzied dancing that died slowly down in their wake. They touched the other bank and stepped off under the tall trees. The coolness of the moist earth floated up under the high, thick branches that seemed to bear as many nightingales as leaves. A distant piano began to play a popular waltz.

Servigny had taken Yvette's arm; very softly he slipped his hand behind her waist and pressed it gently.

"What are you thinking of?" he asked.

"I? . . . Nothing, I'm so happy."

"Then you don't care for me?"

"Yes, I do, Muscade. I care for you, I care for you a great deal; only don't talk about it now. It's too beautiful here to listen to your nonsense."

He clasped her to him, though she strove, with little struggles, to free herself; through the flannel, so soft and fleecy to the touch, he could feel the warmth of her body.

"Yvette," he stammered.

"Yes; what is it?"

"It's . . . I who care for you."

"You . . . don't mean that, Muscade."

"Yes, I do; I've cared for you for a very long time."

She was still struggling to get away, striving to free her arm caught between their two bodies. They walked with difficulty, hampered by this link and by her struggles, zigzagging like a couple of drunkards.

He did not know what to say to her now, well aware that it is impossible to use to a young girl the words one would use to a grown woman; he was worried, wondering what he could do, wondering if she consented or did not understand, at his wits' end for words that would be at once tender, discreet, and unmistakable.

Every second he repeated:

"Yvette! Speak to me, Yvette!"

Suddenly he pressed an audacious kiss on her cheek. She made a little movement of withdrawal, and said in a vexed tone:

"Oh! How absurd you are. Will you leave me alone?"

Her voice revealed nothing of her thoughts and wishes; he saw that she was not too angry, and he stooped his lips to the nape of her neck, on the first few downy golden hairs, the adorable spot he had coveted so long.

Then she struggled with all her might to get free. But he held her firmly, and placing his other hand on her shoulder, forced her head round towards him, and took from her mouth a long, maddening kiss. She slipped between his arms with a quick twist of her whole body, stooped swiftly, and having thus dexterously escaped from his embrace, vanished in the darkness with a sharp rustling of petticoats like the whir of a bird rising.

At first he remained motionless, stunned by her quickness and by her disappearance; then, hearing no further sound, he called in a low voice:

"Yvette!"

There was no answer; he began to walk on, ransacking the darkness with his eyes, searching in the bushes for the white patch that her dress must make. All was dark. He called again more loudly:

" Mam'selle Yvette ! "

The nightingales were silent.

He hurried on, vaguely uneasy, calling ever louder and louder :

" Mam'selle Yvette ! Mam'selle Yvette ! "

Nothing ! He stopped, listened. The whole island was silent ; there was barely a rustle in the leaves overhead. The frogs alone kept up their sonorous croaking on the banks.

He wandered from copse to copse, descending first to the steep wooded slope of the swift main stream, then returning to the bare flat bank of the backwater. He went right up until he was opposite Bougival, then came back to the café La Grenouillère, hunting through all the thickets, constantly crying :

" Mam'selle Yvette, where are you ? Answer ! It is only a joke. Answer me, answer me ! Don't make me hunt like this."

A distant clock began to strike. He counted the strokes ; it was midnight. For two hours he had been running round the island. He thought that she had probably gone home, and, very uneasy, went back, going round by the bridge.

A servant, asleep in an arm-chair, was waiting in the hall. Servigny woke him and asked :

" Is it long since Mademoiselle Yvette came in ? I left her out in the country, as I had to pay a call."

" Oh, yes, your Grace," the fellow replied, " Mademoiselle came in before ten."

He walked up to his room and went to bed. But he lay with his eyes open, unable to sleep. That snatched kiss had disturbed her. What did she want ? he wondered. What did she think ? What did she know ? How pretty she was, how tormenting ! His desire, dulled by the life he had led, by all the women he had known, was reawakened by this strange child, so fresh, provoking, and inexplicable.

He heard one o'clock strike, then two. He realised that he would get no sleep that night. He was hot and wet with sweat ;

he felt in his temples the quick thudding of his heart. He got up to open the window.

A cool breeze came in, and he drew long deep breaths of it. The night was utterly dark, silent, and still. But suddenly, in the darkness of the garden he caught sight of a speck of light, like a little piece of glowing coal. "Ah, a cigar," he thought. "It can't be anyone but Saval. Léon," he called softly.

"Is that you, Jean ?" a voice answered.

"Yes. Wait, I'm coming down."

He dressed, went out, and joined his friend, who was smoking astride an iron chair.

"What are you doing at this time of night ?"

"Having a rest," replied Saval, and laughed.

Servigny shook his head.

"I congratulate you, my dear chap. As for me, I've run my head into a wall."

"You are telling me. . . . ?"

"I am telling you . . . that Yvette is not like her mother."

"What happened ? Tell me all about it."

Servigny recounted his unsuccessful efforts, then continued : "Yes, the child really worries me. Do you realise that I haven't been able to get to sleep ? What a queer thing a girl is. This one looked as simple as possible, and yet she's a complete mystery. One can understand at once a woman who has lived and loved, who knows what life is like. But with a young girl, on the other hand, one can't be sure of anything at all. I'm really beginning to think she's playing the fool with me."

Saval rocked gently on his chair.

"Be careful, my dear chap," he said very slowly ; "she'll get you to marry her. Remember the illustrious examples in history. That was how Mademoiselle de Montijo became Empress, and she was at least of decent family. Don't play the Napoleon."

"Have no fears about that," said Servigny. "I'm neither a

fool, nor an emperor. One has to be one or the other to lose one's head so completely. But, I say, are you sleepy?"

"Not a bit."

"Come for a walk along the river-side, then."

"Very well."

They opened the gate and started off down the river towards Marly.

It was the cool hour just before dawn, the hour of deepest sleep, deepest rest, utter quiet. Even the faint noises of the night were silent now. The nightingales sang no longer, the frogs had finished their croaking; some unknown animal, a bird perhaps, alone broke the stillness, making a feeble sawing noise, monotonous and regular, like the working of a machine. Servigny, who had at times a touch of the poet and of the philosopher too, said abruptly:

"Look here. This girl absolutely maddens me. In arithmetic, one and one make two. In love, one and one ought to make one, but they make two all the same. Do you know the feeling? The savage need of absorbing a woman into oneself, or of being absorbed into her? I don't mean the mere physical desire to embrace her, but the mental and spiritual torment to be one with another human being, to open one's whole soul, one's whole heart, to her, and to penetrate to the uttermost depths of her mind. And never, never do you really know her or discover all the fluctuations of her will, her desires, and her thoughts. Never can you make even the slightest guess at the whole of the secret, the whole mystery of the spirit come so close to you, a spirit hidden behind two eyes as clear as water, as transparent as though there were no secret behind them. A spirit speaks to you through a beloved mouth, a mouth that seems yours because you desire it so passionately; one by one this spirit sends you its thoughts in the guise of words, and yet it remains farther from you than the stars are from one another, farther out of reach than the stars. Strange, isn't it!"

" I do not ask so much," replied Saval. " I do not bother to look behind the eyes. I don't care much for the inside; it's the outside I care for."

" Whatever you say, Yvette's a queer creature," murmured Servigny. " I wonder how she'll treat me in the morning."

As they reached the weir at Marly, they saw that the sky was paling. Cocks began to crow in the farmyards; the sound reached them slightly muffled by thick walls. A bird cried in a park on the left, continually repeating a simple and ridiculous little cadenza.

" Time to go back," said Saval, and they turned round.

When Servigny reached his room, the horizon gleamed rosily through the still open window. He pulled down the Venetian blinds and drew the heavy curtains across, got into bed, and at last fell asleep. And all the time he dreamt of Yvette.

A curious sound awoke him. He sat up and listened, but did not hear it again. Then suddenly there came against his shutters a rattling like hail. He jumped out of bed and ran to the window; throwing it open, he saw Yvette standing on the garden-path, throwing great handfuls of gravel in his face.

She was dressed in pink, and wore a broad-brimmed straw hat surmounted with a military plume; she was laughing with malicious mischief.

" Well, Muscade, still asleep? What *can* you have been doing last night to wake up so late? Did you have any adventures, my poor Muscade?"

" Coming, coming, Mam'selle! Just a moment, while I stick my nose into the water-jug, and I'll be down."

" Hurry up," she cried; " it's ten o'clock. And I've got a scheme to talk over with you, a plot we are going to carry out. Breakfast at eleven, you know."

He found her seated on a bench with a book on her knees, a novel. She took his arm with friendly familiarity, as frankly and gaily as though nothing had happened the night before, and leading him to the far end of the garden, said:

"This is my plan. We're going to disobey mamma, and you shall take me presently to the Grenouillère. I want to see it. Mamma says that decent women can't go there, but I don't care whether I can or I can't. You'll take me, Muscade, won't you? We'll have such sport with the people on the river."

The fragrance of her was delightful, but he could not discover what vague, faint scent it was that hung round her. It was not one of her mother's heavy perfumes, but a delicate fragrance in which he thought he recognised a faint whiff of iris powder and perhaps a touch of verbena.

Whence came this elusive scent—from her dress, her hair, or her skin? He was wondering about this when, as she spoke with her face very close to his, he felt her fresh breath full in his face, and found it quite as delightful. He fancied that the fleeting fragrance he had failed to recognise was the figment of his own bewitched senses, nothing but a delusive emanation from her youth and alluring grace.

"You will, won't you, Muscade?" she said. "It will be so hot after breakfast that mother won't want to go out. She's very lazy when it's hot. We'll leave her with your friend, and you shall be my escort. We'll pretend we are going to the woods. You don't know how I shall enjoy seeing the Grenouillère."

They reached the gate facing the Seine. A flood of sunlight fell on the quiet, gleaming river. A light heat-mist was lifting, the steam of evaporated water, leaving a little glittering vapour on the surface of the stream. From time to time a boat went by, a light skiff or a heavy barge, and distant whistles could be heard, the short notes of the whistles on the Sunday trains that flooded the country with Parisians, and the long warning notes of the steamboats passing the weir at Marly.

But a small bell rang for breakfast, and they went in.

The meal was eaten in silence. A heavy July noon pressed

on the earth and oppressed the spirit. The heat was almost tangible, paralysing both mind and body. The sluggish words would not leave their lips; every movement was an effort, as though the air had acquired power of resistance, and was more difficult to thrust through.

Yvette alone, though silent, was animated, and possessed by impatience. As soon as dessert was finished she said:

"Supposing we went for a walk in the woods. It would be perfectly delightful under the trees."

"Are you mad?" murmured the Marquise, who looked utterly exhausted. "How can one go out in weather like this?"

"Very well," replied the young girl slyly, "we'll leave you here with the Baron to keep you company. Muscade and I will scramble up the hill and sit down and read on the grass."

She turned to Servigny, saying: "That's all right, isn't it?"

"At your service, Mam'selle," he replied.

She ran off to fetch her hat. The Marquise shrugged her shoulders and sighed: "Really, she's quite mad." Indolently she held out her beautiful white hand in a gesture of profound and seductive lassitude; the Baron pressed a lingering kiss upon it.

Yvette and Servigny departed. At first they followed the river, then they crossed the bridge and went on to the island, and sat down under the willows on the bank of the main stream, for it was still too early to go to La Grenouillère.

The young girl at once took a book from her pocket and, laughing, said:

"Muscade, you're going to read to me." And she held out the volume for him to take. He made a deprecatory gesture. "I, Mam'selle? But I can't read."

"Come, now, no excuses, no arguments," she replied severely. "You're a nice lover, you are. 'Everything for nothing'—that's your creed, isn't it?"

He took the book and opened it, and was surprised to find that it was a treatise on entomology, a history of ants by an

English author. He remained silent, thinking that she was making fun of him.

"Go on, read," she said.

"Is this a bet," he asked, "or just a joke?"

"Neither. I saw the book in a shop; they told me it was the best book about ants, and I thought it would be nice to hear about the lives of the little creatures and watch them running about in the grass at the same time. So read away."

She lay down face downwards at full length, her elbows resting on the ground and her head between her hands, her eyes fixed on the grass.

"'Without doubt,'" he read, "'the anthropoid apes are of all animals those which approach most closely to man in their anatomical structure; but if we consider the habits of ants, their organisation into societies, their vast communities, the houses and roads which they construct, their custom of domesticating animals and even at times of having slaves, we shall be forced to admit that they have the right to claim a place near man on the ladder of intelligence.'"

He continued in a monotonous voice, stopping from time to time to ask: "Isn't that enough?"

She signed "no" with a shake of her head, and, having picked up a wandering ant on the point of a blade of grass she had plucked, she amused herself by making it run from one end of the stem to the other, turning it upside-down as soon as the insect reached either end. She listened in silence and with concentrated attention to all the surprising details of the life of these frail creatures, their subterranean establishments, the way in which they bring up, keep, and feed little grubs in order to drink the secret liquor they secrete, just as we keep cows in our byres, their custom of domesticating little blind insects which clean their dwellings, and of going to war in order to bring back slaves to serve the victors, which the slaves do with such solicitude that the latter even lose the habit of feeding themselves.

And little by little, as though a maternal tenderness had awakened in her head for this creature at once so tiny and so intelligent, Yvette let it climb about her finger, watching it with loving eyes, longing to kiss it. And as Servigny read how they live in a community, how they play together in a friendly rivalry of strength and skill, the young girl, in her enthusiasm, tried to kiss the insect, which escaped from her finger and began to run over her face. She shrieked as violently as though a deadly peril threatened her, and with wild gestures she slapped at her cheek to get rid of the creature. Servigny, roaring with laughter, caught it near her hair and, at the spot where he had caught it, pressed a long kiss, from which Yvette did not recoil.

She got up, declaring: "I like that better than a novel. Now let's go to La Grenouillère."

They reached a part of the island which was laid out like a park, shaded with huge trees. Couples wandered under the lofty foliage beside the Seine, over which the boats were gliding. There were girls with young men, working girls with their sweethearts, who were walking in shirt-sleeves, coats on their arms and tall-hats on the back of their heads, looking weary and dissipated; clerks with their families, the wives in their Sunday best, the children running round their parents like a brood of chickens. A continuous distant buzz of human voices, a dull, rumbling clamour, announced the nearness of the establishment beloved of boating parties. Suddenly it came into view, an enormous roofed barge moored to the bank, filled by a crowd of men and women who sat drinking at tables or stood up, shouting, singing, laughing, dancing, capering to the noise of a jingling piano, out of tune and as vibrant as a tin-can. Tall, red-haired girls, displaying before and behind them the swelling, provocative curves of breasts and hips, walked up and down with eager, inviting glances, all three-parts drunk, talking obscenities. Others were dancing wildly in front of young men who were half naked, dressed only in rowing-shorts and zephyrs, and wearing coloured jockey-caps on their heads. There was a pervading odour of sweat and face powder, the combined exhalations of perfumeries and arm-pits. Those who were drinking at the tables were swallowing white and red and yellow and green liquids, screaming and yelling for no reason, yielding to a violent need to make a din, an animal instinct to fill ears and brain with noise. From time to time a swimmer dived from the roof, splashing those sitting near, who yelled at him like savages.

On the river a fleet of boats passed and repassed; long narrow skiffs went by, urged on by the powerful strokes of bare-armed oarsmen, whose muscles worked under the tanned skin. The women in the boats, dressed in blue or red flannel, holding open umbrellas, also blue or red, over their heads, made brilliant splashes of colour under the burning sun they lolled on their seat in the stern and seemed to glide along the water, motionless or drowsy. Heavier boats moved slowly past, loaded with people. A light-hearted student, bent on making himself conspicuous, rowed with a windmill stroke, bumping into all the boats, whose occupants swore at him. He eventually disappeared crestfallen, after nearly drowning two swimmers, followed by the jeers of the crowd jammed together on the floating café.

Yvette, radiant, passed through the middle of this noisy, struggling crowd on Servigny's arm. She seemed quite happy to be jostled by all and sundry, and stared at the girls with calm and friendly eyes.

"Look at that one, Muscade, what lovely hair she's got! They *do* seem to be enjoying themselves."

The pianist, an oarsman dressed in red, whose hat was very like a colossal straw parasol, began a waltz. Yvette promptly seized her companion by the waist and carried him off with the fury she always put into her dancing. They went on so long and with such frenzy that the whole crowd watched them. Those who were sitting drinking stood upon their tables and beat time with their feet, others smashed glasses. The pianist seemed to go mad; he banged at the ivory keys with galloping hands, gesticulating wildly with his whole body, swaying his head and its enormous covering with frantic movements.

Abruptly he stopped, slid down, and lay full length on the ground, buried under his hat, as though dead of exhaustion. There was a burst of laughter in the café, and every one applauded. Four friends rushed up as though there had been an accident, and picking up their comrade, bore him off by all four limbs, after placing on his stomach the roof under which he sheltered his head. Another jester followed, intoning the *De Profundis*, and a procession formed up behind the mock corpse. It went round all the paths in the island, gathering up drinkers, strollers, indeed every one it met.

Yvette ran along enraptured, laughing heartily and talking to every one, wild with the din and the bustle. Young men pushed against her and stared at her excitedly with eyes whose burning glances seemed to strip her naked. Servigny began to be afraid that the adventure might end unfortunately. The procession went on its way, getting faster and faster, for the four bearers had begun to race, followed by the yelling crowd. But suddenly they turned towards the bank, stopped dead at the edge, for an instant swung their comrade to and fro, and then, all letting go of him at once, they heaved him into the water. A great shout of merriment burst from every mouth, while the bewildered pianist splashed about, swearing, coughing, and spitting out the water; stuck fast in the mud, he struggled to climb up the bank. His hat, which was floating down the stream, was brought back by a boat.

Yvette danced with joy and clapped her hands, saying:

"Oh, Muscade, what fun, what fun!"

Servigny, now serious, watched her, a little embarrassed and a little dismayed to see her so much at ease in these vulgar surroundings. He felt a faint disgust born of the instinct that an aristocrat rarely loses, even in moments of utter abandon, the instinct that protects him from unpardonable familiarities and contacts that would be too degrading. "No one will credit you with too much breeding, my child," he said to himself, astounded. He had an impulse to speak to her aloud as familiarly as he always did in his thoughts, with as little ceremony as he would have used on meeting any woman who was common property. He no longer saw her as any different from the red-haired creatures who brushed against them, bawling obscene words in their harsh voices. Coarse, brief, and expressive, these words were the current speech of the crowd; they seemed to flit overhead, born there in the mud like flies in the dunghill over which they hover. No one seemed shocked or surprised; Yvette did not seem to notice them at all.

"Muscade, I want to bathe," she said. "Let's go out into deep water."

"At your service, ma'am," he replied.

They went to the bathing-cabin to get costumes. She was ready first and waited for him on the bank, smiling at all who looked at her. Then they went off side by side in the warm water. She swam with a luxurious abandon, caressed by the stream, quivering with a sensual pleasure; at every stroke she raised herself as though she were ready to leap out of the river. He found difficulty in keeping up with her; he was out of breath and angry at his inferiority. But she slowed down and then turned quickly and floated, her arms crossed, her eyes staring towards the blue sky. He gazed at the soft, supple line of her body as she lay there on the surface of the river, at the rounded form and small, firm tips of the shapely breasts revealed by her thin, clinging garment, the curving sweetness of her belly, the half-submerged thighs, the bare calf gleaming through the water, and the small foot thrust out. He saw every line of her, as though she were deliberately displaying herself to tempt him, offering herself to him or trying to make a fool of him again. He began to desire her with a passionate ardour, every nerve on edge. Abruptly she turned round and looked at him.

"What a nice head you have," she said with a laugh.

He was hurt, irritated by her teasing, filled with the savage fury of the derided lover. He yielded to a vague desire to punish her, to avenge himself; he wanted to hurt her.

"You'd like that sort of life, would you?" he said.

"What sort?" she asked, with her most innocent air.

"Come now, no more nonsense. You know perfectly well what I mean."

"No, honestly, I don't."

"We've had enough of this comedy. Will you or won't you?"

"I don't understand you in the least."

"You're not so stupid as all that. Besides, I told you last night."

"What? I've forgotten."

"That I love you."

"You!"

"Yes, I!"

"What a lie!"

"I swear it's true."

"Prove it, then."

"I ask for nothing better."

"Well, do, then."

"You didn't say that last night."

"You didn't propose anything."

"Oh, this is absurd!"

"Besides, I am not the one to be asked."

"That's very kind of you! Who is, then?"

"Mamma, of course."

He gave way to a fit of laughter.

"Your mother? No, really, that's too much!"

She had suddenly become very serious, and, looking into his eyes, said:

" Listen, Muscade, if you really love me enough to marry me, speak to mamma first, and I'll give you my answer afterwards."

At that he lost his temper altogether, thinking that she was still playing the fool with him.

" What do you take me for, Mam'selle ? An idiot like the rest of your admirers ? "

She continued to gaze at him with calm, clear eyes. After a moment's hesitation she said :

" I still don't understand."

" Now look here, Yvette," he said brusquely, with a touch of rudeness and ill nature in his voice. " Let's have done with this ridiculous comedy, which has already gone on too long. You keep on playing the innocent maiden, and, believe me, the part doesn't suit you at all. You know perfectly well that there can be no question of marriage between us—but only of love. I told you I loved you—it's quite true—I repeat, I do love you. Now don't pretend not to understand, and don't treat me as though I were a fool."

They were upright in the water, face to face, supporting themselves by little movements of the hands. For some seconds more she continued motionless, as though she could not make up her mind to understand his words, then suddenly she blushed to the roots of her hair. The blood rushed in a swift tide from her neck to her ears, which turned almost purple, and without a word she fled landwards, swimming with all her strength, with hurried, powerful strokes. He could not overtake her, and the pursuit left him breathless. He saw her leave the water, pick up her wrap, and enter her cabin, without turning her head.

He took a long time to dress, very puzzled what to do, planning what to say to her, and wondering whether to apologise or persevere.

When he was ready, she had gone, alone. He returned slowly, worried and anxious. The Marquise, on Saval's arm, was strolling along the circular path round the lawn. At sight of Servigny she spoke with the careless air she had assumed on the previous evening:

"Didn't I tell you not to go out in such heat? Now Yvette has sunstroke; she's gone to lie down. She was as scarlet as a poppy, poor child, and has a frightful headache. You must have been walking full in the sun, and up to some mischief or other, Heaven knows what. You have no more sense than she has."

The young girl did not come down to dinner. When asked if she wanted something brought up to her room, she replied through the closed door that she was not hungry—she had locked herself in and wished to be left alone. The two young men left by the ten o'clock train, promising to come again the following Thursday, and the Marquise sat down by the open window and, musing, listened to the far-off sound of dance-music jerked out at La Grenouillère, vibrating in the profoundly solemn silence of night.

Inured and hardened to love by love, as a man is to riding or rowing, she nevertheless had sudden moments of tenderness which attacked her like a disease. These passions seized roughly upon her, swept through her whole being, driving her mad, exhausting her, or depressing her according to their nature, lofty, violent, dramatic, or sentimental.

She was one of those women who were created to love and to be loved. From a very humble beginning she had climbed high through love, of which she had made a profession almost without being aware of it: acting by instinct, by inborn skill, she accepted money as she accepted kisses, naturally, without distinguishing between them, employing her amazing intuition in an unreasoning and utterly simple fashion, as animals, made cunning by the struggle for life, employ theirs. Many lovers had lain in her arms, and she had felt no tenderness for them, but also no disgust at their embraces. She endured all caresses with calm indifference, as a traveller eats anything, because he must live. But from time to time her heart or her flesh caught fire, and she fell into a passion which lasted weeks or months, according to the physical and moral qualities of her lover. These were the delicious moments of her life. She loved with her whole soul, her whole body, with ecstatic abandon. She threw herself into love like a suicide into a river, and let herself be carried away, ready to die if necessary, intoxicated, maddened, infinitely happy. Each time she thought she had never before felt anything like it, and she would have been entirely amazed if she had been reminded of the many different men of whom she had dreamed passionately all night long, gazing at the stars.

Saval had fascinated her, captured her body and soul. She dreamed of him now, soothed by his image and her remembrance of him, in the calm exaltation of a joy fulfilled, of a happiness present and certain.

A noise behind her made her turn round. Yvette had just come in, still in the same dress she had worn all day, but pale now, and with the burning eyes that are the mark of great weariness. She leaned on the ledge of the open window opposite her mother.

" I've something to tell you," she said.

The Marquise, surprised, looked at her. Her love for her daughter was selfish; she was proud of her beauty, as one is proud of wealth; she was herself still too beautiful to be jealous, too careless to make the plans she was commonly supposed to entertain, yet too cunning to be unconscious of her daughter's value.

" Yes, child," she replied, " I'm listening; what is it?"

Yvette gave her a burning look, as though to read the depths of her soul, as though to detect every emotion which her words would rouse.

" This is it. Something extraordinary happened just now."

" What?"

" Monsieur de Servigny told me he loved me."

The Marquise waited, uneasy. But as Yvette said nothing more, she asked:

"How did he tell you? Explain!"

The young girl sat down by her mother's feet in a familiar coaxing attitude and, pressing her hand, said:

"He asked me to marry him."

Madame Obardi made a sudden gesture of amazement, and cried:

"Servigny? You must be mad!"

Yvette's eyes had never left her mother's face, watching sharply for her thoughts and her surprise.

"Why must I be mad?" she asked gravely. "Why should Monsieur de Servigny not marry me?"

"You must be wrong," stammered the Marquise, embarrassed; "it can't be true. You can't have heard properly—or you misunderstood him. Monsieur de Servigny is too rich to marry you, and too . . . too . . . Parisian to marry at all."

Yvette slowly rose to her feet.

"But if he loves me as he says he does?" she added.

Her mother replied somewhat impatiently:

"I thought you were old enough and knew enough of the world not to have such ideas in your head. Servigny is a man of the world and an egoist; he will only marry a woman of his own rank and wealth. If he asked you to marry him . . . it means he wants . . . he wants. . . ."

The Marquise, unable to voice her suspicions, was silent for a moment, then added:

"Now leave me alone, and go to bed."

And the young girl, as though she now knew all she wanted, replied obediently:

"Yes, mother."

She kissed her mother's forehead and departed with a calm step. Just as she was going out of the door, the Marquise called her back:

"And your sunstroke?" she asked.

"I never had one. It was this affair which had upset me."

"We'll have another talk about it," added the Marquise. "But, above all, don't be alone with him again after this occurrence for some time. And you may be quite sure that he won't marry you, do you understand, and that he only wants to . . . to compromise you."

This was the best she could do by way of expressing her thoughts. And Yvette returned to her room.

Madame Obardi began to reflect.

Having lived for years in an amorous and opulent tranquillity, she had carefully guarded her mind from every thought that might preoccupy, trouble, or sadden her. She had always refused to ask herself what would become of Yvette; there was always time enough to think of that when difficulties arose. She knew, with her courtesan's instinct, that her daughter could not marry a rich and really well-born man save by an extremely improbable piece of good fortune, one of those surprises of love which set adventuresses upon thrones. She did not really contemplate this possibility, too much preoccupied to form plans by which she herself would not be directly affected.

Yvette would doubtless follow in her mother's footsteps. She would become a light o' love; why not? But the Marquise had never had the courage to ask herself when, or how, this would come about.

And now here was her daughter suddenly, without any preparation, asking her one of those questions which cannot be answered, and forcing her to take up a definite position in an affair so difficult, so delicate, so dangerous in every sense, which so profoundly troubled her conscience, the conscience any mother must display when her daughter is involved in an affair such as this.

She had too much natural wit, a wit which might nod but was never quite asleep, to be deceived for one moment in Servigny's intentions, for she knew men, by personal experience, especially men of that tribe. And so, at the first words uttered by Yvette, she had cried out, almost involuntarily:

' Servigny marry you? You must be mad!"

What had led him to use the old, old trick—he, the shrewd rake, the jaded man about town? What would he do now? And the child, how was she to be more explicitly warned or even defended? She was capable of any folly. Who would imagine that a great girl like that could be so innocent, so ignorant, and so unwary?

And the Marquise, thoroughly perplexed and already exhausted by her mental efforts, was utterly at a loss, finding the situation truly difficult.

Weary of the whole business, she thought:

" Oh, well, I'll keep a close watch on them and act according to events. If necessary, I'll even talk to Servigny; he's sensitive, and can take a hint."

She did not ask herself what she should say to him, nor what he would reply, nor what sort of an agreement could be made between them, but, happy at being relieved of this anxiety without having had to take a decision, she began again to dream of her adored Saval. Her glance, wandering in the night, turned to the right towards the misty radiance that hovered over Paris; with both hands she threw kisses towards the great city, swift unnumbered kisses that flew into the darkness one after another; and very softly, as though she were still speaking to him, she murmured:

" I love you! I love you!"

III

Yvette also could not sleep. Like her mother, she sat at the open window, resting her elbows on the sill, and tears, her first bitter tears, filled her eyes.

Till now she had lived and grown up in the heedless and

serene self-confidence of happy youth. Why should she have analysed, wondered, reflected? Why should she not have been like all young girls of her age? Why should doubt, fear, painful suspicions have troubled her? Because she seemed to talk about every subject, because she had taken the tone, the manner, the bold speech of those around her, she had seemed to know all about everything. But she knew no more than a girl brought up in a convent; her risky phrases came from her memory, from the faculty women possess of imitation and assimilation, not from a mind already sophisticated and debauched.

She talked of love in the same way that an artist's or musician's son talks of painting and music at ten or twelve years of age. She knew, or rather suspected, the sort of mystery hidden behind this word—too many jests had been whispered in her presence for her innocence to remain completely unenlightened—but how was she to tell from this that every household was not like the one she lived in? Her mother's hand was kissed with apparent respect; all their friends were titled; all were rich, or appeared to be; all spoke familiarly of princes of the blood royal. Two king's sons had actually come several times, in the evening, to the Marquise's house. How was she to know?

And, besides, she was by nature innocent. She did not probe into things, she had not her mother's intuitive judgment of other people. She lived tranquilly, too full of the joy of life to worry about circumstances which might have roused suspicions in people of more quiet, more thoughtful, more secluded ways, who were less impulsive and less radiantly joyous. And now, in a single instant, by a few words whose brutality she had felt without understanding, Servigny had roused in her a sudden uneasiness, an uneasiness at first unreasoning, and now growing into a torturing fear.

She had gone home, had fled from him like a wounded animal; deeply wounded, indeed, by the words she repeated to herself again and again, trying to penetrate their farthest meaning, trying to guess their whole implication: "You know perfectly well that there can be no question of marriage between us—but of love!"

What had he meant? And why this insult? There was something, then, some shameful secret, of which she was in ignorance? Doubtless she was the only one in ignorance of it. What was it? She was terrified, crushed, as at the discovery of a hidden infamy, the treachery of a friend, one of those calamities of the heart which strike at one's very reason.

She had thought, wondered, pored over it, wept, consumed with fears and suspicions. Then her young and buoyant nature calmed her, and she began to imagine an adventure, to build up an unusual and dramatic situation drawn from her remembrance of all the fanciful romances she had read. She recalled exciting changes of fortune, gloomy and heart-rending plots, and mingled them with her own story, to fling a romantic glory round the half-seen mystery which surrounded her.

She was no longer miserable, she was wholly wrapped up in her dreams. She lifted mysterious veils, imagined improbable complications, a thousand curious and terrible ideas, attractive through their very strangeness. Was she, by any chance, the natural daughter of a prince? Had her unfortunate mother been seduced and deserted, created a marquise by a king, King Victor Emmanuel perhaps, and had she even been forced to flee from the wrath of his family?

Or was she not more probably a child abandoned by her parents, very noble and famous parents, as the fruit of a guilty love, and found by the Marquise, who had adopted her and brought her up? A hundred other notions raced through her head; she accepted or rejected them at the dictates of her fancy. She grew profoundly sorry for herself, at once very happy and very sad; above all, she was delighted at becoming the heroine of a romance with emotions to reveal, a part to act, a dignity and nobility to be upheld. And she thought of the part she would have to play in each plot she imagined. She saw it vaguely, as if she were a character in a novel by Scribe or George Sand. It would be compounded of equal parts of devotion, pride, self-sacrifice, magnanimity, tenderness, and fine words. Her volatile heart almost revelled in her new position.

She had continued till nightfall to ponder over her future course of action, wondering how to set to work to drag the truth from the Marquise.

And at the coming of night, so suitable to a tragic situation, she had thought of a trick, a quite simple yet subtle trick, for getting what she wanted ; it was to tell her mother very abruptly that Servigny had asked her to marry him. At this news Madame Obardi, in her surprise, would surely let fall a word, an exclamation, that would illumine her daughter's mind.

So Yvette had promptly put her plan into execution. She expected a burst of astonishment, protests of affection, disclosures, accompanied by tears and every sign of emotion.

And lo and behold ! her mother had not apparently been either surprised or heart-broken, merely annoyed ; from the worried and peevish tone of her reply the young girl, in whose mind every latent power of feminine cunning, wit, and knowledge were suddenly aroused, realised that it was no good insisting, that the mystery was quite other and more painful than she had imagined, and that she must discover it for herself. So she had returned to her room with a sad heart, her spirit distressed, depressed now in the apprehension of a real misfortune, without knowing how or why she was suffering such an emotion. She rested her elbows on the window-sill and wept.

She cried for a long time, not dreaming now ; she made no attempt at further discovery. Little by little she was overcome with weariness, and closed her eyes. She dozed, for a few minutes, in the unrefreshing slumber of a person too exhausted to undress and get into bed ; her sleep was long and fitful, roughly broken whenever her head slipped from between her hands.

She did not go to bed until the earliest gleam of daylight, when the chill of dawn drove her from the window.

During the next day and the next, she kept an air of melancholy and reserve. Her mind was at work ceaselessly and urgently within her; she was learning to watch, to guess, to reason. A gleam, still vague, seemed to throw a new light upon the men and events passing around her; distrust invaded her soul, distrust of every one that she had believed in, distrust of her mother. During those two days she conjectured every conceivable supposition. She envisaged every possibility, making the most extravagant resolutions, in the impulsiveness of her volatile and unrestrained nature. On the Wednesday she fixed on a plan, a whole scheme of conduct and an elaborate plan of espionage. On the Thursday morning she rose with the determination to be more cunning than the most experienced detective, to be armed against all the world.

She even decided to take as her motto the two words "Myself alone," and for more than an hour she wondered how they could with best effect be engraved round her monogram and stamped on her note-paper.

Saval and Servigny arrived at ten o'clock. The young girl held out her hand with reserve, but without embarrassment, and said in a familiar, though serious, tone:

"Good morning, Muscade. How are you?"

"Pretty well, thank you, Mam'selle. And you?"

He watched her narrowly. "What game is she playing now?" he said to himself.

The Marquise having taken Saval's arm, he took Yvette's, and they began to walk round the lawn, disappearing and reappearing behind the clumps of trees.

Yvette walked with a thoughtful air, her eyes on the gravel path, and seemed scarcely to hear her companion's remarks, to which she made no reply.

Suddenly she asked :

" Are you really my friend, Muscade ? "

" Of course, Mam'selle."

" But really, really and truly ? "

" Absolutely your friend, Mam'selle, body and soul."

" Enough not to tell a lie for once, just for once ? "

" Enough not even to tell one for twice, if necessary."

" Enough to tell me the whole truth, even if it's unpleasant ? "

" Yes, Mam'selle."

" Well, what do you really think, really, really think, of Prince Kravalow ? "

" Oh, Lord ! "

" There you are, already getting ready to tell a fib."

" No, I'm searching for the words, the right words. Well, dash it, the Prince is a Russian—a real Russian, who speaks Russian, was born in Russia, and perhaps had a passport to get into France. There's nothing false about him except his name and his title."

She looked into his eyes.

" You mean he's a . . . a . ."

He hesitated ; then, making up his mind, said :

" An adventurer, Mam'selle."

" Thank you. And the Chevalier Valréali is no better, is he ? "

" It's as you say."

" And Monsieur de Belvigne ? "

" Ah, he's rather different. He's a gentleman, provincial of course ; he's honourable . . . up to a point . . . but he's singed his wings through flying too near the candle."

" And you ? "

Without hesitation he replied :

" I ? Oh, I'm what's generally called a gay dog, a bachelor of good family who once had brains and frittered them away on making puns ; who had health, and ruined it by playing the fool ; moderate wealth, and wasted it doing nothing. All

I have left is a certain experience of life, a pretty complete freedom from prejudice, a vast contempt for men, women included, a profound sense of the uselessness of my actions, and a wide tolerance of scoundrels in general. I still have momentary flashes of honesty, as you see, and I'm even capable of affection, as you could see if you would. With these qualities and defects I place myself at your orders, Mam'selle, body and soul, for you to dispose of at your pleasure. There!"

She did not laugh; she listened attentively, carefully scrutinising his words and meanings.

"What do you think of the Comtesse de Lammy?" she continued.

"You must allow me not to give you my opinions on women," he said gaily.

"Not on any?"

"No, not on any."

"Then that means you must have a very low opinion of them, of all of them. Now think, aren't there any exceptions?"

He laughed with the insolent air he almost always wore, and the brutal audacity that was his strength, his armour against life.

"Present company always excepted, of course," he said.

She flushed slightly, but coolly asked:

"Well, what do you think of me?"

"You want to know? Very well, then. I think you're a person of excellent sense, of considerable experience, or, if you prefer it, of great common sense; that you know very well how to mask your battery, amuse yourself at others' expense, hide your purpose, pull the strings and wait, without impatience, for the result."

"Is that all?" she asked.

"That's all," he replied.

"I'll make you alter that opinion Muscade," she said very gravely. Then she went over to her mother, who was walking with bent head and tiny steps, with the languid gait one falls into when murmuring of things sweet and intimate. As she walked she drew designs, letters perhaps, with the tip of her sunshade, and talked to Saval without looking at him, talked long and slowly, resting on his arm, held close against his side. Yvette looked sharply at her, and a suspicion, so vague that she could not put it into words, as if it were a physical sensation only half realised, flitted across her mind as the shadow of a wind-blown cloud flits across the earth.

The bell rang for lunch.

It was silent, almost gloomy.

There was storm in the air, as the saying goes. Vast motionless clouds lay in wait on the horizon, silent and heavy, but loaded with tempest.

When they had taken their coffee on the veranda, the Marquise asked:

"Well, darling, are you going for a walk to-day with your friend Servigny? This is really the weather to enjoy the coolness of the woods."

Yvette threw her a rapid glance, and swiftly looked away again.

"No, mother, I'm not going out to-day."

The Marquise seemed disappointed.

"Do go for a little walk, child," she persisted. "It's so good for you."

"No, mother," said Yvette sharply, "I'm going to stay in the house, and you know quite well why, because I told you the other night."

Madame Obardi had quite forgotten, consumed with her need to be alone with Saval. She blushed, fidgeted, and, distracted by her own desire, uncertain how to secure a free hour or two, stammered:

"Of course; I never thought of it. You're quite right; I don't know where my wits are wandering."

Yvette took up a piece of embroidery which she called the "public welfare," busying herself with it five or six times a year, on days of utter boredom, and seated herself on a low chair beside her mother. The young men sat in deck-chairs and smoked their cigars.

The hours went by in idle conversation that flagged continually. The Marquise threw impatient glances at Saval, seeking for an excuse, any way of getting rid of her daughter. Realising at last that she would not succeed, and not knowing what plan to adopt, she said to Servigny:

"You know, my dear Duc, that you're both going to stay the night here. To-morrow we are going to lunch at the restaurant Fournaise, at Chatou."

He understood, smiled, and said with a bow:

"I am at your service, Marquise."

Slowly the day wore on, slowly and uncomfortably, under the menace of the storm. Gradually the hour of dinner approached. The lowering sky was heavy with dull, sluggish clouds. They could not feel the least movement in the air.

The evening meal was eaten in silence. A sense of embarrassment and restraint, a sort of vague fear, silenced the two men and the two women.

When the table had been cleared, they remained on the veranda, speaking only at long intervals. Night was falling, a stifling night. Suddenly the horizon was torn by a great jagged flame that lit with its dazzling and pallid glare the four faces sunk in the shadows. Followed a distant noise, dull and faint, like the noise made by a cart crossing a bridge; the heat of the atmosphere increased, the air grew still more oppressive, the evening silence more profound.

Yvette rose.

"I'm going to bed," she said. "The storm makes me feel ill."

She bent her forehead for the Marquise to kiss, offered her hand to the two young men, and departed.

As her room was directly above the veranda, the leaves of a large chestnut-tree planted in front of the door were soon gleaming with a green light. Servigny fixed his eyes on this pale gleam in the foliage, thinking now and then that he saw a shadow pass across it. But suddenly the light went out. Madame Obardi sighed deeply.

" My daughter is in bed," she said.

Servigny rose.

" I will follow her example, Marquise, if you will allow me."

He kissed her hand and disappeared in his turn.

She remained alone with Saval, in the darkness. At once she was in his arms, clasping him, embracing him. Then, though he tried to prevent it, she knelt down in front of him, murmuring : " I want to look at you in the lightning flashes."

But Yvette, her candle blown out, had come out on to her balcony, gliding bare-footed like a shadow, and was listening, tortured by a painful and confused suspicion. She could not see, being exactly over their heads on the roof of the veranda. She heard nothing but a murmur of voices, and her heart beat so violently that the thudding of it filled her ears. A window shut overhead. So Servigny had just gone up to bed. Her mother was alone with the other.

A second flash split the sky, and for a second the whole familiar landscape was revealed in a vivid and sinister glare. She saw the great river, the colour of molten lead, like a river in some fantastic dream-country. At the same instant a voice below her said : " I love you." She heard no more ; a strange shudder passed over her, her spirit was drowned in a fearful sea of trouble.

Silence, pressing, infinite, a silence that seemed the eternal silence of the grave, brooded over the world. She could not breathe, her lungs choked by some unknown and horrible weight. Another flash kindled the heavens and for an instant lit up the horizon, another followed on its heels, then another and another.

The voice she had already heard repeated more loudly : " Oh ! How I love you ! How I love you ! " And Yvette knew the voice well ; it was her mother's.

A large drop of warm water fell upon her forehead, and a slight, almost imperceptible quiver ran through the leaves, the shiver of the coming rain.

Then a tumult came hurrying from far off, a confused tumult like the noise of the wind in trees; it was the heavy shower pouring in a torrent upon the earth, the river, and the trees. In a few moments the water was streaming all round her, covering her, splashing her, soaking her like a bath. She did not move, thinking only of what was happening on the veranda. She heard them rise and go up to their rooms. Doors slammed inside the house. And obeying an irresistible longing for certitude, a maddening, torturing desire, the young girl ran down the stairs, softly opened the outer door, ran across the lawn under the furious downpour of rain, and hid in a clump of bushes to watch the windows.

One alone, her mother's, showed a light. And suddenly two shadows appeared on the luminous square, two shadows side by side. Then they drew closer and made only one; another flash of lightning flung a swift and dazzling jet of light upon the house-front, and she saw them embracing, their arms about one another's necks.

At that she was stunned; without thinking, without knowing what she did, she cried out with all her strength, in a piercing voice: "Mother!" as one cries to warn another creature of deadly peril.

Her desperate cry was lost in the clatter of the rain, but the entwined pair started uneasily apart. One of the shadows disappeared, while the other tried to distinguish something in the darkness of the garden.

Fearing to be taken unawares and found by her mother, Yvette ran to the house, hurried upstairs, leaving a trail of water dripping from step to step, and locked herself in her room, determined to open to no one. Without taking off the soaking clothes which clung to her body, she fell upon her knees with clasped hands, imploring in her distress some superhuman protection, the mysterious help of heaven, that unknown aid we pray for in our hours of weeping and despair. Every instant the great flashes threw their livid light into the room, and she saw herself fitfully reflected in her wardrobe-mirror, with her wet hair streaming down her back, so strange a figure that she did not recognise herself.

She remained so for a long time, so long that the storm passed without her noticing its departure. The rain ceased to fall, light flowed into the sky, though it was still dark with clouds, and a warm, fragrant, delicious freshness, the freshness of wet leaves and grass, drifted in at the open window. Yvette rose from her knees, took off her cold sodden clothes, without thinking at all of what she did, and got into bed. She fixed her eyes on the growing daylight, then wept again, then tried to think.

Her mother! With a lover! The shame of it! But she had read so many books in which women, even mothers, abandoned themselves in like fashion, only to rise once more to honour in the last few pages, that she was not utterly dumbfounded to find herself involved in a drama like all the dramas in the stories she read. The violence of her first misery, her first cruel bewilderment, was already slightly lessened by her confused recollections of similar situations. Her thoughts had roamed among so many tragic adventures, gracefully woven into their stories by the authors of romances, that gradually her horrible discovery began to seem the natural continuation of a novelette begun the night before.

"I will save my mother," she said to herself.

Almost calmed by this heroic resolution, she felt herself strong, great, ready upon the instant for sacrifice and combat. She thought over the means she must employ. Only one seemed good to her, and accorded with her romantic nature. And she rehearsed, like an actress before the performance, the interview she would have with her mother.

The sun had risen and the servants were up and about. The

maid came with her chocolate. Yvette had the tray set down on the table, and said :

" Tell my mother that I'm not well, that I shall stay in bed till the gentlemen leave ; tell her I did not sleep last night and that I wish not to be disturbed, because I must try to sleep."

The astonished maid caught sight of the soaked dress, thrown like a rag on the carpet.

" Mademoiselle has been out, then ? " she said.

" Yes, I went for a walk in the rain to clear my head."

The servant picked up the petticoats, stockings, and muddy shoes, and went out carrying them gingerly on her arm with an expression of disgust ; they were dripping like the clothes of a drowned woman.

Yvette waited, knowing well that her mother would come.

The Marquise entered, having leapt out of bed at the first words of the maid, for she had endured a vague uneasiness ever since that cry of " Mother ! " pierced the darkness.

" What's the matter ? " she said.

Yvette looked at her and faltered.

" I . . . I . . ."

Then, overcome by violent and sudden emotion, she began to sob.

The astonished Marquise asked again :

" What's the matter with you ? "

Then, forgetting all her schemes and carefully-prepared phrases, the young girl hid her face in her hands and sobbed :

" Oh, mother ! Oh, mother ! "

Madame Obardi remained standing by the bed, too excited to understand fully, but guessing, with that subtle instinct wherein her strength lay, almost the whole truth.

Yvette, choked with sobs, could not speak, and her mother, exasperated at last and feeling the approach of a formidable scene, asked sharply :

" Come, what's the matter with you ? Tell me."

With difficulty Yvette stammered :

"Oh! last night . . . I saw . . . your window."

"Well, what then?" asked the Marquise, very pale.

Her daughter repeated, still sobbing:

"Oh, mother! Oh, mother!"

Madame Obardi, whose fear and embarrassment were changing to anger, shrugged her shoulders and turned to go.

"I really think you must be mad. When it's all over, let me know."

But suddenly the young girl parted her hands and disclosed her tear-stained face.

"No. . . . Listen. . . . I *must* speak to you. . . . Listen. Promise me . . . we'll both go away, far away, into the country, and we'll live like peasants and no one will know what's become of us. Will you, mother? Please, please, I beg you, mother, I implore you!"

The Marquise, taken aback, remained in the middle of the room. She had the hot blood of the people in her veins. Shame, maternal shame, mingled with a vague sensation of fear and the exasperation of a passionate woman whose love is menaced. She shivered, equally ready to implore forgiveness or to fly into a rage.

"I don't understand you," she said.

"I saw you, mother," continued Yvette, "last night. . . . You must never again . . . Oh, if you knew . . . we'll both go away. . . . I'll love you so much that you'll forget. . . ."

"Listen, my child," said Madame Obardi in a trembling voice, "there are some things you don't yet understand. Well, never forget . . . never forget . . . that I forbid you . . . ever to speak to me . . . of . . . of . . . of those matters."

But the young girl caught desperately at her rôle of saviour and went on:

"No, mother, I'm no longer a child, and I have the right to know. I know all sorts of disreputable people, adventurers, come to our house, and that that's why we are not respected; and I know more than that. Well, it mustn't be, I won't endure it. We'll go away; you can sell your jewels; we'll work if necessary, and we'll live like honest women somewhere far away. And if I manage to get married, so much the better."

Her mother looked at her out of angry black eyes, and answered:

"You're mad. Be good enough to get up and come out to lunch with the rest of us."

"No, mother. There's someone here, you know whom, whom I won't see again. He must go out of this house, or I will. You must choose between us."

She was sitting up in bed, and raised her voice, speaking like a character on the stage; at last she had entered upon the drama so long dreamed of, and her grief was almost forgotten in absorption in her mission.

"You must be mad," repeated the astonished Marquise again, finding nothing else to say.

"No, mother," the young girl added, with dramatic verve, "that man leaves this house or else I go; I shall not weaken."

"And where will you go? . . . What will you do?"

"I don't know; it doesn't matter much . . . I want us to be honest women."

The repetition of that phrase "honest women" aroused in the Marquise the fury of a drab.

"Silence!" she shouted. "I won't be spoken to like that. I'm as good as any other woman, do you hear? I'm a harlot, it's true, and I'm proud of it; I'm worth a dozen of your honest women."

Yvette, overwhelmed, looked at her and stammered:

"Oh, mother!"

But the Marquise became frenzied with excitement.

"Yes, I am a harlot. What then? If I weren't a harlot, you'd be a kitchen-maid to-day, as I was once, and you'd work for thirty sous a day, and you'd wash the dishes, and your mistress would send you out on errands to the butcher's, d'you hear, and kick you out if you were idle ; whereas here you are, idling all day long, just because I *am* a harlot. There ! When you're only a poor servant-girl with fifty francs of savings, you must get away from it somehow if you don't want to rot in the workhouse ; and there's only one way for women, only one way, d'you hear, when you're a servant ! We can't make fortunes on the stock exchange or at high finance. We've nothing but our bodies, nothing but our bodies."

She beat her breast like a penitent at confession, and advanced towards the bed, flushed and excited :

" So much the worse for a pretty girl ; she must live on her looks or grind along in poverty all her lifelong . . . all her life. . . . There's no alternative."

Then, returning hastily to her old idea : " And your honest women, do they go without ? It's they who are sluts, because they're not forced. They've money to live on and amuse themselves with ; they have their lovers out of pure wantonness. It's they who are sluts ! "

She stood beside Yvette's bed ; Yvette, utterly overcome, wanted to scream for help and run away ; she was crying noisily, like a beaten child.

The Marquise was silent, and looked at her daughter ; seeing the girl's utter despair, she was herself overcome by sorrow, remorse, tenderness, and pity ; and falling upon the bed with outstretched arms, she too began to sob, murmuring :

" My poor darling, my poor darling, if you only knew how you hurt me."

And for a long time they both wept.

Then the Marquise, whose grief never lasted very long, rose gently, and said very softly :

" Well, darling, that's how it is ; it can't be helped. It can't be altered now. Life must be taken as it comes."

But Yvette continued to cry ; the shock had been too severe and too unexpected for her to be able to reflect upon it calmly and recover herself.

" Come, get up, and come down to breakfast, so that nothing will be noticed," said her mother.

The young girl shook her head, unable to speak ; at last she said very slowly, her voice choked with sobs :

" No, mother, you know what I said ; I won't change my mind. I will not leave my room till they have gone. I won't see any of those people again, never, never. If they come back, I . . . I . . . you won't see me again."

The Marquise had dried her eyes and, worn out with her emotion, murmured :

" Come now, think it over, be sensible about it." Then again, after a minute's silence : " Yes, you had better rest this morning. I'll come and see you in the afternoon."

She kissed her daughter on the forehead and went away to get dressed, quite calm again.

As soon as her mother had disappeared, Yvette ran to the door and bolted it, so as to be alone, quite alone ; then she began to reflect.

About eleven o'clock the maid knocked at the door and asked :

" Madame la Marquise wishes to know if you want anything, Mademoiselle, and what will you have for lunch ? "

" I'm not hungry," replied Yvette ; " I only want to be left alone."

She stayed in bed as though she were really ill. About three o'clock there was another knock.

" Who's there ? " she asked.

" It's I, darling," answered her mother's voice ; " I've come to see how you are."

She hesitated. What should she do ? She opened the door and got back into bed. The Marquise came close, speaking softly as though to an invalid.

" Well, are you feeling better ? Won't you eat an egg ? "

" No, thank you, nothing."

Madame Obardi had sat down beside the bed. Neither spoke for some time ; then, at last, as her daughter remained immobile, her hands resting inertly on the sheets, the Marquise added :

" Aren't you going to get up ? "

" Yes, presently," answered Yvette. " I've thought a great deal, mother," she continued slowly and seriously, " and this . . . this is my decision. The past is the past ; let us say no more about it. But the future will be different . . . or else . . . or else I know what I shall have to do. And now let us have done with this subject."

The Marquise, who had thought that the scene was all over, felt somewhat irritated. She had had more than enough. This great goose of a girl ought to have understood long ago. But she made no answer, only repeating :

" Are you going to get up ? "

" Yes, I'm ready now."

The mother acted as maid to her daughter, bringing her her stockings, her corset, and her petticoats. Then she kissed her.

" Shall we go for a walk before dinner ? "

" Yes, mamma."

And they walked along the bank of the river, talking almost entirely of the most trivial affairs.

IV

Next morning Yvette went off alone to sit in the place where Servigny had read over the history of the ants.

" I will not leave it," she said to herself, " until I have come to a decision."

The river ran at her feet, the swift water of the main stream ; it was full of eddies and great bubbles which swirled silently past her.

She had already envisaged every aspect of the situation and every means of escape from it. What was she to do if her mother failed to hold scrupulously to the condition she had laid down, if she did not give up her life, her friends, everything, to take refuge with her in some distant region?

She might go alone . . . away. But whither? How? What could she live on? By working? At what? Whom should she ask for work? And the melancholy and humble life of the working girl, of the daughters of the common folk, seemed to be a little shameful, and unworthy of her. She thought of becoming a governess, like the young ladies in novels, and of being loved and married by the son of the house. But for that rôle she should have been of noble descent, so that when an irate parent reproached her for stealing his son's heart, she could have answered proudly:

"My name is Yvette Obardi."

She could not. And besides, it was a rather commonplace, threadbare method.

A convent was no better. Besides, she felt no call towards a religious life, having nothing but an intermittent and fleeting piety. No one—since she was the thing she was—could save her by marrying her, she could not take help from a man, there was no possible way out, no certain resource at all.

Besides, she wanted something violent, something really great, really brave, something that would act as an example: and she decided to die.

She came to this resolution quite suddenly, quite calmly, as though it were a question of a journey, without reflecting, without seeing what death means, without realising that it is an end without a new beginning, a departure without a return, an eternal farewell to earth, to life.

She was attracted immediately by this desperate decision, with all the impulsiveness of a young and ardent spirit. And she pondered over the means she should employ. They all appeared to be painful and dangerous to carry out, and to demand, too, a violence which was repulsive to her.

She soon gave up the idea of dagger or pistol, which might only wound, maim, or disfigure her, and which required a steady and practised hand—rejected hanging as vulgar, a pauper's sort of suicide, ridiculous and ugly—and drowning because she could swim. Poison was all that remained, but which poison? Almost all are painful, and produce vomiting. She did not want to suffer, or to vomit. Then she thought of chloroform, having read in a newspaper of a young woman who suffocated herself by this means.

At once she felt something like pleasure in her resolve, a secret self-praise, a prick of vainglory. They should see the manner of woman she was!

She returned to Bougival and went to the chemist's, where she asked for a little chloroform for an aching tooth. The man, who knew her, gave her a very small phial of the drug. Then she walked over to Croissy, where she procured another little phial of poison. She got a third at Chaton, and a fourth at Rueil, and returned home late for lunch. As she was very hungry after her walk, she ate a hearty meal, with the sharp enjoyment that exercise brings.

Her mother, glad to see her excellent appetite, felt now quite confident, and said to her as they rose from the table:

"All our friends are coming to spend Sunday here. I've invited the prince, the chevalier, and Monsieur de Belvigne."

Yvette turned slightly pale, but made no answer. She left the house almost at once, went to the railway station, and took a ticket to Paris.

Throughout the afternoon she went from chemist to chemist, buying a few drops of chloroform from each.

She returned in the evening, her pockets full of little bottles. Next day she continued her campaign, and happening to go into a druggist's, she was able to buy half a pint all at once. She did not go out on Saturday—it was stuffy and overcast; she spent the whole of it on the veranda, lying in a long cane-chair. She thought about nothing, filled with a placid resolution.

The next day, wishing to look her best, she put on a blue

frock which suited her very well. And as she viewed herself in the mirror she thought suddenly: "To-morrow I shall be dead." A strange shiver ran through her body. "Dead! I shall not speak, I shall not think, no one will see me any more. And I shall never see all this again." She scrutinised her face carefully, as though she had never seen it before, examining, above all, the eyes, discovering a thousand aspects of herself, a secret character in her face that she did not know, astonished to see herself, as though she were face to face with a stranger, a new friend.

"It is I," she said to herself, "it is I, in that glass. How strange it is to see oneself. We should never recognise ourselves, if we had no mirrors. Every one else would know what we looked like, but we should have no idea of it."

She took the thick plaits of her hair and laid them across her breast, gazing at her own gestures, her poses and movements.

"How pretty I am!" she thought. "To-morrow I shall be dead, there, on my bed."

She looked at her bed, and imagined that she saw herself lying on it, white as the sheets.

Dead! In a week that face, those eyes, those cheeks, would be nothing but black rottenness, shut up in a box underground.

A frightful spasm of anguish constricted her heart.

The clear sunlight flooded the landscape, and the sweet morning air came in at the window.

She sat down and thought. Dead—it was as though the world was disappearing for her sake; but no, nothing in the world would change, not even her room. Yes, her room would stay just the same, with the same bed, the same chairs, the same dressing-table, but she would be gone for ever, and no one would be sorry, except perhaps her mother.

People would say: "How pretty she was, little Yvette!" and that was all. And when she looked at her hand resting on the arm of her chair, she thought again of the rottenness, the black and evil-smelling corruption that her flesh would become. And again a long shudder of horror ran through her whole body, and she could not understand how she could disappear without the whole world coming to an end, so strong was her feeling that she herself was part of everything, of the country, of the air, of the sun, of life.

A burst of laughter came from the garden, a clamour of voices, shouts, the noisy merriment of a country-house party just beginning, and she recognised the sonorous voice of Monsieur de Belvigne, singing :

" Je suis sous ta fenêtre,
Ah ! daigne enfin paraître."

She rose without thinking and went to look out. Every one clapped. They were all there, all five of them, with two other gentlemen she did not know.

She drew back swiftly, torn by the thought that these men had come to enjoy themselves in her mother's house, in the house of a courtesan.

The bell rang for lunch.

" I will show them how to die," she told herself.

She walked downstairs with a firm step, with something of the resolution of a Christian martyr entering the arena where the lions awaited her.

She shook hands with them, smiling pleasantly but a little haughtily. Servigny asked her :

" Are you less grumpy to-day, Mam'selle ? "

" To-day," she replied in a strange, grave voice, " I am for the wildest pleasures. I'm in my Paris mood. Take care." Then, turning to Monsieur de Belvigne : " You shall be my pet to-day, my little Malvoisie. After lunch I'm taking you all to the fair at Marly."

Marly fair was indeed in full swing. The two new-comers

were presented to her, the Comte Tamine and the Marquis de Boiquetot.

During the meal she hardly spoke, bending every effort of will to her resolve to make merry all that afternoon, so that none might guess, so that there should be all the more surprise; they would say: " Who would have thought it? She seemed so gay, so happy! One can never tell what is going on in their heads!"

She forced herself not to think of the evening, the hour she had chosen, when they would all be on the veranda.

She drank as much wine as she could get down, to sharpen her courage, and took two small glasses of brandy; when she left the table she was flushed and a little giddy; she felt herself warmed in body and spirit, her courage high, ready for adventure.

" Off we go!" she cried.

She took Monsieur de Belvigne's arm, and arranged the order of the rest.

" Come along, you shall be my regiment. Servigny, I appoint you sergeant; you must march on the right, outside the ranks. You must make the Foreign Legion march in front, our two aliens, the prince and the chevalier, and behind them the two recruits who have joined the colours to-day. Quick march!"

They went off, Servigny playing an imaginary bugle, and the two new arrivals pretending to play the drum. Monsieur de Belvigne, somewhat embarrassed, said to Yvette:

" Do be a little reasonable, Mademoiselle Yvette. You'll get yourself talked about."

" It's you I'm compromising, Raisiné," she replied. " As for myself, I don't care a rap. It will be all the same to-morrow. So much the worse for you; you shouldn't go about with girls like me."

They went through Bougival, to the amazement of the people in the streets. Every one turned round and stared; the local inhabitants came to their doors; the travellers on the little railway which runs from Rueil to Marly yelled at them; the men standing on the platforms shouted:

"To the river! . . . To the river! . . ."

Yvette marched with a military step, holding Servigny by the arm, as if she were leading a prisoner. She was far from laughter; she wore an air of pale gravity, a sort of sinister immobility. Servigny interrupted his bugle solo in order to shout orders. The prince and the chevalier were enjoying themselves hugely, judging it all vastly diverting and very witty. The two recruits played the drum steadily.

On their arrival at the fair ground they caused quite a sensation. The girls clapped, all the young folk giggled; a fat man arm-in-arm with his wife said to her enviously:

"*They're* enjoying life, they are."

Yvette caught sight of a merry-go-round, and made De Belvigne mount a wooden horse on her right, while the rest of the squad clambered on to horses behind them. When their turn was over she refused to get off, making her escort remain upon the back of her childish steed for five turns running. The delighted crowd flung witticisms at them. Monsieur de Belvigne was very white when he got off, and felt sick.

Then she began careering through the stalls. She made each of the men get weighed before the eyes of a large crowd. She made them buy absurd toys, which they had to carry in their arms. The prince and the chevalier very soon had more than enough of the jest; Servigny and the two drummers alone kept up their spirits.

At last they reached the far end, and she looked at her followers with a curious expression, a glint of malice and perversity in her eyes. A strange fancy came into her head; she made them all stand in a row on the right bank overlooking the river, and said:

"Let him who loves me most throw himself into the water."

No one jumped. A crowd had formed behind them;

women in white aprons gaped at them, and two soldiers in red breeches laughed stupidly.

"Then not one of you is ready to throw himself into the water at my request?" she repeated.

"So much the worse, damn it," murmured Servigny, and leapt, upright, into the river.

His fall flung drops of water right up to Yvette's feet. A murmur of surprise and amusement ran through the crowd. Then the young girl bent down, picked up a little piece of wood, and threw it into the river, crying: "Fetch it."

The young man began to swim, and seizing the floating stick in his mouth, like a dog, he brought it to land, clambered up the bank, dropped on one knee, and offered it to her.

"Good dog," she said, taking it, and patting his head.

"How can they do it?" cried a stout lady, vastly indignant.

"Nice goings-on," said another.

"Damned if I'd take a ducking for any wench," said a man.

She took Belvigne's arm again, with the cutting remark: "You're a noodle; you don't know what you've missed."

As they went home she threw resentful glances at the passers-by.

"How stupid they all look," she observed; then, raising her eyes to her companion's face, added: "And you too, for the matter of that."

Monsieur de Belvigne bowed. Turning round, she saw that the prince and the chevalier had disappeared. Servigny, wretched and soaked to the skin, was no longer playing the bugle, but walked with a melancholy air beside the two tired young men, who were not playing the drum now.

She began to laugh dryly.

"You seem to have had enough. That's what you call fun, isn't it? That's what you've come here for. I've given you your money's worth."

She walked on without another word, and suddenly De Belvigne saw that she was crying.

" What's the matter ? " he asked in alarm.

" Leave me alone," she murmured. " It's nothing to do with you."

But he insisted foolishly : " Now, now Mademoiselle, what is the matter with you ? Has anybody hurt you ? "

" Be quiet," she said irritably.

Abruptly, unable to withstand the terrible sorrow flooding her heart, she broke into such a violent fit of sobbing that she could not walk any further. She covered her face with her hands, and gasped for breath, choking, strangled, stifled by the violence of her despair.

Belvigne stood helplessly beside her, repeating :

" I don't understand at all."

But Servigny rushed towards her. " Come along home, Mam'selle, or they'll see you crying in the street. Why do you do these silly things, if they make you so unhappy ? "

He led her forward, holding her arm. But as soon as they reached the gate of the villa she ran across the garden and up to her room, and locked herself in.

She did not reappear until dinner-time ; she was pale and very grave. All the rest were gay enough, however. Servigny had bought a suit of workman's clothes in the neighbourhood, corduroy trousers, a flowered shirt, a jersey, and a smock, and was talking like a peasant.

Yvette was in a fever for the ending of the meal, feeling her courage ebbing. As soon as coffee was over she went again to her room. She heard laughing voices under her window. The chevalier was telling jokes, foreign witticisms and puns, crude and not very savoury. She listened in despair. Servigny, slightly drunk, was imitating a tipsy workman, and was addressing the Marquise as " Mrs. Obardi." Suddenly he said to Saval : " Hullo, Mr. Obardi." Every one laughed.

Then Yvette made up her mind. First she took a sheet of her note-paper and wrote :

"BOUGIVAL, Sunday, 9 P.M.

"I die so that I may not become a kept woman.

"YVETTE."

Then a postscript:

"Good-bye, mother, dear. Forgive me."

She sealed up the envelope, and addressed it to Madame la Marquise Obardi.

Then she moved her arm-chair up to the window, set a little table within reach of her hand, and placed upon it the large bottle of chloroform, with a handful of cotton-wool beside it.

An immense rose-tree in full bloom, planted near the veranda and reaching right up to her window, filled the night with little gusts of faint, sweet fragrance; for some moments she sat breathing in the perfumed air. The crescent moon swung in the dark sky, its left side gnawed away, and veiled now and again with small clouds.

"I'm going to die," thought Yvette. "I'm going to die!" Her heart, swollen with sobs, bursting with grief, choked her. She longed to cry for mercy, to be reprieved, to be loved.

Servigny's voice came up to her; he was telling a shady story, constantly interrupted by bursts of laughter. The Marquise seemed more amused then any of them; she repeated gaily: "No one can tell a story like that as well as he can."

Yvette took the bottle, uncorked it, and poured a little of the liquid on to the cotton-wool. It had a queer, pungent, sweet smell, and as she lifted the pad of cotton-wool to her lips, she swallowed the strong, irritating flavour of it, and it made her cough.

Then, closing her mouth, she began to breathe it in. She took long draughts of the deadly vapour, shutting her eyes, and compelling herself to deaden every impulse of her mind, so that she would no longer think nor realise what she was doing.

At first she felt as though her heart were swelling and growing, as though her spirit, just now heavy and burdened with sorrow, were growing light, as light as if the weight oppressing it had been raised, lessened, removed.

A lively and pleasant sensation filled her whole body, penetrating to the tips of her fingers and toes, entering into her flesh, a hazy drunkenness, a happy delirium.

She saw that the cotton-wool was dry, and was surprised that she was not yet dead. Her senses were sharpened, intensified and more alert. She heard every word uttered on the veranda. Prince Kravalow was relating how he had killed an Austrian general in a duel.

Far away, in the heart of the country, she heard the noises of the night; the intermittent barking of a dog, the short croak of bull-frogs, the faint shiver of the leaves.

She took up the bottle, soaked the little piece of cotton-wool, and began again to breathe it in. For some moments she felt nothing; then the languid, delightful, secure contentment that she had felt at first took hold of her once more.

Twice she poured out more chloroform, greedy now of the physical and mental sensation, the drowsy languor in which her senses were drowning. She felt as though she no longer had bones or flesh or arms or legs. All had been gently taken from her, and she had felt nothing. The chloroform had drained away her body, leaving nothing but her brain, wider, freer, more lively, more alert than she had ever felt it before.

She remembered a thousand things she had forgotten, little details of her childhood, trifles which gave her pleasure. Her mind, suddenly endowed with an agility hitherto unknown to it, leapt from one strange idea to another, ran through a thousand adventures, wandered at random in the past, and rambled through hopes of the future. This rapid, careless process of thought filled her with a sensual delight; dreaming so, she enjoyed a divine happiness.

She still heard the voices, but could no longer distinguish the words, which seemed to her to take on another sense. She sank down and down, wandering in a strange and shifting fairyland.

She was on a large boat which glided beside a very pleasant country filled with flowers. She saw people on the banks, and these people were talking very loudly, and then she found herself on land again, without wondering how she got there, and Servigny, dressed like a prince, came to take her to a bull-fight. The streets were full of people talking, and she listened to their conversations, which did not in the least surprise her, but were as though she had always known them; for through her dreamy intoxication she still heard her mother's friends laughing and chatting on the veranda.

Then all grew dim.

Then she awoke, deliciously sleepy, and had some difficulty in recalling herself to consciousness.

So she was not dead yet.

But she felt so rested, and in such comfort and in such peace of mind, that she was in no hurry to finish the affair. She would have liked this glorious languor to last for ever.

She breathed slowly, and looked at the moon facing her above the trees. Something in her soul was changed. Her thoughts were no longer those of a short while ago. The chloroform, soothing her body and mind, had assuaged her grief, and put to sleep her will to die.

Why not live? Why should she not be loved? Why should she not live happily? Everything now seemed possible, easy, sure. Everything in life was sweet, was good and charming. But because she wished to go on dreaming for ever, she poured more of this dream-water on to the cotton-wool, and again began to breathe it in, occasionally removing the poison from her nostrils, so that she should not take too much, so that she should not die.

She looked at the moon, and saw a face in it, a woman's face. She began once more to roam about the country, adrift in the hazy visions of an opium dream. The face hung in the centre of the sky ; then it began to sing ; in a well-known voice it sang the *Alleluia d'Amour*. It was the Marquise, who had just gone indoors to play the piano.

Yvette had wings now. She was flying through the night, a beautiful, clear night, over woods and rivers. She flew with vast delight, opening and beating her wings, wafted by the wind as by a caressing touch. She whirled through the air, which kissed her skin, and glided along so fast, so fast, that she had no time to see anything below her, and she found herself sitting beside a pond, with a line in her hand—she was fishing.

Something tugged at the line ; she pulled it in and brought up the magnificent pearl necklace she had once desired. She was not in the least astonished at the catch, and looked at Servigny, who had appeared beside her, though she did not know how, and was fishing too ; he was just landing a wooden roundabout horse.

Then once again she felt that she was waking, and heard them calling to her from below.

Her mother had said : " Blow out the candle."

Then Servigny's voice, clear and humorous : " Mam'selle Yvette, blow out your candle."

They all took up the cry in chorus.

" Mam'selle Yvette, blow out your candle."

Again she poured chloroform on to the cotton-wool, but as she did not want to die, she kept it at some distance from her face, so that she could breathe the fresh air while filling her room with the asphyxiating odour of the narcotic, for she knew that someone would come upstairs. So she arranged herself in a charming attitude of abandonment, a mimicking of the abandon of death, and waited.

" I'm a little uneasy," said the Marquise. " The foolish child has gone to sleep leaving the candle alight on the table. I'll send Clémence up to blow it out and to shut her balcony window, which she has left wide open."

In a few moments the maid knocked at the door and called:

"Mademoiselle, Mademoiselle!"

After an interval of silence she began again: "Mademoiselle, Madame le Marquise says please will you blow out your candle and shut the window."

Again she waited, then knocked more loudly and called:

"Mademoiselle, Mademoiselle!"

As Yvette did not answer, the servant departed and told the Marquise:

"Mademoiselle has certainly gone to sleep; her door is bolted and I can't wake her."

"But surely she won't go on sleeping like that?" murmured Madame Obardi.

On Servigny's advice they all assembled under the young girl's window and shouted in chorus:

"Hip, hip, hurrah—Mam'selle Yvette!"

The cry rang out in the still night, piercing the clear moonlit air, and died away in the sleeping country-side; they heard it fade away like the noise of a train that has gone by.

As Yvette did not reply, the Marquise said:

"I hope nothing's the matter with her; I'm beginning to be alarmed."

Then Servigny snatched the red roses and the still unopened buds from the big rose-tree that grew up the wall, and began to hurl them through the window into her room. At the first which struck her, Yvette started and nearly cried out. Some fell on her dress, some in her hair, others flew over her head and landed on the bed, covering it with a rain of flowers.

Once more the Marquise cried in a choking voice:

"Come, Yvette, answer!"

"Really, it's not normal," declared Servigny. "I'll climb up by the balcony."

But the chevalier was indignant.

"Pardon me, pardon me, but that's too much of a favour,

I protest ; it's too good a way—and too good a time—for making a rendezvous ! "

And all the others, thinking that the young girl was playing a trick on them, cried out :

" We protest. It's a put-up affair. He shan't go up, he shan't go up."

But the Marquise repeated in her agitation :

" Someone must go and see."

" She favours the duke ; we are betrayed," declared the prince, with a dramatic gesture.

" Let's toss for the honour," suggested the chevalier, and took a gold hundred-franc piece from his pocket.

He began with the prince. " Tails," he called. It was heads. The prince in his turn threw the coin, saying to Saval :

" Call, please."

" Heads," called Saval.

It was tails.

The prince proceeded to put the same question to all the others. All lost. Servigny, who alone remained facing him, drawled insolently :

" Damn it, he's cheating ! "

The Russian placed his hand on his heart and offered the gold coin to his rival, saying :

" Spin it yourself, my dear duke."

Servigny took it and tossed it, calling : " Heads ! "

It was tails: He bowed, and pointed to the pillar of the balcony.

" Up you go, prince," he said.

But the prince was looking about him with a troubled air.

" What are you looking for ? " asked the chevalier.

" I . . . I should like a . . . a ladder."

There was a general roar of laughter, and Saval came forward, saying : " We'll help you."

He lifted the man in his Herculean arms, with the advice : " Hold on to the balcony."

The prince promptly caught hold of it and, Saval letting go, he remained suspended, waving his legs. Servigny caught hold of the wildly-struggling limbs that were groping for a foothold, and tugged at them with all his strength; the hands loosed their grip and the prince fell like a log on to the stomach of Monsieur de Belvigne, who was hurrying forward to help support him.

" Whose turn now ? " asked Servigny, but no one offered.

" Come on, Belvigne, a little courage."

" No, thank you, my boy. I'd sooner keep my bones whole."

" Well, you, then chevalier ? You should be used to scaling fortresses."

" I leave it to you, my dear duke."

" Well . . . well . . . I don't know that I'm so keen on it as all that." And Servigny walked round the pillar with a scrutinising eye. Then he leapt, caught hold of the balcony, hauled himself up like a gymnast on the horizontal bar, and clambered over the rail.

All the spectators applauded, with uplifted faces. But he reappeared directly, crying: " Come at once! Quickly! Yvette's unconscious! "

The Marquise screamed loudly and dashed up the stairs.

The young girl, her eyes closed, lay like one dead. Her mother rushed wildly into the room and threw herself upon her.

" What is it ? Tell me, what is it ? " she asked.

Servigny picked up the bottle of chloroform which had fallen on the floor. " She's suffocated herself," he said. He set his ear to her heart, then added: " But she's not dead; we'll soon bring her round. Have you any ammonia here ? "

" Any what . . . any what . . . sir ? " said the distracted maid.

" Any sal volatile ? "

" Yes, sir."

" Fetch it at once, and leave the door open, to make a draught."

The Marquise had fallen upon her knees and was sobbing. " Yvette ! Yvette ! My child, my little girl, my child, listen, answer me, Yvette ! My child ! Oh ! my God, my God, what is the matter with her ? "

The frightened men wandered aimlessly about the room, bringing water, towels, glasses, and vinegar.

Someone said : " She ought to be undressed."

The Marquise, who was almost out of her wits, tried to undress her daughter, but she no longer knew what she was doing. Her trembling hands fumbled uselessly at the clothing, and she moaned : " I . . . I . . . I can't, I can't."

The maid had returned with a medicine bottle ; Servigny uncorked it and poured out half of its contents on to a handkerchief. He thrust it under Yvette's nose, and she choked.

" Good ; she's breathing," he said. " It's nothing."

He bathed her temples, her cheeks, and her neck with the strong-smelling liquid. Then he signed to the maid to unlace the young girl, and when nothing but a petticoat was left over her chemise, he took her in his arms and carried her to the bed ; he was shaken, his senses maddened by the fragrance of her half-naked body, by the touch of her flesh, and the softness of the half-seen breasts on which he pressed his lips.

When she was in bed he rose to his feet, very pale.

" She's coming to," he said ; " it's nothing," for he had heard that her breathing was continuous and regular. But seeing the men's eyes fixed upon Yvette stretched across the bed, a spasm of jealous fury seized him. He went up to them, saying :

" Gentlemen, there are too many of us in this room. Be good enough to leave Monsieur Saval and myself alone with the Marquise."

His voice was sharp and authoritative. The other men left at once.

Madame Obardi had seized her lover in her arms and, with her face raised to his, was crying :

" Save her ! . . . Oh, save her ! "

But Servigny, who had turned round, saw a letter on the table. With a swift movement he picked it up and read the address. He guessed the whole affair at once and thought : " Perhaps the Marquise had better not know about this." And tearing open the envelope, he read at a glance the two lines which it contained :

" I die so that I may not become a kept woman.

" YVETTE."

" Good-bye, mother, dear. Forgive me."

" Deuce take it," he said to himself. " This needs thinking over " ; and he hid the letter in his pocket. He returned to the bedside, and at once the thought came to him that the young girl had regained consciousness, but dared not show it out of shame, humiliation, and a dread of being questioned.

The Marquise had fallen on her knees and was weeping, her head resting on the foot of the bed. Suddenly she exclaimed :

" A doctor ! We must have a doctor ! "

But Servigny, who had been whispering to Saval, said to her :

" No, it's all right now. Just go out for a minute and I promise you that she'll be ready to kiss you when you come back."

The baron took Madame Obardi's arm and led her away. Servigny sat down beside the bed and took Yvette's hand.

" Listen to me, Mam'selle," he said.

She did not answer. She felt so happy, so comfortable, so cosy and warm that she would have liked never to move or speak again, but to live on in this state. A sense of infinite well-being possessed her, like no sensation she had ever known. The warm night air drifted into the room in a gentle, caressing breeze. and from time to time its faint breath blew sweetly across her face. It was a caress, the wind's kiss, the soft refreshing breath of a fan made of all the leaves in the wood, all the shadows of the night, all the mists of the river, and all the flowers, for the roses strewn upon the floor and the bed, and the rose-tree that clung to the balcony, mingled their languid fragrance with the healthy tang of the night breeze.

She drank in the good air, her eyes closed, her senses still half adrift in the intoxication of the drug; she no longer felt a wish to die, but a strong, imperious desire to live, to be happy, no matter how, to be loved, yes, loved.

"Mam'selle Yvette, listen to me," repeated Servigny.

She decided to open her eyes. Seeing her thus revived, he went on:

"Come now, what's all this foolishness?"

"I was so unhappy, Muscade," she murmured.

He gave her hand a benevolent squeeze.

"Well, this has been a deuce of a lot of use to you, now, hasn't it? Now promise me not to try again"

She did not answer, but made a little movement of her head, and emphasised it with a smile that he felt rather than saw.

He took from his pocket the letter he had found on the table.

"Am I to show this to your mother?" he asked.

"No," she signed with a movement of her head.

He did not know what more to say, for there seemed no way out of the situation.

"My dear little girl," he murmured, "we must all accept our share of things, however sad. I understand your grief, and I promise. . . ."

"You're so kind . . ." she stammered.

They were silent. He looked at her. There was tenderness and surrender in her glance, and suddenly she raised her arms, as if she wished to draw him to her. He bent over her, feeling that she was calling him, and their lips met.

For a long time they stayed thus with closed eyes. But he, realising that he was on the point of losing control, raised his head and stood up. She was smiling at him now with real tenderness, and gripping his shoulders with both hands, she tried to hold him back.

"I'm going to fetch your mother," he said.

"One more second," she murmured. "I'm so happy."

Then, after a brief interval of silence, she said very softly, so softly that he hardly heard her:

"You will love me very much, won't you?"

He knelt down by the bedside and kissed her wrist, which she held out to him.

"I adore you."

But there were footsteps at the door. He sprang up and cried in his ordinary voice, with its faint note of irony:

"You can come in. It's all over now."

The Marquise flung herself upon her daughter with open arms, and embraced her frantically, covering her face with tears. Servigny, his heart full of joy and his body on fire with love, stepped out on to the balcony to breathe deeply of the cool night air, humming:

"Souvent femme varie;
Bien fol est qui s'y fie."

OUR FRIENDS THE ENGLISH

A SMALL LEATHER-BOUND NOTEBOOK LAY ON THE UPHOLSTERED seat of the railway carriage. I took it up and opened it. It was a traveller's diary, dropped by its owner.

Here are the last three pages of it copied out.

. . . . . .

February 1st. Mentone, capital of the Consumptives, noted for its pulmonary tubercles. Quite different from the potato tubercle, which lives and grows in the earth for the purpose of nourishing and fattening men, this variety lives and grows in man for the purpose of nourishing and fattening the earth.

I got this scientific definition from a friendly doctor here, a very learned man.

Am looking for an hotel. Am directed to the Grrrrand Hotel of Russia, England, Germany, and the Netherlands. Pay homage to the landlord's cosmopolitan intellect and book a room in this caravanserai, which looks empty, it is so big.

Walk round the town, which is pretty and admirably situated at the foot of an imposing mountain peak (see guide-book). Meet various people who look ill, being taken for a walk by others who look bored. Have observed several people wearing comforters (note this, all naturalists who may be becoming anxious at the disappearance of these garments !).

Six p.m. Return for dinner. The tables are laid in an enormous room which could shelter three hundred guests ; as a matter of fact, it holds just twenty-two. They come in one after another. The first is a tall, thin, clean-shaven Englishman. He is wearing a frock-coat with a long skirt, fitting closely at the waist. His thin arms are enveloped in its sleeves like an umbrella sheathed in its cover. This garment reminds me at the same time of an ecclesiastical cassock and of the civilian uniforms worn by ex-army captains and army pensioners. Down the front elevation runs a row of buttons clad in black serge like their master, and sewn very close to one another; they look like an army of wood-lice. The buttonholes stand in a row opposite and have the air of making unseemly advances to the modest little buttons.

The waistcoat fastens on the same system. The owner of the garment does not look precisely a sporty boy.

He bows to me; I return the compliment.

Next item—three ladies, all English, a mother and two daughters. Each wears a helping of whipped white of egg on the top of her head; rather remarkable. The daughters are old, like the mother. The mother is old, like the daughters. All three are thin, flat-chested, tall, stiff, and tired-looking; their front teeth are worn outside, to intimidate plates and men.

Other residents arrive, all English. Only one is fat and red-faced, with white whiskers. Every woman (there are fourteen) has a helping of white of egg on her head. I observe that this crowning delicacy is made of white lace (or is it tulle? I don't know). It appears to be unsweetened. All the ladies look as though they were pickled in vinegar, although there are several young girls, not bad-looking, but with no figures and with no apparent promise of them. I am reminded of Bouilhet's lines:

> "Qu'importe ton sein maigre, ô mon objet aimé!
> On est plus près du cœur quand la poitrine est plate;
> Et je vois comme un merle en sa cage enfermé,
> L'amour entre les os, rêvant sur une patte."

Two young men, younger than the first, are likewise imprisoned in sacerdotal frock-coats. They are lay priests, with wives and children; they are called parsons. They look more serious, less unbending, less kindly than our own priests.

I would not take a hogshead of them for a pint of ours. But that's a matter of taste.

As soon as all the residents are present, the head parson begins to speak, and recites, in English, a sort of long *benedicite ;* the whole table listens to it with that pickled look on their faces.

My dinner being thus dedicated, despite me, to the God of Israel and Albion, all start their soup.

Solemn silence reigns in the huge room—a silence which is surely not normal. I suppose the chaste sheep are annoyed at the invasion of a goat.

The women especially retain a stiff, starched look, as though afraid of dropping their head-dress of whipped cream into the soup.

The head parson, however, addresses a few words to his neighbour, the under parson. As I have the misfortune to understand English, I observe with amazement that they are continuing a conversation, interrupted before dinner, on the texts of the prophets. Every one listens attentively.

I am fed, always against my will, upon unbelievable quotations.

" I will provide water for him that thirsteth," said Isaiah.

I did not know it. I knew none of the truths uttered by Jeremiah, Malachi, Ezekiel, Elijah, and Gagachias. These simple truths crawled down my ears and buzzed in my head like flies.

" Let him that is hungry ask for food ! "

" The air belongeth to the birds, as the sea belongeth to the fish."

" The fig-tree produceth figs, and the date-palm dates."

" He who will not hear, to him knowledge is denied."

How much greater and more profound is our great Henry Monnier, who through the lips of one man, the immortal *Prud'homme*, has uttered more thrilling truths than have been compiled by all the goodly fellowship of the prophets.

Confronted by the sea. he exclaims: "How beautiful is the ocean, but what a lot of good land spoilt!"

He formulates the everlasting policy of the world: "This sword is the light of my life. I can use it to defend the Power that gave it to me, and, if need be, to attack It also."

Had I had the honour to be introduced to the English people surrounding me, I would certainly have edified them with quotations from our French prophet.

Dinner over, we went into the lounge.

I sat alone, in a corner. The British nation appeared to be hatching a plot on the other side of the room.

Suddenly a lady went to the paino.

"Ah," thought I, "a little mew-sic. Good."

She opened the instrument and sat down; the entire colony ranked itself round her like an army, the women in front, the men in the rear rank.

Were they going to sing an opera?

The head parson, now turned choirmaster, raised his hand, then lowered it; a frightful din rose up from every throat. They were singing a hymn.

The women squalled, the men barked, the windows shook. The hotel dog howled in the yard. Another answered him from a room.

I went off in a furious temper. I went for a walk round the town. No theatre. No casino. No place of amusement. I had to go back to the hotel.

The English were still singing.

I went to bed. They went on singing. Till midnight they sang the praises of the Lord in the harshest, most hateful, most out-of-tune voices I ever heard. Maddened by the horrible spirit of imitation which drives a whole nation to such orgies, I buried my head beneath the sheets and sang:

I pity the English Lord
To whom such hymns are outpoured.
If the Lord has a better ear
Than His faithful people here,
If He likes wit and grace
And a pretty face,
Appreciates music and art,
Talent and liveliness,
I pity Him, I confess,
From the bottom of my heart.

When I finally dropped off to sleep, I had fearful nightmares. I saw prophets riding upon parsons, eating white of egg off the heads of corpses.

Horrible! Horrible!

February 2nd. As soon as I was up, I asked the landlord if these barbarian invaders of his hotel made a daily practice of this frightful diversion.

"Oh, no, sir," he answered with a smile. "Yesterday was Sunday, and Sunday is a holy day to them, you know."

I answered:

Nothing is sacred when a parson's near,
The traveller's rest, his dinner or his ear.
But if this caterwauling starts again,
I shall incontinently take the train.

Somewhat surprised, the landlord promised to look into the matter.

During the day I made a delightful excursion in the hills. At night, the same *benedicite*. Then the drawing-room. What will they do? Nothing, for an hour.

Suddenly the same lady who accompanied the hymns the day before, goes to the piano and opens it. I shiver with fright.

She plays . . . a waltz.

The girls begin to dance.

The head parson beats time on his knee from force of habit. The Englishmen one after another invite the ladies; the white of egg whirls round and round and round will it turn into sauce?

This is much better. After the waltz comes a quadrille, then a polka.

Not having been introduced, I remain demurely in a corner.

February 3rd. Another charming walk to the old castle, a picturesque ruin in the hills, on every peak of which remain the remnants of ancient buildings. Nothing could be more beautiful than the ruined castles among the chaos of rocks dominated by Alpine snow-peaks (see guide-book). Wonderful country.

During dinner I introduce myself, after the French fashion, to the lady next to me. She does not answer—English politeness.

In the evening, another English ball.

February 4th. Excursion to Monaco (see guide-books).

In the evening, English ball. I am present, in the rôle of plague-spot.

February 5th. Excursion to San Remo (see guide-books).

In the evening, English ball. Still in quarantine.

February 6th. Excursion to Nice (see guide-books).

In the evening, English ball. Bed.

February 7th. Excursion to Cannes (see guide-books).

In the evening, English ball. Have tea in my corner.

February 8th. Sunday; my revenge. Am waiting for them.

They have resumed their pickled Sunday faces, and are preparing their throats for hymns.

So before dinner I slip into the drawing-room, pocket the key of the piano, and say to the porter: "If the parsons want the key, tell them I have it, and ask them to see me."

During dinner various doubtful points in the Scriptures are discussed, texts elucidated, genealogies of biblical personages explained.

Then they go to the drawing-room. The paino is approached. Sensation.—Discussion; they seem thunderstruck. The white of egg nearly flies off. The head parson goes out, then returns. More discussion. Angry eyes are turned on me; here are the three parsons, bearing down on me in line. They are ambassadorial, really rather impressive. They bow. I get up. The eldest speaks:

"Mosieu, on me avé dit que vô avé pris la clef de la piano. Les dames vôdraient le avoir, pour chanté le cantique."

I answer: "Sir, I can perfectly well understand the request these ladies make, but I cannot concede to it. You are a religious man, sir; so am I, and my principles, stricter, no doubt, than yours, have determined me to oppose this profanation of the divine in which you are accustomed to indulge.

"I cannot, gentlemen, permit you to employ in the service of God an instrument used on weekdays for girls to dance to. We, sir, do not give public balls in our churches, nor do we play quadrilles upon the organ. The use you make of this piano offends and disgusts me. You may take back my answer to the ladies."

The three parsons retired abashed. The ladies appeared bewildered. They sing their hymns without the piano.

February 9th. Noon. The landlord has just given me notice; I am being expelled at the general request of the English people.

I meet the three parsons, who seem to be supervising my departure. I go straight up to them and bow.

"Gentlemen," I say, "you seem to have a deep knowledge of the Scriptures. I myself have more than a little scholarship. I even know a little Hebrew. Well, I should like to submit to you a case which profoundly troubles my Catholic conscience.

"You consider incest an abominable crime, do you not? Very well, the Bible gives us an instance of it which is very disturbing. Lot, fleeing from Sodom, was seduced, as you know, by his two daughters, and yielded to their desires, being deprived of his wife, who had been turned into a pillar of salt. Of this appalling and doubly incestuous connection were born Ammon and Moab, from whom sprang two great peoples, the Ammonites and the Moabites. Well, Ruth, the reaper who disturbed the sleep of Boaz in order to make him a father, was a Moabite.

"Do you not know Victor Hugo's lines?—

> '. . . Ruth, une moabite,
> S'était couchée aux pieds de Booz, le sein nu,
> Espérant on ne sait quel rayon inconnu,
> Quand viendrait du réveil la lumière subite.'

"The 'hidden ray' produced Obed, who was David's ancestor.

"Now then, was not Our Lord Jesus Christ descended from David?"

The three parsons looked at one another in consternation, and did not answer.

"You will say," I went on, "that I speak of the genealogy of Joseph, the lawful but superfluous husband of Mary, mother of Christ. Joseph, as we all know, had nothing to do with his son's birth. So it was Joseph who was descended from a case of incest, and not the Divine Man. Granted. But I will add two further observations. The first is that Joseph and Mary, being cousins, must have had the same ancestry; the second, that it is a disgrace that we should have to read ten pages of genealogical tree for nothing.

" We ruin our eyes learning that A begat B, who begat C, who begat D, who begat E, who begat F, and when we are almost driven off our heads by this interminable rigmarole, we come to the last one, who begat nothing. That, gentlemen, may well be called excess of mystification."

The three parsons, as one man, abruptly turned their backs on me, and fled.

Two p.m. I catch the train for Nice.

. . . . . .

There the diary ended. Although these remarks reveal in their author execrable taste, a cheap wit and much vulgarity, yet I think they might put certain travellers on their guard against the peril of the Englishman abroad.

I should add that there are undoubtedly charming Englishmen ; I have often met them. But they are rarely our fellow-guests at hotels.

ROGER'S METHOD

I WAS WALKING WITH ROGER ONE DAY WHEN A STREET-HAWKER bawled in our ears:

"New method of getting rid of mothers-in-law! Buy, oh buy!"

I stopped, and said to my companion:

"Now that reminds me of a question I've long wanted to ask you. What is this 'Roger's method' your wife talks about so often? She jokes about it in such a gay, knowing way that I take it to be some love-potion of which you hold the secret. Whenever she's told of some young man who is exhausted and has lost his nervous strength, she turns to you and says with a smile: 'Ah, you ought to show him Roger's method.' And the funniest thing of all is that you always blush."

"Well, there's a reason for it," answered Roger. "If my wife really knew what she was talking about, she'd stop it mighty quick. I'll tell you the story in strict confidence. You know I married a widow with whom I was very much in love. Now my wife has always been very free of speech, and before she became my wife we often had rather spicy little talks. After all, that's possible with widows; they have the taste of it in their mouths, you see. She has a perfectly honest liking for good smoking-room stories. The sins of the tongue do very little harm; she's bold, and I'm bashful; and before our wedding she liked to embarrass me with jokes and questions which were not easy for me to answer. Perhaps it was her forwardness which made me fall in love with her. And, talking of love, I was absolutely devoted to her from head to toe, and she knew it too, the little baggage.

"We decided on a quiet wedding and no honeymoon.

After the religious ceremony the witnesses were to lunch with us, and then we were to go for a drive, returning to my house in the Rue du Helder for dinner. Well, the witnesses left, and off we went in the carriage; I told the coachman to take us to the Bois de Boulogne. It was the end of June, and gorgeous weather.

"As soon as were alone, she began to laugh.

"'My dear Roger,' she said, 'now's the time to show yourself gallant. See what you can do.'

"This invitation absolutely paralysed me. I kissed her hand; I told her I loved her. I even had the pluck to kiss the nape of her neck twice, but the passers-by embarrassed me. And she kept on saying with a funny, provoking little air: 'What next? . . . What next? . . .'

"This 'what next?' drained all my strength away. After all, in a carriage, in the Park, in broad daylight, one could hardly . . . well, you know what I mean.

"She was amused by my obvious embarrassment. From time to time she remarked: 'I'm very much afraid I've drawn a blank. You make me very uneasy.'

"I too began to be uneasy—about myself. As soon as I'm scared, I become perfectly useless.

"At dinner she was charming. To pluck up my courage, I'd sent away my servant, who embarrassed me. Oh, we were perfectly well-behaved, but you know how foolish lovers are. We drank from the same glass, we ate off the same plate, with the same fork. We amused ourselves by beginning one biscuit from both ends, so that our lips met in the middle.

"'I should like a little champagne,' she said.

"I had forgotten the bottle on the sideboard. I took it, untwisted the wires, and pressed the cork to make it fly off. It wouldn't go. Gabrielle smiled and murmured: 'An evil omen.'

"I pushed the swollen end of the cork with my thumb,

I twisted it to the right, I twisted it to the left, but in vain, and suddenly I broke it right at the lip of the bottle.

" 'Poor Roger,' sighed Gabrielle.

" I took a corkscrew and screwed it into the piece left in the neck. I couldn't pull it out; I had to call Prosper back. My wife was now shrieking with laughter and saying: 'Well, well; I see I can depend on you.' She was a little tipsy.

" By the time we came to the coffee, more than a little.

" A widow does not need to be put to bed with the maternal solicitude accorded to young girls, and Gabrielle went calmly to her room, saying: 'Smoke your cigar for a quarter of an hour.'

" When I rejoined her, I had lost confidence in myself, I admit. I felt unnerved, worried, ill at ease.

" I took my lawful place. She said nothing. She looked at me with a smile upon her lips, obviously desiring to chaff me. Irony, at such a moment, was the last straw. I must confess that it made me helpless—hand and foot.

" When Gabrielle observed my . . . embarrassment, she did nothing to reassure me. On the contrary, she asked me with an air of detachment: 'Are you always as lively as this?'

" I could not help answering: 'Shut up; you're unbearable.'

" She went on laughing, but in an unrestrained, improper, exasperating way.

" True, I cut a sorry figure, and must have looked a proper fool.

" From time to time, between new fits of merriment, she would say, choking with laughter: 'Come on—be brave—buck up, you poor boy.'

" Then she continued to laugh so immoderately that she positively screamed.

" Finally I was so exhausted, so furious with myself and her, that I realised I should smack her unless I went away.

" I jumped out of bed and dressed myself quickly in a fiendish temper, without a word to her.

" She became grave at once and, seeing that I was angry, asked : ' What are you doing ? Where are you going ? '

" I did not answer, and went down into the street. I wanted to kill someone, to have my revenge, to do some quite insane thing. I strode straight ahead at a great rate, and suddenly the idea came to me to go off with a woman. Who knows ?—it would be a trial, an experience, practice perhaps. At all events it would be revenge. And if I were ever deceived by my wife, I should at least have deceived her first.

" I did not hesitate. I knew of a house not far from my own house ; I ran there and went in like a man who throws himself into deep water to see if he can still swim.

" Well, I *could* swim ; I swam very well. I stayed there a long time, enjoying my secret and subtle revenge. Then I found myself in the street once more, at the cool hour before dawn. I now felt calm and sure of myself, contented, tranquil and still ready, I thought, for deeds of valour.

" I went slowly home, and quietly opened the door of my room.

" Gabrielle was reading, her elbow propped up on the pillow. She raised her head and asked in a frightened voice : ' Ah, there you are ; where have you been ? '

" I made no answer. I undressed with an air of assurance. I returned like a victorious lord to the place whence I had abjectly fled.

" She was amazed, and was convinced that I had made use of some mysterious secret.

" And now on every occasion she speaks of ' Roger's method ' as though she were referring to some infallible scientific device.

" Well, well, it's ten years ago now, and I'm afraid the same attempt would not have much chance of success to-day, for me at any rate.

" But if any friend of yours is nervous about his wedding-night, tell him of my stratagem, and tell him, too, that from twenty to thirty-five there's no better way of loosening the tags, as the squire of Brantôme would have said."

THE CHRISTENING

IN FRONT OF THE FARM-GATE THE MEN WERE WAITING IN THEIR Sunday clothes. The May sun shed its brilliant light on the flowering apple-trees which roofed the whole farmyard with blossom in great, round, fragrant bunches of pink and white. Petals fell round them in a ceaseless shower, fluttering and eddying into the tall grass, where the dandelions glittered like flames and the poppies were splashed in drops of blood.

A sow slumbered on the side of the manure-heap, and a band of little pigs with twisted, cord-like tails ran round her huge belly and swollen dugs.

Far away, through the trees behind the farmhouse, the church-bell suddenly rang out. Its iron voice sent up a faint and distant cry to the radiant heavens. Swallows darted arrow-like across the blue spaces bounded by the still shafts of tall beeches. A faint smell of stables mingled with the soft sweet fragrance of the apple-trees.

One of the men standing by the gate turned towards the house and cried:

" Come quick, Mélina ; t'bell's ringin'."

He was about thirty years of age, a tall young peasant, as yet not bowed or deformed by long labour in the fields. His old father, gnarled like the trunk of an oak, with scarred wrists and crooked legs, announced : " Women, they bean't never ready first."

The two other sons laughed, and one, turning to the eldest brother, who had shouted first, said : " Go fetch 'em, Polyte. They'll not be here before noon."

The young man entered the house.

A flock of ducks near at hand began to quack and flap their wings, and waddled off down to the pond.

Then at the open door appeared a stout woman carrying a two-months-old child. The white strings of her high bonnet hung down her back, streaming over a shawl as violently scarlet as a house on fire. The child, wrapped in white garments, rested against the nurse's protruding stomach.

Next came the mother, a tall, strong girl of barely eighteen, fresh and smiling, holding her husband's arm. The two grandmothers followed, wrinkled like old apples, weariness apparent in their bowed backs, long since bent by rough and patient toil. One was a widow; she took the arm of the grandfather waiting at the gate, and they left at the head of the procession, just behind the child and the midwife. The rest of the family followed, the younger ones carrying paper bags full of sweets.

The little bell rang ceaselessly, calling with all its strength to the tiny mite it awaited. Children clambered on the dikes; heads appeared at gateways; milkmaids set down their pails and stood between them to watch the christening go by.

And the nurse moved on triumphantly with her living burden, stepping between the puddles on the road, which ran between the tree-crowned banks. And the old people advanced with ceremonious steps, walking a little crookedly, because of their age and infirmity. And the young folk were eager to dance, and looked at the girls who came to see them go by; and the father and mother walked with graver mien, following the child who would take their place and carry on their name in the country, the honoured name of Dentu.

They emerged on the plain and struck across the fields, avoiding the long, roundabout road. Now the church came into view, with its pointed steeple. Just below the slate roof was an aperture, within which something swung swiftly backwards and forwards, passing and repassing behind the narrow window. It was the bell, still ringing, calling the new-born child to come for the first time to the house of God.

A dog had begun to follow the procession; they threw sweets to it, and it frisked round their feet.

The church-door was open. By the altar stood the priest, a tall fellow, slim and strong, with red hair. He too was a Dentu, the child's uncle, another brother of the father. And he duly bestowed the name of Prosper-César upon his nephew, who began to cry when he tasted the symbolic salt.

When the ceremony was over, the family waited on the steps while the priest took off his surplice; then they started off once more. They went fast now, for there was the prospect of dinner before them. A crowd of urchins followed, and whenever a handful of sweets was thrown to them they struggled furiously; they fought hand to hand and pulled one another's hair; even the dog dashed into the fight for the sweets, more stubborn than the children who tugged at his tail and ears and paws.

The nurse was tired; she turned to the priest walking beside her, and said: "How'd it be, sir, if you was to carry your nevvy for a stretch? Ah'm that cramped in the belly, ah'd like a bit of a rest, like."

The priest took the child in his arms, the white clothes making a broad white stripe over the black cassock. He was embarrassed by the little burden, not knowing how to carry it or set it down. Every one laughed, and one of the grandmothers shouted; "Aren't ye ever sorry, passon, that ye'll never have one of your own?"

The priest made no answer. He went forward with long strides, gazing intently at the blue-eyed baby, longing to kiss the rounded cheeks. He could no longer restrain the impulse; raising the child to his face, he gave it a long kiss.

The father shouted: "Hey there, passon, if ye'd like one, ye've only to say so."

They began to jest, after the fashion of peasants.

As soon as they were seated at table, the rough peasant merriment broke out like a tempest. The two other sons were also to marry soon; their sweethearts were present, invited just for the meal; the guests perpetually alluded to the future generations foreshadowed by these unions.

Their words were coarse and pungent; the blushing girls giggled, the men guffawed. They shouted and beat upon the table with their fists. The father and grandfather were not behindhand with scandalous suggestions. The mother smiled; the old women took their share in the fun and thrust in drastic remarks.

The priest, inured to these rustic orgies, sat quietly beside the nurse, tickling his nephew's little mouth. He seemed surprised at the child's appearance, as though he had never noticed it. He contemplated it with deliberate intentness, with dreamy gravity, and a tenderness arose in his heart, a strange, unknown tenderness, sharp and a little melancholy, for the frail little creature that was his brother's son.

He heard nothing, saw nothing, but stared at the child. He wanted to take him once more upon his knees, for still in his breast and in his heart he retained the soft pressure of the infant's body, as when he carried him back from the church.

He was touched by that scrap of humanity as by an ineffable mystery of which he had never before thought, a mystery sacred and august, a new spirit made flesh, the great mystery of new-born life, of wakening love, of the undying race of humanity going on for ever and ever.

The nurse was eating; her eyes shone in her red face. She was worried by the child, who prevented her from getting comfortably near the table.

"Give him to me," said the priest; "I'm not hungry." And he took the child. Then everything around him faded and disappeared; his eyes were fixed on the chubby pink face. Little by little the warmth of the tiny body penetrated through the shawls and the cassock to his legs, like a caress, so light, so good, so pure, so sweet, that his eyes filled with tears.

The noise of the revellers became terrific. The child, disturbed by the uproar, began to cry.

A voice sang out: "Hey there, parson, feed your baby."

And a burst of laughter shook the room. But the mother had risen; she took her son and carried him into the next room. She came back a few minutes later announcing that he was fast asleep in his cradle.

The meal went on. From time to time men and women went out into the yard, then returned and sat down again. The meat, the vegetables, the cider, and the wine coursed down their throats, swelled their bellies, excited their spirits.

Night was falling when the coffee came in.

Long before then the priest had vanished, his absence arousing no surprise.

At last the young mother rose to see if the child were still asleep. It was dark now. She entered the room on tiptoe, and advanced with arms outstretched, so as not to knock against the furniture. But a strange noise made her stop, and she hurried out again in a fright, sure that she had heard someone move. Pale and trembling, she regained the dining-room and told her story. The men rose noisily, drunk and angry, and the father, a lamp in his hand, rushed out.

The priest was on his knees beside the cradle, sobbing. His forehead rested on the pillow, beside the child's head.

THE CONFESSION

THE ENTIRE POPULATION OF VÉZIERS-LE-RÉTHEL HAD followed Monsieur Badon-Leremincé to his grave; in every memory lingered still the last words of the prefect's funeral oration: "An honourable man has gone from us."

Honourable he had been in every visible action throughout his life, in his speech, in the example he set, in his appearance, in his bearing, in his gait, in the cut of his beard and the shape of his hats. He had never spoken a word which did not contain a precept, never given alms without adding a piece of advice, never held out his hand without the air of bestowing a benediction.

He left two children, a son and a daughter; his son was on the town council, and his daughter, who had married a solicitor, Monsieur Poirel de la Voulte, moved in the best circles in Véziers.

They were inconsolable at their father's death, for they loved him sincerely.

As soon as the ceremony was over, they returned to the house of death. All three, son, daughter, and son-in-law, shut themselves up in a room and opened the will, which was to be unsealed by them alone, and only after the coffin had been deposited in its resting-place. This request was conveyed to them by a brief note on the envelope.

Monsieur Poirel de la Voulte, as a lawyer accustomed to such proceedings, opened the envelope. After adjusting his spectacles, he read it out to them in a dry voice fitted for the recital of legal details.

"My children, my dear children, I could not rest quietly in my last sleep did I not make this confession to you from beyond the grave. It is the confession of a crime which I have regretted with a bitterness that has poisoned my life. Yes, I am guilty of a crime, a frightful, appalling crime.

" I was twenty-six years old at the time, and had just been called to the bar in Paris. There I lived like any other young provincial stranded in the city without acquaintances, friends, or relatives.

" I took a mistress. How many people there are whom the word ' mistress ' revolts! Yet there are people who cannot live alone. I am one of them. Solitude fills me with a frightful agony, solitude at night, at home by the fireside. At such times I feel as though I were alone on earth, terribly alone, but surrounded with vague dangers, strange, fearful perils. The thin wall which separates me from my neighbour, the neighbour I do not know, keeps me as far from him as from the stars I see from my window. I am overcome with a sort of fever, a fever of impatience and fear, and the silent walls terrify me. It is so deep and so sad, the silence of a room in which one lives alone. It is not only a silence round about the body, but a silence about the soul, and when a piece of furniture creaks, a shiver runs through the heart, for in this sorrowful place any sound comes as a surprise.

" Often, unnerved and distracted by this terrifying silence, I have begun to speak, to babble words without sense or reason, just for the sake of making a noise. At these times my voice sounded so strange that I was afraid of it too. Is there anything more terrifying than talking to oneself in an empty house? One's voice seems to be another's, an unknown voice, speaking without cause, speaking to nobody, in the hollow air, with no human ear to hear. For one knows, even before they escape into the solitude of the room, the words which are about to come from one's mouth, and when they resound mournfully in the silence, they sound no more than an echo, the strange echo of words murmured in an undertone by the brain.

" I took a mistress, a young girl just like all the young girls who work in Paris at a profession too poorly paid to keep them. She was a sweet, good little thing; her parents lived at Poissy. Occasionally she would go to spend a few days with them.

" For a year I lived uneventfully with her, fully intending to leave her as soon as I should find a girl attractive enough for me to marry. I proposed to leave her a small income, for among people of our class it is commonly acknowledged that a woman's love must be paid for, in cash when she is poor, in presents when she is rich.

" But one day she informed me that she was going to have a child. I was aghast; in a flash I foresaw the ruin of my whole life. I saw the chain I was doomed to drag with me till the day of my death, everywhere I went, in my future family life, in my old age, for ever: the chain of the woman bound to my life by the child, the chain of this child which must be brought up, watched, protected, while all the time the secret must be kept from it and from the world. I was utterly cast down by the news, and a vague desire—a desire I never expressed, but felt in my heart ready to leap out, like men hidden behind doors waiting the word to spring—a criminal desire lurked in the recesses of my mind. Supposing there were an accident. So many of these little creatures die before they are born.

" Oh! I had no wish to see my mistress die. Poor girl, I loved her well. But perhaps I desired the death of the other, before I saw it.

" The child was born. In my little bachelor apartment was a family, a sham family with a child; an unnatural thing. The child was like all babies. I did not love it. Fathers, you know, do not love till later. They have not the natural passionate tenderness that belongs to mothers; their affections have to wake little by little, their souls come upon love little by little, through those bonds which each day draws closer between human beings who share each other's lives.

"Another year went by; now I shunned my cramped little house, littered with linen and swaddling-clothes and socks the size of gloves, a thousand objects of all kinds lying on a table, on the arms of a chair, everywhere. Above all I kept away so as not to hear him cry, for he cried on every occasion, when his clothes were changed, when he was washed, when he was put to bed, indeed always.

"I had made some friendships, and in a drawing-room one day I met your mother. I fell in love with her, and the desire to marry her woke in my heart. I wooed her and asked her hand in marriage; it was granted me.

"And there I was, caught in a trap. I must marry this young girl I adored, already having a child of my own—or I must tell the truth and renounce her, my happiness, my future, everything; for her parents, who were very strict, would never have consented to the marriage if they had known all.

"I spent a terrible month of agonising moral torment, a month during which a thousand terrible thoughts haunted me. And ever growing within me I felt a hatred for my son, for that little scrap of living, weeping flesh who barred my way, cut my life in two, and condemned me to a cheerless existence without any one of the vague hopes which are the charm of youth.

"Then my mistress' mother fell ill, and I was left alone with the child.

"It was December, and frightfully cold. What a night! My mistress had just gone; I had dined alone in the little parlour, and softly entered the room where the baby slept.

"I sat before the fire in an arm-chair. A dry, icy wind blew outside and rattled the window panes, and through the window I could see the stars glitter with that keen light they have on frosty nights.

"Then the obsession which for the last month had haunted me entered into my head anew. The moment I sat still it descended upon me and gnawed my brain. It gnawed me as fixed ideas do, as cancer must gnaw the flesh. I felt it there in my head, in my heart, in my whole body ; it devoured me like a wild beast. I tried to hunt it away, to drive it off, to open my mind to other thoughts, to new hopes, as one opens a window in the morning to let out the tainted air of the night ; but not for a single instant could I chase it from my brain. I do not know how to describe this torture. It nibbled at my soul, and I felt every movement of its teeth with horrible pain, a veritable anguish of body and soul.

" My life was over ! How was I to escape from this dilemma ? How draw back and how confess ?

" And I loved your mother madly ; that made the insurmountable obstacle still more frightful.

" A terrible rage grew in me, tightening my throat, a rage which was akin to madness . . . madness ! Yes, I was mad, that night !

" The child was asleep. I rose and watched it sleeping. It was he, that abortion, that mite, that nothing, who condemned me to hopeless misery.

" He slept, with his mouth open, under a heap of blankets, in a cradle near the bed in which *I* could not sleep.

" How did I do what I did ? Do I know ? What force led me on, what evil power possessed me ? Oh, the temptation came to me without my realising how it made its presence known. I remember only that my heart beat furiously, so violently that I heard it like the strokes of a hammer from behind a wall. That is all I remember—my heart beating. In my head was a strange confusion, a tumult, a routing of all reason, all common sense. I was in one of those hours of terror and hallucination wherein man has no longer knowledge of his actions nor control of his will.

" Softly I raised the coverings which hid my child's body ; I threw them on the foot of the cradle, and saw him stark-naked. He did not wake. Then I went to the window, softly, so softly ; and I opened it.

"A blast of icy air rushed in like a murderer, so bitterly cold that I fell back before it; and the two candles flickered. And I remained standing by the window, not daring to turn round, as if not to see what was happening behind me, and always feeling, gliding over my temples, my cheeks, my hands, the deathly air which flowed into the room in a steady stream. It went on a long time.

"I did not think, I considered nothing. Suddenly a little cough sent a dreadful shiver through me from head to foot, a shiver I can feel at this moment, in the roots of my hair. With a wild movement I slammed the window down and, turning round, ran to the cradle.

"He was still asleep, with open mouth, stark-naked. I touched his legs; they were frozen, and I pulled up the coverings.

"My heart suddenly softened, snapped, was filled with pity, tenderness, and love for the poor innocent wretch I had wanted to kill. I pressed a long kiss on his thin hair, then sat down again by the fireside.

"I thought with stupor, with horror, of what I had done; I wondered whence came these tempests of the soul wherein man loses all awareness of things, all control over himself, and acts under a kind of mad intoxication, not knowing what he does, nor where he goes, like a ship in a hurricane.

"The child coughed once more, and my heart was rent in two. If he were to die! Oh, my God! my God! What would become of me?

"I got up to go and look at him; and, a candle in my hand, I bent over him. Seeing him breathing quietly, I was reassured; he coughed a third time, and I was seized with a terrible shudder, and started so violently back—as a man might when distracted at the sight of some frightful happening—that I let the candle fall.

"When I straightened myself after picking it up I observed that my temples were drenched with the sweat of agony, a sweat hot and icy at once, as though some part of the frightful moral suffering and unspeakable torture, which does actually burn like fire and freeze like ice, were oozing out through the skin and bone of my skull.

" Till daybreak I remained beside the cradle, calming my fears when he remained quiet for a long stretch, and enduring terrible agonies when a feeble cough issued from his mouth.

" He awoke with red eyes and a sore throat, obviously ill.

" When the charwoman came, I sent her out at once for a doctor. He came at the end of an hour, and after examining the child, he said :

" ' Has he not been cold ? "

" ' No, I don't think so,' I stammered, trembling like a very old man.

" Then I asked :

" ' What is it ? Is it serious ? '

" ' I cannot tell yet,' he answered. ' I will come back again this evening.'

" He did come back again that evening. My son had lain almost all day in a deep slumber, coughing from time to time.

" During the night inflammation of the lungs set in.

" It lasted ten days. I cannot tell you what I suffered during those interminable hours which separate dawn from dusk and dusk from dawn.

" He died. . . .

" And since then, since that moment, I have not passed an hour, no, not one hour, without that poignant, fearful memory, that memory which gnaws and twists and rends my spirit, stirring within me like a ravenous beast imprisoned in the bottom of my soul.

" Oh, if I had only been able to go mad ! "

. . .

Monsieur Poirel de la Voulte pushed up his spectacles : it was a gesture customary with him when he had finished reading a deed; and the three looked at one another in silence, pale and motionless.

After a moment the lawyer said: "This must be destroyed."

The other two nodded their assent. He lit a candle, carefully separated the pages containing the dangerous confession from those containing the monetary dispositions, then placed them in the flame of the candle and threw them into the grate.

They watched the white pages burn up. Soon they were only a small black heap. Several letters could still be distinguished, standing out white against the blackened paper, so the daughter crushed the thin shrivelled layer of ash with nervous movements of her toe, and stamped it down among the cold cinders.

For some time longer the three of them stayed watching as though they were afraid that the burnt secret would escape up the chimney.

THE MOTHER OF MONSTERS

I WAS REMINDED OF THIS HORRIBLE STORY AND THIS HORRIBLE woman on the sea-front the other day, as I stood watching—at a watering-place much frequented by the wealthy—a lady well known in Paris, a young, elegant, and charming girl, universally loved and respected.

My story is now many years old, but such things are not forgotten.

I had been invited by a friend to stay with him in a small country town. In order to do the honours of the district, he took me about all over the place; made me see the most celebrated views, the manor-houses and castles, the local industries, the ruins; he showed me the monuments, the churches, the old carved doors, the trees of specially large size or uncommon shape, the oak of St. Andrew and the Roqueboise yew.

When, with exclamations of gratified enthusiasm, I had inspected all the curiosities in the district, my friend confessed, with every sign of acute distress, that there was nothing more to visit. I breathed again. I should be able, at last, to enjoy a little rest under the shade of the trees. But suddenly he exclaimed:

"Why, no, there *is* one more. There's the Mother of Monsters."

"And who," I asked, "is the Mother of Monsters?"

He answered: "She is a horrible woman, a perfect demon, a creature who every year deliberately produces deformed, hideous, frightful children, monsters, in a word, and sells them to peep-show men.

"The men who follow this ghastly trade come from time to time to discover whether she has brought forth any fresh abortion, and if they like the look of the object, they pay the mother and take it away with them.

" She has dropped eleven of these creatures. She is rich.

" You think I'm joking, making it up, exaggerating. No, my friend, I'm only telling you the truth, the literal truth.

" Come and see this woman. I'll tell you afterwards how she became a monster-factory."

He took me off to the outskirts of the town.

She lived in a nice little house by the side of the road. It was pretty and well kept. The garden was full of flowers, and smelt delicious. Anyone would have taken it for the home of a retired lawyer.

A servant showed us into a little parlour, and the wretched creature appeared.

She was about forty, tall, hard-featured, but well built, vigorous, and wealthy, the true type of robust peasantry, half animal and half woman.

She was aware of the disapproval in which she was held, and seemed to receive us with malignant humility.

" What do the gentlemen want ? " she inquired.

My friend replied : " We have been told that your last child is just like any other child, and not in the least like his brothers. I wanted to verify this. Is it true ? "

She gave us a sly glance of anger and answered :

" Oh, no, sir, oh dear no ! He's even uglier, mebbe, than the others. I've no luck, no luck at all, they're all that way, sir, all like that, it's something cruel ; how can the good Lord be so hard on a poor woman left all alone in the world ! "

She spoke rapidly, keeping her eyes lowered, with a hypocritical air, like a scared wild beast. She softened the harsh tone of her voice, and it was amazing to hear these tearful high-pitched words issuing from that great bony body, with its coarse, angular strength, made for violent gesture and wolfish howling.

" We should like to see your child," my friend said.

She appeared to blush. Had I perhaps been mistaken? After some moments of silence she said, in a louder voice: "What would be the use of that to you?"

She had raised her head, and gave us a swift, burning glance.

"Why don't you wish to show him to us?" answered my friend. "There are many people to whom you show him. You know whom I mean."

She started up, letting loose the full fury of her voice.

"So that's what you've come for, is it? Just to insult me? Because my bairns are like animals, eh? Well, you'll not see them, no, no, no, you shan't. Get out of here. I know you all, the whole pack of you, bullying me about like this!"

She advanced towards us, her hands on her hips. At the brutal sound of her voice, a sort of moan, or rather a mew, a wretched lunatic screech, issued from the next room. I shivered to the marrow. We drew back before her.

In a severe tone my friend warned her:

"Have a care, She-devil"—the people all called her She-devil—"have a care, one of these days this will bring you bad luck."

She trembled with rage, waving her arms, mad with fury, and yelling:

"Get out of here, you! What'll bring me bad luck? Get out of here, you pack of beasts, you!"

She almost flew at out throats; we fled, our hearts contracted with horror.

When we were outside the door, my friend asked:

"Well, you've seen her; what do you say to her?"

I answered: "Tell me the brute's history."

And this is what he told me, as we walked slowly back along the white high road, bordered on either side by the ripe corn that rippled like a quiet sea under the caress of a small, gentle wind.

. . . . . .

The girl had once been a servant on a farm, a splendid worker, well-behaved and careful. She was not known to have a lover, and was not suspected of any weakness.

She fell, as they all do, one harvest night among the heaps of corn, under a stormy sky, when the still, heavy air is hot like a furnace, and the brown bodies of the lads and girls are drenched with sweat.

Feeling soon after that she was pregnant, she was tormented with shame and fear. Desirous at all costs of hiding her misfortune, she forcibly compressed her belly by a method she invented, a horrible corset made of wood and ropes. The more the growing child swelled her body, the more she tightened the instrument of torture, suffering agony, but bearing her pain with courage, always smiling and active, letting no one see or suspect anything.

She crippled the little creature inside her, held tightly in that terrible machine; she crushed him, deformed him, made a monster of him. The skull was squeezed almost flat and ran to a point, with the two great eyes jutting right out from the forehead. The limbs, crushed against the body, were twisted like the stem of a vine, and grew to an inordinate length, with the fingers and toes like spiders' legs.

The trunk remained quite small and round like a nut.

She gave birth to it in the open fields one spring morning.

When the women weeders, who had run to her help, saw the beast which was appearing, they fled shrieking. And the story ran round the neighbourhood that she had brought a demon into the world. It was then that she got the name "She-devil."

She lost her place. She lived on charity, and perhaps on secret love, for she was a fine-looking girl, and not all men are afraid of hell.

She brought up her monster, which, by the way, she hated with a savage hatred, and which she would perhaps have strangled had not the *curé*, foreseeing the likelihood of such a crime, terrified her with threats of the law.

At last one day some passing showmen heard tell of the frightful abortion, and asked to see it, intending to take it away if they liked it. They did like it, and paid the mother five hundred francs down for it. Ashamed at first, she did not want to let them see a beast of this sort; but when she discovered that it was worth money, that these people wanted it, she began to bargain, to dispute it penny by penny, inflaming them with the tale of her child's deformities, raising her prices with peasant tenacity.

In order not to be cheated, she made a contract with them. And they agreed to pay her four hundred francs a year as well, as though they had taken this beast into their service.

The unhoped-for good fortune crazed the mother, and after that she never lost the desire to give birth to another phenomenon, so that she would have a fixed income like the upper classes.

As she was very fertile, she succeeded in her ambition, and apparently became expert at varying the shapes of her monsters according to the pressure they were made to undergo during the period of her pregnancy.

She had them long and short, some like crabs and others like lizards. Several died, whereat she was deeply distressed.

The law attempted to intervene, but nothing could be proved. So she was left to manufacture her marvels in peace.

She now has eleven of them alive, which bring her in from five to six thousand francs, year in and year out. One only is not yet placed, the one she would not show us. But she will not keep it long, for she is known now to all the circus proprietors in the world, and they come from time to time to see whether she has anything new.

She even arranges auctions between them, when the creature in question is worth it.

My friend was silent. A profound disgust surged in my heart, a furious anger, and regret that I had not strangled the brute when I had her in my hands.

" Then who is the father ? " I asked.

" Nobody knows," he replied. " He or they have a certain modesty. He, or they, remain concealed. Perhaps they share in the spoils."

. . . . . .

I had thought no more of that far-off adventure until the other day, at a fashionable watering-place, when I saw a charming and elegant lady, the most skilful of coquettes, surrounded by several men who have the highest regard for her.

I walked along the front, arm-in-arm with my friend, the local doctor. Ten minutes later I noticed a nurse looking after three children who were rolling about on the sand.

A pathetic little pair of crutches lay on the ground. Then I saw that the three children were deformed, hunch-backed and lame ; hideous little creatures.

The doctor said to me : " Those are the offspring of the charming lady you met just now."

I felt a profound pity for her and for them.

" The poor mother ! " I cried. " How does she still manage to laugh ? "

" Don't pity her, my dear fellow," replied my friend. " It's the poor children who are to be pitied. That's the result of keeping the figure graceful right up to the last day. Those monsters are manufactured by corsets. She knows perfectly well that she's risking her life at that game. What does she care, so long as she remains pretty and seductive ? "

And I remembered the other, the peasant woman, the She-devil, who sold hers.

OLD JUDAS

THE WHOLE OF THIS DISTRICT WAS AMAZING, MARKED WITH A character of almost religious grandeur and sinister desolation.

In the centre of a great ring of bare hills, where nothing grew but whins and a rare, freakish oak twisted by the wind, there lay a vast, wild tarn, in whose black and stagnant waters shivered thousands of reeds.

A solitary house stood on the banks of this gloomy lake, a small low house inhabited by an old boatman, old Joseph, who lived on the proceeds of his fishing. Every week he carried his fish down to the neighbouring villages, and returned with the simple provisions necessary to his existence.

I had the whim to visit this hermit, and he invited me to come and raise his nets with him.

I accepted.

His boat was a worm-eaten old tub. Thin and bony, he rowed with a quiet, monotonous movement which soothed my spirit, already caught up in the melancholy of the enclosing sky.

Amid this ancient landscape, sitting in this primitive boat, steered by this man from another age, I imagined myself transported to one of the early epochs of the world.

He raised his nets, and threw the fish down at his feet with the gestures of a biblical fisherman. Then he consented to take me to the end of the marsh, and suddenly I saw, on the other bank, a ruin, a gutted hovel, on the wall of which was a cross, a huge red cross: under the last gleams of the setting sun it looked as if it were traced in blood.

"What is that?" I asked.

Instantly the man crossed himself, and answered:

"That is where Judas died."

I was not surprised; I felt as though I might have expected this strange reply.

But I persisted:

"Judas? What Judas?"

He added: "The Wandering Jew, sir."

I begged him to tell me this legend.

But it was better than a legend, it was a piece of history, of almost contemporary history, for old Joseph had known the man.

Once upon a time the hut was occupied by a tall woman, a beggar of sorts, who lived on public charity.

From whom she had got this hovel, old Joseph no longer remembered. One night an old man with a white beard, so old that he looked a centenarian twice over, and could hardly drag one foot after the other, passed by and asked this poor old woman for alms.

She answered:

"Sit down, Father, all here is for all the world, for it comes from all the world."

He sat down on a stone in front of the house. He shared the woman's bread, her bed of leaves, and her house.

He never left her. He had finished his travels.

Old Joseph added:

"It was our Lady the Virgin who permitted that, sir, seeing that a woman had opened her door to Judas."

For this old vagabond was the Wandering Jew.

The country-side did not know this at once, but soon suspected it from the fact that he was always walking, the habit was so strong in him.

Another thing had roused their suspicions. The woman who sheltered the unknown man in her house passed for a Jewess, since she had never been seen at church.

For ten leagues around no one called her anything but "the Jewess."

When the little children of the district saw her coming to beg, they cried out:

" Mother, mother, it's the Jewess ! "

She and the old man began to wander round the neighbourhood, holding their hands out at every door, babbling entreaties after every passer-by. They were seen at all hours of the day, on lonely paths, in village streets, or eating a piece of bread in the shade of a solitary tree, in the fierce heat of noon.

And they began to call the beggar " Old Judas."

One day he brought back in his sack two little live pigs which had been given him at a farm because he had cured the farmer of a sickness.

And soon he stopped begging, wholly occupied in leading his pigs about in search of food, guiding them along the tarn, under the solitary oak-trees, and in the little valleys near by. The woman, on the contrary, wandered ceaselessly in quest of alms, but joined him again every evening.

He never went to church, any more than she, and had never been seen to make the sign of the Cross at the wayside shrines. All this caused a deal of gossip.

One night his companion was taken ill with a fever, and began to shake like a rag in the wind. He went to the town to get medicine, then shut himself up with her, and for six days no one saw him.

But the *curé*, having heard that " the Jewess " was about to pass away, came to bring the dying woman the consolations of his religion, and to offer her the last sacrament. Was she a Jewess ? He did not know. In any event, he wished to try and save her soul.

He had scarcely knocked at the door when old Judas appeared on the threshold, panting, his eyes blazing, all his long white beard quivering like running water : he screamed words of blasphemy in an unknown tongue, stretching out his thin arms to hinder the priest's entry.

The *curé* tried to speak, offered him money and assistance, but the old man continued to revile him, making the gesture of stoning him.

And the priest retreated, pursued by the beggar's curses.

Next day, old Judas's companion died. He buried her himself in front of the doorway. They were so poor that no one interfered with them.

Once more the man was seen leading his pigs along the tarn and on the hillsides. And several times he began begging for food again. But now he got next to nothing, so many stories were going round about him. And every one knew in what a fashion he had welcomed the *curé*.

He disappeared. It was during Holy Week. No uneasiness was felt.

But on Easter Monday some boys and girls who had gone for a walk up to the tarn, heard a great noise in the hut. The door was shut; the boys broke it open and the two pigs escaped, leaping like deer. They were never seen again.

They all entered, and saw on the ground a few old rags, the beggar's hat, some bones, some dried blood and remains of flesh in the hollow of a skull.

His pigs had eaten him.

And old Joseph added:

"It had happened on Good Friday, at three in the afternoon."

I asked him: "How do you know?"

He replied: "It cannot be doubted."

I did not try to make him understand how natural it was for the famished beasts to eat their suffering master if he had died suddenly in his hut.

As for the cross on the wall, it appeared one morning, and no one knew what hand had painted it that strange colour.

After that, none doubted that the Wandering Jew had died in that place.

I believed it myself for an hour.

THÉODULE SABOT'S CONFESSION

WHENEVER SABOT CAME INTO THE PUBLIC-HOUSE OF MARTINville, a roar of laughter went up in anticipation. The fellow was as good as a play. He had no love for parsons, not he! He ate them alive.

Sabot (Théodule), master joiner, represented the radical party at Martinville. He was a tall, thin man with a sly, grey eye, hair brushed on to his temples, and a thin mouth. When he said, "Our holy father the wash-out" in a certain way he had, the whole company yelled with laughter. He was careful to work on Sunday while mass was going on. Every year he killed his pig on the Monday in Holy Week, so as to have black puddings till Easter, and when the priest passed he always said merrily:

"There's the fellow who's just been swallowing his God out of a pint-pot."

The priest, a stout man, also very tall, feared him for his chaff, which won him many supporters. The Reverend Maritime had a diplomatic mind, and liked subtle methods. For ten years the struggle went on between these two, secret, bitter, and incessant. Sabot was on the town council, and it was thought that he would be made mayor, which would certainly constitute the definite defeat of the church.

The elections were about to take place, and the religious party in Martinville trembled for its security. One morning the priest went off to Rouen, telling his servant that he was going to the archbishop's palace.

Two days later he returned, looking joyful and triumphant. Next day every one knew that the chancel of the church was to be restored. His Lordship had given six hundred francs towards it out of his own pocket. All the old deal stalls were to be removed and replaced by new ones of oak. It was an important piece of carpentry, and by the evening every one was talking of it.

Théodule Sabot did not laugh.

When he walked through the village next day, neighbours, friends and enemies alike, all asked him jestingly:

"Is it you who's to do the church choir?"

He found nothing to answer, but his heart was black with rage.

"It's a fine job," they added unkindly. "It's worth a good two or three hundred."

Two days later it was known that the work of repair was to be entrusted to Célestin Chambrelan, the joiner at Percheville. Then the rumour was denied, and then it was announced that all the church pews were to be replaced as well. It would cost quite two thousand francs, and they had appealed to the government for the money. There was great excitement.

Théodule Sabot could not sleep. Never, within the memory of man, had a local joiner executed such a task. Then the story ran that the priest was heart-broken at giving this work to a joiner who was a stranger to the village, but that Sabot's opinions were a barrier that prevented the contract from being entrusted to him.

Sabot knew it. At nightfall he betook himself to the rectory. The servant told him that the priest was at church. He went there.

Two lay sisters, sour old spinsters, were decorating the altar for the month of St. Mary, under the direction of the priest. He stood in the middle of the choir, protruding his enormous stomach, and was superintending the labours of the women who, perched on chairs, were arranging flowers round the shrine.

Sabot felt uneasy there, as though he had entered the house of his deadliest foe, but his avarice spurred him on. He came up cap in hand, taking no notice of the lay sisters, who remained motionless upon their chairs, stupefied with amazement.

"Good evening, parson," he stammered.

"Good evening, joiner," replied the priest without turning his head, engrossed in the work at the altar.

Sabot, who had rather lost his bearings, found nothing more to say. After a pause, however, he added:

"You are making preparations?"

"Yes," replied Maritime, "we are drawing near to the month of St. Mary."

"Quite, quite," said Sabot, and was silent.

He was by now anxious to leave without speaking at all, but a glance at the choir restrained him. He saw that there were sixteen stalls to be repaired, six on the right and eight on the left, the vestry door occupying two places. Sixteen oak stalls were to be had for three hundred francs at the outside, and with a little good management a clever workman could make a clear two hundred francs on the job. He managed to stammer:

"I've come for the work."

The priest looked surprised.

"What work?" he asked.

"The work to be done," murmured Sabot, now quite desperate.

At that the priest turned and stared at him, saying:

"Do you mean the repairs to the choir of my church?"

At the tone adopted by the priest, Théodule Sabot felt a shiver run up his spine, and once more he suffered a violent longing to slink away. But he replied meekly:

"Yes, your Reverence."

The priest crossed his arms on his broad paunch, and said as though thunderstruck with surprise:

"And you . . . you . . . you, Sabot . . . come here and ask me that! . . . You . . . the only infidel in my parish. . . .

Why, it would be a scandal, a public scandal. His Lordship would reprimand me; I might even lose the living."

He paused for a few seconds to regain his breath, then proceeded more calmly:

"I quite understand that it pains you to see a work of such importance entrusted to a joiner from a neighbouring parish. But I cannot do otherwise, unless . . . but no . . . that's impossible. You'd never agree to it, and without that . . . never."

Sabot was now looking at the ranks of pews running right to the west door. Mercy! was all that to be restored?

"What must you have?" he asked. "It can't do any harm telling."

"I must have an overwhelming proof of your good intentions," replied the priest firmly.

"I don't say," murmured Sabot, "I don't say but what an understanding mightn't be come to."

"You must communicate publicly at high mass next Sunday," announced the priest.

The joiner felt himself growing pale and, without answering, asked:

"And the pews, are they all to be done too?"

"Yes," replied the priest with emphasis, "but later on."

"Well, I don't say," replied Sabot. "I don't say. I'm no atheist, I'm not; I've no quarrel with religion. What upsets me is the practice of it, but in a case like this I dare say you'd not find me obstinate."

The lay helpers had descended from their chairs and were hidden behind the altar; they were listening, livid with emotion.

The priest, perceiving that he was victorious, became familiar and jolly at once:

"Splendid! Splendid! Now that's very sensible of you, very sensible. Wait and see."

Sabot smiled uncomfortably, and asked:

"Can't this here communion be put off for a bit, just a little bit?"

But the priest resumed his severe expression.

"From the moment that the contract is given to you, I must be certain of your conversion," he said, then continued more mildly:

"You'd better come and confess to-morrow, for I shall have to examine you at least twice."

"Twice? . . ." repeated Sabot.

"Yes," said the priest with a smile. "You see, you need a thorough cleaning, a complete wash. I expect you to-morrow."

"And where'll you do it?" asked the joiner in dismay.

"Why . . . in the confessional."

"What? . . . In that box over there in the corner? Now look here . . . I don't like your box a bit."

"Why not?"

"Why . . . why, I'm not used to it. And I'm a bit hard of hearing too."

The priest showed himself accommodating.

"Very well. Come to my house, to my study. We'll get it done there privately. Does that suit you?"

"Oh, that'll suit me all right, but that box of yours, no!"

"Well, to-morrow then, after the day's work, at six o'clock."

"Right oh! right you are. That's settled. See you to-morrow, parson, and damn the man who goes back on a bargain."

He held out his huge rough hand, on which the priest let his own fall with a loud smack. The echo ran along the vaulted roof and died in the distance behind the organ pipes.

Throughout the following day Théodule Sabot felt uncomfortable. He suffered an apprehension very like the fear one suffers before having a tooth out. At every moment the thought flashed across his mind: "I've got to confess this evening." And his harried soul, the soul of a not very strongly-convinced atheist, was sorely troubled before the vague powerful terror of the divine mystery.

As soon as his work was over he went off to the priest's house. Its owner was waiting for him in the garden, reading his breviary as he walked up and down a small path. He seemed delighted to see him and welcomed him with a hearty laugh.

" Ah—here we are, then! Come in, come in, Monsieur Sabot; no one will eat you."

Sabot entered the house first.

" If it's all the same to you," he faltered, " I'd like to see my little affair through at once like."

" At your service," replied the priest. " My surplice is here. One minute, and I'm ready to listen to you."

The joiner, so distressed that his mind was a blank, watched him put on the white garment with its pleated folds. The priest signed to him:

" Kneel down on that hassock."

But Sabot remained standing, ashamed at having to kneel.

" Does it do any good?" he stammered.

But the priest had become majestic.

" Only upon the knees," he said, " may the tribunal of repentance be approached."

Sabot knelt.

" Recite the Confiteor," said the priest.

" Eh? . . ." asked Sabot.

" The Confiteor. If you no longer know it, repeat one by one the words I am about to utter."

And the priest pronounced the sacred prayer in a slow voice, scanning each word for the joiner, who repeated it after him.

" Now confess," he said.

But Sabot said nothing, not knowing where to begin.

Then the Reverend Maritime came to his aid.

" Since you seem to be rather out of practice, my child, I will question you. We will take the commandments of God one by one. Listen to me and do not distress yourself. Speak very frankly and never be afraid of confessing too much.

" 'Thou shalt worship one God alone and adore Him with all thy heart.' Have you loved anyone or anything as much as God? Have you loved Him with all your soul, with all your heart, with all the strength of your love?"

Sabot perspired with the effort of thought.

"No," he replied. "Oh, no, your Reverence. I love the good God as much as I can. Oh, Lord! Yes, I love Him all right. As for saying I don't love my children, no. I can't say that. As for saying if I had to choose between them and the good God, as for that I won't say. As for saying if I had to lose a hundred francs for love of the good God, as for that I won't say. But I love Him all right, that's quite certain. I love Him just the same."

"You must love Him more than anything," said the priest gravely.

And Sabot, full of goodwill, declared:

"I'll do my best, your Reverence."

" 'Thou shalt not swear vainly by the name of God, nor by any other,'" resumed Maritime. "Have you occasionally sworn oaths?"

"No—oh, no, not that! I never swear, never. Sometimes, in a moment of hot temper like, I may say 'God blast.' But I never swear."

"But that is swearing," said the priest, and added severely: "Don't do it any more. I pass on to the next: 'Thou shalt spend the Sabbath in serving God devotedly.' What do you do on Sundays?"

This time Sabot scratched his ear.

"Well, I serve the good God in the best way I can, your Reverence. I serve Him . . . at home. I work on Sundays. . . ."

The priest magnanimously interrupted him:

"I know you will behave better in the future. I pass over the three next commandments, as I am sure you have not sinned against the two first, and we will take the sixth with the ninth. To proceed: 'Thou shalt not take another's goods, nor retain them wittingly.' Have you ever in any way taken what did not belong to you?"

Théodule Sabot was indignant:

"Certainly not! Certainly not, your Reverence! I'm an honest man, that I swear. As for saying that I've not once or twice taken an extra hour over a job when I could, as for that I won't say. As for saying that I've never put a few centimes on to a bill, only a few centimes, as for that I won't say. But I'm not a thief, oh, Lord, no!"

"Taking a single centime constitutes a theft," answered the priest severely. "Don't do it again.—'Thou shalt not bear false witness nor lie in any way.' Have you told lies?"

"No! that I haven't. I'm not a liar; that's one of the things I pride myself on. As for saying that I've never told a tall story, as for that I won't say. As for saying that I've never tried to make another fellow believe what wasn't true, when it suited me, as for that I won't say. But as for being a liar, well, I'm no liar."

"You must keep a closer watch upon yourself," said the priest simply. Then he pronounced: 'The works of the flesh thou shalt not desire save only in marriage.' Have you ever desired or possessed any woman but your own wife?"

"No!" cried Sabot sincerely. "Certainly not, your Reverence! Deceive my poor wife? No! No! Not so much as with the tip of my finger, and no more in thought than in deed. I swear that." He paused for a few moments, and then continued in a lower voice, as though a sudden doubt had assailed him:

"As for saying that when I go to town I don't ever go to a house—you know what I mean, a gay house—and fool about a bit and have a change of skin for once—as for that I won't say. . . . But I pay, your reverence, I always pay; and if you pay, that's that, eh?"

The priest did not insist, and gave him absolution.

Théodule Sabot is at work on the repairs to the choir, and goes to communion every month.

THE RETURN

THE SEA IS FRETTING THE SHORE WITH SMALL RECURRING waves. Small white clouds pass rapidly across the wide blue sky, swept along like birds by the swift wind; and the village, in a fold of a valley which descends to the sea, lies drowsing in the sun.

By the side of the road, at the very entrance to the village, stands the lonely dwelling of the Martin-Lévesques. It is a little fisherman's cottage with clay walls and a roof of thatch made gay with tufts of blue iris. There is a square patch of front garden the size of a pocket-handkerchief, containing onions, some cabbages, parsley, and *chevril*, and separated from the road by a hedge.

The man is out fishing, and his wife is sitting in front of the house, mending the meshes of a large brown net spread upon the wall like a gigantic spider's web. A little girl of fourteen is sitting near the gate in a cane-chair tilted back and supported against the fence; she is mending linen, miserable stuff already well darned and patched. Another girl a year younger is rocking in her arms a tiny child still too young to walk or talk, and two mites of two and three are squatting on the ground, opposite each other, digging in the earth with clumsy fingers and throwing handfuls of dust in one another's faces.

No one speaks. Only the baby that is being rocked to sleep cries incessantly in a weak, thin, small voice. A cat is asleep on the window-sill; some faded pinks at the foot of the wall make a fine patch of white blossom, over which a swarm of flies is humming.

The little girl sewing by the gate cries out abruptly:

"Mother!"

"What is it?" her mother answers.

"He's here again."

Ever since the morning they have been uneasy, for a man has been prowling round the house, an old man who looks like a beggar. They saw him as they were taking their father to his ship, to see him on board. He was sitting in the ditch opposite their gate. Then, when they came back from the sea-shore, they saw him still looking at the house.

He looked ill and very wretched. For more than an hour he had not stirred; then, seeing that they took him for a bad character, he had got up and gone off, dragging one leg behind him.

But before long they had seen him return with his weary limp, and he had sat down again, a little farther off this time, as though to spy upon them.

The mother and the little girls were afraid. The mother was particularly uneasy, for she was by nature timid, and her husband, Lévesque, was not due back from the sea before nightfall.

Her husband's name was Lévesque, and hers was Martin, and the pair had been baptized Martin-Lévesque. This is why: her first husband had been a sailor named Martin who went every summer to the Newfoundland cod-fisheries. After two years of married life she had borne him a little daughter and was six months gone with another child, when her husband's ship, the *Two Sisters*, a three-masted barque from Dieppe, disappeared.

No news of her was ever heard, no member of the crew returned, and she was believed lost with all hands.

For ten years Madame Martin waited for her man, having a hard struggle to bring up the two children. Then, as she was a fine, strong woman, a local fisherman named Lévesque, a widower with one son, asked her to marry him. She consented, and bore him two other children in three years.

Their life was hard and laborious. Bread was dear, and

meat almost unknown in the household. Sometimes they were in debt to the baker, in the winter, during the stormy months. But the children grew up strong; the neighbours said:

" They're good folk, the Martin-Lévesques. She's as hard as nails, and there's no better fisherman than Lévesque."

The little girl sitting by the fence went on:

" He looks as though he knew us. Perhaps he's some beggar from Épreville or Auzebosc."

But the mother was sure of the truth. No, no, he wasn't a local man, that was certain.

As he remained motionless as a log, his eyes fixed obstinately upon the cottage, Madame Martin lost her temper; fear lending her courage, she seized a spade and went out in front of the gate.

" What are you doing there?" she cried to the vagabond.

" I'm taking the air," he replied in a hoarse voice. " Am I doing you any harm?"

" What are you playing the spy for round my house?" she replied.

" I'm doing no one any harm," he answered. " Can't I sit down by the roadside?"

Not finding an answer, she went back into the house.

Slowly the day dragged by. Round about midday the man disappeared. But near five o'clock he wandered past once more. He was not seen again that evening.

Lévesque came home at nightfall and was told of the affair.

" Some dirty rascal slinking about the place," he decided.

He went to bed with no anxiety, while his wife dreamed of this tramp who had stared at her with such strange eyes.

When dawn came a gale was blowing, and the sailor, seeing that he could not put out to sea, helped his wife to mend the nets.

About nine o'clock the eldest girl, one of Martin's children, who had gone out for some bread, ran in with a scared face, and cried:

" He's back again, mother."

Her mother felt a prick of excitement ; very pale, she said to her husband :

" Go and tell him not to spy on us like this, Lévesque ; it's fairly getting on my nerves."

Lévesque was a big fisherman with a brick-red face, a thick red beard, blue eyes with gleaming black pupils, and a strong neck always well wrapped up in a woollen scarf, to protect him from the wind and rain of the open sea. He went out calmly and marched up to the tramp.

And they began to talk.

The mother and children watched from the distance, trembling with excitement.

Suddenly the unknown man got up and accompanied Lévesque towards the house.

Madame Martin recoiled from him in terror. Her husband said :

" Give him a bit of bread and a mug of cider ; he hasn't had a bite since the day before yesterday."

The two of them entered the cottage, followed by the woman and the children. The tramp sat down and began to eat, his head lowered before their gaze.

The mother stood and stared at him ; the two eldest daughters, Martin's children, leaned against the door, one of them holding the youngest child, and stared eagerly at him. The two mites sitting among the cinders in the fire-place stopped playing with the black pot, as though to join in gaping at the stranger.

Lévesque sat down and asked him :

" Then you've come from far ? "

" From Cette."

" On foot, like that ? "

" Yes. When you've no money, you must."

" Where are you going ? "

" I was going here."

" Know anyone in these parts ? "

" Maybe."

They were silent. He ate slowly, although ravenous, and took a sip of cider between each mouthful of bread. His face was worn and wrinkled, full of hollows, and he had the air of a man who has suffered greatly.

Lévesque asked him abruptly:

"What's your name?"

He answered without raising his head:

"My name is Martin."

A strange shudder ran through the mother. She made a step forward as though to get a closer view of the vagabond, and remained standing in front of him, her arms hanging down and her mouth open. No one spoke another word. At last Lévesque said:

"Are you from these parts?"

"Yes, I'm from these parts."

And as he at last raised his head, his eyes met the woman's and remained gazing at them; it was as though their glances were riveted together.

Suddenly she said in an altered voice, low and trembling:

"Is it you, husband?"

"Yes, it's me," he said slowly.

He did not move, but continued to munch his bread.

Lévesque, surprised rather than excited, stammered:

"It's you, Martin?"

"Yes, it's me," said the other simply.

"Where have you come from?" asked the second husband.

He told his story:

"From the coast of Africa. We foundered on a reef. Three of us got away, Picard, Vatinel, and me. Then we were caught by savages, who kept us twelve years. Picard and Vatinel are dead. An English traveller rescued me and brought me back to Cette. And here I am."

Madame Martin had begun to cry, hiding her face in her apron.

"What are we to do now?" said Lévesque.

" Is it you that's her husband ? " asked Martin.

" Yes, it's me," replied Lévesque.

They looked at one another and were silent.

Then Martin turned to the circle of children round him and, nodding towards the two girls, asked :

" Are those mine ? "

" Yes, they're yours," said Lévesque.

He did not get up ; he did not kiss them. He only said :

" God, they're big ! "

" What are we to do ? " repeated Lévesque.

Martin, perplexed, had no idea. Finally he made up his mind :

" I'll do as you wish. I don't want to wrong you. But it's annoying when I think of the house. I've two children, you've three. Each has his own. As for the mother, is she yours, or shall I have her ? I agree to whatever you like, but as for the house, that's mine, for my father left it me, I was born in it, and the lawyer's got the papers about it."

Madame Martin was still crying, stifling her short gasps in the blue canvas of her apron. The two tall girls had drawn nearer and were looking uneasily at their father.

He had finished eating, and said in his turn :

" What are we to do ? "

Lévesque had an idea :

" We must get the priest. He'll decide."

Martin rose, and as he went towards his wife she flung herself upon his breast, sobbing :

" It's you, husband ! Martin, my poor Martin, it's you ! "

She held him in her arms, suddenly stirred by a breath of the past, by an anguished rush of memories that reminded her of her youth and of her first kisses.

Martin, much affected, kissed her bonnet. The two children by the fire-place both began to cry when they heard their mother cry, and the youngest of all, in the arms of the younger Martin daughter, howled in a shrill voice like a fife out of tune.

Lévesque stood up and waited.

" Come on," he said. " We must get it put straight."

Martin let go of his wife and, as he was looking at his two daughters, their mother said :

" You might kiss your dad."

They came up together, dry-eyed, surprised, a little frightened. He kissed them one after another, on both cheeks, with a loud, smacking kiss. The baby, seeing the stranger draw near, screamed so violently that it nearly fell into convulsions.

Then the two men went out together.

As they passed the Café du Commerce, Lévesque asked :

" How about a little drink ? "

" Yes, I could do with some," declared Martin.

They went in and sat down in the room, which was still empty. Lévesque shouted :

" Hey, there, Chicot, two double brandies, and the best ! It's Martin, he's come back ; Martin, you know, my wife's man ; Martin of the *Two Sisters*, that was lost."

The barman came up, three glasses in one hand and a pitcher of water in the other, a red-faced, podgy, pot-bellied man. In a calm voice he asked :

" Ah ! So here you are, then, Martin ? "

Martin answered :

" Here I am."

THE CASTAWAY

"REALLY, DEAR, I THINK YOU MUST BE MAD TO GO FOR A WALK in the country in this weather. For the last two months you've had the oddest ideas. You drag me willy-nilly to the seaside, though you never thought of such a thing before in all the forty-five years of our married life. You insist on Fécamp, a melancholy hole, and now you've got such a passion for rushing about, you who could never be induced to stir out, that you want to walk about the fields on the hottest day of the year. Tell d'Apreval to go with you, since he falls in with all your whims. As for me, I'm going in to have a rest."

Madame de Cadour turned to her old friend :

"Are you coming with me, d'Apreval ?"

He bowed and smiled with old-world gallantry.

"Where you go, I go," he said.

"Very well, go and get sunstroke," said Monsieur de Cadour, and re-entered the Hôtel des Bains to lie down on his bed for an hour or two.

As soon as they were alone, the old woman and her aged companion started off. She clasped his hand and said very softly :

"At last! At last!"

"You are mad," he murmured. "I assure you you're mad. Think of the risk. If that man. . . ."

She started violently.

"Oh, Henry, don't call him that man."

"Well," he continued in a brusque voice, "if our son has any notions, if he suspects us, he's got you, he's got us both. You've done without seeing him for forty years. What's the matter with you now, then ?"

They had followed the long road which leads from the sea to the town. They turned to the right to climb the hill of Étretat. The white road unwound itself before them under the blazing rain of sunlight. They walked slowly in the burning heat, taking short steps. She had taken her friend's arm and was walking straight ahead with a fixed, haunted stare.

"So you've never seen him again either?" she said.

"No, never."

"Is it possible?"

"My dear friend, don't let us begin this eternal discussion all over again. I have a wife and children, just as you have a husband; so that each of us has everything to fear from public opinion."

She did not answer. She was thinking of her lost youth, of old, unhappy, far-off things.

She had been married by her family, as a young girl is married. She hardly knew her betrothed, a diplomat, and later she lived with him the life of any woman of fashion.

Then, however, a young man, Monsieur d'Apreval, married like herself, fell passionately in love with her; and during a long absence of Monsieur de Cadour on a political mission in India, she yielded to him.

Could she have resisted? Could she have denied herself? Would she have had the courage, the strength, not to yield?—for she loved him too. No, certainly no! It would have been too hard! She would have suffered too deeply! How crafty and cruel is life! Can we avoid these temptations, or fly from inevitable destiny? How can a woman, alone, deserted, without love, without children, continue to run away from a passion surging in her? It is as though she fled from the light of the sun, to live to the end of her life in darkness.

And how plainly she remembered now the little things, his kisses, his smile, the way he stopped at the door to look at her, whenever he came to her house. What happy days, her only happy days, so soon over!

Then she discovered that she was with child; what agony!

Oh! the long terrible journey to the south, her misery, her incessant fear, her life hidden in the lonely little cottage on the shores of the Mediterranean, in the depths of the garden she dared not go beyond.

How well she remembered the long days she spent lying under an orange-tree, her eyes lifted to the round flaming fruit in the green foliage! How she longed to go out, to go down to the sea, whose sweet scent came to her over the wall, whose little waves she heard upon the beach; and dreamed perpetually of its wide blue surface glittering in the sun, flecked with white sails, and rimmed by a mountain. But she dared not go through the gate. Supposing she were recognised, in this state, her altered figure crying her shame!

And the days of waiting, the last few tormenting days! The fears! The threatening pains! Then the awful night! What misery she had endured!

What a night it had been! How she had moaned and screamed! She could see even now the pale face of her lover, kissing her hand every minute, the doctor's smooth countenance, the nurse's white cap.

And what a convulsion she had felt in her heart at the child's shrill feeble cry, the first effort of a man's voice!

And the day after! The day after! The only day of her life on which she had seen and kissed her son, for never afterwards had she as much as set eyes on him!

Then, after that time, the long empty life, the thought of this child floating always in the void of her mind! She had never seen him again, not once, the little being who was her flesh and blood, her son! He had been seized, carried off, and hidden! She knew only that he was being brought up by Norman peasants, that he had himself become a peasant, that he had married, with a good dowry from the father whose name he did not know.

How many times, in the last forty years, she had longed to go away to see him, to kiss him! She did not think of him as grown up. She dreamed always of that scrap of humanity she had held for one day in her arms, clasped to her tortured body.

How many times she had said to her lover: "I can hold out no longer; I must see him; I am going!"

Always he had restrained her, held her back. She would not know how to contain herself, how to master her emotion. The man would guess, and would exploit the secret. She would be ruined.

"How is he?" she said.

"I don't know. I've never seen him again either."

"Is it possible? To have a son and not know him! To be afraid of him, to have cast him away as a disgrace!"

It was horrible.

They were still walking up the long road, oppressed by the blazing sun, still mounting the interminable hillside.

"It's like a judgment, isn't it?" she continued. "I've never had another child. I could no longer fight my desire to see him; it's haunted me for forty years. A man couldn't understand these things. Remember that I am very near death. And I shall not have seen him again . . . never again; is it possible? How can I have waited so long? I've thought of him all my life, and what a terrible existence the thought has made it! Not once have I awakened, not once, do you hear, without my first thought being for him, for my child! How is he? Oh, how guilty I feel before him! Ought one to fear the world in such a case? I should have left all and followed him, brought him up, loved him. I should have been happier then, surely. But I did not dare. I was a coward. How I have suffered! Oh, those poor abandoned creatures, how they must hate their mothers!"

She stopped abruptly, choked with sobs. The whole valley

was deserted and silent in the overpowering blaze of sunlight. Only the crickets uttered their harsh, ceaseless note in the thin brown grass at the roadside.

" Sit down for a little," he said.

She let him lead her to the edge of the ditch, and sank down upon the grass, burying her face in her hands. Her white hair, falling in curls on each side of her face, became dishevelled, and she wept, torn by her bitter grief.

He remained standing in front of her, uneasy, not knowing what to say to her.

" Come . . . be brave," he murmured.

" I will be," she said, rising to her feet. She dried her eyes and walked on with the shaky steps of an old woman.

A little further on the road ran under a group of trees which hid several houses. They could now hear the regular vibrant shock of a blacksmith's hammer on the anvil. Soon they saw, on the right, a cart halted before a kind of low house, and, in a shed, two men shoeing a horse.

Monsieur d'Apreval went up to them.

" Pierre Bénédict's farm ? " he asked.

" Take the road on the left," answered one, " right by the little inn, and go straight on ; it's the third after Poret's. There's a young pine by the fence. You can't miss it."

They turned to the left. She was going very slowly now, her legs flagging, her heart thudding so violently that it snatched her breath away. At every step she muttered, as though it were a prayer :

" My God ! Oh, my God ! "

A violent access of emotion contracted her throat, making her totter on her feet as though she had been hamstrung.

Monsieur d'Apreval, nervous and rather pale, said sharply :

" If you can't control yourself better, you'll betray us at once. Try to master your feelings."

" How can I ? " she faltered. " My child ! When I think that I'm about to see my child ! "

They followed one of those little lanes that run between one farmyard and another, shut in between a double row of beeches along the roadside.

Suddenly they found themselves in front of a wooden gate shaded by a young pine-tree.

"Here it is," he said.

She stopped short and looked round.

The yard, which was planted with apple-trees, was large, stretching right up to the little thatched farmhouse. Facing it were the stables, the barn, the cow-house, and the chicken-run. Under a slate-roofed shed stood the farm vehicles, a two-wheeled cart, a wagon, and a gig. Four calves cropped the grass, which was very green where the trees shaded it. The black hens wandered into every corner of the enclosure.

There was no sound to be heard; the door of the house was open, but no one was in sight.

They entered the yard. At once a black dog leapt out of an old barrel at the foot of a large pear-tree and began to bark furiously.

Against the wall of the house, on the way to the door, four beehives stood upon a plank, the straw domes in a neat line.

Halting in front of the house, Monsieur d'Apreval shouted:

"Is anyone in?"

A child appeared, a little girl of about ten, dressed in a bodice and woollen petticoat, with bare and dirty legs. She looked timid and sullen, and stood still in the doorway, as though to defend the entry.

"What d'you want?" she said.

"Is your father in?"

"No."

"Where is he?"

"I dunno."

"And your mother?"

"She's with the cows."

"Will she be back soon?"

"I dunno."

The old woman cried out abruptly in a hurried voice, as though fearing to be forcibly dragged away:

"I won't go without seeing him."

"We'll wait, my dear."

As they turned round, they caught sight of a peasant woman coming towards the house, carrying two heavy-looking tin pails on which the sun from time to time flashed with a brilliant white flame.

She was lame in the right leg, and her chest was muffled in a rusty brown knitted garment, stained and bleached by rain and sun. She looked like some poor servant, dirty and wretched.

"There's mother," said the child.

When she was near her dwelling she regarded the strangers with an evil, suspicious look; then went into the house as though she had not seen them.

She looked old; her face was hollowed, yellow, hard, the wooden face of rustics.

Monsieur d'Apreval called her back.

"I say, we came in to ask you to sell us two glasses of milk."

Having set down her pails, she reappeared in the doorway and muttered:

"I don't sell milk."

"We're very thirsty. The lady is old and very tired. Can't we get something to drink?"

The peasant woman stared at him with surly, uneasy eyes. At last she made up her mind.

"Seeing you're here, I'll give you some all the same," she said, disappearing into the house.

Then the child came out carrying two chairs, which she set under an apple-tree; and the mother came, in her turn, with two foaming cups of milk that she placed in the visitors' hands.

She remained standing in front of them as though to keep watch on them and guess their intentions.

" You're from Fécamp ? " she said.

" Yes," replied Monsieur d'Apreval, " we're there for the summer."

Then, after a pause, he added : " Could you sell us chickens every week ? "

She hesitated, then replied ;

" I might. Would you be wanting young birds ? "

" Yes, young ones."

" What do you pay for them at market ? "

D'Apreval, who did not know, turned to his companion : " What do you pay for chicken, dear—young ones ? "

" Four francs and four francs fifty," she faltered, her eyes full of tears.

The farmer's wife looked sideways at her, much surprised, and asked :

" Is the poor lady ill, that she's cryin' ? "

He did not know what to answer, and stammered :

" No. . . . No. . . . She . . . she lost her watch on the way, a beautiful watch, and it grieves her. If anyone picks it up, let us know."

Madame Bénédict thought this queer, and did not answer. Suddenly she said :

" Here's my husband."

She alone had seen him come in, for she was facing the gate. D'Apreval started violently ; Madame de Cadour nearly fell as she turned frantically round in her chair.

A man was standing ten paces off, leading a cow at the end of a cord, bent double, breathing hard.

" Damn the brute ! " he mu tered, taking no notice of the strangers.

He passed them, going towards the cowshed, in which he disappeared.

The old woman's tears were suddenly dried up ; she was too bewildered for speech or thought : her son, this was her son !

D'Apreval, stabbed by the same thought, said in a troubled voice:

"That is Monsieur Bénédict, is it not?"

"Who told you his name?" asked the farmer's wife, distrustful of them.

"The blacksmith at the corner of the high road," he replied.

Then all were silent, their eyes fixed on the door of the cow-shed, which made a sort of black hole in the wall of the building. They could see nothing inside, but vague sounds were to be heard, movements, steps muffled in the straw strewn on the ground.

He reappeared on the threshold, wiping his brow, and came back towards the house with a long slow step that jerked him up at every pace he took.

Again he passed in front of the strangers without appearing to notice them, and said to his wife:

"Go and draw me a mug of cider; I be thirsty."

Then he entered his dwelling. His wife went off to the cellar, leaving the two Parisians by themselves.

Madame de Cadour was quite distracted.

"Let us go, Henry, let us go," she faltered.

D'Apreval took her arm, helped her to rise, and supporting her with all his strength—for he felt certain that she would fall—he led her away, after throwing five francs on to one of the chairs.

As soon as they had passed through the gate, she began to sob, torn with grief, and stammering:

"Oh! oh! Is this what you've made of him?"

He was very pale.

"I did what I could," he answered harshly. "His farm is worth eighty thousand francs. Many middle-class children haven't such a marriage-portion."

They walked slowly back, without speaking another word. She was still sobbing; the tears ran unceasingly from her eyes and rolled down her cheeks.

At last they stopped, and the pair reached Fécamp.

Monsieur de Cadour was awaiting them for dinner. He began to laugh and cried out at sight of them:

"There you are, my wife's got a sunstroke. I'm delighted at it. Upon my word, I think she's been off her head for some time past."

Neither answered; and as the husband, rubbing his hands, inquired: "At all events, have you had a nice walk?"

D'Apreval replied:

"Delightful, my dear fellow, perfectly delightful."

WHAT THE COLONEL THOUGHT

"I'M AN OLD MAN NOW," SAID COLONEL LAPORTE. "I'VE GOT the gout, and my legs are as stiff as the posts in a fence, but, damn me, if a woman, a pretty woman, ordered me to go through the eye of a needle, I believe I'd jump into it like a clown through a hoop. That's how I shall die; it's in the blood. I'm a veteran ladies' man, I am, an old buffer of the old school. The sight of a woman, a pretty woman, stirs me to my boots. I give you my word it does.

"And we're all like that, gentlemen, we Frenchmen. We remain knights to our dying day, the knights of love and hazard, now that they've done away with God, whose real body-guard we used to be.

"But no one can take woman from our hearts. There she is and there she stops. We love her, and we'll go on loving her; we'll do any sort of madness for her, so long as France remains on the map of Europe. And even if France is wiped out, there will always be Frenchmen.

"As for me, when a woman, a pretty woman, looks at me, I feel capable of anything. Why, damn me, when I feel her eyes, her damned wonderful eyes, peering into me, sending a flame through my veins, I want to do Lord knows what, to fight, to struggle, to smash the furniture, to show that I'm the strongest, bravest, boldest, and most devoted of mankind.

"And I'm not the only one, not by a long way; the whole French Army's just the same, I swear it. From the private up to the general, we all go forward to the end when there's a woman, a pretty woman, in the case. Remember what Joan of Arc made us do in the old days. Well, I bet you that if a woman, a pretty woman, had taken command of the army the night before Sedan, when Marshal MacMahon was wounded, we'd have crossed the Prussian lines, by God! and drunk our brandy from their cannons.

"We didn't need a Trochu in Paris, but a St. Geneviève.

"That reminds me of a little story of the war which proves that, in a woman's presence, we're capable of anything.

"I was a plain captain in those days, and was commanding a detachment of scouts fighting a rear-guard action in the middle of a district overrun by the Prussians. We were cut off and constantly pursued; we were worn out in body and mind, perishing of exhaustion and hunger.

"Well, before the next day we had to reach Bar-sur-Tain or we were done for, cut off and wiped out. How we had escaped so long I don't know. We had twelve leagues to march during the night, on empty stomachs, through the snow, which was thick on the ground and still falling. I thought: 'This is the end; my poor lads will never get through.'

"We had eaten nothing since the previous day. All day long we stayed hidden in a barn, huddled against one another for greater warmth, incapable of motion or speech, sleeping by fits and starts, as men do when utterly exhausted with fatigue.

"It was dark by five o'clock, with the livid darkness of a snowy day. I shook my men; many refused to rise, unable to move or to stand up, their joints stiff with the cold and so forth.

"In front of us stretched the plain, a perfect hell of a plain, without a scrap of cover, with the snow coming down. It fell and fell, like a curtain, in white flakes, hiding everything under a heavy mantle, frozen, thick and dead, a coverlet of icy wool. It was like the end of the world.

"'Come on, boys. Fall in.'

"They looked at it, the white dust coming down from the sky, and seemed to think: 'We've had enough; as well die here.'

"So I pulled out my revolver, saying:

" 'I shoot the first man who funks.'

" And off they went, very slowly, like men whose legs are utterly done for.

" I sent four scouts on in front, three hundred yards ahead; the remainder followed higgledy-piggledy, a confused column, in an order dictated only by the extent of their exhaustion and the length of their steps. I placed the strongest in the rear, with orders to hurry on the laggards with bayonet thrusts . . . in the back.

" The snow buried us alive, so to speak, powdering caps and capes without thawing upon them, making phantoms of us, as though we were the ghosts of soldiers dead of weariness.

" I said to myself: 'We'll never get out of this without a miracle.'

" From time to time we halted for a few minutes for the sake of those who could not keep up. Then no sound could be heard but the faint whisper of the snow, the almost inaudible murmur made by the rush and swirl of the falling flakes.

" Some of the men shook themselves, others did not move.

" Then I would order them to continue the march. Up went the rifles on to their shoulders, and with drowsy limbs they plodded on again.

" Suddenly the scouts came in; something was alarming them. They had heard voices in front of us. I sent six men and a sergeant. And I waited.

" Suddenly a sharp cry, a woman's scream, pierced the heavy silence of the snow, and in a few minutes two prisoners were brought before me, an old man and a girl.

" I questioned them in a low voice. They were fleeing from the Prussians, who had occupied their house that evening, and who were drunk. The father had been afraid for his daughter, and without even telling their servants, they had both escaped in the dark.

" I at once realised that they were people of the middle class, or even better.

" 'Come with us,' I said to them.

" Off we went. As the old man knew the country, he acted as our guide. The snow stopped falling; the stars came out and the cold grew quite terrible. The young girl, who held her father's arm, walked with tottering steps, in obvious distress. Several times she murmured: 'I can't feel my feet any longer,' and as for me, I suffered worse to see the poor little woman dragging herself so wearily through the snow.

" Suddenly she stopped.

" 'Father,' she said, 'I'm so tired I can go no further.'

" The old man wanted to carry her, but he could not even lift her off the ground, and with a deep sigh she fainted.

" They formed a circle round her. As for me, I marked time where I stood, not knowing what to do, and unable to make up my mind to abandon the man and his child.

" Then one of my men, a Parisian who had been nicknamed Slim Jim, suddenly said:

" 'Come on, you fellows, we must carry the young lady, or damn me if we're decent Frenchmen.'

" I believe I swore with pure pleasure.

" 'By God, that's good of you, boys; I'll take my share in it too.'

" The trees of a small wood were faintly visible on the left through the darkness. Several men fell out and soon returned with a bundle of branches intertwined to form a litter.

" 'Who'll lend his cape?' said Slim Jim. 'It's for a pretty girl, boys.'

" And ten capes fell round his feet. In a second the girl was lying on the warm garments, and lifted on to six shoulders. I was in front on the right, and, by Jove! I was pleased to bear the burden.

" We went off as though we'd had a glass of wine, with more life and fire. I even heard jokes. You see, Frenchmen only need a woman to become electrified.

" The soldiers had almost formed up again in proper ranks,

heartened and warmed. An old irregular who was following the litter, awaiting his turn to replace the first of his comrades who fell out, murmured to his neighbour in a tone loud enough for me to overhear :

" 'I'm not young any longer, but, damn it all, there's nothing like the sex for putting courage into a man's belly.'

" Until three o'clock in the morning we went forward almost without a halt. Then suddenly the scouts doubled back again, and soon the whole detachment was lying down in the snow, a mere vague shadow on the ground.

" I gave orders in a low voice, and behind us I heard the dry metallic crackle of rifles being cocked.

" For out in the middle of the plain something strange was stirring. It looked like an enormous animal moving along, lengthening out like a snake or gathering itself together into a ball, dashing off abruptly, now to the right, now to the left, halting, then starting off again.

" Suddenly this wandering shape approached us, and I saw, coming up at a fast trot, one behind the other, twelve Uhlans who were lost, and looking for their way. They were now so close that I could plainly hear the loud breathing of the horses, the jingling of their accoutrements, and the creaking of their saddles.

" I cried : 'Fire !'

" Fifty shots broke the silence of the night. Then four or five more reports rang out, then one all by itself, and when the blinding glare of the burnt powder had faded, we saw that the twelve men and nine of their horses had fallen. Three animals were galloping wildly away, one of them dragging behind it the body of its rider, hanging from the stirrup by one foot, bumping and bounding furiously.

" Behind me a soldier laughed, a terrible laugh. Another said :

" 'That makes a few widows.'

" Perhaps he was married. A third added :

" 'It didn't take long.'

" A head was thrust out from the litter.

" 'What is happening ?' asked the girl. 'Is there fighting ?'

" 'It's nothing, Mademoiselle,' I replied. 'We have just dispatched a dozen Prussians.'

" 'Poor wretches !' she murmured ; but as she was cold, she disappeared again under the soldiers' capes.

" Off we went again. We marched for a long time, but at last the sky grew pale. The snow became bright, luminous, and gleaming, and a line of warm colour appeared in the East.

" A distant voice cried :

" 'Who goes there ?'

" The whole detachment halted, and I went forward to reassure the sentry. We were arriving in the French lines.

" As my men filed past headquarters, an officer on horseback, to whom I had just told our story, asked in a loud voice, as he saw the litter go by :

" 'What have you got in there ?'

" A fair, smiling little face, with disordered hair, promptly appeared, and replied :

" 'It's me, Monsieur.'

" A laugh went up among the men, and our hearts leaped for pure joy.

" Then Slim Jim, who was marching beside the litter, waved his cap and shouted :

" '*Vive la France !*'

" And I don't know why, but I felt quite stirred, I thought the gesture so brave and gallant.

" I felt as though we had just saved the country, had done something which other men would not have done, something simple, something truly patriotic.

" I'll never forget that little face of hers, and if I were asked for my opinion on the abolition of drums and bugles, I would propose substituting for them a pretty girl in each regiment. It would be better than playing the *Marseillaise*. Good Lord, what a spirit it would put into a private to have a madonna like that, a living madonna, marching beside the colonel."

He paused for a few seconds, then resumed with an air of conviction, nodding his head :

" Yes, we're great lovers of women, we Frenchmen."

A WALK

WHEN OLD LEVAS, BOOK-KEEPER IN THE SERVICE OF MESSRS. Labuze and Company, left the shop, he stood for some moments dazzled by the brilliance of the setting sun. All day long he had worked in the yellow light of a gas-jet, in the depths of the back part of the shop, which looked on to a courtyard as narrow and deep as a well. So dark was the little room in which he had spent his days for the past forty years that, even in the height of summer, artificial light was necessary, except sometimes between eleven and three.

It was always damp and cold there; and the smell from this sort of pit under the window came into the gloomy room, filling it with an odour of decay and drains.

For forty years Monsieur Levas had been arriving at this prison at eight o'clock each morning, and staying there till seven at night, bent over his ledgers, writing with the savage concentration of a good subordinate.

He was now making three thousand francs a year, having begun at fifteen hundred francs. He had remained a bachelor, his means not permitting him to take a wife. And, never having had anything, he did not desire much. From time to time, however, wearying of his monotonous and endless task, he would formulate a Platonic wish: "Lord, if I had five thousand a year, I'd have an easy time of it." But he never had an easy time, having never had anything but his monthly salary.

His life had gone by without adventures, without passions, almost without hopes. The facility of dreaming, planted in every man, had never blossomed in the narrow bed of his ambitions.

At the age of twenty-one he had gone into Labuze and Company. And he had never come out.

In 1856 his father died, and in 1859 his mother. Since then the only event had been a change of lodgings in 1868, his landlord having proposed to raise the rent.

Every day, at six o'clock precisely, his alarm-clock made him leap out of bed with its fearful clatter, like a chain being unwound. Twice, however, once in 1866, and once in 1874, the mechanism had gone wrong, without his ever having found out why. He dressed, made his bed, swept out his room, and dusted his arm-chair and the top of his chest of drawers. These tasks took an hour and a half.

Then he went out, bought a roll at Lahure's bakery, where he had known eleven different proprietors without the shop ever changing its name, and started off, eating his bread.

His entire existence had therefore taken place in the dark, narrow office, always covered with the same wall-paper. He had come into it in his youth as assistant to Monsieur Brument and with the ambition to take his place. He had taken hi place, and hoped for nothing more.

All the harvest of memories which other men gather in the course of life, the unexpected happenings, the happy or tragic loves, the adventurous journeys, all the chances of a free existence, had passed him by. Days, weeks, months, seasons, years, were all alike. At the same hour each day he rose, went out, arrived at the office, lunched, left the office, dined, and went to bed, without anything having ever interrupted the regular monotony of the same actions, the same events, and the same thoughts.

Once upon a time he had looked at his fair moustache and curly hair in the little round mirror left behind by his predecessor. Now, every evening, before going, he contemplated in the same mirror his white moustache and his bald forehead. Forty years had gone by, long and swift, empty as a day of sorrow, alike as the hours of a sleepless night. Forty years of which nothing remained, not even a memory, not even a grief since the death of his parents. Nothing.

On this day Monsieur Levas stood dazzled, at the street-door, by the brilliance of the setting sun; instead of returning home, he thought of taking a little walk before dinner, as he did four or five times a year.

He reached the boulevards, where a flood of people streamed past under the budding trees. It was a spring evening, one of those first evenings of generous warmth which thrill the heart with a madness of life.

Monsieur Levas walked on with the rickety gait of old age. There was a gleam of gaiety in his eye; he was happy because the rest of the world was merry and the air was warm.

He reached the Champs-Élysées and continued to walk, freshened by the gusts of youth with which the wind caressed him.

The whole sky was aflame, and the Arc de Triomphe was a dark bulk silhouetted against the brilliant background of the horizon, like a giant straddling over a house on fire. When he drew near the huge monument, the old book-keeper realised that he was hungry, and entered a restaurant for dinner.

He dined in front of the shop, on the pavement, off sheep's trotters, a salad, and asparagus; and Monsieur Levas had the best meal he had eaten for a long time. He washed down his Brie cheese with half a bottle of good claret; then he took a cup of coffee, which was unusual with him, and after that a small glass of liqueur brandy.

When he had paid, he felt quite lively and merry, even a little excited. He said to himself: "What a glorious night! I'll go on as far as the entrance to the Bois de Boulogne it will do me good."

He started off again. An old song, which a girl who had

been his neighbour used once upon a time to sing, recurred obstinately into his head.

> " Quand le bois reverdit,
> Mon amoureux me dit :
> Viens respirer, ma belle,
> Sous la tonnelle."

He hummed it endlessly, beginning again and again. Night had fallen over Paris, an airless night, as close as an oven. Monsieur Levas walked along the Avenue of the Bois de Boulogne and watched the carriages go by. They came on with their gleaming eyes, one after another, allowing a glimpse of an embracing couple, the woman in a light dress, the man in black.

It was one long procession of lovers, driving under the warm and starry sky. Continually they came, went by, came, went by, side by side in the carriages, silent, clasped to each other, lost in the illusion and fever of their desires, in the shuddering longing for the next embrace. The warm air seemed filled with swift, wandering kisses. They spread a strange tenderness through the air, making it more stifling than ever. A fever spread through the air from these intertwined couples, these people inflamed with the same expectation, the same thought. All these carriages filled with love-making brought with them their own atmosphere, subtle and disturbing.

Monsieur Levas, a little tired at the end of his walk, sat down on a bench to watch the passage of these cabs heavy with love. Almost at once a woman drew near and sat down beside him.

" Hallo, darling," she said.

He made no answer. She continued :

" Let me love you, dearie ; you'll find me so kind."

" You are making a mistake, Madame," he said. She put her arm through his.

"Come on, don't be a silly boy; listen. . . ."

He had risen, and walked away, a feeling of tightness round his heart.

A hundred yards further on another woman accosted him.

"Come and sit beside me for a while, dearie!"

"Why do you follow this trade?" he said to her.

She stood in his way, and her voice was changed, hoarse and bitter.

"God, I don't do it for fun."

"Then what drives you to it?" he insisted gently.

"One must live, worse luck."

And she went off with a little song on her lips.

Monsieur Levas was bewildered. Other women passed him, called to him, invited him. He felt as though something black and oppressive hung above his head.

He sat down on a bench. The carriages were still rolling past.

"I should have done better not to come," he thought; "I'm quite put out."

And he began to think of all this love, venal or passionate, all these kisses, bought or free, which were passing before his eyes.

Love! He knew nothing of it. In all his life he had known but two or three women, chance meetings, unsought; his means had allowed him no luxuries. And he thought of the life he had led, so different from every one else's, so sombre, so gloomy, so dull, so empty.

There are some people who have no luck. And suddenly, as though a thick veil had been torn aside, he saw clearly the misery, the infinite, monotonous misery of his life, past, present, and to come; the last days like the first, nothing before him, nothing behind him, nothing round him, nothing in his heart; nothing anywhere.

Still the line of carriages went by. Always he saw, appearing and disappearing with the swift passage of the open vehicle, the two inside, silently embracing. It seemed to him as though the whole human race was passing by, drunk with joy, pleasure, and happiness. And he watched them alone, alone, all alone. He would still be alone to-morrow, always alone, alone, as no other creature in the world is alone.

He got up, walked a few steps, and, quickly tired, as though he had just finished a long walk, sat down on the next bench.

What was he waiting for? What was he hoping for? Nothing. He thought how good it must seem, in old age, to hear the chatter of little children as you come home at night. It must be sweet to grow old surrounded with those who owe their lives to you, love you, caress you, tell you those ridiculous, delightful things that warm your heart and console you for everything.

And thinking of his empty room, the clean, sad little room into which no one but himself had ever gone, a feeling of distress oppressed his soul. It seemed to him even more melancholy than his little office.

No one ever came to it; no one ever spoke in it. It was dead, dumb; it lacked even an echo of a human voice. It seemed as though walls must hold something of the people who live between them, something of their ways, their faces, their speech. Houses lived in by happy families are more cheerful than the houses of the miserable. His room was empty of memories, like his life. And the thought of returning to it alone, of getting into bed, of going through all the movements and duties of every evening, was horrible to him. And, as though to get further away from this sinister dwelling-place and from the moment when he must return to it, he rose, and, suddenly reaching the first path in the Bois, he turned into a little copse, to sit down on the grass.

He heard, around him, above him, everywhere, a confused, immense, continuous roar, made up of innumerable different noises, a dull roar, near and distant, a vast vague quivering of life: the breath of Paris, breathing like a colossal living creature.

. . . . . .

The sun, already high in the heavens, threw a flood of light upon the Bois de Boulogne. A few carriages were driving up and down, and groups of riders were trotting gaily past.

A young couple walked along a lonely path. Suddenly the woman, lifting her eyes, caught sight of something brown in the branches. She pointed to it, surprised and uneasy.

"Look. . . . What is that?"

Then with a cry she collapsed into the arms of her companion, who had to lower her on to the ground.

The keepers, promptly summoned, let down from the tree the body of an old man, hanged by his braces.

It was discovered that death had taken place the previous evening. Papers found on the man showed that he was a book-keeper at Messrs. Labuze and Company, and that his name was Levas.

Death was attributed to suicide from a cause unknown. Possibly temporary insanity?

MOHAMMED-FRIPOUILLE

"SHALL WE HAVE OUR COFFEE ON THE ROOF?" ASKED THE captain.

"Yes, by all means," I replied.

He rose. It was already dark in the room, lighted only by the inner courtyard, as is the custom in Moorish houses. In front of the high, pointed windows, creepers fell from the wide balcony on which the warm summer evenings were spent. Nothing but fruit remained upon the table, huge African fruits, grapes as large as plums, soft figs with purple flesh, yellow pears, long fat bananas, dates from Tougourt in a basket of esparto-grass.

The Moorish servant opened the door, and I ascended the staircase, sky-blue walls were lit from above by the gentle light of the dying day.

Soon I uttered a deep sigh of contentment, as I reached the balcony. It dominated Algiers, the harbour, the roadstead and the distant coast-line.

The house which the captain had purchased was an ancient Arab dwelling, situated in the centre of the old town, amid the labyrinthine lanes in which swarms the strange population of the coasts of Africa.

Below, the flat square roofs descended like a giant's staircase to the sloping roofs of the European quarter. Beyond these could be seen the masts of the ships at anchor, and then the sea, the open sea, blue and calm under the calm blue sky.

We lay down on mats, our heads supported by cushions; while slowly sipping the delicious native coffee, I watched the earliest stars come out in the darkening blue. They were dimly to be glimpsed, so distant, so pale, as yet scarcely lit.

A light, winged warmth caressed our skins. Sometimes, too, hotter, heavy gusts, instinct with a vague scent, the scent of Africa; they seemed the near-by breath of the desert, come over the peaks of the Atlas Mountains. The captain, lying on his back, observed:

"What a country, my dear fellow! How sweet life is here! How peculiarly delicious rest is here! Nights like these are made for dreaming!"

I was still watching the birth of the stars, with a curiosity at once indolent and lively, with drowsy happiness.

"You really ought to tell me something about your life in the South," I murmured.

Captain Marret was one of the oldest officers in the African Army, a soldier of fortune, formerly a spahi, who had carved out his career with the point of his sword.

Thanks to him, and to his connections and friends, I had been able to make a magnificent trip in the desert; and I had come that night to thank him before returning to France.

"What kind of story would you like?" he said. "I've had so many adventures during my twelve years in the sand that I no longer remember any separate one."

"Tell me about the Arab women," I replied.

He did not answer, but remained lying on his mat, his arms bent back and his hands beneath his head; now and then I caught the scent of his cigar, the smoke of which rose straight up towards the sky in the windless night.

Suddenly he burst out laughing.

"Yes, I'll tell you a funny incident that dates from my earliest days in Algeria. In those days we had some queer specimens in the African Army; they're no longer to be seen, they no longer happen. They'd have interested you enough to make you spend your whole life in this country.

"I was a plain spahi, a little fellow of twenty, a fair-haired young devil, supple and active, a real Algerian soldier. I was attached to the military post at Boghar. You know Boghar, the place they call the balcony of the South. From the summit of the fort you've seen the beginning of that land of fire, devastated, naked, tortured, stony, and reddened. It's the real antechamber of the desert, the superb blazing frontier of that immense stretch of tawny, empty spaces.

"There were forty of us spahis at Boghar, a company of convict soldiers, and a squadron of African lancers, when the news came that the Ould-Berghi tribe had murdered an English traveller. Lord knows how he got into the country; the English are possessed of the devil.

"Justice had to be done for this crime against a European, but the commanding officer hesitated to send out an expedition, thinking that an Englishman really wasn't worth so much fuss.

"Well, as he was talking the matter over with the captain and the lieutenant, a spahi cavalry sergeant, who was waiting to report, suddenly offered to go and punish the tribe if he were given six men only.

"In the South, as you know, things are freer than in a garrison town, and there's a sort of comradeship between the officer and his men which you don't find elsewhere. The captain burst out laughing.

"'You, my lad?'

"'Yes, Captain, and if you like I'll bring back the whole tribe prisoners.'

"The C.O. was a whimsical fellow, and took him at his word.

"'You'll start to-morrow with six men of your own choosing, and if you don't perform your promise, look out for trouble!'

"The sergeant smiled under his moustache.

"'Have no fears, Colonel. My prisoners will be here by noon on Wednesday at the latest.'

"This sergeant, Mohammed-Fripouille, as he was called, was a truly amazing fellow, a Turk, a real Turk, who had entered the service of France after a somewhat obscure and no doubt chequered career. He had travelled in many lands, in Greece, Asia Minor, Egypt, and Palestine, and must have left behind him a pretty thick trail of misdeeds. He was a real bashi-bazouk, a bold rapscallion, ferocious, and gay with a placid Oriental gaiety. He was stout, very stout in fact, but as supple as a monkey, and rode superbly. His moustaches were unbelievably long and thick, and always gave me a confused impression of a crescent moon and a scimitar. He had an exacerbated hatred for the Arabs, and treated them with cunning and horrible cruelty, perpetually inventing new tricks, ghastly turns of calculated treachery.

" He was also incredibly strong and preposterously daring.

" ' Choose your men, my lad,' said the C.O. to him.

" Mohammed took me. The gallant fellow trusted me, and I remained devoted to him, body and soul, as a result of his choice of me, which gave me as much pleasure as the cross of honour that I won later on.

" Well, we started off next morning at dawn, just the seven of us. My comrades, the sort of bandits, of pirates who, after marauding and vagabonding round every possible country, end by taking service in some foreign legion. In those days our army in Africa was full of these rascals, splendid soldiers, but utterly unscrupulous.

" Mohammed had given each of us some ten rope-ends to carry, each about a yard long. I was also loaded, as being the youngest and lightest, with a whole length of rope, a hundred yards long. When he was asked what he proposed to do with all this string, he replied with his sly calm air :

" ' It's for Arab-fishing.'

" And he winked slyly, a trick he had learnt from a veteran Parisian *chasseur d'Afrique*.

" He rode at the head of our troop, his head swathed in the red turban he always wore in the desert, smiling with pleasure under his enormous moustache.

"He was a fine sight, that huge Turk, with his powerful belly, his colossal shoulders, and his placid expression. He was mounted on a white horse, of medium size, but very strong, and the rider seemed ten times too big for his mount.

"We had entered a little ravine, stony, bare, and yellow, which drops down to the valley of the Chélif, and were talking of our expedition. My comrades spoke with every conceivable different accent, for among them were to be found a Spaniard, two Greeks, an American, and three Frenchmen. As for Mohammed-Fripouille, he had an extraordinary stutter of his own.

"The sun, the terrible sun, the sun of the South, quite unknown on the other side of the Mediterranean, fell upon our shoulders; we went forward at a walking pace, as always in those parts.

"All day we advanced without meeting either a tree or an Arab.

"At about one in the afternoon we had halted beside a little spring which flowed between the stones, and eaten the bread and dried mutton which we carried in our haversacks; then, after twenty minutes' rest, we had started off again.

"At last, at about six in the evening, after a long detour imposed upon us by our leader, we discovered a tribe encamped behind a conical hill. The low brown tents made dark spots upon the yellow ground, and looked like large desert mushrooms growing at the foot of the red hillock calcined by the sun.

"They were our men. A little further on, at the edge of a dark-green field of esparto-grass, the tethered horses were feeding.

"'Gallop,' order Mohammed, and we arrived in the centre of the encampment like a hurricane. The frenzied women, clad in white rags which drooped and billowed round them, hastily entered their dens of canvas, crouching and crawling, shrieking like hunted animals. The men, on the contrary, came up from all sides, attempting to defend themselves.

"We rode straight for the loftiest tent, the chief's.

"We kept our swords sheathed, following the example of Mohammed, who was galloping in a curious manner; he remained absolutely immobile, bolt upright on the little horse, which struggled madly to support his mighty bulk. The tranquillity of the rider, with his long moustaches, contrasted strangely with the liveliness of the animal.

"The native chief came out of his tent as we arrived in front of it. He was a tall thin man, black, with a shining eye, a bulging forehead, and eyebrows shaped like the arc of a circle.

"'What do you want?' he cried in Arabic.

"Mohammed reined in his horse with a jerk, and answered in the same language:

"'Was it you that killed the English traveller?'

"'You've no right to question me,' said the agha in a loud voice.

"All around me was a sound like the muttering of a storm. The Arabs came up from all sides, hustled us, made a ring round us, shouted wildly. They looked like fierce birds of prey, with their great hooked noses, their thin bony faces, their wide garments shaken by their gestures.

"Mohammed was smiling, his turban on one side, excitement showing in his eye; I saw little quivers of pleasure run through his sagging fleshy wrinkled cheeks.

"In a voice of thunder which dominated the clamour, he replied:

"'Death to him who has given death.'

"He thrust his revolver into the agha's brown face. I saw a little smoke rise from the barrel; then a pink froth of brains and blood gushed from the chief's forehead. As though struck by lightning he collapsed upon his back, throwing his arms apart, which raised the trailing skirts of his burnous like wings.

" I thought my last hour had come, the tumult around us was so frightful.

" Mohammed had drawn his sabre ; we followed his example. With windmill strokes he held off those who pressed him most closely, shouting :

" ' I'll spare the lives of those who surrender ; death to the rest.'

" And seizing the nearest in his Herculean fists, he laid him across the saddle and bound his hands, shouting to us :

" ' Do as I do, and sabre those who resist.'

" In five minutes we had captured some twenty Arabs, whose wrists we fastened securely. Then we pursued the fugitives, for at sight of our naked swords there had been a general flight. We collected about thirty more captives.

" The plain was filled with white, scurrying figures. The women dragged their children along, uttering shrill screams. The yellow dogs, like jackals, leapt round us, barking and showing their white fangs.

" Mohammed, who seemed out of his wits with joy, dismounted at one bound, and seizing the rope I had brought, said :

" ' Careful, now, boys ; two of you dismount.'

" Then he made a ludicrous and ghastly thing ; a necklace of prisoners, or rather a necklace of hanged men. He had firmly bound the two wrists of the first captive, then he made a noose round his neck with the same cord, with which he next secured the second captive's arms, and then knotted it round that man's neck. Our fifty prisoners soon found themselves bound in such a manner that the slightest attempt to escape on the part of one of them would have strangled both him and his two neighbours, and they were forced to march at an exactly even pace, without altering the gap between each of them by the slightest hair's-breadth, or else be promptly caught like hares in a snare.

" When this curious task was accomplished, Mohammed

began to laugh, the silent laugh which shook his belly without a sound coming from his mouth.

" 'That's the Arab chain,' he said.

"We too began to roar with laughter at the prisoners' scared piteous faces.

" 'Now, boys,' cried our leader, 'fasten a stake at each end.'

" We attached a stake to each end of this ribbon of ghost-like captives, who remained as motionless as though turned to stone.

" 'And now for dinner,' announced the Turk.

" A fire was lit and a sheep roasted, which we divided with our bare hands. Then we ate some dates found in the tents, drank some milk procured in the same way, and picked up some silver jewellery left behind by the fugitives.

" We were peacefully finishing our meal when I perceived, on the hill facing us, a singular assemblage. It was the women who had recently fled, only the women. And they were running towards us. I pointed them out to Mohammed-Fripouille.

" He smiled.

" 'It's our dessert,' he cried.

" 'Quite so, the dessert!'

"They came up, galloping madly, and soon we were bombarded with stones, which they flung at us without pausing in their onrush. We saw that they were armed with knives, tent-pegs, and broken pottery.

" 'Get on your horses,' yelled Mohammed.

"It was high time. The attack was terrible. They were come to free the prisoners, and strove to cut the rope. The Turk, realising the danger, flew into a mad rage and shouted: 'Sabre them!—sabre them!—sabre them!' And as we remained inactive, uneasy at this new sort of attack, hesitating to kill women, he rushed upon the invaders.

" Alone he charged that battalion of ragged females; the brute proceeded to put them to the sword, working like a galley-slave, in such a frenzy of rage that a white form dropped every time his arm swept down.

" His onslaught was so terrible that the frightened women fled as quickly as they had come, leaving behind them a dozen dead or wounded wretches, whose crimson blood stained their white garments.

" Mohammed returned towards us with a distorted face, repeating :

" ' Off with you, boys, off we go ; they're coming back.'

" And we fought a rear-guard action, slowly leading our prisoners, who were paralysed with the fear of being strangled.

" It was striking twelve next day when we arrived at Boghar with our chain of throttled captives. Only six had died on the way. But we had frequently to undo the knots from one end of the convoy to another, for every shock choked ten or more captives at once."

The captain paused. I did not answer. I thought of the strange country wherein such things were to be seen, and gazed at the black sky and its innumerable company of shining stars.

THE KEEPER

AFTER DINNER WE WERE RECOUNTING SHOOTING ADVENTURES and accidents.

An old friend of ours, Monsieur Boniface, a great slayer o beasts and drinker of wine, a strong and debonair fellow, ful of wit, sense, and a philosophy at once ironical and resigned which revealed itself in biting humour and never in melancholy spoke abruptly :

" I know a shooting story, or rather a shooting drama, that' queer enough. It's not in the least like the usual tale of th kind, and I've never told it before ; I didn't suppose tha anyone would be interested in it.

" It's not very pleasant, if you know what I mean. I mear to say that it does not possess the kind of interest which affects or charms, or agreeably excites.

" Anyhow, here it is.

. . . . . .

" In those days I was about thirty-five, and mad on shooting At that time I owned a very lovely piece of land on the out skirts of Jumièges, surrounded by forests and excellent fo hares and rabbits. I used only to spend four or five days ther a year, by myself, the limited accommodation not permittin of my bringing a friend.

" I had installed there as keeper an old retired policeman, good man, hot-tempered and very conscientious in the per formance of his duties, a terror to poachers, and afraid o nothing. He lived by himself, some way out of the village in a little house, or rather a hovel, consisting of two ground-floo rooms, a kitchen and a small storeroom, and of two mor rooms on the first floor. One of these, a sort of box just large enough for a bed, a chest of drawers, and a chair, was reserved for me.

"Old Cavalier occupied the other. In saying that he was alone in this cottage, I expressed myself badly. He had taken with him his nephew, a hobbledehoy of fourteen, who fetched the provisions from the village two miles off, and helped the old man in his daily duties.

"This youth was tall, thin, and somewhat stooping; his hair was so pale a yellow that it looked like the down on a plucked hen, and so thin that he appeared to be bald. He had enormous feet and colossal hands, the hands of a giant.

"He squinted a little and never looked anyone straight in the face. He gave one the impression that he occupied in the human race the place that the musk-secreting beasts hold in the animal kingdom. He was a polecat or a fox, was that boy.

"He slept in a sort of hole at the top of the little staircase which led to the two rooms. But during my short visits to the Pavilion—I called this hovel the Pavilion—Marius gave up his nest to an old woman from Écorcheville named Céleste, who came in to cook for me, old Cavalier's concoctions being by no means good enough.

"Now you know the characters and the setting. Here is the story.

"It was in 1854, the fifteenth of October: I remember the date, and I shall never forget it.

"I left Rouen on horseback, followed by my dog, a big setter from Poitou, broad-chested and heavy-jowled, who rummaged about in the bushes like a Pont Audemer spaniel.

"My bag was on the saddle behind me, and my gun slung round me. It was a cold day, with a high and mournful wind, and dark clouds rode in the sky.

"While ascending the slope of Canteleu I gazed at the broad valley of the Seine, through which the river meandered with serpentine twists as far as the horizon. On the left all the steeples of Rouen lifted to the sky, and on the right the view was blocked by the far-off tree-clad hills. I passed through the forest of Roumare, going now at a trot, now at a walking pace, and at about five o'clock I arrived at the Pavilion, where old Cavalier and Céleste were waiting for me.

" For the last ten years, at the same season, I had been presenting myself in the same way, and the same mouths welcomed me with the same words :

" ' Good day, your honour. Your honour's health is good ? '

" Cavalier had scarcely altered at all. He stood up to the passage of time like an old tree ; but Céleste, especially in the last four years, was becoming almost unrecognisable.

" She was bent nearly double, and although still active, she walked with the upper part of her body so bowed that it formed almost a right angle with her legs.

" The old woman was very devoted to me ; she always seemed much affected at seeing me again, and whenever I left she used to say :

" ' Think, this is maybe the last time, your honour.'

" And the poor servant's heart-broken, frightened farewell, her desperate resignation to inevitable death, so surely close upon her, stirred my heart strangely each year.

" I dismounted, and while Cavalier, with whom I had shaken hands, was leading my horse to the little shed which did duty for a stable, I entered the kitchen, which also served as the dining-room, followed by Céleste.

" Then the keeper joined us again. From the very first I saw that his face had not its customary expression. He seemed preoccupied, ill at ease, worried.

" ' Well, Cavalier,' I said to him, ' is everything going on all right ? '

" ' Yes and no,' he murmured. ' There's something that isn't at all all right.'

" ' Well, what is it, man ? ' I asked. ' Tell me all about it.'

" But he shook his head.

" ' No, Monsieur, not yet. I don't want to pester you with my worries like this, when you've only just arrived.'

" I insisted, but he absolutely refused to tell me about it before dinner. His expression, however, told me that it was serious.

" Not knowing what to say to him, I asked :

" ' And what about the game ? Have we plenty ? '

" ' Oh, yes, there's plenty of game, plenty. I kept my eyes open, thanks be to God.'

" He said this with such desperate seriousness that it was positively comical. His large grey moustaches looked ready to fall off his lips.

" Suddenly I realised that I had not yet seen his nephew.

" ' And Marius, where has he gone to ? Why hasn't he shown up ? '

" The keeper started ; he wheeled sharply and faced me.

" ' Well, Monsieur, I'd sooner tell you the story straight out ; yes, I'd sooner do that. It's about him that this thing's on my mind.'

" ' Ah. Well, where is he ? '

" ' In the stable, Monsieur ; I'm expecting him to turn up any moment.'

" ' Well, what has he been doing ? '

" ' This is the story, Monsieur. . . .'

" But the keeper hesitated none the less, his voice was changed and shook, his face was suddenly graven with deep wrinkles, the wrinkles of old age.

" Slowly he continued :

" ' Here it is. I noticed this winter that someone was laying snares in the wood of Roseraies, but I couldn't catch the man. I spent night after night there, Monsieur ; but no good. And during that time snares began to appear on the Écorcheville side. I grew thin with rage. But as for catching the thief, impossible !

You would have said the scoundrel was warned beforehand of my visits and my plans.

" 'But one day, while brushing Marius's breeches, his Sunday breeches, I found forty sous in his pocket. Now where had the boy got that from?

" 'I thought it over for a week, and I noticed that he was in the habit of going out; he used to go out just when I came back to bed, Monsieur.

" 'Then I watched him, but I never suspected the truth, not for a moment. And one morning, after going to bed before his eyes, I promptly got up again, and tracked him. And as for tracking, there's no one to touch me, Monsieur.

" 'And I caught him, Monsieur, setting snares on your land —Marius, my nephew, your keeper's nephew!

" 'My blood boiled, and I nearly killed him on the spot. I gave him such a thrashing—oh, Lord! how I did beat him; and I promised him that when you came he would have another from me in your presence, for the sake of the lesson.

" 'That's all. I've gone thin with grief. You know what it means to be crossed like that. But what would you have done, now? He's got no father or mother. I'm the only one of his own blood the boy's got; I've brought him up; I couldn't turn him out, could I?

" 'But I've told him that if he does it again, it's the end, the end, more's the pity. There! Was I right, Monsieur?'

" I held out my hand to him, and replied:

" 'You were right, Cavalier; you're a good fellow.'

" He rose.

" 'Thank you, Monsieur. Now I'll go and fetch him; he must be punished, for the sake of the lesson.'

" I knew that it was useless to attempt to dissuade the old man from any plan he had already formed. So I let him have his own way.

" He went off to fetch the lad, and brought him back, holding him by the ear.

" I was seated on a cane-chair, wearing the grave visage of a judge. Marius appeared to me to have grown ; he was even uglier than the year before, with his evil, cunning expression. And his great hands looked monstrous.

" His uncle shoved him in front of me, and said in his military voice :

" ' Ask pardon from the master.'

" The boy did not utter a word.

" Then, seizing him under the arms, the ex-policeman lifted him off the ground and began to thrash him with such violence that I got up to stop the blows.

" The child was now bawling :

" ' Mercy !—mercy !—mercy ! I promise. . .'

" Cavalier lowered him on to the ground and, forcing him on to his knees by pressing upon his shoulders, said :

" ' Ask pardon.'

" ' I ask pardon,' murmured the young scamp, with downcast eyes.

" Thereupon his uncle lifted him to his feet and dismissed him with a blow which nearly knocked him down again.

" He made off, and I did not see him again that evening.

" But Cavalier seemed terribly distressed.

" ' He's a bad character,' he said, and throughout dinner he kept on saying :

" ' Oh ! how it grieves me, Monsieur ; you don't know how it grieves me.'

" I tried to console him, but in vain. I went up to bed early, so as to be out shooting at break of day. My dog was already asleep upon the floor at the foot of my bed, when I blew out my candle.

" I was awakened in the middle of the night by the furious barking of Bock. I realised at once that my room was full of smoke. I leapt out of bed, lit the light, ran to the door, and opened it. A swirl of flames entered. The house was on fire.

" I promptly shut the strong oak door again, and dragging

on my breeches, I first of all lowered my dog from the window with a rope made of twisted sheets; then, throwing down my clothes, my game-bag and my gun, I made my escape in the same way.

"Then I began to shout with all my might:

"'Cavalier! Cavalier! Cavalier!'

"But the keeper did not wake; the old policeman was a heavy sleeper.

"Through the lower windows I saw that the whole ground-floor was nothing but a blazing furnace, and I saw too that it had been filled with straw to assist the fire.

"So it had been purposely fired!

"I resumed my furious shouts:

"'Cavalier!'

"Then the thought came to me that the smoke was suffocating him. An idea leaped into my mind; slipping two cartridges into my gun, I fired straight at his window.

"The six panes crashed into the room in a welter of splintered glass. This time the old man had heard, and his terrified figure appeared at the window, clad in his night-shirt; he was terrified more than anything by the violent glare which lit up the whole front of his dwelling.

"'Your house is on fire,' I shouted. 'Jump out of the window, quick, quick!'

"The flames suddenly darted through the lower windows, licked the wall, reached him, were on the point of surrounding him. He jumped and landed on his feet like a cat.

"It was high time. The thatched roof cracked in the middle, above the staircase, which formed a sort of chimney for the fire below; an immense red sheaf of flame rose in the air, widened, like the jet of a fountain, and sowed a shower of sparks round the cottage. In a few seconds it was nothing but a mass of flames.

"'How did it catch fire?' asked Cavalier, bewildered.

"'Someone set fire to the kitchen,' I replied.

"'Who could have done it?' he murmured.

"Suddenly I guessed.

"'Marius!' I said.

"The old man understood.

"'Oh! Holy Mother of God!' he stammered; 'that's why he didn't come in again.'

"But a horrible thought ran through my brain. I cried:

"'And Céleste? Céleste?'

"He did not answer, but the house collapsed before our eyes, forming nothing but a huge brazier, blinding, bleeding; a terrible pyre in which the poor woman could be no more than a glowing cinder, a cinder of human flesh.

"We had not heard a single cry.

"But, as the fire was reaching the neighbouring shed, I suddenly thought of my horse, and Cavalier ran to set it free.

"He had scarcely opened the stable-door when a swift, supple form passed between his legs, throwing him flat on his nose. It was Marius, running for all he was worth.

"In a second the man picked himself up. He wanted to run after the wretch, but realising that he could not hope to catch him and maddened with an ungovernable rage, he yielded to one of those momentary, thoughtless impulses which can be neither foreseen nor restrained. He picked up my gun, which was lying upon the ground close by, set it to his shoulder, and before I could move, pulled the trigger, without even knowing whether the gun was loaded.

"One of the cartridges which I had put in to give warning of the fire had not gone off; the charge caught the fugitive full in the back, and flung him on his face, covered with blood. He began to scrabble at the ground with hands and knees, as though trying to go on running upon all fours, like mortally-wounded hares when they see the hunter coming up.

"I dashed to him. The child was already in his death-throes. He died before the flames were extinguished, without having uttered a word.

" Cavalier, still in his night-shirt, with bare legs, stood near us, motionless, bewildered.

" When the people arrived from the village, they took away my keeper, who was like a madman.

. . . . . .

" I appeared at the trial as a witness, and narrated the facts in detail, without altering a single incident. Cavalier was acquitted. But he left the district the same day, and disappeared.

" I have never seen him again.

" That's my shooting story, gentlemen."

BERTHE

My old friend—sometimes one has friends much older than oneself—my old friend Doctor Bonnet had often invited me to stay with him at Riom. I did not know Auvergne at all, and I decided to go and see him about the middle of the summer of 1876.

I arrived on the morning train, and the first figure I saw upon the station platform was the doctor's. He was dressed in grey, and wore a round, black, broad-brimmed hat of soft felt, whose high crown narrowed as it rose, like the chimney of an anthracite stove; it was a true Auvergne hat, and positively smelt of charcoal-burning. Clad thus, the doctor had the appearance of an old young man, with his slender body wrapped in the light-coloured coat, and his large head with its white hair.

He embraced me with the manifest pleasure of a provincial greeting the arrival of a long-desired friend. Extending his arm and pointing all round him he exclaimed proudly:

" Here is Auvergne."

I saw nothing but a line of mountains in front of me, whose summits, like truncated cones, must have been extinct volcanoes.

Then, raising his finger towards the name of the town written upon the front of the station, he said:

" Riom, fatherland of magistrates, pride of the law courts, which should rather have been the fatherland of doctors."

" Why ? " I asked.

" Why ? " he answered with a laugh. " Turn the name round and you have '*mori*'—to die: . . . That's why I installed myself in this neighbourhood, young man."

And, delighted with his jest, he led me away, rubbing his hands.

As soon as I had swallowed a cup of coffee, I had to go and see the old city. I admired the chemist's house, and the other notable houses, all black, but as pretty as toy houses, with their fronts of carved stone. I admired the statue of the Virgin, patron saint of butchers, and even heard, in this connection, the story of an amusing adventure which I will relate some other day, when Doctor Bonnet said to me:

"Now I must beg five minutes in which to go and see a patient, and then I will take you up the hill of Châtel-Guyon, so as to show you, before lunch, the general view of the town and of the whole range of the Puy-de-Dôme. You can wait on the pavement; I'm only going straight up and down again."

He left me opposite one of those old provincial mansions, dark, closed, silent, gloomy. This one seemed to me to have a particularly sinister physiognomy, and I soon discovered the reason. All the large windows on the first floor were blocked up to half their height by stout wooden shutters. Only the top halves opened, as though someone had wished to prevent the creatures shut up in this great stone box from seeing into the street.

When the doctor came down again, I told him what I had noticed.

"You were not mistaken," he replied; "the poor creature shut up in there must never see what is going on outside. She's a madwoman, or rather an idiot, or an imbecile—what you Normans call a 'Niente.'

"Yes, it's a sad story, and an extraordinary pathological case into the bargain. Would you like me to tell it you?"

I told him yes.

"All right," he said. "Twenty years ago now, the owners of that house, my employers, had a child, a girl, just like any other girl.

"But I soon saw that although the body of the little creature was developing admirably, her intelligence was remaining dormant.

" She walked at a very early age, but she absolutely refused to speak. At first I thought her deaf ; then, later, I found out that she could hear perfectly, but did not understand. Violent noises made her tremble ; they frightened her, but she could never trace the cause of them.

" She grew up ; she was superb, and dumb, dumb through lack of intelligence. I tried every means to bring a gleam of light into her brain ; nothing was of avail. I fancied that she recognised her nurse ; once weaned, she did not recognise her mother. She never knew how to speak that word, the first uttered by children, the last murmured by soldiers dying on the battle-field : 'Mother.' Sometimes she attempted inarticulate mutterings, but nothing more.

" When the weather was fine, she laughed all the time, uttering gentle cries like the twittering of a bird ; when it rained, she wept and groaned in a melancholy, terrifying way, like the mourning of dogs howling at death.

" She liked to roll in the grass like a young animal, to run about like a mad creature, and every morning she clapped her hands if she saw the sun coming into her room. When the window was opened, she clapped her hands and moved about in her bed, for them to dress her at once.

" She seemed to draw no distinction between people, between her mother and her servant, between her father and me, between the coachman and the cook.

" I was fond of her unhappy parents, and went to see them almost every day. I often dined with them, which made me notice that Berthe (she had been named Berthe) appeared to recognise the dishes and prefer some to others.

" She was twelve years old at that time. She looked like a girl of eighteen, and was taller than I am.

" So the idea came into my head of developing her greed,

and of attempting by this means to introduce a sense of difference into her mind, of forcing her, by the difference between tastes, by the scale of flavours, if not to think, at least to make instinctive distinctions, which would be, if nothing else, a physical stirring of her brain.

"Then, by appealing to her senses, and carefully choosing those which would best serve our purpose, we wanted to produce a sort of reaction of the body upon the intelligence, and thus gradually augment the insentient working of her brain.

"One day, therefore, I set in front of her two plates, one of soup, one of very sweet vanilla custard. I made her taste them alternately. Then I left her free to make a choice. She ate the plateful of custard.

"I soon made her very greedy, so greedy that she seemed to have nothing in her head but the idea, or rather the desire, of eating. She recognised dishes perfectly, holding out her hand towards those which she liked and eagerly seizing them. She cried when they were taken away.

"Then I had the notion of teaching her to come to the dining-room at the sound of the bell. It took a long time, but I succeeded. In her vague understanding became firmly established a connection between the sound and the taste, a relation between two senses, an appeal from one to the other, and consequently a kind of concatenation of ideas, if one can call this sort of instinctive link between two organic functions an idea.

"I carried my experiment still further, and taught her—with what pains!—to recognise meal-times on the dial of the clock.

"For a long time I was unable to call her attention to the hands, but I succeeded in making her notice the striking mechanism. The method I employed was simple: I stopped the ringing of the bell, and every one rose to go to table when the little brass hammer struck twelve.

"I tried in vain to teach her to count the strokes. Every time she heard the chime she ran to the door; but little by little she must have realised that all the chimes had not the same value with regard to meals; and her eye, guided by her ear, was often fixed upon the dial.

"Noticing this, I took care to go every day at twelve and at six, and as soon as it came to the moment she was waiting for, I placed my finger on the figure twelve and on the figure six. I soon observed that she was following attentively the advance of the little brass hands, which I had often pushed round in her presence.

"She had understood! Or, it would be truer to say, she had grasped it. I had succeeded in awakening in her the knowledge, or rather the sensation, of time, as one can do with carp, though they have not the advantage of clocks, by feeding them at exactly the same moment every day.

"Once this result had been attained, all the timepieces in the house occupied her attention to the exclusion of everything else. She spent her life in looking at them, listening to them, waiting for the hours. A rather funny incident happened. The striking mechanism of a pretty Louis XVI clock, that was hanging over the head of her bed, ran down, and she noticed it. For twenty minutes she stared at the hands, waiting for ten o'clock to strike. But when the hand had passed the figure, she was left bewildered at hearing nothing, so bewildered that she remained sitting there, stirred no doubt by one of those strong emotions which lay hold on us in the face of great catastrophies. And she had the curious patience to sit in front of that little instrument until eleven o'clock, to see what would happen. Again she heard nothing, very naturally. Then, seized abruptly with the mad rage of a creature deceived and tricked, or with the terror inspired by a frightful mystery, or with the furious impatience of a passionate creature confronted by an obstacle, she seized the tongs from the fire-place and struck the clock with such force that she smashed it to pieces instantly.

"So her brain worked and calculated, in an obscure way, it is true, and within a very limited range, for I could not make her distinguish between people as she did between hours. In order to produce a stirring of intelligence in her mind, it was necessary to appeal to her passions, in the physical sense of the word.

"We soon had another proof of this; alas! it was a terrible one.

"She had grown into a superb creature; she was a true type of the race, an admirable, stupid Venus.

"She was now sixteen, and I have rarely seen such perfection of form, suppleness, and regularity of features. I said she was a Venus; so she was, a fair, full-figured, vigorous Venus, with large eyes, clear and empty, blue like flax-flowers, and a large mouth with round, greedy, sensual lips, a mouth made for kisses.

"One morning her father came into my room with a curious expression, and sat down without even replying to my greeting.

"'I want to speak to you about a very serious matter,' he said. 'Could . . . Berthe get married?'

"I started with surprise.

"'Berthe get married!' I exclaimed. 'It's impossible!'

"'Yes,' he resumed, 'I know . . . but think, doctor . . . you see . . . perhaps . . . we had hoped . . . if she had children . . . it would be a great shock for her, a great happiness . . . and who knows whether motherhood might not awaken her intelligence?'

"I was very perplexed. It was true. It was possible that the novelty of the experience, the wonderful maternal instinct which throbs in the hearts of beasts as strongly as in the hearts of women, which makes the hen fling herself upon the jaws of the dog in order to protect her little ones, might lead to a revolution, a violent disturbance in that dormant brain, might even set going the motionless mechanism of her mind.

"Suddenly, too, I remembered an example from my own

experience. Some years previously I had owned a little bitch, a retriever, so stupid that I could get nothing out of her. She had puppies, and became in one day, not intelligent, but almost the equal of many poorly-developed dogs.

" I had scarcely perceived this possibility before the longing increased in me to get Berthe married, not so much out of friendship for her and for her poor parents as out of scientific curiosity. What would happen? It was a strange problem.

" So I said to the father:

" 'You may be right . . . we might try . . . try by all means . . . but . . . but . . . you'll never find a man who'll consent to it.'

" 'I have found one,' he said in a low voice.

" I was amazed.

" 'A decent fellow?' I stammered. 'A man in your own walk of life?'

" 'Yes . . . absolutely,' he replied.

" 'Ah. . . . And . . . might I ask you his name?'

" 'I was just coming to tell you and ask your advice. It is Monsieur Gaston du Boys de Lucelles.'

" I nearly exclaimed: 'The swine!' but I kept my mouth shut, and after a pause I murmured:

" 'Yes, quite all right. I see no obstacle.'

" The poor man shook my hand.

" 'They shall be married next month,' he said.

" Monsieur Gaston du Boys de Lucelles was a young scamp of good family who had consumed his paternal inheritance and had run into debt in a thousand disreputable ways; he was now hunting for a new method of obtaining money.

" He had found this one.

" He was a good-looking lad, well set up, but a rake, one of the loathsome tribe of provincial rakes. He seemed to give promise of being an adequate husband, and one that an allowance would easily remove again.

" He came to the house to press his suit and show himself off before the beautiful idiot, whom he seemed to like. He brought her flowers, kissed her hands, sat at her feet and gazed at her with tender eyes; but she took no notice of any of his attentions, and in no way distinguished him from any of the people among whom she lived.

" The marriage took place.

" You will understand to what a degree my curiosity was inflamed.

" The next day I went to see Berthe, to judge from her face whether any inner part of her had been stirred. But I found her just the same as on other days, solely preoccupied with the clock and dinner. Her husband, on the contrary, seemed very fond of her, and tried to rouse her gaiety and affection by little teasing games such as one plays with kittens.

" He had found nothing better.

" I then started to pay frequent visits to the newly-married couple, and I soon perceived that the young woman recognised her husband and directed upon him the greedy looks which hitherto she had lavished only upon sweet things to eat.

" She followed his movements, distinguished his step on the stairs, or in a neighbouring room, clapped her hands when he came in, and her transfigured countenance burned with a flame of profound happiness and desire.

" She loved him with all her body, with all her soul, her poor feeble soul, with all her heart, the poor heart of a grateful animal.

" She was truly an admirable innocent picture of simple passion, of passion at once carnal and modest, such as nature had set in human beings before man complicated and distorted it with all the subtleties of sentiment.

" As for the man, he quickly wearied of the beautiful, passionate, dumb creature. He no longer spent more than a few hours of each day with her, finding it enough to devote his nights to her.

" And she began to suffer.

" From morning to night she waited for him, her eyes fixed on the clock, not even paying attention to meals, for he always went away for his meals, to Clermont, Châtel-Guyon, Royat, anywhere so as not to be at home.

" She grew thin.

" Every other thought, every other desire, every other interest, every other vague hope, vanished from her mind; the hours in which she did not see him became for her hours of terrible torment. Soon he began to sleep away from her. He spent his nights at the Casino at Royat with women, coming home early at the first gleam of day.

" She refused to go to bed before he returned. She stayed motionless on a chair, her eyes vaguely fixed on the little brass hands which turned round and round in slow, regular progress, round the china dial wherein the hours were inscribed.

" She heard the distant trotting of his horse, and would start up with a bound; then, when he came into the room, she would raise her fingers to the clock with a ghostly gesture, as though to say to him: 'Look how late it is!' He began to be afraid in the presence of this loving, jealous idiot; he became possessed of a slow resentment, as an animal might be. One night he struck her.

" I was sent for. She was screaming in a terrible fit of grief, rage, passion, I knew not what. How can one tell what is going on in these rudimentary brains?

" I calmed her with injections of morphine; and I forbade her ever to see the man again, for I realised that the marriage would inevitably end in her death.

" Then she went mad! Yes, my dear fellow, that idiot girl went mad. She thinks of him always, and waits for him. She waits for him all day and all night, every moment, waking or sleeping, perpetually. As I saw her growing thinner and thinner, and as her obstinate gaze never left the faces of the clocks, I had all these instruments for measuring time removed from the house. Thus I have taken from her the possibility of counting the hours, and of for ever searching her dim memory for the moment at which once upon a time he had been wont to come home. I hope in the long run to kill remembrance in her, to extinguish the spark of reason that I took such trouble to set alight.

"The other day I tried an experiment. I offered her my watch. She took it and studied it for some time; then she began to scream in a terrible way, as though the sight of the little instrument had suddenly reawakened the memory that was beginning to slumber.

"She is thin now, pitifully thin, with shining, hollow eyes. She walks up and down unceasingly, like a caged beast.

"I have had two bars put on the windows, have put up high screens, and have fixed the chairs to the floor, to prevent her from looking into the street to see if he is coming back.

"Oh, the poor parents! What a life theirs will have been!"

We had arrived at the top of the hill; the doctor turned round and said to me:

"Look at Riom from here."

The sombre town wore the aspect of an ancient walled city. In the background, as far as the eye could reach, stretched a green, wooded plain, dotted with villages and towns, and drowned in a thin blue vapour which made the horizon a delight to the eyes. On the right, in the distance, was a line of high mountains with a succession of peaks, rounded or cut sharply as with a sword-cut.

The doctor began to enumerate the places and peaks, telling me the history of each.

But I did not listen to him; I thought only of the mad-woman, saw nothing but her. She seemed to hover like a melancholy ghost over all this wide country.

"What has become of the husband?" I asked abruptly.

My friend, somewhat surprised, answered after a pause:

" He's living at Royat on the allowance made to him. He's happy ; he leads a gay life."

As we were walking slowly homewards, both of us saddened and silent, an English dog-cart passed us from behind, a fast-trotting thoroughbred in the shafts.

The doctor gripped my arm.

" There he is," he said.

I saw nothing but a grey felt hat, tilted over one ear, above a pair of broad shoulders, disappearing in a cloud of dust.

MISTI

RECOLLECTIONS OF A BACHELOR

. . . . . .

MY MISTRESS AT THAT TIME WAS A FUNNY LITTLE WOMAN. She was married, of course, for I've a perfect horror of unmarried women. After all, what pleasure can one have in possessing a woman who has the double disadvantage of belonging to no one and belonging to every one? And honestly, quite apart from the moral side of the question, I can't understand love as a profession. It rather disgusts me. It's a weakness, I know, and I confess it.

The chief pleasure a bachelor gets out of having a married woman for his mistress, is that she provides him with a home, a comfortable, pleasant home in which every one looks after him and spoils him, from the husband to the servants. Every pleasure is there united, love, friendship, even fatherhood, the bed and the table, in fact all that makes up the happiness of life, together with the incalculable advantage of being able to change your household from time to time, of installing yourself by turns in every sphere, in the country, during the summer, in the home of workman who lets you a room in his house; in the winter, with the middle classes, or even with the aristocracy, if you are ambitious.

I have another weakness: I like my mistresses' husbands. I admit that there are husbands, vulgar or coarse, who fill me with disgust for their wives, however charming these may be. But when the husband has wit or charm, I fall inevitably desperately in love. I am careful, if I break with the woman, not to break with the husband. In this way I have made my best friends, and in this manner I have oft-times verified the incontestable superiority of the male over the female of the human species. The latter causes you every possible worry, makes scenes, reproaches you, and so forth; the former, who has quite as much right to complain, treats you, on the contrary, as though you were the good angel of his home.

Well, my mistress was a funny little woman, dark, fantastic, capricious, religious, superstitious, credulous as a monk, but charming. Above all, she had a way of kissing which I have never found in another woman . . . but this is not the place. . . . And such a soft skin! I derived infinite pleasure merely from holding her hand! And her eyes. . . . Her gaze passed over you like a slow caress, delicious and endless. Often I laid my head on her knees, and we remained motionless, she bending over me with that faint, enigmatic, disturbing little smile that women have, I lifting my eyes towards her, receiving like wine poured gently and deliciously into my heart, the shining gaze of her blue eyes, bright as though filled with thoughts of love, blue like a heaven of delights.

Her husband, a civil servant, was often away, leaving our evenings free. Often I spent them at her house, lying on the divan, my forehead pressed against one of her legs, while upon the other slept a huge black cat named "Misti," which she adored. Our fingers met on the animal's muscular back, and caressed one another amid its silky hair. I felt against my cheek its warm flank, throbbing with a perpetual "purr-purr." Sometimes it would stretch out a paw to my mouth, or set five unsheathed claws upon my eyelids, whose points pricked my eyes and withdrew in a flash.

Sometimes we went out on what she called our escapades. As a matter of fact they were very innocent. They consisted in supping at an outlying inn, or else, after we had dined at her house or mine, of visiting low taverns, like students on the spree.

We went to the lowest drinking-places and sat down at the

far end of smoky dens, on rickety chairs, at an old wooden table. A cloud of acrid smoke, which smelled still of the fried fish eaten at dinner, filled the room; men in blouses talked noisily and drank brandy; and the astonished waiter served us cherry brandies.

Trembling with delicious terror, she would raise her little black veil, folded double, to the tip of her nose, where it rested, and begin to drink with the pleasure of committing a delightful crime. Each cherry she swallowed gave her the sense of a sin committed, each sip of the coarse liquor ran down her throat like a delicate, forbidden pleasure.

Then she would say to me in a low voice: "Let us go." And we left. She went out quickly, her head lowered, with short steps, between the drinkers who watched her pass with resentful glances; and when we found ourselves out in the street again, she would utter a deep sigh as though we had just escaped from dreadful peril.

Sometimes she asked me with a shudder: "If I were insulted in one of these places, what would you do?" And I would reply in a swaggering tone: "Why, defend you, damn it." And she would squeeze my arm in her happiness, with a vague wish, perhaps, to be insulted and defended, to see men, even men like that, fight me for her.

One evening, as we were seated at a table in a Montmartre den, we saw a ragged old woman come in, holding in her hand a greasy pack of cards. Observing a lady, the old woman promptly came up to us, offering to tell my companion's fortune. Emma, whose mind believed anything and everything, shivered with pleasure and uneasiness, and made room beside her for the hag.

The ancient, wrinkled woman, with rings of raw flesh round her eyes and an empty, toothless mouth, set out her dirty cards on the table. She made them into heaps, picked them up, and set them out again, muttering inaudible words. Emma listened, pale, breathing quickly, panting with distress and curiosity.

The witch began to speak; she made vague predictions: happiness and children, a fair young man, a journey, money, a lawsuit, a dark gentleman, the return of a friend, a success, a death. The announcement of this death struck the young woman. Whose death? When? How?

"As to that," replied the old woman, "the cards are not strong enough; you must come and see me to-morrow. I'll tell you with the coffee-mark, which never fails."

Emma turned anxiously to me.

"We may go to-morrow, mayn't we? Oh, please say yes! If not, you don't know how it will torment me."

I began to laugh.

"We'll go if you want to, darling."

The old woman gave us her address.

She lived on the sixth floor of an awful house behind the Buttes-Chaumont. We went there the next day.

Her room, a garret with two chairs and a bed, was full of strange things—bunches of herbs hanging from nails, dried animals, bottles and phials containing various coloured liquids. On the table a stuffed black cat stared with glass eyes. He looked like the familiar spirit of this sinister dwelling.

Emma, faint with excitement, sat down, and said at once:

"Oh, darling, look at the cat! Isn't he just like Misti?"

And she explained to the old woman that she herself had a cat just like that one; oh, exactly like it.

"If you love a man," replied the witch solemnly, "you must not keep it."

"Why not?" asked Emma, struck with terror.

The old woman sat down beside her in a familiar way, and took her hand.

"It's the sorrow of my life," she said.

My friend was eager to hear. She pressed the old woman to tell her, questioned her, urged her: the superstitious credulity they shared made them sisters in mind and heart. At last the woman made up her mind.

"I loved that cat," she said, "like a brother. I was young in those days, and all alone; I did sewing at home. Monton was all I had. A lodger gave him to me. He was as clever as a child, and gentle too; he idolised me, dear lady, he idolised me more than a fetish. All day long he purred in my lap, all night on my pillow; I felt his heart beat, I did.

"Well, I made friends with a man, a nice boy who worked at a linen-draper's. It went on for three months without my granting him anything. But you know how it is, one weakens —it happens to everybody; and besides, I had begun to love him, that I had. He was so nice, so nice and kind. He wanted us to live together all the time, for economy. At last I let him come and see me one evening. I hadn't made up my mind, oh, dear, no! but I liked the idea of being together for an hour.

"At the beginning he was very well behaved. He said pretty things to me which stirred my heart. Then he kissed me, Madame, gave me a lover's kiss. I had shut my eyes and remained in a sort of paralysis of happiness. Suddenly I felt that he'd made a violent movement, and he screamed, a scream I shall never forget. I opened my eyes and saw that Monton had flown at his face and was tearing his skin with his claws, like a rag of linen. And the blood was streaming down, Madame.

"I tried to pull the cat off, but he held tight, and went on scratching, and even bit me, he was so far out of his senses. At last I got hold of him and threw him out of the window, which was open, since it was summer.

"When I began to wash my poor friend's face, I saw that he had lost his eyes, both eyes.

"He had to go to the hospital. He died of agony a year after. I wanted to have him with me and feed him, but he would not. He seemed to hate me after it had happened.

"As for Monton, he broke his back in the fall. The porter

had picked up the body. I had him stuffed, since I still felt attached to him. If he had done that, it was because he loved me, wasn't it?"

The old woman was silent, and stroked the dead beast with her hand; the carcass shook on its wire skeleton.

Emma, her heart wrung, had forgotten the predicted death. At any rate, she said nothing more about it, and went away after giving the woman five francs.

Her husband came back the next day, and so several days passed before I saw her.

When I visited her again, I was surprised not to see Misti. I asked where he was.

She blushed, and replied:

"I gave him away. I wasn't happy about him."

I was surprised.

"Not happy? Not happy? What about?"

She gave me a long kiss, and murmured in a low voice:

"I was afraid for your eyes, darling."

OLD BONIFACE'S CRIME

AS BONIFACE THE POSTMAN LEFT THE POST OFFICE HE DIScovered that his round that day would not take as long as usual, and felt a sharp pleasure in the knowledge. His task was the rural delivery outside the town of Vireville, and when he returned at night, with long, weary strides, his legs had often more than forty kilometres behind them.

So his delivery would be quickly done! He could even loiter a little on the way and get home about three in the afternoon. What luck!

He left the town by the Sennemare road and began his duties. It was June, the green and flowery month, the month when meadows look their best.

Dressed in a blue blouse, and wearing a black cap with red braid, the postman took the narrow paths across fields of colza, oats, or wheat. The crops were shoulder-high, and his head, passing along above the ears, appeared to float on a calm green sea rippled gently by a little wind.

He entered the farms through wooden gates set in the hedgerows shaded by double rows of beeches, and greeting the peasant by name: "Good morning, Monsieur Chicot," he would offer him his paper, the *Petit Normand*. The farmer would wipe his hand on the seat of his breeches, take the sheet of paper, and slip it into his pocket to read at his leisure after the midday meal. The dog, kennelled in a barrel, at the foot of a leaning apple-tree, would bark furiously and tug at his chain, and the postman, without turning round, would set off again with his military gait, his long legs taking great strides, his left hand in his sack, his right swinging with a quick, ceaseless gesture the stick that kept him company on his round,

He delivered his letters and circulars at the hamlet of Sennemare, and then went on across the fields to deliver his mail to the tax-collector, who lived in a little house half a mile from the village.

He was a new collector, one Monsieur Chapatis, who had arrived the previous week and was but recently married.

He took in a Paris paper, and sometimes postman Boniface, when he had the time to spare, would glance at it before handing it over to its destined owner.

Accordingly he opened his sack, took out the newspaper, slipped off the band, unfolded it, and began to read it as he walked. The first page was of no interest to him; politics left him cold; he never looked at the financial news, but the news items enthralled him.

They were particular that day. He was so strongly affected by the story of a crime committed in a gamekeeper's cottage that he stopped in the middle of a clover-patch to re-read it slowly. The details were appalling. A wood-cutter, passing the keeper's cottage one morning, noticed a little blood on the door-step, as though someone's nose had been bleeding. "He killed a rabbit last night," thought the wood-cutter, but, drawing nearer, he observed that the door was ajar and the lock smashed.

Then, seized with terror, he ran to the village to inform the mayor; the latter brought with him the constable and the schoolmaster as reinforcements, and the four men went back together. They found the keeper lying in front of the fire-place with his throat cut, his wife under the bed, strangled, and their little six-year-old daughter suffocated between two mattresses.

Boniface the postman was so deeply affected at the thought of this murder, the horrible details of which came home to him one by one, that he felt a weakness in his legs, and said out loud:

"Good Lord, there *are* some villains in this world!"

Then he slipped the journal back into its paper belt and set off again, his head full of visions of the crime. Soon he reached Monsieur Chapatis' dwelling ; he opened the gate of the little garden and approached the house. It was a low building, consisting merely of a ground-floor surmounted by a mansard roof. It was at least five hundred yards from the nearest neighbour's.

The postman mounted the two steps up to the entrance, set his hand to the knob, attempted to open the door, and found it locked Then he saw that the shutters had not been opened, and that no one had left the house that day.

He felt uneasy, for ever since his arrival Monsieur Chapatis had been in the habit of rising early. Boniface pulled out his watch. It was only ten past seven, so that he was nearly an hour ahead of his usual time. Still the tax-collector should have been up and about.

So he went round the building, walking with circumspection, as though he were in danger. He observed nothing suspicious, except a man's footprints in a strawberry-bed.

But suddenly he paused, motionless, transfixed with horror, as he passed in front of a window. Groans were coming from inside the house.

He went towards it and, straddling across a border of thyme, set his ear to the shutter to hear the better ; the sound of groans was unmistakable. He could hear plainly long sighs of pain, something like a death-rattle, the sound of a struggle. Then the groans became louder and more frequent, grew even more frenzied, and became screams.

Boniface, no longer in any doubt that a crime was being committed at that very moment in the tax-collector's house, rushed off as fast as his legs could carry him. He fled back through the little garden and dashed across the meadows and cornfields. He ran breathlessly, shaking his sack so that it banged against his back, and arrived, exhausted, panting, and desperate, at the door of the police station.

Inspector Malautour was mending a broken chair with tin-tacks and a hammer. Constable Rantieux was gripping the broken piece of furniture between his legs and holding a nail at the edge of the break; the inspector, chewing his moustache, his eyes round and moist with concentration, hit his subordinate's fingers at every stroke.

As soon as he saw them the postman cried out:

"Come quick, somebody's murdering the tax-collector! Come quick, quick!"

The two men ceased their work and looked up, with the dumbfounded air of men suddenly and amazingly interrupted.

Boniface, seeing that their surprise was greater than their haste, said again:

"Quick! Quick! Thieves are in the house, I heard screams, there's barely time!"

The inspector set down his hammer and asked:

"Who was it who informed you of this deed?"

The postman replied:

"I was going to deliver the paper and two letters when I noticed that the door was shut and that the tax-collector had not yet got up. I walked round the house to try and find out the reason, and heard someone groaning as though he were being strangled or had had his throat cut, so I came away to fetch you as fast as I could go. There's barely time."

The inspector drew himself up to his full height and said:

"You did not render assistance in person?"

"I was afraid that I was not present in sufficient strength," replied the frightened postman.

At that the police official was convinced, and said:

"A moment, while I put my coat on, and I'll follow you."

He went into the police station, followed by his subordinate carrying back the chair.

They reappeared almost immediately and all three set off with vigorous strides for the scene of the crime.

Arriving near the house, they carefully slowed their pace,

and the inspector drew his revolver. Very softly they penetrated into the garden and approached the wall of the house. There were no new signs indicating that the malefactors had departed. The door was still shut, the windows still closed.

"We've got them," murmured the inspector.

Old Boniface, quivering with excitement, made him go round to the side and, pointing to a shuttered window, said:

"It's in there."

The inspector went forward alone, and set his ear to the boards. The two others waited, ready for anything, their eyes fixed upon him.

For a long time he remained motionless, listening. In order to apply his ear closer to the wooden shutter, he had taken off his cocked hat and was holding it in his right hand.

What was he hearing? His impassive face revealed nothing, but suddenly the tips of his moustache turned up, his cheeks were creased as though in silent laughter, and once more straddling across the box-tree border, he came back towards the two men, who stared at him amazed.

Then he signed to them to follow him on tiptoe and, having reached the entrance, bade Boniface slip the paper and letters under the door.

The postman, dumbfounded, obeyed meekly.

"And now off we go," said the inspector.

But as soon as they had passed through the gate, he turned to Boniface, showed the whites of his eyes, gleaming with merriment, and spoke in a bantering tone, with a knowing flicker of his eyelids:

"You're a sly dog, you are."

"What do you mean?" replied the old man. "I heard it, I swear I heard it."

But the policeman, unable to restrain himself any longer burst into a roar of laughter. He laughed as if he would choke bent double, his hands across his belly, his eyes filled with tears the flesh on each side of his nose distorted into a frightful grimace. The two others stared at him in bewilderment.

But as he could neither speak nor stop laughing nor make them understand what was affecting him, he made a gesture, a quite vulgar and scandalous gesture.

As he still failed to make himself understood, he repeated the movement several times, nodding towards the house, still shuttered.

Suddenly his man understood, in his turn, and burst into formidable transports of merriment.

The old man stood stupidly between the other two, who rolled in agonies of mirth.

At last the inspector grew calm; he gave the old man a vigorous chaffing poke in the stomach, and exclaimed:

"Ah, you sly dog, you and your jokes! I shan't forget old Boniface's crime in a hurry."

The postman, his large eyes wide open, said once more:

"I swear I heard it."

The inspector began to laugh again. His constable had sat down on the grass at the roadside to have his laugh out in comfort.

"Ah, you heard it, did you? And is that how you murder your wife, eh, you dirty dog?"

"My wife?" He reflected at some length, then replied:

"My wife. . . . Yes, she hollers when I knock her about . . . but if she does, what's a bit of noise, anyway? Was Monsieur Chapatis beating his?"

At that the inspector, in a delirium of mirth, turned him round like a puppet with his hands on his shoulders, and whispered into his ear something at which the postman was struck dumb with amazement.

At last the old man murmured thoughtfully:

"No. . . . Not like that. . . . Not like that. . . . Not a bit like that. . . . Mine doesn't say anything. . . . I'd never have believed it . . . is it possible? . . . Anyone would have sworn that a murder was taking place."

And filled with shame, confusion, and bewilderment, he went on his way across the fields, while the constable and the inspector, still laughing and shouting pungent barrack jests after him, watched his black cap recede into the distance above the quiet waves of the corn.

ROSE

THE TWO YOUNG WOMEN LOOK AS THOUGH BURIED UNDER A canopy of flowers. They are alone in the huge landau, which is loaded with bouquets like a giant basket. Upon the front seat lie two white satin hampers full of violets from Nice, and on the bearskin which covers their knees is a heap of roses, mimosa, pinks, daisies, tuberoses, and orange-blossom, knotted together with silk rosettes, seeming about to crush the two slender bodies. Nothing emerges from this brilliant, perfumed bed but their shoulders, their arms, and a wisp of the upper half of their gowns, one blue, the other lilac.

The coachman's whip is sheathed in anemones, the horses' traces are covered with wallflowers, the spokes of the wheels blossom with mignonette; where the lamps should be hung two enormous round bouquets that look like the two strange eyes of this wheeled and flower-decked animal.

At a rapid trot the landau passes along the Antibes road, preceded, followed, and accompanied by a crowd of other garlanded vehicles, full of women drowning in a sea of violets. For it is the day of the battle of flowers at Cannes.

When they reach the Boulevard de la Foncière, the battle begins. For the whole length of the immense avenue a double row of garlanded carriages runs up and down like an endless ribbon. Flowers are flung from one to another. They pass through the air like bullets, strike the fresh faces, flutter, and fall in the dust, where a crowd of urchins picks them up.

A tight-packed crowd on the pavement is looking on, noisy but well behaved, kept in order by mounted police, who trot arrogantly up and down, forcing back the over-inquisitive, as though to keep the plebeians from mingling with the rich.

The carriages call to one another, exchange greetings, and discharge volleys of roses. A car full of pretty girls dressed as red devils attracts and seduces all eyes. A debonair young man, who looks like a portrait of Henry IV, is throwing with eager gaiety a bouquet held on an elastic string. Before the menace of its impact the women shade their eyes and the men duck their heads, but the graceful weapon, swift and obedient, describes a curve in the air and returns to its master, who promptly flings it at a fresh face.

The two young women empty their arsenal in handfuls, and receive a hail of bouquets; at last, tired by an hour of combat, they order the coachman to follow the Juan Bay road, which runs along the sea.

The sun disappears behind the Esterel, silhouetting on the flaming western sky the black jagged edge of the long mountain. The quiet waters stretch, blue and clear, to the far horizon where they mingle with the sky: the fleet anchored in the middle of the bay looks like a herd of monstrous beasts, motionless upon the water, apocalyptic animals, breast-plated and hump-backed, topped with masts frail as feathers, with eyes that light up at dusk.

The young women, huddled under the protection of the heavy rug, glance languidly about them. At last one of them speaks:

"There are some marvellous evenings, are there not, Margot, when life seems well worth living?"

"Yes, it's very lovely," replied the other, "but there is something missing, all the same."

"What! I feel perfectly happy; there's nothing I want."

"Yes, but there is. You are overlooking it now. However profound the delight which overmasters our bodies, we demand always one thing more . . . for our hearts."

"To love a little?" said the other, smiling.

"Yes."

They fell into silence, looked straight ahead; then she who was called Marguerite murmured:

"Without love, life seems to me insupportable. I need to be loved, were it only by a dog. We are all like that, whatever you may say, Simone."

"No, my dear. I would rather not be loved at all than by just anyone. Do you think I should enjoy being loved, for instance, by . . . by. . . ."

She searched her mind for someone by whom she might be loved, and her eyes roved over the wide landscape. After raking the horizon, her glance fell upon the two metal buttons gleaming on the coachman's back, and with a laugh she continued: "by my coachman?"

Madame Margot smiled faintly and said in a low voice:

"I assure you it's very good fun to have one of your servants in love with you. It's happened to me two or three times. They roll their eyes so comically that I could die of laughter. Of course, the more loving they are, the more severe you become, until some day you dismiss them on the first excuse that comes into your head, because you'd look so ridiculous if anyone noticed what was going on."

Madame Simone listened with her eyes looking straight in front of her, then declared:

"No, my footman's heart is really not good enough for me. But tell me how you discovered that they were in love with you."

"Why, just as I do with any other man; when they grew stupid."

"Well, *I* don't think my lovers look so stupid."

"Why, they're idiots, my dear, unable to speak, answer, or understand anything at all."

"But what did you feel like when a servant fell in love with you? Were you affected, flattered . . . what?"

"Affected? No. Flattered? Yes, a little. One is always flattered by the love of a man, whoever he may be."

" Really, Margot ! "

" It's quite true, my dear. I'll tell you a strange thing which happened to me. You will see how queer and contradictory one's feelings are in such circumstances.

" Four years ago next autumn I found myself without a maid. I had tried five or six hopeless creatures one after another, and was about despairing of ever finding one, when I read, in the advertisement columns of a paper, that a young girl with knowledge of sewing, embroidery, and hairdressing was looking for a place and that she could supply excellent references. Also, she spoke English.

" I wrote to the address indicated, and next day the person in question came to see me. She was fairly tall, slender, and rather pale, with a very timid bearing. She had beautiful black eyes, a charming complexion, and I was attracted to her at once. I asked her for her references ; she gave me one in English, for she had just left, she said, the service of Lady Rymwell, with whom she had been ten years.

" The letter stated that the girl had left of her own free will in order to go back to France, and that her mistress had found nothing to reproach her with, during her long service, except some slight indications of ' French coquetry.'

" The puritanical flavour of the English phrase made me smile, and I engaged her at once as my maid She began her duties the same day ; her name was Rose.

" By the end of a month I adored her.

" She was a magnificent find, a pearl, a marvel.

" Her taste in hairdressing was perfect ; she could trim a hat better than the best shops, and was a dressmaker into the bargain.

" I was amazed at her ability. Never had I had such a maid.

" She dressed me rapidly, and her hands were uncommonly light. I never felt her fingers on my skin, and there is nothing I dislike so much as the touch of a servant's hand. I grew more and more indolent, it was such a pleasure to be dressed from head to foot, from chemise to gloves, by this tall, timid girl, whose cheeks always wore a faint blush, and who never spoke. After my bath she used to rub me and massage me while I dozed on my sofa; upon my word, I thought of her as a friend of humble rank rather than as a mere servant.

"One morning the porter came with an air of mystery, and asked to speak to me. I was surprised, and told him to come in. He was a very steady man, an old soldier who had been my husband's orderly.

"He seemed embarrassed by what he had to tell, and at last faltered:

"'Madame, the district inspector of police is in the hall.'

"'What does he want?' I asked sharply.

"'He wants to search the house.'

"The police are a useful body, but I loathe them. I don't think it's a noble profession. Irritated and disturbed, I replied:

"'Why this search? What is it for? I won't have them in.'

"'He says there is a criminal here,' replied the porter.

"This time I was frightened, and told him to send up the inspector to explain. He was a fairly well-bred man, decorated with the Legion of Honour. He made excuses and begged my pardon, and eventually announced that one of my servants was a convict!

"I was thoroughly annoyed; I replied that I would vouch for the entire staff of the house, and went through them one after another.

"'The porter, Pierre Courtin, an old soldier.'

"'That's not the man.'

"'The coachman, François Pingau, a peasant from Champagne, the son of one of the farmers on my father's estate.'

"'Not the man.'

"'A stable-boy, also from Champagne, the son of some peasants with whom I am acquainted; and the footman you have just seen.'

"'That's not he.'

"'Then, Monsieur, it must be clear to you that you have made a mistake.'

"'Excuse me, Madame, but I am quite sure that there is no mistake on my part. As the person in question is a dangerous criminal will you have the goodness to have all your servants brought here before you and me?'

"I refused at first, but at last I gave way, and made them all come up, men and women.

"The inspector cast but a single glance at them, and declared:

"'That is not all.'

"'I am sorry, Monsieur; the only one missing is my own maid, a girl whom you could not possibly mistake for a convict.'

"'May I see her too?' he asked.

"'Certainly.'

"I rang for Rose, who promptly appeared. She had scarcely entered the room when the inspector made a sign, and two men whom I had not seen, hidden behind the door, flung themselves upon her, seized her hands, and bound them with cords.

"A cry of rage escaped me, and I was ready on the instant to run to her defence. The inspector stopped me:

"'This girl, Madame, is a man named Jean-Nicolas Lecapet, condemned to death in 1879 for murder preceded by rape. His sentence was commuted to imprisonment for life. Four months ago he escaped. We have been searching for him ever since.'

"I was bewildered, thunderstruck. I could not believe it. With a laugh the inspector continued:

"'I can give you only one proof. His right arm is tattooed.'

" The sleeve was rolled up. It was true. The police officer added, rather tactlessly :

" ' You will have to trust *us* to verify the remaining details.'

" And they led my maid away !

" Now—would you believe it ?—the feeling strongest in me was not anger at the way I had been tricked, duped, and made ridiculous ; it was not the shame of having been dressed and undressed, handled and touched, by that man . . . but a . . . profound humiliation . . . the womanly humiliation. Do you understand ? "

" No, not quite."

" Oh, think. . . . That fellow had been sentenced . . . for rape. . . . I thought, don't you know . . . of the woman he had ravished . . . and it . . . it humiliated me. . . . Now do you understand ? "

Madame Margot did not speak. She gazed straight in front of her with a queer, absent stare, at the two gleaming buttons of the coachman's livery, her lips curved in the inscrutable smile a woman sometimes wears.

THE FATHER

HE WAS EMPLOYED AT THE MINISTRY OF EDUCATION, AND AS he lived in the Batignolles suburb he took the omnibus every morning to go to his office. And every morning he travelled to the centre of Paris facing a girl, with whom he fell in love.

She went to her work in a shop at the same time every day. She was small and dark, one of those brunettes whose eyes are so dark that they are like pitch balls stuck in her face, and whose skin has the gleam of ivory. Every day he saw her appear at the corner of the same street; and she would start running to catch up the heavy vehicle. She ran with short, hurried steps, supple and graceful, and would jump on to the step before the horses had quite stopped. Then she would make her way into the inside, panting a little, and, sitting down, would glance all round her.

The first time that he saw her, François Tessier knew that her face gave him infinite pleasure. Sometimes we meet such women, women whom we desire to seize fiercely in our arms, at first sight, before we even know them. This girl answered all the intimate desires, the secret dreams, the very ideal of love, as it were, which we bear about with us in the subconscious depths of our hearts.

Against his will he stared obstinately at her. His gaze embarrassed her and she blushed. He noticed this, and tried to turn away his eyes, but time and again they returned to her in spite of his efforts to fix his gaze elsewhere.

At the end of a few days they were no longer strangers, although they had never spoken to each other. He gave her his seat when the omnibus was full and went up on the top, in spite of the torture of loss it inflicted upon him. She greeted him now with a little smile; and though she always lowered her eyes under his gaze, which she felt to be too eager, yet she no longer seemed angry at being watched.

At last they began to talk to each other. A sudden, intimate friendship was established between them, an intimacy confined to half an hour each day. And certainly it was the most delightful half-hour of his day. He thought of her all the rest of the time, and never ceased to dwell on the vision of her during his long sojourns at the office, haunted, obsessed, and invaded by the changing, clinging image which the face of a beloved woman leaves with us. It seemed to him that complete possession of that little creature would be for him a wild happiness, almost beyond human realisation.

Every morning now she shook hands with him, and he retained until evening the sense of that contact, the memory in his flesh of the faint pressure of her small fingers; he imagined that he preserved the imprint of them on his skin.

Throughout the rest of his time he looked forward anxiously to the short omnibus journey. And his Sundays seemed heartbreaking.

She loved him too, not a doubt of it, for one Saturday in the spring she consented to lunch with him the next day at Maisons-Laffitte.

She arrived first at the station, and was waiting for him. He was surprised; but she said to him:

"Before we go, I've something to say. We've twenty minutes; that's more than long enough."

She was trembling, leaning on his arm, her eyes lowered and her cheeks pale.

"You must make no mistake about me," she continued. "I'm an honest girl, and I won't come with you unless you promise, unless you'll swear not to . . . not to do anything which isn't . . . which isn't . . . nice."

She had suddenly gone more scarlet than a poppy. She

was silent. He did not know what to reply, happy and disappointed at the same time. At the bottom of his heart he possibly preferred that it should be like this ; yet . . . yet he had lulled himself to sleep, the night before, with dreams that had fired his pulses. Certainly he would have loved her less, had he known her to be of easy virtue ; but then how charming, how delicious it would be for him if she were ! His mind was racked by all the selfish calculations that men make over this business of love.

As he said nothing, she added in a voice shaken with emotion, and tears at the corners of her eyes :

" If you don't promise to respect me, absolutely . . . I'm going back home."

He squeezed her arm affectionately and replied :

" I promise ; you shall do nothing you do not want to do."

She seemed relieved, and asked with a smile :

" Is that really true ? "

He looked into the depths of her eyes.

" I swear it ! "

" Then let's take the tickets," she said.

They could hardly speak a word to one another on the way, as their compartment was full.

Having reached Maisons-Laffitte, they directed their steps towards the Seine.

The warm air quieted their thoughts and their senses. The sun fell full upon the river, the leaves, and the grass, and darted a thousand gleams of happiness into body and mind. Hand in hand they walked along the bank, watching the little fish that glided in shoals under the surface of the water. They wandered along, adrift in happiness, as though transported from the earth in an ecstasy of delight.

At last she said :

" You must think me mad."

" Why ? " he asked.

"Isn't it mad of me to go all alone with you like this?" she went on.

"Why, no; it's quite natural."

"No, no! It's not natural—for me—for I don't want to do anything foolish—and this is just how one does come to do foolish things. But if you only knew! It's so dull, every day the same thing, every day in the month and every month in the year. I live alone with my mother. And since she has had many sorrows in her life, she's not very gay. As for me, I do what I can. I try to laugh, but I don't always succeed. But all the same, it was wrong of me to come. But at least you don't blame me for it?"

For answer he kissed her eagerly upon the ear. But she drew away from him with a swift movement, and said, suddenly vexed:

"Oh, Monsieur François, after what you promised me!"

And they turned back towards Maisons-Laffitte.

They lunched at the Petit-Havre, a low house buried beneath four enormous poplars, and standing on the bank of the river.

The fresh air, the heat, the thin white wine, and the exciting sense of each other's nearness made them flushed, troubled and silent. But after coffee, a sudden tide of joy welled up in them; they crossed the Seine and set off again along the bank towards the village of La Frette.

Suddenly he asked:

"What is your name?"

"Louise."

"Louise," he repeated, and said no more.

The river, describing a long curve, caressed a distant row of white houses mirrored head downwards in the water. The girl picked daisies and arranged them in a huge rustic sheaf; the man sang at the top of his voice, as lively as a colt just put out to grass.

To the left, a slope planted with vines followed the curve

of the river. Suddenly François stopped and remained motionless with astonishment.

" Oh, look ! " he said.

The vineyards had ceased, and all the hillside was now covered with flowering lilac. It was a violet-hued wood, a carpet spread upon the earth, reaching as far as the village two or three kilometres distant.

She too stood spellbound with delight.

" Oh ! How lovely ! " she murmured.

They crossed a field and ran towards this strange hill which every year supplies all the lilac trundled about Paris on the little barrows of the street sellers.

A narrow path lost itself among the shrubs. They took it, and, coming to a small clearing, sat down there.

Legions of flies murmured above their heads, filling the air with a soft, ceaseless drone. The sun, the fierce sun of an airless day, beat down upon the long slope of blossom, drawing from this flower-forest a powerful scent, great heady gusts of perfume, the exhalation of the flowers.

A church-bell rang in the distance.

Quietly they embraced, then drew each other closer, lying in the grass, conscious of nothing but their kisses. She had closed her eyes and held him in her open arms, clasping him tightly, all thought dismissed, all reason abandoned, every sense utterly suspended in passionate expectation. She gave herself utterly to him, without knowing what she was doing, without even realising that she was delivered into his hands.

She came to herself half mad, as from a dreadful disaster, and began to weep, moaning with grief, hiding her face in her hands.

He tried to console her. But she was anxious to leave, to get back, to go home at once. She walked up and down with desperate strides, ceaselessly repeating :

" My God ! My God ! "

" Louise," he begged. " Please stay, Louise."

Her cheeks were burning now, and her eyes sunken. As soon as they arrived at the station in Paris, she left him without even bidding him good-bye.

When he met her next day in the omnibus, she seemed to him to have changed, to have grown thinner.

"I must speak to you," she said to him. "We will get off at the boulevard."

When they were alone on the pavement she said:

"We must say good-bye to one another. I cannot see you again after what has happened."

"But why not?" he stammered.

"Because I cannot. I was to blame. I shall not be guilty a second time."

At that he begged and implored her, tortured with desire, maddened with the need to possess her utterly, in the deep abandon of nights of love.

"No, I cannot," she replied obstinately. "No, I cannot."

He grew more and more eager and excited. He promised to marry her.

"No," she said again, and left him.

He did not see her for eight days. He could not meet her, and, as he did not know her address, he thought her lost for ever.

On the evening of the ninth day his door-bell rang. He went to open the door. It was she. She flung herself into his arms and resisted no longer.

For three months she was his mistress. He began to weary of her, when she told him that she was with child. At that he had only one idea left in his head: to break with her at all costs.

Unable to tell her frankly what he meant to do, not knowing how to deal with the situation or what to say, wild with apprehension, and with the fear of the growing child, he made a desperate move. He decamped one night and disappeared.

The blow was so cruel that she made no search for the man who had deserted her in this fashion. She flung herself at her mother's knees and confessed her misfortune to her; a few months later she gave birth to a son.

The years slipped by. François Tessier grew old, without suffering any change in his manner of life. He led the monotonous and dismal existence of a bureaucrat, without hope or expectation. Every day he rose at the same hour, went down the same streets, walked through the same door past the same hall-porter, entered the same office, sat down on the same seat, and worked at the same task. He was alone in the world, alone by day in the midst of his indifferent colleagues, alone at night in his bachelor lodgings. Every month he saved up a hundred francs for his old age.

Every Sunday he went for a walk along the Champs-Élysées, to watch the world of fashion go by, the carriages and the pretty women.

Next day he would say to his comrades in duress:

"It was a wonderful sight outside the park yesterday."

One Sunday it chanced that he took a new way and went into the Parc Monceau. It was a bright summer morning. Nurses and mothers, seated on the benches at the side of the paths, were watching the children playing in front of them.

Suddenly François Tessier shivered. A woman passed him, holding two children by the hand, a little boy of about ten, and a little girl of four. It was she.

He walked on for another hundred yards, and then sank into a chair, choked with emotion. She had not recognised him. Then he went back, trying to see her again. She was sitting down now. The boy was standing beside her, charmingly decorous, and the little girl was making mud-pies. It was she, it was certainly she. She had the grave demeanour of a lady; her dress was simple, her bearing full of dignity and assurance.

He watched her from a distance, not daring to come close. The little boy raised his head. François Tessier felt himself trembling. This was his son, past all manner of doubt. He gazed at him, and fancied that he recognised himself as he might look in an old photograph.

He stayed hidden behind a tree, waiting for her to go, so that he might follow.

He did not sleep that night. The thought of the child racked him more than any other. His son! Oh! if he could only know, be sure! But what would he have done?

He had seen her house, he made inquiries, he learnt that she was married to a neighbour, a good man of high moral principles, who had been touched by her misery. Knowing her sin and forgiving it, he had even acknowledged the child, his, François Tessier's child.

Every Sunday he revisited the Parc Monceau. Every Sunday he saw her, and each time the mad, irresistible longing came to him to take his son in his arms, cover him with kisses, and carry him off, steal him.

He suffered terribly in his wretched loneliness, an old bachelor with nothing to love; he suffered a frightful anguish, torn by a fatherly love made up of remorse, longing, jealousy, and that need of small creatures to love which nature has implanted in the secret depths of every human being.

At last he decided to make a desperate effort, and, going up to her one day as she was entering the park, stood in her way, and said, with livid face and quivering lips:

"Don't you recognise me?"

She raised her eyes, looked at him, uttered a scream of fear and horror, and, seizing her two children by the hand, fled, dragging them after her.

He went home to weep.

More months went by. He saw her no more. But he suffered day and night, gnawed and devoured by love for his child.

To embrace his son he would have died, would have committed murder, accomplished any task, braved any danger, attempted any perilous enterprise.

He wrote to her. She did not answer. After twenty letters he realised that he could not hope to move her. Then he took a desperate resolution; ready to receive a pistol bullet in his heart if he failed, he wrote a short note to her husband:

"SIR,—

"My name must be an abhorred one to you. But I am so wretched, so tortured with remorse, that I have no hope except in you.

"I ask only for ten minutes' talk with you.

"Yours," etc.

Next day he received the answer:

"SIR,—

"I shall expect you at five o'clock on Tuesday."

As he mounted the staircase, François Tessier paused on every step, so furious was the beating of his heart. It was a hurrying clamour within his chest, a galloping animal, a dull and violent thudding. He could not breathe without an effort, and clung to the banisters to keep himself from falling.

At the third floor he rang. A servant opened the door.

"Monsieur Flamel?" he inquired.

"Yes, sir. Will you come in?"

He entered a middle-class drawing-room. He was alone, and he waited in agony like a man in the grip of disaster.

A door opened. A man appeared. He was tall, grave, and rather stout, and wore a black frock-coat. He pointed to a chair.

François Tessier sat down, then said in a breathless voice:

"Monsieur . . . Monsieur . . . I don't know if you know my name . . . if you know. . . ."

Monsieur Flamel cut him short.

" Do not trouble to explain, Monsieur. I know. My wife has spoken of you."

He had the forthright aspect of a kindly man trying to be severe; and the upstanding dignity of a sober, middle-class citizen.

" You see, Monsieur, it's like this," continued François Tessier. " I am dying of grief, remorse, and shame. All that I long for is that I may once, just once, kiss . . . the child."

Monsieur Flamel rose, went to the fire-place, and rang. The servant appeared.

" Fetch Louis," he said.

She went out. They remained facing one another, silent, having nothing else to say, waiting.

Suddenly a little boy of ten dashed into the room and ran to kiss the man he thought to be his father. But he stopped in confusion when he saw the stranger.

Monsieur Flamel kissed him on the forehead, and then said:

" Now, kiss this gentleman, darling."

The child advanced obediently, looking at the stranger.

François Tessier had risen; he let his hat fall and was himself ready to collapse.

Monsieur Flamel had tactfully turned his back and was looking out of the window at the street.

The child waited in great astonishment. He picked up the hat and restored it to the stranger. Then François, taking the little boy in his arms, began to cover his face with furious kisses, upon eyes, cheeks, mouth, and hair.

The child was frightened by the storm of kisses and tried to avoid them, turning away his head, and with his little hands thrust away the man's greedy lips.

Abruptly François Tessier set him down again.

" Good-bye! Good-bye!" he cried.

And he fled like a thief.

CONFESSING

THE NOON SUN POURED FIERCELY DOWN UPON THE FIELDS. They stretched in undulating folds between the clumps of trees that marked each farmhouse; the different crops, ripe rye and yellowing wheat, pale-green oats, dark-green clover, spread a vast striped cloak, soft and rippling, over the naked body of the earth.

In the distance, on the crest of a slope, was an endless line of cows, ranked like soldiers, some lying down, others standing, their large eyes blinking in the burning light, chewing the cud and grazing on a field of clover as broad as a lake.

Two women, mother and daughter, were walking with a swinging step, one behind the other, towards this regiment of cattle. Each carried two zinc pails, slung outwards from the body on a hoop from a cask; at each step the metal sent out a dazzling white flash under the sun that struck full upon it.

The women did not speak. They were on their way to milk the cows. When they arrive, they set down one of their pails and approach the first two cows, making them stand up with a kick in the ribs from wooden-shod feet. The beast rises slowly, first on its forelegs, then with more difficulty raises its large hind quarters, which seem to be weighted down by the enormous udder of livid pendulous flesh.

The two Malivoires, mother and daughter, kneeling beneath the animal's belly, tug with a swift movement of their hands at the swollen teat, which at each squeeze sends a slender jet of milk into the pail. The yellowish froth mounts to the brim, and the women go from cow to cow until they reach the end of the long line.

As soon as they finish milking a beast, they change its position, giving it a fresh patch of grass on which to graze.

Then they start on their way home, more slowly now, weighed down by the load of milk, the mother in front, the daughter behind.

Abruptly the latter halts, sets down her burden, sits down, and begins to cry.

Madame Malivoire, missing the sound of steps behind her, turns round and is quite amazed.

" What's the matter with you ? " she said.

Her daughter Céleste, a tall girl with flaming red hair and flaming cheeks, flecked with freckles as though sparks of fire had fallen upon her face one day as she worked in the sun, murmurs, moaning softly, like a beaten child :

" I can't carry the milk any further."

Her mother looked at her suspiciously.

" What's the matter with you ? " she repeated.

" It drags too heavy, I can't," replied Céleste, who had collapsed and was lying on the ground between the two pails, hiding her eyes in her apron.

" What's the matter with you, then ? " said her mother for the third time. The girl moaned :

" I think there's a baby on the way." And she broke into sobs.

The old woman now in her turn set down her load, so amazed that she could find nothing to say. At last she stammered :

" You . . . you . . . you're going to have a baby, you clod ! How can that be ? "

The Malivoires were prosperous farmers, wealthy and of a certain position, widely respected, good business folk, of some importance in the district.

" I think I am, all the same," faltered Céleste.

The frightened mother looked at the weeping girl grovelling at her feet. After a few seconds she cried :

" You're going to have a baby ! A baby ! Where did you get it, you slut ? "

Céleste, shaken with emotion, murmured :

" I think it was in Polyte's coach."

The old woman tried to understand, tried to imagine, to realise who could have brought this misfortune upon her daughter. If the lad was well off and of decent position, an arrangement might be come to. The damage could still be repaired. Céleste was not the first to be in the same way, but it was annoying all the same, seeing their position and the way people talked.

" And who was it, you slut ? " she repeated.

Céleste, resolved to make a clean breast of it, stammered :

" I think it was Polyte."

At that Madame Malivoire, mad with rage, rushed upon her daughter and began to beat her with such fury that her hat fell off in the effort.

With great blows of the fist she struck her on the head, on the back, all over her body ; Céleste, prostrate between the two pails, which afforded her some slight protection, shielded just her face with her hands.

All the cows, disturbed, had stopped grazing and turned round, staring with their great eyes. The last one mooed, stretching out its muzzle towards the women.

After beating her daughter till she was out of breath, Madame Malivoire stopped, exhausted ; her spirits reviving a little, she tried to get a thorough understanding of the situation.

"—— Polyte ! Lord save us, it's not possible ! How could you, with a carrier ? You must have lost your wits. He must have played you a trick, the good-for-nothing ! "

Céleste, still prostrate, murmured in the dust :

" I didn't pay my fare ! "

And the old Norman woman understood.

Every week, on Wednesday and on Saturday, Céleste went to town with the farm produce, poultry, cream, and eggs.

She started at seven with her two huge baskets on her arm, the dairy produce in one, the chickens in the other, and went to the main road to wait for the coach to Yvetot.

She set down her wares and sat in the ditch, while the chickens with their short pointed beaks and the ducks with their broad flat bills thrust their heads between the wicker bars and looked about them with their round, stupid, surprised eyes.

Soon the bus, a sort of yellow box with a black leather cap on the top, came up, jerking and quivering with the trotting of the old white horse.

Polyte the coachman, a big, jolly fellow, stout though still young, and so burnt up by sun and wind, soaked by rain, and coloured with brandy that his face and neck were brick-red, cracked his whip and shouted from the distance :

" Morning, Mam'selle Céleste. In good health, I hope ? "

She gave him her baskets, one after the other, which he stowed in the boot ; then she got in, lifting her leg high up to reach the step, and exposing a sturdy leg clad in a blue stocking.

Every time Polyte repeated the same joke : " Well, it's not got any thinner."

She laughed, thinking this funny.

Then he uttered a " Gee up, old girl ! " which started off the thin horse. Then Céleste, reaching for her purse in the depths of her pocket, slowly took out fivepence, threepence for herself and twopence for the baskets, and handed them to Polyte over his shoulder.

He took them, saying :

" Aren't we going to have our little bit of sport to-day ? "

And he laughed heartily, turning round towards her so as to stare at her at his ease.

She found it a big expense, the half-franc for a journey of two miles. And when she had no coppers she felt it still more keenly ; it was hard to make up her mind to part with a silver coin.

One day, as she was paying, she asked :

" From a good customer like me you oughtn't to take more than threepence."

He burst out laughing.

"Threepence, my beauty; why, you're worth more than that."

She insisted on the point.

" But you make a good two francs a month out of me."

He whipped up his horse and exclaimed :

" Look here, I'm an obliging fellow ! We'll call it quits for a bit of sport."

" What do you mean ? " she asked with an air of innocence.

He was so amused that he laughed till he coughed.

" A bit of sport is a bit of sport, damn it ; a game for a lad and a lass, a dance for two without music."

She understood, blushed, and declared :

" I don't care for that sort of game, Monsieur Polyte."

But he was in no way abashed, and repeated, with growing merriment :

" You'll come to it some day, my beauty, a bit of sport for a lad and a lass ! "

And since that day he had taken to asking her, each time that she paid her fare :

" Aren't we going to have our bit of sport to-day ? "

She, too, joked about it by this time, and replied :

" Not to-day, Monsieur Polyte, but Saturday, for certain ! "

And amid peals of laughter he answered :

" Saturday, then, my beauty."

But inwardly she calculated that, during the two years the affair had been going on, she had paid Polyte forty-eight whole francs, and in the country forty-eight francs is not a sum which can be picked up on the roadside; she also calculated that in two more years she would have paid nearly a hundred francs.

To such purpose she meditated that, one spring day as they jogged on alone, when he made his customary inquiry : " Aren't we going to have our bit of sport yet ? " She replied :

" Yes, if you like, Monsieur Polyte."

He was not at all surprised, and clambered over the back of his seat, murmuring with a complacent air :

" Come along, then. I knew you'd come to it some day."

The old white horse trotted so gently that she seemed to be dancing upon the same spot, deaf to the voice which cried at intervals, from the depths of the vehicle : " Gee up, old girl ! Gee up, then ! "

Three months later Céleste discovered that she was going to have a child.

All this she had told her mother in a tearful voice. Pale with fury, the old woman asked :

" Well, what did it cost ? "

" Four months ; that makes eight francs, doesn't it ? " replied Céleste.

At that the peasant woman's fury was utterly unleashed, and, falling once more upon her daughter, she beat her a second time until she was out of breath. Then she rose and said :

" Have you told him about the baby ? "

" No, of course not."

" Why haven't you told him ? "

" Because very likely he'd have made me pay for all the free rides ! "

The old woman pondered awhile, then picked up her milk-pails.

" Come on, get up, and try to walk home," she said, and, after a pause, continued :

" And don't tell him as long as he doesn't notice anything, and we'll make six or eight months' fares out of him."

And Céleste, who had risen, still crying, dishevelled and swollen round the eyes, started off again with dragging steps, murmuring :

" Of course I won't say."

THE NECKLACE

SHE WAS ONE OF THOSE PRETTY AND CHARMING GIRLS BORN, as though fate had blundered over her, into a family of artisans. She had no marriage portion, no expectations, no means of getting known, understood, loved, and wedded by a man of wealth and distinction; and she let herself be married off to a little clerk in the Ministry of Education.

Her tastes were simple because she had never been able to afford any other, but she was as unhappy as though she had married beneath her; for women have no caste or class, their beauty, grace, and charm serving them for birth or family. Their natural delicacy, their instinctive elegance, their nimbleness of wit, are their only mark of rank, and put the slum girl on a level with the highest lady in the land.

She suffered endlessly, feeling herself born for every delicacy and luxury. She suffered from the poorness of her house, from its mean walls, worn chairs, and ugly curtains. All these things, of which other women of her class would not even have been aware, tormented and insulted her. The sight of the little Breton girl who came to do the work in her little house aroused heart-broken regrets and hopeless dreams in her mind. She imagined silent antechambers, heavy with Oriental tapestries, lit by torches in lofty bronze sockets, with two tall footmen in knee-breeches sleeping in large arm-chairs, overcome by the heavy warmth of the stove. She imagined vast saloons hung with antique silks, exquisite pieces of furniture supporting priceless ornaments, and small, charming, perfumed rooms, created just for little parties of intimate friends, men who were famous and sought after, whose homage roused every other woman's envious longings.

When she sat down for dinner at the round table covered with a three-days-old cloth, opposite her husband, who took the cover off the soup-tureen, exclaiming delightedly: "Aha! Scotch broth! What could be better?" she imagined delicate meals, gleaming silver, tapestries peopling the walls with folk of a past age and strange birds in faery forests; she imagined delicate food served in marvellous dishes, murmured gallantries, listened to with an inscrutable smile as one trifled with the rosy flesh of trout or wings of asparagus chicken.

She had no clothes, no jewels, nothing. And these were the only things she loved; she felt that she was made for them. She had longed so eagerly to charm, to be desired, to be wildly attractive and sought after.

She had a rich friend, an old school friend whom she refused to visit, because she suffered so keenly when she returned home. She would weep whole days, with grief, regret, despair, and misery.

One evening her husband came home with an exultant air, holding a large envelope in his hand.

"Here's something for you," he said.

Swiftly she tore the paper and drew out a printed card on which were these words:

> "The Minister of Education and Madame Ramponneau request the pleasure of the company of Monsieur and Madame Loisel at the Ministry on the evening of Monday, January the 18th."

Instead of being delighted, as her husband hoped, she flung the invitation petulantly across the table, murmuring:

"What do you want me to do with this?"

"Why, darling, I thought you'd be pleased. You never go out, and this is a great occasion. I had tremendous trouble to get it. Every one wants one; it's very select, and very few go to the clerks. You'll see all the really big people there."

She looked at him out of furious eyes, and said impatiently:

"And what do you suppose I am to wear at such an affair?"

He had not thought about it; he stammered:

"Why, the dress you go to the theatre in. It looks very nice, to me. . . ."

He stopped, stupefied and utterly at a loss when he saw that his wife was beginning to cry. Two large tears ran slowly down from the corners of her eyes towards the corners of her mouth.

"What's the matter with you? What's the matter with you?" he faltered.

But with a violent effort she overcame her grief and replied in a calm voice, wiping her wet cheeks:

"Nothing. Only I haven't a dress and so I can't go to this party. Give your invitation to some friend of yours whose wife will be turned out better than I shall."

He was heart-broken.

"Look here, Mathilde," he persisted. "What would be the cost of a suitable dress, which you could use on other occasions as well, something very simple?"

She thought for several seconds, reckoning up prices and also wondering for how large a sum she could ask without bringing upon herself an immediate refusal and an exclamation of horror from the careful-minded clerk.

At last she replied with some hesitation:

"I don't know exactly, but I think I could do it on four hundred francs."

He grew slightly pale, for this was exactly the amount he had been saving for a gun, intending to get a little shooting next summer on the plain of Nanterre with some friends who went lark-shooting there on Sundays.

Nevertheless he said: "Very well. I'll give you four hundred francs. But try and get a really nice dress with the money."

The day of the party drew near, and Madame Loisel seemed sad, uneasy and anxious. Her dress was ready, however. One evening her husband said to her :

" What's the matter with you ? You've been very odd for the last three days."

" I'm utterly miserable at not having any jewels, not a single stone, to wear," she replied. " I shall look absolutely no one. I would almost rather not go to the party."

" Wear flowers," he said. " They're very smart at this time of the year. For ten francs you could get two or three gorgeous roses."

She was not convinced.

" No . . . there's nothing so humiliating as looking poor in the middle of a lot of rich women."

" How stupid you are ! " exclaimed her husband. " Go and see Madame Forestier and ask her to lend you some jewels. You know her quite well enough for that."

She uttered a cry of delight.

" That's true. I never thought of it."

Next day she went to see her friend and told her her trouble.

Madame Forestier went to her dressing-table, took up a large box, brought it to Madame Loisel, opened it, and said :

" Choose, my dear."

First she saw some bracelets, then a pearl necklace, then a Venetian cross in gold and gems, of exquisite workmanship. She tried the effect of the jewels before the mirror, hesitating, unable to make up her mind to leave them, to give them up. She kept on asking :

" Haven't you anything else ? "

" Yes. Look for yourself. I don't know what you would like best."

Suddenly she discovered, in a black satin case, a superb diamond necklace ; her heart began to beat covetously. Her hands trembled as she lifted it. She fastened it round her neck, upon her high dress, and remained in ecstasy at sight of herself.

Then, with hesitation, she asked in anguish :

" Could you lend me this, just this alone ? "

" Yes, of course."

She flung herself on her friend's breast, embraced her frenziedly, and went away with her treasure.

The day of the party arrived. Madame Loisel was a success. She was the prettiest woman present, elegant, graceful, smiling, and quite above herself with happiness. All the men stared at her, inquired her name, and asked to be introduced to her. All the Under-Secretaries of State were eager to waltz with her. The Minister noticed her.

She danced madly, ecstatically, drunk with pleasure, with no thought for anything, in the triumph of her beauty, in the pride of her success, in a cloud of happiness made up of this universal homage and admiration, of the desires she had aroused, of the completeness of a victory so dear to her feminine heart.

She left about four o'clock in the morning. Since midnight her husband had been dozing in a deserted little room, in company with three other men whose wives were having a good time.

He threw over her shoulders the garments he had brought for them to go home in, modest everyday clothes, whose poverty clashed with the beauty of the ball-dress. She was conscious of this and was anxious to hurry away, so that she should not be noticed by the other women putting on their costly furs.

Loisel restrained her.

" Wait a little. You'll catch cold in the open. I'm going to fetch a cab."

But she did not listen to him and rapidly descended the staircase. When they were out in the street they could not find a cab ; they began to look for one, shouting at the driver whom they saw passing in the distance.

They walked down towards the Seine, desperate and shivering. At last they found on the quay one of those old night-prowling carriages which are only to be seen in Paris after dark, as though they were ashamed of their shabbiness in the daylight.

It brought them to their door in the Rue des Martyrs, and sadly they walked up to their own apartment. It was the end, for her. As for him, he was thinking that he must be at the office at ten.

She took off the garments in which she had wrapped her shoulders, so as to see herself in all her glory before the mirror. But suddenly she uttered a cry. The necklace was no longer round her neck!

" What's the matter with you?" asked her husband, already half undressed.

She turned towards him in the utmost distress.

" I . . . I . . . I've no longer got Madame Forestier's necklace. . . ."

He started with astonishment.

" What! . . . Impossible!"

They searched in the folds of her dress, in the folds of the coat, in the pockets, everywhere. They could not find it.

" Are you sure that you still had it on when you came away from the ball?" he asked.

" Yes, I touched it in the hall at the Ministry."

" But if you had lost it in the street, we should have heard it fall."

" Yes. Probably we should. Did you take the number of the cab?"

" No. You didn't notice it, did you?"

" No."

They stared at one another, dumbfounded. At last Loisel put on his clothes again.

" I'll go over all the ground we walked," he said, " and see if I can't find it."

And he went out. She remained in her evening clothes, lacking strength to get into bed, huddled on a chair, without volition or power of thought.

Her husband returned about seven. He had found nothing.

He went to the police station, to the newspapers, to offer a reward, to the cab companies, everywhere that a ray of hope impelled him.

She waited all day long, in the same state of bewilderment at this fearful catastrophe.

Loisel came home at night, his face lined and pale ; he had discovered nothing.

"You must write to your friend," he said, "and tell her that you've broken the clasp of her necklace and are getting it mended. That will give us time to look about us."

She wrote at his dictation.

By the end of a week they had lost all hope.

Loisel, who had aged five years, declared :

"We must see about replacing the diamonds."

Next day they took the box which had held the necklace and went to the jewellers whose name was inside. He consulted his books.

"It was not I who sold this necklace, Madame ; I must have merely supplied the clasp."

Then they went from jeweller to jeweller, searching for another necklace like the first, consulting their memories, both ill with remorse and anguish of mind.

In a shop at the Palais-Royal they found a string of diamonds which seemed to them exactly like the one they were looking for. It was worth forty thousand francs. They were allowed to have it for thirty-six thousand.

They begged the jeweller not to sell it for three days. And they arranged matters on the understanding that it would be taken back for thirty-four thousand francs, if the first one were found before the end of February.

Loisel possessed eighteen thousand francs left to him by his father. He intended to borrow the rest.

He did borrow it, getting a thousand from one man, five hundred from another, five louis here, three louis there. He gave notes of hand, entered into ruinous agreements, did business with usurers and the whole tribe of money-lenders. He mortgaged the whole remaining years of his existence, risked his signature without even knowing if he could honour it, and, appalled at the agonising face of the future, at the black misery about to fall upon him, at the prospect of every possible physical privation and moral torture, he went to get the new necklace and put down upon the jeweller's counter thirty-six thousand francs.

When Madame Loisel took back the necklace to Madame Forestier, the latter said to her in a chilly voice:

" You ought to have brought it back sooner; I might have needed it."

She did not, as her friend had feared, open the case. If she had noticed the substitution, what would she have thought? What would she have said? Would she not have taken her for a thief?

Madame Loisel came to know the ghastly life of abject poverty. From the very first she played her part heroically. This fearful debt must be paid off. She would pay it. The servant was dismissed. They changed their flat; they took a garret under the roof.

She came to know the heavy work of the house, the hateful duties of the kitchen. She washed the plates, wearing out her pink nails on the coarse pottery and the bottoms of pans. She washed the dirty linen, the shirts and dish-cloths, and hung them out to dry on a string; every morning she took the dustbin down into the street and carried up the water, stopping on each landing to get her breath. And, clad like a poor woman, she went to the fruiterer, to the grocer, to the butcher, a basket on her arm, haggling, insulted, fighting for every wretched halfpenny of her money.

Every month notes had to be paid off, others renewed, time gained.

Her husband worked in the evenings at putting straight a merchant's accounts, and often at night he did copying at twopence-halfpenny a page.

And this life lasted ten years.

At the end of ten years everything was paid off, everything, the usurer's charges and the accumulation of superimposed interest.

Madame Loisel looked old now. She had become like all the other strong, hard, coarse women of poor households. Her hair was badly done, her skirts were awry, her hands were red. She spoke in a shrill voice, and the water slopped all over the floor when she scrubbed it. But sometimes, when her husband was at the office, she sat down by the window and thought of that evening long ago, of the ball at which she had been so beautiful and so much admired.

What would have happened if she had never lost those jewels. Who knows? Who knows? How strange life is, how fickle! How little is needed to ruin or to save!

One Sunday, as she had gone for a walk along the Champs-Élysées to freshen herself after the labours of the week, she caught sight suddenly of a woman who was taking a child out for a walk. It was Madame Forestier, still young, still beautiful, still attractive.

Madame Loisel was conscious of some emotion. Should she speak to her? Yes, certainly. And now that she had paid, she would tell her all. Why not?

She went up to her.

"Good morning, Jeanne."

The other did not recognise her, and was surprised at being thus familiarly addressed by a poor woman.

" But . . . Madame . . ." she stammered. " I don't know . . . you must be making a mistake."

" No . . . I am Mathilde Loisel."

Her friend uttered a cry.

" Oh ! . . . my poor Mathilde, how you have changed ! . . ."

" Yes, I've had some hard times since I saw you last ; and many sorrows . . . and all on your account."

" On my account ! . . . How was that ? "

" You remember the diamond necklace you lent me for the ball at the Ministry ? "

" Yes. Well ? "

" Well, I lost it."

" How could you ? Why, you brought it back."

" I brought you another one just like it. And for the last ten years we have been paying for it. You realise it wasn't easy for us ; we had no money. . . . Well, it's paid for at last, and I'm glad indeed."

Madame Forestier had halted.

" You say you bought a diamond necklace to replace mine ? "

" Yes. You hadn't noticed it ? They were very much alike."

And she smiled in proud and innocent happiness.

Madame Forestier, deeply moved, took her two hands.

" Oh, my poor Mathilde ! But mine was imitation. It was worth at the very most five hundred francs ! . . ."

HAPPINESS

IT WAS TEA-TIME, JUST BEFORE THE LAMPS WERE BROUGHT IN. The villa overlooked the sea; the vanished sun had left the sky rose-tipped in its passing, and powdered with golden dust; and the Mediterranean, without ripple or faintest movement, smooth, still gleaming with the light of the dying day, spread out a vast shield of burnished metal.

Far to the right, the jagged mountains lifted their black, sharp-cut bulk against the dim purple of the West.

They were speaking of love, retelling an ancient tale, saying over again things already said many, many times before. The soft, melancholy dusk pressed upon their speech, so that a feeling of tenderness welled up in their hearts, and the word "love," constantly repeated, now in a man's strong voice, now in the high, clear tones of a woman, seemed to fill the little room, flitting about it like a bird, hovering like a spirit over them.

Can one love for years without end?

Yes, claimed some.

No, declared others.

They drew a distinction between various cases, made clear the qualities that divided one from another, quoted examples; and all, both men and women, filled with rushing, disquieting memories which they could not reveal and which hovered on their lips, seemed profoundly moved; they spoke of this commonplace yet supreme thing, this mysterious concord between two beings, with the deepest emotion and burning interest.

Suddenly one among them, whose eyes were fixed on the distant scene, exclaimed:

" Oh! Look! What's that, over there?"

Across the sea, on the rim of haze, rose a huge, grey, shapeless mass.

The women had risen and were staring uncomprehendingly at this amazing object, which none of them had ever seen before.

" It's Corsica," said someone. " It can be seen two or three times a year under exceptional atmospheric conditions, when the air is so perfectly clear as not to conceal it with those mists of water-vapour in which distant prospects are always wrapped."

They could distinguish vaguely the mountain peaks, and fancied that they could see the snow on the summits. And every one was surprised, disturbed, almost frightened at this abrupt appearance of a world, at this phantom risen from the sea. Such perilous visions had they, perchance, who set out like Columbus across strange seas.

Then an old gentleman, who had not spoken, remarked:

" Oddly enough, in that island which has just swum into our sight—at the very moment when it would give force to what we have been saying and awaken one of my strangest memories—I came across a perfect instance of faithful love, miraculously happy love.

" Five years ago I made a tour in Corsica. That wild island is farther away from us, and less known to us, than America, although it is somctimes to be seen from the coasts of France, even as to-day.

" Imagine a world still in chaos, a maelstrom of mountains separated by narrow ravines down which foaming torrents rush, not a single level space, but only immense billows of granite and gigantic undulations in the ground, covered with thickets or with lofty forests of chestnut and pine. It is virgin soil, uncultivated, deserted, although an occasional village may be descried, like a pile of rocks perched on the top of a mountain. There is no culture, no industry, no art. Never does one meet with a piece of carved wood, a block of sculptured stone, with any reminder of hereditary taste, rudimentary or refined, for gracious and beautiful things. That is the most striking thing in this superb, harsh country: its inherited indifference to that search for magical loveliness which is called art.

"Italy, where every palace, full of masterpieces, is itself a masterpiece, where marble, wood, bronze, iron, in fact all metals and stones, bear witness to the genius of man, where the tiniest heirlooms in old houses reveal a divine care for beauty, is to each one of us a sacred and beloved land, because she displays and proves to us the strong impulse, the grandeur, the power, and the triumph of the creative intelligence.

"Facing her, wild Corsica has remained just as she was in her earliest days. There man lives in his rude house, indifferent to all that does not affect his mere existence or his family quarrels. He has survived with the defects and qualities of all uncivilised races, violent, strong to hate, instinctively bloodthirsty, but also hospitable, generous, full of true piety, simple-hearted, opening his door to the passer-by and bestowing a loyal friendship in return for the smallest token of sympathy.

"For a month I had been wandering over this magnificent island, feeling as though I were at the end of the world. There are no inns, no taverns, no roads. Mule paths lead to the villages that cling to the flanks of the mountains and overlook the twisting gulfs from whose depths the heavy, muffled, deep roar of the torrent rises ceaselessly in the silence of evening. The traveller knocks at the house doors and asks for shelter for the night and food until next day. He sits down at the humble table and sleeps beneath the humble roof, and in the morning shakes the outstretched hand of his host, who leads him to the edge of the village.

"One evening, after walking for ten hours, I came to a little house standing by itself in the depths of a narrow valley that fell into the sea a league farther on. The two steep slopes of the hillside, covered with thickets, boulders, and tall trees, were like two gloomy walls enclosing this unutterably mournful abyss.

" Round the hovel were a few vines, a small garden, and, further on, some large chestnut-trees ; enough, actually, for a bare existence, a fortune in that poor country.

" The woman who opened the door was old, hard-featured, and clean, which was unusual. The man, seated on a cane-chair, got up to greet me and then sat down without saying a word.

" ' Please excuse him,' said his wife to me. ' He's deaf now. He's eighty-two.'

" She spoke perfect French. I was surprised.

" ' You are not Corsicans ? ' I asked her.

" ' No,' she replied, ' we come from the mainland. But we have lived here for fifty years.'

" A feeling of anguish and terror overwhelmed me at the thought of the fifty years that had rolled by in this dark hole, so far from towns and the life of men. An old shepherd came in, and we began to eat the only course of the dinner, a thick soup in which potatoes, bacon, and cabbage were all boiled together.

" When the short meal was over, I went out and sat before the door, my heart oppressed with the melancholy of that sombre landscape, in the grip of that feeling of wretchedness which sometimes lays hold on the traveller, on sad evenings, in desolate places. It seems as though all things were coming to an end, life itself, and the universe. The dreadful misery of life is revealed in one blinding flash, and the isolation of all things, the nothingness of all things, and the black loneliness of our hearts which soothe and deceive themselves with dreams until the coming of death itself.

" The old woman joined me, and tormented by the curiosity which lives on in the hearts of even the most resigned of mortals, said to me :

" ' So you come from France? '

" ' Yes, I am travelling for pleasure.'

" ' You are from Paris, perhaps? '

" ' No, I come from Nancy.'

" At that it seemed to me that an extraordinary excitement was agitating her. How I saw this, or rather felt it, I do not know.

" ' You are from Nancy? ' she repeated slowly.

" The husband appeared in the doorway, impassive, as are all deaf people.

" ' It does not matter,' she continued. ' He cannot hear.'

" Then, after a few seconds:

" ' Then you know people in Nancy? '

" ' Why, yes, almost everybody.'

" ' The Sainte-Allaize family? '

" ' Yes, very well; they were friends of my father's.'

" ' What is your name? '

" I told her. She stared intently at me, then said in that soft voice evoked by wakening memories:

" ' Yes, yes, I remember quite well. And the Brisenaves, what has become of them? '

" ' They are all dead.'

" ' Ah! And the Sirmonts, do you know them? '

" ' Yes, the youngest is a General.'

" At that she replied, shaking with excitement, with anguish, with I know not what confused powerful and intimate emotion, with I know not how pressing a need to confess, to tell everything, to speak of things she had until this moment kept locked in the secret places of her heart, and of the people whose name troubled the very depths of her soul:

" ' Yes, Henri de Sirmont. I know him well. He is my brother.'

" I lifted my eyes to her, quite dumbfounded with surprise. And suddenly I remembered.

" It had been a great scandal, long ago, in aristocratic Lorraine. As a young girl, beautiful, wealthy, Suzanne de Sirmont had run off with a non-commissioned officer in the hussar regiment of which her father was commander.

" He was a handsome lad ; his parents were peasants, but he wore the blue dolman with a gallant air, this soldier who seduced his colonel's daughter. Doubtless she had seen him, noticed him, fallen in love with him as she watched the squadrons march past. But how had she spoken to him, how had they been able to meet and come to an understanding ? How had she dared to make him realise that she loved him ? This no one ever knew.

" Nothing had been guessed or foreseen. One evening, when the soldier had just completed his term of service, he disappeared with her. A search was made, but they were not found. No news of them was heard, and she was thought of as dead.

" And thus I had found her in this sinister valley.

" Then in my turn I answered :

" ' Yes, I remember well. You are Mademoiselle Suzanne.'

" She nodded ' yes.' Tears poured from her eyes. Then, glancing towards the old man, standing motionless on the threshold of his dwelling, she said to me :

" ' That is he.'

" And I realised that she still loved him, still saw him with eyes blinded by love.

" ' But at least you have been happy ? ' I asked.

" She answered, in a voice that came from her heart :

" ' Oh, yes, very happy. He has made me very happy. I have never had any regrets.'

" I gazed at her, a little sad, surprised, marvelling at the power of love ! This rich girl had followed this man, this peasant. She had stooped to a life without charm, luxury, or refinement of any sort, she had accustomed herself to an entirely simple existence. And she still loved him. She had become the wife of a country clodhopper, with a bonnet and a canvas skirt. She sat on a cane-bottomed chair, she ate broth made of potatoes, cabbage, and bacon, out of an earthen platter set on a deal table. She slept on straw at his side.

" She had never a thought for anything but him. She had regretted neither jewels, nor fine clothes, nor fashion, nor the comfort of arm-chairs, nor the perfumed warmth of tapestry-hung rooms, nor the softness of down whereon the body sinks to rest. She had never needed anything but him ; so only that he was there, she wanted nothing.

" In early youth she had forsaken life and the world and those who had loved and nurtured her. She had come, alone with him, to this wild ravine. And he had been everything to her, all that a woman desires, all that she dreams of, all that she ceaselessly awaits, all for which she never ceases to hope. He had filled her existence with happiness from its beginning to its close.

" She could not have been happier.

" And all night long, as I listened to the hoarse breathing of the old soldier lying on his pallet beside the woman who had followed him so far, I thought of this strange and simple adventure, of her happiness, so complete, built of so little.

" I left next morning, after shaking hands with the old couple."

The teller of the tale was silent. A woman said :

" All the same, her ideal was too easy of attainment, her needs too primitive, her demands on life too simple. She must have been a stupid girl."

Another woman said slowly :

" What does it matter ? She was happy."

In the distance, on the rim of the world, Corsica receded into the night, sinking slowly back into the sea, withdrawing the vast shadow that had appeared as though itself would tell the story of the two humble lovers sheltered by its shores.

THE OLD MAN

THE WARM AUTUMN SUNLIGHT FELL ACROSS THE FARMYARD through the tall beeches at the roadside. Under the turf cropped by the cows, the earth was soft and moist with recent rain, and sank underfoot with a sound of sucked-in water; the apple-trees laden with apples strewed the dark-green herbage with pale-green fruit.

Four young heifers were grazing, tethered in a line; from time to time they lowed towards the house; cocks and hens lent colour and movement to the dungheap in front of the cowshed, running round, cackling noisily, scratching in the dust, while the two cocks crowed without ceasing, looking for worms for their hens, and calling to them with lively clucks.

The wooden gate opened; a man came in, aged perhaps forty, but looking sixty, wrinkled and bent, walking with long strides, weighed down by heavy sabots filled with straw. Arms of abnormal length hung down by the side of his body. As he drew near the farmhouse, a yellow cur, tied to the foot of an enormous pear-tree, beside a barrel which served as his kennel, wagged his tail, and began to bark joyously.

"Down, Finot!" cried the man.

The dog was silent.

A peasant woman came out of the house. Her broad, flat, bony body was plainly visible through a tight-fitting woollen jersey. A short grey skirt reached half-way down her legs, which were hidden in blue stockings; she too wore sabots filled with straw. A yellowing white bonnet covered the sparse hair that clung round her skull, and her face, brown, thin, ugly, toothless, bore the savage and brutalised expression found often in the faces of peasants.

" How is he ? " asked the man.

" Parson says it's the end," replied the woman ; " he won't last through the night."

The two of them went into the house.

After passing through the kitchen, they entered a low, dark room, faintly lit by a window, in front of which hung a rag of Norman chintz. Huge beams in the ceiling, brown with age, dark and smoke-begrimed, ran across the room from one side to the other, carrying the light floor of the loft, where crowds of rats ran about both by day and by night.

The earthen floor, damp and uneven, had a greasy look ; at the far end of the room the bed was a dim white patch. A hoarse, regular sound, a harsh, rattling, and whistling breath, with a gurgling note like that made by a broken pump, came from the darkened couch, where an old man lay dying : the woman's father.

The man and the woman came up and stared at the dying man with their calm, patient eyes.

" This time, it's the end," said the son-in-law ; " he won't even last till nightfall."

" He's been gurgling like that since midday," answered his wife.

Then they were silent. Her father's eyes were closed, his face was the colour of earth, so dry that it looked as though carved of wood. Between his half-open lips issued a laboured, clamorous breathing, and at every breath the grey calico sheet over his chest heaved and fell.

After a long silence the son-in-law declared :

" There's nothing to do but leave him to snuff out. There's nothing we can do. But it's annoying all the same, because of the colzas ; now the weather's good, I'll have to transplant them to-morrow."

His wife seemed uneasy at this idea. She pondered for some moments, then said :

"Seeing that he's going to die, we won't bury him before Saturday; that will leave you to-morrow for the colza."

The peasant meditated.

"Yes," he said, "but then to-morrow I'll have to bid the guests for the funeral; it'll take me a good five or six hours to go and see every one from Tourville to Manetot."

The woman, after pondering for two or three minutes, declared:

"It's barely three, so you could start going round to-night and go all over Tourville way. You may as well say he's dead, seeing that he can't last through the afternoon."

For a few moments the man remained in doubt, pondering over the consequences and the advantages of the idea.

"Very well, I'll go," he said at last.

He made as though to go out, then came back, and said, after a brief hesitation:

"Seeing that you've no work on hand, shake down some cooking-apples, and then you might make four dozen dumplings for the people that will be coming to the funeral; they'll want cheering up. Light the range with the faggot under the shed by the winepress. It's dry."

He left the room, went back into the kitchen, opened the cupboard, took out a six-pound loaf, carefully cut off a slice, gathered the crumbs fallen on to the shelf in the hollow of his hand, and crammed them into his mouth, in order to waste nothing. Then on the tip of his knife he picked up a bit of salt butter from the bottom of a brown earthenware pot and spread it on his bread, which he began to eat, slowly, as he did everything.

He went back across the yard, quieted the dog, who began to bark again, went out on to the road which ran alongside his ditch, and departed in the direction of Tourville.

Left alone, the woman set about her task. She took the lid off the flour-bin and prepared the paste for the dumplings.

For a long time she worked it, turning it over and over, kneading it, squeezing it, and beating it. Then she made a large ball of it, yellowish-white in colour, and left it on the corner of the table.

Then she went to get the apples, and, to avoid injuring the tree with a stick, she climbed into it with the aid of a stool. She chose the fruit with care, taking only the ripest, and heaped them in her apron.

A voice called from the road:

" Hey there! Madame Chicot! "

She turned round. It was a neighbour, Master Osime Favet, the mayor, on his way to manure his fields, seated on the manure-cart, with his legs dangling over the side. She turned round and replied:

" What can I do for you, Master Osime? "

" How's your father getting on? "

" He's practically gone," she shouted. " The funeral's on Saturday at seven, seeing as we're in a hurry to do the colza."

" Right," replied the neighbour. " Good luck to you! Are you well? "

" Thank you, yes," she replied to his polite inquiry. " And you too? "

Then she went on picking her apples.

As soon as she came in, she went to her father, expecting to find him dead. But from the door she could hear his noisy, monotonous death-rattle, and to save time decided that it was useless to go to his bedside. She began to make the dumplings.

She wrapped the apples, one by one, in a thin leaf of paste, then lined them up along the edge of the table. When she had made forty-eight, arranged in dozens one in front of the other, she began to think of getting supper ready, and hung her pot over the fire, to cook the potatoes; for she had reflected that it was useless to light the range that day, having still the whole of the next day in which to complete her preparations for the funeral.

Her husband returned about five o'clock. As soon as he had crossed the threshold he inquired :

" Is it over yet ? "

" Not yet," she replied. " The gurgling's still going on."

They went to the bed. The old man was in exactly the same condition. His raucous breathing, regular as the working of a clock, had become neither quicker nor slower. It came from second to second, with slight variations in the pitch, determined by the passage of the air as it entered and left his chest.

His son-in-law stared at him, then said :

" He'll go out when we're not thinking of it, like a candle."

They went back to the kitchen, and began their supper in silence. When they had swallowed the soup, they ate a slice of bread and butter as well ; then, as soon as the plates were washed, they went back to the dying man's room.

The woman, holding a small lamp with a smoky wick, passed it in front of her father's face. If he had not been breathing he would certainly have been taken for dead.

The bed belonging to the two peasants was hidden at the other end of the room, in a sort of recess. They got into bed without speaking a word, extinguished the light, and closed their eyes ; soon two uneven snores, one deep, the other shriller, accompanied the uninterrupted rattle of the dying man.

The rats ran to and fro in the loft.

The husband awoke with the first pale glimmer of dawn. His father-in-law was still alive. He shook his wife, uneasy at the old man's resistance.

" I say, Phémie, he won't finish it off. What would you do about it ? "

He knew her to be of good counsel.

" He won't get through the day, for certain," she replied. " There's nothing to be afraid of. And then the mayor won't stand in the way of the burial to-morrow just the same, seeing what he did for old Father Rénard, who died just at sowing-time."

He was convinced by the voice of reason, and went off to the fields.

His wife cooked the dumplings, and then finished all the work of the farmhouse.

At midday, the old man was not dead. The day-labourers hired for the transplanting of the colza came in a group to look at the aged man who was so reluctant to take his leave. Each said his say, then went off again to the fields.

At six, when they returned from work, her father was still breathing. His son-in-law at last became alarmed.

"What's to do now, Phémie?"

She had no more idea than he what was best to do. They went to find the mayor. He promised that he would shut his eyes and authorise the burial on the next day. The officer of health, whom they went to see, also undertook, as a favour to Master Chicot, to antedate the death certificate. The man and the woman went home reassured.

They went to bed and slept as on the night before, mingling their sonorous breathing with the fainter breathing of the old man.

When they awoke, he was not dead.

At that they were overwhelmed. They remained standing at the father's bedside, looking at him with distrust, as though he had meant to play a shabby trick on them, to deceive and annoy them for his own amusement; above all, they grudged him the time he was making them waste.

"What are we to do?" asked the son-in-law.

She had no idea, and answered:

"It's vexing, it is."

They could not now put off the guests, who would be arriving at any moment. They decided to wait for them and explain the situation.

About ten to seven the first guests appeared. The women

dressed in black, their heads wrapped in large veils, came in with a melancholy air. The men, ill at ease in their cloth coats, advanced more slowly, two and two, talking business.

Maître Chicot and his wife, dismayed, received them with distressed explanations; as they accosted the first group of guests, both of them burst into sudden premeditated and simultaneous sobs. They explained their story, recounted their embarrassment, offered chairs, ran to and fro, made excuses, tried to prove that anybody would have acted in the same way, talking incessantly, suddenly became so talkative that they gave no one a chance to reply.

They went from one to the next.

"We'd never ha' thought it; it's not to be believed he could ha' lasted like this!"

The bewildered guests, a little disappointed, like people who have been robbed of a long-expected ceremony, did not know what to do, and remained seated or standing. Some were anxious to go. Maître Chicot restrained them.

"We'll break a bit of food together all the same. We've made some dumplings; better make the best of the chance."

Faces brightened at the thought. The guests began to talk in low voices. Gradually the yard filled; the first-comers were telling the news to the new arrivals. They whispered together; every one was cheered at the thought of the dumplings.

The women went in to see the dying man. They crossed themselves at the bedside, stammered a prayer, and came out again. The men, less eager for the spectacle, threw a single glance through the window, which had been set ajar.

Madame Chicot recounted the death agony.

"For two days now he's been like that, neither more nor less, neither higher nor lower. Isn't it just like a pump run dry?"

When everybody had seen the dying man, their thoughts were turned towards the collation; but as the guests were too numerous for the kitchen to hold, the table was carried out in front of the door. The four dozen dumplings, golden and appetising, attracted all eyes, set out in two large dishes. Every one reached forward to take one, fearing that there were not enough. But four were left over.

Maître Chicot, his mouth full, declared:

"If the old man could see us, it'ud be a rare grief to him; he was rare and fond of them in his time."

"He'll never eat any more now," said a fat, jovial peasant. "We all come to it in the end."

This reflection, far from saddening the guests, appeared to cheer them up. At the moment it had come to them to eat the dumplings.

Madame Chicot, heart-broken at the expense, ran ceaselessly to and from the cellar to fetch cider. The jugs came up and were emptied one after another. Every one was laughing now, talking loudly, beginning to shout, as people will shout at meals.

Suddenly an old peasant woman, who had remained near the dying man, held there by a greedy terror of the thing which was so soon to come to herself, appeared at the window and shouted in a shrill voice:

"He's gone! He's gone!"

Every one was silent. The women rose quickly, to go and see.

He really was dead. The rattle had ceased. The men looked at one another with downcast eyes. The old blackguard had chosen his time ill.

The Chicots were no longer crying. It was all over; they were calm. They kept on saying:

"We knew it couldn't last. If only he could have made up his mind last night, we shouldn't have had all this bother."

Never mind, it was all over. They would bury him on Monday, that was all, and would eat more dumplings for the occasion.

The guests departed, talking of the affair, pleased all the same at having seen it, and also at having had a bite to eat.

And when the man and his wife were by themselves, face to face, she said, with her face contracted with anguish:

"All the same, I shall have to make four dozen more dumplings. If only he could have made up his mind last night!"

And her husband, more resigned, replied:

"You won't have to do it every day."

A COWARD

SOCIETY CALLED HIM "HANDSOME SIGNOLES." HIS NAME was Viscount Gontran-Joseph de Signoles.

An orphan, and possessed of an adequate income, he cut a dash, as the saying is. He had a good figure and a good carriage, a sufficient flow of words to pass for wit, a certain natural grace, an air of nobility and pride, a gallant moustache and an eloquent eye, attributes which women like.

He was in demand in drawing-rooms, sought after for *valses*, and in men he inspired that smiling hostility which is reserved for vital and attractive rivals. He had been suspected of several love-affairs of a sort calculated to create a good opinion of a youngster. He lived a happy, care-free life, in the most complete well-being of body and mind. He was known to be a fine swordsman and a still finer shot with the pistol.

"When I come to fight a duel," he would say, "I shall choose pistols. With that weapon, I'm sure of killing my man."

One evening, he went to the theatre with two ladies, quite young, friends of his, whose husbands were also of the party, and after the performance he invited them to take ices at Tortoni's.

They had been sitting there for a few minutes when he noticed a gentleman at a neighbouring table staring obstinately at one of the ladies of the party. She seemed embarrassed and ill at ease, and bent her head. At last she said to her husband:

"There's a man staring at me. *I* don't know him; do you?"

The husband, who had seen nothing, raised his eyes, but declared :

" No, not in the least."

Half smiling, half in anger, she replied :

" It's very annoying ; the creature's spoiling my ice."

Her husband shrugged his shoulders.

" Deuce take him, don't appear to notice it. If we had to deal with all the discourteous people one meets, we'd never have done with them."

But the Viscount had risen abruptly. He could not permit this stranger to spoil an ice of his giving. It was to him that the insult was addressed, since it was at his invitation and on his account that his friends had come to the café. The affair was no business of anyone but himself.

He went up to the man and said :

" You have a way of looking at those ladies, sir, which I cannot stomach. Please be so good as to set a limit to your persistence."

" You hold your tongue," replied the other.

" Take care, sir," retorted the Viscount, clenching his teeth ; " you'll force me to overstep the bounds of common politeness."

The gentleman replied with a single word, a vile word which rang across the café from one end to the other, and, like the release of a spring, jerked every person present into an abrupt movement. All those with their backs towards him turned round, all the rest raised their heads ; three waiters spun round on their heels like tops ; the two ladies behind the counter started, then the whole upper half of their bodies twisted round, as though they were a couple of automata worked by the same handle.

There was a profound silence. Then suddenly a sharp noise resounded in the air. The Viscount had boxed his adversary's ears. Every one rose to intervene. Cards were exchanged.

Back in his home, the Viscount walked for several minutes up and down his room with long quick strides. He was too excited to think. A solitary idea dominated his mind: "a duel"; but as yet the idea stirred in him no emotion of any kind. He had done what he was compelled to do; he had shown himself to be what he ought to be. People would talk of it, would approve of him, congratulate him. He repeated aloud, speaking as a man speaks in severe mental distress:

"What a hound the fellow is!"

Then he sat down and began to reflect. In the morning he must find seconds. Whom should he choose? He searched his mind for the most important and celebrated names of his acquaintance. At last he decided on the Marquis de la Tour-Noire and Colonel Bourdin, an aristocrat and a soldier; they would do excellently. Their names would look well in the papers. He realised that he was thirsty, and drank three glasses of water one after the other; then he began to walk up and down again. He felt full of energy. If he played the gallant, showed himself determined, insisted on the most strict and dangerous arrangements, demanded a serious duel, a thoroughly serious duel, a positively terrible duel, his adversary would probably retire and apologise.

He took up once more the card which he had taken from his pocket and thrown down upon the table, and read it again as he had read it before, in the café, at a glance, and in the cab, by the light of each gas-lamp, on his way home.

"Georges Lamil, 51 rue Moncey." Nothing more.

He examined the grouped letters; they seemed to him mysterious, full of confused meaning. Georges Lamil? Who was this man? What did he do? Why had he looked at the woman in that way? Was it not revolting that a stranger, an unknown man, could thus disturb a man's life, without warning, just because he chose to fix his insolent eyes upon a woman? Again the Viscount repeated aloud:

"What a hound!"

Then he remained standing stock-still, lost in thought, his eyes still fixed upon the card. A fury against this scrap of paper awoke in him, a fury of hatred in which was mingled a queer sensation of uneasiness. This sort of thing was so stupid! He took up an open knife which lay close at hand and thrust it through the middle of the printed name, as though he had stabbed a man.

So he must fight. Should he choose swords or pistols?—for he regarded himself as the insulted party. With swords there would be less risk, but with pistols there was a chance that his adversary might withdraw. It is very rare that a duel with swords is fatal, for mutual prudence is apt to restrain combatants from engaging at sufficiently close quarters for a point to penetrate deeply. With pistols he ran a grave risk of death; but he might also extricate himself from the affair with all the honours of the situation and without actually coming to a meeting.

"I must be firm," he said. "He will take fright."

The sound of his voice set him trembling, and he looked round. He felt very nervous. He drank another glass of water, then began to undress for bed.

As soon as he was in bed, he blew out the light and closed his eyes.

"I've the whole of to-morrow," he thought, "in which to set my affairs in order. I'd better sleep now, so that I shall be quite calm."

He was very warm in the blankets, but he could not manage to compose himself to sleep. He turned this way and that, lay for five minutes upon his back, turned on to his left side, then rolled over on to his right.

He was still thirsty. He got up to get a drink. A feeling of uneasiness crept over him:

"Is it possible that I'm afraid?"

Why did his heart beat madly at each familiar sound in his room? When the clock was about to strike, the faint squeak of the rising spring made him start; so shaken he was that for several seconds afterwards he had to open his mouth to get his breath.

He began to reason with himself on the possibility of his being afraid.

"Shall I be afraid?"

No, of course he would not be afraid, since he was resolved to see the matter through, and had duly made up his mind to fight and not to tremble. But he felt so profoundly distressed that he wondered:

"Can a man be afraid in spite of himself?"

He was attacked by this doubt, this uneasiness, this terror; suppose a force more powerful than himself, masterful, irresistible, overcame him, what would happen? Yes, what might not happen? Assuredly he would go to the place of the meeting, since he was quite ready to go. But supposing he trembled? Supposing he fainted? He thought of the scene, of his reputation, his good name.

There came upon him a strange need to get up and look at himself in the mirror. He relit his candle. When he saw his face reflected in the polished glass, he scarcely recognised it, it seemed to him as though he had never yet seen himself. His eyes looked to him enormous; and he was pale; yes, without doubt he was pale, very pale.

He remained standing in front of the mirror. He put out his tongue, as though to ascertain the state of his health, and abruptly the thought struck him like a bullet:

"The day after to-morrow, at this very hour, I may be dead."

His heart began again its furious beating.

"The day after to-morrow, at this very hour, I may be dead. This person facing me, this me I see in the mirror, will be no more. Why, here I am, I look at myself, I feel myself alive, and in twenty-four hours I shall be lying in that bed, dead, my eyes closed, cold, inanimate, vanished."

He turned back towards the bed, and distinctly saw himself lying on his back in the very sheets he had just left. He had the hollow face of a corpse, his hands had the slackness of hands that will never make another movement.

At that he was afraid of his bed, and, to get rid of the sight of it, went into the smoking-room. Mechanically he picked up a cigar, lit it, and began to walk up and down again. He was cold; he went to the bell to wake his valet; but he stopped, even as he raised his hand to the rope.

"He will see that I am afraid."

He did not ring; he lit the fire. His hands shook a little, with a nervous tremor, whenever they touched anything. His brain whirled, his troubled thoughts became elusive, transitory, and gloomy; his mind suffered all the effects of intoxication, as though he were actually drunk.

Over and over again he thought:

"What shall I do? What is to become of me?"

His whole body trembled, seized with a jerky shuddering; he got up and, going to the window, drew back the curtains.

Dawn was at hand, a summer dawn. The rosy sky touched the town, its roofs and walls, with its own hue. A broad descending ray, like the caress of the rising sun, enveloped the awakened world; and with the light, hope—a gay, swift, fierce hope—filled the Viscount's heart! Was he mad, that he had allowed himself to be struck down by fear, before anything was settled even, before his seconds had seen those of this Georges Lamil, before he knew whether he was going to fight?

He washed, dressed, and walked out with a firm step.

He repeated to himself, as he walked:

"I must be energetic, very energetic. I must prove that I am not afraid."

His seconds, the Marquis and the Colonel, placed themselves at his disposal, and after hearty handshakes discussed the conditions.

" You are anxious for a serious duel ? " asked the Colonel.

" Yes, a very serious one," replied the Viscount.

" You still insist on pistols ? " said the Marquis.

" Yes."

" You will leave us free to arrange the rest ? "

In a dry, jerky voice the Viscount stated:

" Twenty paces ; at the signal, raising the arm, and not lowering it. Exchange of shots till one is seriously wounded."

" They are excellent conditions," declared the Colonel in a tone of satisfaction. " You shoot well, you have every chance."

They departed. The Viscount went home to wait for them. His agitation, momentarily quietened, was now growing minute by minute. He felt a strange shivering, a ceaseless vibration, down his arms, down his legs, in his chest ; he could not keep still in one place, neither seated nor standing. There was not the least moistening of saliva in his mouth, and at every instant he made a violent movement of his tongue, as though to prevent it sticking to his palate.

He was eager to have breakfast, but could not eat. Then the idea came to him to drink in order to give himself courage, and he sent for a decanter of rum, of which he swallowed six liqueur glasses full one after the other.

A burning warmth flooded through his body, followed immediately by a sudden dizziness of the mind and spirit.

" Now I know what to do," he thought. " Now it is all right."

But by the end of an hour he had emptied the decanter, and his state of agitation had once more become intolerable. He was conscious of a wild need to roll on the ground, to scream, to bite. Night was falling.

The ringing of a bell gave him such a shock that he had not strength to rise and welcome his seconds.

He did not even dare to speak to them, to say " Good evening " to them, to utter a single word, for fear they guessed the whole thing by the alteration in his voice.

"Everything is arranged in accordance with the conditions you fixed," observed the Colonel. "At first your adversary claimed the privileges of the insulted party, but he yielded almost at once, and has accepted everything. His seconds are two military men."

"Thank you," said the Viscount.

"Pardon us," interposed the Marquis, "if we merely come in and leave again immediately, but we have a thousand things to see to. We must have a good doctor, since the combat is not to end until a serious wound is inflicted, and you know that pistol bullets are no laughing-matter. We must appoint the ground, near a house to which we may carry the wounded man if necessary, etc. In fact, we shall be occupied for two or three hours arranging all that there is to arrange."

"Thank you," said the Viscount a second time.

"You are all right?" asked the Colonel. "You are calm?"

"Yes, quite calm, thank you."

The two men retired.

When he realised that he was once more alone, he thought that he was going mad. His servant had lit the lamps, and he sat down at the table to write letters. After tracing, at the head of a sheet: "This is my will," he rose shivering and walked away, feeling incapable of connecting two ideas, of taking a resolution, of making any decision whatever.

So he was going to fight! He could no longer avoid it. Then what was the matter with him? He wished to fight, he had absolutely decided upon this plan of action and taken his resolve, and he now felt clearly, in spite of every effort of mind and forcing of will, that he could not retain even the strength necessary to get him to the place of meeting. He tried to picture the duel, his own attitude and the bearing of his adversary.

From time to time his teeth chattered in his mouth with a

slight clicking noise. He tried to read, and took down Châteauvillard's code of duelling. Then he wondered:

"Does my adversary go to shooting-galleries? Is he well known? Is he classified anywhere? How can I find out?"

He bethought himself of Baron Vaux's book on marksmen with the pistol, and ran through it from end to end. Georges Lamil was not mentioned in it. Yet if the man were not a good shot, he would surely not have promptly agreed to that dangerous weapon and those fatal conditions?

He opened, in passing, a case by Gastinne Renette standing on a small table, and took out one of the pistols, then placed himself as though to shoot and raised his arm. But he was trembling from head to foot and the barrel moved in every direction.

At that, he said to himself:

"It's impossible. I cannot fight in this state."

He looked at the end of the barrel, at the little, black, deep hole that spits death; he thought of the disgrace, of the whispers at the club, of the laughter in drawing-rooms, of the contempt of women, of the allusions in the papers, of the insults which cowards would fling at him.

He was still looking at the weapon, and, raising the hammer, caught a glimpse of a cap gleaming beneath it like a tiny red flame. By good fortune or forgetfulness, the pistol had been left loaded. At the knowledge, he was filled with a confused inexplicable sense of joy.

If, when face to face with the other man, he did not show a proper gallantry and calm, he would be lost for ever. He would be sullied, branded with a mark of infamy, hounded out of society. And he would not be able to achieve that calm, that swaggering poise; he knew it, he felt it. Yet he was brave, since he wanted to fight! . . . He was brave, since. . .

The thought which hovered in him did not even fulfil itself in his mind; but, opening his mouth wide, he thrust in the barrel of his pistol with savage gesture until it reached his throat, and pressed on the hammer.

When his valet ran in, at the sound of the report, he found him lying dead upon his back. A shower of blood had splashed the white paper on the table, and made a great red mark beneath these four words :

" This is my will "

THE DRUNKARD

I

A NORTHERLY GALE WAS BLOWING, SWEEPING ACROSS THE sky vast wintry clouds, black and heavy, which in their passage flung furious showers of rain upon the earth.

The raging sea roared and shook the coast, hurling shorewards great, slow-moving, frothing waves, which were shattered with the noise of a cannon. They came on quite quietly, one after another, mountain-high ; at each squall they flung in the air the white foam of their crests like the sweat from monstrous heads.

The hurricane was sucked into the little valley of Yport ; it whistled and moaned, tearing the slates from the roofs, smashing the shutters, throwing down chimneys, hurling such violent gusts along the streets that it was impossible to walk without clinging to the walls, and children would have been swept away like leaves and whisked over the houses into the fields.

The fishing-boats had been hauled up on dry land, for fear of the sea that at high tide would strip the beach clean, and some sailors, sheltered behind the round bellies of the vessels lying on their sides, were watching the fury of sky and sea.

Gradually they went away, for night was falling on the storm, wrapping in darkness the raging ocean and all the strife of angry elements.

Two men still remained, their hands in their pockets, their backs stooped under the squalls, their woollen caps crammed down to their eyes, two tall Norman fishermen, their necks fringed with bristling beards, their skins burnt by the salt gusts of the open sea, their eyes blue, with a black speck in the centre, the piercing eyes of sailors who see to the edge of the horizon, like birds of prey.

"Come along, Jérémie," said one of them. "We'll pass away the time playing dominoes. I'll pay."

But the other still hesitated, tempted by the game and the brandy, knowing well that he would get drunk again if he went into Parmelle's, and held back, too, by the thought of his wife left all alone in the cottage.

"Anyone would say you'd made a bet to fuddle me every night. Tell me, now, what good does it do you, for you always pay?" he asked.

He laughed none the less at the idea of all the brandy he had drunk at another's expense; he laughed the happy laugh of a Norman getting something for nothing.

His friend Mathurin still held him by the arm.

"Come along, Jérémie. It's no night to go home with nothing warm in your belly. What are you afraid of? Won't your old woman warm your bed for you?"

"Only the other night I couldn't find the door at all," replied Jérémie. "They pretty well fished me out of the brook in front of our place."

The old scoundrel laughed again at the thought of it, and went quietly towards Parmelle's café, where the lighted windows gleamed; Jérémie went forward, dragged by Mathurin and pushed by the wind, incapable of resisting the double force.

The low room was full of sailors, smoke, and clamour. All the men, clad in woollen jerseys, their elbows on the tables, were shouting to make themselves heard. The more drinkers that came in, the louder it was necessary to yell through the din of voices and the click of dominoes on marble, with the inevitable result that the uproar grew worse and worse.

Jérémie and Mathurin went and sat down in a corner and began a game; one after another the glasses of brandy disappeared in the depths of their throats.

Then they played more games, drank more brandy. Mathurin went on pouring it out, winking at the proprietor, a stout man with a face as red as fire, who was chuckling delightedly as if he were enjoying an interminable joke; and Jérémie went on swallowing the brandy, nodding his head, giving vent to a laughter like the roaring of a wild beast, staring at his comrade with a besotted, happy air.

All the company went home. Each time that one of them opened the outer door to leave, a gust of wind entered the café, driving the thick smoke from the pipes into mad swirls, swinging the lamps at the end of their chains until the flames flickered; and then suddenly they would hear the heavy shock of a breaking wave and the howling of the gale.

Jérémie, his collar unfastened, was lolling drunkenly, one leg thrust out and one arm hanging down; in the other hand he held his dominoes.

They were by now left alone with the proprietor, who had come up to them with the sharpest interest.

"Well, Jérémie," he asked, "does it feel good, inside? Has all the stuff you've poured down freshened you up, eh?"

"The more goes down," spluttered Jérémie, "the drier it gets, in there."

The innkeeper cast a sly glance at Mathurin.

"And what about your brother, Mathurin?" he said. "Where is he at the moment?"

"He's warm all right, don't you worry," replied the sailor, shaking with silent laughter.

And the two of them looked at Jérémie, who triumphantly put down the double six, announcing:

"There's the boss."

When they had finished their game, the proprietor announced:

"Well, boys, I'm going to pack up. I'll leave you the lamp and the bottle; there's a franc's worth of stuff still left in it. Lock the street door, Mathurin, won't you, and slip the key under the shutter like you did the other night?"

"Right you are, don't worry," replied Mathurin.

Parmelle shook hands with his two belated customers, and stumped up the wooden stairs. For several minutes his heavy step resounded through the little house; then a loud bump announced that he had got into bed.

The two men went on playing; from time to time the fury of the gale momentarily increased in violence; it shook the door and made the walls tremble. The two tipplers would raise their heads as though someone were coming in; then Mathurin would take the bottle and fill up Jérémie's glass. But suddenly the clock over the counter struck twelve. Its husky chime resembled the clashing of saucepans, and the strokes resounded for a long time, jingling like old iron.

Promptly Mathurin rose, like a sailor whose watch is finished:

"Come alone, Jérémie, we must get along."

The other set himself in motion with more difficulty, got his balance by leaning on the table; then reached the door and opened it while his companion was turning out the lamp.

When they were in the street Mathurin locked up the tavern and said:

"Well, good night; see you to-morrow."

And he vanished in the darkness.

II

Jérémie advanced three steps, then wavered, thrust out his hands, found a wall to hold him upright, and went on again with tottering steps. Now and then a squall, rushing up the narrow street, hurled him forward into a run for several paces; then, when the violence of the swirling blast died down, he halted abruptly, his forward impulse lost, and began to waver drunkenly again upon his wayward legs.

Instinctively he went towards his own home, as birds towards their nest. He recognised his door at last and began to fumble at it in order to find the lock and put his key in it. He could not find the hole, and began to swear in a low voice. Then he knocked upon the door with his fists, calling to this wife to come and help him.

" Mélina ! hi ! Mélina ! "

As he leant against the door to keep himself from falling, it yielded and swung open, and Jérémie, losing his support, collapsed into his house, and rolled on to his nose in the middle of his own dwelling-place. He felt something heavy pass over his body and escape into the night.

He did not move, overwhelmed with fright, bewildered, in terror of the devil, of ghosts, of all the mysterious works of darkness ; for a long time he waited without daring to stir. But as he saw there were no further signs of movement, he recovered a little of his wits, the muddled wits of a hard drinker.

He sat up very softly. Again he waited for a long time, and at last, plucking up courage, murmured :

" Mélina ! "

His wife did not answer.

A sudden misgiving crossed his darkened brain, an undefined misgiving, a vague suspicion. He did not move, he stayed there sitting on the ground, in the dark, ransacking his thoughts, brooding over unfinished speculations as unsteady as his feet.

Again he asked :

" Tell me who it was, Mélina. Tell me who it was. I won't do anything to you."

He waited. No voice rose in the darkness. He was thinking aloud, now.

" I've had a drop to drink, I have. I've had a drop to drink. It was him that treated me, the lubber ; he did it, so as I wouldn't go home. I've had a drop to drink."

And then he went on in his former manner.

" Tell me who it was, Mélina, or I'll do you a mischief."

After another pause of waiting, he went on with the slow, obstinate logic of a drunken man.

"It was him that kept me at that swab Parmelle's place; and all the other nights too, so as I mightn't go home. He's plotting with someone. Oh, the stinking swine!"

Slowly he rose to his knees. Blind rage was taking possession of him, mingling with the fumes of the liquor.

"Tell me who it was, Mélina!" he repeated, "or I'll bash your head in, I give you fair warning!"

He was standing upright now, shaking all over in a blaze of fury, as though the alcohol in his body had caught fire in his veins. He made a step forward, bumped into a chair, snatched it up, walked on, reached the bed, fumbled at it, and felt under the clothes the warm body of his wife.

Then, mad with rage, he snarled:

"Oh! so you were there all the time, you slut, and wouldn't answer!"

And, raising the chair he grasped in his strong fist, the sailor dashed it down in front of him with exasperated fury. A scream came wildly from the bed, a mad piercing scream. Then he began to beat at it like a thresher in a barn. Soon nothing stirred. The chair broke to pieces, but one leg remained in his hand, and he went on, panting.

Suddenly he stopped and asked:

"Now will you say who it was?"

Mélina did not answer.

At that, worn out with fatigue, besotted by his own violence, he sat down again on the ground, stretched himself to his full length, and went to sleep.

When dawn appeared, a neighbour, noticing that the door was open, came in. He found Jérémie snoring on the floor, where lay the remains of a chair, and, in the bed, a mess of blood and flesh.

A VENDETTA

PAOLO SAVERINI'S WIDOW LIVED ALONE WITH HER SON IN A poor little house on the ramparts of Bonifacio. The town, built on a spur of the mountains, in places actually overhanging the sea, looks across a channel bristling with reefs, to the lower shores of Sardinia. At its foot, on the other side and almost completely surrounding it, is the channel that serves as its harbour, cut in the cliff like a gigantic corridor. Through a long circuit between steep walls, the channel brings to the very foot of the first houses the little Italian or Sardinian fishing-boats, and, every fortnight, the old steamboat that runs to and from Ajaccio.

Upon the white mountain the group of houses form a whiter patch still. They look like the nests of wild birds, perched so upon the rock, dominating that terrible channel through which hardly ever a ship risks a passage. The unresting wind harasses the sea and eats away the bare shore, clad with a sparse covering of grass ; it rushes into the ravine and ravages its two sides. The trailing wisps of white foam round the black points of countless rocks that everywhere pierce the waves, look like rags of canvas floating and heaving on the surface of the water.

The widow Saverini's house held for dear life to the very edge of the cliff ; its three windows looked out over this wild and desolate scene.

She lived there alone with her son Antoine and their bitch Sémillante, a large, thin animal with long, shaggy hair, of the sheep-dog breed. The young man used her for hunting.

One evening, after a quarrel, Antoine Saverini was treacherously slain by a knife-thrust from Nicolas Ravolati, who got away to Sardinia the same night.

When his old mother received his body, carried home by bystanders, she did not weep, but for a long time stayed motionless, looking at it; then, stretching out her wrinkled hand over the body, she swore vendetta against him. She would have no one stay with her, and shut herself up with the body, together with the howling dog. The animal howled continuously, standing at the foot of the bed, her head thrust towards her master, her tail held tightly between her legs. She did not stir, nor did the mother, who crouched over the body with her eyes fixed steadily upon it, and wept great silent tears.

The young man, lying on his back, clad in his thick serge coat with a hole torn across the front, looked as though he slept; but everywhere there was blood; on the shirt, torn off for the first hasty dressing; on his waistcoat, on his breeches, on his face, on his hands. Clots of blood had congealed in his beard and in his hair.

The old mother began to speak to him. At the sound of her voice the dog was silent.

" There, there, you shall be avenged, my little one, my boy, my poor child. Sleep, sleep, you shall be avenged, do you hear! Your mother swears it! And your mother always keeps her word; you know she does."

Slowly she bent over him, pressing her cold lips on the dead lips.

Then Sémillante began to howl once more. She uttered long cries, monotonous, heart-rending, horrible cries.

They remained there, the pair of them, the woman and the dog, till morning.

Antoine Saverini was buried next day, and before long there was no more talk of him in Bonifacio.

He had left neither brothers nor close cousins. No man

was there to carry on the vendetta. Only his mother, an old woman, brooded over it.

On the other side of the channel she watched from morning till night a white speck on the coast. It was a little Sardinian village, Longosardo, where Corsican bandits fled for refuge when too hard pressed. They formed almost the entire population of this hamlet, facing the shores of their own country, and there they awaited a suitable moment to come home, to return to the maquis of Corsica. She knew that Nicolas Ravolati had taken refuge in this very village.

All alone, all day long, sitting by the window, she looked over there and pondered revenge. How could she do it without another's help, so feeble as she was, so near to death? But she had promised, she had sworn upon the body. She could not forget, she could not wait. What was she to do? She could no longer sleep at night, she had no more sleep nor peace; obstinately she searched for a way. The dog slumbered at her feet and sometimes, raising her head, howled into the empty spaces. Since her master had gone, she often howled thus, as though she were calling him, as though her animal soul, inconsolable, had retained an ineffaceable memory of him.

One night, as Sémillante was beginning to moan again, the mother had a sudden idea, an idea quite natural to a vindictive and ferocious savage. She meditated on it till morning, then, rising at the approach of day, she went to church. She prayed, kneeling on the stones, prostrate before God, begging Him to aid her, to sustain her, to grant her poor worn-out body the strength necessary to avenge her son.

Then she returned home. There stood in the yard an old barrel with its sides stove in, which held the rain-water; she overturned it, emptied it, and fixed it to the ground with stakes and stones; then she chained up Sémillante in this kennel, and went into the house.

Next she began to walk up and down her room, taking no

rest, her eyes still turned to the coast of Sardinia. He was there, the murderer.

All day long and all night long the dog howled. In the morning the old woman took her some water in a bowl, but nothing else ; no soup, no bread.

Another day went by. Sémillante, exhausted, was asleep. Next day her eyes were shining, her hair on end, and she tugged desperately at the chain.

Again the old woman gave her nothing to eat. The animal, mad with hunger, barked hoarsely. Another night went by.

When day broke, Mother Saverini went to her neighbour to ask him to give her two trusses of straw. She took the old clothes her husband had worn and stuffed them with the straw into the likeness of a human figure.

Having planted a post in the ground opposite Sémillante's kennel, she tied the dummy figure to it, which looked now as though it were standing. Then she fashioned a head with a roll of old linen.

The dog, surprised, looked at this straw man, and was silent, although devoured with hunger.

Then the woman went to the pork-butcher and bought a long piece of black pudding. She returned home, lit a wood fire in her yard, close to the kennel, and grilled the black pudding. Sémillante, maddened, leapt about and foamed at the mouth, her eyes fixed on the food, the flavour of which penetrated to her very stomach.

Then with the smoking sausage the mother made a collar for the straw man. She spent a long time lashing it round his neck, as though to stuff it right in. When it was done, she unchained the dog.

With a tremendous bound the animal leapt upon the dummy's throat and with her paws on his shoulders began to rend it. She fell back with a piece of the prey in her mouth, then dashed at it again, sank her teeth into the cords, tore away a few fragments of food, fell back again, and leapt once more, ravenous.

With great bites she rent away the face, and tore the whole neck to shreds.

The old woman watched, motionless and silent, a gleam in her eyes. Then she chained up her dog again, made her go without food for two more days, and repeated the strange performance.

For three months she trained the dog to this struggle, the conquest of a meal by fangs. She no longer chained her up, but launched her upon the dummy with a sign.

She had taught the dog to rend and devour it without hiding food in its throat. Afterwards she would reward the dog with the gift of the black pudding she had cooked for her.

As soon as she saw the man, Sémillante would tremble, then turn her eyes towards her mistress, who would cry "Off!" in a whistling tone, raising her finger.

When she judged that the time was come, Mother Saverini went to confession and took communion one Sunday morning with an ecstatic fervour; then, putting on a man's clothes, like an old ragged beggar, she bargained with a Sardinian fisherman, who took her, accompanied by the dog, to the other side of the straits.

In a canvas bag she had a large piece of black pudding. Sémillante had had nothing to eat for two days. Every minute the old woman made her smell the savoury food, stimulating her hunger with it.

They came to Longosardo. The Corsican woman was limping slightly. She went to the baker's and inquired for Nicolas Ravolati's house. He had resumed his old occupation, that of a joiner. He was working alone at the back of his shop.

The old woman pushed open the door and called him:

"Hey! Nicolas!"

He turned round; then, letting go of her dog, she cried:

"Off, off, bite him, bite him!"

The maddened beast dashed forward and seized his throat.

The man put out his arms, clasped the dog, and rolled upon the ground. For a few minutes he writhed, beating the ground with his feet; then he remained motionless while Sémillante nuzzled at his throat and tore it out in ribbons.

Two neighbours, sitting at their doors, plainly recollected having seen a poor old man come out with a lean black dog which ate, as it walked, something brown that its master was giving to it.

In the evening the old woman returned home. That night she slept well.

COCO

THROUGHOUT THE NEIGHBOURHOOD THE LUCASES' FARM WAS known as the "Métairie," no one could say why. The peasants no doubt connected this word "Métairie" with an idea of wealth and size, for the farm was certainly the largest, most prosperous, and best-managed in the district.

The yard was very large, and was encircled by five rows of magnificent trees, planted to shelter the short, delicate apple-trees from the strong wind of the plain. It contained long, tile-roofed buildings in which the hay and grain were stored, fine cowsheds built of flints, stabling for thirty horses, and a dwelling-house of red brick, that looked like a small country-seat.

The manure heaps were well kept; the watch-dogs lived in kennels, a crowd of chickens ran to and fro in the high grass.

Every day at noon fifteen persons, master, men, and maids, took their places at the long kitchen table on which the soup steamed in a great delf bowl with a pattern of blue flowers.

The animals, horses, cows, pigs, and sheep were fat, clean, and well kept; and Lucas, a tall man who was beginning to acquire a paunch, made his rounds three times a day, watching over all and taking thought for all.

At the far end of the stable they kept, out of charity, a very old white horse that the mistress was anxious to have cared for until it died a natural death, because she had raised and always kept it, and because it stirred memories in her heart.

This old pensioner was looked after by a fifteen-year-old lad named Isidore Duval, called Zidore for short, who, during the winter, gave him his ration of oats and his straw and, in the summer, was obliged to go four times a day and change the position where he was tied up, so that he might have plenty of fresh grass.

The animal, which was almost crippled, could hardly lift its heavy legs, thick at the knees and swollen above the hoofs. Its coat, which was no longer groomed, looked like white hair, and its long eyelashes gave its eyes a melancholy air.

When Zidore took it out to grass, he had to tug at the halter, so slowly did the animal walk; and the boy, stooping, panting, swore at it, exasperated at having the ancient nag to look after.

The farm-hands, noticing the boy's anger towards Coco, laughed at it; they were always talking to Zidore about the horse, just to exasperate the lad. His friends chaffed him. In the village he was called Coco-Zidore.

The boy was furious, and felt growing in himself a desire to be revenged on the horse. He was a thin child, long in the leg, very dirty, and with a mop of red, thick, coarse, bristling hair. He seemed stupid, spoke with a stammer, and with infinite labour, as though ideas were born with difficulty into his dull, brutish soul.

For a long time he had felt surprised that Coco was still kept, angry at seeing good stuff wasted on a useless beast. From the moment that it ceased working, it seemed to him wrong to feed it, revolting to waste good oats, expensive oats, on this paralysed jade. Often, in spite of Farmer Lucas' orders, he economised on the horse's food, supplying it with no more than half its ration, keeping back litter and hay. The hatred in his confused, primitive mind grew sharper, the hatred of a grasping peasant, cunning, ferocious, brutal, and cowardly.

When summer came round again, he had to go and move the beast from place to place on its sloping meadow. It was a long way from the farm. More furious each morning, the lad plodded off across the cornfields. The men working in the fields shouted to him in jest:

"Hey! Zidore! Give my kind regards to Coco."

He never answered, but on the way he would break off a

stick from a hedge, and as soon as he had tethered the old horse in a new place, he would allow it to resume its grazing and then, coming up treacherously, begin to thwack its hocks. The animal would try to escape, to rush away, to avoid the blows, and ran round at the end of its halter as though it were in a circus ring. The boy beat it savagely, running relentlessly after it, his teeth shut hard in anger.

Then he would go slowly away, without looking back, while the horse watched him go with its old eyes, its flanks heaving, out of breath after so much trotting, and it would not lower its bony white head again until it had seen the young peasant's blue blouse vanish in the distance.

As the nights were warm, Coco was now left to sleep out of doors, away at the edge of the valley, beyond the wood. Zidore alone went to see the animal.

The boy had a further habit of amusing himself by throwing stones at it. He would sit down ten paces away on a bank and stay there for half an hour, from time to time flinging a jagged pebble at the old nag, which remained standing, chained up in front of its enemy and looking steadily at him, not daring to crop the grass until he was gone.

But one thought remained firmly planted in the lad's mind: Why feed this horse which did no work? It seemed to him as if this wretched jade were stealing another's victuals, the possessions of mankind, the property of the good God, were stealing even from himself, Zidore, who had to work for his food.

Little by little, every day, the boy lessened the circle of pasture which he gave it by moving the stake to which its halter was fixed.

The animal went without food, grew thin, pined away. Too weak to break the cord, it stretched out its head towards the broad expanse of green, shining grass so near at hand; the smell of it reached its nostrils but it could not touch it.

Then one morning Zidore had an idea: he decided not to

go on moving Coco. He had had enough of walking so far for the sake of this miserable carcass.

But he came all the same, to enjoy his revenge. The anxious beast stared at him. He did not beat it that day. He walked round it, his hands in his pockets. He even pretended to change its position, but thrust the stake back into the same hole, and went away, delighted with his invention.

The horse, seeing him go, neighed to remind him; but the lad began to run, leaving it all alone in the valley, well tied up, and without a blade of grass within range of its jaws.

Famished, it tried to reach the thick verdure that it could touch with the tip of its nostrils. It went down on its knees, stretching its neck, thrusting forward its slobbering lips. All in vain. Throughout the day, the old beast wore itself out with useless, terrible struggles. Hunger ravaged it, a hunger rendered more frightful by the sight of all that good green food stretched out on every side.

The boy did not return that day. He roamed about the woods after birds' nests.

He reappeared the next day. Coco was lying down, exhausted. It rose at the sight of the boy, expecting that at last its position would be changed.

But the young peasant did not even touch the mallet lying in the ground. He came up, stared at the animal, flung a clod of earth at its muzzle, which splashed the white hair, and went away again, whistling.

The horse remained standing as long as it could still keep him in sight; then, feeling only too well that its attempts to reach the near by grass would be useless, lay down once more upon its side and closed its eyes.

Next day Zidore did not come.

When, the following day, he drew near to Coco, who was still lying down, he saw that the horse was dead.

He remained standing, looking at it, pleased with his work, and at the same time surprised that it was already finished.

He touched it with his foot, lifted one of its legs and then let it fall back again, sat down on the body and stayed there, his eyes fixed on the grass, without thinking of anything.

He returned to the farm, but did not mention the accident, for he wanted to go on playing truant at the times when he had been accustomed to go and change the horse's position.

He went to see it the next day. Crows took flight at his approach. Innumerable flies were crawling about the body and buzzing all round it.

On his return he announced the event. The beast was so old that no one was surprised. The master said to two hands:

"Get your spades and dig a hole where it lies."

The men buried the horse just at the spot where it had died of hunger.

The grass came up lush, verdant, and vigorous, nourished by the poor body.

THE HAND

A CIRCLE HAD BEEN FORMED ROUND MONSIEUR BERMUTIER, examining magistrate, who was giving his opinion on the mysterious Saint Cloud affair. For the past month all Paris had been wildly excited over this inexplicable crime. No one could make head or tail of it.

Monsieur Bermutier was standing with his back to the fireplace, and was talking, threading the evidence together, discussing the various theories, but drawing no conclusions.

A number of women had risen to draw near to him, and were still standing up, their eyes fixed on the magistrate's clean-shaven lips, whence his grave observations issued. They shivered and trembled, their nerves on edge with inquisitive terror, with that greedy and insatiate desire to be terrified which haunts their souls and tortures them like a physical hunger.

One of them, paler than the rest, remarked during an interval of silence:

"It's horrible. It verges upon the supernatural. No one will ever get to the bottom of it."

The magistrate turned to her.

"Yes, Madame," he said, "probably no one ever will. As for the word 'supernatural' which you have just used, it has nothing to do with the case. We are dealing with a crime planned with the greatest skill and executed skilfully, so well entangled in mystery that we cannot unravel it from its attendant circumstances. But once upon a time I myself had to deal with an affair in which an element of fantasy did really appear to be involved. We had to let that one go too, for we were never able to clear it up."

Several women cried at the same time, so rapidly that their voices sounded as one:

"Oh, do tell us the story!"

Monsieur Bermutier smiled gravely, as an examining magistrate ought to smile.

"But please do not believe," he resumed, "that I could for one moment imagine that there was anything supernatural about this adventure. I only believe in normal causes. But if, instead of employing the word 'supernatural' to express that which we do not understand, we use merely the word 'inexplicable,' it will be much more useful. At any rate, in the affair which I am going to relate to you, it is more especially the attendant circumstances, the preliminary circumstances, which appealed to me. Here are the facts of the case:

"In those days I was examining magistrate at Ajaccio, a little white town lying on the shores of a delightful bay entirely surrounded by high mountains.

"The affairs with which I was most particularly concerned in those parts were the affairs of vendetta. There are some magnificent vendettas, as dramatic as they could well be, ferocious, heroic. In this district we come across the finest stories of revenge that you could possibly imagine, hatred centuries old, appeased for a moment, never wiped out, abominable plots, murders become massacres, and almost deeds to boast of. For two years I heard tell of nothing but the price of blood, of the terrible Corsican custom which obliges a man to revenge every wrong upon the person who committed it, upon his descendants and those near to him. I have seen old men's throats cut, and their children's and their cousins'; my head was filled with these stories.

"Now one day I learnt that an Englishman had just taken, for a number of years, a small villa at the end of the bay. He had brought with him a French manservant whom he had engaged at Marseilles on his way out.

"Soon everybody began to take an interest in this strange

person, who lived alone in his house, never going out except to shoot or fish. He spoke to no one, never went into the town, and, every morning, spent an hour or two at pistol and carbine practice.

" Legends grew up about him. People suggested that he was an important personage who had left his native land for political reasons; then it was stated that he was hiding after having committed an abominable crime. They even quoted circumstances of a peculiarly horrible nature.

" I was anxious, in my position as examining magistrate, to get some information about this man; but I found it impossible to discover anything. His name he gave as Sir John Rowell.

" I was content, then, with keeping him under close watch; but in fact I had no cause to believe in any suspicious circumstances connected with him.

" But as the rumours about him continued and grew, and became common property, I resolved to try and see this stranger for myself, and I made a habit of shooting regularly in the neighbourhood of his property. For a long time I waited my chance. At last it presented itself in the form of a partridge which I shot at and killed under the Englishman's nose. My dog brought it to me, but, taking it with me, I went to make excuses for my discourteous act and to request Sir John Rowell to accept the bird.

" He was a big man with red hair and a red beard, very tall and very stout, a polite and placid Hercules. There was about him no trace of the so-called British stiffness, and he thanked me warmly for my civility in French of which the accent was unmistakably from the other side of the English Channel.

At the end of a month we had chatted together five or six times.

" At last one evening, as I was passing his gate, I saw him smoking a pipe, straddling a chair in his garden. I greeted him, and he asked me to come in and drink a glass of beer. I did not oblige him to repeat his invitation.

"He received me with every mark of the true, meticulous English courtesy, spoke enthusiastically of France and Corsica, declaring that he was delighted with '*cette pays*' and '*cette rivage*.'

"Thereupon, with the greatest care and under the form of a lively curiosity, I asked him some questions about his life and his plans. He answered without a sign of embarrassment, and told me that he had travelled a great deal in Africa, India, and America. He added with a laugh:

"'Oh, yes, I've had plenty of adventures.'

"Then he began to tell me hunting-stories, and gave me most interesting details about hunting hippopotami, tigers, and even gorillas.

"'They are all formidable animals,' I observed.

"'Oh, no,' he said with a smile, 'the worst is man.' And his smile changed to a laugh, the pleasant laughter of a hearty, happy Englishman.

"'I've hunted man a lot, too.'

"Then he began to speak of weapons, and invited me to come in and see his various types of guns.

"His drawing-room was hung with black—black silk embroidered with gold. Large yellow flowers twisted upon the dark material, gleaming like flames.

"'It's a Japanese material,' he told me.

"But in the centre of the largest panel a strange thing caught my eye. Upon a square of red velvet a black object lay in sharp relief: I went up to it; it was a hand, a man's hand. Not the hand of a skeleton, white and clean, but a black, dried hand, with yellow nails, the muscles laid bare, and traces of stale blood, like dirt, on the bones, that had been cut clean off, as though with a blow from an axe, at the centre of the forearm.

"Round the wrist an enormous iron chain, riveted and

welded on this foul limb, fastened it to the wall by a ring strong enough to hold an elephant.

"'What is that?' I asked.

"'That's my best enemy,' answered the Englishman, calmly. 'It came from America. It was cut off with a sabre and the skin torn off with a sharp stone and dried in the sun for eight days. Oh, it was a fortunate thing for me.'

"I touched this human relic, which must have belonged to a colossus. The fingers, excessively long, were attached by enormous muscles which in places still retained shreds of flesh. The hand was frightful to see; flayed in this wise, it instinctively made me think of the revenge of some savage.

"'The man must have been very strong,' I said.

"'Oh, yes,' said the Englishman sweetly, 'but I was stronger than he. I put that chain on to hold him.'

"I thought the man was jesting, and said:

"'The chain is quite useless now; the hand will not escape.'

"Sir John Rowell replied in a grave voice:

"'It was always trying to get away. The chain is necessary.'

"With a swift glance I examined his face, asking myself:

"'Is the man mad, or has he merely a poor taste in jokes?'

"But his face remained impenetrable, placid and kindly. I began to speak of other matters, and expressed my admiration for his guns.

"I noticed, however, that three loaded revolvers were lying about on various pieces of furniture, as though the man lived in constant fear of an attack.

"I revisited him on several occasions. Then I went there no more. People had grown accustomed to his presence. They were all completely indifferent to him.

"A whole year went by. Then one morning near the end

of November my servant woke me and announced that Sir John Rowell had been murdered during the night.

" Half an hour later I entered the Englishman's house with the commissioner-general and the chief of police. The valet, quite desperate and at his wits' end, was weeping in front of the door. At first I suspected this man, but he was innocent.

" The criminal was never discovered.

" As I entered Sir John's drawing-room, I saw at the first glance the body, lying on its back, in the centre of the room.

" The waistcoat was torn, and a rent sleeve hung down; everything pointed to the fact that a terrible struggle had taken place.

" The Englishman had died of strangulation. His face, black and swollen, a terrifying sight, wore an expression of the most appalling terror; he held something between his clenched teeth; and his neck, pierced with five holes which might have been made with iron spikes, was covered with blood.

" A doctor joined us. He made a long examination of the finger-prints in the flesh and uttered these strange words:

" ' It's just as if he had been strangled by a skeleton.'

" A shiver ran down my spine, and I turned my eyes to the wall, to the spot where I had formerly seen the horrible flayed hand. It was no longer there. The chain, broken, hung down.

" I stooped over the dead man, and I found in his distorted mouth one of the fingers of the vanished hand, cut, or rather sawn, in two by his teeth just at the second joint.

" We proceeded with the formal investigations. Nothing was discovered. No door had been forced, no window, no article of furniture. The two watch-dogs had not awakened.

" Here, in a few words, is the servant's deposition:

" For the past month his master had seemed to be very agitated. He had received many letters, which he burnt as soon as they arrived.

"Often he would take up a horse-whip, in a rage which savoured of madness, and beat furiously the dried hand which had been sealed to the wall and removed, no one knew how, at the very hour of the crime.

"He had a habit of going to bed very late, and carefully locked all the doors and windows. He always had weapons within the reach of his arm. Often, at night, he would speak in a loud voice, as though quarrelling with someone.

"That night it happened that he had made no noise, and it was only when he came to open the windows that the servant had found Sir John murdered. He suspected no one.

"I communicated what I knew of the death to the magistrates and public officials, and a detailed inquiry was made over the entire island. Nothing was discovered.

"Then, one night, three months after the crime, I had a fearful nightmare. It seemed to me that I saw the hand, the horrible hand, run like a scorpion or a spider along my curtains and my walls. Three times I awoke, three times I fell asleep again, three times I saw the hideous relic career round my room, moving its fingers like paws.

"Next day the hand was brought to me; it had been found in the cemetery, on the tomb in which Sir John Rowell was buried, for we had been unable to discover his family.

"The index-finger was missing.

"There, ladies, that is my story. I know nothing more."

The ladies, horror-stricken, were pale and trembling.

"But that is not a *dénouement*, nor an explanation!" exclaimed one of them. "We shall not sleep if you do not tell us what really happened, in your opinion."

The magistrate smiled austerely.

"Oh, as for me, ladies," he said, "I shall certainly spoil your bad dreams! I simply think that the lawful owner of the hand was not dead, and that he came to fetch it with the one that remained to him. But I certainly don't know how he did it. It was a kind of vendetta."

"No," murmured one of the ladies, "that can't be the explanation."

And the judge, still smiling, concluded:

"I warned you that my theory would not appeal to you."

THE TRAMP

HE HAD KNOWN BETTER DAYS, IN SPITE OF HIS POVERTY AND his infirmity.

At the age of fifteen both his legs had been crushed by a carriage on the Varville high road. Ever since then he had been a beggar, dragging himself along the roads and across the farmyards, balanced on his crutches, which had forced his shoulders to the level of his ears. His head looked as though buried between two hills.

As a child, he had been found in a ditch by the rector of Billettes, on the eve of All Souls' Day, and for that reason had been christened Nicolas Toussaint (All Saints). He was brought up by charity, and remained a stranger to any form of education. It was after drinking some brandy given him by the village baker that he was lamed, which was considered an excellent joke; since then he had been a vagabond, not knowing how to do anything except hold out his hand for alms.

In earlier days the Baroness d'Avary had given him a sort of kennel filled with straw to sleep in, next to the chicken-house on the farm belonging to her country-house; and in the times of famine he was always certain of finding a piece of bread and a glass of cider in the kitchen. Often he received there a few coppers as well, thrown down by the old lady from the top of the terrace steps or from the windows of her room. Now she was dead.

In the village he was given scarcely anything; he was too well known; people were tired of him after forty years of seeing him drag his deformed and ragged body round from hovel to hovel on his two wooden paws. Yet he would not leave the neighbourhood, for he knew no other thing on earth but this corner of the country, these three or four hamlets in which he had dragged out his miserable life. He had set boundaries to his begging, and would never have passed over the frontiers within which he was used to keep himself.

He did not know if the world extended far beyond the trees which had always bounded his view. He had no curiosity in the matter. And when rustics, weary of meeting him continually at the edges of their fields or beside their ditches, shouted to him : " Why do you never go to the other villages, instead of always hobbling round these parts ? " he would not answer and would go away, seized with a vague fear of the unknown, the fear of a poor man in confused terror of a thousand things, new faces, rough treatment, the suspicious looks of people who did not know him, and the policemen who went two by two along the roads, and sent him ducking instinctively into the bushes or behind the heaps of stones.

When he saw them in the distance, glittering in the sun, he acquired suddenly a strange, monstrous agility in getting himself into some hiding-place. He tumbled off his crutches, letting himself fall like a rag, and rolled up into a ball, becoming quite small, invisible, flattened like a hare in its form, blending his brown rags with the brown earth.

As a matter of fact he had never had anything to do with them. But he carried it in his blood, as though he had received this terror from the parents he had never seen.

He had no refuge, no roof, no hut, no shelter. He slept anywhere in the summer, and in the winter he slipped under barns or into cowsheds with remarkable adroitness. He always decamped before his presence was discovered. He knew the holes by which buildings might be entered ; and the handling of his crutches had given surprising strength to his arms ; by the strength of his wrists alone he would climb up into hay-lofts, where he sometimes stayed for four or five days without stirring out, when he had collected sufficient provisions during his rounds.

He lived like the beasts of the woods, surrounded by men, knowing no one, loving no one, arousing in the peasants no emotion but a sort of indifferent contempt and resigned hostility. He had been nicknamed " Bell," because he swung between his two props like a bell between its two hammers.

For the past two days he had had nothing to eat. No one gave him anything now. People were at last quite tired of him. The peasant women at their doors shouted at him from the distance when they saw him coming :

" Be off with you, you clod! Why, I gave you a bit of bread only three days ago ! "

And he swivelled round on his props and went off to the next house, where he was welcomed in the same fashion.

The women declared to their next-door neighbours :

" After all, we can't feed the lazybones all the year round."

The lazybones, however, needed food every day.

He had roamed all over Saint Hilaire, Varville, and Les Billettes without harvesting a solitary centime or an old crust. No hope remained, except at Tournolles ; but that required of him a journey of two leagues on the high road, and he felt too weary to drag himself along, with his belly as empty as his pocket.

But he set off.

It was December ; a cold wind ran over the fields and whistled in the bare branches, and the clouds galloped across the low, dark sky, hastening to an unknown goal. The cripple went slowly on, painfully moving his crutches one after the other, steadying himself on the one twisted leg that remained to him, terminated by a club-foot swathed in a rag.

From time to time he sat down at the roadside and rested for a few minutes. Hunger was overwhelming his confused and stupid wits with utter misery. He had only one idea, to eat, but he did not know how it was to be brought about.

For three hours he struggled along the long road ; then,

when the trees of the village came into sight, he hastened his movements.

The first peasant whom he met, and of whom he asked alms, replied:

"Here you are back again at your old trade! Shall we never be rid of you?"

And "Bell" departed. At every door he was roughly treated and sent away without being given anything. But he continued his round, patient and obstinate. He did not garner a halfpenny.

Then he visited the farms, dragging himself across fields soft with rain, so exhausted that he could not lift his sticks. Everywhere he was driven away. It was one of those cold, melancholy days on which hearts are hardened, and tempers hasty, on which the soul is dark, and the hands open neither to give nor to succour.

When he had visited every house with which he was acquainted, he went and lay down in the corner of a ditch which ran alongside Maître Chiquet's farmyard. He unhooked himself—this is the best way of expressing the manner in which he let himself fall down between the high crutches that he slipped under his arms. For a long time he remained motionless, tortured by hunger, but too much of an animal fully to comprehend his fathomless misery.

He waited for he knew not what, in that vague state of expectation which lives on, deathless, in all of us. There in the corner of the yard, in the icy wind, he awaited the mysterious aid from heaven or mankind which a wretched victim will always hope for, without wondering how, or why, or by whose agency it can possibly arrive.

A flock of black hens was passing, seeking their sustenance in the earth, which gives food to all creatures. At every moment their sharp beaks found a bit of grain or an invisible insect, after which the birds would continue their slow, sure search.

"Bell" watched them, thinking of nothing; then there came to him, into his belly if not into his head, the feeling, rather than the thought, that one of those birds would make excellent eating, grilled over a fire of dead wood.

The idea that he was about to commit a theft never touched him. Taking up a stone which lay within his reach, he threw it at the nearest hen, and, being an expert shot, killed it outright. The bird fell on its side, beating its wings. The rest fled, swaying from side to side on their thin legs, and "Bell," clambering once more into his crutches, started off to retrieve his booty, his movements resembling those of the hens.

As he arrived beside the little black corpse stained on the head with blood, he was given a violent blow in the back which made him loose hold of his sticks and sent him rolling for ten paces in front of him. Maître Chiquet, exasperated, rushed upon the marauder and showered blows upon him, beating him furiously, with the fury of a peasant who has been robbed, belabouring with fist and knee the entire body of the cripple, who could not defend himself.

The farm-hands came up in their turn, and joined their master in battering the beggar. When they were weary of beating him, they picked him up, carried him off, and shut him up in the wood-shed while someone went to fetch the police.

"Bell," half dead, bleeding, and fainting with hunger, remained lying on the ground. Evening came, the night, then dawn. He had still had nothing to eat.

About midday the police appeared and opened the door with great care, expecting to meet with some resistance, for Maître Chiquet had given them to understand that he had been attacked by the beggar and had defended himself with great difficulty.

"Come on! Up you get!" shouted the sergeant.

But "Bell" could not move. He tried hard to hoist himself on to his sticks, but did not succeed. They thought he was shamming, trying to trick them, acting with the obstinate ill will common to malefactors, and the two armed men laid rough hands on him and set him on his crutches by main force.

Terror had gripped him, his instinctive terror of all wearers of the yellow shoulder-belt, the terror of the hunted before the hunter, of the mouse before the cat. With a superhuman effort he managed to remain upright.

" Off we go ! " said the sergeant. He walked. All the farm-hands watched him go. The women shook their fists at him ; the men sniggered and abused him : he was caught at last ! Good riddance !

He went off between his two guards. He succeeded in finding the desperate energy necessary to keep going until evening, stupefied, no longer even realising what was happening to him, too frightened to understand anything.

The people they met on the way stopped to watch him go by, and the peasants murmured :

" It's some thief or other."

Towards nightfall they reached the capital of the canton. He had never been so far as this. He hardly realised at all what was going on, nor what might hsppen to him afterwards. All these terrible, unforeseen events, these faces and and strange houses, bewildered him.

He did not utter a word, having nothing to say, for he no longer understood anything. And besides, it was so many years since he had spoken to anyone that he had very nearly lost the use of his tongue ; moreover, his thoughts were too confused to find expression in words.

He was locked up in the town jail. The policemen never imagined that he might need something to eat, and he was left until next day.

But when they came down to question him, they found him lying dead upon the floor. What a surprise !

A PARRICIDE

COUNSEL FOR THE DEFENCE HAD PLEADED INSANITY. How else was this strange crime to be accounted for?

One morning, in the reeds near Chatou, two bodies had been found locked in each other's arms, those of a man and his wife. They were a couple well known in society, wealthy, no longer young, and only married the previous year, the woman having lost her first husband three years before.

They were not known to have any enemies, and they had not been robbed. They had apparently been thrown into the river from the bank, after having been struck, one after the other, with a long iron spike.

The inquest did not lead to any discovery. The watermen who were questioned knew nothing; the affair was on the point of being abandoned, when a young joiner from a neighbouring village, named Georges Louis, known as The Gentleman, gave himself up.

To all interrogation he refused to make any other answer than:

"I had known the man for two years, the woman for six months. They often came to me to have old furniture mended, because I am good at the work."

And when he was asked: "Why did you kill them?" he would reply obstinately:

"I killed them because I wanted to kill them."

Nothing more could be got out of him.

The man was doubtless an illegitimate child formerly put out to nurse in the district and afterwards abandoned. He had no name except Georges Louis, but since, as he grew up, he had shown himself unusually intelligent, with tastes and a natural delicacy quite foreign to his comrades, he had been nicknamed "The Gentleman," and was never called anything else. He was known to be remarkably clever as a joiner, the profession he had adopted. He even did a little carving in wood. He was also said to have ideas above his station, to be a follower of communistic doctrines, even of nihilism, a great reader of novels of adventure and bloodthirsty romances, an influential elector and a clever speaker at working-men's or peasants' meetings.

Counsel for the defence had pleaded insanity.

How, in truth, could it be supposed that this workman should have killed his best clients, clients who were both rich and generous (he admitted this), who in two years had given him work which had brought in three thousand francs (his books testified to it)? There was only one explanation: insanity, the obsession of a man who has slipped out of his class and avenges himself on society as a whole by the murder of two gentlefolk; and counsel made a neat allusion to his nickname of "The Gentleman," given to this outcast by the whole neighbourhood.

"Consider the irony of the situation!" he exclaimed. "Was it not capable of still more violently exciting this unhappy youth with no father nor mother? He is an ardent republican; nay, he even belongs to that political party whose members the State was once wont to shoot and deport, but which to-day she welcomes with open arms, the party to whom arson is a first principle and murder a perfectly simple expedient.

"These lamentable doctrines, nowadays acclaimed in debating-societies, had ruined this man. He has listened to men of the republican party, yes! and even women too, demanding the blood of Monsieur Gambetta, the blood of Monsieur Grévy; his diseased brain has succumbed, he has thirsted for blood, the blood of nobility!

" It is not this man, gentlemen, whom you should condemn, it is the Commune ! "

Murmurs of approval ran to and fro. It was generally felt that counsel for the defence had won his case. The public prosecutor did not reply.

Then the judge asked the prisoner the customary question :

" Prisoner at the bar, have you nothing to add in your defence ? "

The man rose.

He was small in stature, with flaxen hair and grey eyes, steady and bright. A strong, frank, sonorous voice came from the throat of this slender youth, and his very first words altered at once the view that had been formed of him.

He spoke loudly, in a declamatory tone, but so clearly that his slightest words carried to the ends of the large court :

" Your Worship, as I do not wish to go to a madhouse, and even prefer the guillotine, I will tell you all.

" I killed the man and the woman because they were my parents.

" Now hear me and judge me.

" A woman, having given birth to a son, sent him out to nurse. It had been well if she had known to what district her accomplice had carried the little creature, innocent, but condemned to lasting misery, to the shame of illegitimate birth, to worse than that : to death, since he was abandoned, since the nurse, no longer receiving the monthly allowance, might well have left him, as such women often do, to pine away, to suffer from hunger, to perish of neglect.

" The woman who suckled me was honest, more honest, more womanly, greater of soul, a better mother, than my own mother. She brought me up. She was wrong to do her duty. It is better to leave to their death the wretches who are flung out into provincial villages, as rubbish is flung out at the roadside.

" I grew up with the vague impression that I was the bearer

of some dishonour. One day the other children called me 'bastard.' They did not know the meaning of the word, which one of them had heard at home. Neither did I know its meaning, but I sensed it.

"I was, I can honestly say, one of the most intelligent children in the school. I should have been an honest man, Your Worship, perhaps a remarkable man, if my parents had not committed the crime of abandoning me.

"And it was against me that this crime was committed. I was the victim, they were the guilty ones. I was defenceless, they were pitiless. They ought to have loved me: they cast me out.

"I owed my life to them—but is life a gift? Mine, at any rate, was nothing but a misfortune. After their shameful desertion of me, I owed them nothing but revenge. They committed against me the most inhuman, the most shameful, the most monstrous crime that can be committed against a human being.

"A man insulted, strikes; a man robbed takes back his goods by force. A man deceived, tricked, tormented, kills; a man whose face is slapped, kills; a man dishonoured, kills. I was more grievously robbed, deceived, tormented, morally slapped in the face, dishonoured, than all the men whose anger you condone.

"I have avenged myself, I have killed. It was my lawful right. I took their happy lives in exchange for the horrible life which they imposed on me.

"You will call it parricide! Were they my parents, those people to whom I was an abominable burden, a terror, a mark of infamy; to whom my birth was a calamity and my life a threat of shame? They sought their selfish pleasure; they brought forth the child they had not counted on. They suppressed that child. My turn has come to repay them in kind.

"And yet, even at the eleventh hour, I was prepared to love them.

"It is now two years, as I have already told you, since the

man, my father, came to my house for the first time. I suspected nothing. He ordered two articles of furniture. I learnt later that he had obtained information from the village priest, under the seal of a secret compact.

"He often came; he gave me work and paid me well. Sometimes he even chatted with me on various subjects. I felt some affection for him.

"At the beginning of this year he brought his wife, my mother. When she came in she was trembling so violently that I thought she was the victim of a nervous disorder. Then she asked for a chair and a glass of water. She said nothing; she stared at my stock with the expression of a lunatic, and to all the questions he put to her she answered nothing but yes and no, quite at random! When she had gone, I thought her not quite right in the head.

"She came back the following month. She was calm, mistress of herself. They remained talking quite a long time that day, and gave me a big order. I saw her again three times without guessing anything; but one day, lo and behold! she began to talk to me about my life, my childhood, and my parents. I answered: 'My parents, Madame, were wretches who abandoned me.' At that she set her hand to her heart and dropped senseless. I thought at once: 'This is my mother!' but was careful not to give myself away. I wanted her to go on coming.

"So I in my turn made inquiries. I learned that they had been married just the previous July, my mother having been only three years a widow. There had been rumours enough that they had been lovers during her first husband's lifetime, but no proof had been forthcoming. I was the proof, the proof they had first hidden, and hoped ultimately to destroy.

"I waited. She reappeared one evening, accompanied, as always, by my father. She seemed to be in a very agitated state that day, I do not know why. Then, just as she was going, she said to me:

" 'I wish you well, because I believe you are an honest lad and a good worker; doubtless you will be thinking of getting married some day; I have come to make it possible for you to choose freely any woman you prefer. I myself married the first time against the desires of my heart, and I know how much suffering it brings. Now I am rich, childless, free, mistress of my fortune. Here is your marriage portion.'

" She held out to me a large envelope.

" I stared fixedly at her, then said:

" 'Are you my mother?'

" She drew back three paces and hid her eyes in her hand, so that she could see me no more. He, the man, my father, supported her in his arms and shouted at me:

" 'You are mad!'

" 'Not at all,' I replied. 'I know very well that you are my parents. I am not to be deceived so easily. Admit it, and I will keep your secret; I will bear no malice, I will remain what I am now, a joiner.'

" He recoiled towards the door, still supporting his wife, who was beginning to sob. I ran and locked the door, put the key in my pocket, and continued:

" 'Look at her, then, and continue to deny that she is my mother!'

" At that he lost his self-control and turned very pale, terrified by the thought that the scandal hitherto avoided might suddenly come out; that their position, their good name, their honour would be lost at a blow.

" 'You're a scoundrel,' he stammered, 'trying to get money out of us. And yet they tell us to be good to the common people, the louts, to help them and succour them!'

" My mother, bewildered, was repeating over and over again:

" 'Let us go. Let us go.'

" Then, as the door was locked, he exclaimed:

" 'If you don't open the door immediately, I'll have you jailed for blackmail and assault!'

"I had kept my self-control; I opened the door, and saw them disappear in the darkness.

"At that I felt suddenly as though I had just been orphaned, abandoned, cast into the gutter. A dreadful sadness, mingled with rage, hatred, and disgust overwhelmed me. I felt a swollen rush of emotion through my whole being, a rising tide of justice, righteousness, honour, and spurned affection. I set off running in order to catch them up on the bank of the Seine, which they must follow in order to reach Chatou station.

"I overtook them before long. The night became pitch-dark. I slunk along on the grass, so that they did not hear me. My mother was still crying. My father was saying:

"'It is your own fault. Why did you insist on seeing him? It was madness, in our position. We might have done him kindness by stealth, without showing ourselves. Seeing that we could not hope to recognise him, what was the use of these perilous visits?'

"Then I threw myself in their path, a suppliant.

"'Clearly you *are* my parents,' I stammered. 'You have already cast me off once; will you reject me a second time?'

"At that, Your Worship, he raised his hand to me, I swear it on my honour, on the law, on the State. He struck me, and as I seized him by his coat-collar, he drew a revolver from his pocket.

"I saw red, I no longer knew what I did. I had my callipers in my pocket; I struck him, struck him with all my force.

"Then the woman began to cry: 'Help! Murder!' and tore at my beard. Apparently I killed her too. How can I know what I did at that moment?

"Then, when I saw them both lying on the ground, I threw them into the Seine, without thinking.

"That is all. Now judge me."

The prisoner sat down again. After this revelation the trial was postponed until the following session. It will soon come on again. If you and I were the jury, what should we do with this parricide?

THE LITTLE ONE

MONSIEUR LEMONNIER HAD REMAINED A WIDOWER WITH ONE child. He had loved his wife madly, with a noble and tender love that never failed, throughout the whole of their life together. He was a good, honest fellow, simple, very simple in fact, free from diffidence and malice.

Having fallen in love with a poor neighbour, he asked for her hand and married her. He was in a fairly prosperous drapery business, was making quite a good amount of money, and did not for one moment imagine that the girl might not have accepted him for himself alone.

At all events she made him happy. He had no eyes for anybody or anything but her, thought only of her, and looked at her continually in an abandon of adoration. During meals he would commit a thousand blunders rather than look away from the beloved face ; he would pour the wine into his plate and the water into the salt-cellar, and then would burst out laughing like a child, declaring :

" There, you see I love you too much ; it makes me do such a lot of silly things."

And she would smile, with an air of calm resignation, and then would turn away her eyes, as though embarrassed by her husband's worship, and would try to make him talk, to chat on any subject ; but he would reach across the table and take her hand, and, holding it in his, would murmur :

" My little Jeanne, my dear little Jeanne."

She would end by growing vexed and exclaiming :

" Oh, do be reasonable ; get on with your dinner, and let me get on with mine ! "

He would utter a sigh and break off a mouthful of bread, which he would proceed slowly to munch.

For five years they had no children. Then suddenly she found herself with child. It was a delirious happiness for them. He would never leave her during the whole of her pregnancy; to such an extent, in fact, that her maid, an old nurse who had brought her up and was given to speaking her mind to them, would sometimes thrust him out of the house and lock the door, so as to force him to take the air.

He had formed an intimate friendship with a young man who had known his wife since her childhood, and who was second head clerk at the Prefecture. Monsieur Duretour dined three times a week at the Lemonniers', brought flowers for Madame and sometimes secured a box at the theatre; and often, during dessert, the kind, affectionate Lemonnier would turn to his wife and exclaim:

"With a comrade like you and a friend like him, one is perfectly happy on earth."

She died in childbed. He nearly died too. But the sight of the child gave him courage: a little shrivelled creature that moaned.

He loved the baby with a passionate and grief-stricken love, a morbid love, wherein remained the remembrance of death, but wherein survived something of his adoration of the dead woman. The boy was his wife's flesh, her continued being, a quintessence of her, as it were. He was her very life poured into another body; she had disappeared that he might exist. . . . And the father embraced him frantically. . . .

But also the child had killed her, had taken, stolen that adored existence, had fed upon it, had drunk up her share of life. . . . And Monsieur Lemonnier replaced his son in the cradle and sat down beside him to contemplate him. He remained there for hours and hours, watching him, musing of a thousand sad or sweet things. Then, as the child was sleeping, he stooped over his face and wept into his coverings.

The child grew. The father could not forgo his presence for an hour; he would prowl about the nursery, take him out for walks, put on his clothes, wash him, give him his meals. His friend, Monsieur Duretour, also seemed to cherish the baby, and would embrace him with rapture, with those frenzies of affection which are a parent's property. He would make him leap in his arms or ride a cockhorse for hours upon his leg, and suddenly, overturning him upon his knees, would raise his short frock and kiss the brat's fat thighs and round little calves.

"Isn't he a darling, isn't he a darling!" would Monsieur Lemonnier murmur in delight, and Monsieur Duretour would clasp the child in his arms, tickling his neck with his moustache.

Only Céleste, the old nurse, seemed to have no affection for the little one. She was vexed at his pranks, and seemed exasperated by the cajolery of the two men.

"Is that any way to bring up a child?" she would exclaim. "You'll make a perfect monkey of him."

More years went by, and Jean attained the age of nine. He could scarcely read, he had been so spoilt, and he always did exactly as he liked. He had a stubborn will, a habit of obstinate resistance, and a violent temper. The father always gave way and granted him everything. Monsieur Duretour was perpetually buying and bringing for the little one the toys he coveted, and fed him on cakes and sweets.

On these occasions Céleste would lose her temper, and exclaim:

"It's a shame, Monsieur, a shame. You'll be the ruin of the child, the ruin of him, do you hear! But it's got to be stopped, and stopped it shall be, yes, I promise it shall, and before long, too."

"Well, what about it, my good woman?" Monsieur Lemonnier would answer with a smile. "I'm too fond of him, I can't go against his will. It's up to you to take your share in his upbringing."

Jean was weak and somewhat ailing. The doctor declared him to be anæmic, and ordered iron, red meat, and strong broth.

But the little one liked nothing but cakes, and refused all other nourishment; and his father, in despair, stuffed him with cream tarts and chocolate éclairs.

One evening, as the two sat down to table alone together, Céleste brought in the soup-tureen with an assurance and an air of authority unusual in her. She abruptly took off the lid, plunged the ladle into the middle of it, and announced:

" There's broth such as I've never made before; the little one really must have some, this time."

Monsieur Lemonnier, terrified, lowered his head. He saw that this was not going down well.

Céleste took his plate, filled it herself, and placed it back in front of him.

He immediately tasted the soup and declared:

" Yes, it is excellent."

Then the servant took the little boy's plate and poured into it a whole ladleful of soup. She retired two paces and waited.

Jean sniffed it, pushed away the plate, and uttered a " pah " of disgust. Céleste, grown pale, went swiftly up to him and, seizing the spoon full of soup, thrust it forcibly into the child's half-open mouth.

He choked, coughed, sneezed, and spat, and, yelling, grasped his glass in his fist and flung it at his nurse. It caught her full in the stomach. At that, exasperated, she took the brat's head under her arm and began to ram spoonful after spoonful of soup down his gullet. He steadily vomited it back, stamping his feet with rage, writhing, choking, and beating the air with his hands, as red as though he were dying of suffocation.

At first the father remained in such stupefaction that he made no movement at all. Then suddenly he rushed forward with the wild rage of a madman, took the servant by the throat, and flung her against the wall.

"Get out! . . . out! . . . out! . . . brute!" he stammered.

But with a vigorous shake she repulsed him, and with dishevelled hair, her cap hanging down her back, her eyes blazing, cried:

"What's come over you now? You want to beat me because I make the child eat his soup, when you'll kill him with your spoiling!"

"Out! . . . be off with you . . . off with you, brute!" he repeated, trembling from head to foot.

Then in a rage she turned upon him, and facing him eye to eye, said in a trembling voice:

"Ah! . . . You think . . . you think you're going to treat me like that, me, me? . . . No, never. . . . And for whose sake, for whose sake? . . . For that snotty brat who isn't even your own child! No . . . not yours! . . . No! not yours! . . . not yours! . . . not yours! Why, everybody knows it, by God, except you. . . . Ask the grocer, the butcher, the baker, every one, every one. . . ."

She faltered, choked with anger, then was silent and looked at him.

He did not stir; livid, his arms waving wildly. At the end of several seconds he stammered in a feeble, tremulous voice, in which strong emotion still quivered:

"You say? . . . you say? . . . What do you say?"

Then she answered in a calmer voice:

"I say what I know, by God! What every one knows."

He raised his two hands and, flinging himself upon her with the fury of a brute beast, tried to fell her to the ground. But she was strong, in spite of her age, and agile too. She slipped through his arms and, running round the table, once more in a violent rage, screeched:

"Look at him, look at him, you fool, and see if he isn't the living image of Monsieur Duretour; look at his nose and eyes, are *your* eyes like that? Or your nose? Or your hair? And were *hers* like that? I tell you everybody knows it, everybody, except you! It's the laughing-stock of the town! Look at him! Look at him! . . ."

She passed in front of the door, opened it, and disappeared.

Jean, terrified, remained motionless, staring at his soup-plate.

At the end of an hour she returned, very softly, to see. The little one, after having devoured the cakes, a dish of custard, and a dish of pears in syrup, was now eating jam out of a pot with his soup-spoon.

The father had gone out.

Céleste took the child, embraced him, and, with silent steps, carried him off to his room and put him to bed. And she returned to the dining-room, cleared the table, and set everything in order, very uneasy in her mind.

No sound whatever was to be heard in the house. She went and set her ear to her master's door. He was not moving about the room. She set her eye to the keyhole. He was writing and seemed calm.

Then she went back to sit in her kitchen, so as to be ready for any circumstance, for she realised that something was in the air.

She fell asleep in her chair, and did not wake until daybreak.

She did the household work, as was her custom every morning; she swept and dusted, and, at about eight o'clock, made Monsieur Lemonnier's coffee.

But she dared not take it to her master, having very little idea how she would be received; and she waited for him to ring. He did not ring. Nine o'clock went by, then ten o'clock.

Céleste, alarmed, prepared the tray, and started off with a beating heart. In front of the door she stopped and listened. Nothing was stirring. She knocked, there was no answer.

So, summoning up all her courage, she opened the door and went in; then, uttering a terrible shriek, she dropped the breakfast-tray which she held in her hands.

Monsieur Lemonnier was hanging right in the middle of his room, suspended by the neck from a ring in the ceiling. His tongue protruded in ghastly fashion. The slipper had fallen off his right foot and lay on the floor; the other slipper had remained upon the foot. An overturned chair had rolled to the bedside.

Céleste, at her wits' end, fled shrieking. All the neighbours ran up. The doctor discovered that death had taken place at midnight.

A letter, addressed to Monsieur Duretour, was found upon the suicide's table. It contained this solitary line:

"I leave and entrust the little one to you."

IX

GUILLEMOT ROCK

THIS IS THE SEASON FOR GUILLEMOTS.

From April until the end of May, before the bathers arrive from Paris, one may observe, at the little watering-place called Étretat, the sudden appearance of certain old gentlemen in top-boots and tight shooting-coats. They spend four or five days at the Hôtel Hanville, disappear, come again three weeks later; then, after a second stay, depart for good.

The following spring, they appear again.

They are the last hunters of the guillemot, the survivors of those of the old days; for thirty or forty years ago there were some twenty of these fanatics, but now they are but a few fanatical sportsmen.

The guillemot is a rare migrant whose habits are strange. For almost the whole of the year it lives in the neighbourhood of Newfoundland, and off the islands of Saint-Pierre and Miquelon; but at the nesting season a band of migrants crosses the Atlantic and, every year, comes to lay its eggs and hatch them out on the same spot, the rock called Guillemot Rock, near Étretat. They are never to be found in any other spot than this. They have always come thither, they have always been shot, and they still keep coming back; they always will come back. As soon as the young birds have been raised, they go away again, and disappear for a year.

Why do they never go elsewhere, choose some other point in the long white cliff, which runs unchanged from the Pas de Calais to Le Havre? What force, what unconquerable instinct, what age-long custom impels these birds to return to this spot? What was the manner of their first migration, or the nature of the tempest which may long since have cast their sires upon this rock? And why have the children, the grandchildren, all the descendants of the first-comers, always returned thither?

They are not numerous; a hundred at the most, as though a solitary family possessed this tradition, performed this annual pilgrimage.

And every spring, as soon as the little wandering tribe is reinstalled upon its rock, the same hunters reappear in the village. Once, as young men, they were familiar to the inhabitants; to-day they are old, but still faithful to the regular meeting-place that for the past thirty or forty years they have appointed for their gathering.

For nothing in the world would they fail to keep the appointment.

It was an April evening in one of the last years. Three of the old guillemot-shooters had just arrived; one of them was missing, Monsieur d'Arnelles.

He had written to no one, given no news! But he was not dead, like so many others; it would have been known. At last, weary of waiting, the first-comers sat down to table; dinner was nearly over when a carriage rolled into the yard of the hostelry; and soon the late arrival entered.

He sat down, in excellent spirits, rubbing his hands, ate with a good appetite, and, as one of his companions expressed surprise at his wearing a frock-coat, replied calmly:

"Yes, I had not time to change."

They went to bed as soon as they rose from the table, for, in order to surprise the birds, it is necessary to start well before daybreak.

Nothing is pleasanter than this sport, this early morning expedition.

At three in the morning the sailors wake the sportsmen by throwing gravel at their window-panes. In a few minutes all are ready and down on the shingle beach. Although no twilight is yet visible, the stars have paled a little; the sea screams over the pebbles, the breeze is so cold that they shiver a little, despite their thick clothes.

Soon the two boats, pushed out by the men, rush down the slope of rounded pebbles, with a noise as of tearing canvas; then they are swaying upon the first waves. The brown sails are hoisted up the masts, swell slightly, tremble, hesitate, and, bulging once more, round-bellied, sweep the tarred hulls away towards the wide opening down the river, dimly visible in the gloom.

The sky grows clear; the darkness seems to melt away; the coastline appears, still veiled in mist, the long white coastline, straight as a wall. They pass the Manne-Porte, an enormous arch through which a ship could go, double the point of La Courtine, run past the vale of Antifer and the cape of the same name; and suddenly there rushes into sight a beach on which are hundreds of gulls. It is Guillemot Rock.

It is merely a small hump of cliff, and on the narrow ledges of rock the heads of birds are visible, watching the boats.

They are there, motionless, waiting, not daring as yet to fly away. Some, settled upon the extreme edges, look as though they are sitting on their hind parts, upright like bottles, for their legs are so short that, when they walk, they appear to be gliding on wheels, and, when they want to fly away, they are unable to start with a run, and are obliged to let themselves fall like stones, almost on top of the men watching for them.

They are aware of their weakness and the danger it entails, and do not readily decide to fly.

But the sailors begin to shout and beat the gunwales with the wooden thole-pins, and the birds, terrified, one by one launch out into the void, and drop to the very level of the waves; then, their wings beating with swift strokes, they gather way, dart off, and reach the open spaces, unless a hail of shot casts them into the water.

For an hour they are slaughtered thus, one after another being forced to make off; and sometimes the females on their nests, utterly devoted to the business of hatching, refuse to leave, and ever and anon receive a volley which splashes their white plumage with spots of rosy blood, and the bird dies, still faithfully guarding her eggs.

On the first day, Monsieur d'Anelles shot with his customary enthusiasm; but, when they went off home at about ten o'clock, beneath the high and radiant sun which threw great triangles of light into the white clefts in the cliffs, he appeared somewhat distracted, and now and then he seemed lost in thought, unlike his usual self.

As soon as they were back on land, some sort of servant, clad in black, came and whispered with him. He appeared to reflect, to hesitate; then he replied:

"No, to-morrow."

And, next day, the shooting was resumed. This time Monsieur d'Anelles often missed his birds, though they let themselves fall almost on to the end of his gun-barrel, and his friends, laughing, asked him if he was in love, if any secret trouble were tormenting his heart and brain. At last he admitted it.

"Yes, as a matter of fact I must be off directly, and that's upsetting me."

"What, you're going away? Why?"

"Oh, urgent business. I can't stay any longer."

Then they began to talk of other things.

As soon as lunch was over, the servant in black reappeared. Monsieur d'Anelles ordered him to harness the horses, and the fellow was on the point of going out when the three other sportsmen intervened, insisting on an explanation, with many entreaties and demands that their friend should stay.

At last one of them said:

"But, look here, this business of yours can't be so very serious, if you've already waited two days."

The fourth, altogether perplexed, reflected, plainly a prey to conflicting ideas, torn between pleasure and duty, unhappy and ill at ease.

After a long period of meditation, he murmured with some hesitation :

" You see . . . you see, I am not alone here ; I have my son-in-law with me."

There were cries and exclamations.

" Your son-in-law ? . . . But where is he ? "

At that he appeared suddenly confounded, and blushed.

" What ? Didn't you know ? Why . . . why . . . he is out in the barn. He's dead."

Stupefied silence reigned.

More and more distressed, Monsieur d'Anelles continued :

" I have had the misfortune to lose him ; and, as I was taking the body to my home at Briseville, I made a slight detour just to keep our appointment here. But you will realise that I can delay no longer."

Then one of the sportsmen, bolder than the rest, suggested :

" But . . . since he is dead . . . it seems to me . . . that he might very well wait one more day."

The two others hesitated no longer.

" You can't deny that," they said.

Monsieur d'Arnelles seemed relieved of a great weight, but, still somewhat uneasy, he inquired :

" You . . . you honestly think . . . ? "

As one man, the three others replied :

" Dash it all ! dear boy, two days more or less won't make any difference to him in his condition."

Thereupon, perfectly at ease, the father-in-law turned round to the undertaker.

" Very well, my good man, let it be the day after to-morrow."

TIMBUCTOO

THE BOULEVARD, THAT RIVER OF LIFE, SWARMED WITH PEOPLE in the golden dust of the setting sun. The whole sky was a blinding red ; and, behind the Madeleine, an immense blazing cloud flung along the great avenue an oblique shower of fire, quivering like the vapour above a brazier.

The gay, throbbing crowd went by under this flaming mist, and seemed transfigured. Faces were gilded, black hats and clothes took on purple gleams ; the polish on their shoes darted flames across the asphalt pavement.

In front of the cafés a throng of men were drinking gleaming, coloured beverages, which looked like precious stones melted into the crystal.

In this crowd of people with their light or sombre clothes, sat two officers in full uniform, and the dazzling brilliance of their gold lace made every eye glance at them. They were talking gaily and aimlessly, in the midst of all this radiant, vibrant life, in the glowing splendour of the evening ; and they were watching the throng, the sauntering men and the hurrying women who left behind them a divine and disquieting perfume.

Suddenly an enormous negro, dressed in black, pot-bellied, bedizened with trinkets on his waistcoat of ticking, his face shining as though it had been polished with blacking, passed in front of them with an air of triumph. He laughed at the passers-by, he laughed at the newspaper-vendors, he laughed at the blazing sky, he laughed at the whole of Paris. He was so tall that his head overtopped all others ; and, behind him, all the loungers turned round to stare at his back.

But suddenly he caught sight of the officers, and, jostling through the crowd of drinkers, he rushed up to them. As soon as he was in front of their table, he fixed his gleaming, delighted eyes upon them, and the corners of his mouth rose to his ears, disclosing his white teeth, bright as a crescent moon in a black sky. The two men, bewildered, stared at this ebony giant, unable to make head or tail of his merriment.

And he cried out, in a voice which drew a burst of laughter from every table :

" Mawnin', Lieutenant."

One of the officers was a lieutenant-colonel, the other a colonel. The former said :

" I don't know you, sir. I am quite unable to imagine what you want of me."

The negro replied :

" Me like you much, Lieutenant Védié, siege of Bézi, we hunt much grapes."

The officer, quite at a loss, stared fixedly at the fellow, groping in the depths of his memory ; and exclaimed abruptly :

" Timbuctoo ! "

The negro, radiant, smacked his thigh, uttered a laugh of unbelievable violence, and roared :

" Ya, ya, my Lieutenant, remember Timbuctoo, ya, mawnin' ! "

The Major gave him his hand, laughing heartily himself. Then Timbuctoo became serious again. He took the officer's hand and, so swiftly that the other could not prevent him, he kissed it, according to the custom of the negroes and the Arabs. The embarrassed officer said to him in a severe voice :

" Come, Timbuctoo, we are not in Africa. Sit down there and tell me how it is that I find you here."

Timbuctoo stretched his paunch, and, speaking so fast that he stammered, announced :

" Make much money, very much, big rest'rant, good eat, Prussians, me, steal much, very much, F'ench cooking, me get hund'ed thousand f'ancs. Ha ! Ha ! Ha ! Ha ! "

And he writhed with laughter, bellowing with a gleam of mad merriment in his eyes.

When the officer, who understood his strange language, had questioned him for some time, he said to him :

" Well, good-bye, Timbuctoo ; see you again soon."

The negro promptly rose, shook, this time, the outstretched hand, and, still laughing, exclaimed :

" Mawnin', mawnin', Lieutenant ! "

And he departed, so happy that he gesticulated as he walked, and the crowd took him for a lunatic.

" Who was that brute ? " inquired the Colonel.

" A good lad and a good soldier," replied the Major. " I will tell you what I know about him ; it is funny enough.

" You know that at the beginning of the war of 1870 I was shut up in Bézières, the place the negro calls Bézi. We were not besieged, but blockaded. The Prussian lines surrounded us on every side, out of range of cannon-shot, and not firing on us, but gradually starving us out.

" I was a lieutenant at the time. Our garrison was composed of troops of every sort, the remnants of decimated regiments, fugitives and marauders separated from their army corps. We even had eleven Turcos, who arrived one evening, no one knows how or whence. They had turned up at the gates of the town, worn out, ragged, starving, and drunk. They were entrusted to me.

" I very soon realised that they detested every form of discipline ; they were always getting out of the town, and were always drunk. I tried the police station, even a dose of prison ; nothing did any good. My men would disappear for whole days, as though they had burrowed underground, and then would reappear so tipsy that they could not stand. They had no money. Where did they drink ? And how, and by what means ?

" The problem began to fascinate me, especially as these

savages interested me, with their perpetual laugh and their natures of overgrown, naughty boys.

"I noticed at last that they obeyed blindly the biggest of the lot; the one you have just seen. He ruled them absolutely as he chose, and prepared their mysterious enterprises with the undisputed authority of an omnipotent chief. I made him come and see me, and questioned him. Our conversation lasted a good three hours, so much trouble did it take me to comprehend his surprising rigmarole. As for him, poor devil, he made the most extraordinary efforts to be understood, invented words, gesticulated, perspired with the effort, wiped his brow, panted, stopped, and abruptly began again when he fancied he had discovered a new means of explaining himself.

"Eventually I gathered that he was the son of a great chief, a sort of negro king in the neighbourhood of Timbuctoo. I asked him his name. He answered something like 'Chavaharibouhalikhranafotapolara.' I thought it simpler to give him the name of his country: 'Timbuctoo.' And a week later the entire garrison knew him by no other name.

"But we were consumed by a frantic desire to know how this African ex-prince managed to get hold of drink. I discovered it in strange fashion.

"I was on the ramparts one morning, scanning the horizon, when I saw something moving in a vineyard. It was getting near the vintage season, and the grapes were ripe, but I never thought of that. I imagined that a spy was approaching the town, and I organised an entire expedition to seize the prowler. I took command myself, after getting permission from the General.

"I had sent out, through three different gates, three little bands which were to meet near the suspected vineyard and surround it. In order to cut off the spy's retreat, one of the detachments had to march for a good hour. A man who remained on the watch upon the walls indicated to me by signs that the fellow I had noticed had not left the field. We went on our way in complete silence, crawling, almost lying flat in the ruts. At last we reached the appointed spot; swiftly I deployed my men, who dashed into the vineyard and found . . . Timbuctoo, going on all fours through the middle of vines, and eating the grapes, or rather lapping them up like a dog lapping soup, taking them straight off the plants in large mouthfuls, tearing down the bunches with his teeth.

"I tried to make him stand up; it was not to be dreamed of, and I realised then why he was crawling thus on his hands and knees. Set on his legs, he tottered for a few seconds, threw out his arms, and fell flat on his nose. I have never seen a man so drunk as he was.

"He was carried home on two vine-poles. He never stopped laughing all the way back, and waved his arms and legs.

"That was the whole mystery. My rascals drank from the grape itself. Then, when they were so tight that they could not move, they went to sleep where they were.

"As for Timbuctoo, his love of the vines passed all belief and measure. He lived among them like the thrushes, which, by the way, he hated with the hatred of a jealous rival. He repeated constantly:

"'Th'ushes eat all the g'apes, d'unkards!'

"One evening I was sent for. Something was seen approaching us across the plain. I had not brought my spyglass, and could make out very little. It was like a great serpent uncoiling, a convoy, I don't know what.

"I sent some men forward to meet this strange caravan, which soon made its triumphal entry. Timbuctoo and nine of his comrades were carrying, upon a kind of altar made of rustic chairs, eight severed heads, bleeding and grimacing. The tenth Turco was leading a horse, to whose tail a second was attached, and six more animals followed, secured in the same fashion.

"This is what I learned. Setting off to the vineyards, my Africans had suddenly noticed a Prussian detachment drawing near to a village. Instead of fleeing, they hid; then, when the officers had dismounted in front of an inn, in search of refreshments, the gallant eleven charged, put to flight the Uhlans, who thought they were seriously attacked, and killed the two sentries, in addition to the Colonel and the five officers with him.

"That day I embraced Timbuctoo. But I noticed that he found difficulty in walking. I thought he was wounded; he burst out laughing, and told me:

"'Me, p'ovisions for count'y.'

"For Timbuctoo had no idea of going to war for glory; he did it for profit. Everything he found, everything which appeared to him to have any value, everything, especially, which sparkled, he thrust into his pocket. And what a pocket! It was a gulf which began at his hip and ended at his ankle. He had picked up a piece of army slang, and called it his 'deep,' and deep it was, in very truth!

"He had consequently stripped off the gilt from the Prussian uniforms, the brass from their helmets, the buttons, etc., and thrown the whole collection into his 'deep,' which was full to overflowing.

"Every day he cast into it every shining object which caught his eye, pieces of tin or silver coins; the outline of his figure became remarkably quaint.

"He was determined to carry it all back to the land of ostriches, whose brother this king's son seemed to be in his devouring passion for acquiring glittering articles. If he had not had his 'deep,' what would he have done? Doubtless he would have swallowed them.

"Every morning his pocket was empty. He must have had a central dump where his riches were heaped together. But where was it? I was never able to find out.

"The General, informed of Timbuctoo's great feat, ordered

the bodies which had been left in the neighbouring village to be buried at once, so that it might not be discovered that they had been decapitated. The Prussians returned there the next day. The mayor and seven prominent residents were shot on the spot by way of reprisals, for having given away the presence of the Germans.

"Winter had come. We were worn out and desperate. We fought now every day. The famished men could no longer march. Only the eight Turcos (three had been killed) remained fat and glossy, vigorous and always ready for a fight. Timbuctoo was positively growing fatter. One day he said to me:

"'You, much hung'y, me good meat.'

"And, as a matter of fact, he did bring me an excellent steak. But of what? We had no more cows, sheep, goats, donkeys, or pigs. It was impossible to get horseflesh. I thought of all this after I had eaten the meat. It was then that a horrible thought came to me. These negroes had been born very near the district where men are eaten! And every day so many soldiers were slain in the town. I questioned Timbuctoo. He refused to answer. I did not insist, but from that time onward I refused his presents.

"He adored me. One night we were caught in a snowstorm out at the advanced pickets. We were sitting on the ground. I cast looks of pity on the poor negroes shivering under the white, frozen dust. As I was very cold myself, I began to cough. I instantly felt something fall on me, like a large, warm covering. It was Timbuctoo's coat which he was throwing over my shoulders.

"I rose and, giving him back his garment, said:

"'Keep that, my lad; you need it more than I do.'

"'No,' he replied, 'for you, Lieutenant; me not need, me warm, warm."

"And he looked at me with entreaty in his eyes.

"'Come now, obey me,' I went on. 'Keep your coat; I wish you to.'

"Thereupon the negro rose, drew his sabre, which he knew how to make as sharp as a scythe, and holding in his other hand the wide cloak which I would not take, declared:

"'If you not keep coat, me cut; nobody have coat.'

"He would have done it. I gave in.

"Eight days later we had capitulated. Some of us had been able to escape. The rest were about to march out of the town and surrender to the victors.

"I directed my steps towards the Place d'Armes, where we were to muster, when I stopped, bewildered with amazement, in front of a gigantic negro clad in white duck, and wearing a straw hat. It was Timbuctoo. He looked radiant, and was walking to and fro with his hands in his pockets, in front of a small shop in whose window were displayed two plates and two glasses.

"'What are you doing?' I said to him.

"'Me not gone,' he replied. 'Me good cook, me make eat Colonel, Alge'ia; me eat P'ussians, steal much, much.'

"There were ten degrees of frost. I shivered at sight of this duck-clad negro. Then he took my arm and made me go inside. I noticed an enormous sign, which he was going to hang up at his door as soon as we were gone, for he had some traces of shame.

"And I read, traced by the hand of some accomplice, the following announcement:

M. TIMBUCTOO'S MILITARY KITCHEN
LATE COOK TO H.M. THE EMPEROR
PARISIAN ARTIST —— MODERATE PRICES

"In spite of the despair gnawing at my heart, I could not help laughing, and I left my negro to his new profession.

"Was it not better than having him taken prisoner?

"You have just seen that the rascal has succeeded.

"To-day Bézières belongs to Germany. The Restaurant Timbuctoo is the beginning of our revenge."

A TRUE STORY

A GALE WAS BLOWING OUT OF DOORS; THE AUTUMN WIND moaned and careered round the house, one of those winds which kill the last leaves and carry them off into the clouds.

The shooting-party were finishing their dinner, still in their boots, flushed, animated, and inflamed. They were Normans, of a class between the nobles and the yeomen, half country-squires, half peasants, rich and strong, capable of breaking the horns of the bulls when they catch hold of them at fairs.

All day long they had been shooting over the land of Maître Blondel, the mayor of Éparville, and were now at their meal round the large table, in the sort of half farmhouse, half country-seat owned by their host.

They spoke as ordinary men shout, laughed like wild beasts roaring, and drank like cisterns, their legs outstretched, their elbows on the table-cloth, their eyes shining beneath the flame of the lamps, warmed by a huge fire which cast blood-coloured gleams over the ceiling; they were talking of shooting and of dogs. But they had reached the period when other ideas come into the heads of half-drunk men, and all eyes were turned on a sturdy, plump-cheeked girl who was carrying the great dishes of food in her red hands.

Suddenly a hefty fellow, named Séjour, who, after studying for the Church, had become a veterinary surgeon, and looked after all the animals in the locality, exclaimed:

" By Gad, Blondel, there's no flies on that filly you've got there! "

There was a resounding laugh. Then an old nobleman, Monsieur de Vernetot, who had lost caste through taking to drink, lifted up his voice:

"Once upon a time I had a funny affair with a girl like that. I really must tell you the tale. Whenever I think of it, it reminds me of Mirza, the bitch I sold to the Comte d'Haussonnel: she returned every day as soon as she was unchained, she found it so hard to leave me. In the end I grew angry, and asked the Comte to keep her chained up. Well, do you know what the poor beast did? She died of grief.

"But, to return to my maid, here's the story.

"I was twenty-five at the time, and was living a bachelor life on my Villebon estate. When a man's young, you know, and has money, and bores himself to tears every evening after dinner, he keeps his eyes open on every side.

"I soon discovered a young thing in service with Déboultot of Canville. You knew Déboultot, Blondel, didn't you? In short, the hussy took my fancy to such an extent that one day I went off to see her master, and suggested a bit of business to him. He was to let me have his servant, and I was to sell him my black mare, Cocote, which he'd been wanting for close on two years. He gave me his hand, with a 'Put it there, Monsieur de Varnetot.' The bargain was struck, the little girl came to my house, and I myself took my mare to Canville and let her go for three hundred crowns.

"At first everything went swimmingly. No one suspected anything; the only thing was that Rose loved me a little too much for my liking. She wasn't of the common stock, I tell you. There was no ordinary blood in her veins; it must have come from some other girl who went wrong with her master.

"In short, she adored me. It was all coaxing and billing and cooing, and calling me pet names as if I were her little dog; so many pretty loving ways that I began to think rather seriously.

"I said to myself: 'This mustn't go on, or I'll let myself be caught.' But I'm not easily caught, I'm not. I'm not the sort of fellow to be wheedled with a couple of kisses. In fact, my eyes were very much open, when she told me that she was in the family way.

" Crash! Bang! It was as though someone had fired a couple of shots into my chest. And she kissed me, kissed me and laughed and danced, fairly off her head with delight! I said nothing the first day, but I reasoned it out at night. 'Well, that's that,' I thought, 'but I must avoid the worst and cut her adrift; it's high time.' You see, my father and mother were at Barneville, and my sister, who was the wife of the Marquis d'Yspare, at Rollebec, two leagues from Villebon. I couldn't take any chances.

" But how was I to extricate myself? If she left the house, suspicions would be aroused, and people would talk. If I kept her, the cat would soon be out of the bag; and besides, I could not let her go like that.

" I spoke about it to my uncle, the Baron de Créteuil, an old buck who had had more than one such experience, and asked him for a word of advice. He replied calmly:

" 'You must get her married, my boy.'

" I jumped.

" 'Get her married, Uncle! But to whom?'

" He quietly shrugged his shoulders:

" 'Anyone you like; that's your business, and not mine. If you're not a fool, you can always find someone.'

" I thought over this advice for a good week, and ended by saying to myself: 'My uncle's quite right.'

" So I began to rack my brains and search for a man; when one evening the justice of the peace, with whom I had been dining, told me:

" 'Old Mother Paumelle's son has just been up to his larks again; he'll come to a bad end, will that boy. It's true enough that like father like son.'

" This Mother Paumelle was a sly old thing whose own youth had left something to be desired. For a crown she would assuredly have sold her soul, and her lout of a son into the bargain.

"I went to find her, and, very carefully, I made her understand the situation.

"As I was becoming embarrassed in my explanations, she suddenly asked me:

"'And what are you going to give the girl?'

"She was a cunning old thing, but I was no fool, and had made all my preparations.

"I had just three little bits of land away out near Sasseville, which were let out from my three Villebon farms. The farmers were always complaining that they were a long way off; to make a long story short, I had taken back these three fields, six acres in all, and, as my peasants were making an outcry about it, I let them all off their dues in poultry until the end of each lease. By this means I put the business through all right. Then I bought a strip from my neighbour, Monsieur d'Aumonté, and had a cottage built on it, all for fifteen hundred francs. In this way I made a little bit of property which did not cost me much, and I gave it to the girl as a dowry.

"The old woman protested: this was not enough; but I held to it, and we parted without settling anything.

"Early next morning the lad came to see me. I had almost forgotten what he looked like. When I saw him, I was reassured; he wasn't so bad for a peasant; but he looked a pretty dirty scoundrel.

"He took a detached view of the affair, as though he had come to buy a cow. When we had come to terms, he wanted to see the property, and off we went across the fields. The rascal kept me out there a good three hours; he surveyed the land, measured it, and took up sods and crushed them in his hands, as though he were afraid of being cheated over the goods. The cottage was not yet roofed, and he insisted on slate instead of thatch, because it required less upkeep!

"Then he said to me:

"'But what about the furniture? You're giving that!'

"'Certainly not,' I protested; 'it's very good of me to give you the farm.'

"'Not half,' he sniggered; 'a farm and a baby.'

"I blushed in spite of myself.

"'Come,' he continued, 'you'll give the bed, a table, the dresser, three chairs, and the crockery, or there's nothing doing.'

"I consented.

"And back we went. He had not yet said a word about the girl. But suddenly he asked, with a cunning, worried air:

"'But if she died, who would the stuff go to?'

"'Why, to you, of course,' I replied.

"That was all he had wanted to find out that morning. He promptly offered me his hand with a gesture of satisfaction. We were agreed.

"But, oh! I had some trouble to convince Rose, I can tell you. She grovelled at my feet, sobbed and repeated: 'You suggest this, you! you!' She held out for more than a week, in spite of my reasoning and my entreaties. Women are silly things; once love gets into their heads, they can't understand anything. Common sense means nothing to them: love before all, all for love!

"At last I grew angry and threatened to turn her out. At that she gradually yielded, on condition that I allowed her to come and see me from time to time.

"I myself led her to the altar, paid for the ceremony, and gave the wedding breakfast. I did the thing in style. Then it was: 'Good night, children!' I went and spent six months with my brother in Touraine.

"When I returned, I learnt that she had come to the house every week and asked for me. I hadn't been back an hour when I saw her coming with a brat in her arms. Believe me or not, as you like, but it meant something to me to see that little mite. I believe I even kissed it.

"As for the mother, she was a ruin, a skeleton, a shadow. Thin, and grown old. By God, marriage didn't suit her!

"'Are you happy?' I inquired mechanically.

"At that she began to cry like a fountain, hiccuping and sobbing, and exclaimed:

"'I can't, I can't live without you, now! I'd rather die! I can't!'

"She made the devil of a noise. I consoled her as best I could, and led her back to the gate.

"I found out that her husband beat her, and that the old harpy of a mother-in-law made life hard for her.

"Two days later she came back again; she took me in her arms and grovelled on the ground.

"'Kill me, but I won't go back there any more,' she implored. Exactly what Mirza would have said if she had spoken!

"All this fuss was beginning to get on my nerves, and I cleared out for another six months. When I returned . . . when I returned, I learnt that she had died three weeks before, after having come back to the house every Sunday . . . still just like Mirza. The child too had died eight days later.

"As for the husband, the cunning rascal, he came into the inheritance. He's done well for himself since, so it seems; he's a town councillor now."

Then Monsieur de Varnetot added with a laugh:

"Anyhow, I made his fortune for him."

And Monsieur Séjour, the veterinary surgeon, raising a glass of brandy to his lips, gravely concluded the story with:

"Say what you like, but there's no place in this world for that sort of woman!"

FAREWELL

THE TWO FRIENDS WERE FINISHING DINNER. FROM THE CAFÉ window they saw the boulevard, covered with people. They felt the caress of the warm airs that drift through Paris on calm summer nights, making a man raise his eyes towards the passers-by, rousing in him a desire to get away, far away to some distant place, no one knows where, under green leaves ; making him dream of moonlit rivers and glow-worms and nightingales.

One of the two, Henri Simon, sighing deeply, said :

"Ah ! I'm getting old. It's sad. Once, on nights like this, I felt the devil in my bones. To-day I feel nothing but regrets. Life goes so fast ! "

He was already somewhat fat, aged perhaps forty-five, and very bald.

The other, Pierre Carnier, a shade older, but slimmer and more lively, replied :

"As for me, my dear chap, I've grown old without noticing it in the least. I was always a gay dog, a jolly fellow, vigorous and all that. But when a man looks in his mirror every day, he does not see old age doing its work, for it is slow and regular, and changes the face so gradually that the transitions are imperceptible. That is the only reason why we do not die of grief after only two or three years of its ravages. For we cannot appreciate them. In order to realise them, we should have to go without looking at our faces for six months on end—then what a blow it would be !

"And women, my dear chap, how sorry I am for the poor things ! The whole of their happiness, the whole of their power, the whole of their lives, lies in their beauty, which lasts ten years.

" Well, I have grown old without suspecting it, and thought myself almost an adolescent when I was nearly fifty. Not feeling within myself any infirmity of any sort, I went on my way, happy and care-free.

" The revelation of decay came to me in a simple but terrible manner, and prostrated me for nearly six months . . . then I resigned myself to my lot.

" I have often been in love, like all men, but once more than usual.

" I met her at the seaside, at Étretat, about twelve years ago now, shortly after the war. There is nothing so charming as the beach there, in the morning, at the bathing-hour. It is small, curved like a horseshoe, framed in the high white cliffs pierced with those curious holes known as the Gates, one very large, stretching its gigantic limb into the sea, the other opposite it, low and round; the crowd of women gathers together within the frame of high rocks, thronging the narrow tongue of shingle, covering it with a brilliant garden of bright frocks. The sun falls full upon the slopes, on sunshades of every hue, on the greenish-blue sea; everything is gay and charming, a smiling scene. You go and sit right at the edge of the water, and watch the ladies bathing. They come down the beach draped in a flannel wrap which they cast off with a pretty gesture as they reach the foamy fringe of the small waves; and go into the sea with swift little steps, sometimes interrupted by a shiver of delicious cold, a brief catching of the breath.

" Very few stand this bathing-test. There they can be judged, from the calf to the throat. Above all, when they leave the water, their weaknesses are plain to see; although the sea-water is a powerful stimulant to flabby bodies.

" The first time that I saw this young woman under these conditions, I was ravished and seduced. She stood the test triumphantly. There are faces, too, whose charm comes home to us instantaneously, conquers us at sight. We think we have found the woman we were born to love. I suffered that sensation, that shock of emotion.

"I got an introduction to her, and was soon caught as I had never been. She played havoc with my heart. It is a dreadful and glorious experience thus to submit oneself to a woman's power. It is almost a torture, and, at the same time, an incredible happiness. Her look, her smile, the hair on the nape of her neck lifted by the breeze, all the tiniest lines of her face, the faintest movements of her features, ravished me, overwhelmed me, and maddened me. She possessed me with the whole of herself, her gestures, her attitudes, even the clothes she wore, which acquired magical powers. I thrilled at the sight of her veil on a piece of furniture, or her glove thrown down on an arm-chair. Her dresses seemed to me inimitable. No woman's hats were as delightful as hers.

"She was married, but the husband came down every Saturday and went away again on the Monday. In other respects he left me quite indifferent. I was not in the least jealous, I do not know why; never has any human being seemed to me of less importance in life, or occupied less of my attention, than that man.

"How I loved her! And how beautiful she was, how graceful and young! She was youth, elegance, and freshness personified. I had never really felt what a pretty creature a woman is, how fine, distinguished, and delicate, fashioned of charm and grace. I had never realised the seductive beauty that lies in the curve of a cheek, in the quiver of a lip, in the round folds of a little ear, in the shape of the absurd organ we call a nose.

"It lasted three months, and then I went off to America, my heart crushed with despair. But the thought of her dwelt with me, presistent, triumphant. She possessed me from the distance as she had possessed me close at hand. Years passed. I never forgot her. The charming image of her remained before my eyes and in my heart. And my affection for her remained faithful, a calm affection now, a feeling like the loved remembrance of all that was most beautiful and seductive in my experience of life.

" Twelve years are so little in the life of a man! He never feels them pass! They go by one after the other, gently and swiftly, slow and hurried, each so long, and yet so soon finished! And they add up together so promptly, leave so little trace behind them, fade so utterly that when he turns to look at the time that has run by he sees nothing, and cannot understand how it has come about that he is old.

" It really seemed to me as though a mere few months separated me from that charming season on the beach at Étretat.

" Last spring I went to dine with some friends of mine at Maisons-Laffitte.

" Just as the train was starting, a stout lady got into my compartment, escorted by four little girls. I scarcely troubled to glance at this mother-hen with her brood, very wide and very round, her full-moon face framed in a ribbon-decked hat.

" She breathed hard, out of breath after walking fast. The children began to chatter. I opened my paper and began to read.

" We had just gone through Asnières when my neighbour suddenly said to me:

" ' Excuse me, Monsieur, but are you not Monsieur Carnier?'

" ' Yes, Madame.'

" Then she began to laugh, with the happy laughter of a contented woman, yet with a touch of sadness in it.

" ' You do not recognise me?'

" I hesitated. I certainly thought I had seen that face somewhere; but where? When?

" ' Yes . . . and no . . .' I replied. ' I certainly know you, but I can't think of your name.'

" She blushed slightly, and said:

" 'Madame Julie Lefèvre.'

"I had never had such a shock. In a single instant I felt as though all were over with me! I felt that a veil had been torn from before my eyes, and that I was on the point of making frightful and heart-rending discoveries.

" This was she! This fat, ordinary woman, she? And she had hatched out these four daughters since I had last seen her. The little creatures caused me more astonishment than their mother herself. They had come from her body; they were already big; they had taken their place in life. While she no longer counted, she, that marvel of fascinating exquisite grace. I had seen her only yesterday, it seemed, and now had found her thus! Was it possible? Violent grief oppressed my heart, and a protest, too, against Nature herself, an unreasoning exasperation at this brutal, infamous work of destruction.

" I looked at her in awe. Then I took her hand, and tears came into my eyes. I wept for her youth, I wept for her death. For I did not know this fat woman.

" She, also affected, faltered:

" 'I am greatly changed, am I not? But time goes by, doesn't it? You see, I have become a mother, just a mother, a good mother. Farewell to the rest, it is all over. Oh! I thought you would not recognise me if we ever met. And you have changed too; it took me some time to be sure that I was not making a mistake. You've gone quite white. Think of it; it is twelve years ago! Twelve years! My eldest girl is ten already.'

" I looked at the child. And I found in her something of her mother's old charm, but as yet a sense of immaturity, of something early and unformed. And life seemed to me swift as a passing train.

" We arrived at Maisons-Laffitte. I kissed my old friend's hand. I had found nothing to say to her but the most appalling commonplaces. I was too overcome to speak.

" That evening, when all alone in my house, I looked for a long time into the mirror, a long, long time, and I ended by recalling myself as I had been, by seeing again, in my mind's eye, my brown moustache and my black hair, and the youthful outlines of my face. Now I was old. Farewell."

A MEMORY

HOW MANY MEMORIES OF MY YOUTH CAME TO ME UNDER THE gentle caress of the earliest summer sun! It is an age wherein all is good, glad, charming, and intoxicating. How exquisite are the memories of lost springs!

Do you recall, my old friends, my brothers, those years of gladness in which life was but triumph and laughter? Do you recall the days when we roamed disreputably about Paris, our radiant poverty, our walks in the woods newly clad in green, our revels under the open sky outside the taverns on the banks of the Seine, and our love adventures, so commonplace and so delicious?

I should like to relate one of those adventures. It dates from twelve years ago, and already feels so old, so old, that it seems now at the other end of my life, before the turning, the ugly turning whence suddenly I saw the end of the journey.

I was twenty-five in those days. I had just come to Paris; I worked in a government office, and Sundays seemed to me extraordinary festivals, full of exuberant happiness, although nothing remarkable ever happened on them.

Every day is Sunday now. But I regret the times when I had only one a week. How good it was! I had six francs to spend!

I awoke early, that particular morning, with that feeling of freedom well known to clerks, the feeling of deliverance, rest, tranquillity, and independence.

I opened my window. The weather was glorious. The clear blue sky was spread above the city, full of sunshine and swallows.

I dressed very quickly and went out, eager to spend the

day in the woods, to breathe the odour of the leaves; for I come off country stock, and spent my childhood on the grass and under the trees.

Paris was waking joyfully, in the warmth and the light. The fronts of the houses shone, the concierges' canaries sang furiously in their cages, and gaiety ran down the street, lighting up faces and stirring laughter everywhere, as though a mysterious happiness filled all animate and inanimate life in that radiant dawn.

I reached the Seine, to catch the *Swallow*, which was to take me to Saint-Cloud.

How I loved waiting for the boat upon the landing-stage! I felt as though I were off to the end of the world, to new and wonderful countries. I watched the boat come into sight, away in the distance under the arch of the second bridge, very small, with its plume of smoke, then larger, larger, always growing; and to my mind it took on the airs and graces of a liner.

It came alongside the stage, and I embarked.

A crowd of people in their Sunday clothes were already on board, with gay dresses, brilliantly coloured ribbons, and fat scarlet faces. I placed myself right in the bows, and stood there watching quays, trees, houses, and bridges go by. And suddenly I saw the great viaduct of Point-du-Jour barring the stream. It was the end of Paris, the beginning of the country, and at once beyond the double line of arches the Seine widened out, as though space and liberty had been granted to it, becoming suddenly the lovely peaceful river that flows on across the plains, at the foot of the wooded hills, through the meadows, and along the edge of the forest.

After passing between two islands, the *Swallow* followed the curve of a slope whose green expanse was covered with white houses. A voice announced: "Bas-Meudon"; then, farther on: "Sèvres," and, still farther on: "Saint-Cloud."

I disembarked. And I hurried through the little town

along the road to the woods. I had brought a map of the surroundings of Paris, lest I lost myself on the paths which run in every direction across the woods where the people of Paris go for their expeditions.

As soon as I was in the shade, I studied my route, which seemed perfectly simple. I was to turn to the right, then to the left, then to the left again, and I should arrive at Versailles by nightfall, for dinner.

And I began to walk slowly, beneath the fresh leaves, drinking in the fragrant air, perfumed with the odour of buds and sap. I walked with short steps, unmindful of the stacks of old paper, of the office, of my chief and my colleagues, and of files, and dreaming of the happy adventures that must assuredly be waiting for me in the stretches of that veiled, unknown future. I was filled with a thousand memories of childhood awakened in me by the scents of the country, and I went on, sunk in the fragrant, living, throbbing loveliness of the woods, warmed by the powerful June sun.

Sometimes I sat down by a bank and looked at the little flowers of every kind, whose names I had long known. I knew them all again, just as though they were the very ones I had once seen in my own country. They were yellow, red, and violet, delicate and dainty, lifted on high stalks or huddled close to the earth. Insects of every colour and shape, short and squat or long and thin, extraordinary in their construction, frightful microscopic monsters, peacefully mounted the blades of grass, which bent under their weight.

Then I slept for some hours in a ditch, and went on again, rested and strengthened by my sleep.

In front of me opened a delightful alley, whose rather sparse leafage allowed drops of sunlight to shower everywhere upon the soil, and gleamed on the white daisies. It ran on endlessly, calm and empty. A solitary great hornet buzzed down it, pausing at times to sip a flower that stooped beneath it, and flying off again almost at once to come to rest again a little farther on. Its fat body looked like brown velvet striped with yellow, borne on wings that were transparent and inordinately small.

Suddenly I saw at the end of the path two people, a man and a woman, coming towards me. Annoyed at being disturbed in my quiet walk, I was on the point of plunging into the undergrowth when I fancied I heard them calling to me. The woman was actually waving her sunshade, and the man, in his shirt-sleeves, his frock-coat over one arm, was raising the other as a signal of distress.

I went towards them. They were walking hurriedly, both very red, she with little rapid steps, he with long strides. Ill humour and weariness were visible on their faces.

The woman asked me at once:

"Monsieur, can you tell me where we are? My idiotic husband has lost us, after saying that he knew this district perfectly."

"Madame," I replied confidently, "you are going towards Saint-Cloud, and Versailles is behind you."

"What!" she continued, glancing with angry pity towards her husband. "Versailles is behind us? But that is precisely where we mean to have dinner!"

"So do I, Madame; I am going there."

"Oh dear, oh dear, oh dear!" she repeated, in the tone of overwhelming contempt with which women express their exasperation.

She was quite young, pretty, and dark, with a shadow of a moustache on her lip.

As for the man, he was perspiring and mopping his brow. Without doubt they were Parisian shopkeepers. The man looked overcome, tired out and miserable.

"But, my dear girl," he murmured, "it was you. . . ."

She did not permit him to finish the sentence.

"It was I! . . . Ah! it is I now. Was it I who wanted to go off without inquiries, declaring that I could always find my way? Was it I who wanted to turn to the right at the top of the hill, declaring that I remembered the way? Was it I who undertook to look after Cachou. . . ."

She had not finished speaking when her husband, as though he had suddenly gone out of his mind, uttered a piercing cry, a long, wild cry, which cannot be written in any language, but which was something like *teeeteeet*.

The young woman seemed neither surprised nor excited, and continued:

" No, upon my word, some people are too silly, always pretending to know everything. Was it I who took the Dieppe train last year instead of the Havre train? Tell me, was it I? Was it I who betted that Monsieur Letournier lived in the Rue des Martyrs? . . . Was it I who wouldn't believe that Céleste was a thief? . . ."

And she continued furiously, with amazing rapidity of speech, piling up the most heterogeneous, unexpected, and grievous charges, furnished by all the intimate situations in their existence together, blaming her husband for all his actions, ideas, manners, experiments, and efforts, his whole life, in fact, from their wedding day up to the present moment.

He tried to stop her, to calm her, and faltered:

" But, my dear girl . . . it's no use . . . in front of the gentleman . . . we're making an exhibition of ourselves. It is of no interest to the gentleman."

And he turned his melancholy eyes upon the thickets, as though eager to explore their peaceful and mysterious depths, to rush into them, escape and hide from every eye. From time to time he again uttered his cry, a prolonged, very shrill *teeeteeet*. I imagined this habit was a nervous disorder.

The young woman abruptly turned to me and, changing her tone with remarkable rapidity, remarked:

" If Monsieur will be good enough to permit us, we will go with him, in order not to lose ourselves again and risk having to sleep in the wood."

I bowed; she took my arm and began to talk of a thousand things, of herself, her life, her family, and her business. They kept a glove-shop in the Rue Saint-Lazare.

Her husband walked beside her, continually throwing wild glances into the thick of the trees, and every now and then shouting, *teeeteeet*.

At last I asked him:

" Why do you shout like that?"

" It's my poor dog that I've lost," he replied with an air of consternation and despair.

" What? You have lost your dog?"

" Yes. He was barely a year old. He had never gone out of the shop. I wanted to take him for a walk in the woods. He had never seen grass or leaves before, and it pretty well sent him off his head. He began to run about, barking, and has disappeared in the forest. I should also tell you that he was very frightened of the railway; it may have made him lose his senses. I have called and called in vain; he has not come back. He will die of hunger in there."

Without turning towards her husband, the woman remarked:

" If you had kept him on the lead, it wouldn't have happened. People as silly as you have no business to have dogs."

" But, my dear girl, it was you. . . ."

She stopped short; and looking into his eyes as though she were going to tear them out, she began once more her innumerable reproaches.

Night was falling. The veil of mist which covers the country-side at twilight was slowly unfolding; romance hovered around, born of the strange, delightful coolness that fills the woods at the approach of night.

Suddenly the young man stopped, and, feeling about himself frantically, exclaimed:

" Oh! I believe I have. . . ."

" Well, what?" she asked, looking at him.

" I did not realise that I was carrying my frock-coat on my arm."

" Well? "

" I have lost my letter-case . . . my money is in it."

She quivered with rage and choked with indignation.

" That is the last straw. How idiotic you are, how perfectly idiotic! How can I have married such a fool? Well, go and look for it, and take care that you find it. I will go on to Versailles with this gentleman. I don't want to spend the night in the woods."

" Yes, dear," he replied meekly; " where shall I find you? "

A restaurant had been recommended to me. I told him of it.

The husband turned back and, bending down towards the ground, scanning it with anxious eyes, he walked away, continually shouting *teeeteeet*.

It was a long time before he disappeared; the shades of evening, thicker now, obscured him at the far end of the path. Soon the outline of his body was seen no more, but for a long time we heard his melancholy *teeeteeet*, *teeeteeet*, becoming shriller as the night grew darker.

As for me, I walked on with lively, happy steps through the sweetness of the twilight, with the unknown woman leaning on my arm.

I racked my brain in vain for compliments. I remained silent, excited and enraptured.

But suddenly a high road cut across our path. I saw that on the right, in a valley, there was quite a town.

What was this place?

A man was passing; I questioned him.

" Bougival," he replied.

I was thunderstruck.

" Bougival! Are you sure? "

" Damn it all, I live there! "

The little woman laughed uproariously.

I suggested taking a cab to Versailles.

"Certainly not!" she replied. "This is too funny, and I'm so hungry. I'm not a bit anxious; my husband will always find his way all right. It's a pleasure for me to be relieved of him for a few hours."

We accordingly entered a restaurant by the waterside, and I was bold enough to engage a private room.

She got thoroughly tipsy, I can assure you; sang, drank champagne, and did all sorts of crazy things . . . even the craziest of all.

That was my first adultery!

THE CONFESSION

MARGUERITE DE THÉRELLES WAS DYING. ALTHOUGH SHE was only fifty-six, she looked at least seventy-five. She was gasping, paler than her sheets, shaken with frightful shudders, her face distorted, her eyes haggard, as though they saw some frightful thing.

Her elder sister, Suzanne, who was six years older than she, was sobbing on her knees at the bedside. A little table had been drawn up to the dying woman's couch, and on the tablecloth stood two lighted candles, for they were waiting for the priest, who was to administer the extreme unction and the last sacrament.

The apartment wore the sinister aspect of all chambers of death, their air of despairing farewell. Medicine bottles stood on the tables, cloths lay about in corners, kicked or swept out of the way. The disordered chairs themselves looked frightened, as though they had run in every direction. For Death, the victor, was there, hidden, waiting.

The story of the two sisters was very touching. It had been told far and wide, and had filled many eyes with tears.

Suzanne, the elder, had once been deeply in love with a young man who loved her. They were betrothed, and were only awaiting the day fixed for the wedding, when Henry de Sampierre died suddenly.

The young girl's despair was terrible, and she declared that she would never marry. She kept her word. She put on widow's weeds and never gave them up.

Then her sister, her little sister Marguerite, who was only twelve years old, came one morning and threw herself into her elder sister's arms, saying :

" Sister, I don't want you to be unhappy. I don't want you to cry all your life long. I will never leave you, never, never! I won't marry either. I will stay with you for ever and ever."

Suzanne kissed her, touched by her childish devotion, believing in it not at all.

But the little sister kept her word, and, despite her parents' prayers and her sister's entreaties, she never married. She was pretty, very pretty; she refused several young men who seemed to love her; she never left her sister.

They lived together all the days of their lives, and were never parted. They lived side by side, inseparable. But Marguerite always seemed sad and depressed, more melancholy than the elder, as though crushed, perhaps, by her sublime self-sacrifice. She aged more rapidly, had white hair at the age of thirty, and, often ill, seemed the victim of some secret gnawing malady.

Now she was to be the first to die.

She had not spoken for twenty-four hours. She had only said, at the first glimmer of dawn:

" Go and fetch the priest; the time has come."

Since then she had lain still on her back, shaken with fits of shuddering, her lips trembling as though terrible words had risen from her heart and could not issue forth, her eyes wild with terror, a fearful sight.

Her sister, mad with grief, was crying brokenly, her forehead pressed against the edge of the bed, and repeating:

" Margot, my poor Margot, my little one! "

She had always called her " my little one," just as the younger had always called her " Sister."

Steps sounded on the staircase. The door opened. A choir-boy appeared, followed by the old priest in his surplice. As soon as she saw him, the dying woman sat up with a convulsive movement, opened her lips, babbled two or three words, and fell to scraping her nails together as though she meant to make a hole in them.

The Abbé Simon went up to her, took her hand, kissed her on the brow, and said gently:

"God forgive you, my child; be brave, the time has come: speak."

Then Marguerite, shivering from head to foot, shaking the whole bed with her nervous movements, stammered:

"Sit down, sister, and listen."

The priest bent down to Suzanne, still lying at the foot of the bed, raised her, placed her in an arm-chair, and, taking in each hand the hand of one of the sisters, murmured:

"O Lord God, give them strength, grant them Thy pity!"

And Marguerite began to speak. The words came from her throat one by one, hoarse, deliberate, as though they were very weary.

"Mercy, mercy, sister, forgive me! Oh, if you knew how all my life I have dreaded this moment! . . ."

"What have I to forgive you, little thing?" stammered Suzanne, her tears choking her. "You have given me everything, sacrificed everything for me; you are an angel."

But Marguerite interrupted her:

"Hush, hush! Let me speak . . . do not stop me . . . it is horrible . . . let me tell all . . . the whole story, without faltering. . . . Listen. . . . You remember . . . you remember . . . Henry. . . ."

Suzanne shuddered and looked at her. The younger sister continued:

"You must hear it all, if you are to understand. I was twelve, only twelve, you remember that, don't you? And I was spoilt, I did everything that came into my head! . . . Don't you remember how spoilt I was? . . . Listen. . . . The first time he came he wore high shining boots; he dismounted in front of the steps, and he apologised for his clothes, saying he had come with news for Father. You remember, don't you? . . . Don't speak . . . listen. When I saw him I was quite overcome, I thought him so handsome; and I remained standing in a corner of the drawing-room all the time he was speaking. Children are strange . . . and terrible. . . . Oh, yes . . . I have dreamed of it!

"He came back . . . many times. . . . I gazed at him with all my eyes, with all my soul. . . . I was big for my age . . . and far more sophisticated than people supposed. He came again often. . . . I thought of nothing but him. I used to repeat very softly: 'Henry . . . Henry de Sampierre!'

"Then they said that he was going to marry you. It was a sore grief to me, sister, oh, a sore, sore grief! I cried for three whole nights, without sleeping. He used to come every day, in the afternoon, after lunch, you remember, don't you? Don't speak . . . listen. You made him cakes, of which he was very fond . . . with flour, butter and milk. . . . Oh! I knew just how you made them. . . . I could make them this moment, if I had to. He would swallow them in a single mouthful, and then he would toss down a glass of wine . . . and then say: 'Delicious!' Do you remember how he used to say it?

"I was jealous, jealous. . . . The day of your wedding was drawing near. There was only a fortnight. I was going mad. I used to say to myself: 'He shall not marry Suzanne, no, I won't have it. . . . It is I who will marry him, when I am grown up. I shall never find a man I love so much.' . . . And then one evening, ten days before the wedding, you went out with him to walk in front of the house, in the moonlight . . . and out there . . . under the pine-tree, the big pine-tree . . . he kissed you . . . held you . . . in his arms . . . for such a long time. . . . You haven't forgotten, have you? . . . It may have been the first time . . . yes . . . you were so pale when you came back into the drawing-room!

"I saw you; I was there, in the copse. I grew wild with

rage! If I could have done it, I would have killed you both!

"I said to myself: 'He shall not marry Suzanne, never! He shall not marry anyone. . . . I should be too unhappy. . . .' Suddenly I began to hate him terribly.

"Do you know what I did then? . . . Listen. I had seen the gardener make little balls with which to kill stray dogs. He crushed a bottle with a stone, and put the ground glass in a little ball of meat.

"I took a little medicine-bottle from Mother's room, I smashed it up with a hammer, and hid the glass in my pocket. It was a glittering powder. . . . Next day, as soon as you had made the little cakes, I split them open with a knife and put the glass in. . . . He ate three of them . . . and I, too, ate one. . . . I threw the other six into the pond . . . the two swans died three days later. . . . Don't speak . . . listen, listen. I was the only one who did not die. . . . But I have always been ill . . . listen. . . . He died . . . you know . . . listen . . . that was nothing. . . . It was afterwards, later . . . always . . . that it was most terrible . . . listen. . . .

"My life, my whole life . . . what torture! I said to myself: 'I will never leave my sister. And I will tell her all, in the hour of my death.' . . . There! And since then I have thought every moment of this hour, the hour when I shall have to tell you all. . . . Now it has come . . . it is terrible. . . . Oh! . . . Sister!

"Every moment the thought has been with me, morning and evening, day and night: 'I shall have to tell her, some day. . . .' I waited. . . . What torment! . . . It is done. . . . Do not say anything. . . . Now I am afraid. . . . I am afraid. . . . Oh, I am afraid! If I were to see him again, presently, when I am dead . . . see him again . . . do you dream of seeing him? . . . See him before you do! . . . I shall not dare. . . . I must . . . I am going to die. . . . I want you to forgive me. I want you to. . . . Without it, I cannot come into his presence. Oh, tell her to forgive me, Father, tell her. . . . I beg you. I cannot die without it. . . ."

She was silent, and lay panting, still clawing at the sheet with her shrivelled fingers. . . .

Suzanne had hidden her face in her hands, and did not stir. She was thinking of the man she might have loved so long! What a happy life they would have had! She saw him again, in the vanished long-ago, in the distant past for ever blotted out. Oh, belovèd dead, how you tear our hearts! Oh, that kiss, her only kiss! She had kept it in her soul. And then, nothing more, nothing more in all her life! . . .

Suddenly the priest stood up and cried out in a loud shaken voice:

" Mademoiselle Suzanne, your sister is dying! "

Then Suzanne let her hands fall apart and showed a face streaming with tears, and, falling upon her sister, she kissed her fiercely, stammering:

" I forgive you, I forgive you, little one. . . ."

A HUMBLE DRAMA

MEETINGS CONSTITUTE THE CHARM OF TRAVELLING. Who does not know the joy of coming, five hundred leagues from one's native land, upon a Parisian, a college friend, or a neighbour in the country? Who has not spent a night, unable to sleep, in the little jingling stage-coach of countries where steam is still unknown, beside a strange young woman, half seen by the gleam of the lantern when she clambered into the carriage at the door of a white house in a little town?

And, when morning comes, and brain and ears are still numbed by the perpetual ringing of the bells and the noisy clatter of the windows, how charming to see your pretty tousled neighbour open her eyes, look about her, arrange her rebellious tresses with the tips of her slim fingers, adjust her hat, feel with her skilful hand whether her corsets have not slipped, whether her person is as it should be, and her skirt not too crushed!

She gives you, too, a single cold, inquisitive glance. Then she settles herself into her corner and seems to have no eyes for anything but the landscape.

In spite of yourself, you stare at her all the time: you think of her the whole time in spite of yourself. What is she? Where has she come from? Where is she going to? In spite of yourself, you sketch a little romance in your mind. She is pretty; she seems charming! Happy man! . . . Life might be exquisite by her side. Who knows? Perhaps she is the woman necessary to our emotions, our dreams, our desires.

And how delicious, too, is the regret with which you see her get off at the gate of a country-house. A man is waiting there with two children and two servants. He takes her in his arms and kisses her as he helps her down. She stoops and takes up the little ones who are stretching out their hands, and caresses them lovingly; they go off down a path while the maids take the boxes which the conductor is handing down from the roof.

Good-bye! It is finished. You will never see her again. Good-bye to the woman who has spent the night at your side. You never knew her, never spoke to her; still, you are a little sad when she goes. Good-bye!

I have many of these memories of travel, grave and gay.

I was in Auvergne, wandering on foot among those delightful French mountains, not too high, not too wild, but friendly and homely. I had climbed the Sancy, and was just going into a little inn, near a pilgrims' chapel named Notre Dame de Vassivière, when I noticed an old woman, a strange, absurd figure, lunching by herself at the table inside.

She was at least seventy, tall, withered, and angular, with white hair arranged in old-fashioned sausage curls on her temples. She was dressed in the quaint and clumsy style of the wandering Englishwoman, like a person to whom clothes were a matter of complete indifference; she was eating an omelette and drinking water.

She had an odd expression, with restless eyes, the face of one whom life has treated harshly. I stared at her in spite of myself, wondering: "Who is she? What sort of thing is this woman's life? Why is she wandering all alone in these mountains?"

She paid, then rose to go, readjusting upon her shoulders an extraordinary little shawl, whose two ends hung down over her arms. She took from a corner a long alpenstock covered with names engraved in the rusty iron, then walked out, straight and stiff, with the long strides of a postman setting off on his round.

A guide was waiting for her at the door. They moved off.

I watched them descend the valley, along the road indicated by a line of high wooden crosses. She was taller than her companion, and seemed to walk faster than he.

Two hours later I was climbing up the brim of that deep funnel in the heart of which, in a vast and wonderful green cavity filled with trees, bushes, rocks, and flowers, lies Lake Pavin, so round that it looks as though it had been made with a compass, so clear and blue that one might suppose it a flood of azure poured down from the sky, so charming that one would like to live in a hut on the slope of the wood overlooking this crater where, quiet and cool, the water sleeps.

She was standing there motionless, gazing at the transparent water lying at the bottom of the dead volcano. She was standing as though she would peer beneath it, into its unknown depths, peopled, it is said, by trout of monstrous size who have devoured all the other fish. As I passed close to her, I fancied that two tears welled in her eyes. But she walked away with long strides to rejoin her guide, who had stopped in a tavern at the foot of the rise leading to the lake.

I did not see her again that day.

Next day, as night was falling, I arrived at the castle of Murol. The old fortress, a giant tower standing upon a peak in the centre of a large valley, at the crossing of three dales, rises towards the sky, brown, crannied, and battered, but round from its broad circular base to the crumbling turrets of its summit.

It is more impressive than any other ruin in its simple bulk, its majesty, its ancient air of power and austerity. It stands there solitary, high as a mountain, a dead queen, but still a queen of the valleys crouching under it. The visitor approaches by a pine-clad slope, enters by a narrow door, and stops at the foot of the walls, in the first enclosure, high above the whole country-side.

Within are fallen rooms, skeleton staircases, unknown pits, subterranean chambers, oubliettes, walls cleft through the middle, vaults still standing, none knows how, a maze of stones and crannies where grass grows and animals creep.

I was alone, roaming about this ruin.

Suddenly, behind a piece of wall, I caught sight of a human being, a sort of phantom, as if it were the spirit of the ancient ruined building.

I started in amazement, almost in terror. Then I recognised the old woman I had already met twice.

She was weeping. She was weeping big tears, and held her handkerchief in her hand.

I turned to go. She spoke to me, ashamed at having been discovered unawares.

"Yes, Monsieur, I am crying. . . . It does not happen often."

"Excuse me, Madame, for having disturbed you," I stammered in confusion, not knowing what to answer. "Doubtless you are the victim of some misfortune."

"Yes—no," she murmured, "I am like a lost dog."

And putting her handkerchief over her eyes, she burst into sobs.

I took her hands and tried to console her, touched by her very moving grief. And abruptly she began to tell me her history, as if she did not want to be left alone any longer to bear her grief.

"Oh! . . . Oh! . . . Monsieur. . . . If you knew . . . in what distress I live . . . in what distress. . . .

"I was happy. . . . I have a home . . . away in my own country. I cannot go back again, I shall never go back again, it is too cruel.

"I have a son. . . . It is he! It is he! Children do not know. . . . One has so short a time to live! If I saw him now, I might not know him! How I loved him! How I loved him! Even before he was born, when I felt him stir in my body. And then afterwards! How I embraced him, caressed him, cherished him! If you only knew how many nights I have spent watching him sleep, thinking of him! I was mad about him. He was eight years old when his father sent him away to a boarding-school. It was all over. He was no longer mine. Oh! my God! He used to come every Sunday, that was all.

"Then he went to school in Paris. He only came four times a year; and each time I marvelled at the changes in him, at finding him grown bigger without having seen him grow. I was robbed of his childhood, his trust, the love he would never have withdrawn from me, all my joy in feeling him grow and become a little man.

"I saw him four times a year! Think of it! At each of his visits his body, his eyes, his movements, his voice, his laugh, were no longer the same, were no longer mine. A child alters so swiftly, and, when you are not there to watch him alter, it is so sad; you will never find him again!

"One year he arrived with down upon his cheeks! He! My son! I was amazed . . . and—would you believe it?—sad. I scarcely dared to kiss him. Was this my baby, my wee thing with fair curls, my baby of long ago, the darling child I had laid in long clothes upon my knee, who had drunk my milk with his little greedy lips, this tall brown boy who no longer knew how to caress me, who seemed to love me chiefly as a duty, who called me 'mother' for convention's sake, and who kissed me on the forehead when I longed to crush him in my arms?

"My husband died. Then it was the turn of my parents. Then I lost my two sisters. When Death enters a house, it is as though he hastened to finish as much work as possible so that he need not return for a long time. He leaves but one or two alive to mourn the rest.

"I lived alone. In those days my big son was dutiful enough. I hoped to live and die near him.

"I went to join him, so that we might live together. He had acquired a young man's ways; he made me realise that I worried him. I went away; I was wrong; but I suffered so to feel that I, his mother, was intruding. I went back home.

"I hardly saw him again.

"He married. What joy! At last we were to be united again for ever. I should have grandchildren! He had married an English girl who took a dislike to me. Why? Perhaps she felt that I loved him too much?

"I was again forced to go away. I found myself alone. Yes, Monsieur.

"Then he went to England. He was going to live with them, his wife's parents. Do you understand? They have him, they have my son for their own! They have stolen him from me! He writes to me every month. At first he used to come and see me. Now he comes no more.

"It is four years since I have seen him. His face was wrinkled and his hair was turning white. Was it possible? This man, who would soon be an old man, my son? My little pink baby of long ago? Doubtless I shall not see him again.

"And I travel all the year. I go to the right and to the left, as you see, all by myself.

"I am like a lost dog. Good-bye, Monsieur. Do not stay near me, it hurts me to have told you all this."

And, as I walked down the hill again, I turned round, and saw the old woman standing on a cracked wall, gazing at the mountains, the long valley, and Lake Chambon in the distance.

The skirts of her dress and the queer little shawl on her thin shoulders fluttered in the wind like a flag.

MASTER BELHOMME'S BEAST

THE HAVRE STAGE-COACH WAS JUST LEAVING CRIQUETOT and all the passengers were waiting in the yard of the Commercial Hotel, kept by young Malandain, for their names to be called out.

The coach was yellow, on wheels that once were yellow too, but now turned almost grey with accumulated layers of mud. The front wheels were quite small: those at the back, large and rickety, bore the well of the coach, which was unshapely and distended like the paunch of an animal.

Three white hacks harnessed in tandem, whose huge heads and large round knees were the most noticeable things about them, had to pull this conveyance, which had something monstrous in its build and appearance. The horses seemed asleep already in front of this strange vehicle.

The driver, Césaire Horlaville, a corpulent little man but agile enough nevertheless, by virtue of continually mounting the wheels and climbing on to the roof of his coach, with a face reddened by the open air of the country-side, by rain and storm and many brandies, and eyes always blinking as if still under the lash of wind and hail, appeared at the door of the hotel, wiping his mouth with the back of his hand. Large round hampers, full of scared poultry, stood in front of the solid countrywomen. Césaire Horlaville took these one by one and put them up on the roof of his vehicle; then, more carefully, he put up those which were filled with eggs: finally he tossed up from below a few little sacks of seed and small parcels wrapped in handkerchiefs, bits of cloth or paper. Then he opened the door at the back and, taking a list from his pocket, he called out from it:

"The reverend Father from Gorgeville."

The priest came forward, a tall powerful man, broad, stout, purple in the face, and kindly. He lifted up his cassock to free his foot for stepping up, just as women lift up their skirts, and climbed into the rickety old coach.

"The schoolmaster from Rollebosc-les-Grinets."

The schoolmaster hurried forward, a tall and hesitating fellow, with a frock-coat down to his knees; and disappeared in his turn through the open door.

"Master Poiret, two seats."

Poiret takes his place, tall and stooping, bent with drudgery, grown thin through lack of food, bony, and with a skin all withered from neglected ablutions. His wife followed him, small and wizened, looking very like a tired mare, and clutching in both hands a huge green umbrella.

"Master Rabot, two seats."

Rabot, by nature irresolute, hesitated. He asked:

"Was it me you were calling?"

The driver, who had been nicknamed "Foxy," was going to make a joking reply, when Rabot took a header towards the door of the coach, thrust forward by a shove from his wife, a tall, buxom wench with a belly as big and round as a barrel, and hands as large as a washerwoman's beetle.

And Rabot slipped into the coach like a rat into his hole.

"Master Caniveau."

A huge peasant, more beefy than a bull, summoned all his energy and was, in his turn, swallowed up inside the yellow well of the coach.

"Master Belhomme."

Belhomme, a tall skeleton of a man, drew near, his neck awry, his aspect dolorous, a handkerchief applied to his ear as if he was suffering from very severe toothache.

All of them wore blue smocks over antique and peculiar jackets of black or green cloth, garments, worn on special occasions, which they would uncover in the streets of Havre; and their heads were covered with caps made of silk, as high as towers—the final elegance in that Norman country-side.

Césaire Horlaville shut the door of his coach, climbed on to his box, and cracked his whip.

The three horses seemed to wake up, and, shaking their necks, made audible a vague murmur of tiny bells.

Then the driver, bawling out " Gee up ! " from the bottom of his lungs, lashed the animals with a sweep of the arm. They roused themselves, made an effort, and set off along the road at a slow and halting jog-trot. And behind them the vehicle, jolting its loose panes and all the old iron of its springs, made an astounding jangle of tin and glassware, whilst each row of passengers, tossed and rocked by the jolts, surged up and down with every fall or rise of their uneven progress.

At first silence reigned, out of respect for the parish priest, whose presence put a restraint on their loquacity. He made the first remark, being of a garrulous and friendly disposition.

" Well, Master Caniveau," he said, " are you getting on all right ? "

The big countryman, whose similarity of build, appearance, and paunch formed a bond between the priest and himself, replied, smiling :

" Much as usual, Father, much as usual, and how's yourself ? "

" Oh, as for me, I can always get along ! "

" And you, Poiret ? " asked the reverend gentleman.

" I'd be all right, except for the colzas which have had nothing at all of a crop this year, and in business it is by the crops of colza that we make up our losses, as a rule."

" Well, well, times are hard ! "

" Lord, yes, they're hard ! " declared Rabot's hefty wife, in a voice like a policeman.

As she came from a neighbouring village, the priest knew nothing of her but her name.

" Are you the Blondel girl ? " he asked.

" Yes, that's me. I married Rabot."

Rabot, skinny, nervous, and complacent, saluted the priest with a smile; he saluted him by bowing his head deeply forward, as if to say: "Yes, this is really Rabot, whom the Blondel girl has married."

Abruptly, Master Belhomme, who kept his handkerchief over his ear, began to groan in a lamentable manner. He ground his teeth horribly, stamping his feet to express the most frightful suffering.

"Your toothache seems to be very bad?" demanded the priest.

The peasant stopped moaning for an instant to reply:

"Not a bit of it, Father. It's not my teeth, it's my ear, right down inside my ear."

"What's the matter with your ear then? An abscess?"

"I don't know whether it's an abscess, but I know it's a beast, a filthy beast, which got itself inside me when I was asleep on the hay in the loft."

"A beast! Are you sure?"

"Am I sure? As sure as heaven, Father, seeing it's gnawing away the inside of my ear. It'll eat out my head, for sure, it'll eat out my head. Oh, ger-ow, ger-ow, ger-ow! . . ." And he began stamping his feet again.

His audience was roused to the keenest interest. Each of them proffered different advice. Poiret would have it that it was a spider, the schoolmaster that it was a caterpillar. He had seen such a case before at Campemuret, in the Orme county, where he had lived for six years; though in this case the caterpillar had got into the head and come out through the nose. But the man had remained deaf in that ear, because the ear-drum was split.

"It must have been a worm," declared the priest.

Master Belhomme, his head tilted on one side, and leaning it against the carriage door, for he had been the last to get in, went on groaning:

"Oh, ger-ow, ow, ow, I'm scared to death it's an ant,

a big ant, it's gnawing so. There, Father, it's galloping and galloping . . . oh . . . ow . . . ow . . . ow . . . it hurts like the devil ! "

" Haven't you seen the doctor ? " demanded Caniveau.

" Lord, no ! "

" What for haven't you ? "

Fear of doctors seemed to cure Belhomme.

He sat up, without however removing his handkerchief.

" What for haven't I ? You've got money to waste on them, have you, for them good-for-nothings ? You take yourself to them, once, twice, three times, four times, five times. And for that, a couple of crowns of a hundred sous apiece, two crowns at least. And you tell me what he'd have done for me, the good-for-nothing, you tell me what he'd have done ! D'you know that ? "

Caniveau laughed.

" Now how would I know ? Where are you going anyway ?"

" I'm off to Havre to see Chambrelan."

" What Chambrelan ? "

" The healer, of course."

" What healer ? "

" The healer who cured my dad."

" Your dad."

" Yes, my dad, in his time."

" What was the matter with your dad ? "

" A great wind in his back, so as he could move nor foot nor leg."

" And what did your Chambrelan do for him ? "

" He kneaded his back as if he was going to make bread of it, with both his hands. And it was all right again in a couple of hours."

Belhomme was quite sure in his mind that Chambrelan had also pronounced certain words over it, but he dared not say as much before the priest.

Laughing, Caniveau persisted :

" How d'you know it's not a rabbit you've got in your ear ? It might have taken that earhole of yours for its burrow, seeing the undergrowth you've got growing outside. You wait. I'll make it run for its life."

And Caniveau, shaping his hands into a speaking-trumpet, began to imitate the crying of hounds hot on the scent. He yelped, howled, whimpered, and bayed. Everybody in the coach began to laugh, even the schoolmaster who never laughed.

However, as Belhomme appeared irritated at being made fun of, the priest turned the conversation, and speaking to Rabot's lusty wife, said :

" I dare say you have a big family ? "

" Yes, indeed, Father. And how hard it is to rear them ! "

Rabot nodded his head, as if to say : " Oh, yes, it's hard to rear them."

" How many children have you ? "

She stated magisterially, in a harsh deliberate voice :

" Sixteen children, Father. Fifteen of them by my good man."

And Rabot's smile broadened, as he knuckled his forehead. He managed fifteen children all by himself, he, Rabot. His wife said so. And there was no doubting her. He was proud of it, by George !

By whom was the sixteenth ? She did not say. Probably it was the first. Perhaps every one knew about it, for no one was surprised. Even Caniveau remained unmoved.

But Belhomme began to groan.

" Oh, ow . . . ow . . . ow . . . it fair tears me to bits. Hell ! "

The coach drew up outside the Café Polyte. The priest said :

" If we were to drop a little water in your ear, it might bring the thing out with it. Would you like to try it ? "

" For sure. I'm willing."

Every one got down to assist at the operation.

The priest called for a basin, a napkin, and a glass of water ;

and he ordered the schoolmaster to hold the patient's head well over to one side, and then, as soon as the liquid should have penetrated into the passage, to swing it rapidly over the other way.

But Caniveau, who had straightway applied himself to Belhomme's ear to see whether he could not discover the beast with his naked eye, cried out:

"God bless my soul, what a sticky mess! You'll have to get that out, my boy. No rabbit could get out through that conglomeration of stuff. He'd stick fast with all four feet."

The priest examined the passage in his turn and realised that it was too narrow and too stuffed with wax to attempt the expulsion of the beast. It was the schoolmaster who cleared the path with a match and a bit of rag. Then, amid general anxiety, the priest poured down this scoured channel half a glass of water which ran over Belhomme's face and hair and down his neck. Then the schoolmaster turned the head sharply back over the basin, as if he were trying to unscrew it. A few drops fell out into the white vessel. All the travellers flung themselves upon it. No beast had emerged.

However, Belhomme announcing: "I can't feel anything," the priest, triumphant, cried:

"It is certainly drowned!"

Every one was pleased. They all got back into the coach.

But hardly had they got under way again when Belhomme burst out with the most terrible cries. The beast had wakened up and had become quite frantic. He even swore that it had now got into the head, that it was devouring his brain for him. He accompanied his howls with such contortions that Poiret's wife, believing him possessed of the devil, began to cry and make the sign of the cross. Then, the pain abating a little, the afflicted man related that *it* was now careering round his ear. He described with his finger the movements of the beast, seeming to see it, and follow it with a watchful eye.

" Look at it now, there it goes up again! . . . ow . . . ow . . . ow . . . oh, hell!"

Caniveau lost patience.

" It's the water has sent it crazy, that beast of yours. Likely it's more used to wine."

His listeners burst out laughing. He added:

" As soon as you and me reach the Café Bourboux, give it a small brandy and I'll warrant it'll worry you no more."

But Belhomme could no longer endure his misery. He began to cry out as if his very inside was being torn out. The priest was obliged to support his head for him. His companions begged Césaire Horlaville to stop at the first house on the way.

It turned out to be a farm, lying near the roadside. Belhomme was carried to it; then they stretched him out on the kitchen table to begin the operation again. Caniveau persisted in advising Memboux brandy with the water, in order to make the beast either tipsy or drowsy, or perhaps kill it outright. But the priest preferred vinegar.

This time they poured in the liquid drop by drop, so that it would reach the farthest corner; then they left it for some minutes in the inhabited organ.

Another basin having been brought, Belhomme was turned bodily over by that lusty pair, the priest and Caniveau, while the schoolmaster banged with his finger on the healthy ear, the better to empty out the other.

Césaire Horlaville himself, whip in hand, had come in to watch.

All at once they saw in the bottom of the basin a small brown speck, no bigger than an onion seed. It was moving, however. It was a flea! Cries of surprise burst forth, then shouts of laughter. A flea! Oh, this was rich, this was very rich! Caniveau slapped his thigh, Césaire Horlaville cracked his whip, the priest burst into guffaws like the braying of an ass, the schoolmaster gave vent to a laugh like a sneeze, and the two women uttered little cries of merriment like nothing but the clucking of hens.

Belhomme was sitting on the table, and, resting the basin on his knees, he contemplated with grave intentness, and a gleam of angry joy in his eye, the vanquished beastie which turned and twisted in its drop of water.

He grunted : " So there you are, you swine," and spit at it.

The driver, beside himself with amusement, repeated :

" A flea, a flea ! Oh, look at it, the little devil of a flea, the little devil of a flea ! "

Then, his exuberance wearing off a little, he cried :

" Come now, let's be off. We've wasted enough time."

And the travellers, still laughing, made their way to the coach.

But Belhomme, last to come, declared :

" I'm off back to Criquetot. I've nowt to do at Havre."

The driver told him :

" Never mind that, pay your fare."

" I don't owe no more than half, seeing I've not done half the journey."

" You owe as much as if you'd done the lot."

And a dispute began, which very soon became a furious quarrel. Belhomme swore that he would pay no more than twenty sous, Césaire Horlaville declared that he would have forty.

They shouted at each other, thrusting their faces close together and glaring into each other's eyes.

Caniveau clambered out of the coach.

" In the first place you owe forty sous to the priest, d'ye hear, and then drinks round to every one, that makes it fifty-five, and out of that you'll have to give Césaire twenty. How's that, Forty ? "

The driver, delighted at the idea of Belhomme's having to screw out three francs seventy-five, replied :

" Right you are."

" Now then, pay up."

" I'll not pay. The priest's not a doctor, anyhow."

" If you don't pay, I'll put you back in the coach with Césaire and take you to Havre."

And seizing Belhomme round the waist, the giant lifted him up as if he had been a child.

The other realised that he would have to give in. He drew out his purse and paid.

Then the coach set off again for Havre, while Belhomme turned back towards Criquetot and all the travellers, silent now, watched his blue peasant's smock, rolling along on his long legs down the white road.

FOR SALE

TO SET OUT ON FOOT, WHEN THE SUN IS JUST RISING, AND WALK through the dew, by the side of the fields, at the verge of the quiet sea, what ecstasy!

What ecstasy! It enters in through the eyes with the radiant light, through the nostrils with the sharp air, through the skin with the caressing wind.

Why do we retain, so clear, so precious, so sharp a memory of a few moments of passionate union with the Earth, the memory of a swift, divine emotion, of the almost caressing greeting of a country-side revealed by a twist of the road, at the mouth of a valley, at the edge of a river, just as if we had come upon a charming and complaisant young girl?

I remember one day, among many. I was walking along the coast of Brittany towards the out-thrust headland of Finistère. I walked quickly, thinking of nothing at all, along the edge of the water. This was in the neighbourhood of Quimperlé, in the loveliest and most adorable part of Brittany.

It was a morning in spring, one of those mornings in which one is again just twenty, a morning to revive dead hopes and give back the dreams of first youth.

I walked between the cornfields and the sea, along a road that was no better than a path. The corn was quite motionless, and the waves lifted very gently. The air was filled with the fragrance of ripening fields and the salt scent of the seaweed. I walked without a thought in my head, straight forward, continuing a journey I had begun fifteen days before, a tramp round the coast of Brittany. I felt gloriously fit, content, light of feet and light of heart. I just walked.

I thought of nothing. Why think of anything in hours filled

by an instinctive happiness, a profound physical happiness, the happiness of the beasts of the fields and the birds soaring in the blue spaces beneath the sun? I heard the far-off sound of hymn-singing. A procession perhaps, since this was Sunday. Then I rounded a little headland, stood still, amazed with delight. Five large fishing-boats came into sight, filled with people, men, women, and children, on their way to the Indulgence at Plouneven.

They hugged the coast, moving slowly, helped scarcely at all by the soft, timid wind which swelled the brown sails faintly and then, as if wearied out, let them fall, all slack, round the masts.

The clumsy boats moved slowly, filled with such a crowd of folk. And the whole crowd was singing. The men standing against the sides of the boats, their heads covered with wide hats, sang their deep notes lustily, the women shrilled the treble air, and the thin voices of the children pierced that devout and monstrous uproar like the tuneless squeak of fifes.

The voyagers in all five boats shouted the same hymn, whose monotonous rhythm rose to the quiet sky, and the five boats sailed one behind the other, close together.

They passed close by in front of me, and I saw them draw away, I heard their song sink and die upon the air.

And I fell dreaming delightful dreams, as youth will dream, absurd divine dreams.

How swiftly it is gone, the age of dreams, the only happy age in a whole lifetime. No one is ever lonely, ever sad, ever gloomy or cast down, who bears within himself that most wonderful power of wandering, as soon as he is left to himself, into a world of happy dreams. What faery world, where anything may happen in the audacious imagination of the dreamer who roams therein! How adorable life appears covered in the gold dust of dreams!

Alas, those days are done!

I fell dreaming. Of what? Of all that a man never ceases to hope for, all that he desires, riches, honour, women.

And I walked on, taking great strides, my hand caressing the yellow locks of the corn, which bowed itself under my fingers and thrilled my skin as if I had touched living hair.

I made my way round a little promontory and saw, at the end of a narrow open beach, a white-walled house built above three terraces that came down to the shore.

Why does this house send through me a shiver of delight? Do I know it? Sometimes, in such wanderings, we come upon corners of the country that we seem to have known for a very long time, so familiar are they to us, so do they wake a response in our hearts. Is it possible that we have never seen them before, that we have not lived in them in some former life? Everything about them stirs us, fills us with the most profound delight, the gentle swell of the horizon, the ordered trees, the colour of the soil.

A charming house, rising from its high steps. Large fruit-trees had established themselves along the terraces which came down to the water, like giant stairs. And on the rim of each terrace, like a crown of gold, ran a border of Spanish broom in full flower.

I halted in my tracks, possessed with a sudden love for this dwelling-place. How I would have liked to own it, to live there, for ever!

I drew near the door, my heart beating quickly with envious desire, and saw, on one of the pillars of the gate, a big placard: " For Sale."

I felt a sharp thrill of delight, as if this dwelling had been offered to me, as if I had been given it. Why, yes, why? I do not know.

" For Sale." Then it no longer belonged to any special person, could belong to anyone on earth, to me, to me! Why this joy, this sense of utter delight, deep incomprehensible delight? I knew well enough, however, that I could not buy it. How could I pay for it? No matter, it was for sale. The caged bird belongs to its owner, the bird in the air is mine, not being man's.

I went into the garden. Oh, what a delightful garden, with its terraces lifted one above the other, its espaliers with arms stretched out like crucified martyrs, its clumps of golden broom, and two old fig-trees at the end of each terrace!

When I stood on the last, I looked all round me. The shore of the little bay stretched at my feet, curved and sandy, separated from the open sea by three massive brown rocks, which closed the entry to the bay and must have acted as a breakwater on rough days.

On the headland, right opposite, two great stones, one upright, the other lying in the grass, a menhir and a dolmen, like two strange beings, husband and wife, turned to stone by an evil spell, seemed to watch unwinkingly the small house that they had seen built—they who for centuries had known this one-time solitary cove—the small house that they would see fall, crumple, vanish little by little and altogether disappear, the little house that was for sale.

Oh, old dolmen and old menhir, how I love you!

I knocked at the door as if I had been knocking at my own door. A woman came to open it, a servant, a little old servant, black-gowned, white-bonneted, looking like a working nun. It seemed to me as if I knew her too, this woman.

I said to her:

"You are not a Breton woman, are you?"

She answered:

"No, sir, I come from Lorraine."

She added:

"You have come to look over the house?"

"Oh, yes, certainly."

And I went in.

It seemed to me that I knew it all, the walls, the furniture.

I was almost surprised not to find my own walking-sticks in the hall.

I made my way into the drawing-room, a charming drawing-room carpeted with rush-mats, which looked out over the sea through its three large windows. On the mantel-shelf, Chinese vases and a large photograph of a woman. I went to it at once, convinced that I recognised her too. And I did recognise her, although I was certain that I had never met her. It was she, the inexpressible she, she for whom I was waiting, whom I desired, she whom I summoned, whose face haunted my dreams. She, she whom one seeks always, in every place, she whom one is every moment just going to see in the street, just going to discover on a country road the instant one's glance falls on a red sunshade over the cornfield, she who must surely already be in the hotel when I enter it on my travels, in the railway carriage I am just getting into, in the drawing-room whose door is just opening to me.

It was she, assuredly, past all manner of doubt, it was she. I recognised her by her eyes which were looking at me, by her hair arranged English fashion, but above all by her mouth, by that smile which long ago I had surmised.

I asked at once:

"Who is this lady?"

The nun-like servant answered dryly:

"That is Madame."

I continued:

"She is your mistress?"

In her austere conventional fashion, she replied:

"Oh, no, sir."

I sat down and said firmly:

"Tell me about her."

She stood amazed, motionless, obstinately silent.

I persisted:

"She is the owner of the house, then?"

"Oh, no, sir."

" Then whose is this house ? "

" It belongs to my master, Monsieur Tournelle."

I pointed a finger towards the photograph.

" And this lady, who is she ? "

" That is Madame."

" Your master's wife ? "

" Oh, no, sir."

" His mistress, then ? "

The nun had nothing to say. I went on, pricked by a vague jealousy, by a confused anger against this man who found this woman first.

" Where are they now ? "

The servant murmured :

" Monsieur, the gentleman is in Paris, but about Madame I know nothing."

I shivered.

" Ah. They are no longer together ? "

" No, sir."

I became wily, and said solemnly :

" Tell me what happened, probably I could be of service to your master. I know this woman, she's a bad lot."

The old servant looked at me, and seeing my honest expression, she trusted me.

" Oh, sir, she did my master a bad turn. He made her acquaintance in Italy and he brought her away with him as if he had married her. She sang beautifully. He loved her so much, sir, that it was pitiful to see him. They were travelling in this district last year. And they discovered this house which had been built by a fool, an old fool who wanted to settle five miles from the village. Madame wanted to buy it outright, so that she could stay here with my master. And he bought the house to please her.

" They lived here all last summer, sir, and almost all the winter.

"And then, one morning at breakfast-time, Monsieur called me.

" ' Césaire, has Madame come in ? '

" ' No, sir.'

" We waited for her the whole day. My master was like a madman. We sought everywhere ; we did not find her. She had gone, sir, we never knew where or how."

Oh, what a tide of joy surged in me ! I would have liked to embrace the nun, to seize her round the waist and make her dance in the drawing-room.

Oh, she had gone, she had escaped, she had left him, utterly wearied, disgusted with him ! How happy I was !

The old woman went on :

" Monsieur almost died of grief, and he has gone back to Paris, leaving me here with my husband to sell the house. He is asking twenty thousand francs for it."

But I was no longer listening. I was thinking of her. And all at once it struck me that I had only to set out again to come upon her, that this very springtime she would have been driven to come back to the place, to see the house, this charming house that she must have loved so dearly, to see it emptied of him.

I flung ten francs into the old woman's hand. I snatched the photograph and rushed off at a run, pressing desperate kisses on the adorable face that looked up from the cardboard.

I regained the road and began to walk on, looking at her, her very self. How glorious that she was free, that she had got away ! Without doubt I should meet her to-day or to-morrow, this week or next, now that she had left him. She had left him because my hour had come.

She was free, somewhere, in the world. I had only to find her now that I knew her.

And all the while I touched caressingly the bowed locks of ripe corn, I drank in the sea air that filled out my lungs, I felt the sun kissing my face. I had walked on, I walked on wild with joy, drunk with hope. I walked on, certain that I was going to meet her soon and lead her back to enjoy our turn in that charming home " For Sale." How she would revel in it, this time !

THE UNKNOWN

We were talking of lucky adventures and each of us had an odd happening to relate, delightful and unexpected encounters, in a railway carriage, in a hotel, abroad, on a seashore. Seashores, said Roger des Annettes, were uncommonly propitious for a love-affair.

Gontran, who had said nothing, was appealed to.

" Paris is still the happiest hunting-ground of all," said he. " With a woman, as with a book, we appreciate one more highly in a place where we never expected to find one ; but the finest specimens are found only in Paris."

He was silent for some moments, then added :

" God, how adorable they are ! Go out into our streets on any spring morning. They look as if they had come up like flowers, the little darlings pattering along beside the houses. What a charming, charming, charming sight ! The scent of violets reaches us from the pavement ; the bunches of violets that pass us in the slow-moving carts pushed by the hawkers. The town is alive with spring, and we look at the women. Christ, how tempting they are in their light frocks, thin frocks through which their skin gleams ! One strolls along, nose down to the scent and senses on fire ; one strolls along and one sniffs them out and waylays them. Such mornings are utterly divine.

" You notice her approaching in the distance, a hundred paces away you can find out and recognise the woman who will be delightful at close range. By a flower in her hat, a movement of her head, the swing of her body, you know her. She comes. You say to yourself : 'Attention, eyes front !' and walk past her with your eyes devouring her.

"Is she a slip of a girl running errands for a shop, a young woman coming from church or going to visit her lover? What's the odds? Her breast shows rounded under her transparent bodice. Oh, if only one might thrust a finger down beneath it—a finger, or one's lips! Does she look shy or bold, is her head dark or fair? What's the odds? The swift passage of this woman, as she flits past, sends a thrill down your spine. And how desire haunts us until evening for the woman we have met in such a fashion! I'll swear I've treasured the memory of a round twenty of the dear creatures seen once or ten times like this, and I would have fallen madly in love with them if I had known them more intimately.

"But there you are, the women we cherish most fiercely are the ones we never know. Have you noticed it? It's very odd. Every now and then one catches a glimpse of women the mere sight of whom rouses in us the wildest desire. But one never more than glimpses them. For my part, when I think of all the adorable creatures whom I have jostled in the streets of Paris, I could hang myself for rage. Where are they? Who are they? Where could I find them again, see them again? There is a proverb which says that we are always rubbing elbows with happiness, and I'll take my oath that I've more than once walked past the woman who could have snared me like a linnet with the allurement of her fragrant body."

Roger des Annettes had been listening with a smile, and answered:

"I know all that as well as you. Listen what happened to me, yes, to me. About five years ago I met for the first time, on the Pont de la Concorde, a tall and rather sturdy young woman who made on me an impression . . . oh, an altogether amazing impression! She was a brunette, a plump brunette, with gleaming hair growing low on her forehead and eyebrows that bracketed both eyes under their high arch that stretched from temple to temple. The shadow of a moustache on her lip set one dreaming . . . dreaming . . . as the sight of a bunch of flowers on a table stirs dreams of a beloved wood. She had a shapely figure, firm rounded breasts held proudly like a challenge, offering themselves as a temptation. Her eyes were like ink-stains on the gleaming white of her skin. This girl's eyes were not eyes, but shadowed caverns, deep open caverns in her head, through which one saw right into her, entered into her. What a veiled empty gaze, untroubled by thought and utterly lovely!

" I imagined her to be a Jewess. I followed her. More than one man turned to look after her. She walked with a slightly swaggering gait, a little graceless but very disturbing. She took a cab in the Place de la Concorde. And I stood there like a stuck pig, beside the Obelisk; I stood transfixed by the fiercest passion of longing that had ever assailed me in my life.

" I remembered her for at least three weeks, then I forgot her.

" Six months later I saw her again in the Rue de la Paix, and at sight of her my heart leaped as if I had caught sight of some mistress whom I had loved to distraction. I halted the better to watch her approach. As she passed me, almost touching me, I seemed to be standing in the mouth of a furnace. Then, as she drew away, I felt as if a cool wind were blowing across my face. I did not follow her. I was afraid of committing some folly, afraid of myself.

" Again and again I saw her in my dreams. You know what such obsessions are.

" It was a year before I found her again; then, one evening at sunset, about the month of May, I recognised her in a woman who was walking in front of me up the Champs-Élysées.

" The Arc de l'Étoile lifted its sombre outline against the flaming curtain of the sky. A golden dust, a mist of rosy light hung in the air, it was one of those splendid evenings which are the immortal glory of Paris.

" I followed her, wild with the longing to speak to her, to kneel at her feet, to tell her of the emotion which was choking me.

" Twice I walked past her in order to turn and meet her

again. Twice, as I passed her, I experienced again that sensation of fiery heat which had come over me in the Rue de la Paix.

" She looked at me. Then I saw her enter a house in the Rue de Presbourg. I waited two hours in a doorway. She did not come out. At last I decided to question the concierge. He did not appear to understand me. 'She must have been a caller,' he said.

" And it was eight months before I saw her again.

" Then one January morning, during a spell of Arctic cold, I was on my way down the Boulevard Malesherbes and running to warm myself, when at the corner of a street I collided so violently with a woman that she dropped a small parcel.

" I began apologies. It was she!

" For a moment I stood still, stunned by the suddenness of the shock; then, giving her back the parcel she had been carrying in her hand, I said abruptly:

" 'I am distressed and overjoyed, Madame, to have rushed into you like this. Will you believe me that for more than two years I have noticed you, admired you, longed cruelly to make your acquaintance, and I could not manage to find out who you were nor where you lived? Pardon words like these, ascribe them to my passionate desire to be numbered among those who have the right to speak to you. Such a feeling could not wrong you, could it? You do not know me. I am Baron Roger des Annettes. Make your own inquiries: you will be told that I am a man you can admit to your house. If you refuse my request now, you will make me the most miserable wretch alive. I implore you, be kind, give me, allow me the chance to visit you.'

" She regarded me intently, out of her strange lustreless eyes, and answered smiling:

" 'Give me your address. I will come to your house.'

" I was so utterly dumbfounded that I must have shown it. But I am never long in recovering from such shocks and I hastened to give her a card, which she slipped into her pocket with a swift gesture, with a hand evidently used to manipulating clandestine letters.

"Becoming bold, I stammered:

"'When shall I see you?'

"She hesitated, as if she had to make a complicated calculation, no doubt trying to recollect just what she had to do with each hour of her time; then she murmured:

"'Sunday morning, is that all right for you?'

"'I am quite sure that it is all right.'

"Then she went away, after she had searched my face, judged me, summed me up, dissected me with that heavy insensible stare that seemed to leave something on one's skin, a kind of viscous fluid, as if her glance flung out on to human beings one of those dense liquids which devil-fish use to cloud the water and lull their prey to sleep.

"All the time until Sunday, I gave myself up to the most desperate cudgelling of my wits, in the effort to make up my mind what she was and ascertain the correct attitude to adopt to her.

"Ought I to give her money? How much?

"I decided to buy a piece of jewellery, an uncommonly charming piece of jewellery too, and I placed it, in its case, on the mantel-shelf.

"I waited for her, after a restless night.

"She arrived about ten o'clock, quite calm, quite placid, and gave me her hand as if we were old friends. I offered her a seat, I relieved her of her hat, her veil, her furs, her muff. Then, slightly embarrassed, I began to press her somewhat more hardily, for I had no time to lose.

"She asked for nothing better, and we had not exchanged twenty words before I began to undress her. She herself continued this ticklish business that I never succeed in finishing: I prick myself on pins, I twist strings into inextricable knots instead of undoing them; I mismanage and confuse everything, I delay it all and I lose my head.

"Do you know any moment in life, my friend, more marvellous than the moments when you are watching—standing just far enough away and using just enough discretion to avoid startling that ostrich modesty all women affect—a woman who is stripping herself for you of all the rustling garments that fall round her feet, one after another?

"And what is prettier, too, than the gestures with which they put off those adorable garments that slip to the ground, empty and stretched indolently out as if they had just been struck dead? How glorious and intoxicating is the revelation of her flesh, her naked arms and breasts after her bodice is off, and how disturbing the lines of her body glimpsed under the last veil of all!

"But all at once I saw an amazing thing, a black stain between her shoulders; for she had turned her back to me: a wide stain standing vividly out, black as night. I had promised, moreover, not to look at her.

"What was it? I had not the least doubt what it was, however, and the memory of that clearly visible moustache, the eyebrows joined above the eyes, of that mop of hair which covered her head like a helmet, ought to have prepared me for this shock.

"I was none the less dumbfounded and my mind was thronged suddenly with swift thoughts and strange remembered things. I imagined that I was looking at one of those enchantresses from the Thousand and One Nights, one of those fatal and faithless creatures who exist only to drag mortal men into unknown abysses. I thought of Solomon making the Queen of Sheba walk over a mirror to assure himself that she had not a cloven hoof.

"And . . . and when it came to the point of singing her my song of love, I discovered that I had no voice left, not even a trickle of sound, my dear. Or let's say I had a voice like a eunuch, which at first astonished and at last thoroughly displeased her, for she remarked, clothing herself with all dispatch:

" 'There was not much point in putting me to this trouble, was there ?'

" I wanted her to accept the ring bought for her, but she said deliberately and very stiffly : 'What do you take me for, Monsieur ?' so that I crimsoned to the ears under this accumulation of humiliations. And she departed without adding another word.

" And that is all there is to my adventure. But the worst of it is that, now, I am in love with her, and madly in love.

" I cannot see a woman without thinking of her. All others repel me, disgust me, in so far as they do not resemble her. I cannot press a kiss on another cheek without seeing her cheek beside the one I am caressing, and without suffering agonies from the unappeased desire which torments me.

" She is present at all my rendezvous, at all the caresses, that she spoils for me and renders hateful to me. She is always there, pressed close to the other woman, standing or lying down, visible and unattainable. And I believe now that she was in very truth a woman under a spell, bearing between her shoulders a mysterious talisman.

" Who is she ? Even now I do not know. I have met her twice again. I bowed to her. She made not the slightest return to my greeting, she pretended not to know me at all. Who is she ? An Asiatic perhaps ? Most likely an Eastern Jewess. Yes, a Jewess. I am convinced she is a Jewess. But why ? Yes, why indeed ? I do not know."

THE SECRET

THE LITTLE BARONESS DE GRANGERIE WAS DROWSING ON HER couch, when the little Marquise of Rennedon entered abruptly, looking very disturbed, her bodice a little rumpled, her hat a little on one side, and dropped into a chair, exclaiming:

"Ouf, I've done it!"

Her friend, who had never seen her anything but placid and gentle, sat bolt upright in amazement. She demanded:

"What is it? What have you done?"

The Marchioness, who did not seem able to remain in one place, got to her feet, and began to walk about the room; then she flung herself on the foot of the couch where her friend was resting and, taking her hands, said:

"Listen, darling, promise me never to repeat what I am going to tell you."

"I promise."

"On your immortal soul."

"On my immortal soul."

"Well, I have just revenged myself on Simon."

The other woman exclaimed:

"Oh, you've done right!"

"Yes, haven't I? Just think, during the past six months he has become more intolerable than ever, intolerable beyond words. When I married him, I knew well enough how ugly he was, but I thought he was a kindly man. What a mistake I made! He must certainly have thought that I loved him for himself, with his fat paunch and his red nose, for he began to coo like a turtle-dove. You can imagine that it made me laugh, I nicknamed him 'Pigeon' for it. Men really do have the oddest notions about themselves. When he realised that I felt no more than friendship for him, he became suspicious, he began to speak bitterly to me, to treat me as if I were a coquette or a fast woman, or I don't know what. And then it became more serious because of . . . of . . . it's not very easy to put it into words. . . . In short, he was very much in love with me, very much in love . . . and he proved it to me often, far too often. Oh, my dearest, what torture it is to be . . . made love to by a clown of a man! . . . No, really, I couldn't bear it any longer . . . not any longer at all . . . it is just like having a tooth pulled every evening . . . much worse than that, much worse. Well, imagine among your acquaintances someone very ugly, very ridiculous, very repellent, with a fat paunch—that's the frightful part—and great hairy calves. You can just imagine him, can't you? Now imagine that this someone is your husband . . . and that . . . every evening . . . you understand. No, its loathsome! . . . loathsome! It made me sick, positively sick . . . sick in my basin. Really, I can't bear it any longer. There ought to be a law to protect wives in such cases. Just imagine it yourself, every evening! . . . Pah, it's beastly!

"It's not that I have been dreaming of romantic love-affairs—never. There aren't any nowadays. All the men in our world are like stable-boys or bankers; they care for nothing but horses or money; and if they love women, they love them only as they love horses, just to display them in their drawing-rooms as they show off a pair of chestnuts in the Bois. Nothing else. Life to-day is such that romantic feelings can play no part.

"We should show ourselves merely as matter-of-fact and unemotional women. Intercourse is now no more than meetings at stated times, at which the same thing is always repeated. Besides, for whom could one feel any affection or tenderness? Men, our men, are generally speaking only correct tailors' dummies altogether wanting in intelligence and sensibility. If we look for any intellectual graces, as a man looks for water in a desert, we call the artists to our side; and we behold the arrival of intolerable *poseurs* or underbred Bohemians. As for me, like Diogenes, I have been looking for a man, one real man in the whole of Parisian society; but I am already quite convinced that I shall not find him, and it will not be long before I blow out my lantern. To return to my husband, since it fairly turned my stomach to see him coming into my room in his shirt and drawers, I used all means, all, you understand me, to alienate him and to . . . disgust him with me. At first he was furious, and then he became jealous, he imagined that I was deceiving him. In the early days he contented himself with watching me. He glared like a tiger at all the men who came to the house, and then the persecution began. He followed me everywhere. He used abominable means to take me off my guard. Then he never left me alone to talk with anyone. At all the balls, he remained planted behind me, poking out his clumsy hound's head as soon as I said a word. He followed me to the buffet, forbidding me to dance with this man and that man, taking me away in the very middle of the cotillion, making me look foolish and ridiculous, and appear I don't know what sort of a person. It was after this that I ceased to go anywhere.

"In this intimacy, he became worse still. Would you believe that the wretch treated me as . . . as . . . I daren't say it . . . as a harlot.

"My dear! . . . he said to me one evening: 'Whose bed have you been sharing to-day?' I wept and he was delighted.

"And then he became worse still. The other week he took me to dine in the Champs-Élysées. Fate ordained that Baubiguac should be at the neighbouring table. Then, if you please, Simon began to tread furiously on my feet and growl at me over the melon: 'You have given him a rendezvous, you slut! Just you wait!' Then—you could never guess what he did, my dear—he had the audacity to pull my hatpin gently out and he drove it into my arm. I uttered a loud cry.

Everybody came running up. Then he staged a detestable comedy of mortification. You can imagine it.

"At that very moment I said to myself: 'I'll have my revenge, and before very long, too.' What would you have done?"

"Oh, I would have revenged myself!"

"Very well, that's what I've done to him."

"How?"

"What! Don't you understand?"

"But, my dear . . . still . . . well, yes."

"Yes, what? Gracious, just think of his head! Can't you just see him, with his fat face, his red nose, and his sidewhiskers hanging down like dog's ears."

"Yes."

"Well, I said to myself: 'I shall revenge myself for my own pleasure and Marie's,' for I always intended to tell you, but never anyone but you, mind. Just think of his face and then remember that he . . . that he . . . he is. . . ."

"What . . . you've. . . ."

"Oh, darling, never, never tell a soul, promise me again! But think how funny it is . . . think. . . . He has looked quite different to me since that very moment . . . and I burst out laughing all alone . . . all alone. . . . Just think of his head."

The Baroness looked at her friend, and the wild laughter that welled up in her breast burst between her lips; she began to laugh, but she laughed as if she were hysterical, and with both hands pressed to her breast, her face puckered up, her breath strangled in her throat, she leaned forward as if she would fall over on her face.

Then the little Marquise herself gave way to a stifling outburst of mirth. Between two cascades of little cries she repeated:

"Think . . . do think . . . isn't it funny? Tell me . . . think of his head . . . think of his sidewhiskers! . . . of his nose . . . just think . . . isn't it funny? but whatever you do, don't tell anyone . . . don't . . . tell . . . about it . . . ever!"

They continued for some minutes very nearly suffocated, unable to speak, weeping real tears in their ecstasy of amusement.

The Baroness was the first to recover her self-control, and still shaking:

"Oh! . . . tell me how you did it . . . tell me . . . it's so funny . . . so funny!"

But the other woman could not speak . . . she stammered:

"When I had made up my mind . . . I said to myself: . . . 'Now . . . hurry up . . . you must make it happen at once.' . . . And I . . . did it . . . to-day. . . ."

"To-day!"

"Yes . . . right at once . . . and I told Simon to come and look for me at your house for our especial amusement. . . . He's coming . . . at once . . . he's coming. . . . Just think . . . think . . . think of his head when you see him. . . ."

The Baroness, a little sobered, panted as if she had just finished running a race. She answered:

"Oh, tell me how you did it . . . tell me."

"It was quite easy. I said to myself: 'He is jealous of Baubiguac; very well, Baubiguac it shall be. He is as clumsy as his feet, but quite honourable; incapable of gossiping.' Then I went to his house after breakfast."

"You went to his house. On what excuse?"

"A collection . . . for orphans. . . ."

"Tell me the whole tale . . . quickly . . . tell me the whole tale. . . ."

"He was so astounded to see me that he could not speak. And then he gave me two louis for my collection, and then as I got up to go away, he asked news of my husband; then I pretended to be unable to contain my feelings any longer, and I told him everything that was on my mind. I painted him even blacker than he is, look you. . . . Then Baubiguac was very touched, he began to think of ways in which he might help me . . . and as for me, I began to cry . . . but I cried as a woman cries . . . when she is crying on purpose. . . .

He comforted me . . . he made me sit down . . . and then, as I didn't stop, he put his arm round me. . . . I said : 'Oh, my poor friend . . . my poor friend ! ' He repeated : 'My poor friend, my poor friend ! ' and he went on embracing me . . . all the time . . . until we reached the closest embrace of all. . . . There.

" When it was over, I made a terrible display of despair and reproaches. Oh, I treated him, I treated him as if he were the lowest of the low . . . . But I wanted to burst out laughing madly. I thought of Simon, of his head, of his sidewhiskers. Imagine it . . . just imagine it ! I've done it to him. And he was so afraid of it happening. Come wars, earthquakes, epidemics, even if we all die . . . I've done it to him. Nothing can ever prevent it now ! Think of his head . . . and say to yourself that I've done it to him ! "

The Baroness, who was almost choking to death, demanded :

" Shall you see Baubiguac again ? "

" No, never. Certainly not. . . . I've had enough of him . . . he's no more desirable than my husband."

And they both began to laugh again so violently that they reeled like epileptics.

The ringing of a bell silenced their mirth.

The Baroness murmured :

" It's he . . . look closely at him."

The door opened, and a stout man appeared, a ruddy-faced man with thick lips and drooping sidewhiskers ; he rolled incensed eyes.

The two young women regarded him for a moment ; then they flung themselves wildly down on the couch, in such a delirium of laughter that they groaned as if they were in the most dreadful agony.

And he repeated in a stupefied voice :

" Upon my word, are you mad ? . . . are you mad ? . . . are you mad ? "

THE CHRISTENING

"Now, Doctor, a little cognac."

"With pleasure."

And the old naval doctor, holding out his little glass, watched the precious liquor rising to the brim, flecked with golden gleams.

Then he lifted it to the level of his eye, passed it in front of the light from the lamp, sniffed it, sucked in a few drops that he rolled a long time on his tongue and on the moist, sensitive flesh of his palate, then said :

"Oh, the divine poison ! Or rather, the seductive assassin, the adorable destroying angel !

"You know nothing about it, you people. You have read, it is true, that excellent book called *L'Assommoir*, but you have not seen, as I have, drink exterminate a whole tribe of savages, a small Negro kingdom, drink carried in kegs landed, with the most peaceful air, by red-bearded English sailors.

"But now listen. I have seen, with my own eyes, the strangest and most amazing drama of strong drink, and quite near here, in Brittany, in a little village in the neighbourhood of Pont l'Abbé.

"I was living at the time, on a year's leave, in a country-house left me by my father. You know that flat coast where the wind whistles day and night over the gorse bushes, and where one still sees here and there, upright and lying along the ground, those monstrous stones which were once gods, and which have retained something disturbing in their attitude, in their aspect, their shape. They always look to me as if they were just going to come alive, and I should see them set out across the country-side, with slow, heavy steps, the steps of granite giants, or fly off on vast wings, stone wings, towards a Druid heaven.

"The sea encloses and dominates the horizon, the restless sea, full of black-headed rocks, always covered with a slaver of foam, like dogs who lie in wait for the fishermen.

"And they, these men, they go down to this terrible sea which overturns their fishing-cobbles with one shake of his blue-green back, and swallows them down like pellets. They go out in their small boats, day and night, brave, anxious, and drunk. Drunk they most often are. 'When the bottle is full,' they say, 'you see the reef; but when it's empty, you see it no more.'

"Go into the thatched cottages. You'll never find the father there. And if you ask the wife what has become of her man, she stretches her arm towards the sombre sea, muttering and frothing out its white saliva along the shore. He slept below it one evening when he had drunk a little too deeply. And the eldest son as well. She has four boys left, four tall striplings, fair-skinned and sturdy. Their turn next.

"I was living, then, in a country-house near Pont l'Abbé. I lived alone with my servant, an old sailor, and a Breton family who took care of the property in my absence. It consisted of three people, two sisters and the man who had married one of them, and who looked after my garden.

"This same year, about Christmas-time, my gardener's wife was brought to bed of a boy.

"The husband came to ask me to stand godfather. I could hardly refuse, and he borrowed ten francs, for christening-expenses, he said.

"The ceremony was arranged for the second of January. For a week past the ground had been covered with snow, a vast carpet, colourless and sombre, which seemed, in this low flat country, to stretch out over illimitable wastes. The sea, far beyond the white plain, looked black; and we could see it moving restlessly, shaking its back, rolling its waves, as if it wanted to fling itself on its pale neighbour, who seemed dead, so quiet, so sad, so cold she lay.

" At nine o'clock in the morning, Papa Kérandec arrived in front of my door with his sister-in-law, the big Kesmagan, and the nurse who was carrying the child rolled up in a quilt.

" And then we all set out for the church. It was cold enough to split the dolmens, one of those piercing cold days which crack the skin and cause frightful pain with their bitter cold that burns like fire.

" As for me, I was thinking of the poor little creature who was being carried in front of us, and I thought to myself that this Breton race really was made of iron, since children were able, from the moment they were born, to survive such excursions.

" We arrived in front of the church, but the door was still shut. The priest was late.

" Thereupon the nurse, resting herself on one of the boundary stones near the porch, began to undress the infant. I thought at first that he had wetted his napkin, but I saw that they were stripping him naked, the poor little wretch, stark-naked, in the icy air. I ran forward, horrified at the insensate act.

" ' Are you mad ! You'll kill him.'

" The woman answered placidly :

" ' Oh, no, honoured sir, he must come before the good God quite naked.'

" The father and the aunt looked on at the performance with the utmost calm. It was the custom. If it were not followed, ill luck would befall the infant.

" I worked myself up into a rage, I cursed the man, I threatened to go home, I tried forcibly to cover up the frail little body. It was all no use. The nurse escaped from me, running through the snow, and the poor little devil's body turned purple.

" I was just going to leave the cruel wretches when I saw the priest coming across the fields, followed by the sacristan and a country lad.

" I ran to meet him, and expressed my indignation to him, without mincing my words. He was not surprised, he did not quicken his pace, he made no attempt to hurry himself. He answered :

" 'What do you expect, sir ? It's the custom. They all do it, we can't hinder them.'

" 'But at least get a move on ! ' I shouted.

" He replied :

" 'I can't come any quicker.'

" And he entered the vestry, while we remained on the threshold of the church, where I swear I suffered more than the little creature howling under the lash of the bitter cold.

" The door opened at last. We went in. But the child had to remain naked throughout the whole ceremony.

" It was interminable. The priest blundered on through the Latin syllables that issued from his mouth, falsely scanned. He walked with a slow gait, with the slow gait of a pious tortoise, and his white surplice froze my heart, like another fall of snow in which he had wrapped himself to torture, in the name of a cruel and barbarous God, this human grub racked by the cold.

" The christening was at last accomplished according to the proper rites, and I saw the nurse roll the frozen child, who was moaning in a thin pitiful voice, up again in its wide quilt.

" The priest said to me :

" 'Will you come and sign the register ? '

" I turned to my gardener :

" 'Now get back as quickly as you can, and get that child warm at once.'

" And I gave him some advice how to ward off inflammation of the lungs if there were still time to do it.

" The man promised to carry out my recommendation, and he went away with his sister-in-law and the nurse. I followed the priest into the vestry.

" When I had signed, he demanded five francs of me for expenses.

" Having given the father ten francs, I refused to pay again. The priest threatened to tear out the leaf and annul the ceremony. I threatened him, on my side, with the Public Prosecutor.

" The quarrel lasted a long time. I ended by paying.

" The instant I got home, I wanted to make sure that no further misfortune had happened. I ran to Kerandec's house, but the father, the sister-in-law, and the nurse had not yet returned.

" The woman who had given birth to the child, left all alone, was sobbing with cold in her bed, and she was hungry, having had nothing to eat since the night before.

" ' Where the devil have they gone ? ' I said.

" She answered, without surprise or resentment :

" ' They've gone off to celebrate the occasion.'

" It was the custom. Then I remembered my ten francs, which ought to have paid for the christening but were doubtless now paying for drink.

" I sent in some soup for the mother and I ordered a good fire to be made in her fire-place. I was anxious and angry, promising myself to let those devils have it hot and strong, and asking myself with horror what would become of the wretched brat.

" At six o'clock in the evening they had not returned.

" I ordered my servant to wait for them and I went to bed.

" I fell asleep very quickly, for I sleep like an old sea-dog.

" I was roused about daybreak, by my servant, who brought me some warm water for shaving.

" As soon as I had my eyes open, I demanded :

" ' And Kerandec ? '

" The man hesitated, then he stammered :

" ' Oh, he came back, sir, after midnight, so drunk he could not walk, and the big Kesmagan woman too, and the nurse too.

I verily believe they had slept in a ditch, so that the little baby was dead, which they hadn't even noticed.'

" I leaped out of bed, shouting :

" ' The child is dead ! '

" ' Yes, sir. They carried it to Mother Kerandec. When she saw it, she began to cry ; then they made her drink to comfort her.'

" ' What, they made her drink ? '

" ' Yes, sir. But I only learned that this morning, just now. As Kerandec had neither brandy nor money, he took the lamp oil that you had given them, sir, and all four of them drank it, as much as was left in the bottle. And now the Kerandec woman is very ill.'

" I had flung on my clothes with all haste, and, snatching up a stick, with the determination to thrash all these human beasts, I ran to my gardener's house.

" The woman in the bed was rolling in agony, stupefied with paraffin, beside the blue corpse of the child.

" Kerandec, the nurse, and the big Kesmagan woman were snoring on the ground.

" I had to look to the wife, who died towards noon."

The old doctor was silent. He took up the bottle of brandy, poured out a fresh glass and, once more flashing the lamplight across the tawny liquor so that it seemed to fill his glass with the translucent essence of dissolved topazes, he swallowed the treacherous and gleaming liquid at a gulp.

INDISCRETION

BEFORE MARRIAGE, THEY HAD LOVED EACH OTHER WITH A pure love, their heads in the stars. It had begun in a pleasant acquaintance made on a sea front. He had found her entirely charming, this young girl, like a rose, with her transparent sunshades and her pretty gowns, drifting past the vast background of the sea. He had loved her, fair and delicately slender, in her frame of blue waves and illimitable sky. And he confounded the compassionate tenderness roused in him by this virginal child with the vague, powerful emotion stirred in his soul, his heart, his very veins, by the sharp salt air and the wide country-side filled with sun and sea.

As for the girl, she had loved him because he wooed her, because he was young, rich enough, well-bred and fastidious. She had loved him because it is natural for young girls to love young men who speak to them of love.

Then for three months they had spent their time together, eyes looking into eyes and hand touching hand. The mutual happiness that they felt—in the morning before the bath, in the freshness of a new day, and their farewells at night, on the shore, under the stars, in the soft warm of the quiet night, farewells murmured softly, very softly—had already the character of kisses, though their lips had never met.

They dreamed of one another in the instant of sleep, thought of one another in the instant of waking, and, without a word exchanged, called to each other, and desired each other with all the force of their souls and all the force of their bodies.

After their marriage, their adoration had come to earth. It had been at first a kind of sensuous and insatiable fury of possession, then an exalted affection wrought of flesh and blood romance, of caresses already a little sophisticated, of ingenious and delicately indelicate love-making. Their every glance had a lascivious significance, all their gestures roused in them thoughts of the ardent intimacy of their nights.

Now, without acknowledging it, perhaps without yet realising it, they had begun to weary of one another. They loved each other dearly, still ; but there were no longer any revelations to share, nothing to do that they had not done many times, nothing to discover about one another, not even a new word of love, an unpremeditated ecstasy, an intonation that might make more poignant the familiar words, so often repeated.

None the less they made every effort to feed the dying flame of their first fierce caresses. Every day they invented affectionate pretences, artless or subtle little comedies, a whole series of desperate attempts to re-awake the insatiable ardour of first love in their hearts, and the burning desire of the bridal month in their blood.

Sometimes, by dint of exciting their passions, they enjoyed again an hour of unreal ecstasy, followed at once by a mood of fatigue and aversion.

They had tried moonlit nights, walks under the trees in the gentle air of evening, the poetry of riversides veiled in mist, the excitement of public festivities.

Then, one morning, Henrietta said to Paul :

" Will you take me to dine in a cabaret ? "

" Of course, darling."

" In a really well-known cabaret ? "

" Of course."

He looked at her, with a questioning air, quite aware that she was thinking of something that she did not care to say aloud.

She added :

" You know, in a cabaret . . . how shall I put it ? . . . in a really gay cabaret . . . in the sort of cabaret where people arrange to meet each other alone ? "

He smiled.

" Yes, I understand. In a private room of a fashionable café."

" That's it. But a fashionable café where you are known, where you have perhaps already had supper . . . no . . . dinner . . . and don't you know . . . you know . . . I should like . . . no, I'll never dare say it."

" Tell me, darling; what can anything matter, between you and me? We don't hide little things from each other."

" No, I dare not."

" Really now, don't pretend to be shy. What is it? "

" Well . . . well . . . I would like . . . I would like to be taken for your mistress . . . and that the waiters, who don't know that you are married, should suppose me your mistress, and you too . . . that you should think me your mistress, for one hour, just in that room which must have memories for you . . . Don't you see? And I shall believe, myself, that I am your mistress . . . I shall be doing a dreadful thing . . . I shall be deceiving you . . . with yourself. Don't you see? It is very wicked. . . . But I should like . . . don't make me blush . . . I feel myself blushing. . . . You can't imagine how it would . . . would excite me to dine like that with you, in a place that's not quite nice . . . in a *cabinet particulier* where people make love . . . every evening. . . . It is very wicked . . . I'm as red as a peony. Don't look at me."

He laughed, very amused, and answered:

" Yes, we'll go, this evening, to a really smart place, where I am known."

About seven o'clock they walked up the staircase of a fashionable boulevard café, he all smiles like a conqueror, she shy, veiled, delighted. As soon as they had entered a private room furnished with four arm-chairs and a vast couch of red velvet, the head waiter, black-clad, came in and presented the card. Paul offered it to his wife.

" What would you like to eat? "

" Oh, but I don't know what's the right thing to order here."

So he read down the list of dishes as he took off his overcoat, which he handed to the footman. Then he said :

" A very spicy dinner—*potage bisque*—*poulet à la diable*, *râble de lièvre*, *homard à l'américaine*, *salade de légumes bien épicée*, and dessert. We will drink champagne."

The head waiter turned a smiling regard on the young woman. He picked up the card, murmuring :

" Will Monsieur Paul have sweet or dry ? "

" Champagne, very dry."

Henrietta was delighted to observe that this man knew her husband's name.

They sat side by side on the couch, and began to eat.

They had the light of ten wax candles, reflected in a large mirror marked all over by thousands of names traced on it by diamonds : they flung over the gleaming crystal what looked like an immense spider's web.

Henrietta drank steadily, to enliven her, though she felt giddy after the first glass. Paul, excited by his memories, kissed his wife's hand every moment. His eyes shone.

She was oddly excited by this not very reputable place, disturbed, happy, a little wanton but very thrilled. Two grave, silent waiters, accustomed to see all and forget all, to present themselves only when necessary, and to remove themselves at moments when emotions ran dangerously high, came and went swiftly and deftly.

By the middle of the dinner Henrietta was half drunk, more than half drunk, and Paul, very merry, was madly pressing her knee. She was babbling wildly now, impudently gay, with flushed cheeks and suffused burning eyes.

" Now, Paul, own up, don't you know I simply must know everything ? "

" Well, darling ? "

" I daren't say it."

" Say anything you want to."

" Have you had mistresses . . . many mistresses . . . before me ? "

He hesitated, a little dubious, not sure whether he ought to keep quiet about his triumphs or boast of them.

She added :

" Oh, I implore you, do tell me, have you had ever so many ? "

" Well, I've had several."

" How many ? "

" Well, I really don't know . . . a man can't really be sure about these things, don't you know ? "

" You didn't keep count of them ? "

" Of course not."

" Oh, so you must have had ever so many."

" Of course."

" But about how many ? . . . only just about ? "

" But I haven't the least idea, darling. Some years I had ever so many, and there were other years when I had very few."

" How many a year, do you suppose ? "

" Sometimes twenty or thirty, sometimes only four or five."

" Oh, that makes more than a hundred women altogether."

" Well, yes, about that "

" Oh, it's revolting ! "

" Why do you call it revolting ? "

" Because of course it is revolting, when you think of it . . . all those women . . . naked . . . and always . . . always the same thing. Oh, how revolting it is, all the same, more than a hundred women ! "

He was shocked that she found it disgusting, and answered her with that superior manner which men assume to make women realise that they are talking nonsense.

" Well, upon my word, that's a queer thing to say ; if it's disgusting to have a hundred women, it is just as disgusting to have one."

" Oh, no, nothing of the kind."

" Why not ? "

" Because one woman, that is a real union, a real love which holds you to her, while a hundred women is just lust or misconduct. I don't understand how a man can press himself against all those dirty wenches . . ."

" They're not, they are very clean."

" It's impossible for them to be clean, living the life they do."

" But, on the contrary, it is just because of the life they live that they are so clean."

" Oh, fie, when you think that only the night before they were doing the same thing with another man ! It's shameful."

" It's no more shameful than drinking out of this glass which was drunk from this morning by goodness knows who, which you may be sure has at any rate been well washed. . . ."

" Oh, be quiet, you disgust me."

" Then why did you ask me if I had had mistresses ? "

" Tell me, these mistresses of yours, were they all girls of that sort ? "

" No, no, of course not."

" What were they, then ? "

" Well, actresses . . . some . . . some little shop-girls . . . and some . . . several society women."

" How many society women ? "

" Six."

" Only six ? "

" Yes."

" Were they pretty ? "

" Of course."

" Prettier than the girls ? "

" No."

" Which did you like best, the girls or the society women ? "

" The girls."

" Oh, what nasty tastes you have ! Why ? "

" Because I don't care for amateur performers."

" Oh, horrible ! You really are detestable, you know. But tell me, did it amuse you to go from one to the other ? "

"Of course."

"Very much?"

"Very much."

"What is it that amused you? Aren't they all alike?"

"Of course not."

"Oh, women are not all alike?"

"Not at all alike."

"Not in anything?"

"Not in anything."

"How odd! How do they differ?"

"Altogether."

"In their bodies?"

"Yes, of course, in their bodies."

"All over their bodies?"

"All over their bodies."

"And what else?"

"Well, in their way of . . . of making love, of talking, of saying even little things."

"And . . . and it is very amusing to have a change?"

"Of course."

"And do men, too, vary?"

"I couldn't tell you that."

"You can't tell me?"

"No."

"They must vary."

"Yes . . . no doubt. . . ."

She sat sunk in thought, the glass of champagne in her hand. It was full, she drank it off at a gulp; then, placing it on the table, she flung both arms round her husband's neck, murmuring against his heart:

"Oh, my darling, I love you so! . . ."

He took her in a passionate embrace. A waiter who was entering withdrew, shutting the door; and the serving of the courses was suspended for about five minutes.

When the head waiter reappeared, solemn and dignified,

carrying the sweet, she was holding another full glass between her fingers, and, peering into the tawny translucent depths of the liquid, as if she saw there strange imagined things, she was murmuring in a reflective tone :

" Yes, it must be very amusing, all the same."

A MADMAN

HE DIED A HIGH-COURT JUDGE, AN UPRIGHT MAGISTRATE WHOSE irreproachable life was held up to honour in every court in France. Barristers, young puisne judges, judges, greeted with a low bow that marked their profound respect, his thin white impressive face, lighted up by two fathomless gleaming eyes.

He had given up his life to the pursuit of crime and the protection of the weak. Swindlers and murderers had had no more formidable enemy, for he seemed to read, in the depths of their souls, their most secret thoughts, and penetrate at a glance the dark twistings of their motives.

He had died, in his eighty-second year, everywhere honoured, and followed by the regrets of a whole nation. Soldiers in scarlet trousers had escorted him to his grave, and men in white ties had delivered themselves round his coffin of grief-stricken speeches and tears that seemed sincere.

And then came the strange document that the startled solicitor discovered in the desk where he had been accustomed to keep the dossiers of famous criminals.

It had for title:

"WHY?"

. . . . . .

June 20th, 1851. I have just left the court. I have condemned Blondel to death. Why did this man kill his five children? Why? One often comes across people to whose temperaments the taking of life affords a keen physical pleasure. Yes, yes, it must be a physical pleasure, perhaps the sharpest of all, for is not killing an act more like the act of creation than any other? To *make* and to *destroy*. In these two words is contained the history of the universe, the history of all worlds, of all that exists, all. Why is it so intoxicating to kill?

June 25th. To think that there is a living being in there—a creature who loves, walks, runs! A living being. What is a living being? This thing possessed of life, bearing within itself the vital power of motion and a will that orders this motion. It is kin to nothing, this human being. Its feet do not belong to the ground. It is a germ of life wandering over the earth; and this germ of life, come I know not whence, can be destroyed at will. Then nothing, for ever nothing. It decays, it is ended.

June 26th. Then why is it a crime to kill? Yes, why? It is, on the contrary, a law of nature. The ordained purpose of every being is to kill: he kills to live, and he kills for the sake of killing. To kill is in our nature: we must kill. The beasts kill continually, every day, at every moment of their existence. Man kills continually to feed himself, but as he must also kill for sheer sensual satisfaction, he has invented sport. A child kills the insects that he finds, the little birds, all the little animals that come his way. But that does not satisfy the irresistible lust for wholesale killing which is in us. It is not enough to kill beasts; we must kill men too. In other days, we satisfied this need by human sacrifice. To-day the necessities of communal life have made murder a crime. We condemn it and punish the assassin. But since we cannot live without yielding to the innate and imperious instinct of death, we assuage it from time to time by wars in which one whole race butchers another. War is a debauch of blood, a debauch in which the armies sate themselves and on which not only plain citizens are drunken, but women, and the children who every evening read under the lamp the hysterical recital of the massacres.

One would have imagined that scorn would be meted out to those destined to accomplish these slaughterings of men. No. They are heaped with honours. They are clad in gold and gorgeous raiment; they wear feathers on their heads, decorations on their breasts; and they are given crosses, rewards, honours of all kinds. They are haughty, respected, adored of women, acclaimed by the mob, and solely because their mission in life is to shed human blood. They drag through the streets their instruments of death, which the black-coated passer-by regards with envy. For killing is the glorious law thrust by nature into the profoundest impulse of our being. There is nothing more lovely and more honourable than to kill.

June 30th. To kill is the law; because nature loves immortal youth. She seems to cry through all her unconscious acts: "Hasten! Hasten! Hasten!" As she destroys, so she renews.

July 2nd. Being—what is being? All and nothing. Through thought, it is the reflection of all things. Through memory and for science, it is an epitome of the world, the tale of which it bears within itself. Mirror of things, and mirror of deeds, each human being becomes a little universe within the universe.

But travel; look at the people swarming everywhere, and man is nothing now, nothing now, nothing! Get into a ship, put a wide space between yourself and the crowded shore, and you will soon see nothing but the coast. The infinitesimal speck of being disappears, so tiny it is, so insignificant. Traverse Europe in a swift train and look out through the window. Men, men, always men, innumerable, inglorious, swarming in the fields, swarming in the streets; dull-witted peasants able to do no more than turn up the earth; ugly women able to do no more than prepare food for their men, and breed. Go to India, go to China, and you will see scurrying about more thousands of creatures, who are born, live, and die without leaving more trace than the ant crushed to death on the road. Go to the country of black men, herded in their mud huts; to the country of fair-skinned Arabs sheltered under a brown canvas that flaps in the wind, and you will understand that the solitary individual being is nothing, nothing. The race is all. What is the individual, the individual member of a wandering desert tribe? And men who are wise do not trouble themselves overmuch about death. Man counts for nothing with them. A man kills his enemy: it is war. That, in the old days, was the way of the world, in every great house, in every province.

Yes, journey over the world and watch the swarming of the innumerable and nameless human beings. Nameless? Aye, there's the rub! To kill is a crime because we have enumerated human beings. When they are born, they are registered, named, baptized. The law takes charge of them. Very well, then! The man who is not registered is of no account: kill him in the desert, kill him in the hills or in the plain, what does it matter! Nature loves death: she will not punish it.

What is verily sacred, is the social community. That's it! It is that which protects man. The individual is sacred because he is a member of the social community. Homage to the social state, the legal God. On your knees!

The State itself can kill because it has the right to alter the social community. When it has had two hundred thousand men butchered in a war, it erases them from the community, it suppresses them by the hands of its registrars. That is the end of it. But we who cannot alter the records of the town halls, we must respect life. Social community, glorious divinity who reigns in the temples of the municipalities, I salute you. You are stronger than nature. Ha, ha!

July 3rd. To kill must be a strange pleasure and of infinite relish to a man. To have there, standing before him, a living, thinking being: to thrust in him a little hole, only a little hole, to see pouring out that red stuff which we call blood, which makes life, and then to have in front of one only a lump of nerveless flesh, cold, inert, emptied of thought.

August 5th. I who have spent my life in judging, condemning, in killing by uttered words, in killing by the guillotine such as have killed by the knife, I, I, if I did as do all the assassins whom I have struck down, I, I, who would know it?

August 10th. Who would ever know it? Who would suspect me, me, especially if I chose a creature in whose removal I have no interest?

August 15th. The temptation. The temptation has entered into me like a worm that crawls. It crawls, it moves, it roves through my whole body, in my mind, which thinks only of one thing—to kill; in my eyes, which lust to see blood, to see something die; in my ears, where there sounds continually something strange, monstrous, shattering, and stupefying, like the last cry of a human creature; in my legs, which tingle with desire to go, to go to the spot where the thing could come to pass; in my hands, which tremble with lust to kill. What a glorious act it would be, a rare act, worthy of a free man, greater than other men, captain of his soul, and a seeker after exquisite sensations!

August 22nd. I could resist no longer. I have killed a small beast just to try, to begin with.

Jean, my man, had a goldfinch in a cage hung in a window of the servant's room. I sent him on an errand and I took the little bird in my hand, in my hand where I felt the beating of his heart. He was warm. I went up to my room. From time to time, I clutched him harder, his heart beat faster; it was frightful and delicious. I all but choked him. But I should not have seen the blood.

Then I took the scissors, short nail-scissors, and I cut his throat in three strokes, so cleverly. He opened his beak, he struggled to escape me, but I held him fast, oh, I held him; I would have held a mad bulldog, and I saw the blood run. How beautiful blood is, red, gleaming, clear! I longed to drink it. I wetted the end of my tongue with it. It was good. But he had so little of it, the poor little bird! I had no time to enjoy the sight of it as I would have liked. It must be glorious to see a bull bleed to death.

And then I did all that assassins do, that real ones do. I washed the scissors, I washed my hands, I threw out the water, and I carried the body, the corpse, into the garden to bury it. I hid it in the strawberry bed. It will never be found. Every day I shall eat a strawberry from that plant. In very truth, how one can enjoy life when one knows how!

My man wept; he supposed that his bird had flown. How could he suspect me? Ha, ha!

Aug. 25th. I must kill a man. I must.

Aug. 30th. It is done. What a simple thing it is!

I went to take a walk in the Bois de Vernes. I was thinking of nothing, no, of nothing. And there was a child on the road, a little boy eating a slice of bread and butter.

He stood still to let me pass and said:

"Good day, Monsieur le Président."

And the thought came into my head: "Suppose I were to kill him?"

I replied:

"Are you all alone, my boy?"

"Yes, sir."

"All alone in the wood?"

"Yes, sir."

The desire to kill intoxicated me like strong drink. I approached him stealthily, sure that he would run away. And then I seized him by the throat . . . I squeezed him, I squeezed him with all my strength. He looked at me with terrified eyes. What eyes! Quite round, fathomless, clear, terrible. I have never experienced so savage an emotion . . . but so short. He clutched my wrists with his little hands, and his body writhed like a feather in the fire. Then he moved no more.

My heart thudded, ah ! the bird's heart ! I flung the body in a ditch, then grasses over him.

I went home again ; I dined well. What an utterly simple affair !

That evening I was very gay, light-hearted, young again. I spent the rest of the evening at the Prefect's house. They found me good company.

But I have not seen blood. I am calm.

Aug. 30th. The corpse has been found. They are searching for the murderer. Ha, ha !

Sept. 1st. They have arrested two tramps. Proofs are lacking.

Sept. 2nd. The parents have been to see me. They wept. Ha, ha !

Oct. 6th. They have discovered nothing. Some wandering vagabond must have struck the blow. Ha, ha ! If I had only seen the blood flow, I think I should now be quiet in my mind.

Oct. 10th. The lust to kill possesses my every nerve. It is like the furious passions of love that torture us at twenty.

Oct. 20th. Yet another. I was walking along the river, after breakfast. And I saw, under a willow, a fisherman fast asleep. It was high noon. A spade was stuck, it might have been for the purpose, in a near-by field of potatoes.

I took it, I came back ; I lifted it like a club and, cutting through it with a single blow, I split the fisherman's head right open. Oh, how he bled ! Crimson blood, full of brains. It trickled into the water, very gently. And I went on my way at a solemn pace. If anyone had seen me! Ha, ha! I should have made an excellent assassin.

Oct. 25th. The affair of the fisherman has roused a great outcry. His nephew, who used to fish with him, has been accused of the murder.

Oct. 26th. The examining magistrate declares that the nephew is guilty. Every one in the town believes it. Ha, ha!

Oct. 27th. The nephew has put up a poor defence. He declares that he had gone to the village to buy bread and cheese. He swears that his uncle was killed in his absence. Who believes him?

Oct. 28th. The nephew has partially confessed, so utterly have they made him lose his head. Ha, ha! Justice!

Nov. 15th. Crushing evidence accumulates against the nephew, who will inherit from his uncle. I shall preside at the assizes.

Jan. 25th. To death! To death! To death! I have condemned him to death. Ha, ha! The Solicitor-General spoke like an angel. Ha, ha! Yet another. I shall go to see him executed.

March 20th. It is done. He was guillotined this morning. He made a good end, very good. It gave me infinite pleasure. How sweet it is to see a man's head cut off! The blood spurted out like a wave, like a wave. Oh, if I could, I would have liked to have bathed in it! What intoxicating ecstasy to crouch below it, to receive it in my hair and on my face, and rise up all crimson, all crimson! Ah, if people knew!

Now I shall wait, I can afford to wait. So little a thing might trip me up.

. . . . . .

The manuscript contained several more papers, but without relating any fresh crime.

The alienists, to whom it was entrusted, declare that there exist in the world many undetected madmen, as cunning and as redoubtable as this monstrous maniac.

LITTLE ROQUE

MÉDÉRIC ROMPEL, POSTMAN, FAMILIARLY ADDRESSED AS Méderi by the country-folk, left the post office of Roüy-le-Tors at his usual hour. He passed through the little town with the long strides of an old campaigner, and cut across the meadows of Villaumes to reach the bank of the Brindille. Following the course of the stream, he reached the village of Carvelin, where his delivery began.

He went at a rapid pace, keeping alongside the narrow brook, which threaded its way, frothing, gurgling, and eddying, over a weedy bed, beneath an arch of willows. The great boulders that blocked its passage were each encircled by a little noose of water, a kind of cravat finished off with a knot of foam. Occasionally there were cascades a foot deep, often unseen, but falling on a sonorous note, fretful yet soothing, under the green roof of leaves and creepers. Further on, the banks widened out into a small, quiet lake, where the trout swam through green tresses of weed that waved under the gentle current.

Médéric went steadily forward, observing nothing, and thinking only: " My first letter is for the Poivrons, and then I have one for Monsieur Renardet; I shall have to go through the copse, then."

His blue blouse, caught tightly round his waist in a black leather belt, moved with steady speed past the green line of willows; his stick, a stout branch of holly, moved at his side with the same action as his legs.

He crossed the Brindille by a bridge made of a single tree-trunk, thrown across from one bank to the other; its only rail was a rope supported by stakes sunk into the banks.

The copse belonged to Monsieur Renardet, the Mayor of

Carvelin, and the most important landowner in the district. It was a sort of wood of huge old trees, as straight as pillars, and stretched the length of half a league along the brook, that bounded this vast leafy vault. Along the waterside large shrubs had sprung up under the sun's heat, but deep in the copse nothing was to be found but moss, thick, sweet, and soft, filling the still air with a faint odour of decay and rotten wood.

Médéric slowed down, took off his black cap with its scarlet trimming, and wiped his brow, for, though it was not yet eight o'clock in the morning, it was already hot in the meadows. He had just put on his hat, and was resuming his rapid stride, when he noticed, at the foot of a tree, a small knife, a child's knife. As he picked it up, he found a thimble too, then, two steps farther on, a needle-case.

He picked them up and thought: "Better give them to the mayor"; and continued his journey, but now with his eyes wide open, expecting all the time to find something more.

Suddenly he stopped dead, as though he had bumped into a wooden barrier, for ten paces in front of him there lay upon its back the body of a child, stark-naked on the moss. It was the body of a little girl about twelve years old; her arms were flung wide apart, her feet were separated, and her face was covered with a handkerchief. A little blood stained her legs.

Médéric crept forward on tiptoe, as though he feared to make a sound, scenting danger. His eyes were wide open.

What was this? She must be asleep. Then he reflected that people do not sleep naked like that at half-past seven in the morning, in a cold wood. She was dead, then, and he was in the presence of a crime. At this thought, old soldier as he was, a cold shiver ran up his back. Murder, and child-murder at that, was so rare a happening in the district that he could not believe his eyes. But there was no wound upon her, nothing but the blood congealed upon her leg. How long had she been dead?

He had stopped quite close to her, and was looking at her,

leaning on his stick. He must know her, since he knew all the local inhabitants, but, not being able to see her face, he could not guess her name. He bent down to remove the handkerchief from her face, then stopped, with outstretched hand, restrained by a sudden thought.

Had he the right to interfere in any way with the disposition of the body before the judicial inquiry? He imagined the law as a kind of General, whose notice nothing can escape, and who attaches as much importance to a lost button as to a stab in the stomach. Beneath that handkerchief damning evidence might be found; a real clue, which might well lose its value if touched by a clumsy hand.

So he rose, to run to the mayor's house. A second thought held him back. Suppose that by any chance the little girl were still alive, he could not leave her like this. Quickly he knelt down at a discreet distance from her and, thrusting out his hand, touched her foot. It was cold, frozen into that ghastly chill that makes dead flesh so terrifying, and leaves no room for doubt. The touch of it turned his stomach, as he expressed it later, and the saliva dried in his mouth. He rose at once and began to run through the wood towards Monsieur Renardet's house.

He ran at the regulation double, his stick under his arm, his fists closed, his head thrust forward; his leather bag, full of letters and newspapers, pounded rhythmically against his back.

The mayor's house was at the end of the wood, whose trees served as its park. One corner of the surrounding wall was washed by the Brindille, which here ran into a small pond.

It was a large, square house of grey stone. It was very old, and had stood siege in the old days; at the far end of it was a huge tower, sixty feet high and built in the water. Once, from the summit of this keep, watch had been kept over all the district. It was called the Tower of Renard, no one knew quite why. It was doubtless from this name that the name Renardet came, borne by all the owners of this property, which had been in the same family, it was said, for more than two hundred years. For the Renardets belonged to that almost noble yeoman class so often found in the country before the Revolution.

The postman rushed into the kitchen where the servants were having breakfast, shouting: " Is the Mayor up? I must speak to him at once."

Médéric was known for a man of weight and authority, and they knew at once that something serious had happened.

Monsieur Renardet was notified, and ordered the man to be brought in. Pale and out of breath, the postman, cap in hand, found the mayor seated at a long table covered with scattered papers.

He was a tall, stout man, with an unwieldy figure and a ruddy skin. He was as strong as a bull, and much loved in the locality, for all his quick temper. About forty years of age, and for the past six months a widower, he lived on his land in the style of a country nobleman. His impetuous nature had landed him in many awkward places, from which he had always been rescued by his indulgent and tactful comrades, the magistrates of Roüy-le-Tors. Was it not he, indeed, who one fine day threw the driver of the mail-coach from his box, because the fellow had almost run over his pointer Micmac? Had he not broken the ribs of a gamekeeper who prosecuted him for carrying his gun across a piece of land belonging to a neighbour? Had he not even arrested the sub-prefect when he stopped in the village in the pursuit of his administrative duties—styled by Monsieur Renardet an electioneering campaign, because it was opposed to the good old tradition of government by the family?

" What's the matter, Médéric?" asked the mayor.

" I've found a little girl in your wood, dead."

Renardet rose, his face brick-red.

" What did you say . . . a little girl?"

" Yes, sir, a little girl, quite naked, lying on her back, and there was some blood; she's dead as a door-nail."

"My God," swore the mayor, "that must be Madame Roque's little girl! I've just been told that she never came home to her mother's last night. Where did you find her?"

The postman began a detailed explanation, and offered to guide the mayor to the spot.

But Renardet turned gruff. "No, I don't need you. Send the constable, the town clerk, and the doctor to me as soon as you can, and go on with your delivery. Hurry, man, hurry, and tell them to meet me in the wood."

The postman, accustomed to discipline, obediently withdrew, angry and disgusted at being excluded from the inquiry.

The mayor went out too, taking his hat, a large soft hat of grey felt, with a very broad brim. He halted a moment upon the threshold of his dwelling. Before him stretched a wide lawn where gleamed three great splashes of red, blue, and white, three monstrous baskets of flowers in full bloom, one straight opposite the house, the other two at the sides. In the background the first trees of the wood stood up to the sky; on the left, on the far side of the Brindille, which widened here into a pool, a wide expanse of meadows lay open to his view, a green, flat landscape intersected by ditches and hedges of pollard willows. These fantastic tree-creatures, standing there like ghosts or hunchbacks, bore upon their short, thick trunks a waving fan of little branches.

On the right were the stables, the outhouses, and all the buildings dependent upon the property; behind them began the village, a prosperous little place chiefly inhabited by cattle-breeders.

Renardet walked slowly down his steps and, turning to the left, reached the bank of the stream, which he followed at a slow pace, his hands behind his back. His head was bent, and from time to time he sent a piercing glance round him in search of the men he had sent for.

When he reached the shelter of the trees, he stopped, took off his hat, and wiped his brow, as Médéric had done; for the blazing

July sun fell like a rain of fire upon the earth. Then the mayor resumed his journey, stopped once more, and retraced his steps. Suddenly he bent down and soaked his handkerchief in the stream which ran at his feet. He spread it upon his head, under his hat; drops of water trickled over his temples, over his purple ears, over his strong red neck, and, one after another, ran beneath the white collar of his shirt.

As no one had yet appeared, he began to tap with his foot; then he shouted: "Hey! Hey!"

From the right a voice answered: "Hey! Hey!"

The doctor appeared under the trees. He was a small, thin man, once an army surgeon, with a local reputation for great skill. He was lame, having been wounded on active service, and walked with a stick. The constable and the town clerk appeared next; they arrived together, having both received the news at the same time. They ran up panting, with scared faces, walking and running by turns in their haste, and waving their arms so wildly that they seemed to do more work with them than with their legs.

"You know what the trouble is?" said Renardet to the doctor.

"Yes, a dead child found in the wood by Médéric."

"That's right. Come along."

They set off side by side, following the other pair. Their steps made no sound upon the moss, their eyes continually searched the ground in front of them.

Suddenly Doctor Labarbe stretched out his arm: "There it is."

Far off, under the trees, something bright could be seen. Had they not known what it was, they would never have guessed. So shining white did it look that anyone would have thought it a sheet dropped on the ground, for a sunbeam came through the branches and lit up the pale flesh with a great ray flung obliquely over the stomach of the corpse. As they drew near, they gradually made out the form, the veiled head turned towards the water, and the two arms flung wide apart as in a crucifixion.

"I'm damned hot," said the mayor, and, stooping down to the Brindille, he again wetted his handkerchief and replaced it on his head.

The doctor hurried on, interested by the discovery. As soon as he reached the corpse, he bent down to examine it, without touching it. He had put on his glasses, as one does when studying a curiosity, and he walked quietly round it.

Without rising he said: "Rape and murder. We'll verify it directly. The girl's almost a woman too: look at her throat."

The two breasts, already well formed, sagged on the bosom that death had robbed of its firmness.

Carefully the doctor lifted the handkerchief that covered the head. The face was black and ghastly, with tongue and eyes protruding. "Strangled," he said, "as soon as the job was done."

He felt the neck: "Strangled with the bare hands; there's no special trace, no nail-mark or finger-print. That's that, and it *is* Madame Roque's little girl."

Gingerly he replaced the handkerchief. "I can do nothing; she's been dead for at least twelve hours. The police must be told."

Renardet was standing up with his hands behind his back, gazing at the little body laid upon the ground. "Poor little thing!" he muttered. "We must find her clothes."

The doctor felt her hands, her arms, her legs. "She'd just had a bathe," he said. "They must be on the river-bank."

The mayor gave his orders. "You, Principe"—this to the town clerk—"you hunt along the stream for her clothes. And you, Maxim"—this to the constable—"you run to Roüy-le-Tors and fetch me the examining magistrate and the police. They must be here within an hour. You understand?"

The two men departed quickly, and Renardet said to the doctor: "What blackguard in the district could do such a thing?"

"Who can say?" the doctor murmured. "Anyone is capable of it. Anyone in general, and no one in particular. It must have been a tramp, some fellow out of work. Now we're a Republic, they are the only people you meet on the roads."

Both were supporters of the Bonapartist cause.

"Yes," answered the mayor, "it must have been a passing stranger, a vagabond without hearth or home."

"Or wife," added the doctor with a faint smile. "Having neither supper nor bed, he got himself the rest. There are I don't know how many men on this earth who are capable, at any moment, of committing a crime. Did you know that the little girl was missing?"

With the end of his stick he touched, one after another, the dead child's stiffened fingers, pressing on them as on the keys of a piano.

"Yes. The mother came to see me last night, about nine o'clock, as the child had not come in at seven for her supper. We shouted for her on the roads till midnight, but we never thought of the wood. Besides, we needed daylight to make a really effective search."

"Have a cigar," said the doctor.

"No, thanks. I don't want to smoke. This business has given me rather a turn."

The two remained standing, in front of the frail young body, so pale upon the dark moss. A great blue-bottle walked up one thigh, stopped at the blood-stains, and went on up the body, running over the hip with its hurried, jerky little steps. It climbed up one breast, then came down again and explored the other, seeking for something to drink. The two men watched the roving black speck.

"How pretty it is," said the doctor, "a fly on human skin!

The ladies of the last century were quite right to wear them on their faces. I wonder why the custom has gone out."

The mayor, lost in thought, appeared to hear nothing. Abruptly, he swung round, startled by a noise. A woman in a blue bonnet and apron came running through the trees. It was the mother, Madame Roque. As soon as she caught sight of Renardet she began to scream: " My little darling, where's my little darling?" so wild with grief that she never looked down. Suddenly she saw her darling, and stopped dead. She clasped her hands and flung up her arms: piercing and heart-rending screams came between her lips, the screams of a wounded animal.

She flung herself upon her knees beside the body, and snatched at the handkerchief with a violent gesture. When she saw that dreadful face, black and distorted, she drew back shuddering, then buried her face in the moss, her body shaken with ceaseless, heart-breaking sobs.

The clothes clung round her tall, bony frame, that heaved and shook. They could see the ghastly quivering of her thin, ugly ankles and her withered calves, in their coarse blue stockings. Her crooked fingers burrowed in the earth as though she would make a hole and hide in it.

The doctor, deeply moved, murmured: " Poor old thing!"

Renardet felt a curious disturbance in his stomach; then he uttered a sort of violent sneeze, vented simultaneously from nose and mouth. He pulled his handkerchief from his pocket and cried noisily into it, choking, sobbing, and blowing his nose. " M—m—m—my God," he blubbered, " I'd I—I—like to see them g—guillotine the swine that did it!"

But Principe returned empty-handed and disconsolate. " I've found nothing, sir," he muttered to the mayor, " nothing anywhere."

" What can't you find?" the other demanded thickly.

" The little girl's clothes."

"W—well, go on looking . . . and . . . and f—find them, or you'll get into trouble with me."

Knowing that there was no opposing the mayor, the fellow went off again with a discouraged air, casting a timid sideways glance at the body.

Distant voices were heard among the trees, a confused din, the uproar of an approaching crowd; for on his round Médéric had spread the news from door to door. The country-folk, at first dumbfounded, had talked it over in the street on one another's door-steps. Then they gathered together, and, after twenty minutes' chattering, discussion, and comment, were coming to see it for themselves.

They arrived in groups, a little hesitant and uneasy, fearing their own feelings at first sight of the body. When they saw it they stopped, not daring to come closer, and talking in low tones. Then they grew bold, advanced a few steps, stopped again, advanced a few more, and soon grouped themselves round the dead child, the mother, the doctor, and Renardet. They formed a deep circle, swaying and clamorous, and pushed ever closer by the sudden onrush of the late-comers. In a few moments they were touching the body; some of them even bent down to handle it. The doctor kept them at a distance. But the mayor, roused suddenly from his stupor, became furious; seizing Doctor Labarbe's stick, he fell upon his subjects, stammering: "Clear out! . . . Clear out! . . . Pack of beasts! . . . Clear out! . . ." In one second the circle of inquisitive spectators widened by two hundred yards.

Madame Roque had risen and turned round, and was now sitting weeping, with her hands in front of her face.

The crowd was discussing the affair, and the boys' greedy eyes devoured the nude young body. Renardet noticed it and, hastily tearing off his linen coat, he threw it over the girl's form, which was completely hidden by that huge garment.

The inquisitive spectators drew quietly nearer; the wood

was getting fuller and fuller; a continuous murmur of voices rose to the thick foliage of the tall trees.

The mayor stood there in his shirt-sleeves, stick in hand, in a pugnacious attitude. He seemed exasperated by the curiosity of the crowd, and repeated: " If one of you comes a step nearer, I'll break his head like a dog's."

The peasants had a wholesome dread of him, and kept clear. Doctor Labarbe, who was smoking, sat down beside Madame Roque and talked to her, trying to distract her attention. The old woman promptly took her hands from her face and answered him in a rush of tearful words, venting her grief in the sheer flood of her speech. She told him her whole life-history, her marriage, the death of her husband, a cowherd, gored to death, her daughter's childhood, her wretched existence as a widow with a child and no resources. She was all she had, was little Louise, and now she'd been killed, killed here in this wood. Suddenly she felt a wish to see her child again and, dragging herself to the body upon her knees, she lifted a corner of the garment that covered it; then let it fall again and broke into fresh sobs. The crowd was silent, gazing eagerly at the mother's every movement.

There was a sudden disturbance; and a cry of " The police, the police! "

Two policemen appeared in the distance, advancing at a rapid trot, escorting their captain and a short, ginger-whiskered gentleman, who bobbed up and down like a monkey on his big white mare.

The constable had found Monsieur Pictoin, the examining magistrate, at the very moment when he was mounting his horse to take his daily ride; it was his ambition to be taken for a smart young fellow, which vastly amused the officers.

He and the captain dismounted and shook hands with the mayor and the doctor, casting a sneaking glance at the linen coat on the ground, filled out as it was by the body lying beneath it.

When he had been thoroughly acquainted with the facts of the case, his first act was to disperse the crowd. The police cleared it out of the wood, but it soon reappeared in the meadow and formed a hedge, a long hedge of excited, moving heads, all along the Brindille, on the far side of the brook.

In his turn the doctor made his statement, and Renardet wrote it down with a pencil in his notebook. All the verifications were made, registered, and commented upon, but no new discovery was made. Maxim had returned also, without finding a trace of the missing clothes.

Every one was amazed at their disappearance ; no one could explain it except by the theory of robbery, and, since the rags were not worth a shilling, even this theory was inadmissible.

The examining magistrate, the mayor, the captain, and the doctor searched in couples, looking between even the smallest twigs along the waterside.

" How is it," said Renardet to the magistrate, " that the wretch hid or stole the clothes, yet left the body right in the open, in full view ? "

The other was crafty and sagacious. " Aha," he answered, " possibly a trick. This crime was committed either by a brute or by a very sly dog. Anyhow, we'll soon find him all right."

The sound of carriage wheels made them turn their heads. The Deputy, the doctor, and the clerk of the police station were arriving. The search continued, amid animated conversation.

Renardet said suddenly : " You know you're all lunching with me ? "

Every one accepted with smiles ; the examining magistrate, thinking that they had had enough, for that day, of Madame Roque's little girl, turned to the mayor.

" I can have the body taken to your house, can't I ? You have a room there where it can be kept till to-night."

The mayor was distressed, and stammered : " Yes . . . no, no. To tell you the truth, I'd sooner not have it . . . on account of the servants, you know. They're already talking of . . .

of ghosts and things . . . in my tower, the tower of Renard. You know what it is. . . . I couldn't get one to stay on. . . . No . . . I'd sooner not have it in the house."

The magistrate smiled : "Very well. . . . I'll get it taken straight to Roüy for the inquest." And turning to the Deputy, he said : "I may have the use of your carriage, may I not ?"

"Certainly."

They all came back to the body. Madame Roque was seated beside her daughter now, holding her hand and staring in front of her with wild, blurred eyes. The two doctors tried to lead her away, so that she should not see the child taken from her. But she understood at once what they were about to do and, throwing herself upon the body, seized it with both arms. Lying beside it, she shrieked : "You shan't have it, it's mine, mine now. They've killed my child ; I'll keep her, you shan't have her."

The men, disturbed and irresolute, stood round her. Renardet went down on his knees to speak to her. "Listen, we must have her, so as to know who killed her. Otherwise we shan't know ; we must find him to punish him. You shall have her back when we've found him, I promise you."

This reason moved her ; hate burned in her crazed eyes. "Then he'll be caught ?" she said.

"Yes, I promise you he will."

She rose, determined to let them have their own way. But, hearing the captain murmur, "Curious that her clothes can't be found," a new and strange idea entered the peasant woman's brain.

"Where are her clothes ?" she asked. "They're mine, I want 'em. Where've they been put ?"

It was explained to her that they were still lost, whereupon she persisted with despairing obstinacy, weeping and moaning, demanding : "They're mine, I want 'em. Where are they ? I want 'em."

The more they tried to calm her, the more obstinately she

sobbed. She did not want the body any longer, only the clothes, her daughter's clothes, perhaps less from maternal affection than from the blind cupidity of a wretch to whom a single coin represents a fortune.

And when the little body, rolled in a wrap fetched from Renardet's house, disappeared into the carriage, the old woman stood under the trees, supported by the mayor and the captain, and cried: "I've got nothing, nothing, nothing at all, nothing, not even her li'l bonnet! I've got nothing, nothing, nothing, not even her li'l bonnet!"

The parish priest had now come on the scene; he was still quite young, but already very plump. He undertook to get Mother Roque away, and they set off together towards the village. The mother's grief abated under the honeyed consolation of God's servant, who promised her a thousand assuagements. But she repeated incessantly: "If only I had her li'l bonnet," clinging stupidly to this thought, which now completely obsessed her.

Renardet shouted after them: "You'll lunch with us, Father? In an hour's time."

The priest turned his head and replied: "With great pleasure. I'll be there about twelve."

All the guests made their way towards the house, that lifted over the trees its grey front and the great tower built beside the Brindille.

The meal was a long one: they talked about the crime. Every one there held the same theory: it had been the work of some tramp, who had happened to wander that way while the child was bathing.

Then the magistrates returned to Roüy, after announcing that they would return early next day; the doctor and the parish priest went home, while Renardet took a long walk through the meadows and came back to the copse, where he walked up and down until nightfall, with slow steps, his hands clasped behind his back.

He went to bed very early, and the next morning he was still asleep when the examining magistrate entered his bedroom. He was rubbing his hands, and his face expressed great satisfaction.

"Ah," he said, "you're still in bed. Well, my dear fellow, we've news this morning."

The mayor sat up in bed.

"What is it?"

"Oh, an odd enough thing. You'll remember that yesterday, the mother was making a terrible fuss about wanting something to remind her of her daughter, particularly her little bonnet. Well, when she opened her door this morning, she found on the door-step the child's two little wooden shoes. This proves that the crime was committed by someone in the district, by someone who now feels sorry for her. Besides, postman Médéric has brought me the dead girl's thimble, knife, and needle-case. There's no doubt that the man was carrying off her clothes to hide them when he dropped the things that were in the pocket. For my part, I attach especial importance to the incident of the wooden shoes, which points to a degree of moral sensibility and a quality of compassion in the murderer. If you are ready, we will therefore consider in turn the leading people of your district."

The mayor got out of bed. He rang for hot water to shave himself. "Very well," he said, "but it will be a long job, and we can begin at once."

Monsieur Pictoin straddled across his chair, indulging his passion for equestrian exercises even indoors.

Renardet, staring at himself in the glass, was now covering his chin with a white foam; then he drew his razor over the skin and went on: "The name of the leading citizen of Carvelin is Joseph Renardet, mayor, well-to-do landowner, a hot-tempered man who beats keepers and drivers. . . ."

The examining magistrate laughed aloud: "That's enough; go on to the next."

"The next in importance is Monsieur Pelledent, deputy mayor, cattle farmer, also a well-to-do landowner, a shrewd peasant, uncommonly tricky, uncommonly sharp in money matters, but in my opinion incapable of such a monstrous crime."

"Next," said Monsieur Pictoin.

So Renardet shaved and washed, and went through his inspection of the morals of all the inhabitants of Carvelin. After debating for two hours, their suspicions narrowed down to three sufficiently dubious characters: a poacher called Cavalle, one Paquet, a fisherman of trout and crabs, and a cowherd called Clovis.

II

The investigations went on all summer: the criminal was not discovered. The men suspected and arrested were easily able to prove their innocence, and the police had to abandon their search for the culprit.

But this murder seemed in some strange fashion to have stirred the whole country-side. An uneasy feeling lurked in people's hearts, a vague fear, an inexplicable sense of terror, sprung not only from the impossibility of discovering any clue, but also and in a special degree from that strange discovery of the wooden shoes at Mother Roque's door-step on the next morning. The certainty that the murderer had been present at the discussions, that he must still be living in the village, haunted and obsessed all minds, seemed to hover over the country-side like a perpetual menace.

The copse had become a terrifying place; it was avoided, and they believed it haunted. Before the murder, the villagers used to walk there every Sunday afternoon. They sat on the moss below great tall trees, or wandered contentedly along the stream, peering at the trout gliding under the grasses. The lads played at bowls, skittles, cork pool, and ball in special places which they had taken for themselves, levelling the ground and treading it down hard and firm ; and the girls walked up and down, arms linked, in groups of four and five, twittering their village romances in shrill voices that grated on the ear : the tuneless notes shivered the quiet air and set the listeners' teeth on edge like drops of vinegar. Nowadays the villagers ventured no more under the high, thick vault, as if they expected to find dead bodies lying there every day.

Autumn came, the leaves were falling. Day and night they fell, curled and fluttering, twirling as they came down past the great trees. Sometimes, when a gust of wind swept over the tops of the trees, the slow, ceaseless rain grew suddenly heavier and became a confused and rushing downpour which covered the moss with a thick yellow carpet that crackled faintly under the feet. The almost inaudible murmuring, the fluttering, ceaseless murmur of their falling, so sweet and so sad, seemed a lament, and these ever-dropping leaves seemed tears, great tears poured out by the great, sad trees which wept day and night for the end of the year, for the end of warm dawns and quiet dusks, for the end of hot breezes and blazing suns, and perhaps, too, for the crime they had seen committed under their shadow, for the child violated and killed at their feet. They wept in the silence of the deserted, empty wood, the shunned, forsaken wood, where the soul, the little soul of the dead child surely wandered, lonely.

Tawny and angry-looking, swollen by the storms, the Brindille ran swifter between its dried-up banks, between two rows of slender bare willows.

Suddenly Renardet took to walking in the copse again. Every day at nightfall he left his house, slowly descended the steps of the terrace, and disappeared between the trees with a dreamy air, his hands in his pockets. He strode for a long time over the soft, wet moss, while an army of crows who had gathered from the country round to roost in the lofty tree-tops, swept out across the sky like a vast mourning veil floating in the wind, with a monstrous, sinister clamour.

Sometimes they settled, a horde of black spots clustered on the tangled branches against the red sky, the blood-red sky of autumn twilight. Then all at once they flew off again, cawing frenziedly and spreading above the wood again the long sombre line of flying wings.

They sank at last in the highest tops, and little by little ceased their crying, while the advancing darkness merged their black feathers with the blackness of the hollow night.

Still Renardet wandered slowly under the trees; then, when the shadows drew so thickly down that he could no longer walk about, he returned home and fell heavily into his big chair before the glowing chimney-piece, stretching towards the hearth his damp feet, that steamed in front of the flames for hours.

Then, one morning, startling news ran through the countryside: the mayor was having his copse cut down.

Twenty wood-cutters were already at work. They had begun with the corner nearest the house, and under the master's eye they made rapid progress.

First, the men who were to lop off the branches scrambled up the trunk.

Fastened to the tree by a rope round their bodies, they first take a grip of it with their arms, then raise one leg and drive the steel spike fixed to the soles of their boots firmly into the trunk. The point pierces the tree, and is wedged there, and as if he were walking the man raised himself and drives in the spike of the other foot: then he supports himself on this one and makes a fresh advance with the first foot.

And at each step he carries higher the rope that holds him to the tree; at his waist the steel hatchet dangles and glitters. He climbs gently and steadily, like a parasitic animal attacking a giant, he mounts clumsily up the vast column, twining his arm round it and digging in his spurs till he can decapitate it.

As soon as he reaches the first branches, he stops, detaches the sharp axe from his thigh, and strikes. He strikes with slow, regular blows, severing the limb close to the trunk; and all of a sudden the branch cracks, bends, hangs, tears apart, and rushes down, brushing past the surrounding trees in its fall. Then it is dashed on the earth with a crash of shattered wood, and for a long time all its smallest twigs quiver and shake.

The earth is covered with fallen branches, that the rest of the men take and saw into smaller pieces, fastening them in bundles and piling them in heaps, while the trees still left standing look like monstrous pillars of wood, gigantic stakes amputated and shorn by the sharp steel of the axes.

And when the last branch has fallen, the woodman leaves the noose of rope he has carried up with him fastened to the peak of the straight, slender pillar; then, digging in his spurs, he climbs down the pillaged trunk, and the wood-cutters proceed to attack it at the foot, striking heavy blows that echo all through the forest.

When the cut at the foot seems deep enough, a number of men haul on the rope fastened to the top, shouting all together with each heave, and the great mast suddenly cracks and falls to the earth with the hollow, vibrating roar of a distant cannon-shot.

And day by day the wood grew less, losing its felled trees as an army loses its soldiers.

Renardet never left it; he stayed there from morning to evening, immobile, his hands clasped behind his back, contemplating the slow death of his forest. When a tree had fallen, he placed his foot on it as if it were a dead body. Then he turned his gaze to the next with a kind of secret and dispassionate impatience, as if he expected something, hoped that something would come of this massacre.

Meanwhile, they drew near the place where little Roque had been found. They came to it at last, one evening, at dusk.

As the shadows were drawing down under a darkened sky, the wood-cutters wanted to stop work, and put off until to-morrow the felling of an enormous beech, but the owner refused to allow it, and insisted that they should forthwith lop off its branches and haul down the monstrous tree that had lent its shadow to the crime.

When the man had stripped it bare of all its branches and made it ready for its doom, when the wood-cutters had undermined its base, five men began to haul on the rope fastened to the summit.

The tree resisted; hacked half through as it was, the powerful trunk was rigid as an iron girder. The workmen, lying right back on the rope, pulled all together, heaving steadily, and accompanied every pull with a breathless shout.

Two wood-cutters stood near the giant, grasping their axes, like two executioners ready to strike another blow, and Renardet, motionless, his hand on the bark, waited for the fall in the grip of a nervous agitation.

One of the men said to him: "You are standing too close, sir; when it falls, you might get hurt."

He neither replied nor drew back; he looked prepared to fling himself upon the beech with both arms and throw it like a wrestler throwing his man.

At the foot of the great wooden column, there was a sudden rending that seemed to run through it to the very top like a mournful shudder; and it swayed a little, on the verge of falling, but resisting still.

With tense bodies and straining arms, the men gave another and mightier heave; and as the shattered tree swayed over, Renardet made a sudden step forward, then stopped, his shoulders braced to take the inevitable shock, the fatal shock that would crush him to the ground.

But the tree, falling a little to one side, only grazed his body, flinging him face downwards five yards away.

The workmen rushed forward to lift him up; he had already

raised himself on his knees; he was dazed, with eyes staring wildly, and he drew his hand across his forehead as if he had come to his senses after an access of madness.

When they had helped him to his feet, the astonished men questioned him, unable to understand what he had done. Stammering, he told them that for a moment he had lost his head, or, rather, slipped for a second back into his childhood, and he had imagined that he had time to cross beneath the tree as youngsters rush across in front of hurrying carriages, that he had played at taking risks, that for a week he had felt the desire to do it growing in him, and every time a tree cracked as it fell had wondered if one could run under it without being touched. It was a fool's trick, he admitted; but every one has these moments of insanity and these puerile and idiotic temptations.

He explained all this very slowly in a muffled voice, hesitating for words; then he went off, saying: "We'll be here again to-morrow, my men, to-morrow."

As soon as he reached his room, he sat down at his table, flooded with light reflected from the shade of the lamp, and wept, his face between his hands.

He wept for a long time, then he dried his eyes, lifted his head, and looked at his clock. It was not yet six. He thought: "I have time before dinner," and he went and locked his door. Then he came back and sat down again at his table. He pulled out the middle drawer, took a revolver from inside, and placed it on his papers, in the full glare of the lamp. The steel of the weapon gleamed, and threw out flashes of light like flames.

Renardet stared at it for a time with the uncertain eye of a drunken man; then he stood up and began to walk about.

He walked from one end of the room to the other, and from time to time he stopped, to begin again at once. Suddenly he opened the door of his dining-room, soaked a napkin in the water-jug, and wiped his forehead, as he had done on the morning of the crime. Then he began to walk about again.

Every time he walked past his table, the shining weapon attracted his glance, almost fitted itself into his hand ; but he kept his eye on the clock and thought : " I have still time."

Half-past six struck. Then he grasped the revolver, and, his face twisted into a horrible grimace, he opened his mouth and thrust the barrel inside as if he wanted to swallow it. He stood so for some moments, motionless, finger on the trigger ; then, seized with a sudden shuddering horror, he spat the pistol out on to the carpet.

He dropped into his chair, shaken with sobs : " I can't. I daren't. My God, my God ! What shall I do to get the courage to kill myself ? "

There was a knock at the door ; he leaped to his feet in a frenzy. A servant said : " Dinner is ready, sir." " Very well," he answered, " I'm coming down."

So he picked up the weapon, shut it away in the drawer again, then looked at himself in the glass over the chimney-piece to assure himself that his face was not too convulsed. He was flushed, as always, a little more flushed perhaps. That was all. He went downstairs and sat down to dinner.

He ate slowly, like a man anxious to prolong a meal, anxious not to be left alone with himself. Then he smoked several pipes in the dining-room while the table was cleared. Then he went back to his room.

As soon as he had shut himself in it, he looked under his bed, opened every cupboard, explored every corner, moved every piece of furniture to look behind it. After that he lit the wax candles on the chimney-piece, and swung round time and again, his eyes peering into every corner of the room in an agony of fear that distorted his face, for he knew that he would assuredly see, as he saw her every night, little Roque, the little girl he had violated and afterwards strangled.

Every night, the horrible scene enacted itself. It began with a sort of muttering in his ears, like the noise of a grinding-machine or the sound of a distant train crossing a bridge.

Then his breath came in gasps ; he stifled, and had to unbutton the collar of his shirt, and his belt. He walked about to stir the blood in his veins, he tried to read, he tried to sing ; it was all in vain ; willy-nilly, his mind went back to the day of the murder and forced him to live it over again in every secret detail, and to suffer again all its most violent emotions from the first minute of the day to the last.

When he had risen that morning, the morning of that dreadful day, he had felt a slight dizziness and a headache which he attributed to the heat, and for that reason remained in his room until he was called for lunch. The meal over, he had taken a nap ; then, towards the end of the afternoon, he had gone out to enjoy the fresh and cooling breeze under the trees of the copse.

But as soon as he was outside the house, the heavy, burning air of the flat country-side had oppressed him more than ever. The sun, still high in the sky, poured floods of blazing sunshine down on the burnt-up earth, dry and dying of thirst. No breath of wind stirred the leaves. Beasts, birds, even the grasshoppers were silent. Renardet reached the great trees and began to walk over the moss where a faint, fresh odour rose from the Brindille under the vast roof of branches. But he felt ill at ease. It seemed to him that an unknown, invisible hand was clutching his throat ; and he hardly thought of anything, having at all times very few ideas in his head. Only one vague thought had been obsessing him for three months : the thought of marrying again. He suffered from his solitary life, suffered in body and soul. Accustomed for ten years to feel a woman near him, accustomed to her constant presence, to her daily embrace, he felt the need, a confused and overmastering need, of her perpetual nearness and her habitual kiss. Since Madame Renardet's death, he suffered all the time, hardly understanding why ; he suffered because he missed her dress brushing past his leg every hour of the day, and especially because he could no longer find peace and ease of body in her arms. He had been a widower for barely six months and already he was looking round the neighbourhood for some young girl or some widow he might marry when his period of mourning was at an end.

His soul was chaste, but it was housed in the powerful body of a Hercules, and carnal visions began to trouble his sleep and the hours when he lay awake. He drove them from him; they returned; and now and then he murmured, smiling to himself: "I'm a Saint Anthony, I am."

On that particular morning he had had several of these persistent visions, and a sudden desire had seized him to bathe in the Brindille to refresh himself and cool the heat of his blood.

A little farther on, he knew a wide deep stretch of river where the country-folk sometimes came to dip themselves in summer. He went there.

Thick-grown willows hid this clear pool, where the current paused and drowsed a little before rushing on again. As he drew near, Renardet thought he heard a slight sound, a faint, lapping sound which was not the river lapping against its banks. He parted the leaves carefully and looked through. A very young girl, quite naked, showing white through the translucent water, was splashing the water with both hands, making little dancing movements in the water, turning and swaying with gracile gestures. She was no longer a child, and she was not yet a woman grown; she was plump and shapely, and had withal the air of a precocious child, developed beyond her years, almost mature. He did not stir, transfixed with amazement and a dreadful pain, the breath strangled in his throat by a strange and poignant emotion. He stood there, his heart beating as if one of his sensual dreams had just come to life, as if an evil faery had conjured up before him this disturbing and too youthful creature, this little peasant Venus, rising from the ripples of the stream as that other diviner Venus from the sea waves.

The child finished her bathe suddenly; she did not see him, and came towards him to get her clothes and dress herself. As she came nearer and nearer to him, taking little delicate steps to avoid the sharp stones, he felt himself driven towards her by an irresistible force, a mad animal lust that pricked his flesh, filled his mind with madness, and made him tremble from head to foot.

For a moment she stood still behind the willow where he was hiding. Then he lost all self-control, and, parting the branches, he flung himself on her and seized her in his arms. She fell down, too terrified to resist, too stunned to call out, and he possessed her without realising what he was doing.

He woke from his criminal madness like a man waking from a nightmare. The child began to cry.

" Hush," he said, " hush then. I'll give you some money."

But she did not listen ; she went on sobbing.

He began again : " Now hush then. Hush then. Hush then."

She screamed and writhed in the effort to escape.

Abruptly he realised that he was lost ; and he seized her by the throat to silence on her lips those terrible rending sounds. As she went on struggling with the desperate strength of a creature trying to fly from death, he tightened his great hand on the little throat swelling with her cries, and so savagely did he grip her that he had strangled her in a few seconds without ever dreaming of killing her, wanting only to silence her.

Then he got to his feet, dazed with horror.

She lay stretched out before him, stained with blood, and her face black. He was on the point of rushing away, when the confused mysterious instinct that prompts all human beings in their moments of peril, stirred in his distraught mind.

He was about to throw the body in the water, but a second impulse drove him to make a small parcel of the clothes. He had some string in his pockets, and he tied it up and hid it in the stream in a deep hole under the trunk of a tree whose foot was washed by the waters of the Brindille.

Then he strode rapidly away, reached the meadows, made a wide detour in order to be seen by the peasants living far from the place at the other side of the district, and returned home for dinner at the usual hour, telling his servants where his walk had taken him.

That night he slept; he fell into a profound, sodden sleep, such a sleep as must sometimes visit men condemned to death. He did not open his eyes until the first gleams of dawn, and, tortured by fear of the discovery of the hideous crime, lay waiting for the hour at which he always rose.

Afterwards he had to be present at all the investigations. He went through these like a somnambulist, in a half-crazed state in which he saw men and things like the figments of a dream, his clouded mind hardly conscious, in the grip of that sense of unreality which oppresses all our faculties in times of appalling disaster.

Nothing but the mother's agonised cry found its way to his heart. At that moment he was ready to fling himself at the old woman's knees and cry: "I did it." But he stifled the impulse. He did, however, go during the night to fish out the dead girl's sabots and carry them to her mother's door-step.

So long as the inquest lasted, and so long as he had to direct and mislead justice, he was calm, master of himself, cunning and smiling. With the magistrates he discussed placidly all the theories which they conceived, disputed their opinions, confounded their reasoning. He even found a certain bitter and melancholy pleasure in upsetting their examinations of the accused, in confusing their ideas on the subject, and proving the innocence of the men they suspected.

But from the very day when the inquiries were given up, he became gradually more nervous, more excitable than ever before, carefully as he controlled his bursts of rage. Sudden noises made him start fearfully; he shuddered at the least thing, sometimes shaking from head to foot when a fly settled on his face. Then an overmastering desire for movement seized on him, impelled him to long, violent walks, kept him walking about his room through whole nights.

It was not that he was torn with remorse. His gross and unreasoning mind was not susceptible to any refinement of sentiment or moral fear. A man of action, even a violent man, born to fight, to ravage conquered countries and massacre the conquered, full of the savage instincts of the hunter and the soldier, he had little or no respect for human life. Although for political reasons he supported the Church, he believed neither in God nor the Devil, and consequently did not look to any life after death for either punishment or reward for his deeds in this life. He believed in nothing but a vague philosophy made up of all the notions of the Encyclopædists of the previous century; and he regarded religion as a moral sanction of the law, both of them having been invented by men to regulate social relationships.

To kill a man in a duel, or in war, or in a quarrel, or by accident, or for revenge, or even in an ambush, he found an amusing and laudable affair, and it would have left no more impression on his mind than a shot fired at a hare; but the murder of this child had stirred the very depths of his heart. He had done the deed in a madness of uncontrollable lust, in something like a storm of physical desire that swept aside his reason. And he had kept still in his heart, kept in his flesh, kept on his lips, kept even in his murderous fingers, something like a gross and brutal love and a frightful horror of this young girl surprised and foully killed by him. His thoughts recurred perpetually to the horrible scene; and although he compelled himself to dismiss the vision, although he rejected it in terror and disgust, he felt it wandering in his mind, twisting in his thoughts, waiting relentlessly for the chance to reappear.

Then he grew afraid of the evenings, afraid of the darkness creeping round him. He did not know yet why he found the shadows terrifying; but he had an instinctive dread of them; he felt that they were peopled with frightful things. The light of day did not encourage horrors. Things and creatures alike were clearly visible in it; moreover, only such things and creatures as can show themselves in full light are ever encountered by day. But night, shadowy night, thicker than walls and empty, infinite night, so black, so vast, was filled with frightful things that brushed his skin in passing; he felt that a mysterious horror was abroad and roving about at night, and he thought the darkness hid an unknown danger, imminent and threatening. What was it?

Before long he knew. Late one sleepless night, as he sat in his chair, he thought he saw the curtains at his window move. He waited, uneasy, with a beating heart; the hangings stirred no more; then, all at once, they shook again; at least he thought they shook. He dared not rise from his chair; he did not dare even to breathe; and yet he was a brave man; he had fought many times and he would have rejoiced at finding thieves in the house.

Had the curtains really moved? He asked himself the question, afraid that his eyes were playing him tricks. Besides, it was the very least movement, a faint quiver of the drapery, a sort of trembling of the folds rather than such a lifting movement as the wind makes. Renardet sat there with staring eyes and out-thrust neck; and abruptly, ashamed of his fear, he stood up, took four steps, seized the hangings in both hands and drew them wide apart. At first he saw nothing but the black panes, as black as squares of gleaming ink. Night, the vast, impassable space of night, stretched beyond them to the unseen horizon. He stood thus looking out on to illimitable darkness; and suddenly he noticed a gleam, a gleam that moved and seemed a long way off. Then he pressed his face against the glass, thinking that a crab-fisher must be poaching in the Brindille, for it was past midnight, and this gleam was moving along the edge of the water under the trees of the copse. Renardet was still unable to make it out and he shaded his eyes with his hands; in a flash the gleam became a bright light, and he saw little Roque naked and bleeding on the moss.

He shrank back, convulsed with horror, hurling his chair

aside and falling on his back. He lay there for some minutes, his brain reeling, then he sat up and began to reflect. He had had an hallucination, that was all, an hallucination caused by nothing more alarming than a night robber prowling along the edge of the stream with his lantern. What could be less surprising, indeed, than that the memory of his crime should sometimes call up in his mind the image of the dead girl?

He got up, drank a glass of water, and seated himself in his chair. He thought: "What shall I do, if it begins again?" And it would begin again: he felt it, he was sure of it. Even now the window was tempting him to lift his eyes, calling to them, drawing them. He turned his chair round so that he should not see it; then he took up a book and tried to read; but soon he thought he heard something moving behind him, and he swung his chair round violently on one leg. The curtain was moving again; there was no doubt this time that it had moved; he could doubt it no longer; he rushed at it and grasped it so violently that he tore it down, rod and all, then he pressed his face desperately against the pane. There was nothing to see. All outside was dark; and he drew his breath again as gladly as a man rescued from imminent death.

Then he went back and sat down again; but almost at once he was seized with a desire to look out of the window again. Now that the curtain was down, it looked like a shadowy hole opening on to the darkened country-side; it fascinated and terrified him. To keep himself from yielding to this fatal temptation, he undressed, blew out his light, lay down in bed, and closed his eyes.

Hot and wet with sweat, he lay there stiff on his back and waited for sleep. Suddenly a bright light fell on his eyelids. He opened them, thinking the house was on fire. All was dark, and he lifted himself on one elbow, and tried to make out the window, that still beckoned him relentlessly. Straining his eyes to see it, he saw at last a few stars; and he got out of bed, groped across the room, found the window-panes with his outstretched hands, and rested his forehead against them. There below, under the trees, the body of the young girl shone with a phosphorescent glow, lighting up the shadows round it.

With a great cry, Renardet rushed back to his bed, where he remained until morning, his head hidden under the pillow.

From that night, his life was intolerable. His days were filled with dread of his nights ; and every night the vision came again. As soon as he had shut himself in his room, he tried to struggle against it ; but in vain. An irresistible force dragged him to his feet and thrust him to the window as if to summon the phantom, and he saw it at once, lying at first in the place where he had committed the crime, lying with arms outstretched and legs apart, just as the body had lain when it was found. Then the dead child rose and drew near with little delicate steps, just as the child had done when she came out of the river. She drew near, very lightly, her straight, small limbs moving over the grass and the carpet of drooping flowers ; then she rose in the air towards Renardet's window. She came towards him, as she had come on the day of the crime, towards her murderer. The man drew back before the apparition, he drew back as far as his bed and there collapsed, well knowing that the little girl had come in and now was standing behind the curtain, that would move in a moment. He watched the curtain until daybreak, with staring eyes, waiting all the time to see his victim emerge. But she showed herself no more ; she stayed there, behind the hangings, and now and then a faint trembling shook them. Renardet, his fingers twisted in the bed-clothes, gripped them as he had gripped little Roque's throat. He listened to the striking of the hours : in the silence he heard the ticking of his clock and the loud beating of his heart. And he suffered, poor wretch, more than any man had ever suffered before.

Then, when a streak of light crept across the ceiling and announced the coming of day, he felt himself released, alone at last, alone in his room ; and he lay down to sleep. He slept now for some hours, a restless, fevered sleep, and often in his dreams he saw again the frightful vision of his waking nights.

Afterwards, when he came downstairs for lunch, he felt bowed down like a man who has been enduring the most exhausting labour ; he ate little, perpetually haunted by dread of what he would see when night fell again.

At the same time he knew quite well that it was not an apparition, that the dead do not return, and that it was his sick mind, obsessed by one thought and by one unforgettable memory, his mind alone that evoked the dead child itself had raised from the dead, had summoned and had set before his eyes, branded as they were with an ineffaceable sight. But he knew, too, that he would not be made whole again, that he would never escape from the frightful lash of this memory, and he determined to die rather than endure these torments any longer.

He began to seek a means of killing himself. He wanted to find some simple natural way that would not rouse suspicions of a suicide. For he valued his reputation and the name handed down by his ancestors, and if people found the manner of his death suspicious they would certainly recall the inexplicable crime, and the undiscovered murderer, and it would not be long before they were accusing him of the vile deed.

A strange thought came into his head : he would have himself crushed to death by the tree at whose foot he had killed little Roque. So he decided to have his copse cut down, and to stage an accident. But the beech refused to break his back.

Back in his house, he had endured a frightful despair ; he had seized his revolver and then he had been afraid to fire.

Dinner-time came, he had eaten, and then come upstairs again. And he did not know what he was going to do. After escaping once, he felt a coward now. In that moment by the beech, he was ready, strengthened, resolute, master of his courage and his determination ; now he was weak and as afraid of death as of the dead.

He stammered : " I daren't do it now, I daren't do it now," and he looked with equal horror at the weapon on the table and the curtain that hid his window. He thought, too, that some frightful thing would have happened as soon as life had left him. Some thing? What? Perhaps he would have met her again? She was spying on him, waiting for him, calling him, and it was because she wanted to trap him now, to take him in the snare of her revenge and force him to die, that she showed herself to him like this every evening.

He began to cry like a child, repeating : "I daren't do it now, I daren't do it now." Then he fell on his knees, stammering : " My God, my God ! " Yet he did not believe in God. And now he dared neither look at the window where he knew the apparition crouched, nor at the table on which his revolver lay gleaming.

He stood up again and said aloud : "This can't go on, I must put an end to it." A shudder of fear ran through his limbs at the sound of his voice in the silent room ; but he decided to make no more resolutions, knowing too well that the fingers of his hand would always refuse to press the trigger of the weapon, and so he took refuge with his head under the bed-clothes, and considered what to do.

He must find some expedient that would compel him to die, he must plan a trick against himself that would remove every possibility of further hesitation, delay, or regret. He envied the condemned led to the scaffold under a guard of soldiers. Oh, if he could but implore someone to shoot him, if he could but confess his state of mind, confess his crime to some friend who would never divulge it, and take at his hands the boon of death! But from what man could he ask so terrible a service? What man? He sought among all the men he knew. The doctor? No. Wouldn't he be sure to tell the whole story later? And all at once a fantastic thought flashed across his mind. He would write to the examining magistrate, who was his intimate friend, and denounce himself. He would tell him everything in the letter, the crime, the tortures he endured, his resolution to die, his hesitation, and the means he was employing to stimulate his weakening courage. He would beg him in the name of their old friendship to destroy the letter as soon as the news was brought him that the guilty man had done justice on himself. Renardet could count on the magistrate, he knew him steadfast, discreet, absolutely incapable of a careless speech. He was one of those men whose inflexible conscience is controlled and directed and ordered by pure reason.

The plan had hardly taken shape in his mind when a fantastic joy flooded his heart. Now he was at peace. He would write his letter, leisurely, then when day broke he would put it in the box nailed to the wall of his farm, then he would climb to the top of his tower so that he could see the postman come, and when that blue-bloused man had gone, he would throw himself head-first on to the rocks from which the foundations of the tower rose. He would take care to be seen first by the workmen who were cutting down his wood. Then he would climb out on to the jutting platform that carried the flagstaff for the flags on holidays. He would break the flagstaff with a sudden shake and crash to the ground along with it. Who would doubt that it was an accident? And considering his weight and the height of the tower, he would be killed on the spot.

He rose from his bed at once, went to his table, and began to write; he forgot nothing, no detail of the crime, no detail of his life of agony, no detail of the tortures his heart had endured, and he ended by declaring that he had sentenced himself to death, that he was going to execute the criminal, and he begged his friend, his old friend, to take care that no one ever insulted his memory.

As he finished the letter, he saw that day had come. He closed it, sealed it, wrote the address, then walked lightly downstairs and almost ran to the little white box nailed to the wall at the corner of the farm. The paper was heavy in his hand;

he dropped it inside the box, came quickly back, drew the bolts of the great door, and climbed to the top of his tower to wait for the coming and going of the postman who would carry away his death sentence.

Now he felt calm, liberated, saved!

A cold, dry wind, an icy wind, blew in his face. He drew a deep, greedy breath, his mouth open, drinking in its bitter caress. The sky was red, with the fiery red of a winter sky, and all the white, frost-bound plain glittered in the early rays as though it were powdered with crushed glass. Upright, bare-headed, Renardet looked out over the wide country-side; there were meadows on his left hand, and on his right lay the village; from its chimneys spirals of smoke rose from the fires lit for breakfast.

He saw the Brindille running below him, between the rocks where he would very soon lie crushed. He felt new-born in this lovely, frozen dawn, full of vigour and full of life. He was bathed in light, wrapped round in it, filled with it as with hope. A thousand memories assailed him, memories of other such mornings, of swift walks over the hard earth that rang under his feet, of good sport on the edge of the marshes where the wild duck nested. All the pleasant things he loved, the pleasant things of life, rushed through his memory, stabbed him with fresh desires, woke all the sharp appetites of his powerful active body.

And he was going to die? Why? Was he going to kill himself violently because he was afraid of a shadow? Afraid of nothing? He was rich and still young. What madness! All he needed to help him to forget was some distraction, to go away for a while, to travel. This very night he had not seen the child, because his mind had been preoccupied and lost itself in other thoughts. Perhaps he would never see her again? And if she continued to haunt him in this house, she would certainly not follow him anywhere alse. The earth was wide and the future long. Why should he die?

His glance wandered over the meadows, and he caught sight of a blue patch in the path that ran by the Brindille. It was Médéric coming to deliver the letters from town and take away the village letters.

Renardet started violently as a pang of grief ran through him, and he rushed down the winding staircase to take back his letter, to make the postman give it to him. Little he cared now whether he was seen or not; he ran across the grass covered with the frozen crystals of the night's frosts and he reached the box at the corner of the farm at the same moment as the postman.

The man had opened the little wooden box and was taking out several letters put there by the people of the parish.

"Good day, Médéric," Renardet said to him.

"Good day, Mr. Mayor."

"I say, Médéric, I've dropped a letter in the box that I want. I've come to ask you to give it me back."

"Certainly, Mr. Mayor, I'll give it to you."

And the postman raised his eyes. He was thunderstruck at the sight of Renardet's face; his cheeks were purple, his eyes were restless, black-rimmed, and sunk in his head, his hair wild, his beard tangled, his tie awry. It was evident that he had not been to bed.

"Are you ill, Mr. Mayor?" the man demanded.

The other man realised in a flash that he must present an odd appearance; he became confused and stammered: "No . . . no. It's only that I jumped out of bed to ask you for that letter. . . . I was asleep. . . . Don't you see?"

A vague suspicion crossed the old soldier's mind.

"What letter?" he answered.

"The one you're going to give me back."

Médéric was hesitating now; he did not think the mayor's manner was natural. Perhaps there was a secret, a political secret in the letter. He knew that Renardet was not a republican, and he knew all about the queer shifts and all about the underhand dealings in use at elections.

"Who's this letter addressed to?" he demanded.

"To Monsieur Pictoin, the examining magistrate. You know him quite well, my friend Monsieur Pictoin."

The postman sought among the letters and found the one he was being asked to return. Then he began to scrutinise it, turning it over and over in his fingers, very perplexed, very disturbed between his fear of committing a serious fault and his fear of making an enemy of the mayor.

Seeing his hesitation, Renardet made a movement to seize the letter and snatch it from him. This abrupt gesture convinced Médéric that he had stumbled on an important secret, and he decided to carry out his duty at all costs.

So he threw the envelope in his bag, shut it up, and answered:

"No, I can't, Mr. Mayor. As soon as ever it's been posted to the judge, I can't do anything about it."

Renardet's heart contracted with a frightful anguish.

"But you know me quite well," he babbled. "You can recognise my writing itself. I need that letter, I tell you."

"I can't do it."

"Come, Médéric, you know that I'm not the sort of man to deceive you, and I tell you I need it."

"No, I can't."

A sudden anger clouded Renardet's violent mind.

"You'd better mind what you're doing, damn you: I mean what I say and well you know it, and I can lose your job for you, my good man, and that before you're much older, too. Besides, I'm mayor of the district after all, and I order you now to give me that letter."

The postman answered firmly: "No, I can't do it, Mr. Mayor."

Then Renardet lost his head; he seized him by the arm and tried to snatch his bag; but the man shook himself free and, stepping back, lifted his thick holly stick. He was quite unmoved. "Don't lay a hand on me, Mr. Mayor," he said deliberately, "or I'll lay this across you. Be careful. I intend to do my duty."

Renardet felt that he was lost; suddenly he became humble, soft-voiced, imploring like a tearful child.

"Come, come, my friend, give me that letter, I'll reward you, I'll give you some money, wait, wait, I'll give you a hundred francs—do you hear?—a hundred francs."

The man swung on his heels and began to walk off.

Renardet followed him, panting, babbling.

"Médéric, Médéric, listen, I'll give you a thousand francs—do you hear?—a thousand francs."

The other man held on his way, without a word. Renardet went on: "I'll make your fortune . . . do you hear? I'll give you anything you like. . . . Fifty thousand francs. . . . Fifty thousand francs for that letter. . . . What do you say to that? You don't want it? Well, a hundred thousand francs . . . do you understand? . . . a hundred thousand francs . . . a hundred thousand francs."

The postman turned round, his face hard and his glance unrelenting. "And that'll do, and I'll take care to repeat to the judge all you've been saying to me."

Renardet stopped dead. It was all over. He had no hope left. He turned round and rushed towards the house, running like a hunted animal.

And now Médéric himself stood still and regarded his flight in amazement. He saw the mayor re-enter his house, and he went on waiting in the certain expectation of some astonishing happening.

And before long, indeed, the tall figure of Renardet appeared at the summit of Renard's tower. He ran round the flat parapet like a madman; then he grasped the flagstaff and shook it furiously without managing to break it; then all at once, his hands flung out like a swimmer making a dive, he leaped into space.

Médéric rushed to his help. As he crossed the park, he saw the wood-cutters going to work. He hailed them with shouts of the accident; and at the foot of the walls they found a bleeding body with its head crushed on a rock. The Brindille flowed round the rock, and just here, where its waters widened out, clear and calm, they saw, trickling through the water, a long scarlet thread of blood mixed with brains.

MONSIEUR PARENT

LITTLE GEORGES, ON ALL FOURS ON THE PATH, WAS MAKING sand castles. He shovelled the sand together with both hands, heaped it up into a pyramid, and planted a chestnut leaf on the top.

His father, seated on an iron chair, was watching him with concentrated and loving attention, and had no eyes for anyone else in the small crowded park.

All along the circular path which runs past the lake, encircles the lawn, and comes back again by way of the Church of the Trinity, other children were thus busied, like young animals at their sport, while the bored nursemaids gazed into the air with their dull, stupid eyes, or the mothers talked together, casting incessant, watchful glances on the troop of youngsters.

Nurses walked gravely up and down, two by two, trailing behind them the long bright ribbons of their caps, and carrying in their arms white objects wrapped in lace, while little girls in short dresses which revealed their bare legs held grave conversations between two hoop races, and the keeper of the garden, in a green tunic, wandered through this crowd of children, constantly stepping aside lest he should demolish the earthworks and destroy the ant-like labours of these tiny human larvæ.

The sun was sinking behind the roofs of the Rue Saint-Lazare, and throwing its great, slanting rays upon the myriad-hued crowd of children. The chestnut-trees were lit up with gleams of yellow, and the three cascades in front of the lofty portals of the church looked as though they ran liquid silver.

Monsieur Parent watched his son squatting in the dust;

he followed lovingly his slightest gestures, and seemed to throw kisses from his lips to Georges's every movement.

But raising his eyes to the clock on the steeple, he discovered that he was five minutes slow. Thereupon he rose, took the little boy by the arm, shook his earthy garments, wiped his hands, and led him away towards the Rue Blanche. He hastened his steps, anxious not to reach home later than his wife, and the youngster, who could not keep up with him, trotted along at his side.

His father accordingly took him in his arms and, quickening his pace still more, began to pant with exhaustion as he mounted the sloping pavement. He was a man of forty, already grey, somewhat stout, and he bore uneasily before him the round, jolly paunch of a gay bachelor rendered timid by circumstances.

Some years earlier he had married a young woman whom he had loved tenderly, and who was now treating him with insolence and authority of an all-powerful despot. She was incessantly scolding him for everything he did, and everything he omitted to do, bitterly upbraiding him for his slightest actions, his habits, his simple pleasures, his tastes, his ways, his movements, the rotundity of his figure, and the placid tones of his voice.

He still loved her, however, but he loved yet more the child she had given him, Georges, now three years old, the greatest joy and the most precious burden of his heart. Possessed of a modest income, he lived at home on his twenty thousand francs a year, and his wife, who had had no marriage portion, lived in a state of perpetual fury at her husband's inaction.

At last he reached his house and, setting the child down on the first step of the staircase, wiped his forehead and began to ascend.

At the second story, he rang the bell.

An old servant who had brought him up, one of those servant-mistresses who become family tyrants, came and opened the door.

" Has Madame come in yet ? " he asked in an agony of fear.

The servant shrugged her shoulders.

" When has Monsieur ever known Madame to be in by half-past six ? " she answered.

He replied with some embarrassment :

" That's good, so much the better : it gives me time to change my clothes, for I'm very hot."

The servant stared at him with angry and contemptuous pity.

" Oh, yes, I can see that," she grumbled ; " Monsieur is streaming with perspiration ; Monsieur has been running ; carrying the little one, very likely, and all in order to wait for Madame till half-past seven. As for me, no one will ever persuade me to be ready to time, now. I get dinner for eight o'clock, and if people have to wait, so much the worse for them ; a joint must not be burnt ! "

Monsieur Parent pretended not to listen.

" Very good, very good," he murmured; " Georges's hands must be washed ; he's been making sand castles. I will go and change. Tell the maid to give the little one a thorough cleaning."

And he went to his room. Once there, he thrust home the bolt, so as to be alone, quite alone. He was so accustomed by now to seeing himself bullied and ill-used that he only judged himself safe when under the protection of a lock. He no longer even dared to think, to reflect, or to reason with himself, unless he felt secured against the eyes and imaginations of others, by the turn of a key. He collapsed into a chair in order to get a little rest before putting on a clean shirt, and realised that Julie was beginning to be a new peril in the house. She hated his wife, that was plainly to be seen. Above all, she hated his chum, Paul Limousin, who had continued to be that rare thing, an intimate and familiar friend in the home, after having been the inseparable comrade of his bachelor life. It was Limousin who acted as oil and buffer between Henriette and himself, who even defended him with vigour and sternness against the undeserved reproaches, the painful scenes, all the miseries which made up his daily existence.

For nearly six months now, Julie had been constantly indulging in malicious remarks and criticisms of her mistress. She was perpetually condemning her, declaring twenty times a day: "If I were Monsieur, I wouldn't let myself be led by the nose like that. Well, well . . . there it is . . . every one according to his own nature."

One day she had even insulted Henriette to her face, who had been contented with saying to her husband that night: "You know, the first sharp word I get from that woman, out she goes." She seemed, however, to be afraid of the old servant, though she feared nothing else; and Parent attributed this meekness to her esteem for the nurse who had brought him up and had closed his mother's eyes.

But this was the end; things could not go on any longer, and he was terrified at the thought of what would happen. What was he to do? To dismiss Julie seemed to him a decision so formidable that he dared not let his thoughts dwell upon it. It was equally impossible to admit her right and his wife wrong; and before another month had gone by, the situation between the two of them would become insupportable.

He sat there, his arms hanging down, vaguely searching his mind for a method of complete conciliation, and finding none. "Luckily I have Georges," he murmured. "Without him I should be utterly wretched."

Then the idea came to him of asking Limousin for his advice; he decided to do so, but immediately the remembrance of the enmity between his servant and his friend made him fear that his friend would suggest her dismissal; and he fell once more into an agony of indecision.

The clock struck seven. He started. Seven o'clock, and he had not yet changed his shirt! Scared and panting, he undressed, washed, put on a white shirt, and dressed again hurriedly, as though he were being awaited in the next room on a matter of urgent importance.

Then he went into the drawing-room, happy to feel that he needn't be afraid of anything now.

He glanced at the newspaper, went and looked into the street, and came back and sat down on the sofa; but a door opened and his son came in, washed, his hair combed, and smiling. Parent took him in his arms and kissed him with passionate emotion. He kissed him first on the hair, then on the eyes, then on the cheeks, then on the mouth, and then on the hands. Then he made him jump up in the air, lifting him up to the ceiling, at the full stretch of his arms. Then he sat down again, tired by these exertions, and, taking Georges on his knee, he made him play " ride a-cock-horse."

The child laughed with delight, waved his arms, and uttered shrieks of joy, and his father laughed as well, and shrieked with pleasure, shaking his great paunch, enjoying himself even more than the little boy.

This poor, weak, resigned, bullied man loved the child with all his kind heart. He loved him with wild transports of affection, with violent, unrestrained caresses, with all the shamefaced tenderness hidden in the secret places of his heart that had never been able to come into the light and grow, not even in the first few hours of his married life; for his wife had always been cold and reserved in her bahaviour.

Julie appeared in the doorway, her face pale and her eyes gleaming, and announced, in a voice trembling with exasperation:

" It is half-past seven, Monsieur."

Parent threw an anxious and submissive glance at the clock, and murmured:

" Yes, it certainly is half-past seven."

" Well, dinner's ready now."

Seeing the storm imminent, he tried to dispel it:

"But didn't you tell me, when I came in, that you would not have dinner ready till eight?"

"Eight! . . . Why, you can't be thinking what it means! You don't want to give the child his dinner at eight! One says eight, but, Lord, that's only a manner of speaking. Why, it would ruin the child's stomach to make him eat at eight. Oh, if it were only his mother that was concerned! She takes good care of her child! Oh, yes, talk of mothers, she's a mother, she is! It's downright pitiful to see a mother like that!"

Parent, positively quivering with anguish, felt that he must cut short this threatening scene.

"Julie," he said, "I will not have you speak of your mistress like that. You hear, don't you? Don't forget for the future."

The old servant, breathless with astonishment, turned on her heel and went out, pulling the door to with such violence that all the crystals on the chandelier jingled. For a few seconds a sound like the soft murmurous ringing of little invisible bells fluttered in the silent air of the drawing-room.

Georges, surprised at first, began to clap his hands with pleasure, and, puffing out his cheeks, uttered a loud "Boom" with all the strength of his lungs, in imitation of the noise of the door.

Then his father began to tell him stories; but his mind was so preoccupied that again and again he lost the thread of his narrative, and the child, no longer understanding, opened his eyes wide in amazement.

Parent's eyes never left the clock. He fancied he could see the hand moving. He would have liked to stop the clock, to make time stand still until his wife returned. He did not blame Henriette for being late, but he was afraid, afraid of her and Julie, afraid of everything that might happen. Ten minutes more would suffice to bring about an irreparable catastrophe, revelations, and scenes of violence that he dared not even imagine. The mere thought of the quarrel, the sudden outbursts of voices, the insults rushing through the air like bullets, the two women staring into one another's eyes, hurling bitter remarks at one another, made his heart beat and his mouth feel as dry as if he were walking in the sun ; it made him as limp as a rag, so limp that he lost the strength to lift up the child and make him jump upon his knee.

Eight o'clock struck ; the door reopened and Julie reappeared. She no longer wore her air of exasperation, but an air of cold, malicious resolution that was still more formidable.

" Monsieur," she said, " I served your mother till her last day ; I brought you up from your birth to this very day. I may say that I'm devoted to the family. . . ."

She awaited a reply.

" Why, yes, my good Julie," stammered Parent.

" You know very well," she continued, " that I've never done anything for the sake of money, but always in your interests, that I've never deceived you or lied to you ; that you've never had any fault to find with me. . . ."

" Why, yes, my good Julie."

" Well, Monsieur, this can't go on any longer. It was out of friendship for you that I never spoke, that I left you in your ignorance ; but it is too much ; the neighbourhood is making too merry at your expense. You can do what you like about it, but everybody knows ; and I must tell you too, though it goes sore against the grain. If Madame comes home at these absurd hours, it's because she's doing abominable things."

He sat there bewildered, not understanding. He could only stammer :

" Be silent. . . . You know I forbade you. . . ."

She cut him short with ruthless determination.

" No, Monsieur, I must tell you all now. For a long time now Madame has been deceiving you with Monsieur Limousin. More than twenty times I've caught them kissing behind doors. Oh, don't you see ? If Monsieur Limousin had been rich, it would not have been Monsieur Parent that Madame married.

If Monsieur would only remember how the marriage came about, he would understand the business from beginning to end."

Parent had risen, livid, stammering:

"Be silent. . . . Be silent . . . or . . . ."

"No," she continued, "I will tell you all. Madame married Monsieur for his money; and she has deceived him from the very first day. Why, Lord-a-mercy, it was an understood thing between them; a minute's thought is enough to realise that. Then, as Madame was not pleased at having married Monsieur, whom she did not love, she made his life a burden to him, such a burden that it broke my heart to see it. . . ."

He advanced two steps, his fists clenched, repeating:

"Be silent. . . . Be silent . . ." for he could find no reply.

The old servant did not draw back; she looked ready to go to any lengths.

But Georges, at first bewildered, then frightened by these harsh voices, began to utter shrill cries. He stood there behind his father, and howled, with his mouth wide open and his face puckered up.

Parent was exasperated by his son's uproar; it filled him with courage and rage. He rushed upon Julie with uplifted arms, prepared to smite with both hands, and crying:

"You wretch! You'll turn the child's brain."

His hands were almost on her; she flung the words in his face.

"Monsieur can strike me if he likes, me that brought him up: it won't stop his wife deceiving him, nor her child not being his."

He stopped dead, and let his arms fall to his sides; and stood facing her, so astounded that he no longer understood what she was saying.

"You've only to look at the little one to recognise the father," she added. "Why, Lord-a-mercy, he's the living image of Monsieur Limousin. You've only to look at his eyes and his forehead. Why, a blind man wouldn't be deceived. . . ."

But he had seized her by the shoulders and was shaking her with all his strength, muttering:

"Viper . . . viper! Out of here, viper! . . . Be off, or I'll kill you! . . . Be off! . . . Be off! . . ."

With a desperate effort he flung her into the next room. She fell upon the table set for dinner, and the glasses tumbled and smashed; then she got up again and put the table between herself and her master, and while he pursued her in order to seize her again, spat hideous remarks at him.

"Monsieur has only to go out . . . this evening, after dinner . . . and come back again at once. . . . He will see! . . . he will see if I have lied! . . . Let Monsieur try . . . he will see."

She had reached the door of the kitchen and fled through it. He ran after her, rushed up the backstairs to her bedroom, where she had locked herself in, and, beating on the door, cried out:

"You will leave the house this instant."

"You may be sure I shall," she replied through the panel. "Another hour, and I'll be gone."

At that he slowly descended the stairs again, clinging to the banisters to keep from falling, and went back to the drawing-room where Georges was crying, sitting on the floor.

Parent collapsed into a chair and stared dully at the child. He could not understand anything now; he was no longer conscious of anything; he felt dazed, stupefied, crazy, as though he had just fallen on to his head; he could scarcely remember the horrible things his servant had told him. Then, little by little, his reason, like a turbid pool, grew calm and clear, and the revolting secret he had learned began to turn and twist in his breast.

Julie had spoken so clearly, with such vigour, certainty, and sincerity, that he did not question her good faith, but he persisted in questioning her perspicacity. She might well have been mistaken, blinded by her devotion to him, impelled by an unconscionable hatred of Henriette. But the more he tried to reassure and convince himself, a thousand little facts awakened in his memory, remarks made by his wife, glances of Limousin's, a host of trifles, unnoticed, almost unperceived, departures late at night, simultaneous absences, even gestures, almost insignificant, but strange, movements he had not been able to see or understand, which now assumed vast importance in his eyes, and became evidence of complicity between them. Everything which had occurred since his wedding rose up suddenly in a memory sharpened by pain. It all recurred to him, the strange intonations, the suspicious attitudes. The slow mind of this quiet, kindly man, harassed now with doubt, displayed to him as certainties things which could not as yet be more than suspicions.

With furious pertinacity he rummaged amid the five years of his married life, striving to recall everything, month by month, day by day; and each disturbing fact he discovered pierced his heart like a wasp's sting.

He gave no thought to Georges, who was quiet now, lying on his back on the carpet. But, seeing that no attention was being paid to him, the child began to cry again.

His farther started up, seized him in his arms, and covered his head with kisses. His child, at any rate, remained to him! What did the rest matter? He held him, clasped him, his mouth buried in the fair hair, comforted, consoled, murmuring: "Georges . . . my little Georges, my dear little Georges! . . ." But suddenly he remembered what Julie had said! . . . Yes, she had said that he was Limousin's child. . . . Oh, it was not possible, it couldn't be possible! No, he could not believe it, could not even suspect it for one moment. This was one of the odious infamies that germinate in the mean minds of servants! "Georges," he repeated, "my dear Georges!" The boy was silent again now, under his caresses.

Parent felt the warmth of his little breast penetrate through the clothes to his own. It filled him with love, with courage, with joy; the child's sweet warmth caressed him, strengthened him, saved him.

Then he thrust the beloved head with its curly hair a little further from him, and gazed at it passionately. He stared at it hungrily, desperately; the sight of it intoxicated him.

"Oh, my little one . . . my little Georges!" he repeated over and over again.

Suddenly he thought: "Supposing he were like Limousin . . . all the same!"

The thought was a strange cruel thing entering into him, a poignant, violent sensation of cold through his body, in all his limbs, as though his bones were suddenly turned to ice. Oh, if he were like Limousin! . . . and he continued to gaze at Georges, who was laughing now. He gazed at him with wild, distressed, haggard eyes. And he searched his features, the brow, the nose, the mouth, the cheeks, to see whether he could not find in them something of Limousin's brow, nose, mouth, or cheeks.

His thoughts wandered, like the thoughts of a man going mad; and the face of his child altered beneath his eyes, and took on strange appearances and preposterous resemblances.

Julie had said: "A blind man would not be deceived." There must be something striking, something quite undeniable! But what? The brow? Yes, perhaps. But Limousin's brow was narrower! The mouth, then? But Limousin wore a full beard! How could one establish a resemblance between the child's fat chin and this man's hairy one?

Parent thought: "I cannot see it, I cannot look at it any longer; I am too distressed; I could not recognise anything now. . . . I must wait; I must look properly to-morrow morning, when I get up."

Then he thought: "But if he were like *me*, I should be saved, saved!"

X

He crossed the room in two strides, in order to examine his child's face side by side with his own in the mirror.

He held Georges seated on his arm, in order that their faces might be close together, and spoke out loud, so great was his bewilderment.

" Yes . . . we have the same nose . . . the same nose . . . perhaps . . . I'm not sure . . . and the same eyes. . . . No, his eyes are blue. . . . Then . . . Oh, my God ! . . . my God ! . . . my God ! . . . I'm going mad. . . . I will not look any more. . . . I'm going mad ! "

He fled from the mirror to the other end of the room, fell into an arm-chair, set the child down in another, and burst into tears. He wept with great, hopeless sobs. Georges, frightened by the sound of his father's moans, began to cry too.

The front-door bell rang. Parent bounded up as though pierced by a bullet.

" There she is," he said. " What am I to do ? "

He ran and shut himself up in his room, so as to have time at least to wipe his eyes. But after some moments, another peal at the bell gave him a second shock ; then he remembered that Julie had left and that the housemaid had not been told. So no one would go and open the door ? What was to be done ? He went himself.

Suddenly he felt brave, resolute, able to play his own part and face the inevitable scene. The appalling shock had matured him in a few moments. And, besides, he wanted to know, he wanted the truth with the fury of a timid man, with the obstinacy of an easy-going man come to the end of his patience.

Nevertheless, he was trembling. Was it with terror ? Yes. . . . Perhaps he was still afraid of her ? Who knows how much goaded cowardice has gone to the making of a bold move ?

He stopped behind the door that he had reached with furtive steps, and listened. His heart was beating furiously, and he could hear nothing but the sound of it, great dull blows in his chest, and the shrill voice of Georges still crying in the drawing-room.

Suddenly the noise of the bell ringing over his head shook him like an explosion ; at that he seized the door-handle and, panting, fainting, turned the knob and opened the door.

His wife and Limousin were standing facing him, on the staircase.

" So you are opening the door, now," she said with an air of astonishment in which a trace of irritation was apparent ; " then where is Julie ? "

His throat was contracted and his breathing hurried ; he strove to answer, unable to utter a word.

" Have you gone dumb ? " she continued. " I asked you where Julie was."

At that he stammered :

" She . . . she . . . she has gone."

His wife was beginning to be angry.

" What, gone ? Where ? Why ? "

He was gradually regaining his balance, and felt stirring in him a mordant hatred of this insolent woman standing before him.

" Yes, gone for good. . . . I dismissed her."

" You have dismissed her ? . . . Julie ? . . . You must be mad. . . ."

" Yes, I dismissed her because she was insolent . . . and because she . . . because she ill-treated the child."

" Julie ? "

" Yes. . . . Julie."

" What was she insolent about ? "

" About you."

" About me ? "

" Yes . . . because dinner was burnt and you had not come in."

" She said . . . ? "

" She said . . . offensive things about you . . . which I should not . . . which I could not listen to. . . ."

" What things ? "

" It is of no use to repeat them."

" I want to know."

" She said that it was very sad for a man like me to marry a woman like you, unpunctual, with no sense of order, careless, a bad housekeeper, a bad mother, and a bad wife. . . ."

The young woman had entered the hall, followed by Limousin, who remained silent before this unexpected situation. She shut the door abruptly, threw down her coat on a chair, and walked up to her husband, stammering in exasperation:

" You say . . . you say . . . that I'm . . . ?"

He was very pale, very calm.

" I say nothing, my dear," he replied ; " I am only telling you what Julie said, because you wanted to know ; and I want you to realise that it was precisely on account of these remarks that I dismissed her."

She trembled with her violent desire to tear out his beard and rend his cheeks with her nails. She felt his revulsion from her in his voice, in his expression, in his manner, and she could not outface it ; she strove to regain the offensive by some direct and wounding phrase.

" Have you had dinner ? " she asked.

" No, I waited."

She shrugged her shoulders impatiently.

" It is stupid to wait after half-past seven. You ought to have known that I was detained, that I was busy, engaged."

Then, suddenly, she felt the need to explain how she had passed the time, and related, in short, haughty words, that, having been obliged to get some articles of furniture a long way off, a very long way, in the Rue de Rennes, she had met Limousin, after seven o'clock, in the Boulevard Saint-Germain, on her way home, and had asked him to come in with her and have something to eat in a restaurant which she did not like to enter by herself, although she was faint with hunger. That was how she came to have dinner with Limousin, if it could be called a dinner, for they had only had soup and half a chicken, they were in such haste to get home.

"But you were quite right," replied Parent simply; "I was not blaming you."

Then Limousin who had remained silent hitherto, almost hidden behind Henriette, came up and offered his hand, murmuring:

"You are well?"

"Yes, quite well," replied Parent, taking the outstretched hand and shaking it limply.

But the young woman had seized upon a word in her husband's last sentence.

"Blame . . . why do you say 'blame'? One might think you meant. . . ."

"No, not at all," he said, excusing himself. "I simply meant to say that I was not at all uneasy at your lateness and was not trying to make a crime of it."

She took it haughtily, seeking a pretext for a quarrel:

"My lateness? . . . Anyone would think it was one o'clock in the morning and I had been out all night."

"No, my dear, I said 'lateness' because I had no other word. You were due home by half-past six, and you come in at half-past eight. That is being late! I quite understand; I . . . I'm not . . . not even surprised. . . . But . . . but . . . it is difficult for me to use any other word."

"But you pronounce it as though I had slept away from home."

"No . . . not at all."

She saw that he meant to go on yielding the point and was about to enter her room when at last she noticed that Georges was crying.

"What is the matter with the child?" she asked, with a troubled look on her face.

"I told you that Julie had been rather rough with him."

"What has the creature been doing to him?"

" Oh, hardly anything ! She pushed him and he fell."

She was eager to see her child, and rushed into the dining-room ; then stopped dead at sight of the table covered with spilt wine, broken bottles and glasses, and overturned salt-cellars.

" What is the meaning of this scene of destruction ? "

" Julie. . . ."

But she cut short his utterance in a rage :

" This is too much, the last straw ! Julie treats me as though I were a dissolute woman, beats my child, breaks my crockery, and turns my house upside down, and you seem to think it perfectly natural."

" No, I don't. . . . I dismissed her."

" Really ! . . . You actually dismissed her ! Why, you ought to have put her in charge. The police are the people to go to on these occasions ! "

" But, my dear," he stammered, " I . . . couldn't very well . . . there was no reason. . . . It was really very awkward."

She shrugged her shoulders in infinite contempt.

" Ah, well, you'll never be anything but a limp rag, a poor, miserable creature with no will of your own, no energy, no firmness. Your precious Julie must have been pretty outrageous for you to have made up your mind to get rid of her. How I wish I could have been there for a minute, just a single minute ! "

She had opened the drawing-room door, and ran to Georges, lifted him up, and clasped him in her arms, kissing him and murmuring : " Georgy, what's the matter, my lamb, my little love, my duck ? "

He stopped crying, at his mother's caresses.

" What's the matter ? " she repeated.

The frightened eyes of the child perceived that there was trouble.

" It was Zulie, who beat daddy," he replied.

Henriette turned to her husband, bewildered at first. Then

a wild desire to laugh woke in her eyes, quivered on her thin cheeks, curled her lip, curled the outer edges of her nostrils, and finally issued from her mouth in a clear bubbling rush of merriment, a cascade of gaiety, as melodious and lively as the trill of a bird.

"Ha! Ha! Ha!" she repeated, with little malicious cries that escaped between her white teeth and inflicted a biting agony on Parent. "She b . . . b . . . beat you. . . . Ha! Ha! Ha! Ha! . . . How funny! . . . how funny! . . . Do you hear, Limousin? Julie beat him . . . beat him . . . Julie beat my husband. . . . Ha! . . . Ha! . . . Ha! . . . How funny!"

"No! No!" stammered Parent. "It's not true . . . it's not true. . . . It was I, on the contrary, who flung her into the dining-room, so hard that she knocked the table over. The child couldn't see. It was I who beat her."

"Tell me again, ducky," said Henriette to her son. "It was Julie who beat Papa?"

"Yes, it was Zulie," he replied.

Then, passing suddenly to another thought, she went on:

"But hasn't the child had his dinner? Haven't you had anything to eat, darling?"

"No, mummy."

At that she turned furiously upon her husband.

"You're mad, absolutely crazy! It's half-past eight and Georges has not had his dinner!"

He made excuses, hopelessly lost in the scene and his explanation, crushed at the utter ruin of his life.

"But we were waiting for you, my dear. I did not want to have dinner without you. You always come in late, so I thought you would come in any moment."

She threw her hat, which she had kept on until this point, into an arm-chair and broke out in a tone of exasperation:

"Really, it's intolerable to have to deal with people who can't understand anything or guess anything or do anything for themselves. If I had come home at midnight, I suppose the child would not have had anything to eat at all. As if you could not have understood, when it was half-past seven, that I'd been hindered, delayed, held up! . . ."

Parent was trembling, feeling his anger getting the upper hand; but Limousin intervened, and, turning to the young woman, remarked:

"You are quite unjust, dear. Parent could not guess that you would be so late, for you never have been; and, besides, how could he manage everything by himself, after dismissing Julie?"

But Henriette had thoroughly lost her temper, and replied:

"Well, he'll have to manage somehow, for I won't help him. Let him get out of the mess as best he can!"

And she ran into her room, having already forgotten that her son had had nothing to eat.

Limousin became suddenly strenuous in aiding his friend. He gathered up and removed the broken glass with which the table was covered, put the knives and forks back, and settled the child in his little high chair, while Parent went in search of the housemaid and told her to serve dinner.

She arrived in some surprise; she had been working in Georges's room and had heard nothing.

She brought in the soup, an overcooked leg of mutton, and mashed potatoes.

Parent had sat down beside his child, his brain in a whirl, his reason undermined by the catastrophe. He gave the little boy his food, and tried to eat himself; he cut up the meat, chewed it, and swallowed it with an effort, as though his throat were paralysed.

Then, little by little, there awoke in his soul a wild longing to look at Limousin, who was sitting opposite him, rolling little pills of bread. He wanted to see if he were like Georges. But he dared not raise his eyes. He made up his mind, however, and looked abruptly up at the face he knew so well, although it seemed to him that he had never studied it, so much did it differ from his imagination of it. Time and again he cast a swift glance over the man's face, trying to recognise the faintest lines and features and their significance; then, instantly, he would look at his son, pretending that he was merely giving him his food.

Two words roared in his ears: "His father! His father! His father!" They hummed in his temples with every beat of his heart. Yes, that man, that man sitting calmly on the other side of the table, was perhaps the father of his son, Georges, his little Georges. Parent stopped eating; he could eat no longer. A frightful pain, the sort of pain that makes a man cry out, roll on the ground, and bite the furniture, tore at the very depths of his body. He longed to take his knife and plunge it into his belly. It would be a relief, it would save him; all would be over.

For how could he go on living now? How could he live, get up in the morning, eat his meals, walk along the streets, go to bed in the evening, and sleep at night, with this thought drilled into him, as with a gimlet: "Limousin, Georges's father?" No, he would no longer have strength to walk one step, put on his clothes, think of anything, speak to anyone! Every day, every hour, every second, he would be asking himself that question, seeking to know, to guess, to surprise the horrible secret. And the child, his dear child—he could no longer see him without enduring the fearful agony of this uncertainty, without feeling himself torn to the bowels, tortured to the marrow of his bones. He would have to go on living here, stay in this house, side by side with the child he would love and hate. Yes, assuredly he would end by hating him. What torment! Oh, if only he were certain that Limousin was the father, perhaps he might succeed in growing calm, in falling asleep amid his misery, his grief! But not to know was intolerable!

Not to know, always to be trying to find out, always suffering, and every moment embracing the child, another man's child, taking him for walks in the town, carrying him in his arms, feeling the caress of his soft hair against his lips, adoring him, and endlessly thinking: " Perhaps he is not mine? " Would it not be better to see no more of him, to abandon him, lose him in the streets, or flee far away, so far that he would never again hear anyone speak of anything?

He started, as the door opened. His wife came in.

" I'm hungry," she said: " are you, Limousin? "

" Yes, by Jove, I am," replied Limousin with some hesitation.

She had the mutton brought back.

" Have they had dinner," Parent wondered, " or were they late because they've been love-making? "

Both were now eating with an excellent appetite. Henriette, quite calm, was laughing and joking. Her husband kept her under observation too, looking quickly at her and as quickly away again. She wore a pink tea-gown trimmed with white lace, and her fair hair, her white neck, and her plump hands emerged from the pretty, dainty, scented gown as from a sea-shell edged with foam. What had she been doing all day long with that man? Parent saw them kissing, murmuring passionate words. How was it possible for him not to know, not to guess, seeing them thus side by side, facing him?

How they must be mocking at him, if he had been their dupe since the very first day! Was it possible that a man, a good man, should be thus tricked, merely because his father left him a little money? Why were such things not visible in the sinners' souls, how was it possible that nothing revealed the deceit of the wicked to the upright heart, that the same voice should lie and adore, and the sly eyes of deceit look the same as the eyes of truth?

He watched them, waiting for a gesture, a word, an intonation. Suddenly he thought: " I will surprise them this evening."

" My dear," he said, " as I have just dismissed Julie, I must start to-night to try and find another servant. I'm going out directly, so as to get someone for to-morrow morning. I may be back rather late."

" Very well, go," she replied, " I shan't move from here. Limousin will keep me company. We will wait for you." And, turning to the housemaid, she added:

" Put Georges to bed, then you can clear the table and go to bed yourself."

Parent had risen. He was swaying upon his legs, dazed, tottering. " See you again presently," he murmured, and reached the door by dint of leaning against the wall, for the floor was heaving like a ship.

Georges had gone off in the arms of the maid. Henriette and Limousin passed into the drawing-room.

" Are you mad," he said, as soon as the door was shut, " that you bully your husband so? "

She turned to him.

" You know, I'm beginning to find your long established habit of setting up Parent as a martyr rather trying."

Limousin sat down in an arm-chair and, crossing his legs, replied:

" I'm not setting him up as a martyr in the least, but I do think that, as things are, it's preposterous to defy the man from morning to night."

She took a cigarette from the mantelpiece, lit it, and answered:

" But I don't defy him—on the contrary; only he irritates me by his stupidity . . . and I treat him as he deserves."

" What you are doing is extraordinarily silly," replied Limousin impatiently, " but all women are alike. Here you have an excellent fellow, too good, idiotic in his faith and goodness, who in no way annoys us, does not for one instant suspect us, and leaves us as free and easy as we could wish; and you do all that you can to make him lose his temper and ruin our lives."

"You disgust me," she said, turning towards him. "You're a coward, like all men! You're afraid of the fool!"

He sprang up, and burst out furiously:

"If it comes to that, I should very much like to know how he has treated you, and what possible grudge you can have against him! Does he make you unhappy? Does he beat you? Does he deceive you? No, it really is too much to make that poor chap suffer just because he's too kind, and have a grudge against him simply because you are deceiving him."

She went up to Limousin and, staring into his eyes, answered:

"And it is you who blame me for deceiving him—you, you? Must you be utterly beastly too?"

He defended himself, rather shamefacedly.

"But I don't blame you at all, my dear, I only ask you to treat your husband with a little consideration, because we both of us need his trust. I thought you would realise that."

They were standing close to one another; he, tall and dark, with drooping whiskers, and the rather vulgar carriage of a good-looking fellow who is very pleased with himself; she, dainty, pink and fair, a little Parisian, half *cocotte* and half suburban young woman, born in the back room of a shop, brought up to stand on its door-step and entice customers with her glances, and married off, by the happy chance of this accomplishment, to the innocent passer-by who fell in love with her because he saw her standing there at the door every day as he went in the morning and came home in the evening.

"But, you great booby," she said, "you don't understand that I hate him just because he married me, because he bought me, in fact; because everything that he says, everything that he does, everything that he thinks, gets on my nerves. Every instant he exasperates me by the stupidity you call his kindness, by the dullness you call his trust, and, above all, because he is my husband, instead of you. Although he hardly troubles us, I feel him between us. And then? . . . And then? . . . No, he really is too big a fool to suspect anything. I wish he were at least a little jealous; there are moments when I long to shout at him: 'Can't you see anything, you ass? Don't you realise that Paul is my lover?'"

Limousin burst out laughing.

"In the meantime you would do better to keep your mouth shut, and leave our existence untroubled."

"Oh, I won't trouble it. There is nothing to fear from that imbecile. But it really is incredible that you should not realise how hateful he is to me, how he grates on my nerves. You always seem to love him, to shake hands frankly with him. Men are extraordinary creatures at times."

"One must know how to dissemble, my dear."

"It's not a question of dissimulation, dear, but of feeling. When you men deceive another man, anyone would think you immediately began to like him better; we women hate him from the very moment that we have deceived him."

"I don't in the least see why a man should hate a good sort of fellow whose wife he's taking."

"You don't see? . . . you don't see? All you men are lacking in decent feeling. Well, it's one of those things one feels and cannot express. And, anyhow, I oughtn't to try. . . . No, it's no use, you wouldn't understand. You've no intuition, you men."

She smiled, the gay, malicious smile of a wanton, and set her hands upon his shoulders, holding up her lips to his; he bowed his head to hers as he caught her in his arms, and their lips met. And as they were standing in front of the mirror on the mantelpiece, another couple exactly like them embraced behind the clock.

They had heard nothing, neither the sound of the key nor the creaking of the door; but suddenly Henriette uttered a shrill scream and thrust Limousin away with both arms; and they saw Parent watching them, livid, with clenched fists, his shoes off, and his hat over his brow.

He looked at them, first at one and then at the other, with a quick movement of the eyes, without turning his head. He seemed mad ; without uttering a word he rushed at Limousin, took him in his arms as though to crush the breath out of him, and flung him into the corner of the drawing-room with such a furious onslaught that the other, losing his footing and clawing the air with his hands, struck his head roughly against the wall.

But when Henriette realised that her husband was going to murder her lover, she threw herself on Parent and seized him by the throat. With demented strength she sent her thin pink fingers into his flesh, and squeezed so tightly that the blood spurted from beneath her nails. She bit his shoulder as though she wanted to rend it to pieces with her teeth. Parent, choked and stifling, let go of Limousin, in order to shake off the woman clinging to his throat ; putting his arms round her waist he hurled her with one mad effort to the other end of the room.

Then, with the short-lived rage of the easy-going and the quickly spent strength of the weak, he remained standing between the two of them, panting, exhausted, not knowing what he ought to do. His brutal fury had escaped in his effort like the froth of an uncorked bottle, and his unwonted energy ended in mere gasping for breath.

" Get out ! " he stammered, as soon as he could speak. " Get out, both of you, at once ! "

Limousin remained motionless in his corner, huddled against the wall, too bewildered to understand anything as yet, too frightened to move a finger. Henriette, her hands resting on a table, her head thrust forward, her hair dishevelled, and her dress torn so that her bosom was bared, was waiting, like an animal about to spring.

" Get out at once ! " repeated Parent more loudly. " Get out ! "

Seeing that his first fury was calmed, his wife plucked up courage, stood up, took two paces towards him, and said, in a voice already almost insolent :

"Have you lost your wits? . . . What's the matter with you? . . . Why this unjustifiable assault?"

He turned on her, raising his fist as though to strike her down.

"Oh! . . . Oh!" he faltered. "This is too much . . . too much! I . . . I . . . I heard all . . . all . . . do you understand? . . . all! You vile creature! . . . you vile creature! . . . You are both vile! . . . Get out! . . . both of you! . . . At once! . . . I could kill you! . . . Get out!"

She realised that it was all over, that he knew, that she could no longer play the innocent, but must give way. But all her impudence had come back to her, and her hatred for the man, doubled now, urged her to boldness, and woke in her an impulse to defiance and bravado.

"Come, Limousin," she said in a clear voice, "since I am to be turned out, I will go home with you."

But Limousin did not move. Parent, attacked by a fresh access of rage, cried:

"Clear out, then! . . . Get out, you vile creatures . . . or else . . . or else! . . ."

He snatched up a chair and whirled it above his head.

Henriette rapidly crossed the drawing-room, took her lover by the arm, dragged him away from the wall, to which he appeared to be fixed, and led him to the door, repeating:

"Come along, dear, come along. . . . You can see that the man is mad . . . come along!"

In the doorway she turned to her husband, trying to think what she could do, what she could imagine, that would wound him to the heart, as she left the house. And an idea came to her, one of those venomous, deadly ideas in which the sum of feminine treachery ferments.

"I want to take my child away," she said firmly.

"Your . . . your child?" stammered Parent in bewilderment. "You dare to speak of your child . . . after . . . after . . . Oh! oh! oh! it is too much! . . . You dare? . . . Clear out, you scum! Clear out!"

She went up to him, almost smiling, almost revenged already, and defied him at close quarters, face to face.

"I want my child . . . and you have no right to keep him, because he's not yours. . . . Do you hear? . . . He's not yours. . . . He's Limousin's."

"You're lying, wretch, you're lying!" cried Parent desperately.

"You idiot," she replied, "every one knows it except you. I tell you that that man there is his father. You've only to look to see. . . ."

Parent recoiled before her, tottering. Then suddenly he turned round, snatched up a candle, and dashed into the next room.

He came back almost immediately, carrying little Georges wrapped in his bed-clothes. The child, awakened with a start, was crying with terror. Parent flung him into his wife's hands and, without adding a word, thrust her roughly out on to the staircase where Limousin was prudently awaiting her.

Then he shut and double-locked the door and thrust home the bolts. He had scarcely regained the drawing-room when he fell full length upon the floor.

II

Parent lived alone, entirely alone. During the first few weeks following his separation, the strangeness of his new life prevented him from thinking much. He had resumed his bachelor life, his loafing habits, and had his meals at a restaurant, as in the old days. Anxious to avoid scandal, he made his wife an allowance regulated by their lawyers. But, little by little, the remembrance of the child began to haunt his thoughts. Often, when he was alone at home in the evenings, he would imagine that he suddenly heard Georges cry "Daddy." In a moment his heart would begin to beat and he would promptly rise and open the front door, to see if by any chance the little boy had returned. Yes, he might have come home again as dogs and pigeons do. Why should a child have less natural instinct than an animal?

Then, realising his error, he would return and sit down in his arm-chair and think of the child. He thought of him for whole hours, whole days. It was no mere mental obsession, but a yet stranger physical obsession as well, a need of the senses and the nerves to embrace him, hold him, feel him, take him on his knee and dandle him. He grew frantic at the feverish remembrance of past caresses. He felt the little arms clasping his neck, the little mouth pressing a great kiss on his beard, the little hair tickling his cheek. The longing for these sweet, vanished endearments, for the delicate, warm, dainty skin held to his lips, maddened him like the desire for a woman beloved and departed.

He would suddenly burst into tears in the street as he thought that he might have had fat little Georgy trotting along beside him on his little legs, as in the old days when he took him for walks. Then he would go home and sob till evening, his head between his hands.

Twenty times, a hundred times a day, he asked himself this question: "Was he, or was he not, Georges's father?" But it was chiefly at night that he gave himself up to interminable speculation on this subject. As soon as he was in bed, he began, every evening, the same series of desperate arguments.

After his wife's departure he had at first had no doubts: the child was assuredly Limousin's. Then, little by little, he began to hesitate again. Henriette's statement certainly had no value. She had defied him in an attempt to make him desperate. When he came coolly to weigh the pros and the cons, there was many a chance that she was lying.

Limousin alone, perhaps, could have told the truth. But how was he to know it, to question him, to get him to confess?

Sometimes Parent would get up in the middle of the night,

resolved to go and find Limousin, to beseech him, to offer him anything he wanted, if he would only put an end to his abominable anguish. Then he would return hopelessly to bed, reflecting that doubtless the lover would lie too! It was positively certain that he would lie in order to hinder the real father from taking back his child.

Then what was he to do? Nothing!

He was heart-broken that he had precipitated events like this, that he had not reflected or been more patient, had not had the sense to wait and dissemble for a month or two, until his own eyes might have informed him. He ought to have pretended to have no suspicions, and have left them calmly to betray themselves. It would have been enough for him to have seen the other man kiss the child to guess, to understand. A friend's kiss is not the same as a father's. He could have spied on them from behind doors. Why had he not thought of it? If Limousin, left alone with Georges, had not promptly seized him, clasped him in his arms, and kissed him passionately, if he had left him to play without taking any interest in him, no hesitation would have been possible; it would have meant that he was not the father, did not believe himself or feel himself to be the father.

With the result that Parent could have turned out the mother and kept his son, and he would have been happy, perfectly happy.

He would go back to bed, perspiring and tormented, ransacking his memory for Limousin's behaviour with the child. But he could remember nothing, absolutely nothing, no gesture, no glance, no word, no suspicious caress. Nor did the mother take any notice of her child. If he had been the fruit of her lover, doubtless she would have loved him more.

He had been separated from his son, then, out of revenge, out of cruelty, to punish him for having surprised them.

He would make up his mind to go at dawn and ask the magistrate to give him the right to claim Georgy.

But he had scarcely formed this resolve when he would feel himself overcome by a certainty of the contrary. From the moment that Limousin had been Henriette's lover, her beloved lover from the first day, she must have given herself to him with the passionate, ardent abandon that makes a woman a mother. And was not the cold reserve which she had always brought to her intimate relations with himself an obstacle against the likelihood of his having given her a child?

So he was about to claim, take home, and perpetually cherish another man's child? He could never look at him, kiss him, hear him say "daddy" without being struck and torn by the thought: "He is not my son at all." He was about to condemn himself for all time to this torture, this miserable existence! No, better to dwell alone, live alone, grow old alone, and die alone!

Every day and every night saw the renewal of these abominable uncertainties and sufferings that nothing could assuage or end. Above all he dreaded the darkness of the falling dusk, the melancholy of twilight. It was then that there fell upon his heart with the darkness a shower of grief, a flood of despair drowning him, maddening him. He was afraid of his thoughts, as a man fears criminals, and he fled before them like a hunted animal. Above all he dreaded his empty dwelling, so dark and dreadful, and the streets, also deserted, where here and there a gas-lamp glimmers, and the lonely passer-by heard in the distance is like a prowling marauder and your pace quickens or slackens as he follows you or comes towards you.

In spite of himself, Parent instinctively sought out the main streets, well lighted and populous. The lights and the crowds attracted him, occupied his mind and dulled his senses. When he was weary of wandering idly through the throng, when the passers-by became fewer and the pavements emptier, the terrors of solitude and silence drove him to some large café full of customers and glare. He would rush to it like a moth to the flame, sit down at a little round table, and order a bock. He would drink it slowly, disturbed in mind by every customer who rose to leave. He would have liked to take him by the arm, to hold him back, to beg him to stay a little longer, so afraid was he of the moment when the waiter would stand in front of him and remark with a wrathful air : " Closing-time, Monsieur."

For, every evening, he was the last to go. He saw the tables carried inside, and, one by one, the gas-jets turned down, all except two, his own and the one at the counter. Miserably he would watch the cashier count the money and lock it up in the drawer ; and he would depart, thrust out by the staff, who would mutter : " There's a limpet for you ; anyone might think he had nowhere to sleep."

And as soon as he found himself in the street once more, he would begin to think of little Georges again, ransacking his tortured brain to discover whether he was or was not the father of his child.

In this way he caught the beer-house habit ; there the perpetual jostling of the drinkers keeps you familiar but silent company, and the heavy smoke of the pipes quiets uneasy thoughts, while the heavy beer dulls the mind and calms the heart.

He lived in these places. As soon as he got up, he went off thither to find neighbours to distract his eyes and his thoughts. Then, out of laziness, he soon took to having his meals there. At about midday he would rap his saucer on the marble table, and the waiter would speedily bring a plate, a glass, a napkin, and that day's lunch. As soon as he had finished eating, he would slowly drink his coffee, his eyes fixed on the decanter of brandy which would soon give him an hour of blessed sottishness. First of all he would moisten his lips with the brandy, as though to take the taste of it, merely culling the flavour of the liquor with the tip of his tongue. Then he would pour it into his mouth, drop by drop, letting his head fall back ; he would let the strong liquor run slowly over his palate, over his gums, over the membrane of his cheeks, mingling it with the clear saliva which flowed freely at its contact. Then, refreshed by the mixture, he swallowed it unctuously, feeling it run all the way down his throat to the pit of his stomach.

After every meal he would spend more than an hour in sipping thus three or four glasses, which numbed his brain little by little. Then he would sink his head on to his chest, close his eyes, and doze. He would wake up in the middle of the afternoon and promptly reach for the bock which the waiter had set before him while he was asleep ; then, having drunk it, he would sit up straight on the red velvet seat, pull up his trousers and pull down his waistcoat so as to cover up the white line which had appeared between them, shake his coat collar, pull down his cuffs, and then would take up the papers he had already read in the morning. He went through them again from the first line to the last, including the advertisements, the "situations wanted" column, the personal column, the stock exchange news and the theatre programmes.

Between four and six he would go for a walk along the boulevards, to take the air, as he used to say ; then he would come back to the seat which had been kept for him and order his absinthe.

Then he would chat with the regular customers whose acquaintance he had made. They would comment on the topics of the day, the news items and the political events ; this led up to dinner. The evening passed like the afternoon, until closing-time. This was for him the terrible moment when he had to go home in the dark to his empty room, full of terrible memories, horrible thoughts and agonising griefs. He no longer saw any of his old friends, any of his relations, anyone who might remind him of his past life.

But as his lodgings became a hell to him, he took a room in a big hotel, a large room on the ground floor, so that he could see the passers-by. He was no longer alone in this vast public dwelling-place ; he felt people swarming round him ; he heard voices behind the partitions; and when his old grief harassed him too cruelly, between his bed with the sheet drawn back and his lonely fireside, he would go out into the broad passages and walk up and down like a sentry, past all the closed doors, looking sadly at the pairs of boots in couples before each of them, the dainty boots of the women squatting beside the strong ones of the men; and he would reflect that all these people were happy, no doubt, and sleeping lovingly, side by side or in each other's arms, in the warmth of their beds.

Five years went by in this fashion, five mournful years with no events but an occasional two hours of bought love.

One day, as he was going for his customary walk between the Madeleine and the Rue Drouot, he suddenly noticed a woman whose bearing struck him. A tall man and a child were with her. All three were walking in front of him. "Where have I seen those people?" he wondered, and all of a sudden he recognised a gesture of the hand: it was his wife, his wife with Limousin and with his child, his little Georges.

His heart beat so that he was almost stifled, but he did not stop; he wanted to see them, and he followed them. Anyone would have said that they were a family party, a decent family of decent middle-class people. Henriette was leaning on Paul's arm, talking softly to him and occasionally looking at him from beside him. At these times Parent saw her profile, and recognised the graceful line of her face, the movements of her mouth, her smile, and the caress of her eyes. The child in particular drew his attention. How big he was and strong! Parent could not see his face, but only the long fair hair which fell upon his neck in curling locks. It was Georges, this tall bare-legged boy walking like a little man beside his mother.

As they stopped in front of a shop, he suddenly saw all three. Limousin had gone grey, older, and thinner; his wife, on the contrary, was younger than ever, and had put on flesh; Georges had become unrecognisable, so different from the old days!

They set off again. Parent followed them once more, then hurried past them in order to turn back and see their faces at close quarters. When he passed the child, he felt a longing, a mad longing to seize him in his arms and carry him off. He touched him, as though by chance. The child turned his head and looked angrily at this clumsy fellow. At that Parent fled, struck, pursued, wounded by his glance. He fled like a thief, overcome by the horrible fear that he had been seen and recognised by his wife and her lover. He raced to his beer-house and fell panting into his chair.

That evening he drank three absinthes.

For four months he bore the scar of that meeting on his heart. Every night he saw them all again, happy and care-free, father, mother, and child, walking along the boulevard before going home to dinner. This new vision effaced the old one. It was a new thing, a new hallucination, and a new grief, too. Little Georges, his little Georges, whom he had loved so well and kissed so much in the old days, was vanishing into a distant and ended past, and he saw a new Georges, like a brother of the old one, a little boy with bare calves, who did not know him! He suffered terribly from this thought. The child's love was dead; there was no longer any bond between them; the child had not stretched out his arms at sight of him. He had given him an angry look.

Then little by little his soul grew calm again; his mental torments grew less keen; the image which appeared before his eyes and haunted his nights became vague, rarer. He began to live more like the rest of the world, like all the men of leisure who drink their bocks at marble-topped tables and wear out the seats of their trousers on the thread-bare velvet seats.

He grew old amid the pipe-smoke, and bald in the gas-light, made quite an event of his weekly bath, his fortnightly hair-cut, the purchase of new clothes or a new hat. When he arrived at the beer-house wearing a new hat, he would contemplate himself in the mirror for a long time before sitting down, would take it off and put it on several times in succession, would set it at different angles, and would finally ask his friend, the lady at the counter, who was looking at it with interest: "Do you think it suits me?"

Two or three times a year he would go to the theatre; and, in the summer, he would sometimes spend the evening at an open-air concert in the Champs-Élysées. He carried the tunes in his head; they sang in the depths of his memory for weeks; he would even hum them, beating time with his foot, as he sat at his bock.

The years followed one another, slow and monotonous, and short because they were empty.

He did not feel them slipping over his head. He advanced towards death without stirring, without exciting himself, sitting at a beer-house table; only the great mirror against which he leaned a head that every day was a little balder, witnessed to the ravages of time, who runs swift-footed, devouring man, poor man.

By this time he seldom thought of the terrible drama in which his life had been wrecked, for twenty years had gone by since that ghastly evening.

But the life he had fashioned for himself ever since had worn him out, enervated him, exhausted him; often the proprietor of the beer-house, the sixth proprietor since his first coming to the place, would say to him: "You need shaking up a bit, Monsieur Parent; you ought to get fresh air, go to the country; I assure you you've changed a great deal in the last few months."

And as his client left, the man would pass on his reflections to the cashier: "Poor Monsieur Parent is in a bad way; staying in Paris all the time is doing him no good. Get him to go out into the country and have a fish dinner from time to time; he thinks a lot of your opinion. Summer's coming soon; it'll put some life into him."

And the cashier, full of pity and kindly feeling for the

obstinate customer, would every day repeat to Parent: "Now, Monsieur, make up your mind to get into the open air. It's so lovely in the country when the weather's fine! If I only could, I'd spend all my life there, I would."

And she would tell him her dreams, the simple and poetical dreams of all the poor girls who are shut up from one year's end to another behind the windows of a shop, and watch the glittering, noisy stream of life go by in the street outside, and dream of the calm, sweet life of the fields, of life under the trees, under the radiant sun falling upon the meadows, the deep woods, the clear rivers, the cows lying in the grass, and all the various flowers, all the wild, free blossoms, blue, red, yellow, violet, lilac, pink, and white, so charming, so fresh, so sweet-scented, all the flowers of Nature waiting there to be picked by the passer-by and heaped into huge bunches.

She found pleasure in talking to him always of her perpetual longing, unrealised and unrealisable; and he, poor hopeless wretch, found pleasure in listening to her. He came and sat now beside the counter, so as to talk to Mademoiselle Zoé and discuss the country with her. Little by little a vague desire came over him to go and see, just once, whether it really was as nice as she said it was, outside the walls of the great city.

One morning he asked her:

"Do you know any place in the suburbs where one can get a good lunch?"

"Yes," she replied; "go to La Terrasse at Saint-Germain. It's so pretty."

He had been there long ago, when he was engaged to Henriette. He decided to go again.

He chose a Sunday, for no particular reason, but merely because the usual thing is to go off for the day on a Sunday, even when the whole week is unoccupied.

So one Sunday morning he went off to Saint-Germain.

It was early in July, a hot, sunny day. Sitting in the corner of the railway carriage, he watched the passing of the trees and the strange little houses on the outskirts of Paris. He felt sad, annoyed with himself for having yielded to this new desire and broken his habits. The landscape, changing, yet always the same, wearied him. He was thirsty ; he would gladly have got off at every station in order to sit down in the café that he saw outside, drink a bock or two, and take the next train back to Paris. And the journey seemed to him to be long, very long. He used to spend whole days sitting still with the same motionless objects before his eyes, but he found it enervating and wearisome to remain seated while moving about, to watch the country moving while he himself did not stir.

He took some interest in the Seine, nevertheless, whenever they crossed it. Under the bridge at Chatou he saw skiffs darting along at the powerful strokes of bare-armed oarsmen, and thought : " Those chaps must be having a good time."

The long ribbon of river that unrolls from both sides of the bridge of Pecq aroused a vague desire in the depths of his heart to walk along the banks. But the train plunged into the tunnel which precedes Saint-Germain Station and soon stopped at the arrival platform.

Parent got out and, weighed down by fatigue, went off in the direction of La Terrasse, his hands behind his back. Having reached the iron railing, he stopped to look at the view. The vast plain was spread out before him, boundless as the sea, a green expanse dotted with large villages as populous as towns. White roads ran across this wide country, patches of forest wooded it in various places, the pools of the Vésinet gleamed like silver medals, and the distant slopes of Sannois and Argenteuil hovered behind the light bluish mist like shadows of themselves. The warm, abundant light of the sun was bathing the whole broad landscape, faintly veiled by the morning mist, by the sweat of the heated earth exhaled in thin fog, and by the damp vapours of the Seine, gliding endlessly like a serpent across the plains, encircling the villages, and skirting the hills.

A soft breeze, laden with the odour of leaves and sap, caressed the skin, penetrated deep into the lungs, and seemed to rejuvenate the heart, ease the mind, and invigorate the blood.

Parent, surprised, drank deeply of it, his eyes dazzled by the vast sweep of the landscape.

"Yes, it's very nice here," he murmured.

He walked forward a few steps, and stopped again to stare. He fancied he was discovering new and unknown things, not the things which his eyes saw, but those of which his soul foretold him, events of which he was unaware, glimpses of happiness, unexplored pleasures, a whole view of life whose existence he had not suspected, suddenly revealed to him as he gazed at this stretch of boundless plains.

All the appalling melancholy of his existence appeared to him, brilliantly illumined by the radiance flooding the earth. He saw the twenty years of café life, drab, monotonous, heartbreaking. He might have travelled like other men, gone hither and thither among strange peoples in little-known lands across the seas, taken an interest in everything that fascinates other men, in art and in science; he might have lived life in a thousand forms, life the mysterious, delightful, agonising, always changing, always inexplicable and strange.

But now it was too late; he would go on swilling beer till the day of his death, without family, without friends, without hope, without interest in anything. Infinite wretchedness overwhelmed him, and a longing to run away, hide, go back to Paris, to his beer-house and his sottishness. All the thoughts, all the dreams, all the desires slumbering in the sloth of a stagnant heart had been awakened, stirred to life by this ray of country sunlight.

He felt that he would go out of his mind if he stayed any longer in this place, and hastened to the Pavillon Henri IV for lunch, to dull his mind with wine and spirits and at least to talk to someone.

He chose a small table in one of the arbours, whence he

could overlook all the surrounding country, chose his meal, and asked to be served at once.

Other excursionists arrived and sat down at near-by tables. He felt better; he was no longer alone. In another arbour three persons were lunching. He had glanced at them several times without really seeing them, as one looks at strangers.

Suddenly the voice of a woman gave him one of those thrills which penetrate to the very marrow.

"Georges," said the voice, "will you carve the chicken?"

"Yes, Mother," answered another voice.

Parent raised his eyes; he realised, guessed at once who these people were! He would never have known them again. His wife was very stout and quite white-haired, a grave, virtuous old lady. She thrust her head forward as she ate, for fear of staining her dress, although she had covered her bosom with a napkin. Georges had become a man. He had a beard, the uneven, almost colourless beard that lies like soft curling down upon the cheeks of youths. He wore a high hat, a white waistcoat, and a monocle, no doubt for fashion's sake. Parent stared at him in amazement! Was this his son Georges? No, he did not know this young man; there could be nothing in common between them.

Limousin's back was turned towards him; he was busy eating, his shoulders rather bowed.

Well, they all three seemed happy and contented; they had come to lunch in the country at a well-known restaurant. Their existence had been calm and pleasant, they had lived like a happy family in a nice, warm, well-filled house, filled with all the trifles that make life pleasant, all the delights of affection, all the tender words constantly exchanged by those who love each other. And it was thanks to him that they had lived thus, thanks to his money, after deceiving, robbing, and ruining him. They had condemned him, the innocent, simple, kind-hearted victim, to all the horrors of loneliness, to the revolting life he led between pavement and bar, to every form of moral torment and physical misery. They had made of him a useless, ruined creature, lost in the world, a poor old man without any possible happiness or expectation of it, with no hope left in any thing or person. For him the earth was empty, for there was nothing on earth that he loved. He might pass through crowds or along streets, go into every house in Paris, open every room, but never would he find, on the other side of the door, a face beloved or desired, the face of a woman or child that would smile at the sight of him. It was this idea above all that worked upon his mind, the image of a door that one opens in order to find and embrace someone behind it.

And it was all the fault of these three wretches; of that vile woman, that treacherous friend, and that tall fair lad with his assumption of haughtiness.

He bore as great a grudge now against the child as against the two others! Was he not Limousin's son? If not, would Limousin have kept him, loved him? Would not Limousin have speedily dismissed the mother and the child, had he not known full well that the child was his? Does anyone bring up another man's child?

And there they were, the three malefactors who had made him suffer so much.

Parent gazed at them, tormenting and exciting himself by the recollection of all his woes, all his agony, all the moments of despair he had known. He was exasperated, above all, by their air of placid self-satisfaction. He longed to kill them, to throw his siphon of soda-water at them, to smash in Limousin's head, which every moment bobbed down towards his plate and instantly rose again.

And they would continue to live in this fashion, free from care, free from any sign of uneasiness. No, no! It was too much! He would have his revenge, have it now, since he had them here at hand. But how? He ransacked his mind, dreaming of appalling deeds such as happen in sensational novels, but could think of nothing practical. He drank glass after glass, to excite and encourage himself, so that he should not let slip an opportunity that certainly would never return.

Suddenly he had an idea, a terrible idea ; he stopped drinking, in order to mature it. A smile creased his lips. "I've got them. I've got them," he murmured. "We shall see. We shall see."

"What would Monsieur like to follow?" asked a waiter.

"Nothing. Coffee and brandy, the best."

He watched them as he sipped his liqueur. There were too many people in the restaurant for his purpose ; he would wait ; he would follow them ; they were sure to go for a walk on the terrace or in the woods. When they had gone some distance away he would join them, and then he would have his revenge ; yes, he would have his revenge! It was none too soon, after twenty-three years of suffering. Ah, they didn't suspect what was going to befall them!

They were quietly finishing their lunch, chatting with no sense of anxiety. Parent could not hear their words, but he could see their calm gestures. The face of his wife was particularly exasperating to him. She had acquired a haughty air, the appearance of a fat and unapproachable nun, armour-plated with moral principles, casemated in virtue.

They paid their bill and rose. Then he saw Limousin. He looked for all the world like a retired diplomat, he wore such an air of importance, with his handsome whiskers, soft and white, whose points fell to the lapels of his frock-coat.

They departed. Georges was smoking a cigar, and wore his hat over one ear. Parent promptly followed them.

At first they walked along the terrace, regarding the landscape with the placid admiration of the well-fed ; then they went into the forest.

Parent rubbed his hands and continued to follow them, at a distance, concealing himself so as not to rouse their notice too soon.

They walked with short steps, basking in the warm air and

the greenery. Henriette was leaning on Limousin's arm and was walking, very upright, at his side, like a wife sure and proud of herself. Georges was knocking leaves down with his cane, and occasionally leapt lightly over the ditches at the side of the road, like an eager young horse on the point of dashing into the foliage.

Little by little Parent caught them up, panting with emotion and weariness, for he never walked now. Soon he came up with them, but a confused, inexplicable fear had seized hold of him, and he went past them, so as to turn round and meet them face to face.

He walked on with a beating heart, feeling them now behind him, and kept saying to himself: "Come! Now is the time; courage, courage! Now is the time!"

He turned round. All three had sat down at the foot of a large tree, and were still chatting.

At that he made up his mind, and went back with rapid steps. Stopping in front of them, he stood in the middle of the road and stammered in a voice broken with emotion.

"It is I! Here I am! You were not expecting me, were you?"

All three stared at the man, whom they thought mad.

"Anyone might think you did not know me," he continued. "Look at me! I am Parent, Henri Parent. You were not expecting me, eh? You thought it was all over; that you would never see me again, never. But no, here I am again. Now we will have it out."

Henriette, terrified, hid her face in her hands, murmuring: "Oh, my God!"

Seeing this stranger apparently threatening his mother, Georges had risen, ready to take him by the throat.

Limousin, dumbfounded, was looking with terrified eyes at this man come from the dead, who waited for a few seconds to regain his breath and went on:

"So now we'll have it out. The moment has come! You

deceived me, condemned me to the life of a convict, and you thought I should never catch you ! "

But the young man took him by the shoulders and, thrusting him away, said :

" Are you mad ? What do you want ? Get along with you at once or I'll lay you out ! "

" What do I want ? " replied Parent. " I want to tell you who those people are."

But Georges, furious now, shook him and raised his hand to strike him.

" Let go," he said. " I am your father. . . . Look and see if those wretches recognise me now ! "

Horribly startled, the young man loosened his grasp and turned to his mother.

Parent, freed, walked up to her.

" Well ? Tell him who I am ! Tell him that my name is Henri Parent, and that I am his father, since his name is Georges Parent, since you are my wife, since all three of you are living on my money, on the allowance of ten thousand francs which I have been giving you ever since I threw you out of my house. And tell him also why I threw you out of my house. Because I surprised you with that wretch, that scoundrel, your lover !— Tell him what I was, I, a good man whom you married for his money, and deceived from the first day. Tell him who you are and who I am. . . ."

He stammered and panted, overcome with rage.

" Paul, Paul ! " cried the woman in a piercing voice. " Stop him ; make him be silent ! Stop him saying these things in the presence of my son ! "

Limousin had risen in his turn.

" Be silent, be silent," he murmured in a very low voice. " Realise what you are doing."

" I know what I am doing ! " replied Parent furiously. " That is not all. There is one thing I want to know, a thing which has been tormenting me for twenty years."

He turned towards Georges, who was leaning against a tree, bewildered.

" Listen," he continued. " When she left my house, she thought it was not enough to have betrayed me ; she wanted to leave me hopeless too. You were my only consolation ; well, she took you away, swearing that I was not your father, but that he was ! Was she lying ? I do not know. For twenty years I have been wondering."

He went right up to her, a tragic, terrible figure, and, tearing away the hand with which she covered her face, cried :

" Well ! I summon you to-day to tell me which of us is this young man's father—he or I : your husband or your lover. Come, come, tell me ! "

Limousin flung himself upon him. Parent thrust him back.

" Ah ! " he sniggered furiously ; " you are brave to-day ; braver than the day when you fled on to the staircase because I was going to strike you. Well, if she won't answer, answer yourself. Tell me, are you the boy's father ? Come, speak ! "

He turned back to his wife.

" If you will not tell me," he said, " at least tell your son. He is a man now. He has a perfect right to know who his father is. I do not know, I never have known, never ! I cannot tell you, my boy."

He grew more and more furious, and his voice grew shrill. He waved his arms like a man in an epileptic fit.

" Now ! . . . Answer. . . . She does not know. . . . I'll wager she does not know. . . . No . . . she does not know. . . . By God ! she slept with both of us ! Ha ! Ha ! Ha ! . . . Nobody knows . . . nobody . . . do people know these things ? . . . You will not know either, my boy, you will not know any more than I do . . . ever . . . ask her ! . . . Ask her ! You will see that she does not know. Nor do I . . . nor does he . . . nor do you . . . nobody knows. . . . You can take your choice . . . yes . . . you can take your choice . . . him or me. . . . Choose. . . . Good-bye . . . that is all. . . . If she decides to tell you, let me know, won't you, at the Hôtel des Continents. . . . I should like to know. . . . Good-bye. . . . I wish you every happiness. . . ."

And he departed gesticulating, talking to himself, under the tall trees, in the cool, quiet air filled with the fragrance of rising sap. He did not turn round to look at them. He walked on, spurred on by fury, in an ecstasy of passion, his mind completely overturned by his obsession.

Suddenly he found himself at the station. A train was starting. He boarded it. During the journey his anger cooled, he regained his senses, and arrived back in Paris amazed at his boldness.

He felt crushed, as though his bones were broken. Nevertheless he went and had a look at his beer-house.

Seeing him come in, Mademoiselle Zoé, surprised, inquired :

" Back already ? Are you tired ? "

" Yes," he replied. " . . . yes very tired . . . very tired. . . . You see . . . when a man's not used to going out ! It's the end ; I'll never go to the country again. I should have done better to stay here. From this time forward I'll never stir out."

And she was unable to get him to tell her about his excursion, though she was very eager to hear.

That evening, for the first time in his life, he got completely drunk, and had to be carried home.

COUNTRY COURTS

THE COURT-HOUSE OF THE GORGEVILLE JUSTICE OF THE Peace is full of country-folk, seated impassively round the walls, awaiting the opening of the Court.

Among them are large and small, ruddy, fat fellows and thin ones who look as though they were carved out of a block of apple-wood. They have placed their baskets on the ground, and there they sit placidly, silent, absorbed in their own affairs. They have brought with them the smells of the stable, of sweat, of sour milk and manure. Flies are buzzing about under the white ceiling. Through the open door you can hear the cocks crowing.

On a kind of platform stands a long table, covered with a green cloth. Seated at the very end on the left, a wrinkled old man is writing. At the end on the right, a policeman, stiffly erect in his chair, is gazing vacantly into space. On the bare wall, a large wooden Christ, writhing in an anguished attitude, seems still to offer up His eternal agony on behalf of these louts who smell of beasts.

His Honour, the Justice of the Peace, at length enters the Court. Corpulent and ruddy-complexioned, with every quick step of his fat, hurried body he jerks his large black magistrate's robe: he sits down, places his cap on the table, and looks round the assembled company with an air of deep disgust.

He is a provincial scholar, a local wit, one of those who translate Horace, relish the minor verse of Voltaire, and know "Vert-Vert" by heart as well as the obscene poems of Parny.

He opens proceedings.

"Now then, Monsieur Potel, call the cases."

Then, with a smile, he murmurs:

" *Quidquid tentabam dicere versus erat.*"

The Clerk of the Court, raising his bald head, stammers out in an unintelligible voice: " Madame Victorie Bascule versus Isidore Paturon."

A huge woman comes forward, a country woman, a woman from the county town, wearing a beribboned hat, a watch-chain festooned across her stomach, rings on her fingers, and ear-rings shining like lighted candles.

The Justice of the Peace greets her with a glance of recognition not without a gleam of mockery, and says:

" Madame Bascule, enumerate your complaints."

The defence stands on the opposite side of the Court. It is represented by three people. In the middle a young peasant, twenty-five years of age, chubby as an apple and red as a poppy in the corn. On his right, his wife, quite young, puny, slight, very like a bantam-hen, with a flat narrow head, crowned as with a crest by a rose-coloured bonnet. She has a round eye, apprehensive and choleric, which looks out sideways like a bird's. On the boy's left stands his father, an old bent man, whose twisted body is lost in his starched smock, as if it were under a bell-glass.

Madame Bascule holds forth:

" Your Honour, for fifteen years I have looked after this boy here. I have brought him up and loved him like a mother, I have done everything for him, I have made a man of him. He had promised me, he had sworn never to leave me, he even drew up a deed to say so, in return for which I have given him a small property, my bit of land in Bec-de-Mortin, which is valued in the six thousands. And now that baggage, that low-down good-for-nothing, that dirty hussy. . . ."

The Justice of the Peace: " Restrain yourself, Madame Bascule."

Madame Bascule: " A miserable . . . a miserable . . . I know quite well she has turned his head, has done I don't know what to him, no, I really don't know what . . . and he is going to marry her, the fool, the great blockhead, and he will bring her my property as a dowry, my bit of land in Bec-de-Mortin. . . . But not if I know it, not if I know it . . . I have a paper, there it is. . . . Let him gave me back my property, then. We made a lawyer's deed for safety's sake, and a private agreement on paper for friendship's sake. One is as good as the other. Each has his rights, isn't that true?" (She holds out to the Justice of the Peace a stamped paper opened out wide.)

Isidore Paturon: "It's not true."

The Justice: "Silence! You shall speak in due course." (He reads.)

> "I, the undersigned, Isidore Paturon, promise by these presents to my benefactress, Madame Bascule, never to leave her during my life, and to serve her with devotion.
>
> "GORGEVILLE, *August 5th*, 1883."

The Justice: "There is a cross for signature: you don't know how to write, then?"

Isidore: "No. Can't write at all."

The Justice: "It was you who made it—this cross?"

Isidore: "No. Not me."

The Justice: "Who did make it, then?"

Isidore: "She did."

The Justice: "You are prepared to take your oath that you did not make this cross?"

Isidore (in an outburst): "By my dad's head, my ma's, my grandfer's, my gran'ma's, and the good God's, who hears me, I swear it isn't me." (He raises his hands and spits aside to emphasise his oath.)

The Justice (smiling): "What then were your relations with Madame Bascule, here present?"

Isidore: "She served me for a whore." (Laughter in Court.)

The Justice: "Restrain your language. You mean that your relations were not so innocent as she claims."

Paturon, Senior (breaking in): " He wasn't fifteen, not fifteen, your Honour, when she debouched him. . . ."

The Justice : " You mean ' debauched ' ? "

The Father : " How do I know ? He wasn't fifteen years old. And she'd fed him out of her own hand for four years then, stuffed him like a fatted fowl, crammed him with food fit to burst, saving your Honour. And then when the time came that he seemed to her ready, she disrupted him. . . ."

The Justice : " Corrupted. . . . And you let it happen ? "

The Father : " It was her or some other woman, it was bound to happen ! . . ."

The Justice : " Very well, then, what do you complain of ? "

The Father : " Nothing ! Oh, I've nothing to complain of myself, nothing, only that he doesn't want any more of it himself, and he is quit of her. I demand protection according to the law."

Madame Bascule : " These people are heaping lies on me, your Honour. I made a man of him."

The Justice : " Quite ! "

Madame Bascule : " And he is going back on me, deserting me, stealing my property. . . ."

Isidore : " It isn't true, your Honour. I wanted to leave her five years ago, because she had fattened beyond all bounds, and that didn't suit me a bit. That displeased me, and why not ? Didn't I say to her then I was going to leave her ? And then she wept like a gutter-spout and promised me her property at Bec-de-Mortin to stay a few more years, only four or five. Of course I said ' Yes,' for sure. What would you have done yourself ?

" So I stayed five years, every day and every hour of it. I had kept my promise. Give the Devil his due ! That was full value, that was ! "

Isidore's wife, silent till then, cries out with the piercing scream of a parrot :

" Just look at her, look at her, your Honour, the old haystack, and say if that wasn't full value ! "

The father nods with an air of conviction, and repeats :

" Lor', yes, full value that ! " (Madame Bascule subsides on the bench behind her, and begins to weep.)

The Justice (in a fatherly tone) : " What did you expect, my good woman ? I can do nothing. You have given him your bit of land at Bec-de-Mortin by deed in a perfectly legal way. It is his, absolutely his. He has an indisputable right to do what he has done, and to bring it to his wife as dowry. I am not going to embark on questions of . . . of . . . delicacy. I can only regard the facts from the point of view of the law. I can do absolutely nothing in the matter."

Father Paturon (proudly) : " It'll be all right to get back home, then ? "

The Justice : " Certainly." (They go out, followed by the sympathetic looks of the country-folk, with the air of people who have won their case. Madame Bascule sobs on her bench.)

The Justice (smiling) : " Compose yourself, my good woman. Come now, come now, compose yourself . . . and . . . and if I have any advice to give you, it is, look for another . . . another pupil. . . ."

Madame Bascule (in the midst of her tears) : " I shall never find one . . . never. . . ."

The Justice : " I am sorry I cannot put you in the way of one." (She throws a look of despair towards the Christ, suffering and writhing on the Cross, then she rises and goes out, with mincing steps, hiccuping her discomfiture, hiding her face in her handkerchief.)

The Justice turns towards his clerk, and in a bantering voice : " Calypso could not console herself for the departure of Ulysses." Then, in solemn tones :

" Call the next case."

The Clerk of the Court stammers out :

" Célestin Polyte Lecacheur—Prosper Magloire Dieulafait. . . ."

THE HAIRPIN

I WILL NOT RECORD THE NAME EITHER OF THE COUNTRY OR OF the man concerned. It was far, very far from this part of the world, on a fertile and scorching sea-coast. All morning we had been following a coast clothed with crops and a blue sea clothed in sunlight. Flowers thrust up their heads quite close to the waves, rippling waves, so gentle, drowsing. It was hot—a relaxing heat, redolent of the rich soil, damp and fruitful: one almost heard the rising of the sap.

I had been told that, in the evening, I could obtain hospitality in the house of a Frenchman, who lived at the end of a headland, in an orange grove. Who was he? I did not yet know. He had arrived one morning, ten years ago; he had bought a piece of ground, planted vines, sown seed; he had worked, this man, passionately, furiously. Then, month by month, year by year, increasing his demesne, continually fertilising the lusty and virgin soil, he had in this way amassed a fortune by his unsparing labour.

Yet he went on working, all the time, people said. Up at dawn, going over his fields until night, always on the watch, he seemed to be goaded by a fixed idea, tortured by an insatiable lust for money, which nothing lulls to sleep, and nothing can appease.

Now he seemed to be very rich.

The sun was just setting when I reached his dwelling. This was, indeed, built at the end of an out-thrust cliff, in the midst of orange-trees. It was a large plain-looking house, built four-square, and overlooking the sea.

As I approached, a man with a big beard appeared in the doorway. Greeting him, I asked him to give me shelter for the night. He held out his hand to me, smiling.

"Come in, sir, and make yourself at home."

He led the way to a room, put a servant at my disposal, with the perfect assurance and easy good manners of a man of the world; then he left me, saying:

"We will dine as soon as you are quite ready to come down."

We did indeed dine alone, on a terrace facing the sea. At the beginning of the meal, I spoke to him of this country, so rich, so far from the world, so little known. He smiled, answering indifferently.

"Yes, it is a beautiful country. But no country is attractive that lies so far from the country of one's heart."

"You regret France?"

"I regret Paris."

"Why not go back to it?"

"Oh, I shall go back to it."

Then, quite naturally, we began to talk of French society, of the boulevards, and people, and things of Paris. He questioned me after the manner of a man who knew all about it, mentioning names, all the names familiar on the Vaudeville promenade.

"Who goes to Tortoni's now?"

"All the same people, except those who have died."

I looked at him closely, haunted by a vague memory. Assuredly I had seen this face somewhere. But where? but when? He seemed weary though active, melancholy though determined. His big fair beard fell to his chest, and now and then he took hold of it below the chin and, holding it in his closed hand, let the whole length of it run through his fingers. A little bald, he had heavy eyebrows and a thick moustache that merged into the hair covering his cheeks. Behind us the sun sank in the sea, flinging over the coast a fiery haze. The orange-trees in full blossom filled the air with their sweet, heady scent. He had eyes for nothing but me, and with his intent gaze he seemed to peer through my eyes, to see in the depths of my thoughts the far-off, familiar, and well-loved vision of the wide, shady pavement that runs from the Madeleine to the Rue Drouot.

"Do you know Boutrelle?"

"Yes, well."

"Is he much changed?"

"Yes, he has gone quite white."

"And La Ridamie?"

"Always the same."

"And the women? Tell me about the women. Let me see. Do you know Suzanne Verner?"

"Yes, very stout. Done for."

"Ah! And Sophie Astier?"

"Dead."

"Poor girl! And is . . . do you know. . . ."

But he was abruptly silent. Then in a changed voice, his face grown suddenly pale, he went on:

"No, it would be better for me not to speak of it any more, it tortures me."

Then, as if to change the trend of his thoughts, he rose.

"Shall we go in?"

"I am quite ready."

And he preceded me into the house.

The rooms on the ground floor were enormous, bare, gloomy, apparently deserted. Napkins and glasses were scattered about the tables, left there by the swart-skinned servants who prowled about this vast dwelling all the time. Two guns were hanging from two nails on the wall, and in the corners I saw spades, fishing-lines, dried palm leaves, objects of all kinds, deposited there by people who happened to come into the house, and remaining there within easy reach until someone happened to go out or until they were wanted for a job of work.

My host smiled.

" It is the dwelling, or rather the hovel; of an exile," said he, " but my room is rather more decent. Let's go there."

My first thought, when I entered the room, was that I was penetrating into a second-hand dealer's, so full of things was it, all the incongruous, strange, and varied things that one feels must be mementoes. On the walls two excellent pictures by well-known artists, hangings, weapons, swords and pistols, and then, right in the middle of the most prominent panel, a square of white satin in a gold frame.

Surprised, I went closer to look at it and I saw a hairpin stuck in the centre of the gleaming material.

My host laid his hand on my shoulder.

" There," he said, with a smile, " is the only thing I ever look at in this place, and the only one I have seen for ten years. Monsieur Prudhomme declared : ' This sabre is the finest day of my life ! ' As for me, I can say : ' This pin is the whole of my life ! ' "

I sought for the conventional phrase ; I ended by saying :

" Some woman has made you suffer ? "

He went on harshly :

" I suffer yet, and frightfully. . . . But come on to my balcony. A name came to my lips just now, that I dared not utter, because if you had answered ' dead,' as you did for Sophie Astier, I should have blown out my brains, this very day."

We had gone out on to a wide balcony looking towards two deep valleys, one on the right and the other on the left, shut in by high sombre mountains. It was that twilight hour when the vanished sun lights the earth only by its reflection in the sky.

He continued :

" Is Jeanne de Limours still alive ? "

His eye was fixed on mine, full of shuddering terror.

I smiled.

" Very much alive . . . and prettier than ever."

" You know her ? "

"Yes."

He hesitated:

"Intimately?"

"No."

He took my hand:

"Talk to me about her."

"But there is nothing I can say: she is one of the women, or rather one of the most charming and expensive gay ladies in Paris. She leads a pleasant and sumptuous life, and that's all one can say."

He murmured: "I love her," as if he had said: "I am dying." Then abruptly:

"Ah, for three years, what a distracting and glorious life we lived! Five or six times I all but killed her; she tried to pierce my eyes with that pin at which you have been looking. There, look at this little white speck on my left eye. We loved each other! How can I explain such a passion? You would not understand it.

"There must be a gentle love, born of the swift mutual union of two hearts and two souls; but assuredly there exists a savage love, cruelly tormenting, born of the imperious force which binds together two discordant beings who adore while they hate.

"That girl ruined me in three years. I had four millions which she devoured quite placidly, in her indifferent fashion, crunching them up with a sweet smile that seemed to die from her eyes on to her lips.

"You know her? There is something irresistible about her. What is it? I don't know. Is it those grey eyes whose glance thrusts like a gimlet and remains in you like the barb of an arrow? It is rather that sweet smile, indifferent and infinitely charming, that dwells on her face like a mask. Little by little her slow grace invades one, rises from her like a perfume, from her tall, slender body, which sways a little as she moves, for she seems to glide rather than walk, from her lovely, drawling voice that seems the music of her smile, from the very motion of her body, too, a motion that is always restrained, always just right, taking the eye with rapture, so exquisitely proportioned it is. For three years I was conscious of no one but her. How I suffered! For she deceived me with every one. Why? For no reason, for the mere sake of deceiving. And when I discovered it, when I abused her as a light-o'-love and a loose woman, she admitted it calmly. 'We're not married, are we?' she said.

"Since I have been here, I have thought of her so much that I have ended by understanding her: that woman is Manon Lescaut come again. Manon could not love without betraying; for Manon, love, pleasure, and money were all one."

He was silent. Then, some minutes later:

"When I had squandered my last sou for her, she said to me quite simply: 'You realise, my dear, that I cannot live on air and sunshine. I love you madly, I love you more than anyone in the world, but one must live. Poverty and I would never make good bedfellows.'

"And if I did but tell you what an agonising life I had lead with her! When I looked at her, I wanted to kill her as sharply as I wanted to embrace her. When I looked at her . . . I felt a mad impulse to open my arms, to take her to me and strangle her. There lurked in her, behind her eyes, something treacherous and for ever unattainable that made me execrate her; and it is perhaps because of that that I loved her so. In her, the Feminine, the detestable and distracting Feminine, was more puissant than in any other woman. She was charged with it, surcharged as with an intoxicating and venomous fluid. She was Woman, more essentially than any one woman has ever been.

"And look you, when I went out with her, she fixed her glance on every man, in such a way that she seemed to be giving each one of them her undivided interest. That maddened me and yet held me to her the closer. This woman, in the mere act of walking down the street, was owned by every man in it, in spite of me, in spite of herself, by virtue of her very nature, although she bore herself with a quiet and modest air. Do you understand?

"And what torture! At the theatre, in the restaurant, it seemed to me that men possessed her under my very eyes. And as soon as I left her company, other men did indeed possess her.

"It is ten years since I have seen her, and I love her more then ever."

Night had spread its wings upon the earth. The powerful scent of orange-trees hung in the air.

I said to him:

"You will see her again?"

He answered:

"By God, yes. I have here, in land and money, from seven to eight hundred thousand francs. When the million is complete, I shall sell all and depart. I shall have enough for one year with her—one entire marvellous year. And then good-bye, my life will be over."

I asked:

"But afterwards?"

"Afterwards, I don't know. It will be the end. Perhaps I shall ask her to keep me on as her body-servant."

THE WOODCOCKS

My Dearest, you ask me why I do not come back to Paris; you are amazed, and you are almost angry. The reason that I am going to offer will doubtless disgust you: Can a sportsman return to Paris at the beginning of the woodcock season?

I understand, of course, and am fond enough of the life of the town, which revolves between house and street, but I prefer a free life, the simple autumn life of the sportsman.

In Paris I feel as if I were never in the open air; for the streets are, after all, no more than vast public apartments, without ceilings. Is a man in the open air, held between two walls, his feet on stone or wooden pavements, his outlook everywhere bounded by buildings, without any prospect of meadow, plain, or wood? Thousands of fellow-creatures elbow you, push you, greet you, and talk to you; and the mere fact of receiving the rain on an umbrella when it rains is not enough to give me the impression and the sense of space.

Here I remark very sharply and delightfully the distinction between inside and outside. . . . But that is not what I want to say to you. . . .

It is the woodcock season.

I must tell you that I live in a big Norman house, in a valley, near a little stream, and that I get some shooting almost every day.

Other days, I read. I read just the books that Parisians have no time to know, very serious, very profound, very strange books written by a brilliant and inspired scientist, a foreigner who has spent the whole of his life in studying the one problem, and has observed all the facts relative to the influence on our minds of the functioning of our physical organism.

But I want to tell you about the woodcock. My two friends, then, the d'Orgemol brothers and I, live here during the shooting-season, waiting for the first frost. Then, as soon as it freezes, we set out for their farm at Cannetot, near Fécamp, because there, there is a delightful little wood, a divine little wood, where all the woodcocks halt in their flight.

You know the d'Orgemols, both of them giants, both real early Normans, both of them men of that old powerful race of conquerors who invaded France, took and held England, settled themselves along every coast of the old world, built towns everywhere, passed like a wave over Sicily, leaving behind the monuments of a marvellous art, pulled down kings, pillaged the proudest cities, engaged popes in priestly intrigues and, craftier than those Italian pontiffs, beat them at their own game; and, more important to the world than all, left children behind them in the beds of every race. The d'Orgemols are two Normans of the purest and oldest stock, they have every Norman characteristic, voice, accent, manner, fair hair, and eyes the hue of the sea.

When we are together, we talk in the dialect, we live, and act like Normans, we become landed Normans more peasant-like than our farmers.

Well, we waited a fortnight for the woodcock.

Every morning Simon, the eldest, would say to me:

"Hullo, the wind's coming round to the east, it'll freeze. They'll be here in two days."

The younger, Gaspard, more cautious, waited until the frost came to announce its arrival.

Well, last Friday, he came into my room at daybreak, shouting:

"It's come, the ground is covered with white! Two more such days, and we go to Cannetot!"

Two days later, indeed, we did set out for Cannetot. You

would have laughed to see us. We move in a strange hunting-coach which my father had constructed some time ago. " Construct " is the only word I can use to speak of this travelling tomb, or rather this moving earthquake. It contains everything: holds for the stores, holds for the weapons, holds for the trunks, boxes with peep-holes for the dogs. Everything is in shelter, except the human passengers, perched on railed seats outside as high as a three-storied house and carried on four gigantic wheels. You scramble up there as best you can, using feet, hands, and even teeth on occasion, for no ladder gives access to that erection.

Very well, the two d'Orgemols and I reach this mountain, rigged out like Laplanders. We are clad in sheepskins, we wear enormous woollen stockings over our breeches, and gaiters over our woollen stockings; we have black fur caps and white fur gloves. When we are installed, Jean, my man, throws us up three basset-hounds, Pif, Paf, and Moustouche. Pif belongs to Simon, Paf to Gaspard, and Moustouche to me. They are like three small hairy crocodiles. They are long, low, hollow in the back, and bow-legged, and so shaggy that they look like yellow bushes. Their black eyes are hardly visible under their eyebrows, or their white teeth under their beards. We never shut them in the rolling kennels in the coach. Each of us keeps his own dog under his feet for the sake of warmth.

And so we set off, shaken almost to pieces. It is freezing, freezing hard. We are happy. We arrive about five o'clock. The farmer, Monsieur Picot, is waiting for us in front of the door. He is a jovial fellow, not very tall, but plump, thick-set, active as a mastiff, cunning as a fox, always smiling, always happy and very sharp after the money.

It is a fine holiday for him, in the woodcock season.

The farm is immense, an old building in an orchard, encircled by four rows of beech-trees which struggle the year round against the sea wind.

We enter the kitchen, where a monstrous fire is blazing in our honour.

Our table is set close to the lofty fire-place, where, in front of the limpid flames, a plump bird is turning and roasting, while the juice drips into an earthen plate.

The farmer's wife greets us now, a tall, silent woman, always busied with household cares, her head full of deals and calculations, of sheep and cattle. She is a methodical woman, level-headed and austere, highly respected in the district.

Along the end of the kitchen runs the big table where the hired men and women of every class, ploughmen, labourers, farm wenches, shepherds, will shortly seat themselves; and all those folk eat in silence under the quick eye of the mistress and watch us dine with Farmer Picot, who lets off jests that make us all laugh. Then, when all her household has been fed, Madame Picot will take, alone, her hasty and frugal meal on a corner of the table, keeping an eye on the servant-girl meanwhile.

On ordinary days, she dines with her household.

The three of us, the d'Orgemols and I, sleep in a white room, bare, whitewashed, and containing only our three beds, three chairs, and three basins.

Gaspard always wakes first and sounds a ringing reveille. And in half an hour every one is ready and we set off with old Picot, who shoots with us.

Monsieur Picot prefers me to his masters. Why? Doubtless because I am not his master. Then you may see us both making for the wood from the right, while the two brothers advance on it from the left. Simon has the dogs in his charge, leading them, all three held at the end of a cord.

For we are not out after woodcock but rabbits. We are convinced that we must not look for woodcock, but just come across them. We stumble on them and kill them, don't you know! When you specially want to find them, you never set eyes on one. It is a strange and lovely thing to hear in the clear morning air the sharp report of the gun, then Gaspard's thunderous voice filling the whole country-side and roaring: " Woodcock—here they come ! "

I am wily. When I have brought down a woodcock, I call out: " Rabbit ! " And I rejoice exceedingly when we lay out the bag at lunch.

There we are, old Picot and I, in the little wood where the leaves fall with a soft, ceaseless murmur, a harsh murmur, a little sad; they are dead. It is cold, a thin, sharp cold that pricks eyes, nose, ears, and has powdered the edges of the grass and the brown ploughed fields with a fine white moss. But we are warm in all our limbs, under the thick sheepskin. The sun sparkles in the blue air; it has little or no warmth, but it sparkles. It is good to shoot over the woods on a keen winter morning.

Yonder a dog breaks into a shrill barking. It is Pif. I know his thin voice. Then, silence. Now another outburst, then another; and Paf gives tongue in his turn. But what is Moustouche doing? Ah, there he goes whimpering like a chicken whose neck is being wrung. They have started a rabbit. Now, Farmer Picot!

They draw apart, then close in, separate again, then run back; we follow their haphazard goings, running along narrow paths, every sense on the alert, fingers on the triggers of our guns.

They make back towards the common, we make back too. Suddenly a grey streak, a shadow crossed the path. I bring my gun to my shoulder and fire. The faint smoke clears away in the blue air, and I see on the grass a morsel of white fur that moves. Then I shout at the top of my voice: " Rabbit, rabbit ! Here it is ! " And I show it to the three dogs, to the three shaggy crocodiles, who congratulate me with wagging tails; they then go off in search of another.

Old Picot has rejoined me. Moustouche begins to yelp. The farmer says:

"That's surely a hare, let's go to the edge of the common."

But just as I emerged from the wood, I saw, standing ten paces from me, Gargan, the deaf-mute, Monsieur Picot's herdsman, wrapped round in a voluminous yellowish cloak, with a woollen bonnet on his head, and knitting away at a stocking, as all the shepherds of these parts do.

"Good morning, shepherd," I said, as we always do.

And he lifted his head in greeting, although he had not heard my voice, but he had seen my lips moving.

I have known this shepherd for fifteen years. For fifteen years I have seen him every autumn, standing on the edge or in the middle of a field, his body motionless and his hands ceaselessly knitting. His flock follow him like a pack of hounds, seeming to obey his eye.

Old Picto grasped my arm:

"You know that the shepherd has killed his wife?"

I was dumbfounded.

"Gargan? The deaf-mute?"

"Yes, this last winter, and he was brought to trial at Rouen. I will tell you about it."

And he drew me into the copse, for the herdsman was able to pick up the words from his master's lips as if he had heard them. He understood no one else; but, face to face with him, he was no longer deaf; and his master, on the other hand, read like a wizard every meaning of the mute's dumb show, all the gestures of his fingers, the wrinklings of his cheeks, and the flashes of his eyes.

Listen to this simple story, a melancholy piece of news, just such a one as happens in the country, time and again.

Gargan was the son of a marl-digger, one of those men who go down into the clay pits to dig out that sort of soft stone, white and viscous, that we scatter on the fields. Deaf and dumb from birth, he had been brought up to keep the cows along the roadside ditches.

Then, employed by Picot's father, he had become a shepherd

at the farm. He was an excellent shepherd, zealous and honest, and he could set dislocated limbs, though he had not been taught anything of the kind.

When Picot came into the farm in his time, Gargan was thirty years old, and looked forty. He was tall, thin, and bearded, bearded like a patriarch.

Then, just about this time, Martel, an honest country woman, died, leaving a young girl of fifteen, who had been nicknamed "A Wee Drop," because of her immoderate liking for brandy.

Picot took in this ragged young wretch and employed her in light tasks, feeding her without paying her wages, in return for her work. She slept in the barn, in the cattle-shed or in the stable, on straw or dung, any place, no matter where, for no one bothers to find a bed for these ragamuffins. She slept anywhere, with anyone, perhaps with the carter or the labourer. But it soon came about that she attached herself to the deaf-mute and formed a more lasting union with him. How did these two poor wretches come together? How did they understand each other? Had he ever known a woman before this barn rat, he who had never talked to a soul? Was it she who sought him out in his rolling hut and seduced him at the edge of the road, a hedge-side Eve? No one knows. It only became known, one day, that they were living together as man and wife.

No one was surprised. And Picot even found this union quite natural.

But now the parish priest learned of this union without benefit of clergy, and was angry. He reproached Madame Picot, made her conscience uneasy, menaced her with mysterious penalties. What was to be done? It was quite simple. They were taken to the church and the town hall to be married. Neither of them had a penny to his name; he not a whole pair of trousers, she not a petticoat that was all of a piece. So nothing hindered the demands of State and Church from being satisfied. They were joined together, before mayor and priest, within one hour, and everything seemed arranged for the best.

But would you believe that, very soon, it became a joke in the country-side (forgive the scandalous word) to cuckold poor Gargan? Before the marriage, no one thought of lying with the Wee Drop; and now, every one wanted his turn just for fun. For a brandy she received all comers, behind her husband's back. The exploit was even so much talked of in the district round that gentlemen came from Goderville to see it.

Primed with a pint, the Wee Drop treated them to the spectacle with anyone, in a ditch, behind a wall, while at the same time the motionless figure of Gargan was in full view a hundred paces away, knitting a stocking and followed by his bleating flock. People laughed fit to kill themselves in all the inns in the country-side; in the evening, round the fire, nothing else was talked about; people hailed each other on the roads, asking: "Have you given your drop to the Wee Drop?" Every one knew what that meant.

The shepherd seemed to see nothing. But then one day young Poirot from Sasseville beckoned Gargan's wife to come behind a haystack, letting her see a full bottle. She understood and ran to him, laughing; then, hardly were they well on the way with their evil work when the herdsman tumbled on them as if he had fallen from a cloud. Poirot fled, hopping on one leg, his trousers about his heels, while the mute, growling like a beast, seized his wife's throat.

People working on the common came running up. It was too late; her tongue was black and her eyes starting out of her head; blood was running out of her nose. She was dead.

The shepherd was tried by the Court at Rouen. As he was dumb, Picot served him as interpreter. The details of the affair were very amusing to the audience. But the farmer had only one idea, which was to get his herdsman acquitted, and he went about it very craftily.

He told them first the whole history of the deaf-mute and of his marriage; then, when he came to the crime, he himself cross-examined the murderer.

The whole Court was silent.

Picot said slowly:

"Did you know that she was deceiving you?"

And at the same time, he conveyed his question with his eyes.

The other made a sign, "no," with his head.

"She was lying in the haystack when you found her?"

And he gesticulated like a man who sees a revolting sight.

The other made a sign, "yes," with his head.

Then the farmer, imitating the gestures of the mayor performing the civil ceremony and of the priest uniting them in the name of God, asked his servant if he had killed his wife because she was joined to him before man and God.

The shepherd made a sign, "yes," with his head.

Picot said to him:

"Now, show us how it happened."

Then the deaf-mute himself acted the whole scene. He showed how he was sleeping in the haystack, how he had been awakened by feeling the movement of the straw, how he had looked round carefully, and had seen the thing.

He was standing stiffly between two policemen, and all at once he imitated the obscene actions of the criminal pair clasped together in front of him.

A great shout of laughter went up in the Court, then stopped dead; for the shepherd, his eyes wild, working his jaws and his great beard as if he had been gnawing something, his arms stretched out, his head thrust forward, repeated the ghastly gesture of a murderer strangling his victim.

And he howled horribly, so maddened with rage that he imagined himself still grasping her, and the policemen were forced to seize him and push him forcibly into a seat to quiet him.

A profound and agonised shudder ran through the Court. Then Farmer Picot, placing his hand on his servant's shoulder, said simply :

" He has his honour, this man before you."

And the shepherd was acquitted.

As for me, my dearest, I was listening with deep emotion to the end of this strange affair that I have told you, crudely enough, so as not to alter the farmer's way of telling it, when a gunshot rang out in the middle of the wood ; and Gaspard's great voice roared through the wind, like the thunder of a cannon :

" Woodcock ! Here they come ! "

And that is how I spend my time, watching for the arrival of the woodcock while you too go out to watch the first winter dresses arrive in the Bois.

IN A RAILWAY CARRIAGE

THE SUN WAS VANISHING BEHIND THE VAST CHAINS OF HILLS whose loftiest peak is the Puy de Dôme, and the shadow of the crests filled the deep valley of Royat.

Several people were strolling in the park, round the bandstand. Others were still sitting together in groups, in spite of the sharp evening air.

In one of these groups an animated discussion was in progress, for a grave problem had arisen, and one which seriously perturbed Mesdames de Sarcagnes, de Vaulacelles, and de Bridoie. In a few days the holidays would begin, and the discussion centred round the means of bringing home their sons, now at Jesuit and Dominican colleges.

Now, these ladies had not the least desire to undertake a journey to bring back their offspring, and they did not know exactly who could be entrusted with this delicate task. The last days of July were already on them. Paris was empty. They tried in vain to recall any name which offered the necessary guarantees.

Their concern was the greater because an unsavoury episode had occurred in a railway carriage some few days before. And these ladies were firmly convinced that all the women of the town spent their whole time in the express trains between Auvergne and the Gare de Lyon in Paris. According to Madame de Bridoie, the columns of personal gossip in *Gil Blas*, moreover, announced the presence at Vichy, at Mont Dore, and La Bourboule of every known and unknown pretty lady. The fact that they were there, was proof that they must have come in a railway carriage; and they would assuredly return in a railway carriage; they must indeed be compelled to go on returning in order to come back again every day. It was a continual coming and going of damaged goods on this abominable line. The ladies lamented that access to the stations was not forbidden to disreputable women.

Roger de Sarcagnes was fifteen years old, Gontran de Vaulacelles thirteen, and Roland de Bridoie eleven years. What was to be done? They could not, under any circumstances, expose their darlings to the risk of meeting such creatures. What might they hear, what might they see, and what might they find out if they were to spend a whole day, or a night, in a compartment which held also one or two of these vicious women with one or two of their companions!

There seemed no way out of the difficulty, and then Madame de Martinsec happened to come past. She stopped to greet her friends, who poured their woes into her ears.

"But what could be easier?" she cried. "I'll lend you the abbé. I can quite well spare him for forty-eight hours. Rodolphe's education will not suffer during that short time. He will go for your children and bring them home."

So it was arranged that Father Lecuir, a young and cultured priest, and Rodolphe de Martinsec's tutor, should go to Paris the following week to take charge of the young people.

So the priest set out on Friday; and on Sunday morning he was at the Gare de Lyon, ready, with his three youngsters, to take the eight o'clock express, the new through express which had started to run only a few days before, in response to the unanimous demands of all the people taking the waters in Auvergne.

He walked down the platform, followed by his schoolboys, like a hen and her chicks, in search of a compartment either empty or occupied by people whose appearance was quite irreproachable, for his mind retained a lively sense of all the meticulous commands laid upon him by Mesdames de Sarcagnes, de Vaulacelles, and de Bridoie.

Suddenly he saw, standing outside the door of one compartment, an old gentleman and an old white-haired lady talking to another lady seated inside the carriage. The old gentleman was an officer of the Legion of Honour, and they were all unmistakably gentlefolk. "This is the place for me," thought the abbé. He helped his three pupils in and followed them.

The old lady was saying:

"Be sure to take the greatest care of yourself, my child."

The younger lady answered:

"Oh, yes, mamma, don't be anxious."

"Call in the doctor as soon as ever you feel yourself in pain."

"Yes, yes, mamma."

"Then good-bye, my daughter."

"Good-bye, mamma."

They embraced each other warmly, then a porter shut the door and the train began to move.

They were alone. The abbé, in high delight, congratulated himself on his clever management, and began to talk to the young people entrusted to his care. The day he left, it had been arranged that Madame de Martinsec should allow him to give the three boys lessons during the whole of the holidays, and he was anxious to test the abilities and dispositions of his new pupils.

The eldest, Roger de Sarcagnes, was one of those tall schoolboys who have shot up too rapidly, thin and pale, with joints that seemed to fit badly. He spoke slowly, with an air of simplicity.

Gontran de Vaulacelles, on the contrary, had remained short in stature, and squat; he was spiteful, sly, mischievous, and queer-tempered. He made fun of every one, talked like a grown man, making equivocal answers that caused his parents some uneasiness.

The youngest, Roland de Bridoie, did not seem to have any

aptitude for anything at all. He was a jolly little animal and resembled his father.

The abbé had warned them that they would be under his orders during the two summer months, and he read them a carefully-worded lecture on their duty to him, on the way in which he intended to order their ways, and on the manner that he would adopt towards them.

He was an upright and simple-minded priest, somewhat sententious and full of theories.

His conversation was interrupted by a loud sigh uttered by their fair neighbour. He turned his head towards her. She was sitting still in her corner, her eyes staring in front of her, her cheeks slightly pale. The abbé turned back to his disciples.

The train rushed on at full speed, running through plains and woods, passing under bridges and over bridges, and in its shuddering onrush shaking violently the long chain of travellers shut up in the carriages.

Meanwhile Gontran de Vaulacelles was questioning Father Lecuir about Royat and the amusements the place had to offer. Was there a river? Could you fish in it? Would he have a horse, as he had last year? And so on.

Abruptly, the young woman uttered something like a cry, an " Oh " of pain, quickly smothered.

Uneasy, the priest asked her:

" You are feeling unwell, Madame? "

She answered:

" No, no, Father, it is nothing, a passing indisposition, nothing at all. I have been ailing for some time, and the motion of the train wearies me."

Her face had indeed become livid.

He insisted:

" Is there anything I can do for you, Madame? "

" Oh, no, nothing at all, Father. Thank you so much."

The priest returned to his conversation with his pupils, accustoming them to his methods of teaching and discipline.

The hours went by. Now and then the train stopped and went on once more. The young woman seemed to be sleeping now, and she never moved, ensconced in her corner. Although the day was more than half gone, she had not yet eaten anything. The abbé thought: "This young lady must be very ill indeed."

The train was only two hours away from Clermont-Ferrand, when all at once the fair traveller began to moan. She looked as if she might fall from her seat, and, supporting herself on her hands, with wild eyes and distorted face, she repeated: "Oh, my God! Oh, my God!"

The abbé rushed to her.

"Madame . . . Madame . . . Madame, what is the matter?"

She stammered:

"I . . . I . . . think that . . . that . . . that my baby is going to be born." And thereupon she began to cry out in the most terrifying fashion. From her lips issued a long-drawn and frantic sound which seemed to tear its way through her throat, a shrill, frightful sound, with an ominous note in it that told her agony of mind and bodily torture.

The unfortunate priest, dazed, stood in front of her, and did not know what to do or what to say or what effort to make; he murmured: "My God, if I had only known! . . . my God, if I had only known!" He had crimsoned to the very whites of his eyes; and his three pupils stared in utter bewilderment at this outstretched moaning woman.

Suddenly, she writhed, lifting her arms over her head, and a strange shuddering seized her limbs, a convulsion that shook her from head to foot.

The abbé thought that she was going to die, to die there before him, deprived of help and care by his incompetence. So he said in a resolute voice:

"I will help you, Madame. I don't know what to do . . . but I will help you as best I can. I owe aid to all suffering creatures."

Then, swinging round on the three youngsters, he cried :

" As for you, you are going to put your heads out of the windows, and if one of you turns round, he will copy out a thousand lines of Virgil for me."

He lowered the three windows himself, pushed the three heads into their places, drew the blue curtains round their necks, and repeated :

" If you stir as much as once, you shall not be allowed a single outing during the whole of the holidays. And don't forget that I never change my mind."

And he turned back to the young woman, rolling up the sleeves of his cassock.

Her moans came ceaselessly, with now and then a scream. The abbé, his face crimson, helped her, exhorted her, spoke words of comfort to her, and lifted his eyes every minute towards the three youngsters, who kept turning swift glances, quickly averted, towards the mysterious task performed by their new tutor.

" Monsieur de Vaulacelles, you will copy out for me the verb ' to disobey ' twenty times ! " he cried.

" Monsieur de Bridoie, you shall have no sweets for a month ! "

Suddenly the young woman ceased her monotonous wailing, and almost in the same instant a strange, thin cry, like a yelp or a miaow, brought the three schoolboys round in one wild rush, sure that they had just heard a newly born puppy.

In his hands the abbé was holding a little naked babe. He regarded it with startled eyes ; he seemed at once satisfied and abashed, near laughter and near tears ; he looked like a madman, so expressively distorted was his face by the rapid movement of his eyes, his lips, and his cheeks.

He observed, as if he were announcing an amazing piece of news to his pupils :

" It's a boy."

Then he added immediately :

" Monsieur de Sarcagnes, pass me the bottle of water in the rack. That's right. Take out the stopper. That's quite right. Pour me out a few drops in my hand, only a few drops. . . . That's enough."

And he scattered the water on the bald forehead of the little creature he was holding, and announced :

" I baptize thee in the name of the Father, of the Son, and of the Holy Ghost. Amen."

The train drew into the station of Clermont. The face of Madame de Bridoie appeared in the doorway. Then the abbé, quite losing his head, presented her with the tiny human animal that he had just acquired, and murmured :

" This lady has had a slight accident on the journey."

He conveyed the impression that he had picked the child up in a gutter ; and, his hair wet with sweat, his bands round on his shoulder, his gown soiled, he repeated :

" They saw nothing . . . nothing at all—I'll answer for that. . . . All three of them looked out of the window. . . . I'll answer for that . . . they saw nothing."

And he descended from the compartment with four boys instead of the three he had gone to fetch, while Mesdames de Bridoie, de Vaulacelles, and de Sarcagnes, very pale, exchanged stupefied glances and found not a word to utter.

That evening, the three families dined together to celebrate the home-coming of the schoolboys. But no one had anything much to say ; fathers, mothers, and children alike seemed preoccupied.

Suddenly the youngest, Roland de Bridoie, asked :

" Tell me, mamma, where did the abbé find that little boy ? "

His mother evaded a direct answer :

" Come, get on with your dinner, and let us alone with your questions."

He was silent for some minutes, and then went on :

" There was no one there except the lady who had stomachache. The abbé must be a conjurer, like Robert Houdin who made a bowl full of fishes come under a cloth."

"Be quiet now. It was God who sent him."

"But where did God put him? I didn't see anything. Did he come in by the door? Tell me."

Madame de Bridoie, losing patience, replied:

"Come now, that's enough, be quiet. He came from under a cabbage, like all little babies. You know that quite well."

"But there wasn't a cabbage in the carriage."

Then Gontran de Vaulacelles, who was listening with a sly look on his face, smiled and said:

"Yes, there was a cabbage. But no one saw it except the abbé."

ÇA IRA

I HAD ALIGHTED AT BARVILLES ONLY BECAUSE I HAD READ IN a guide (I don't know which): "Fine gallery, two Rubenses, one Teniers, one Ribera."

So I thought: Let's go and see it. I will dine at the Hôtel de l'Europe, which the guide declares to be admirable, and set out again to-morrow.

The gallery was closed: it was opened only when travellers asked to see it; it was opened now at my request, and I could contemplate some obscure daubs attributed by a highly-imaginative caretaker to the finest masters of painting.

Then I found myself all alone, in the long street of a small town quite strange to me, built in the very middle of illimitable plains; and, having absolutely nothing to do, I walked the whole length of this *artery*, I investigated several uninteresting shops; then, as it was only four o'clock, I was seized by one of those despondent moods which overwhelm the most spirited of us.

What could I do? Heaven help me, what could I do? I would have given twenty pounds for the suggestion of any conceivable amusement. Finding my mind barren of ideas, I decided merely to smoke a good cigar, and I went in search of the tobacconist's. I recognised it very shortly by its red lantern, and I went in. The saleswoman proffered me several boxes to choose from; having glanced at the cigars, which I perceived to be as bad as possible, I directed my attention, quite by chance, to the woman in charge.

She was a woman of about forty-five years of age, stout and turning grey. She had a plump, decent-looking face, which seemed to me somehow familiar. However, I did not know this lady. No, most assuredly I did not know her. But could it be that I had met her? Yes, that was possible. The face in front of me must be an acquaintance known only to me by sight, an old acquaintance since lost to view, changed now, and certainly grown much stouter.

I murmured:

"Forgive me, Madame, for staring at you like this, but I seem to have known you for a long time."

She answered, blushing:

"It's funny. I feel the same."

I gave a cry:

"Oh! Ça ira!"

She flung up both hands in exaggerated despair, absolutely overwhelmed by my words, and stammered:

"Oh, suppose someone hears you."

Then she herself cried suddenly:

"Well, I never! It's you, George!"

Then she looked round in terror lest anyone were listening. But we were alone, quite alone.

"Ca ira." How ever had I succeeded in recognising Ca ira, the skinny Ça ira, the forlorn Ça ira, in this placid and stout official of the Government?

Ca ira. What memories woke to sudden life in my heart: Bougival, La Grenouillère, Chatou, the Restaurant Fournaise, long days spent in skiffs along the riverside, ten years of my life spent in this corner of the country, on this delightful stretch of river.

At that time we were a company of twelve, living in Galopois' place, at Chatou, and leading there a queer enough life, always half naked and half drunk. The habits of the present-day boating man are considerably changed. Nowadays these gentlemen wear monocles.

In our set we had a score of river girls, regulars and casuals. Some Sundays we had four; on other Sundays they were all there. Some of them were, so to speak, members of the family;

the others came when they had nothing better to do. Five or six lived in communal fashion on the men who had no women, and among these was Ça ira.

She was a thin and wretched girl, and walked with a limp. This lent her the charms of a grasshopper. She was nervous, awkward, graceless in everything she did. She attached herself fearfully to the meanest, the most insignificant, the most poverty-stricken of us, who would keep her for a day or a month, according to his means. How she came to be one of us no one knew. Had we met her one Sunday evening, at the Rowing-Club ball, and rounded her up in one of those drives of women that we often made? Had we asked her to a meal, seeing her sit lonely at a little table in a corner? None of us could have said; but she was one of the gang.

We had christened her Ça ira, because she was always bewailing her fate, her misfortune, and her mortifications. Every Sunday we said to her:

"Well, Ça ira, is life treating you better?"

And she made an unvarying reply:

"No, not much, but we'll hope things will get better one of these days."

How came this wretched, unattractive, and graceless creature to be following a profession that demands infinite attractions, confidence, skill, and beauty? A mystery. But Paris is full of harlots ugly enough to disgust a policeman.

What did she do during the remaining six days of the week? She had told us on several occasions that she went to work. At what? We did not care to know; we were quite indifferent to the way in which she managed to exist.

Later, I had almost lost sight of her. Our little company gradually dispersed, leaving the way open for another generation, to whom we also left Ça ira. I heard about it on the odd occasions when I went to lunch at the Fournaise.

Our successors, unaware of our reason for bestowing that name upon her, had supposed it to be an Oriental name and they named her Zaïra: then in their turn they bequeathed their canoes and some of their river girls to the next generation. (Generally speaking, one generation of boating men lives on the water for three years, and then leaves the Seine to take up law, medicine, or politics.)

Zaira then became Zara, and, later still, Zara was modified into Sarah. By this time, she was supposed to be a Hebrew.

The latest of all, the gentlemen with the monocles, now called her simply, "The Jewess."

Then she disappeared.

And here I had found her again, selling tobacco at Barvilles.

I said to her:

"Well, things are better now, eh?"

She answered:

"A little better."

I was seized with curiosity about this woman's life.

In those earlier days, I had cared nothing at all about it; to-day I felt intimately concerned, held, vividly interested. I asked her:

"How did you manage to find an opportunity?"

"I don't know. It happened just when I was least expecting it."

"Was it at Chatou that you came upon it?"

"Oh, no."

"Then where was it?"

"At Paris, in the boarding-house where I lived."

"Ah, so you did have a place in Paris?"

"Yes, I was with Madame Ravelet."

"And who is Madame Ravelet?"

"You don't know Madame Ravelet? Oh!"

"Indeed I don't."

"The dressmaker, the fashionable dressmaker in the Rue de Rivoli."

Whereupon she began to tell me about a thousand little phases of her old life, a thousand hidden phases of Parisian life, the inside working of a fashionable dressmaker's, the life led by these wenches, their adventures, their notions, the intimate psychology of a workgirl, that street hawk flitting along the sidewalks in the morning on her way to the shop, strolling bare-headed after the midday meal, and on her way home in the evening.

Delighted to talk of old times, she said :

" If you knew how terrible we were . . . and what awful things we did ! We used to tell each other our adventures every day. We don't think much of men, I can tell you.

" As for me, the first trick I pulled off was over an umbrella. I had an old alpaca one, a disgraceful object. As I came in one rainy day, shutting it up, tall Louise says to me :

" ' I don't know how you dare go out with that thing.'

" ' But I haven't another, and at the moment funds are low.'

" Funds were always low !

" ' Go and pick one up at the Madeleine,' she answers.

" That surprises me.

" She goes on :

" ' That's where we all get them : there are as many as you want.'

" She explains the method to me. It is simple enough.

" So off I go with Irma to the Madeleine. We find the verger and explain to him that the week before we forgot an umbrella. Then he asks us if we remember what the handle was like, and I describe to him a handle with an agate knob. He takes us into a room where there were more than fifty lost umbrellas ; we look through them all and we don't find mine, but I choose a fine one, a very fine one with a handle of carved ivory. Louise went and claimed it some days later. She described it before she saw it, and they gave it to her without the least suspicion.

" For this sort of work, we dressed ourselves very smartly."

And she laughed, opening and dropping the hinged lid of the big tobacco box.

She went on :

" Oh, we played our little games, and very queer some of them were too. You see, there were five of us in the work-room, four ordinary girls and one quite different, Irma, lovely Irma. She looked like a gentlewoman, and she had a lover in the State Council. That did not prevent her from being very friendly with the rest of us. There was one winter when she said to us :

" ' You don't know what a jolly good thing we're going to pull off.'

" And she unfolded her idea to us.

" Irma, you know, was so shapely that she simply went to men's heads, and she had such a figure too, and hips that made your mouth water. And now she had thought of a way for each of us to wangle a hundred francs to buy ourselves rings, and she planned it out like this :

" You know I wasn't well off just then, and the others were no better ; we hardly made a hundred francs a month in the workshop, no more. We had to make the rest on the side.

" Of course each of us had two or three regular lovers who gave us a little money, but only a little. Sometimes during our noonday stroll we managed to catch the eye of a gentleman who came back again next day ; we'd play him up for a fortnight and then give in. But these fellows didn't bring in much. And the fellows at Chatou were merely recreation. Oh, if you knew the tricks we were up to ! They'd make you die of laughing. So when Irma said she'd thought of a way for us to make a hundred francs, we were wild with joy. It's a disgraceful tale I'm going to tell you, but I don't care ; you know a thing or two, since you've lived at Chatou for four years. . . .

" Well, she said to us :

" ' We are going to pick up at the Opera Ball the very best, most distinguished, and richest specimen of manhood in Paris. I know them all.'

" At first we couldn't believe it would come off, because

that sort of man isn't really open to dressmakers ; to Irma, yes, but not to us. Oh, she had style, had Irma. You know, we always said in the workroom that if the Emperor had known her, he would certainly have married her.

" For this business, she made us put on our smartest clothes, and she said :

" ' Now you won't come to the ball, you are each of you going to wait in a cab in one of the streets near by. A gentleman will come and get into your carriage. As soon as he gets in, you will embrace him as enticingly as you know how, and then you will scream to make him understand you've made a mistake and are expecting someone else. The pigeon will be thoroughly excited to think he's taking another man's place and he'll want to insist on staying ; you'll resist him, you'll struggle like the devil to get out . . . and then . . . you will go and have supper with him. . . . Then of course he'll have to give you something for your trouble.'

" You still don't understand ? Well, this is what she did, the sly little devil.

" She made all four of us get into four carriages, real private carriages, very swagger carriages, and then she sent us into the streets near the Opera. Then she went to the ball by herself. As she knew all the most famous men in Paris by name, because Madame dressed their wives, she picked one of them out and played him. She said all kinds of things to him ; my word, she was witty too. When she saw that he was well worked up, she dropped her mask and there he was caught in a noose. Then he wanted to take her off with him at once, and she gave him an appointment in half an hour's time in a carriage standing opposite Number 20 in the Rue Taitbout. In the carriage was me ! I was all wrapped up and my face veiled. Suddenly a gentleman put his head in at the window and said :

" ' Is it you ? '

" I answered softly :

" ' Yes, it's me, come in quickly.'

"He comes in, and I take him in my arms and hug him, hug him until he couldn't breathe ; then I go on :

"'Oh, how happy I am, how happy I am!'

"And then all at once I cry :

"'But it's not you! Oh, heavens! Heavens!'

"And I begin to weep.

"Imagine how embarrassed the man is! At first he tries to console me ; he apologises, and protests that he has made a mistake himself.

"I went on weeping, but less bitterly, and then sighed deeply. Then he talked tenderly to me. He was everything a gentleman should be, and how he was delighted to see my tears gradually stopping.

"In short, one thing led to another, and he suggested my going to supper with him. I refused ; I tried to jump out of the carriage ; he caught me round the waist, and then held me, as I had held him when he came in.

"And then . . . and then . . . we had . . . we had supper . . . you understand . . . and he gave me . . . guess, just guess . . . he gave me five hundred francs. . . . Believe me, some men are free with their money!

"Well, it came off all right with every one of us. Louise did least well with two hundred francs. But, you know, Louise really was too thin."

The tobacco-shop woman chattered on, pouring out in one wild rush all the memories stored so long in her heart, the cautiously closed heart of a Government licensee. All the days of poverty and adventure stirred in her memory. She thought with regret of the gay bohemian life of the Paris streets, a life of privation and sold kisses, of laughter and misery, of trickery and love that was not always feigned.

I said to her :

"But how did you get your licence to sell tobacco?"

She smiled :

"Oh, that's quite a story. I must tell you that in my

boarding-house I had right next door to me a law student; one of those students, you know, who never study. This one lived in cafés from morning to night, and he adored billiards, as I have never known anyone adore it.

"When I was alone we sometimes spent the evening together. It was by him that I had Roger."

"Who's Roger?"

"My son."

"Oh."

"He allowed me a little money to bring up the brat, but I knew very well that the fellow wouldn't be any real good to me; I was the surer of it because I'd never seen a man so slack, except him, never. At the end of ten years he hadn't got through his first exam. When his people saw that he would never come to anything, they sent for him to come back home somewhere in the provinces; but we kept up a correspondence about the child. And then—would you believe it?—at the last election, two years ago, I heard that he had been made a Deputy for his district. And then he spoke in the Chamber. It's quite true what they say, that in the kingdom of the blind. . . . Well, to cut the story short, I sought him out and made him get a tobacco shop for me at once, on the strength of my being the daughter of a deported man. It's quite true that my father was deported, but I never thought that would be any use to me.

"In short . . . but here's Roger."

There came in a tall young man, a correct, serious, self-conscious young man.

He dropped a kiss on his mother's forehead, and she said to me:

"Now, Monsieur, this is my son, head clerk at the town hall. You know what that means . . . future Sub-Prefect."

I greeted this functionary with all proper respect, and departed to go to my hotel after gravely pressing the hand held out to me by Ça ira.

UNMASKED

THE BOAT WAS CROWDED WITH PEOPLE. THE CROSSING promised to be calm, and the ladies of Havre were going to make an excursion to Trouville.

The ropes were cast off; a final shriek from the whistle announced our departure, and at the same moment the ship shuddered through her whole body, and along her flanks rose the sound of water rushing.

The paddles revolved for some seconds, stopped, and started again slowly: then the captain, standing on his bridge, shouted into the telephone that goes down into the bowels of the engine-room, "Right away," and they began to churn up the sea at full speed.

We glided along past the crowded quay. The people on the boat waved their handkerchiefs as if they were setting out for America, and their friends on shore waved back in like manner.

The burning July sun poured down on red sun-shades, on light frocks, on happy faces, on the almost unruffled sea. Once outside the harbour, the little boat swung sharply round, turning her narrow nose towards the far-off coast half seen through the morning haze.

On our left gaped the mouth of the Seine, twenty kilometres across. Here and there large buoys marked the position of the sandbanks, and from this distance we could see the smooth discoloured waters of the river, that did not mix with the salt water, but stretched out in long yellow ribbons across the vast, light-green spaces of the open sea.

As soon as I am aboard a ship, I feel an irresistible impulse to stride up and down, like a sailor keeping his watch. Why?

I don't know. So I begin to tramp round the bridge through the crowd of travellers.

Suddenly I heard my name. I turned round. It was an old friend of mine, Henri Sidoine, whom I had not seen for ten years.

We shook hands and, talking of one thing and another, we began to prowl up and down again together like bears in a cage, much as I had been doing alone just before. And as we talked we eyed the two rows of travellers seated along both sides of the bridge.

All at once Sidoine, his face distorted with anger, exclaimed :

" This boat is full of English people ! The swine ! "

It really was full of English people. The men stood up and looked at the horizon through their glasses, with a portentous air, as who should say : " We, we English, are the rulers of the waves. Boom, boom, look at us now ! "

And all the white sun-veils floating from their white hats looked like the waving flags of their complete self-sufficiency.

The gawky young ladies, whose footgear resembled their country's dreadnoughts, clasped shawls of many colours round their stiff bodies and skinny arms, and smiled vacantly at the brilliant seascape. Their tiny heads, pushed out at the ends of these long bodies, bore queer-shaped English hats, and the meagre rolls of hair resting on the nape of their necks looked like coiled snakes.

And the ancient spinsters, even skinnier, exposing their British jawbones to the widest extent, looked as if they were threatening the universe with their monstrous yellow teeth.

Walking past them, one caught a whiff of india-rubber and mouth-wash.

With growing indignation, Sidoine repeated :

" The swine ! Why can't we stop their coming into France ? "

I smiled and asked him :

" Why do you want to do that ? As far as I'm concerned, they're a matter of complete indifference."

He retorted :

" It's all very well for you. But I, I married an Englishwoman. And there you have it."

I stood still and laughed in his face.

" Oh, the devil you did ! Tell me about it. She makes you very unhappy, does she ? "

He shrugged his shoulders.

" No, not exactly."

" Then . . . she . . . she . . . deceives you ? "

" Unfortunately, no. That would give me grounds for divorce and I should be vastly relieved thereby."

" Well, I don't understand it, then."

" You don't understand ? That doesn't surprise me. Well, it's nothing more than the fact that she has learned French ! Listen :

" I had not the least desire in the world to get married when two years ago I went to spend the summer at Étretat. There's nothing so fatal as these seaside towns. One overlooks the fact that slips of girls look their best in these places. Paris suits women and the country suits young girls.

" The donkey rides, the morning bathe, picnic luncheons, are so many matrimonial snares. And really there is nothing more charming than an eighteen-year-old child running across a field or gathering flowers by the roadside.

" I made the acquaintance of an English family staying at the same hotel as I was. The father looked like the men you see over there, and the mother like all other Englishwomen.

" There were two sons, the type of bony youth that plays violent games from morning to evening, with balls, sticks, or rackets ; then two girls, the eldest a dry stick, another of those Englishwomen like preserved fruits ; the younger a marvellous creature. A fair, or rather a flaxen-haired girl, with a head conceived in heaven. When these pretty rogues make themselves charming, they are divine. This one had blue eyes,

eyes of that blue which seems to hold all the poetry, all the romance, all the ideals, all the joy of earth.

"What a world of infinite dreams is opened to you by a woman's eyes, such eyes as those! How it calls to the eternal longings and confused desires of our hearts!

"You must remember, too, that we French adore foreigners. As soon as we meet a Russian, Italian, Swedish, Spanish, or English woman with the least claims to beauty, we instantly fall in love. Everything that comes from abroad delights us extravagantly—broadcloth, hats, gloves, guns, and—women.

"We are wrong, however.

"But I believe that what attracts us most in strange women is their broken speech. Immediately a woman speaks our language badly, we find her charming; if she uses quite the wrong French words, she is entrancing, and if she babbles a quite unintelligible dialect she becomes irresistible.

"You cannot imagine how charming it is to hear an adorable rosy mouth say: '*J'aime bôcoup la gigotte.*'

"My little English Kate spoke a language like nothing on earth. For the first few days I couldn't understand it at all, she invented so many amazing words; then I became completely infatuated with this absurd, light-hearted jargon.

"In her mouth all the old, mangled, and ridiculous phrases became utterly fascinating; and every evening on the terrace of the Casino we held long conversations which were no more than a succession of enigmatic phrases.

"I married her! I loved her to distraction, as a dream can be loved. For what your true lover adores is always a dream in the form of a woman.

"You remember the admirable verses of Louis Bouilhet:

> 'What hadst thou been without me? 'Twas but I
> Woke thy mute, senseless strings to melody.
> 'Twere my dream's song, thine empty heart within,
> As music in a hollow violin.'

" Ah, well, my dear friend, the only mistake I made was in giving my wife a French teacher.

" As long as she murdered our vocabulary, and tortured our grammar, I was fond of her.

" Our conversations were simple. They revealed to me the amazing beauty of her person, the incomparable grace of her gestures ; they presented her to me in the guise of a wonderful speaking toy, a flesh-and-blood puppet made for kisses, able to stammer a few words to tell what she loved, sometimes to utter quaint exclamations, and to express in a fashion that was adorable because so incomprehensible and unexpected, her emotions and her unsophisticated sensations.

" She was like nothing but those pretty playthings that say 'papa' and 'mamma,' pronouncing them *Bah-ba* and *Mah-ma*.

" How could I have believed that. . . .

" She can speak, now. . . . She can speak . . . badly . . . very badly. . . . She makes quite as many mistakes. . . . But she can make herself understood . . . yes, I understand her . . . I know what she says . . . I know her. . . .

" I have broken my doll to look at her inside. . . . I have seen it. . . . And still I have to go on talking to her, my dear !

" Oh, you can have no idea of the opinions, the notions, the theories of a young, well brought-up English girl, whom I have no cause to reproach, and who recites to me from morning to night all the phrases out of a phrase-book for the use of schoolgirls and young persons.

" You have seen those cotillion favours, those pretty gilded paper packets which contain utterly detestable bon-bons. I got one of them. I tore it open. I wanted to eat the contents, and now I am all the time so savagely disgusted that I feel a positive nausea at the mere sight of one of her countrymen.

" I have married a woman who is like nothing but a parrot that an old English governess has taught to speak French : do you understand ? "

We were in sight of the crowded wooden quays of Trouville Harbour.

I said:

"Where is your wife?"

"I have taken her to Étretat," he declared.

"And you, where are you going?"

"I? I am going to Trouville to distract my mind."

Then, after a pause, he added:

"You simply cannot imagine how utterly stupid some women can be."

SOLITUDE

IT WAS AFTER A MALE DINNER-PARTY. THE EVENING HAD been hilarious. One of the guests, an old friend of mine, said to me:

"Would you like to walk up the Avenue des Champ-Élysées?"

So we set off, walking slowly up the long sidewalk, under trees that showed their first sparse leaves. There was no sound but the confused, ceaseless murmuring of Paris. A fresh wind blew across our faces, and the dark sky was sown with a golden dust by the myriad stars.

My companion said to me:

"I don't know why, but I breathe better here at night than anywhere else in the world. At these times my spirit seems freed. For a moment, I have one of those sudden inward gleams of light that for a fraction of time deceive us with the thought that we have penetrated the divine secret of the universe. Then the window closes again. The moment is gone."

From time to time we see two shadows slipping along under the walls; we walk past a bench where, pressed close together, two human beings are merged into one dark blur.

The man at my side murmured:

"Poor wretches! They rouse in me no disgust, but only a profound pity. Of all the mysteries of human life, I have pierced one: the terrible unhappiness of mortal life has its roots in the lifelong loneliness of every one of us: all our strivings, all our acts have one end only, escape from this loneliness. Those poor creatures, making love on public benches in the open air, are trying, as we try, as all mortal wretches try, to end their isolation, if only for a moment or less ; but they remain, they will always remain solitary, and so shall we also.

" Some days we realise it more sharply, some less, that's all.

" For some time now I have been suffering the unspeakable torment born of my realisation, my vision of the frightful solitude in which I spend my life, and I know that nothing can end it, nothing, I tell you. Whatever our strivings, whatever our deeds, whatever the wild desire of our hearts, the demands of our lips and the clutch of our arms, we are always solitary.

" I persuaded you to walk along here with me this evening because I suffer horribly, these days, from the loneliness of my rooms. What good will this do me ? I talk to you, you listen to me, and we are alone together, side by side, but alone. Do you understand ?

" Blessed are the poor in spirit, says the Scripture. They keep the illusion of happiness. Such as they do not endure a solitary bitterness, they do not, as I do, drift through life and never touch it but to jostle elbows with it, with no joy but a self-centred satisfaction in understanding, observing, guessing, and enduring without end the knowledge of our eternal isolation.

" You think me a little mad, don't you ?

" Listen to me. Since I have been conscious of the solitude of my spirit, I have felt that day by day I penetrate a little further into a subterranean darkness, whose bounds I cannot find, whose end I do not know, which perhaps has no end. I go my way through it with no companion, with no one near me, and no living soul is walking along the same shadowy road. This subterranean passage is life. Sometimes I hear sounds, voices, cries. . . . I grope towards these confused murmurs. But I never know exactly whence they come ; I never meet any other person, I never touch another hand in the darkness that surrounds me. Do you understand ?

" At times men have caught a glimpse of this frightful anguish.

" Musset wrote :

> ' Who comes ? Who calls ? No voice.
> 'Twas but the ticking clock
> My solitude to mock.'

" But, for him, it was only a fleeting uneasiness, and not, as for me, a hard certainty. He was a poet ; he peopled life with phantoms and dreams. He was never truly alone. I, I am alone !

" Did not Gustave Flaubert, one of the great seers and therefore one of the great tragic figures of this world, write to a friend these despairing words ?—' We are all of us in a wilderness. No man understands any other.'

" No, no man understands any other, whatever he thinks, whatever he says, whatever he tries to do. Does the earth know what is happening in those stars we see, flung out in space like a seed of fire, so distant that we see the light of a few only, while the innumerable company of the others is lost in infinity, so near that they are perhaps one whole like the molecules of a body ?

" Even so, man has no more knowledge of what is taking place in another man. We are farther from each other than these stars, and even more isolated, since thought is an impassable barrier.

" Do you know anything more dreadful than the swift and endless passing by of human beings whose minds we cannot reach ? We love each other as if we were chained fast, close together, with outstretched arms that just cannot touch. We are torn with a desire for union, but all our efforts are barren, our moments of passionate abandon futile, our caresses vain. We reach out towards an intimate union, we strain towards each other, and achieve no more than the violent impact of our bodies.

" I never feel more solitary than when I open my heart to a friend, because it is then that I realise most sharply the impassable barrier. He is beside me, this man; I see his clear eyes fixed on me, but of his soul, behind them, I know nothing at all. He listens to me. What is he thinking? You don't understand this agony of mind? Perhaps he hates me? or despises me? or is jeering at me? He thinks over what I am saying, he judges me, he rails at me, he condemns me, considers me commonplace or a fool. How do I know what he is thinking? How do I know whether he loves me as I love him? And what is passing through that small round head? What mysterious things are the secret thoughts of a human being, these thoughts that are at once hidden and free, that we can neither know, nor direct, nor rule, nor vanquish!

"And I, even I, who have all the will in the world to give my whole being, to fling open all the doors of my soul, cannot surrender myself. In the deepest recesses of my being, I guard the secret hiding-place of this I where no man can enter in. No man can discover it, nor enter therein, because no other man is made in my likeness, because no man understands any other.

"Even now, as I speak, do you at least understand me? No, you think me mad! You watch me curiously, you guard yourself from me! You say to yourself: 'What is the matter with him this evening?' but if ever there comes to you a moment of insight, and you feel in all its horror the subtle and unbearable suffering I endure, come to me and say only, 'I understand you,' and you will give me perhaps one second of happiness.

"There are women who make me realise my solitude even more vividly.

"Wretched! Most wretched! How I have suffered through them, because more often than men do, they have deluded me into thinking that I do not live alone.

"When we enter the dominion of Love we feel a sudden sense of freedom. An unearthly happiness pervades us. Do you know why? Do you know whence comes this sense of profound well-being? It is born of nothing more than a dream that we are no longer solitary. The isolation, the forsaken loneliness of the human spirit seems ended. What folly!

"Even more cruelly driven are we by the undying craving for love which gnaws at our lonely hearts; woman is the dream's supremest cheat.

"You know those glorious hours spent in the company of this long-haired creature whose form enchants us and whose glance inflames us. What ecstasy it is that confounds our minds! What false dream that sweeps us away!

"Can it be that any moment now she and I will be one, one whole? But this 'any moment now' never comes, and after weeks of waiting, of hope and deceitful joy, one day I find myself suddenly more alone than I have ever been before.

"After each kiss, after each embrace, the isolation grows. And how overwhelming, how monstrous it is!

"Sully-Prudhomme, the poet, wrote:

> 'Vain, vain are our embraces, vain our love;
> Vainly we strive with arms that clasp and yearn
> To blend our souls, alone for evermore.'

And then, good-bye. It is the end. You hardly recognise this woman who for an instant of time has been everything to you, and whose inmost—and probably quite commonplace—soul has remained a mystery to you.

"In the very hours when it seemed that, in a mysterious harmony of spirit, a perfect mingling of your desires and all your longings, you had reached down to the very depths of her soul, a word, sometimes only one word, reveals your error and, like a bright light in darkness, shows you the black pit opened between you.

"Nevertheless, the dearest thing in the world still is to spend an evening in the presence of a beloved woman, without words, almost entirely content in the mere sense of her nearness. Ask for nothing more, for never will your soul meet another's.

"As for me, I have shut up the gates of my spirit. I no longer talk to anyone of what I believe, what I think, and what I love. Knowing myself condemned to a frightful solitude, I look out on life as a spectator, and make no comments. Of what account are opinions, quarrels, pleasures, beliefs? Unable to share my life with any other creature, I stand apart from all. My spirit, unseen, keeps its undiscovered house. I have conventional phrases with which to reply to the day's questions, and a smile that signifies 'Yes' when I do not want even to take the trouble to speak.

"Do you understand?"

We had walked up the long avenue as far as the Arc de Triomphe at the Étoile end, and now come back to the Place de la Concorde, for he had delivered himself of all this without haste and added to it a great deal more that now I do not remember.

He halted; and flinging out his arm in an abrupt gesture towards the tall granite obelisk that rears itself from the stones of Paris and loses its lofty Egyptian profile in the stars, an exiled monument bearing the history of its country written in strange signs on its flank, my friend cried: "Look, we are all as that stone!" and left me on the instant without another word.

Was he drunk? Was he mad? Was he inspired? Even now I do not know. Sometimes I think that he was right; sometimes I think that he had lost his mind.

BESIDE THE BED

A great fire blazed on the hearth. On the Japanese table two tea-cups faced each other, and the teapot steamed on one side, near a sugar-basin flanked by a decanter of rum.

The Comte de Sallure threw his hat, his gloves, and his fur coat on a chair, while the Comtesse, her evening-cloak flung off, smoothed her hair lightly in front of the mirror. She was smiling happily to herself, and tapping the hair that curled above her temples with the tips of her slender fingers, gleaming with rings. Then she turned towards her husband. He looked at her for some minutes, in a hesitating way, as if a secret thought were troubling him.

At last he said :

" And are you satisfied with the homage paid to you this evening ? "

She gave him a direct glance, a glance on fire with triumph and defiance, and answered :

" I should hope so ! "

Then she seated herself in the chair. He sat down facing her and, crumbling a roll, went on :

" It was almost ridiculous . . . for me."

She asked :

" Is this a scene ? Do you intend to reproach me ? "

" No, my dear, I am only saying that this Monsieur Burel has been dancing attendance on you in a rather unnecessary way. If . . . if . . . if I had any rights in the matter, I should be angry."

" My dear, be honest. It is merely that you do not feel to-day as you felt last year. When I discovered that you had a mistress, a mistress of whom you were very fond, you did not trouble yourself whether anyone paid homage to me or not. I told you how grieved I was; I said, as you have said this evening, but with more justice on my side: 'My friend, you are compromising Madame de Servy, you are hurting me and you are making me ridiculous.' What did you reply? Oh, you gave me quite clearly to understand that I was free, that between intelligent people marriage was only an association of common interests, a social tie, but not a moral tie. Isn't that so? You gave me to understand that your mistress was infinitely better than I, more seductive, more of a woman. That is what you said: more of a woman. This was all hedged about, of course, with the tact of a well-bred man, wrapped up in compliments, conveyed with a delicacy to which I offer my profound respect. It was none the less perfectly clear to me.

"We agreed that thenceforward we would live together, but quite separated. We had a child who formed a link between us.

"You practically gave me to understand that you cared only for appearances, that I could, if I pleased, take a lover, so long as the liaison remained a secret one. You held forth at great length and quite admirably on women's subtle tact, on the ease with which they steered their way through the decencies of society.

"I understood, my friend, I understood perfectly. In those days you loved Madame de Servy so very passionately, and my legitimate affection, my legal tenderness, bored you. No doubt I reduced your opportunities. Since then we have lived separate lives. We go about together, we return together, and then we go each our own way.

"And now, for the past month or two, you have assumed airs of jealousy. What does it all mean?"

"My dear, I am not at all jealous, but I am afraid of seeing you compromise yourself. You are young, gay, adventurous. . . ."

"Pardon me, but if we are talking of adventures, I insist upon a balance being struck between us."

"Come now, don't joke about it, I beg you. I am speaking

to you as a friend, your true friend. As for all that you have just been saying, it is very exaggerated."

"Not at all. You confessed, you confessed your liaison to me, which is equivalent to giving me leave to go and do likewise. I have not done it. . . ."

"Allow me!"

"Please let me speak. I have not done it. I have no lover, and I have not had one . . . yet. I wait . . . I look . . . I find no one. I must have someone really splendid, finer than you. . . . I am paying you a compliment, and you do not seem to appreciate it."

"My dear, all these witticisms are quite out of place."

"But I am not attempting to be witty at all. You talked to me about the eighteenth century. You gave me to understand that you had the morals of the Regency. I have forgotten nothing. On the day when it suits me to cease being what I am, whatever you do will be quite useless, you understand, you will be a cuckold like the others, and you will never even suspect it."

"Oh . . . how can you take such words on your lips?"

"Such words! . . . But you laughed heartily enough when Madame de Gers said that Monsieur de Servy looked like a cuckold in search of his horns."

"What may seem witty in the mouth of Madame de Gers becomes unseemly in yours."

"Not at all. But you find the word 'cuckold' very amusing when it is applied to Monsieur de Servy, and you think it has an ugly sound when it is applied to yourself. Everything depends on the point of view. Besides, I don't insist upon the word, I only threw it out to see if you were ripe."

"Ripe . . . for what?"

"To be it, of course. When a man is annoyed at hearing that word spoken, it means that he . . . is asking for it. In two months' time you will be the first to laugh if I speak of a

. . . head-dress. Then . . . yes . . . when one actually is it, one doesn't feel it."

"You are behaving in the worst possible taste this evening. I have not seen you like this."

"Ah, well, you see . . . I have changed . . . for the worse. It is your fault."

"Come, my dear, let us talk seriously. I beg you, I implore you not to permit Monsieur Burel's unpleasant assiduity, as you did this evening."

"You are jealous. I was quite right."

"No: not at all. I am only anxious not to look ridiculous. I don't want to look ridiculous. And if I see that gentleman making further conversation against your . . . shoulders, or rather between your breasts. . . ."

He was looking for a channel to make his words carry.

"I . . . I shall box his ears."

"Are you by any chance in love with me?"

"A man might be in love with far less attractive women."

"Stop where you are, please. To tell the truth, I'm no longer in love with you."

The Comte stands up. He makes his way round the little table and, walking behind his wife, presses a kiss on the nape of her neck. She jumps to her feet with a movement of repulsion, and giving him a penetrating glance:

"No more of these pleasantries between us, please. We live apart. It's all over."

"Come now, don't be offended. I have been finding you adorable for a long time."

"Then . . . then . . . it means that I have improved. You too . . . you find me . . . ripe."

"I find you ravishing, my dear; you have arms, a skin, shoulders. . . ."

"Which will please Monsieur Burel."

"You are cruel. But there . . . frankly . . . I don't know another woman so uncommonly attractive as you are."

" You have been fasting."

" What ? "

" I say, you have been fasting."

" Why do you say that ? "

" When a man fasts, he is hungry, and when he is hungry, he is prepared to eat things that at any other time he could not stomach. I am the dish, previously rejected, that you would not be sorry to feel between your teeth . . . this evening."

" Oh, Marguerite ! Who has taught you to speak like this ? "

" You. Think : since your break with Madame de Servy, you have had, to my knowledge, four mistresses, *cocottes* all of them, and perfect of their kind. So how do I suppose I can explain your . . . airy nonsense of this evening, except as the consequence of a temporary abstinence ? "

" I will be brutally frank, without mincing words. I have fallen in love with you again. Really and madly. That's all."

" Oh, indeed ! Then you would like to . . . begin again ? "

" Yes, Madame."

" This evening ! "

" Marguerite ! "

" Good. You shall be still further scandalised. My dear, let us understand each other. We are no longer anything to each other, are we ? I am your wife, it is true, but your wife . . . set free. I am about to take up an engagement elsewhere ; you demand to be given preference. I will give it you . . . at the same price."

" I don't understand."

" Let me make myself clear. Am I as good as your *cocottes* ? Be honest about it."

" A thousand times better."

" Better than the best of them ? "

" A thousand times."

" Well, how much did the best of the lot cost you in three months ? "

" I don't follow you."

"I say, how much did three months of your most charming mistress cost you, in money, jewellery, suppers, dinners, theatres, etc.—the whole business, in short?"

"How on earth do I know?"

"You must know. Let's see now, the average cost, a moderate estimate. Five thousand francs a month: is that about right?"

"Yes . . . just about."

"Well, my friend, give me five thousand francs now, and I am yours for a month, including this evening."

"You are mad."

"So you look at it that way: good night."

The Comtesse goes out of the room into her bedroom. The curtains of the bed are half drawn. A dim fragrance fills the air, it clings to the coverings of the bed itself.

The Comte appears in the doorway.

"That's a delightful scent."

"Really? . . . It's no different, you know. I always use *peau d'Espagne*."

"Amazing! . . . It smells delightful."

"Possibly. But do me the kindness of leaving me now, because I am going to bed."

"Marguerite."

"Go at once."

He comes right into the room, and sits down in the arm-chair.

The Comtesse:

"So that's it? Well, so much the worse for you."

She slowly puts off her dance-frock, slipping out her bare white arms. She lifts them above her head to take down her hair before the glass; and something rosy gleams under a froth of lace at the edge of her black corset.

The Comte springs to his feet and comes towards her.

The Comtesse:

"Don't come near me, or I shall be angry."

He takes her bodily into his arms and feels for her lips.

Then, with an agile twist of her body, she snatches from her dressing-table a glass of the perfumed water she uses for her mouth and flings it over her shoulder full in her husband's face.

He leaps back, dripping with water, furious, murmuring:

"That's a silly trick."

"That may be. But you know my conditions, five thousand francs."

"But that's absolutely insane."

"Why insane?"

"What, why? A husband to pay for sleeping with his wife!"

"Oh . . . what unpleasant words you use!"

"Possibly. I repeat that a man would be insane to pay his wife, his legal wife."

"It is much stupider, when one has a legal wife, to pay *cocottes*."

"Maybe so, but I don't care to be ridiculous."

The Comtesse is sitting on a couch. She draws her stockings slowly down, turning them inside out like the skin of a snake. Her rosy leg emerges from its sheath of mauve silk, and her adorable little foot rests on the carpet.

The Comte draws a little nearer, and in a soft voice:

"What has put this mad idea into your head?"

"What idea?"

"To ask me for five thousand francs."

"Nothing could be more natural. We are strangers to each other, aren't we? And now you want me. You can't marry me, since we are married. So you buy me, a little more cheaply than anyone else perhaps.

"Think now. This money, instead of passing into the hands of a hussy to be used for goodness knows what, will remain in your own house, in your household. Moreover, an intelligent man should find it rather original to pay for his own wife. In an illicit love-affair, the sweetest pleasures are those that cost dearly, very dearly. You give your love . . .

your quite legitimate love, a new value, a savour of vice, a spice of . . . dissipation, when you . . . put a price on it as if it were bought love. Isn't that so?"

She rises to her feet, almost naked, and turns towards a bathroom.

"Now, sir, please go at once, or I shall ring for my maid."

The Comte stands still, puzzled, ill at ease, and looks at her, and abruptly, throwing his pocket-book at her:

"There you are, you baggage, there's six thousand in it. . . . But you understand?"

The Comtesse picks up the money, counts it, and drawls:

"What?"

"Don't make a habit of this."

She breaks into laughter, and going towards him:

"Every month, sir, five thousand, or back I send you to your *cocottes*. And . . . if you are satisfied . . . I shall even demand a rise."

THE LITTLE SOLDIER

EVERY SUNDAY, AS SOON AS THEY WERE OFF DUTY, THE TWO little soldiers set out for a walk.

On leaving the barracks, they turned to the right, crossed Courbevoie with quick strides as if they were marching on parade ; then, as soon as they had left the houses behind, they walked at a quieter pace down the bare, dusty high road to Bezons.

They were small, thin, lost in army coats that were too large and too long, with sleeves falling over their hands, and embarrassed by red trousers so uncomfortably baggy that they were compelled to stretch their legs wide apart in order to walk at a good pace. And under the tall, stiff shakos, hardly a glimpse was visible of their faces, two humble, sunken Breton faces, innocent like the faces of animals, with gentle, placid blue eyes.

They spoke no word during the whole journey, walking straight on, with the same thought in both their heads, which did instead of conversation, for on the edge of the little wood of Champioux they had found a spot that reminded them of their own country, and they felt happy nowhere else.

At the cross-roads from Colombes to Chatou, where the trees begin, they took off the hats that crushed their heads, and mopped their brows.

They always stopped for a short while on Bezons bridge to look at the Seine. They lingered there two or three minutes, bent double, hanging over the parapet ; they looked long at the wide reaches of Argenteuil, where the white, leaning sails of the clippers raced over the water, bringing to their minds perhaps the Breton sea, the port of Vannes near their own homes, and the fishing-boats sailing across the Morbihan to the open sea.

As soon as they had crossed the Seine, they bought their provisions from the pork butcher, the baker, and the man who sold the light wine of the district. A piece of black pudding, four ha'p'orth of bread, and a pint of cheap claret made up their rations, and were carried in their handkerchiefs. But, once beyond the village, they sauntered on very slowly, and at last began to talk.

In front of them a stretch of poor land, dotted with clumps of trees, led to the wood, to the little wood which they had thought like Kermarivan wood. Corn and oats bordered the narrow path, which was lost under the green shoots of the crops, and every time they came, Jean Kerderen said to Luc Le Ganidec:

" It is just like Plounivon."

" Yes, just like it."

They wandered on, side by side, their minds filled with vague memories of their own place, filled with new-awakened pictures, crude and simple pictures like those on cheap picture post-cards. They saw in thought a corner of a field, a hedge, an edge of moor, a cross-roads, a granite cross.

Each time they came, they stopped beside the stone marking the boundaries of an estate, because it had a look of the dolmen at Locneuven.

Every Sunday, when they reached the first clump of trees, Luc Le Ganidec cut himself a switch, a hazel switch; he began carefully peeling off the thin bark, thinking all the time of people at home.

Jean Kerderen carried the provisions.

Now and then Luc mentioned a name, recalled an incident of their childhood, in words that, few as they were, woke long thoughts. And by slow degrees their country, their beloved, far-off country, took them back to herself, filled their thoughts and senses, sent them across the space between, her shapes, her sounds, her familiar horizons, her scents, the scent of green plains swept by the salt sea air.

No longer did they feel the smoky breath of Paris that feeds the trees of her suburbs, but the scent of gorse drawn up on the salt breeze and carried out to the wide sea. And the sails of the pleasure-boats, seen above the banks, looked to them like the sails of the small coasting-boats, seen beyond the wide plain that stretched from their door-step to the very edge of the waves.

They walked slowly on, Luc Le Ganidec and Jean Kerderen, happy and sad, filled with a sweet melancholy, the dull, deep-seated melancholy of a caged beast that remembers.

And by the time Luc had finished stripping the slender switch of its skin, they reached the corner of the wood where every Sunday they ate their lunch.

They found again the two bricks they had hidden in a coppice, and they lit a little fire of branches to cook their black puddings on the point of their knife.

And when they had lunched, eaten their bread to the last crumb, and drunk their wine to the last drop, they remained sitting side by side in the grass, silent, gazing absently into space, eyes drowsily half closed, stretched out beside the field poppies; the leather of their shakos and the leather of their buttons gleamed under the burning sun and fascinated the larks that hovered singing above their heads.

As it drew towards noon, they began to throw occasional glances in the direction of Bezons village, for it was nearly time for the cow-girl to come.

She came past them every Sunday, on her way to milk her cow and take it back to its shed; it was the only cow in the district that was out at grass; it was pastured in a narrow meadow further along, on the fringe of the wood.

Very soon they caught sight of the servant-girl, the only human being walking across the fields, and they were filled with joy by the dazzling flashes of light reflected from the tin pail in the blazing sunshine. They never talked about her. They were content just to see her, without understanding why.

She was a tall, lusty wench, auburn-haired and burnt by the heat of days spent in the open air, a tall bold wench of the Parisian country-side.

Once, seeing them always sitting in the same spot, she said to them :

" Good morning ; d'you always come here ? "

Luc Le Ganidec, the more daring, stammered :

" Yes, we come for a rest."

That was all. But next Sunday she laughed when she saw them, she laughed in the protective, good-humoured fashion of an experienced woman fully conscious of their timidity, and she cried :

" What d'you sit there for ? Are you watching the grass grow ? "

Luc smiled joyously back :

" Maybe so."

She retorted :

" Well, it's slow enough."

He replied, laughing all the time :

" It is that."

She went on. But when she came back with her pail full of milk, she stopped again in front of them, and said :

" Would you like a drop ? It'll remind you of your home."

With the instinctive understanding of a woman of their own class, herself far from her native place perhaps, she had put into words their deepest emotions.

They were both touched. Then, not without difficulty, she poured a little milk down the narrow neck of the pint bottle in which they carried their wine ; and Luc drank first, in little gulps, stopping every moment to see whether he was taking more than his share. Then he gave the bottle to Jean.

She remained standing in front of them, hands on hips, her pail resting on the ground at her feet, happy in the pleasure she was giving them.

Then she went off, crying :

"Well, good-bye! See you next Sunday."

And as long as they could see it, their eyes followed her tall figure getting farther away and smaller, as if it were merging itself in the green shadows of the trees.

When they left the barracks on the Sunday after that, Jean said to Luc:

"Oughtn't we to buy her something nice?"

They could not make up their minds in this exceedingly awkward matter of choosing a delicacy for the cow-girl.

Luc was in favour of a scrap of chitterlings, but Jean preferred caramels, for he loved sweets. His advice carried the day, and they bought a penny-worth of red and white sweets at the grocer's.

They ate their lunch faster than usual, excited by the thought of what was coming.

Jean saw her first.

"There she is," he said.

Luc added:

"Yes, there she is."

She began laughing a long way off, as soon as she saw them, and cried:

"And how are you? All right?"

They answered in one breath:

"How's yourself?"

Then she chatted away, she talked of the simple things that interested them, of the weather, the crops, of her employers.

They dared not offer their sweets, which were melting nicely in Jean's pocket.

At last Luc plucked up heart and murmured:

"We've brought something."

She demanded:

"What is't, then?"

So Jean, red to the ears, drew out the tiny twist of paper and offered it to her.

She began eating the little bits of sugar, rolling them from one cheek to the other and forming little swollen lumps under the flesh. The two soldiers sat in front of her and watched her, excited and very pleased.

Then she went on to milk her cow, and, as she came back, gave them some milk again.

They thought of her all week and spoke of her more than once. Next Sunday she sat down beside them for a longer chat, and the three of them, sitting side by side, stared absently into space, hugging their knees with clasped hands, and told each other little tales and little details of the villages where they were born, while farther off the cow, seeing the servant-girl pausing on her way, stretched towards her its clumsy head with its moist nostrils, and lowed patiently to attract her attention.

Before long the girl consented to eat a bite with them and drink a mouthful of wine. Often she brought them plums in her pocket, for the plum season had begun. Her presence set the two little Breton soldiers very much at their ease, and they chattered away like two birds.

Then one Wednesday, Luc Le Ganidec applied for a pass out of barracks, a thing which he had never done before, and he did not come in until ten o'clock at night.

Thoroughly disturbed, Jean racked his brains to imagine why his comrade had dared to go out like that.

On the following Friday, Luc borrowed ten sous from the man who slept next him, and again asked and got leave to absent himself for some hours.

And when he set out with Jean for their Sunday walk, he wore a very sly, preoccupied, and altogether different air. Kerderen did not understand it, but he was vaguely suspicious of something, without guessing what it might be.

They never said a word until they reached their accustomed resting-place, where they had worn away the grass by sitting always in the same spot; and they ate their lunch slowly. Neither of them was hungry.

Very soon the girl came into sight. They watched her coming as they did every Sunday. When she was quite near them, Luc got up and took two steps. She placed her pail on the ground and hugged him. She hugged him violently, throwing her arms round his neck, quite regardless of Jean, not dreaming he was there, not even seeing him.

Poor Jean sat there bewildered, so bewildered that he did not understand it at all, his mind in a turmoil, his heart broken, still unable to realise it.

Then the girl sat down beside Luc, and they began to chatter. Jean did not look at them; he guessed now why his comrade had gone out twice during the week, and he felt within himself a burning anguish, a sort of wound, the dreadful tearing agony of betrayal.

Luc and the girl got up and went off together to see to the cow. Jean followed them with his eyes. He saw them getting farther and farther away, side by side. His comrade's scarlet trousers formed a dazzling patch on the road. It was he who took up the mallet and hammered in the stake to which the beast was fastened.

The girl squatted down to do the milking, while he caressed the animal's bony spine with a careless hand. Then they left the pail on the grass and withdrew into the wood.

Jean saw nothing but the leafy wall through which they had gone; and he felt so distressed that if he had tried to get up, he would certainly have dropped where he stood.

He sat perfectly still, quite senseless with amazement and misery, a profound unreasoning misery. He longed to cry, to run away, to hide himself, never to see anyone again.

Suddenly he saw them coming out of the coppice. They walked back happily, hand in hand, like village sweethearts. It was Luc who carried the pail.

They embraced again before they parted, and the girl went

off, throwing Jean a friendly good night and a knowing smile. To-day she never remembered to give him any milk.

The two little soldiers remained there side by side, motionless as always, silent and calm, their placid faces revealing nothing of the emotions that raged in their hearts. The sun went down on them. Now and then the cow lowed, watching them from far off.

They got up to go back at the usual hour.

Luc peeled a switch. Jean carried the empty bottle. He left it with the wine-seller in Bezons. Then they made for the bridge, and, as they did every Sunday, halted half-way across to watch the water slip past a while.

Jean leaned over, leaned farther and farther over the iron railing, as if he had seen something in the rushing stream that fascinated him. Luc said to him:

"Do you want to drink a mouthful?"

As the last word left his mouth, the rest of Jean followed his head, his lifted legs described a circle in the air, and the little blue and red soldier dropped like a stone, struck the water, and disappeared in it.

Luc's throat contracted with agony and he tried vainly to shout. Farther down-stream he saw something move; then his comrade's head rose to the surface of the river to sink again.

Farther down still he caught one more glimpse, a hand, only a hand thrust out of the water and sucked down again. Then nothing more.

The watermen who came running up did not find the body that day.

Luc returned to barracks alone, running, completely distracted, and related the accident, eyes and voice full of tears, and blowing his nose furiously.

"He leaned over . . . he . . . he leaned over . . . so far . . . so far that his head did a somersault . . . and . . . and . . . there he was fallen over . . . fallen over. . . ."

Emotion choked him and he could not say any more. If he had only known. . . .

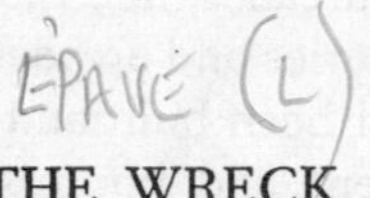

THE WRECK

IT WAS YESTERDAY, DECEMBER THE THIRTY-FIRST.

I had just lunched with my old friend, Georges Garin. The servant brought him a letter covered with seals and foreign stamps.

" May I ? " asked Georges.

" Certainly."

And he began to read eight pages written in a large English hand and crossed in all directions. He read it slowly with a grave intentness, and the deep interest we take in the things that lie near our hearts.

Then he placed the letter on a corner of the chimney-piece and said :

" Well, that's a queer story and one I've never told you ; a love story too, and it happened to me. A queer New Year's Day I had, that year. It's twenty years since. . . . I was thirty then, and now I'm fifty !

" In those days I was an inspector of the Maritime Insurance Company that to-day I direct. I had arranged to spend New Year's Day on holiday in Paris, since it's usual to keep holiday that day, when I had a letter from the director ordering me to set out immediately for the Island of Ré, where a three-master of St. Nazaire, insured by us, had run aground. It was then eight o'clock in the morning. I reached the Company's offices at ten to receive my orders, and the same evening I took the express, which landed me at La Rochelle the following day, December the thirty-first.

" I had two hours to spare before going aboard the Ré boat, the *Jean-Guiton*. I took a walk round the town. La Rochelle is a most fantastic and strangely individual town, with its twisting, labyrinthine streets, where the pavements run under endless galleries with covered arcades, like those of the Rue de Rivoli; but these stooping galleries and arcades are low and mysterious, and look as if they had been built and left there as a setting for conspirators, the ancient and impressive setting of old wars, heroic, savage wars of religion. It is the old Huguenot city, grave, discreet, not superbly built, and with none of those splendid monuments that make Rouen so magnificent, but remarkable by virtue of its whole air of austerity, mingled with a certain lurking cunning; a city of stubborn fighters, a mother of fanatics, the town where Calvinism grew strong and the conspiracy of the four sergeants was hatched.

"When I had wandered for some time through these odd streets, I went aboard a little steam tug, black and tubby, which was to take me to the Island of Ré. She moved out, in an irritated sort of way, her whistle blowing off, slipped between the two old towers that guard the harbour, crossed the roadstead, got through the breakwater built by Richelieu, with enormous stones that are visible at the surface of the water and shut in the town like a vast collar; then she veered to the right.

"It was one of those melancholy days that oppress and crush the mind, weigh on the heart, and deaden in us all strength and energy; a grey, bitter day, darkened by a thick fog, as wet as rain, as cold as ice, and as unhealthy to breathe as a whiff from the sewers.

"Under this roof of low-hanging, sinister haze, the yellow sea, the shallow sandy sea of these endless beaches, lay without a ripple, motionless, lifeless, a sea of discoloured, oily, stagnant water. The *Jean-Guiton* drove forward, rolling a little, out of force of habit; she cut through the sleek, cloudy surface, leaving behind her a few waves, a brief heaving of the water, a slight rippling that soon died away.

"I began to talk to the captain, a short, almost limbless man, as tubby as his ship and with just such a rolling gait. I wanted to gather some details of the loss that I was going to examine. A big, square-built three-master of St. Nazaire, the *Marie-Joseph*, had run aground during a wild night, on the sandy shore of the Island of Ré.

"The owner wrote that the storm had flung the vessel so high up that it had been impossible to refloat her, and that it had been necessary to take everything removable out of her at once. It was my duty to examine the situation of the wreck, to form an opinion as to what must have been her condition before the disaster, and to judge whether every effort had been made to get her off. I had come as the Company's agent, to be a witness to the contrary, if need be, in the legal inquiry.

"On receiving my report, the director had to take such measures as he judged necessary to protect our interests.

"The captain of the *Jean-Guiton* knew all the details of the affair, having been summoned to help, with his boat, in the attempts at salvage.

"He told me the story of the loss, a perfectly simple story. The *Marie-Joseph*, running before a furious gale, lost in the darkness, steering as best she could through a foaming sea—'a milk-soup sea,' the captain called it—had run aground on the vast sandbanks which at low tide turn the coasts of these parts into endless Saharas.

"As I talked, I looked round me and in front of me. Between the sea and the louring sky was a clear space that gave a good view ahead. We were hugging a coast.

"'Is this the Island of Ré?' I asked.

"'Yes, sir.'

"And all at once the captain stretched his right hand in front of us and showed me an almost indistinguishable object lying right out at sea.

"'Look, there's your ship,' he said.

"'The *Marie-Joseph?*'

"'Yes, that's her.'

"I was astounded. This almost invisible object, which

I had taken for a reef, seemed to me to lie at least three kilometres from land.

"'But, Captain,' I answered, 'there must be a hundred fathoms of water at the place you're pointing out.'

"He burst out laughing.

"'A hundred fathoms, my friend! . . . There aren't two, I tell you.'

"He was from Bordeaux. He went on:

"'It will be high tide at twenty minutes to ten. You go out on the shore, your hands in your pockets, after you've lunched at the Dauphin, and I promise you that at ten to three, or three at the latest, you'll be able to walk dryfoot to the wreck, my friend, and you'll have an hour and three-quarters to two hours to stay on board, not more, mind: you'd be caught by the tide. The farther out the sea goes, the faster it comes in. This coast is as flat as a louse. Mark my words and start back at ten to five; at half-past seven you come on board the *Jean-Guiton*, which will land you this same evening on the quay at La Rochelle.'

"I thanked the captain, and I went and sat down in the bows of the tug to look at the little town of Saint-Martin with which we were rapidly coming up.

"It was like all the miniature ports that serve as chief towns to every barren little island lying off the coasts of continents. It was a large fishing-village, one foot in the sea, one foot on land, living on fish and poultry, vegetables and cockles, turnips and mussels. The island is very low-lying, and sparsely cultivated; it seems to be thickly peopled none the less, but I did not penetrate inland.

"After lunch, I crossed a little headland; then, as the tide was rapidly going out, I walked across the sands to a sort of black rock which I could see above the water, far, far away.

"I walked quickly on this yellow plain, which had the resilience of living flesh and seemed to sweat under my feet. A moment ago the sea had been there; now I saw it slipping out of sight in the distance, and I could no longer distinguish the verge that separated sand and sea. I felt that I was watching a gigantic and supernatural transformation scene. One moment the Atlantic was in front of me, and then it had disappeared in the shore, as stage scenery disappears through trapdoors, and now I was walking through a desert. Only the scent and the breath of the salt sea was still round me. I caught the smell of seaweed, the smell of salt water, the sharp, healthy smell of the land. I walked quickly: I was no longer cold; I looked at the stranded wreck, which grew larger as I approached and now looked like a huge stranded whale.

"She seemed to spring from the ground, and in this vast, flat, yellow plain she assumed surprising proportions. She lay over on her side, split, broken, and through her sides, like the sides of a beast, showed her broken bones, bones of tarred wood pierced with great nails. The sand had already invaded her, entering by all the rents; it held her, possessed her, would never let her go again. She looked as if she had taken root in it. Her bows were deeply buried in this soft treacherous beach, while her stern, lifted clean off the ground, seemed to fling to heaven, like a desperate and appealing cry, the two white words on the black bulwarks: *Marie-Joseph*.

"I scrambled into this corpse of a ship over the lower side; then I reached the bridge and explored below. The daylight, coming in through the shattered hatches and the rents in the sides, flooded the long, sombre, cave-like spaces, full of smashed woodwork, with a dim light. There was nothing left inside her but the sand that formed the flooring of this wooden-walled underworld.

"I began to make notes on the state of the vessel. I sat down on an empty broken barrel, and I wrote by the light of a large port-hole through which I could see the boundless stretch of shore. Every now and again, I felt my skin contract with a strange shudder of cold and loneliness; and sometimes I stopped writing to listen to the vague, mysterious sounds of the wreck: the sound of crabs scratching at the bulwarks with their hooked claws, the sound of a thousand small sea-creatures already at work on the body of this corpse, and the gentle, regular sound of the teredo-worm ceaselessly gnawing, like the grinding of a gimlet, in every part of the old timbers, eating out their insides and devouring them all together.

"Suddenly I heard human voices quite near me. I leaped up as if I had seen a ghost. For a brief moment I verily thought I was going to see two drowned men rising from the bottom of this sinister shell to tell me the manner of their death. You may be sure it did not take me long to climb in all haste to the bridge, and I saw standing beside the ship a tall gentleman with three young girls, or rather, a tall Englishman with three little English girls. They were certainly far more frightened than I had been, when they saw a man rush violently up from the depths of the deserted three-master. The youngest of the little girls ran away; the two others clutched their father with both arms; as for him, his mouth opened; he gave no sign of surprise.

"Then, after a brief pause, he spoke:

"'Are you the owner of this vessel, sir?'

"'Yes, sir.'

"'Can I look over her?'

"'Yes, sir.'

"He then delivered himself of a long sentence in English, of which I could distinguish only the one word 'gracious,' recurring several times.

"He looked round for a place to climb on board and I pointed him out the best place and offered him a hand. He got up; then we helped up the three little girls, now recovered from their fright. They were charming, especially the eldest, a fair-haired girl of eighteen, fresh as a flower, and so dainty, so adorably slender. Upon my word, a pretty English girl is like nothing so much as a frail sea flower. This one might just have sprung from the sand, and kept its gold in her hair.

The exquisite freshness of these English girls makes one think of the faintly lovely colours of rosy shells, of mother-of-pearl, rare and mysterious, hidden in the fathomless depths of the seas.

"She spoke French a little better than the father, and interpreted between us. I had to tell the story of the wrecking in all its details, which I extemporised as if I had been present at the disaster. Then the whole family descended into the interior of the wreck. Little cries of astonishment broke from them as soon as they entered this dim, shadowy gallery; and in a moment father and all three daughters were displaying sketch-books which they had doubtless had concealed in their bulky waterproofs, and they all set themselves forthwith to make four pencil sketches of this strange and gloomy place.

"They sat side by side on a jutting beam, and the four sketch-books supported on eight knees were covered with little black lines which evidently represented the gaping belly of the *Marie-Joseph*.

"The eldest girl talked to me as she worked, and I continued my inspection of the skeleton of the ship.

"I learned that they were spending the winter at Biarritz and that they had come to the Island of Ré on purpose to look at this foundered three-master. These people had none of the English insolence; they were just jolly, kind-hearted idiots, born wanderers such as England sends out over the whole world. The father, lank, lean, his red face encased in drooping white whiskers, for all the world like an animated sandwich, a slice of ham in the shape of a human head, between two little hair cushions; the daughters, long-legged, like half-grown storks, as lean as their father, except the eldest, and all three of the girls charming, but especially the eldest.

"She had such a quaint way of speaking, of describing things, of understanding and failing to understand, of lifting to question me eyes as blue as the deep sea, of stopping the sketch to study the scene of her efforts, of setting to work again, and of saying 'Yes' or 'No,' that time went unheeded while I stood there watching and listening to her.

" Suddenly she murmured :

" 'I hear something moving lightly on this boat.'

" I listened carefully, and at once I heard a faint sound, a strange, regular sound. What was it ? I got up and went to look out of the port-hole, and a wild shout broke from me. The sea had come up with us ; it was on the point of surrounding us.

" We rushed to the bridge. It was too late. The sea was all round us, and running in towards the shore at a terrific speed. No, it didn't run, it slid, it glided over the ground, spread out like a monstrous stain. Only a few inches of water covered the sand, but the swiftly moving verge of the stealthy flood was already beyond our sight.

" The Englishman was in favour of plunging through it, but I restrained him ; flight was impossible, on account of the deep pools that we had had to pick our way round as we came, and into which we should fall on the way back.

" We felt a sudden pang of mortal agony. Then the little English girl managed to smile and murmured :

" 'We're shipwrecked now.'

" I wanted to laugh ; but I was paralysed with fear, a frightful cowardly fear, as vile and treacherous as this advancing sea. In one moment of insight I saw all the dangers we were running. I wanted madly to cry : 'Help !' But who was there to hear me ?

" The two smaller English girls huddled against their father, who was looking in consternation at the vast stretch of water round us.

" And night was falling, as swiftly as the sea was swelling, a heavy, damp, icy night.

" 'There's nothing for it but to stay on the boat,' I said.

" 'Oh, yes,' the Englishman answered.

" We stayed up there a quarter of an hour, half an hour,

I really don't know how long, watching the yellow water that deepened all round us, and swirled and seemed to boil and leap for joy over the wide recaptured shore.

" One of the little girls was cold, and we conceived the idea of going below to shelter from the small but icy wind that blew lightly in our faces and pricked our skin.

" I leaned over the hold. The ship was full of water, so we were forced to crouch against the aft bulwark, which afforded us a little shelter.

" Now the shadows of night were falling round us, and we pressed close together, surrounded by the darkness and the waters. I felt the English girl's shoulder trembling against my shoulder ; her teeth chattered a little ; but I felt too the gentle warmth of her body through her clothes, and this warmth thrilled me like a caress. We did not talk now ; we stayed there motionless, mute, crouching as beasts in a ditch crouch against a storm.

" And yet, in spite of everything, in spite of the night, in spite of the terrible and growing damp, I began to feel glad to be there, glad of cold and danger, glad to be spending long hours of darkness and terror on this narrow hulk, close to this pretty and adorable young girl.

" I wondered why I was filled with so strange a sense of well-being and joy.

" Why ? Who knows ? Because she was there ? And who was she ? An unknown little English girl. I did not love her, I did not know her, and a passion of pity for her filled me, overwhelmed me. I longed to save her, to devote myself to her, to commit a thousand follies. A strange thing ! How is it that the nearness of a woman bowls us over like this ? Is it her grace that enslaves and enfolds us ? The seductive charm of youth and beauty mounting to our heads like wine ?

" Isn't it rather a fugitive touch of love, this mysterious love that never ceases to drive human beings into each other's arms, that tries its power the moment a man and a woman meet, piercing their hearts with a vague and deep and secret emotion, as the earth is given water that it may bear flowers?

"But the silence of the night and the sky grew terrifying, for we heard surging faintly round us the gentle swishing of wide waters, the hollow murmur of the rising sea, and the monotonous lapping of the tide against the boat.

"Suddenly I heard sobs. The smallest of the English girls was crying. Then the father tried to comfort her, and they began to talk in their own tongue, which I did not understand. I guessed that he was reassuring her, and that she was still afraid.

"'You are not too cold?' I asked my neighbour.

"'Oh, I'm dreadfully cold.'

"I wanted to give her my cloak; she declined it, but I had taken it off. I wrapped it round her in spite of her protests. In the brief struggle, I touched her hand and a marvellous thrill ran through my whole body.

"For some little time the air had been growing sharper and the water surging with more violence against the sides of the boat. I stood up; a great gust of wind blew in my face. The wind was rising.

"The Englishman noticed it at the same moment, and said simply:

"'This is bad for us, this is.'

"It was bad indeed; it was certain death if a swell, even a light swell, got up to batter and shake the boat, already so broken and knocked about that the first fair-sized wave would carry it away in fragments.

"Our misery increased every moment as the gusts of wind grew more and more violent. The waves were breaking a little now, and through the shadows I saw white lines, lines of foam, rise and vanish, while each surge struck the hulk of the *Marie-Joseph* and sent through her a brief shudder that communicated itself to us.

"The English girl was trembling; I felt her shivering against me, and I felt a wild desire to seize her in my arms.

" In the distance, ahead of us, to the left and right of us, and behind us, the lamps of lighthouses shone out down the coasts, white lights, yellow lights, red lights, revolving lights, like enormous eyes, like giant eyes watching us, spying on us, waiting hungrily to see us disappear. I found one of them particularly maddening. It went out and flashed on again every third second; it really was an eye, with an ever-winking eyelid dropping over its fiery glance.

" Every now and then the Englishman struck a match to look at the time; then he replaced the watch in his pocket. All at once he spoke to me over his daughters' heads, with the utmost seriousness:

" ' Sir, I wish you a happy New Year.'

" It was midnight. I held out my hand, and he shook it; then he spoke a few words of English, and suddenly he and his daughters began to sing " God Save the King "; the sound rose in the darkness, in the silent air, and died in the vast gulf of space.

" For a moment I wanted to laugh; then a strange, fierce emotion seized me.

" There was something at once menacing and superb in this song sung by these doomed and shipwrecked people; it was a prayer and it was magnificent, and worthy of that ancient, glorious *Ave, Cæsar, morituri te salutant.*

" When they had finished, I asked my neighbour to sing something alone, a song, a hymn, anything she liked, to help us forget our woes. She consented, and a moment later her clear young voice sounded out in the darkness. She sang what must have been a plaintive song, for the notes were long-drawn, fell slowly from her lips and fluttered like wounded birds above the waves.

" The sea was rising: it was flinging itself against the wreck now. But I was conscious of nothing but this voice. I thought of the sirens too. If a boat had passed close by us, what would the sailors have said? My troubled mind lost itself in a dream. A siren. Was she not in very truth a siren, this sea maiden, who had kept me on this worm-eaten ship and in a little time would plunge with me into the waters? . . .

"The whole five of us were flung violently across the bridge, for the *Marie-Joseph* had rolled over on her right side. The English girl fell on top of me; I had seized her in my arms and I pressed passionate kisses on her cheek, the hollow of her temple, her hair, madly, not knowing or realising what I was doing, thinking my last moment had come. The boat did not roll again; nor did we stir hand or foot.

"'Kate,' said her father. The girl in my arms answered, 'Yes,' and made a movement to draw away. I swear that at that moment I could have wished the boat to break in two, so that she and I might fall into the water together.

"'A little see-saw,' the Englishman added. 'It's nothing. I have my three daughters safe.'

"Not seeing the eldest, he had at first believed her lost.

"I stood up slowly, and all at once I saw a light on the sea, quite near us. I shouted: there was an answering shout. It was a boat in search of us: the landlord of the hotel had foreseen our imprudence.

"We were saved. I was very sorry for it. They got us off our raft and took us back to Saint-Martin.

"The Englishman was rubbing his hands, and muttering:

"'Now for a good supper! Now for a good supper!'

"We had supper. I was not happy. I was regretting the *Marie-Joseph*.

"Next day we had to go our separate ways, after many embraces and promises to write. They set off for Biarritz. For two pins I'd have followed them.

"I was a silly ass: I all but asked that young girl to marry me. I give you my word that if we had spent a week together, I should have married her. How weak and incomprehensible man often is!

"Two years passed before I heard a word about them; then I received a letter from New York. She was married, and wrote to tell me so. And since then we have written every year, on the first of January. She tells me of her life, talks to me about her children, her sisters, never about her husband. Why? Ah, why? . . . As for me, I write to her of nothing but the *Marie-Joseph*. She is perhaps the only woman that I have loved . . . no . . . that I would have loved. . . . Ah, well . . . who knows? . . . Life hurries us on. . . . And then . . . and then . . . nothing is left. . . . She must be old now. . . . I shouldn't recognise her. . . . Ah, the girl of those days . . . the girl of the wreck . . . what a woman . . . divine! She wrote to me that her hair is quite white. . . . My God . . . that hurts me intolerably. . . . Her hair white. . . . No, the girl I knew no longer exists. . . . How sad it is . . . all this! . . ."

THE HERMIT

WE HAD BEEN WITH SOME FRIENDS TO SEE THE OLD HERMIT who lived on an ancient tumulus, covered with great trees, in the midst of the vast plain that stretches from Cannes to La Napoule.

On the way back, we talked about these strange lay hermits, once so numerous, whose kind have now almost disappeared from the earth. We sought for the moral motives, and made an effort to realise what could be the nature of the sorrows that formerly drove men into solitary places.

One of our companions said abruptly:

"I've known two recluses, a man and a woman. The woman must be still alive. For five years she lived at the summit of an absolutely deserted hill on the Corsican coast, fifteen or twenty miles from any other house. She lived there with a nurse; I went to see her. She must undoubtedly have been a well-known woman of the world. She received us with courtesy, even with pleasure, but I knew nothing about her, and I discovered nothing.

"The man, now, well, I'll tell you his unfortunate fate.

"Turn round. Away over there, you see the peaked and wooded hill that stands out behind La Napoule, thrust up by itself in front of the peaks of the Esterel; its local name is the Hill of Serpents. That's where my recluse lived for about twelve years, within the walls of a small ancient temple.

"When I heard of him, I decided to make his acquaintance, and one March morning I set out for Cannes on horseback. I left my mount at the Napoule inn, and began to climb this strange conical hill on foot; it is perhaps a hundred and fifty or two hundred yards high and covered with aromatic plants, mostly cytisus, whose scent is so strong and pungent that it is quite overpowering and makes you feel positively ill. The ground is stony, and you often see long vipers slithering over the stones and disappearing in the grass. That's what gives the place its well-merited nickname of the Hill of Serpents. There are some days when the ground under your feet seems to give birth to these reptiles as you climb the bare, sun-scorched slope. They are so numberless that you daren't walk any farther; you are conscious of a strange uneasiness, not fear, for the creatures are harmless, but a kind of mystic terror. Several times I have had an odd sense that I was climbing a hill sacred of old, a fantastic hill, scented, mysterious, covered with and peopled by serpents and crowned with a temple.

"The temple is still there. At least, I am told that it was a temple. And I have refrained from trying to find out more about it, because I don't want to destroy the emotional appeal it has for me.

"Well, I climbed it that March morning, ostensibly to admire the scenery. As I approached the top I did indeed see walls, and, sitting on a stone, a man. He was hardly more than forty-five years old, although his hair was quite white; but his beard was still almost black. He was stroking a cat that curled on his knees, and he appeared to take no interest in me. I explored the ruins; a corner of them, roofed over, enclosed behind a construction of branches, straw, grass, and stones, formed his dwelling-place; then I returned and stood beside him.

"The view from the hill is splendid. On the right the Esterel hills lift their strange, truncated peaks; beyond them the rimless sea stretches to the far-off Italian coast with its innumerable headlands, and over against Cannes the flat green islands of Lerins seem to float on the water, the further of them thrusting into the open sea a massive great castle, ancient and battlemented, its walls rising from the waves.

"Then the Alps, their heads still hooded in the snows, rear their great bulk and dominate the green coast with its string of villas and white tree-fast towns that at this distance look like innumerable eggs laid on the edge of the shore.

" I murmured : ' Gad, what a view ! '

" The man lifted his head and said : ' Yes, but when you see it every day and all day, it gets monotonous.'

" So he could speak, my recluse, he could talk and he was bored. I had him.

" I did not stay very long that day, and I did not try to do more than find out the form his misanthropy took. The impression he made on me was that of a man utterly weary of his fellow creatures, tired of everything, hopelessly disillusioned, and disgusted with himself and with the rest of mankind.

" I left him after half an hour's conversation. But I came back a week later, and once again the following week, and then every week ; so that long before the end of two months we were friends.

" Then, one evening in late May, I decided that the moment had come, and I carried up some food to have dinner with him on the Hill of Serpents.

" It was one of those southern evenings heavy with the mingled perfume of flowers that this country-side grows, as the north grows corn, to make almost all the scents that women use for their bodies and their clothes : an evening when old men's senses stir and swoon in dreams of love born of the fragrance of innumerable orange-trees that fill the gardens and all the folds of the valley.

" My recluse greeted me with obvious pleasure, and willingly consented to share my dinner.

" I made him drink a little wine, to which he had long been unused ; it exhilarated him and he began to talk of his past life. I got the impression that he had always lived in Paris, and the life of a gay bachelor.

" I asked him abruptly : ' What mad impulse made you come and perch on this hill-top ? '

" He answered readily : ' Oh, because I had the severest

blow a man could have. But why should I hide my unhappy fate from you? It might make you pity me, perhaps. And besides . . . I have never told anyone . . . never . . . and I should like to know . . . just once . . . how it struck another person . . . what he thought of it.

" 'I was born in Paris, educated in Paris, and I grew up and lived in that city. My parents had left me a few thousand francs income, and I had enough influence to get a quiet subordinate post which made me well off, for a bachelor.

" 'Since early youth I had led the life of a bachelor. You know what that's like. Free, with no family ties, determined never to burden myself with a wife, I spent now three months with one woman, now six months with another, then a companionless year, sipping honey among the multitude of girls on offer or on sale.

" 'This easy-going manner of life, call it commonplace if you like, suited me well enough, and satisfied my natural love of change and novelty. I lived on the boulevard, in theatres and cafés, always out, almost homeless, although I had a comfortable house. I was one of the thousands of people who let themselves drift through life, like corks, for whom the walls of Paris are the walls of the world, who trouble themselves for nothing, since there is nothing they ardently desire. I was what you call a good sort, with no outstanding virtues and no vices. There you have me. And I've a quite accurate knowledge of myself.

" 'So, from the time I was twenty to my fortieth year, my life ran on, slow or fast, with nothing to disturb its even flow. They go so quickly, those uneventful Parisian years when nothing ever happens that the mind remembers as a turning-point, those long, crowded years, gay, trivial years when you eat and drink and laugh without knowing why, and desiring nothing, yet touch your lips to all the savour of life and every kiss that offers. You were young; and then you are old without having done any of the things that other men do, without any ties, any roots, any place in life, almost without friends, without parents, without wives, without children.

" 'Well, I reached the fortieth year of my easy, pleasant life; and to celebrate this anniversary I invited myself to a good dinner in one of the best restaurants. I was alone in the world; it pleased my sense of what was fitting to celebrate the day alone.

" 'Dinner over, I could not decide what to do next. I felt inclined to go to a theatre; and then I was struck with the idea of making a pilgrimage to the Quartier Latin, where I had studied law. So I made my way across Paris and wandered unthinkingly into one of those cafés where you are served by girls.

" 'The one who looked after my table was very young, pretty, and bubbling over with laughter. I offered her a drink, which she readily accepted. She sat down opposite me and looked me over with an expert eye, unable to make out what kind of masculine creature she had to deal with. She was fair-haired, fair altogether; she was a clear-skinned, healthy girl, and I guessed her to be plump and rosy under the swelling folds of her bodice. I murmured all the meaningless gallantries that one always says to these girls, and as she was really very charming, the whim suddenly seized me to take her out . . . just to celebrate my fortieth birthday. It was neither long nor difficult to arrange. She was unattached . . . had been for a fortnight, she told me . . . and she at once agreed to come and have supper with me at the Halles when her work was over.

" 'As I was afraid that she wouldn't stick to me—you never know what will happen, nor who'll come into these beershops, nor what a woman will take into her head to do—I stayed there the whole evening, waiting for her.

" 'I had been unattached myself for a month or two, and as I watched this adorable neophyte of Love flitting from table to table, I wondered if I shouldn't do well to take her on for a time. What I'm describing to you is one of the daily commonplace adventures in a Parisian's life.

" ' Forgive these crude details ; men who have never known an ideal love take and choose their women as they choose a chop at the butcher's, without bothering about anything but the quality of their flesh.

" ' Well, I went with her to her house—for I've too much respect for my own sheets. It was a workgirl's tiny room, on the fifth floor, clean and bare ; I spent two delightful hours there. She had an uncommonly graceful and charming way with her, that little girl.

" ' When I was ready to go, I walked towards her mantel-shelf to deposit thereon the usual present. I had arranged a day for a second interview with the little wench, who was still lying in bed. I saw dimly a clock under a glass case, two vases of flowers, and two photographs, one of which was very old, one of those negatives on glass called daguerreotypes. I bent casually to look at this portrait, and I stood there paralysed, too surprised to understand. . . . It was myself, my first portrait, one that I had had made long ago when I was a student living in the Quartier Latin.

" ' I snatched it up to examine it more closely. I'd made no mistake . . . and I felt like laughing, it struck me as so queer and unexpected.

" ' " Who is this gentleman ? " I demanded.

" ' " That's my father, whom I never knew," she answered. " Mamma left it to me and told me to keep it, because it would be useful to me some day. . . ."

" ' She hesitated, burst out laughing, and added : " I don't know what for, upon my word. It's not likely he'll come and recognise me."

" ' My heart leaped madly, like the galloping of a runaway horse. I laid the picture on its face on the mantel-shelf, put two hundred-franc notes that I had in my pocket on top of it, without at all thinking what I was doing, and hurried out crying: " See you again soon! . . . Good-bye, my dear . . . good-bye!"

"'I heard her answer: " On Wednesday." I was on the darkened stairs and groping my way down them.

"'When I got outside, I saw that it was raining, and I set off with great strides, taking the first road.

"'I walked straight on, dazed, bewildered, raking my memory. Was it possible? Yes, I suddenly remembered a girl who had written to me, about a month after we had broken off relations, that she was with child by me. I had torn up or burned the letter, and forgotten the whole thing. I ought to have looked at the photograph of the woman on the little girl's mantel-shelf. But should I have recognised her? I had a vague memory of it as the photograph of an old woman.

"'I reached the quay. I saw a bench and sat down. It was raining. Now and then people hurried past under umbrellas. Life had become for me hateful and revolting, full of miserable, shameful things, infamies willed or predestined. My daughter . . . perhaps I had just possessed my own daughter. And Paris, vast, sombre Paris, gloomy, dirty, sad, black, with all its shuttered houses, was full of such-like things, adulteries, incests, violated children. I remembered all I'd been told of bridges haunted by vicious and degraded wretches.

"'Without wishing or knowing it, I had sunk lower than those vile creatures. I had climbed into my daughter's bed.

"'I could have thrown myself in the water. I was mad. I wandered about until daybreak, then I went back to my house to think things out.

"'I decided on what seemed to me the most prudent course. I would have a solicitor send for the girl and ask her under what circumstances her mother had given her the portrait of the man she believed to be her father: I would tell him that I was acting on behalf of a friend.

"'The solicitor carried out my instructions. It was on her death-bed that the woman had made a statement about the father of her child, and before a priest whose name I was given.

"'Then, always in the name of this unknown friend, I made half my fortune over to this child, about a hundred and forty thousand francs, arranging it so that she could only touch the interest of it; then I sent in my resignation, and here I am.

"'I was wandering along this coast, and I found this hill and stopped here . . . since . . . I have forgotten how long since that was.

"'What do you think of me? . . . and of what I did?'

"I gave him my hand and answered:

"'You did the right thing. There are plenty of men who would have attached less importance to such a vile accident.'

"'I know that,' he replied, 'but I almost went mad. I must have had a tender conscience without ever guessing it. And I'm afraid of Paris now, as believers must be afraid of hell. I've had a blow on the head, that's all, a blow like a tile falling on you as you walk down the street. Time is making it more bearable.'

"I left my recluse. His story disturbed me profoundly.

"I saw him again twice, then I went away, because I never stay in the south after the end of May.

"When I came back the following year, the man was no longer living on the Hill of Serpents, and I have never heard a word about him since.

"That's the story of my hermit."

MADEMOISELLE PEARL

I

IT REALLY WAS AN ODD NOTION OF MINE TO CHOOSE Mademoiselle Pearl for queen that particular evening.

Every year I went to eat my Twelfth Night dinner at the house of my old friend Chantal. My father, whose most intimate friend he was, had taken me there when I was a child. I had continued the custom, and I shall doubtless continue it as long as I live, and as long as there is a Chantal left in the world.

The Chantals, moreover, lead a strange life; they live in Paris as if they were living in Grasse, Yvetot, or Pont-á-Mousson.

They own a small house with a garden, near the Observatory. There they live in true provincial fashion. Of Paris, of the real Paris, they know nothing and suspect nothing; they are far, very far away. Sometimes, however, they made a journey, a long journey. Madame Chantal went to the big stores, as they called it among themselves. And this is the manner of an expedition to the big stores:

Mademoiselle Pearl, who keeps the keys of the kitchen cupboards—for the linen cupboards are in the mistress's own charge—Mademoiselle Pearl perceives that the sugar is coming to an end, that the preserves are quite finished, and that there's nothing worth talking about left in the coffee-bag.

Then, put on her guard against famine, Madame Chantal passes the rest of the stores in review, and makes notes in her memorandum book. Then, when she has written down a quantity of figures, she first devotes herself to lengthy calculations, followed by lengthy discussions with Mademoiselle

Pearl. At last, however, they come to an agreement and decide what amount of each article must be laid in for a three months' supply: sugar, rice, prunes, coffee, preserves, tins of peas, beans, crab, salt and smoked fish, and so on and so forth.

After which they appoint a day for making the purchases, and set out together in a cab, a cab with a luggage rack on top, to a big grocery store over the river in the new quarters, with an air of great mystery, and return at dinner-time, worn out but still excited, jolting along in the carriage, its roof covered with packages and sacks like a removal van.

For the Chantals, all that part of Paris which lies on the other side of the Seine constituted the new quarters, quarters inhabited by a strange, noisy people, with the shakiest notions of honesty, who spent their days in dissipation, their nights feasting, and threw money out of the windows. From time to time, however, the young girls were taken to the theatre, to the Opéra-Comique or the Française, when the play was recommended by the paper Monsieur Chantal read.

The young girls are nineteen and seventeen years old to-day; they are two beautiful girls, tall and clear-skinned, very well trained, too well trained, so well trained that they attract no more attention than two pretty dolls. The idea never occurred to me to take any notice of them or to court the Chantal girls; I hardly dared speak to them, they seemed so unspotted from the world; I was almost afraid of offending against the proprieties in merely raising my hat.

The father himself is a charming man, very cultured, very frank, very friendly, but desirous of nothing so much as repose, quiet, and tranquillity; he has been largely instrumental in mummifying his family into mere symbols of his will, living and having their being in a stagnant peacefulness. He reads a good deal, from choice, and his emotions are easily stirred. His avoidance of all contact with life, common jostlings and violence has made his skin, his moral skin, very sensitive and delicate. The least thing moves and disturbs him, hurts him.

The Chantals have their friends all the same, but friends admitted to their circle with many reserves, and chosen carefully from neighbouring families. They also exchange two or three visits a year with relatives living at a distance.

As for me, I dine at their house on the Fifteenth of August and on Twelfth Night. That is as sacred a duty to me as Easter Communion to a Catholic.

On the Fifteenth of August a few friends are asked, but on Twelfth Night I am the only guest outside the family.

II

Well, this year, as in every other year, I had gone to dine at the Chantals' to celebrate Epiphany.

I embraced Monsieur Chantal, as I always did, Madame Chantal, and Mademoiselle Pearl, and I bowed deeply to Mesdemoiselles Louise and Pauline. They questioned me about a thousand things, boulevard happenings, politics, our representatives, and what the public thought of affairs in Tonkin. Madame Chantal, a stout lady whose thoughts always impressed me as being square-cut like blocks of stone, was wont to enunciate the following phrase at the end of every political discussion: "All this will produce a crop of misfortunes in the future." Why do I always think that Madame Chantal's thoughts are square? I don't really know why; but my mind sees everything she says in this fashion: a square, a solid square with four symmetrical angles. There are other people whose thoughts always seem to me round and rolling like circles. As soon as they begin a phrase about something, out it rolls, running along, issuing in the shape of ten, twenty, fifty round thoughts, big ones and little ones, and I see them running behind each other out of sight over the edge of the sky. Other persons have pointed thoughts. . . . But this is somewhat irrelevant.

We sat down to table in the usual order, and dinner passed without any remarkable conversation. With the sweets, they brought in the Twelfth Night cake. Now, each year, Monsieur Chantal was king. Whether this was a series of chances or a domestic convention I don't know, but invariably he found the lucky bean in his piece of cake, and he proclaimed Madame Chantal queen. So I was amazed to find in a mouthful of pastry something very hard that almost broke one of my teeth. I removed the object carefully from my mouth and I saw a tiny china doll no larger than a bean. Surprise made me exclaim : " Oh ! " They all looked at me and Chantal clapped his hands and shouted : " Gaston's got it. Gaston's got it. Long live the king ! Long live the king ! "

The others caught up the chorus : " Long live the king ! " And I blushed to my ears, as one often does for no reason whatever, in slightly ridiculous situations. I sat looking at my boots, holding the fragment of china between two fingers, forcing myself to laugh, and not knowing what to do or what to say, when Chantal went on : " Now he must choose a queen."

I was overwhelmed. A thousand thoughts and speculations rushed across my mind in a second of time. Did they want me to choose out one of the Chantal girls ? Was this a way of making me say which one I liked the better ? Was it a gentle, delicate, almost unconscious feeler that the parents were putting out towards a possible marriage ? The thought of marriage stalks all day and every day in families that possess marriageable daughters ; it takes innumerable shapes and guises and adopts every possible means. I was suddenly dreadfully afraid of compromising myself, and extremely timid too, before the obstinately correct and rigid bearing of Mesdemoiselles Louise and Pauline. To select one of them over the head of the other seemed to me as difficult as to choose between two drops of water ; and I was horribly disturbed at the thought of committing myself to a path which would lead me to the altar willy-nilly, by gentle stages, and incidents as discreet, as insignificant, and as easy as this meaningless kingship.

But all at once I had an inspiration, and I proffered the symbolic little doll to Mademoiselle Pearl. At first every one was surprised, then they must have appreciated my delicacy and discretion, for they applauded furiously, shouting: "Long live the queen! Long live the queen!"

As for the poor old maid, she was covered with confusion; she trembled and lifted a terrified face. "No . . . no . . . no . . ." she stammered; "not me . . . I implore you . . . not me . . . I implore you."

At that, I looked at Mademoiselle Pearl for the first time in my life, and wondered what sort of a woman she was.

I was used to seeing her about this house, but only as you see old tapestried chairs in which you have been sitting since you were a child, without ever really noticing them. One day, you couldn't say just why, because a ray of sunlight falls across the seat, you exclaim: "Why, this is a remarkable piece of furniture!" and you discover that the wood has been carved by an artist and that the tapestry is very uncommon. I had never noticed Mademoiselle Pearl.

She was part of the Chantal family, that was all; but what? What was her standing? She was a tall, thin woman who kept herself very much in the background, but she wasn't insignificant. They treated her in a friendly fashion, more intimately than a housekeeper, less so than a relative. I suddenly became aware now of various subtle shades of manner that I had never troubled about until this moment. Madame Chantal said: "Pearl." The young girls: "Mademoiselle Pearl," and Chantal never called her anything but "Mademoiselle," with a slightly more respectful air perhaps.

I set myself to consider her. How old was she? Forty? Yes, forty. She was not old, this maiden lady, she made herself look old. I was suddenly struck by this obvious fact. She did her hair, dressed herself, and got herself up to look absurd, and in spite of it all she was not at all absurd, so innately graceful was she, simply and naturally graceful, though she did her best to obscure it and conceal it. What an odd creature she was, after all! Why hadn't I paid more attention to her? She did her hair in the most grotesque way, in ridiculous little grey curls; under this crowning glory of a middle-aged Madonna, she had a broad, placid forehead, graven with two deep wrinkles, the wrinkles of some enduring sorrow, then two blue eyes, wide and gentle, so timid, so fearful, so humble, two blue eyes that were still simple, filled with girlish wonder and youthful emotions, and griefs endured in secret, softening her eyes and leaving them untroubled.

Her whole face was clear-cut and reserved, one of those faces which have grown worn without being ravaged or faded by the weariness and the fevered emotions of life.

What a pretty mouth, and what pretty teeth! But she seemed as if she dared not smile.

Abruptly, I began to compare her with Madame Chantal. Mademoiselle Pearl was undoubtedly the better of the two, a hundred times better, nobler, more dignified.

I was astounded by my discoveries. Champagne was poured out. I lifted my glass to the queen and drank her health with a pretty compliment. I could see that she wanted to hide her face in her napkin; then, when she dipped her lips in the translucent wine, every one cried: "The queen's drinking, the queen's drinking!" At that she turned crimson and choked. They laughed; but I saw clearly that she was well liked in the house.

III

As soon as dinner was over, Chantal took me by the arm. It was the hour for his cigar, a sacred hour. When he was alone, he went out into the street to smoke; when he had someone to dinner, he took them to the billiard-room, and he played as he smoked. This evening they had lit a fire in the billiard-room, since it was Twelfth Night; and my old friend took his cue, a very slender cue which he chalked with great care; then he said:

"Now, sonny."

He always spoke to me as if I were a little boy: I was twenty-five years old but he had known me since I was four.

I began to play; I made several cannons; I missed several more; but my head was filled with drifting thoughts of Mademoiselle Pearl, and I asked abruptly:

"Tell me, Monsieur Chantal, is Mademoiselle Pearl a relative of yours?"

He stopped playing, in astonishment, and stared at me.

"What, don't you know? Didn't you know Mademoiselle Pearl's story?"

"Of course not."

"Hasn't your father ever told you?"

"Of course not."

"Well, well, that's queer, upon my word, it's queer. Oh, it's quite an adventure."

He was silent, and went on:

"And if you only knew how strange it is that you should ask me about it to-day, on Twelfth Night!"

"Why?"

"Why, indeed! Listen. It's forty-one years ago, forty-one years this very day, the day of Epiphany. We were living then at Roüy-le-Tors, on the ramparts; but I must first tell you about the house, if you're to understand the story properly. Roüy is built on a slope, or rather on a mound which thrusts out of a wide stretch of meadow land. We had there a house with a beautiful hanging garden, supported on the old ramparts. So that the house was in the town, on the street, while the garden hung over the plain. There was also a door opening from this garden on to the fields, at the bottom of a secret staircase which went down inside the thick masonry of the walls, just like a secret staircase in a romance. A road ran past this door, where a great bell hung, and the country-people brought their stuff in this way, to save themselves going all the way round.

"Can you see it all? Well, this year, at Epiphany, it had been snowing for a week. It was like the end of the world. When we went out on to the ramparts to look out over the plain, the cold of that vast white country-side struck through to our very bones; it was white everywhere, icy cold, and gleaming like varnish. It really looked as if the good God had wrapped up the earth to carry it away to the lumber-room of old worlds. It was rare and melancholy, I can tell you.

"We had all our family at home then, and we were a large family, a very large family: my father, my mother, my uncle and my aunt; my two brothers and my four cousins; they were pretty girls; I married the youngest. Of all that company, there are only three left alive: my wife, myself, and my sister-in-law at Marseilles. God, how a family dwindles away: it makes me shiver to think of it. I was fifteen years old then, and now I'm fifty-six.

"Well, we were going to eat our Twelfth Night dinner and we were very gay, very gay. Everybody was in the drawing-room waiting for dinner, when my eldest brother, Jacques, took it into his head to say: 'A dog's been howling out in the fields for the last ten minutes; it must be some poor beast that's got lost.'

"The words were hardly out of his mouth when the garden bell rang. It had a heavy clang like a church bell and reminded you of funerals. A shiver ran through the assembled company. My father called a servant and told him to go and see who was there. We waited in complete silence, we thought of the snow that lay over the whole country-side. When the man came back, he declared he had seen nothing. The dog was still howling: the howls never stopped, and came always from the same direction.

" We went in to dinner, but we were a little uneasy, especially the young ones. All went well until the joint was on the table, and then the bell began to ring again ; it rang three times, three loud, long clangs that sent a thrill to our very finger-tips and stopped the breath in our throats. We sat staring at each other, our forks in the air, straining our ears, seized by fear of some supernatural horror.

" At last my mother said : 'It's very queer that they've been so long coming back ; don't go alone, Baptiste ; one of the gentlemen will go with you.'

" My uncle François got up. He was as strong as Hercules, very proud of his great strength and afraid of nothing on earth. 'Take a gun,' my father advised him. 'You don't know what it might be.'

" But my uncle took nothing but a walking-stick, and went out at once with the servant.

" The rest of us waited there, shaking with terror and fright, neither eating nor speaking. My father tried to comfort us. 'You'll see,' he said, 'it'll be some beggar or some passer-by lost in the snow. He rang once, and when the door wasn't opened immediately, he made another attempt to find his road : he didn't succeed and he's come back to our door.'

" My uncle's absence seemed to us to last an hour. He came back at last, furiously angry, and cursing :

" 'Not a thing, by God, it's someone playing a trick. Nothing but that cursed dog howling a hundred yards beyond the walls. If I'd taken a gun, I'd have killed him to keep him quiet.'

" We went on with out dinner, but we were still very anxious ; we were quite sure that we hadn't heard the last of it ; something was going to happen, the bell would ring again in a minute.

" It did ring, at the very moment when we were cutting the Epiphany cake. The men leaped to their feet as one man. My uncle François, who had been drinking champagne, swore that he was going to murder IT, in such a wild rage that my mother and my aunt flung themselves on him to hold him back. My father was quite calm about it; he was slightly lame, too (he dragged one leg since he had broken it in a fall from his horse), but now he declared that he must know what it was, and was going out. My brothers, who were eighteen and twenty years old, ran in search of their guns, and as no one was paying any attention to me, I grabbed a rook rifle and got ready to accompany the expedition myself.

"It set off at once. My father and my uncle led off, with Baptiste, who was carrying a lantern. My brothers Jacques and Paul followed, and I brought up the rear, in spite of the entreaties of my mother, who stayed behind in the doorway, with her sister and my cousins.

"Snow had been falling again during the last hour and it lay thick on the trees. The pines bent under the heavy ghostly covering, like white pyramids or enormous sugar-loaves; the slighter shrubs, palely glimmering in the shadows, were only dimly visible through the grey curtain of small hurrying flakes. The snow was falling so thickly that you couldn't see more than ten paces ahead. But the lantern threw a wide beam of light in front of us. When we began to descend the twisting staircase hollowed out of the wall, I was afraid, I can tell you. I thought someone was walking behind me and I'd be grabbed by the shoulder and carried off; I wanted to run home again, but as I'd have had to go back the whole length of the garden, I didn't dare.

"I heard them opening the door on to the fields; then my uncle began to swear: 'Blast him, he's gone. If I'd only seen his shadow, I wouldn't have missed him, the b——!'

"The look of the plain struck me with a sense of foreboding, or rather the feel of it in front of us, for we couldn't see it; nothing was visible but a veil of snow hung from edge to edge of the world, above, below, in front of us, to left of us and right of us, everywhere.

"'There, that's the dog howling,' added my uncle. 'I'll

show him what I can do with a gun, I will. And that'll be something done, at any rate.'

"But my father, who was a kindly man, answered: 'We'd do better to go and look for the poor animal: he's whining with hunger. The wretched beast is barking for help; he's like a man shouting in distress. Come on.'

"We started off through the curtain, through the heavy, ceaseless fall, through the foam that was filling the night and the air, moving, floating, falling; as it melted, it froze the flesh on our bones, froze it with a burning cold that sent a sharp, swift stab of pain through the skin with each prick of the little white flakes.

"We sank to our knees in the soft, cold, feathery mass, and we had to lift our legs right up to get over the ground. The farther we advanced, the louder and clearer grew the howling of the dog.

"'There he is!' cried my uncle.

"We stopped to observe him, like prudent campaigners coming upon the enemy at night.

"I could see nothing; then I came up with the others and I saw him; he was a terrifying and fantastic object, that dog, a great black dog, a shaggy sheep-dog with a head like a wolf, standing erect on his four feet at the far end of the long track of light that the lantern flung out across the snow. He didn't move; he stared at us with never a sound.

"'It's queer he doesn't rush at us or away from us,' said my uncle. 'I've the greatest mind to stretch him out with a shot.'

"'No,' my father said decidedly, 'we must catch him.'

"'But he's not alone,' my brother Jacques added. 'He has something beside him.'

"He actually had something behind him, something grey and indistinguishable. We began to walk cautiously towards him.

"Seeing us draw near, the dog sat down on his haunches.

He didn't look vicious. He seemed, on the contrary, pleased that he had succeeded in attracting someone's attention.

"My father went right up to him and patted him. The dog licked his hands; and we saw that he was fastened to the wheel of a small carriage, a sort of toy carriage wrapped all round in three or four woollen coverings. We lifted the wrappings carefully; Baptiste held his lantern against the opening of the carriage—which was like a kennel on wheels—and we saw inside a tiny sleeping child.

"We were so astonished that we couldn't got out a single word. My father was the first to recover: he was warm-hearted and somewhat emotional; he placed his hand on the top of the carriage and said: 'Poor deserted thing, you shall belong to us.' And he ordered my brother Jacques to wheel our find in front of us.

"'A love-child,' my father added, 'whose poor mother came and knocked at my door on Epiphany night, in memory of the Christ-child.'

"He stood still again, and shouted into the darkness four times, at the top of his voice, to all the four corners of the heavens: 'We have got him safe.' Then he rested his hand on his brother's shoulder and murmured: 'Suppose you'd fired at the dog, François?'

"My uncle said nothing, but crossed himself earnestly in the darkness; he was very devout, for all his swaggering ways.

"We had loosed the dog, who followed us.

"Upon my word, our return to the house was a pretty sight. At first we had great difficulty in getting the carriage up the rampart staircase; we succeeded at last, however, and wheeled it right into the hall.

"How comically surprised and delighted and bewildered mamma was! And my poor little cousins (the youngest was six) were like four hens round a nest. At last we lifted the child, still sleeping, from its carriage. It was a girl about six weeks old. And in her clothes we found ten thousand francs in gold, yes, ten thousand francs, which papa invested to bring her in a dowry. So she wasn't the child of poor parents . . . she may have been the child of a gentleman by a respectable young girl belonging to the town, or even . . . we made innumerable speculations, and we never knew anything . . . never a thing . . . never a thing. . . . Even the dog wasn't known to anyone. He didn't belong to the district. In any event, the man or woman who had rung three times at our door knew very well what sort of people my parents were, when they chose them for their child.

" And that's how Mademoiselle Pearl found her way into the Chantal house when she was six weeks old.

" It was later that she got the name of Mademoiselle Pearl. She was first christened Marie Simone Claire, Claire serving as her surname.

" We certainly made a quaint entry into the dining-room with the tiny, wide-awake creature, who looked round her at the people and the lights, with wondering, troubled blue eyes.

" We sat down at the table again, and the cake was cut. I was king and I chose Mademoiselle Pearl for queen, as you did just now. She hadn't any idea that day what a compliment we were paying her.

" Well, the child was adopted, and brought up as one of the family. She grew up : years passed. She was a charming, gentle, obedient girl. Every one loved her and she would have been shamefully spoiled if my mother had not seen to it that she wasn't.

" My mother had a lively sense of what was fitting and a proper reverence for caste. She consented to treat little Claire as she did her own children, but she was none the less insistent that the distance between us should be definitely marked and the position clearly laid down.

" So as soon as the child was old enough to understand, she

told her how she had been found, and very gently, tenderly even, she made the little girl realise that she was only an adopted member of the Chantal family, belonging to them but really no kin at all.

" Claire realised the state of affairs with an intelligence beyond her years and an instinctive wisdom that surprised us all ; and she was quick to take and keep the place allotted to her, with so much tact, grace, and courtesy that she brought tears to my father's eyes.

" My mother herself was so touched by the passionate gratitude and timid devotion of this adorable and tender-hearted little thing that she began to call her ' My daughter.' Sometimes, when the young girl had shown herself more than commonly sweet-natured and delicate, my mother pushed her glasses on to her forehead, as she always did when much moved, and repeated : ' The child's a pearl, a real pearl.' The name stuck to little Claire : she became Mademoiselle Pearl for all of us from that time and for always."

IV

Monsieur Chantal was silent. He was sitting on the billiard-table, swinging his feet ; his left hand fiddled with a ball and in his right hand he crumpled the woollen rag we called " the chalk rag," and used for rubbing out the score on the slate. A little flushed, his voice muffled, he was speaking to himself now, lost in his memories, dreaming happily through early scenes and old happenings stirring in his thoughts, as a man dreams when he walks through old gardens where he grew up, where each tree, each path, each plant, the prickly holly whose plump red berries crumble between his fingers, evoke at every step some little incident of his past life, the little insignificant delicious incidents that are the very heart, the very stuff of life.

I stood facing him, propped against the wall, leaning my hands on my idle billiard-cue.

After a moment's pause he went on: "God, how pretty she was at eighteen—and graceful—and perfect! Oh, what a pretty—pretty—pretty—sweet—gay—and charming girl! She had such eyes . . . blue eyes . . . limpid . . . clear . . . I've never seen any like them . . . never."

Again he was silent. "Why didn't she marry?" I asked.

He didn't answer me: he answered the careless word "marry."

"Why? Why? She didn't want to . . . didn't want to. She had a dowry of thirty thousand francs too, and she had several offers . . . she didn't want to marry. She seemed sad during those years. It was just at the time I married my cousin, little Charlotte, my wife, to whom I'd been engaged for six years."

I looked at Monsieur Chantal and thought that I could see into his mind, and that I'd come suddenly upon the humble, cruel tragedy of a heart at once honourable, upright, and pure, that I'd seen into the secret, unknown depths of a heart that no one had really understood, not even the resigned and silent victims of its dictates.

Pricked by a sudden savage curiosity, I said deliberately:

"You ought to have married her, Monsieur Chantal."

He started, stared at me, and said:

"Me? Marry whom?"

"Mademoiselle Pearl."

"But why?"

"Because you loved her more than you loved your cousin."

He stared at me with strange, wide, bewildered eyes, then stammered:

"I loved her? . . . I? . . . how? What are you talking about?"

"It's obvious, surely? In fact, it was on her account that you delayed so long before marrying the cousin who waited six years for you."

The cue fell from his left hand, and he seized the chalk rag in both hands and, covering his face with it, began to sob into its folds. He wept in a despairing and ridiculous fashion, dripping water from eyes and nose and mouth all at once, like a squeezed sponge. He coughed, spat, and blew his nose on the chalk rag, dried his eyes, choked, and overflowed again from every opening in his face, making a noise in his throat like a man gargling.

Terrified and ashamed, I wanted to run away, and I did not know what to say, or do, or try to do.

And suddenly Madame Chantal's voice floated up the staircase : " Have you nearly finished your smoke ? "

I opened the door and called : " Yes, ma'am, we're coming down."

Then I flung myself on her husband, seized him by the elbows, and said : " Monsieur Chantal, Chantal my friend, listen to me ; your wife is calling you, pull yourself together, pull yourself together, we must go downstairs ; pull yourself together."

" Yes . . . yes . . ." he babbled. " I'm coming . . . poor girl . . . I'm coming . . . tell her I'm just coming."

And he began carefully drying his face on the rag that had been used to rub the score off the slate for two or three years ; then he emerged, white and red in streaks, his forehead, nose, cheeks, and chin dabbled with chalk, his eyes swollen and still full of tears.

I took his hands and led him towards his bedroom, murmuring : " I beg your pardon, I humbly beg your pardon, Monsieur Chantal, for hurting you like this . . . but . . . I didn't know . . . you . . . you see."

He shook my hand. " Yes . . . yes . . . we all have our awkward moments."

Then he plunged his face in his basin. When he emerged, he was still hardly presentable, but I thought of a little ruse. He was very disturbed when he looked at himself in the glass, so I said " You need only tell her you've got a speck of dust in your eye, and you can cry in front of every one as long as you like."

He did at last go down, rubbing his eyes with his handkerchief. They were all very concerned ; every one wanted to look for the speck of dust, which no one could find, and they related similar cases when it had become necessary to call in a doctor.

I had betaken myself to Mademoiselle Pearl's side and I looked at her, tormented by a burning curiosity, a curiosity that became positively painful. She really must have been very pretty, with her quiet eyes, so big, so untroubled, so wide that you'd have thought they were never closed as ordinary eyes are. Her dress was a little absurd, a real old maid's dress, that hid her real charm but could not make her look graceless.

I thought that I could see into her mind as I had just seen into the mind of Monsieur Chantal, that I could see every hidden corner of this simple humble life, spent in the service of others ; but I felt a sudden impulse to speak, an aching, persistent impulse to question her, to find out if she too had loved, if she had loved him ; if like him she had endured the same long, bitter, secret sorrow, unseen, unknown, unguessed of all, indulged only at night in the solitude and darkness of her room. I looked at her, I saw her heart beating under her high-necked frock, and I wondered if night after night this gentle, wide-eyed creature had stifled her moans in the depths of a pillow wet with tears, sobbing, her body torn with long shudders, lying there in the fevered solitude of a burning bed.

And like a child breaking a plaything to see inside it, I whispered to her : " If you had seen Monsieur Chantal crying just now, you would have been sorry for him."

She trembled : " What, has he been crying ? "

" Yes, he's been crying."

" Why ? "

She was very agitated. I answered :

" About you."

" About me ? "

" Yes. He told me how he loved you years ago, and what it had cost him to marry his wife instead of you."

Her pale face seemed to grow a little longer; her wide, quiet eyes shut suddenly, so swiftly that they seemed closed never to open again. She slipped from her chair to the floor and sank slowly, softly, across it, like a falling scarf.

" Help, quick, quick, help ! " I cried. " Mademoiselle Pearl is ill."

Madame Chantal and her daughters rushed to help her, and while they were bringing water, a napkin, vinegar, I sought my hat and hurried away.

I walked away with great strides, sick at heart and my mind full of remorse and regret. And at the same time I was almost happy; it seemed to me that I had done a praiseworthy and necessary action.

Was I wrong or right ? I asked myself. They had hidden their secret knowledge in their hearts like a bullet in a healed wound. Wouldn't they be happier now ? It was too late for their grief to torture them again, and soon enough for them to recall it with a tender, pitying emotion.

And perhaps some evening in the coming spring, stirred by moonlight falling through the branches across the grass under their feet, they will draw close to one another and clasp each other's hands, remembering all their cruel hidden suffering. And perhaps, too, the brief embrace will wake in their blood a faint thrill of the ecstasy they have never known, and in the hearts of these two dead that for one moment are alive, it will stir the swift, divine madness, the wild joy that turns the least trembling of true lovers into a deeper happiness than other men can ever know in all their lives.

ROSALIE PRUDENT

There was in this affair an element of mystery which neither the Jury, nor the President, nor the Attorney-General himself ever quite fathomed.

The girl Prudent (Rosalie), a maid employed by the Varambot family, of Mantes, became pregnant unknown to her employers, was brought to bed during the night in her attic bedroom, then killed and buried her child in the garden.

It was the ordinary story of a servant's infanticide. But one fact remained inexplicable. The investigations conducted in the girl Prudent's bedroom had led to the discovery of a complete set of baby clothes, made by Rosalie herself, who for three months had spent her nights in cutting out and sewing them. The grocer, from whom, out of her own wages, she had bought the candles burned in this long labour had come forward as a witness. Moreover, it was known that the local midwife, whom the girl had informed of her condition, had given her all instructions and practical advice necessary in case her time happened to come at a moment when no help was at hand. She had further sought a place at Poissy for the girl Prudent, who foresaw her dismissal, since the Varambot couple took questions of morality very seriously.

The man and his wife were present at the assizes : an ordinary provincial middle-class couple of small means, very angry with this slut who had defiled their house. They would have liked to see her guillotined on the spot, without a trial, and they overwhelmed her with malicious evidence that in their mouths became veritable accusations.

The accused, a fine, strapping girl from Basse-Normandie,

rather superior for her station, wept incessantly and made no reply.

There was nothing for it but to suppose that she had committed this barbarous action in a moment of despair and madness, since everything pointed to the fact that she had hoped to keep and rear her child.

The President made one more attempt to get her to speak, to wring a confession from her. He urged her with the utmost kindliness, and at last made her understand that all these men come together to judge her did not wish for her death and could even pity her.

Then she made up her mind.

" Come," he asked, " tell us first who is the father of this child."

So far she had obstinately withheld this information.

She answered suddenly, staring angrily at the employers who had spoken with much malice against her.

" It was Monsieur Joseph, Monsieur Varambot's nephew."

The couple started violently and cried out with one voice: " It's a lie! She's lying! It's a vile slander!"

The President silenced them and added: " Go on, please, and tell us how it happened."

Then she poured out a sudden flood of words, comforting her shut heart, her poor, lonely, bruised heart, spilling out her grief, the full measure of her grief, before the severe men whom until this moment she had looked upon as enemies and inflexible judges.

" Yes, it was Monsieur Joseph Varambot, when he came on leave last year."

" What does Monsieur Joseph Varambot do?"

" He's an N.C.O. in the artillery, sir. He spent two months in the house, you see. Two summer months. I didn't think anything of it, I didn't, when he began staring at me, and then saying sweet things to me, and then coaxing me all day long. I let myself be taken in, I did, sir. He kept on telling me that I was a fine girl, that I was nice to look at . . . that I was his sort. . . . I was pleased with this ; I was, for sure. What'ud you expect ? You listen to these things when you're alone . . . all alone . . . like me. I'm alone in the world, sir. . . . I've no one to talk to . . . no one to tell about things that vexed me. . . . I haven't a father, or mother, or brother, or sister, no one. I felt as if he was a brother who'd come back when he began talking to me. And then he asked me to go down to the river bank with him one evening, so we could talk without being heard. I went. I did. . . . How did I know what I was doing ? How did I know what I did after that ? He put his arm round me. . . . I'm sure I didn't want to . . . no . . . no. . . . I couldn't. . . . I wanted to cry, it was such a lovely night . . . the moon was shining. . . . I couldn't . . . he did what he wanted. . . . It went on like that for three weeks, as long as he stayed. . . . I would have followed him to the end of the world . . . he went away. . . . I didn't know I was going to have a baby, I didn't . . . I didn't know until a month after."

She broke into such a passion of weeping that they had to give her time to control herself again.

Then the President spoke to her like a priest in the confessional : "Come now, tell us everything."

She went on with her tale :

"When I saw I was pregnant, I went and told Madame Boudin, the midwife, who's there to tell you I did, and I asked her what I ought to do supposing it happened when she wasn't there. And then I made all the little clothes, night after night, until one o'clock in the morning, every night ; and then I looked out for another place, for I knew quite well I'd be dismissed, but I wanted to stay in the house up to the very last, to save my bit of money, seeing I hardly had any and I had to have all I could, for the little baby. . . ."

"So you didn't want to kill it ?"

"Oh, for sure I didn't, sir."

" Then why did you kill it ? "

" It's like this. It happened sooner than I'd have believed. The pains took me in my kitchen, as I was finishing my washing-up.

" Monsieur and Madame Varambot were asleep already ; so I went upstairs, not without pain, dragging myself from step to step. And I lay down on the floor, on the boards, so I shouldn't soil my bed. It lasted maybe an hour, maybe two, maybe three—I don't know, it hurt me so dreadful ; and then I pressed down with all my strength, I felt him coming out, and I gathered him up.

" Oh, I was so pleased, I was. I did everything that Madame Boudin had told me, everything. And then I put him on my bed. And then, if I hadn't another pain, a mortal pain ! If you knew what it was like, you men, you'd think a bit more about doing it, you would. I fell on my knees, then on my back, on the floor ; and I had it all over again, maybe another hour maybe two, all by myself, there . . . and then another one came out . . . another little baby . . . two—yes, two . . . think of it ! I took him up like the first and laid him on the bed, side by side . . . two. Could I do with it now ? Two children. Me that earns a pound a month. Tell me . . . could I do with it ? One, yes, could be managed, with scraping and saving, but not two. It turned my head. I didn't know what I was doing, I didn't. How do you think I could choose one ?

" I didn't know what I was doing ! I thought my last hour had come. I put the pillow over them, without knowing what I was doing. . . . I couldn't keep two . . . and I lay down again on top of it. And then I stayed there tossing and crying until I saw the light coming in at the window ; they were dead under the pillow for sure. Then I took them under my arm, I got down the stairs, I went out into the kitchen garden, I took the garden spade, and I buried them in the ground, as deep as I could, one in one place, the other in another, not together, so that they couldn't speak about their mother, if little dead babies can speak. I don't know about it, I don't.

"And then I was so ill in my bed that I couldn't get up. They fetched the doctor and he knew all about it. It's the truth, your Worship. Do what you like, I'm ready."

Half the jury were blowing their noses violently, to keep back their tears. Women were sobbing in the Court.

The President questioned her.

"Where did you bury the other one?"

"Which did you find?" she asked.

"Well . . . the one . . . the one who was in the artichokes."

"Oh, well. The other one is among the strawberries—at the edge of the well."

And she began to sob so dreadfully that her moans were heart-breaking to hear.

The girl Rosalie Prudent was acquitted.

SAUVÉE

SAVED

I

THE LITTLE MARQUISE DE RENNENDON BURST INTO THE ROOM like a ball crashing through a window, and began to laugh before she had said a word; she laughed until she cried, just as she had laughed a month before when she came to tell her friend that she had deceived the Marquis to revenge herself, for no reason but to revenge herself, and only once, because he really was too stupid and too jealous.

The little Baronne de Grangerie had thrown down on her vast couch the book she was reading, and she stared curiously at Annette, laughing already herself.

At last she asked:

"What have you done now?"

"Oh . . . my dear . . . my dear . . . it's too funny . . . too funny . . . think of it . . . I'm saved . . . saved . . . saved."

"What do you mean, saved?"

"Yes, saved."

"From what?"

"From my husband, darling, saved! Delivered! Free! . . . free! . . . free!"

"How are you free? In what way?"

"In what way? Divorce! Yes, divorce! I can get a divorce."

"You're divorced?"

"No, not yet. How silly you are! You can't get divorced in three hours! But I've got evidence . . . evidence . . . evidence that he is deceiving me . . . absolutely caught in the act . . . think! . . . in the act. . . . I can prove it. . . ."

"Oh, tell me about it. So he has deceived you?"

"Yes . . . that's to say, no . . . yes and no. Oh, I've been clever, vastly clever. For the last three months he has been detestable, utterly detestable, brutal, coarse, tyrannical, simply impossible. I said to myself: This can't go on, I must get a divorce! But how? It wasn't easy. I tried to get him to beat me. He wouldn't. He crossed me from morning to night, made me go out when I didn't want to, and stay at home when I was longing to drive in town; he made my life unbearable from one week's end to another, but he didn't beat me.

"Then I tried to find out if he had a mistress. Yes, he had one, but he took every precaution when he went to visit her. It simply wasn't possible to take them together. So, guess what I did."

"I can't guess."

"Oh, you'd never guess. I begged my brother to get me a photograph of his girl."

"Of your husband's mistress?"

"Yes. It cost Jacques fifteen louis, the price of one evening, from seven o'clock to twelve, dinner included, three louis an hour. He got the photograph thrown in."

"I should have thought he could have got it cheaper by any other method, and without—without—without being obliged to take the original as well."

"Oh, but she's pretty. Jacques didn't mind it at all. And besides, I wanted to know all sorts of physical details about her figure, her breast, her skin, and all that."

"I don't understand."

"You will in a minute. When I had found out all I wanted to know, I went to a man . . . what shall I call him? . . . a very clever man . . . you know . . . one of those men who arrange things of all . . . of all kinds . . . one of those agents who can get you detectives and accomplices . . . one of those men . . . now do you understand?"

" Yes, I think so. And what did you say to him ? "

" I showed him the photograph of Clarisse (she's called Clarisse) and I said : ' I want a lady's maid like this photograph. She must be pretty, graceful, neat, clean. I'll pay any price you like. If it costs me ten thousand francs, so much the worse for me. I shan't need her for more than three months.'

" The man looked most surprised. ' You want a girl with a good character, Madame ? ' he asked.

" I blushed and stammered : ' She must be honest about money.'

" ' And what about morals ? ' he added. I didn't dare answer. I could only shake my head to mean ' No.' And all at once I realised that he had a dreadful suspicion, and I lost my head and cried : ' Oh, Monsieur, it's for my husband . . . he is deceiving me . . . he's deceiving me up in town . . . and I want . . . I want him to deceive me at home . . . you see . . . so that I can catch him at it.'

" Then the man burst out laughing. And I saw by his face that I had regained his opinion of me. He even thought me rather splendid. I'd have been ready to bet that he wanted to shake hands with me on the spot.

" ' I'll arrange it for you within the week, Madame,' he said. ' And if necessary we'll change the attraction. I'll guarantee success. You won't pay me until we have been successful. . . . So this is the photograph of your husband's mistress ? '

" ' Yes.'

" ' She's got a good figure, not so thin as she appears. And what scent ? '

" I didn't understand. ' How do you mean, what scent ? ' I repeated.

" He smiled. ' Yes, Madame, scent is of the first importance in seducing a man ; because it stirs hidden memories that prepare his mind for the necessary impulse ; scent works a subtle confusion in his mind, disturbs him and weakens his defence by reminding him of past pleasures. You should also try to find out what your husband usually eats when he dines with this lady. You could arrange to give him the same dishes the evening you catch him. Ah, we'll pull it off, Madame, we'll pull it off!'

"I went away delighted. I really had discovered a most intelligent man."

II

"Three days later, a tall, dark girl presented herself before me; she was very beautiful, with an expression at once demure and provocative, a strangely sophisticated expression. Her manner towards me was correctness itself. As I didn't know quite on what footing to put her, I called her 'Mademoiselle'; then she said: 'Oh, Madame need not call me anything but Rose.' We began to talk.

"'Well, Rose, you know why you are here?'

"'I know quite well, Madame.'

"'Excellent, my girl. . . . And you . . . you don't mind at all?'

"'Oh, Madame, this is the eighth divorce I've helped to arrange; I'm used to it.'

"'That's splendid. Will it take you long to bring it off?'

"'Oh, Madame, that depends entirely on the gentleman's temperament. As soon as I have seen him alone for five minutes, I shall be able to tell you with some certainty.'

"'You shall see him at once, my child. But I warn you that he's not beautiful.'

"'That doesn't matter to me, Madame. I've come between wives and some very ugly husbands before this. But I must ask Madame if she has ascertained what scent I ought to use.'

"'Yes, my good Rose . . . vervain.'

"'So much the better, Madame: I'm very fond of that scent.'

" 'And perhaps Madame can also tell me if her husband's mistress wears silk.'

" 'No, my child ; very fine lawn trimmed with lace.'

" 'Oh, she must be very smart. Silk is beginning to be so common.'

" 'I quite agree with you.'

" 'Very well, Madame, I'll begin my duties.'

" She did begin her duties on the spot, as if she had never done anything else in all her life.

" An hour later my husband came in again. Rose didn't even look at him, but he looked at her. She was already smelling strongly of vervain. After five minutes she left the room.

" 'Who's that girl ?' he asked me at once.

" 'That . . . oh, that's my new maid.'

" 'Where did you get her ?'

" 'The Baronne de Grangerie sent her to me, with an excellent recommendation.'

" 'Well, she's pretty enough.'

" 'You think so ?'

" 'I do . . . for a lady's maid.'

" I was overjoyed. I was sure he was nibbling already.

" The same evening Rose said to me : 'I can now promise Madame that it won't take a fortnight. The gentleman is very easy.'

" 'Ah, you've tried already ?'

" 'No, Madame, but its obvious at a glance. Even now he'd like to put his arms round me as he walks past.'

" 'He hasn't said anything to you ?'

" 'No, Madame, he has only asked my name . . . to hear the sound of my voice.'

" 'Excellent, my good Rose. Get on as quickly as you can.'

" 'Don't be afraid of that, Madame. I shall resist just long enough not to make myself cheap.'

" By the end of the week my husband hardly left the house

at all. I used to see him all afternoon wandering about the house; and what was more significant than anything else of his state of mind, was that he no longer stopped me from going out. I was out all day, I was . . . to . . . to leave him free.

"On the ninth day, as Rose was undressing me, she said meekly:

"'It's happened, Madame—this morning.'

"I was a little surprised, even a little distressed, not by the thing itself, but by the way in which she had said it to me. I stammered:

"'And . . . and . . . it went off all right?'

"'Oh, very well, Madame. He has been urging me for three days now, but I didn't want to go too quickly. Perhaps Madame will tell me what time she would like the *flagrante delicto*.'

"'Yes, my girl; let's see . . . we'll make it Friday.'

"'Friday then, Madame. I'll not allow any more liberties until then, so as to keep Monsieur eager.'

"'You're sure you won't fail?'

"'Oh, yes, Madame, quite sure. I'll go on keeping Monsieur from the point, so that he's just ready to come to it at any hour Madame likes to fix.'

"'Let's say five o'clock, my good Rose.'

"'Five o'clock, Madame; and where?'

"'Well—in my room.'

"'Right, in Madame's room.'

"Well, my dear, you see what I did. I went and brought papa and mamma first, and then my uncle d'Orvelin, the president, and then Monsieur Raplet, the judge, a friend of my husband's. I didn't warn them what I was going to show them. I made them all creep on tiptoe to the door of my room. I waited until five o'clock, exactly five o'clock. Oh, how my heart was beating! I made the concierge come up too, so as to have one more witness. Then . . . then, the moment the clock began to strike, bang, I flung the door open. . . . Oh, oh, oh, there they were in the very middle of it, my dear! . . . Oh, what a face . . . what a face, if you had only seen his face! . . . And he turned round, the fathead. Oh, it was funny! I laughed, and laughed. . . . And papa was furious and wanted to whip my husband. And the concierge, an excellent servant, helped him to dress himself again . . . in front of us . . . in front of us . . . he buttoned his braces for him . . . it was wildly funny. . . . As for Rose, she was perfect, quite perfect. . . . She cried . . . she cried beautifully. She's a priceless girl . . . if ever you want a girl like that, remember her!

"And here I am. . . . I came away at once to tell you all about it . . . at once—I'm free. Hurrah for divorce!"

She began to dance in the middle of the drawing-room, while the little Baronne murmured, in a voice full of dreamy disappointment:

"Why didn't you invite me to see it?"